Journey through a da...

Call him Brown. He runs this railroad. This is your ticket to ride his rails. It's a passenger train, but it carries a lot of freight, too, and there are frequent stops. Your ticket doesn't specify a destination. There are many travel options. Brown owns the entire line; he built it from the ground up— the rails and switches, the depots with the sandwich shops and magazine racks, the shabby little towns full of secrets, and the murky barrooms where the drifters float in a whisky haze and the cigarette smoke swirls with desperate conversation. . . and laughter. Brown opens the club car as soon the train departs the station, and he likes to play chess with the passengers. Forget about beating him. Just enjoy the game. Whenever the train stops, you can get out and take a stroll around the station, or wander into town for a beer. Look nonchalant while loitering on the platform and try to fit in. Go ahead, play the part—but don't wander too far, and for pity sake don't lose your ticket. Hold it tight, and stay on the edge of the shadows, just beyond the halo of moths and the soft breathing of the ventilator shafts. You'll be all right, though, so don't worry. He'll be with you the whole way. Brown will. This is his railroad and you're his guest. You got it made.

Turning this page means that you're committed, that you're ready for the journey to Brownsville, but before I punch your ticket I want to know that you'll keep an open mind about the things you'll see, that you won't pull that cord for an emergency stop just so's you can escape into some safe-looking cow pasture. If you feel a little skittish, brace yourself with a shot of liquid courage. The point is, you have stay aboard for the entire ride; otherwise, you'll miss something. Something important. Something that finally convinces you that Fredric Brown was one of the finest writers of crime fiction in the 20th century. Yeah, it's going to be that kind of a ride. You see, I got a point to prove, and I mean to prove it.

Hear that? The locomotive's built up a head of steam. It's time to go, but before departure, a brief stop at the Information Desk is required by Management. Through those doors. . .

Fredric Brown 1906 - 1972

Miss Darkness

The Great Short Crime Fiction of
Fredric Brown

Bruin Books   The Emerald Empire   Eugene, Oregon

Miss Darkness, The Great Short Crime Fiction of Fredric Brown

Published by Bruin Books, LLC June 2012

Visit the scene of the crime at www.bruinbookstore.com

All stories published by expressed permission of the Estate of Fredric Brown

All right reserved. No part of this book may be reproduced or transmitted in any part or by any means, electronic or mechanical, without written permission of the Publisher, except where permitted by law.

Stories selected and edited by Jonathan Eeds

Cover design by Michelle Policicchio

Special thanks to Barry N. Malzberg, who has been great to work with. Also thanks goes to Stephen Haffner of the The Haffner Press, who graciously spotted Bruin Books a couple of hard to find stories.

Printed in the United States of America

ISBN 978-09826339-9-1

Original publication dates: *Miss Darkness*, 1947 Avon Books, Avon Detective Mysteries, No. 3 1947 ; *Little Boy Lost* © 1941 by Frank A. Munsey, Detective Fiction Weekly, August 1941; *Good Night, Good Knight* © 1949 by New Publications Inc., published as *Last Curtain* in New Detective, July 1949; *A Matter of Death* © 1944 by Standard Magazines, Inc., Thrilling Detective, November 1944; *Get Out of Town* © 1942 by Standard Magazines, Inc., Thrilling Detective, September 1942; *Granny's Birthday* © 1960 Alfred Hitchcock's Mystery Magazine, June 1960; *Nightmare in Yellow* ©1961, Dude Magazine, May 1961; *Cry Silence*, © Black Mask, November 1948; *I'll Cut Your Throat Again, Kathleen* © 1948 Mystery Club, Inc., Mystery Book Magazine, winter 1948 ; *A Little White Lye* © 1942, 10 Detective Aces, September 1942; *The Joke* © 1948 by Popular Publications, Inc. published as *If Looks Could Kill*, Detective Tales, October 1948; *Little Apple Hard to Peel* © 1942 by Popular Publications, Inc., Detective Tales, February 1942; *Don't Look Behind You* © 1947 Ellery Queen's Mystery Magazine, May 1947; *Life and Fire*, © 1941 by Frank A. Munsey, Detection Fiction Weekly, March 1941; *The Shaggy Dog Murders*, © 1944 by Popular Publications, Inc. published as *To Slay a Man About a Dog* in Detective Tales Magazine; *The Spherical Ghoul* © 1943 by Standard Magazines, Thrilling Mystery, January 1943; *Moon Over Murder* © 1942 by Standard Magazines, Inc., The Masked Detective, spring 1942; *The Djinn Murder* © 1942 Ellery Queen's Mystery Magazine, January 1942; *Handbook for Homicide* © 1942, renewed 1970, by Popular Publications, Inc., Detective Tales, March 1942;, © 1944 by Standard Magazines, Thrilling Mystery, Summer 1944 ; *The Cat from Siam* © 1949 by Standard Magazines, Inc., Popular Detective, September 1949; *Satan One-and-a-Half* © 1942 by Popular Publications, Inc. Dime Mystery, November 1942; *The Case of the Dancing Sandwiches* © 1948 Mystery Club, Inc., Mystery Book Magazine, spring 1948 ; *The Laughing Butcher* © 1948 by Mystery Club, Inc., Mystery Book Magazine, spring 1948; *Death is a Noise* © 1943, Popular Detective, February 1943; *The Little Lamb* © 1953 Manhunt, August 1953; *Murder Set to Music* © 1956 by King-Size Publications, The Saint Detective Magazine, January 1957; *The Freak Show Murders* © by Street and Smith Publications, Inc., Street & Smith Mystery Magazine, May 1943; *The Wench is Dead* © 1953 Manhunt, July 1953; *The Pickled Punks* © 1953 by King-Size Publications, The Saint Detective Magazine, June/July 1953; *Obit for Obie* © 1946 by Mystery Club, Inc., Mystery Book Magazine, October 1946

Miss Darkness

Introduction i-iv

The Human Comedies

Miss Darkness 1

Little Boy Lost 14

Good Night, Good Knight 22

A Matter of Death 33

Get Out of Town 56

Tinglers

Granny's Birthday 85

Nightmare in Yellow 88

Cry Silence 90

I'll Cut Your Throat Again, Kathleen 95

A Little White Lye 112

The Joke 128

Little Apple Hard to Peel 137

Don't Look Behind You 149

Shaggy Dogs

Life and Fire 163

The Shaggy Dog Murders 177

The Spherical Ghoul 199

Moon Over Murder 223

Saturday Matinees

    The Djinn Murder 237

    Handbook for Homicide 251

    The Jabberwocky Murders 289

    The Cat from Siam 329

Puzzles

    Satan One-and-a-Half 363

    The Case of the Dancing Sandwiches 382

    The Laughing Butcher 434

Slumming

    Death is a Noise 453

    The Little Lamb 475

    Murder Set to Music 487

    The Freak Show Murders 527

Maturity

    The Wench is Dead 595

    The Pickled Punks 621

    Obit for Obie 675

Information Desk

"Please check in prior to departure..."

It was a bad year for the boy, a year of losses. He was the only child of middle class parents, Emma and Karl Brown. Karl was a reporter for a Cincinnati paper. Emma stayed home to run the household. It was Emma who passed first, succumbing to cancer and leaving Karl a widower and the boy motherless. As the end drew near the boy knew he should pray for his mother, and he did so—fervently, but his prayers did nothing to spare her. The futility of it singed his heart with bitterness. The praying was so pointless, intangible. The only tangible thing was the emptiness he felt after his mother was gone, and prayer did nothing to allay that pain. Within the year, his father was dead as well.

It was 1921. Fredric Brown was only 15, slight for his age, small-boned, delicate, prone to illness—especially respiratory ailments—and he suddenly found himself orphaned in an insecure world. A real stew of misfortune was churning in the cauldron. The horror of World War I was a lingering nightmare for the nation. Youth no longer held the promise of innocence, and it wasn't only the returning doughboys who were mentally and physically scarred. The great influenza pandemic tore through the population, killing nearly 130 million people worldwide—3% of the world's population. On the geo-political front, amid the rubble of a broken Europe, the young Adolf Hitler vented his spleen for the time in the Munich beer halls; and on Wall Street, optimism ran high as financiers broke ground on the house of cards that would soon collapse and plunge western civilization into economic ruin. This was the world bequeathed to Fredric Brown, aged 15, orphan.

Although little is mentioned of his parents' deaths, these events, compacted as they were, must have had an enormous impact upon him and probably did as much as anything to shape his views of the world and influence his writing. Was it the shock of abandonment that made him in turn abandon God and declare himself an atheist? Was this the reason why children rarely appear in his writing, as if they didn't even exist? (More cats appear in his stories than children.) Would his quirky imagination, hunger for wordplay and love of paradoxical situations still have developed had his parents survived? Would a completed childhood have actually suppressed Brown's genius and reduced the spark of his creativity? And how did he suffer so much tragedy so young and still develop his trademark sense of humor? That is the true wonderment of it all. Brown's writing is happy-go-lucky and exquisitely sad—one of the many paradoxes we shall encounter.

Certainly, his stories can be enjoyed at face value—this is pulp fiction, after all, but a deeper evaluation will reward the reflective reader. There is a reason Brown is considered a writer's writer, and we should peel back the layers to find out why this is. Brown's signature shock-endings always come to the fore in book introductions and fan appreciations. People love to be surprised and Brown knew that. He was trying to sell stories to popular magazines after all, but as fun and clever as the twist-endings are, they are not the reason we love to read Fredric Brown, nor should his reputation as a writer rest upon them. Brown wasn't an especially keen scene-setter, either. Not a lot of attention is paid to how things look—the color of things, the shape and texture of the stage he sets. For a writer whose own name is a color, he hardly mentions a rainbow, a green tree, an amber field or a bluebird. His settings exist in an essentially colorblind world. He is economic in the use of props: guns, cars, chairs, booze; and if he mentions an object he's damn well going to use it. Little extraneous detail is given. He pays scant regard to the weather, nor does he dwell long enough on the five senses to note the smoke and haze of a dimly-lit barroom, or describe the cheap scent of a salesman's hair tonic, or elaborate of the furnishings in a swanky lobby. In this regard, Brown is a minimalist. Don't look for the flourishes of Flaubert in Fredric Brown. That stuff just doesn't matter.

Only the people matter. It's all about the people: character, dialog, inner monolog, aspirations, self-doubts, affections, afflictions, addictions and, of course, actions. People are indeed the canvas and the source for all the conflict. Brown's sparse descriptive style and focus on dialog and inner thought has the same effect on a reader as a radio play does on a listener. He has the uncanny ability to tickle the reader's imagination just enough that the mind's eye takes over and completes the stage, fills it with props, lighting, backdrops—the flourishes. Brown's voice does this. Without question, his plotting is top drawer, his surprise endings are satisfying, his pacing is electrifying, his puzzles are intriguing and charming, but it's the allure of Brown's voice that brings us back again and again to his fiction. It befriends us.

Biographical information is frustratingly thin, and I confess that I have nothing fresh to offer in the way of facts. The curious may take the quest on upon themselves to ferret out the particulars of his life (Jack Seabrook's *Martians and Misplaced Clues* is a good place to start,) but I would first like to acquaint the biographiles out there—those who prefer to get cozy with an author's background before diving into the main attraction—with the gold mine of insight Brown left behind for us in his stories and novels.

Brown is alive in his fiction. Details of his life and experiences continuously bubble to the surface and are reengineered to suit the dramatic purpose. His narrative voice (again I return to his voice!)—knowing, sympathetic yet edgy, ironic and cynical—is every bit a character as the people he wrote about. He even makes personal appearances from time to time, although not in name, materializing as the impish alter-ego in Pince-nez or wire-rim glasses who can pop up just about anywhere in any story. Regardless of the occasional oblique guest appearance, his personality shines through in every scene—so much so that an attentive and practiced reader will learn to recognize a Brown story without looking at the title or author—just as one recognizes an old friend's voice an aisle away in the supermarket. His love of chess, cats, music, puzzles, Lewis Carroll, Shakespeare, poetry, women, and drinking—bodacious amounts of drinking—are all part of who he was. If a character is drinking the hard stuff, playing chess or cards and cynically shooting the breeze about T.S. Eliot, or Charles Fort, or abnormal psychology, or jazz, or carneys we are likely in company with the man himself.

Fredric Brown is a joy to read. His character driven stories can be appreciated on many levels. His style is unique, engaging and quirky in the best sense of the word. The irony is that he won his only Edgar Award for his first novel and then went on to write his best stuff. When Brown physically weakened in his late fifties and could no longer write, his fiction fell out of favor and remained in limbo. It wasn't until the mid-1980's, when renewed attention was placed on his work, that Brown's popularity enjoyed a resurgence that carries through to this day. His books are highly collectable, fetching hundreds of dollars for first editions. Fans will never let his work slip into obscurity again.

So. . . why hasn't The Eminent Mr. Brown taken his rightful place beside the likes of Dashiell Hammett and Raymond Chandler? This is possibly because he is a victim of his own success. Simply put, he wrote too damn much. He was one of the few writers of that period, or in any period for that matter, who was actually able to pay the rent with his words. He wrote more novels and stories than Hammett and Chandler combined...more by a long shot. He also received the back-alley treatment from Hollywood. The few movies based on his work were abysmal treatments, doing more harm to his reputation than good. (By comparison, Chandler had Bogart as a star and Faulkner as a screen writer.) The failure of Hollywood to properly capitalize on the rich Brownian terrain prevented his stories and characters from ever entering the collective consciousness. Had he refined his output a little more, controlled his craft and art a little better . . . had he written thirty stories instead of over 300, ten novels instead of twenty-nine, stuck to one genre (sorry, science fiction fans,) balanced his energy as a writer so that it did not flicker out just as he was reaching new levels. . . *(Sigh)* . . . but we should be thankful that Fredric Brown was such a generous writer. We have so much to enjoy. The orphan created a very big family indeed.

Miss Darkness is a tribute to the great short crime fiction of Fredric Brown. Its publication marks the 40th anniversary of his passing. –JE

". . .but with a bottle in my pocket and good company waiting for me there, my old tried-and-true friends in the bookcase. Reading a book is almost like listening to the man who wrote it talk. Except that you don't have to be polite. You can take your shoes off and put your feet up on the table and drink and forget who you are." –FB

The Human

Comedies

Miss Darkness

IT WAS LATE in the afternoon, almost dinner time, when Miss Darkness came to stay at Mrs. Prandell's boarding house. The evening papers had just come, and—while Mrs. Prandell was taking Miss Darkness upstairs to show her the advertised vacant room—Mr. Anstruther, in the sitting room downstairs, was saying, "Quite a bit of excitement downtown this afternoon, Miss Wheeler. Did you see any of it?"

"You mean the bank robbery, Mr. Anstruther? No, I was at the main library all afternoon, doing my research." Miss Wheeler's research, of course, was for her magnum opus, a study of Elizabethan poets, a project which had engaged all of her thoughts since her retirement two years before as a teacher of high school English. A strange thing, Miss Wheeler's affinity for Elizabethans; in the flesh those robustious fellows would have shocked her past measure. "Did *you* see any of it?"

"I heard the sirens," said Mr. Anstruther, and he wondered why Miss Wheeler—who had a sudden picture of Mr. Anstruther, as Ulysses, tied to the mast of a ship—giggled a little.

But upstairs, Mrs. Prandell was opening the door of the vacant room. "Fifteen dollars," she said, "with breakfast and dinner. We don't serve lunches. Or it's ten dollars, just with breakfast." Her tone of voice added that if Miss Darkness didn't want it, plenty of others would.

"I—I'll take it," said Miss Darkness. "Just with breakfast."

"Linens once a week; no cooking in rooms; no guests, of course, except in the sitting room downstairs; no pets; no radios after ten o'clock; you furnish your own soap, towels, light bulbs; and breakfast either at seven-thirty or eight-thirty, whichever you prefer. Some go to work earlier than others so we have the two times. Which do you want?"

"Eight-thirty, please."

"And—" Mrs. Prandell glanced down at the small, cheap cardboard suitcase which Miss Darkness had brought, "payable in advance, please." She unbent a little when Miss Darkness had fumbled in her purse and handed over a ten dollar bill. "I'll make you out your receipt after dinner; I've got to help the cook now. What did you say your name is, Miss—?"

"Westerman," said Miss Darkness. "Mary Westerman."

So Mrs. Prandell went downstairs to supervise the cooking, and Miss Darkness (who had not yet, of course, been named that) went into her room and shut the door.

A little while later, about the time Mrs. Prandell was preparing to tinkle the dinner bell, Miss Darkness left her room. At the turn in the stairs, she almost ran head on into Mr. Barry, ascending for a pre-prandial wash-up.

Mr. Barry, insurance salesman, was—by the consensus of Mrs. Prandell's paying guests—a very nice young man. Certainly he was the most presentable male within a radius of blocks. He was not tall, but then neither was Miss Darkness. And he had dark curly hair and humorous eyes and a nice mouth that started, involuntarily, to purse into a whistle when he saw Miss Darkness.

Funny about that. I mean, Miss Wheeler and Miss Gaines, sitting in the sitting room awaiting the call to dinner, could see the turn of the stairs and Miss Darkness standing there. But they saw only a rather mousy-looking girl in a cheap, ready-made dress, whereas Mr. Barry saw much more than that. One might say that he saw the girl herself *through* the inexpensive dress (in a nice way, of course, for he was a nice young man) and he liked what he saw. Miss Darkness was small-boned and delicate, beautifully wrought. Her face was pale, to Misses Wheeler-Gaines; milk-white, to Mr. Barry. Her eyes were big and dark (like moonlit pools) and a little frightened.

Mr. Barry smiled at her. He said, "Nobody tells me these things." (A misleading statement, for everybody told everything at Mrs. Prandell's; the only reason Mr. Barry hadn't heard was that he had just come in.) "You're staying here? A new guest?"

"Yes," said Miss Darkness, and her eyes were wary now, but not so frightened.

"Then may I introduce myself? Walter Barry."

"Mary Westerman," said Miss Darkness. "And may I pass, please? I'm almost late for a dinner appointment."

There wasn't room on the stairs, of course, for Mr. Barry to step aside and bow, but he approximated it pretty well. He stood there watching as she went on down the stairs and out the door. In the sitting room Miss Wheeler looked at Miss Gaines and Miss Gaines looked at Miss Wheeler. And the dinner bell tinkled. An hour later Miss Darkness returned and went directly to her room. Going upstairs shortly after that, Miss Wheeler saw that the light was out in Miss Darkness' room and wondered. It was scarcely eight o'clock.

That was Tuesday.

It was Thursday night, at dinner, that gossip grew. Oh, you may be sure that she had been discussed Tuesday night and Wednesday night, but mildly and with reservations because young Mr. Barry had been present at both of those meals and had shown an inclination to leap to the breach in defense at the slightest word against the new guest.

It was Thursday night that Miss Gaines said, "There's *something* wrong with her, Mrs. Prandell. She's afraid of something. She's even afraid of the light."

"Of the light?" Mr. Anstruther asked. "What do you mean?"

"She sits in the dark, up in that room. And she stays away from our sitting room downstairs here. Why, the first night she was here, I went past her door at eight, and she was sitting in the dark, and again last night. You can see the crack of light under the door when it's on inside the room, you know."

"Perhaps," said Mrs. Prandell, "she goes to bed early."

"Not that early, surely. At least, she'd turn on the light to prepare for bed, and she didn't. I know because I went up to my room for a handkerchief last night just a minute after she came in, and she was in the dark in there."

"How strange," said Miss Wheeler. "Mrs. Prandell, did she say anything to you that would explain . . . ?"

Mrs. Prandell shook her head wonderingly.

"What could explain it?" Miss Gaines asked.

Mr. Anstruther cleared his throat pontifically. "Oh, there are any number of possible explanations. I could think of half a dozen off-hand. She might have trouble with her eyes, for one thing, and be ordered by a doctor to avoid electric lights."

"Then wouldn't she wear dark glasses—at least, when she wasn't in her room?" asked Miss Gaines. "No, it couldn't be that, Mr. Anstruther.

Why, last night when she was coming down the stairs she stopped to think, part way down, as though she was deciding whether to go back or go on, and she was staring right into the bright light at the foot of the stairs while she stood there. She wouldn't have done that."

"Or perhaps," said Mr. Anstruther, "she is afraid, hiding from someone. And hers is front room. Yes, I know there's a shade on the window. Does the shade work properly, Mrs. Prandell?"

"I believe so. I'll check tomorrow."

"Or perhaps," said Mr. Anstruther, "she is a religious fanatic, given to meditation whenever alone. . . No, I don't really think that, I was just suggesting possibilities."

"And you have three to go," said Miss Gaines. "You said you could think of half a dozen."

"Perhaps she works or is associated with blind people, or expects to be. She is learning, deliberately, to get their point of view, as it were, by practicing being blind when she is alone."

"She isn't working with or for the blind," said Mrs. Prandell. "She isn't working at all. And she volunteers no information about herself."

"She could avoid the window," said Miss Wheeler, "without having to stay in the dark. Even if the shade is broken."

"Number five," said Mr. Anstruther. "She is a believer in spirits. She is trying to establish contact with someone she loved who has just died. Perhaps she thinks she has powers as a medium. And darkness is conducive—"

The outer door opened, and Miss Wheeler, seated at the end of the table opposite Mrs. Prandell's end, turned her head so she could see into the hallway. She turned back and whispered, "Here comes *Miss Darkness* now," and nothing more was said until they had heard her footsteps go on up the stairs.

Miss Gaines pushed back her chair a little. She said, "I do believe—"

"That you have forgotten your handkerchief again," said Mr. Anstruther "Am I right, Miss Gaines?"

There was a general laugh at the table, and Miss Gaines reddened very slightly, but she went upstairs. When she came back, everyone at the table looked at her, and she nodded.

There was a moment's silence after that and before the topic was reopened, young Mr. Barry came in, which was a shame. Mrs. Prandell's boarders hadn't had so mystifying a thing to talk about in years.

That was Thursday. On Friday at the earlier of the two breakfast times Miss Wheeler glanced across the table at Mr. Anstruther and said, "Have you heard the latest about the bank robbery last Tuesday?"

"No, Miss Wheeler. What is it?"

"One of the two bandits was caught at the time, you know, and the other got away—with the money. Now they think a woman drove the getaway car."

"Indeed?" said Mr. Anstruther, and his graying, bushy eyebrows rose a full centimeter. "And do they have a description of the woman?"

Mr. Barry put down his fork.

"No," said Miss Wheeler, and you could tell there was disappointment in her voice. "The witness who thinks he saw the car start up, around the corner from the bank, was quite a distance from it. He thinks that it was a young woman, though."

"Indeed?" said Mr. Anstruther, more hopefully. "And that was Tuesday afternoon, was it not?"

Mr. Barry asked, "What do you mean by that, Mr. Anstruther?"

Mr. Anstruther's eyebrows climbed back down again. But before he could formulate an answer, Miss Gaines saved the day by asking for details of just what *had* happened during the robbery; she hadn't read about it.

"Two men entered the bank, with guns," explained Miss Wheeler. "They wore masks; they must have put them on in the entryway, between the inner doors and the outer doors. One of them had a small valise and they held up the bank and put all the bills from the cashiers' cages into it, and got away—got outside, anyway. Of course the alarm went in while they were leaving."

"And one was caught right outside?"

"Not right outside, no. But the police cars, closing in, picked up a man known to be a bank robber two blocks away, on foot. One of the police recognized him. He had a gun, although he'd got rid of the mask, and he wasn't the one who had the satchel of money. They arrested him, of course, and they're holding him, but only on the charge of having a gun; they can't prove any more than that, unless they find the other man—or woman."

"And the witness?" asked Mr. Anstruther, glad that attention had been diverted from his remark about Tuesday.

"Someone the police found the next day. A man who, from some distance, remembers a man carrying a small satchel get into a car parked around the corner from the bank, right after the holdup. He says there was a woman behind the wheel, but he couldn't identify either man or woman. But the police figure the two men split up right outside the bank, one going one way and the other—the one with the money—to where a getaway car had been waiting. That, I believe, is what they call a getaway car."

Mr. Barry smiled at her. He said, "Yes, Miss Wheeler. That's what they call it. I think you missed your vocation, Miss Wheeler."

"That isn't true, Mr. Barry. I would have made a very poor detective, if that's what you mean?"

Mr. Barry smiled at her and stood up. He said, "You'll excuse me, Mrs. Prandell? And, Miss Wheeler, that wasn't what I meant."

That night after dinner, Mr. Barry sat on the porch steps until the others had gone to their rooms, except Mr. Anstruther, who went downtown to a movie.

Miss Darkness, he thought, that's what they call her.

Oddly, the name seemed, to him, to fit quite well without a sinister connotation. Miss Darkness, with dark hair and dark eyes.

But, too, there was a dark mystery. Why *did* she sit in darkness, evening after evening? It wasn't because she retired right away; she'd been heard moving about the room. Hiding?

Mr. Barry rose from the steps and strolled down to the corner and back so he could see her window without seeming to. It was dark all right, and the shade was down. But the shade alone would have been sufficient, especially for a second-floor room.

He saw a cat pad-foot across the shadowed yard. Cats, he thought, see in darkness. And he could think of Mary Westerman as a cuddly kitten, if not a cat, but that still explained nothing. Surely she could not actually see in the dark. . .

Saturday morning, in the sitting room, Miss Gaines watched Miss Darkness go out to eat her lunch, wherever she ate it. Then Miss Gaines strode resolutely into Mrs. Prandell's kitchen.

"She just went out," Miss Gaines said. By this time, of course, the pronoun needed no antecedent.

Mrs. Prandell glanced at the clock. "Well, it's almost noon. She always goes out a while at this time, doesn't she?"

"Yes, but—Far be it from me, Mrs. Prandell, to suggest *snooping*, but have you thought that she really might be—somebody dangerous to have around? What if she has the money from that bank robbery, for instance?"

"She hasn't, Miss Gaines. Don't you think that I didn't—for the protection of all of us—search her room and her belongings the first chance, after what Miss Wheeler told us."

Miss Gaines leaned forward eagerly. "And—?"

"Just a few cheap things in a dime-store cardboard suitcase. That's all. But just the same she's leaving Tuesday, when her week is up. I don't like mysteries, Miss Gaines. I won't take another week's rent from her."

"I'm glad of that, Mrs. Prandell." Miss Gaines leaned forward confidentially. "Did Mr. Anstruther tell you? About yesterday?"

"No. What?"

"Why, he just happened to leave here, at noon, about the time she did. Just after her. He was walking right behind her for several blocks. Then she turned around and saw him and acted as though she thought she was being followed. She stared at him and then turned a corner and walked fast and was out of sight by the time he got to the corner."

Mrs. Prandell sniffed. "Just what I'd have thought," she said. "Well, after next Tuesday—"

It was that night, Saturday night, that Mr. Barry passed up his dinner in order to be sitting on the porch steps when Miss Darkness went out.

"Good evening," he said. "Beautiful night out." It wasn't; it wasn't actually raining, but the sky was a bit cloudy and the air was hot and muggy.

She actually smiled at him, but she answered briefly and went on before he could think of what to say, or ask, next. He watched as she went on down the street, and saw that she looked around behind her, twice. He thought, something is wrong; she's afraid of something. She's in danger, somehow.

It was Sunday evening that Death came to Mrs. Prandell's rooming house. It rang the doorbell at eight forty-five.

Mrs. Prandell was just coming into the sitting room from the kitchen when the bell rang. Mr. Anstruther and Mr. Barry had both stood up to go to answer the door, but she said, "I'll get it," and walked on past them. Miss Gaines put down her magazine to listen.

They heard the door open and Mrs. Prandell's voice say, "Yes?" and a lower, rumbly voice say, "I'm William Thorber, city detective. Do you have a Melissa Carey staying here?"

Nobody in the living room made a sound. They heard Mrs. Prandell say, "Not under that name, Mr. Thorber. But—won't you come in?"

The detective said, "Thank you," and came in. Mr. Barry stood up again, then, and started for the hallway, but Mrs. Prandell and Mr. Thorber were heading for the sitting room, he saw, and he sat back down again.

Mrs. Prandell said, "We do have a mysterious young lady here whom we—well, whom we suspect of not using her right name. Will you tell us something of this—uh—Melissa Carey? She might be the one. And won't you sit down, Mr. Thorber?"

"Thank you, Mrs.—"

"Prandell."

"Thank you, Mrs. Prandell. Melissa Carey is five-five, slender, dark, twenty-three."

"Miss Darkness," said Miss Gaines, a bit breathlessly. "I was *sure*, Mrs. Prandell, that—"

"Darkness?" the detective interrupted. "Is that actually the name she gave?"

"No, Mr. Thorber," said Mrs. Prandell. "She is using the name Mary Westerman. We called her Miss Darkness because she always sits in the dark upstairs."

"Sits in the dark?" Mr. Thorber frowned. "I don't see— Uh, when did she come here?"

"Late Tuesday afternoon, a few hours after the bank robbery downtown. Is she wanted in connection with that, Mr. Thorber? Is she the woman who drove the getaway car? We read about that, of course."

Mr. Thorber smiled. "Not quite that bad, ma'am. She was a clerk in the bank that was robbed. We need her as a material witness."

"A clerk?" Miss Gaines looked disappointed. "You mean she only worked there? But why would she run away and hide here?" A more hopeful look came into her face. "Perhaps she was an accomplice?"

"We're afraid her running away might indicate that, ma'am. Is she here now?"

"Please tell us a little more about it," Miss Gaines begged. "You mean you think she—tipped off the robbers, or something like that?"

The detective frowned. "We're a bit in the dark ourselves, ma'am, just why she ran away like that, from the police. But here's what we do know. The two robbers stopped between the inner and the outer doors to put on the masks they wore into the bank. Miss Carey was working where she, alone of all the people in the bank, could see into that entryway, and she saw the two men as they were putting on their masks, so she alone can identify them. She admitted that right after the robbery, when the chief was talking to her, just before I got there.

"Then we learned Garvey and Roberts had picked up a suspect called John Brady a couple blocks from the bank and had taken him to headquarters. The chief asked Miss Carey if she'd go around to headquarters to see if she could identify him, see? She said sure, and it was only a few blocks and on account of the excitement and everything she'd like some fresh air, and could she walk? And the chief said sure, because we had some more to do at the bank and weren't ready to leave. So she never got there."

Miss Gaines leaned forward. "She disappeared between the bank and headquarters?"

"That's it. And she never went home. She has a little apartment on Dovershire Street, but she never went there either. We been looking for her since, and got a tip tonight that led us here."

Mr. Anstruther, who had been silent until now, cleared his throat. "Is there any reward, Mr. Thorber?"

The detective looked at him. "You're Anstruther? Well, there may be if it turns out that she is implicated, and this leads to recovery of the money. That's up to the insurance company."

"Look," said Mr. Barry. They looked at him, but he reddened a little and couldn't think of what to say. "Are you sure? I mean—"

"We're not sure of anything," said Thorber. "But I'll have to take her to headquarters. If she can explain her actions, of course we won't hold her. And we must have her look at John Brady and either identify him or not. It was lucky for us he had a gun on him, or we couldn't have held him this long."

He stood up. "Is she here now, Mrs. Prandell?"

"Yes, her room is just opposite the head of the stairs. She's up there now, sitting in the dark."

"Thank you," said the detective. He stood up and so did Mr. Barry, Mr. Anstruther, Mrs. Prandell, and Miss Gaines. "Uh—will you all please wait here?"

All of them sat down again except Mr. Barry. He took a step toward the door and his hands clenched at his sides as the detective started up the stairs.

Mrs. Prandell said sharply, "Don't be a fool, Mr. Barry."

But a higher power than Mrs. Prandell had already made Mr. Barry a fool. He stood there, glaring at the staircase, until he heard the detective knock on the door upstairs, and then, as though something was pushing him, he started for the staircase, and up.

Had the carpeting on the stairs not muffled the sound of his footsteps, although he had not tried to walk quietly, things might have happened differently. As it was, he was making the turn in the stairs when the door of Miss Darkness' room opened—to darkness, with a slim, terrified girl silhouetted against it, the back of her hand going to her mouth as though to stifle a scream.

But what propelled Mr. Barry up the last few steps was that he saw both of the detective's hands come out of his pockets as the door opened, and there was a gun in *each* of them. There was a flat thirty-two automatic in his right hand and, almost hidden, a smaller fancier revolver—a woman's pistol—in his left.

There are times when one asks questions afterward, and for Mr. Barry this was one of them. Thorber was pushing Melissa Carey back into the darkness and three things happened almost at once—Mr. Barry's headlong tackle of Thorber's left hand, and Melissa Carey's scream.

The roar of the other gun was seconds later, while the others from below were fearfully coming up the stairs, fearfully led by Mr. Anstruther, who might never have reached the top had not Miss Gaines kept pushing him from behind. The automatic roared again, and that was the last shot of the melee, and there was silence in the room of darkness.

~§~

"I still don't understand *all* of it," Mrs. Prandell was saying the next evening at dinner. "And I do wish you weren't going to leave us, Mr. Barry. I know we all judged the girl wrongly, but after all, she *did* give a false name and all, and—how could we have known?"

Mr. Barry, with a bandage across his forehead where the chopping blow of a pistol barrel had removed an area of epidermis, looked quite dashing and romantic despite, or perhaps because of, a badly blackened eye.

He said, "My dear Mrs. Prandell, I don't blame any of you in the least. It is merely that I want to find a room on the other side of town, because—well, because Miss Carey lives there, or will live there again as soon as they release her from the hospital, where she is being treated for shock, in a few days. I am going to see her again this evening and, in fact, if she accepts a suggestion I have to offer, I won't even need to hunt a room, as she already has an apartment there."

"You—you don't mean—"

"No, I don't mean," said Mr. Barry patiently. "I merely mean that Melissa Barry would be a very nice name, and there *is* a shortage of apartments, you know."

"We all wish you luck," said Mr. Anstruther. "But I still don't see why this detective Thorber, bank robber or not, brought the two guns with him."

"He had to make it look as though she were resisting arrest," said Mr. Barry. "He had to kill her to keep her from identifying him or this John Brady, because—well, even if she wasn't able to identify *him* as one of the robbers, she might have identified Brady and Brady might have squealed."

"I see," said Miss Gaines. "You mean that Thorber, even though he was a real detective, had planned the robbery with Brady, who was a bank robber. Using, I suppose, information he could obtain as a detective?"

Mr. Barry nodded. "And, unluckily for her, Miss Carey was in a position to see them come into the bank entry, without their masks. And after the robbery, when the cops were coming around in droves, she saw

Thorber, and *thought*, but wasn't absolutely sure, that he was one of the men who robbed the bank."

"But why didn't she just say so?"

"She wasn't absolutely sure," Mr. Barry explained. "And that put her on a terrible spot. Either she had to accuse a man who might be innocent, or else her life was in terrible danger, because Thorber knew by then that she'd seen him and his partner, and that if she identified Brady, he was pretty likely to be sunk, too. The only thing she could think of doing was to hide out until—well, her brightest hope was that the police would solve it without her and leave her safe again."

"But the two guns—?" asked Miss Wheeler.

Mr. Anstruther said, "I see that part now, Miss Wheeler. He came prepared to kill her, and to make it look as though she had resisted arrest, and that she'd had the smaller gun and fired at him with it first. So he would be in the clear, on self-defense."

"Oh," said Miss Wheeler, a bit faintly. "Well, I'm glad, Mr. Barry, that you killed him."

Mr. Barry colored faintly. "I'm not sure that I did, Miss Wheeler, you see we were fighting for the gun, and it was in his hand and his finger was on the trigger, but I had an arm-lock on him with the gun pointing diagonally up his own back, and I guess—well, he probably didn't pull the trigger on purpose at all, just a spasmodic reaction from the pain of his arm being broken. I guess it's lucky I did wrestling in college."

For a second or two there was silence broken only by the sound of Mr. Anstruther's celery. And then Miss Wheeler remembered.

"Mr. Barry," she said. "We *still* don't know why Miss Dark—Miss Carey sat in the dark all the time in her room. You talked to her this afternoon, you say. Did she tell you that?"

"Of course she told me. When she ran away from danger that afternoon, she didn't dare go back to her room, you know. Thorber might have been waiting for her there. She had only twenty dollars with her, and for half of it she managed to buy a cheap case and a few things that would let her get by for a week, and when she came here, Mrs. Prandell, she had only exactly ten dollars left. That's why she took only breakfasts."

"You mean that's all she's been eating?"

"Of course. She took walks around, right in the neighborhood, so you wouldn't know that she wasn't eating. She was too proud to let you know that. Or to borrow or steal fifteen cents."

"Fifteen cents?" asked Mrs. Prandell blankly. "For what?"

"For a light bulb," said Mr. Barry.

Avon Detective Mysteries No. 3, 1947

Little Boy Lost

THERE WAS A KNOCK on the door. Gram put the sock she was mending back into the work basket in her lap and then moved the work basket to the table, ready to get up.

But by that time Ma had come out of the kitchen and, wiping her hands on her apron, opened the door. Her eyes went hard.

The smile on the sleek young man in the hallway outside the door showed two gold teeth. He shoved his hat back from his forehead and said: "How ya, Mrs. Murdock? Tell Eddie I'm—"

"Eddie ain't here." Ma's voice was hard like her eyes.

"Ain't, huh? Said he'd be at the Gem. Wasn't there so I thought—"

"Eddie ain't here." There was a finality in Ma's repetition. A tense finality that the man in the hallway couldn't pretend to overlook.

His smiled faded. "If he comes in, you remind him. Tell him I said nine-thirty's the time."

"The time for what?" There wasn't any rising inflection in Ma Murdock's voice to stamp those four words as a question.

There was a sudden narrowing of the eyes that looked at Ma. The man with the gold teeth said, "Eddie'll know that." He turned and walked to the stairs.

Ma closed the door slowly.

Gram was working on the sock again. Her high voice asked: "Was that Johnny Everard, Elsie? Sounded a bit like Johnny's voice."

Ma still faced that closed door. She answered without turning around. "That was Butch Everard, Gram. No one calls him Johnny anymore."

Gram's needle didn't pause.

"Johnny Everard," she said. "He had curls, Elsie, a foot long. I 'member when his dad took him down to the barber shop, had 'em cut off. His ma cried. He had the first scooter in the neighborhood, made with roller-skate wheels. He went away for a while, didn't he?"

"He did," said Ma. "For five years. I wish—"

"Used to be crazy about chocolate cake," said Gram. "When he'd leave our paper, I'd give him a slice every time I'd baked one. But, my, he was in eighth grade when Eddie was just starting in first. Isn't he a bit old to want to play with Eddie? I used to say your father—"

The querulous voice trailed off into silence. Ma glanced at her. Poor Gram, living in a world that was neither past nor present, but a hodgepodge of them both. Eddie was a man now—almost. Eddie was seventeen. And sliding away from her. She couldn't seem to hold him any longer.

Butch Everard and Larry and Slim. Yes, and the crooked streets that ran straight, and the dark pool halls that were brightly lighted, and the things that Eddie hid from her but that she read in his eyes. There were things you didn't know how to fight against.

Ma walked to the window and looked down on the street three floors below. A few doors down, at the opposite curb, stood Eddie's recently acquired jalopy. He'd told her he'd bought it for ten bucks, but she knew better than that. It wasn't much of a car, as cars go, but it had cost him at least fifty. And where had that money come from?

Steady *creak-creak* of Gram's rocker. Ma almost wished she were like Gram, so she wouldn't lie awake nights worrying herself sick until she had to take a sleeping powder to get some sleep. If there was only some way she could make Eddie want to settle down and get a steady job and not run around with men like—

Gram's voice cut across her thoughts. "You ain't lookin' so well, Elsie. Guess none of us are, though. It's the spring, the damp air and all. I made up some sulfur and molasses for us. Your pa, he used to swear by it, and he never had a sick day until just the week before he died."

Ma's tone was lifeless. "I'm all right, Gram. I—I guess I worry about Eddie. He—"

Gram nodded her gray head without looking up. "Has a cold coming on. He don't get outdoors enough daytimes. Boy ought to play out more. But you look downright peaked, Elsie. Used to be the purtiest girl on Seventieth Street. You worry about Eddie. He's a good boy."

Ma whirled. "Gram, I never said I thought he wasn't—"

Gram chuckled. "Brought home a special merit star on his report card, didn't he? And I met his teacher on the street, and she say, says she: 'Mrs. Garvin, that there grandson of yours—' "

Ma sighed and turned to go back to the kitchen to finish the dishes. Gram was back in the past again. It was eight years ago, when he was nine, that Eddie'd brought home that report card with the special merit star on it. That was when she'd hoped Eddie would—

"Elsie, you take a big spoonful of that sulfur 'n' molasses. Over the sink there. I took mine for today a'ready."

"All right, Gram." Ma's steps lagged. Maybe she'd failed Eddie; she didn't know. What else could she do? How could she make Butch Everard let him alone? What did Butch want with him?

There was a dull ache in her head and a heavy weight in her chest. She glanced up at the clock over the door of the kitchen, and her feet moved faster. Eight-forty, and she wasn't through with the supper dishes.

~§~

Eddie Murdock awoke with a start as the kitchen door closed. It was dark. Golly, he hadn't meant to fall asleep. He lifted his wrist quick to look at the luminous dial of his watch, and then felt a quick sense of relief. It was only eight-forty. He had time. Then he grinned in the darkness, a bit proud that he *had* been able to take a nap. Tonight of all nights, and he'd been able to fall asleep.

Why, tonight was *the* night. Lucky he'd waked up. Butch sure wouldn't have liked it if he'd been late or hadn't showed up. But if it was only eight-forty he had lots of time to meet the boys. Nine-thirty they met, and ten o'clock was *it*.

Suppose his wrist watch was wrong, though. It was a cheap one. With a sudden fear he jumped off the bed and ran to the window to look at the big clock across the way. Whew! Eight-forty it was—on the dot.

Everything was ducky then. Golly, if he'd overslept or anything, Butch would have thought he was yellow. And—why, he wasn't even worried. Hell, he was, one of the gang now, a regular, and this was his first crack at something big. Real money.

Well, not *big* money, maybe, but that box office ought to have enough dough to give them a couple hundred apiece. And that wasn't peanuts.

Butch had all those angles figured. He'd picked the best night, the night the most dough came in that window, and he'd timed the best hour—ten o'clock—just before the box office closed. Sure, they were being smart, waiting until all the money had come in that was coming in. And the getaway was a cinch, the way Butch had planned it.

Eddie turned on the light and then crossed over to the mirror and examined himself critically as he straightened his necktie and ran the comb through his hair. He rubbed his chin carefully, but he didn't seem to need a shave.

He winked at his reflection in the glass. That was a smart guy in there looking back at him. A guy that was going places. If a guy proved to Butch that he was a right guy and had the nerve, he could get in on all kinds of easy money.

He pulled out the shoe box from under his dresser and gave his already shiny shoes another lick with the polisher to make them shinier. The leather was a little cracked on one side. Well, after tonight he'd get new shoes and a couple of new suits. A few more jobs, and he'd get a new car like Butch's and scrap the old jalop'.

Then—although the door of his room was closed—he looked around carefully before he reached down into the very bottom of the shoe box and took out something which was carefully concealed by being wrapped in the old polishing cloth, the one that wasn't used any more.

It was a little nickel-plated thirty-two revolver, and he looked at it proudly. It didn't matter that the plating was worn off in a few spots. It was loaded and it would shoot all right.

Just yesterday Butch had given it to him. "Sail right, kid," Butch had said. "It'll do for this here job. There ain't gonna be no shootin' anyway. Just one bozo in the box office that'll fold up the minute he sees guns. He'll shell out without a squawk. And outa your share get yourself something good. A thirty-eight automatic like mine maybe, and a shoulder holster."

The gun in his hand felt comfortingly heavy. Good little gun, he told himself. And *his*. He'd sure keep it even after he'd got himself a better one.

He dropped it into his coat pocket before he went out into the living room. As he walked through the door, the revolver in his pocket hit the wooden door frame with a metallic clunk that the cloth of his coat muffled. He straightened up and buttoned his coat shut. He'd have to watch that. Good thing it happened the first time where it didn't matter.

Ma came in out of the kitchen. She smiled at him and he grinned back. "Hiya, Ma. Didn't think I'd drop off. Should have told you to wake me, but 'sall right. I got time."

Ma's smile faded. "Time for what, Eddie?"

He grinned at her. "Heavy date." The grin faded a bit. "What's the matter, Ma?"

"*Must* you go out, Eddie? I—I just got through the dishes and I thought maybe you'd play some double solitaire with me when you woke up."

It was her tone of voice that made him notice her face. It came to him, quite suddenly, that Ma looked *old*. He said, "Gee, Ma, I wish I could, but—"

Gram's rocker creaked across the silence.

"Johnny was here, Eddie," said Gram's voice. "He said—"

Ma cut in quickly. She'd seen the puzzled look on Eddie's face at the name "Johnny." He didn't know who Johnny was; and Gram thought Butch Everard was still little Johnny, who'd played out front in a red wagon—

"Johnny Murphy," said Ma, blanketing out whatever Gram was going to say. "He's—you don't know him, I guess. Just here on an errand." She tried to make it sound casual. She managed a smile again. "How about that double solitaire, Eddie boy? Just a game or two."

He shook his head. "Heavy date, Ma," he said again. He really felt sorry he couldn't. Well, maybe from now on he'd be able to make it up to Ma. He could buy her things, and—well, if he really got up there he could buy a place out at the edge of town and put her and Gram in it, in style. Bigshots did things like that for their folks, didn't they?

Gram was walking out to the kitchen. Eddie's eyes followed her because they didn't quite want to meet Ma's eyes, and then Eddie remembered what Gram had started to say about some Johnny.

"Say," he said, "Johnny—Gram didn't mean Butch, did she? Was Butch here for me?"

Ma's eyes were on him squarely now, and he forced himself to meet them. She said, "Is your 'heavy date' with Butch, Eddie? Oh, Eddie, he's—" Her voice sounded a little choked.

"Butch is all right, Ma," he said with a touch of defiance. "He's a good guy, Butch is. He's—"

He broke off. Damn. He hated scenes.

"Eddie boy," Gram spoke from the kitchen doorway.

It was a welcome interruption. But she had a tablespoon of that awful sulfur and molasses of hers. Oh, well, good old Gram's goofy ideas were saving him from a scene this time. He crossed over and took the vile stuff off the spoon.

"Thanks, Gram. 'Night, Ma. Don't wait up."

He started for the door. But it wasn't that easy. She caught at his sleeve. "Eddie, please. Listen—"

Hell, it would be worse if he hung around and argued. He jerked his sleeve free and was out of the door before she could stop him again. He could have hung around for half an hour almost, but not if Ma was going to take on like that. He could sit in the jalop' till it was time to go meet the bunch.

Ma started for the door and then stopped. She put her hands up to her eyes, but she couldn't cry. If she could only bawl or— But she couldn't talk to Gram. She couldn't share her troubles, even.

"You take your tonic, Elsie?"

"Yeah," said Ma dully. Slowly she went to the table and sat down before it. She took a deck of cards from its drawer and began to pile them for a game of solitaire. She knew there was no use her even thinking about trying to go to bed until Eddie came home. No matter how late it was.

Gram came back and went over to the window. Sometimes she'd look out of that window for an hour at a time. When you're old it doesn't take much to fill in your time.

Ma looked at Gram and envied her. When you were old you didn't mind things, because you lived mostly in the past, and the present went over and around you like water off a duck's back.

Almost desperately, Ma tried to keep her mind on beating the solitaire game. There were other games you didn't know how to try to beat.

She failed. Then she played out a game. Then she was stuck without even an ace up. She dealt them out again.

She was putting a black ten on a red jack, and then her hand jerked as she heard footsteps coming up the stairs. Was Eddie coming back?

But no, not Eddie's footsteps. Ma glanced up at the clock before she turned back to the game. Ten-thirty. It was about Gram's bedtime.

The footsteps that weren't Eddie's were coming toward the door. They stopped outside. There was a heavy knock.

Ma's hand went to her heart. She didn't trust her legs to stand on. She said, "Come in."

A policeman came in and closed the door behind him. Ma saw only that uniform, but she heard Gram's voice:

"It's Dickie Wheeler. How are you, Dickie?"

The policeman smiled briefly at Gram. "Captain Wheeler now, Gram," he said, "but I'm glad it's still Dickie to you."

Then his face changed as he turned to Ma. "Is Eddie here, Mrs. Murdock?"

Ma stood up slowly. "No—he—" But there wasn't any answer she could make that was as important as *knowing*. "Tell me! What?"

"Half hour ago," said Captain Wheeler, "four men held up the Bijou box office, just as it was closing. Squad car was going by, and—well, there was shooting. Two of the men were killed, and a third is dying. The other got away."

"Eddie—"

He shook his head. "We know the three. Butch Everard, Slim Ragoni, a guy named Walters. The fourth one— They were wearing masks. I hoped I'd find Eddie was home. We know he's been running with those men."

Ma stood up. "He was here at ten. He left just a few minutes ago. He—"

Wheeler put a hand on her shoulder. "Don't say that, Ma." He didn't call her Mrs. Murdock now, but neither of them noticed. "The man who got away was wounded, in the arm. If Eddie comes home sound, he won't need any alibi."

"Dickie," Gram said, and the rocker stopped creaking. "Eddie—he's a good boy. After tonight he'll be all right."

Captain Wheeler couldn't meet her eyes. After tonight—well, he hadn't told them quite all of it. One of the squad-car cops had been killed too. The man who got away would burn for that.

But Gram's voice prattled on. "He's just a little boy, Dickie. A little boy lost. You take him down to headquarters and he'll get a scare. Show him the men who were killed. He needs a lesson, Dickie."

Ma looked at her. "Hush, Gram. Don't you see, it's— Why didn't I stop him tonight, somehow?"

"He had a gun in his pocket tonight, Elsie," said Gram. "When he came out of his room I heard it hit the door. And with what you said about Johnny Everard—"

"Gram," said Ma wearily, "go to bed." There wasn't any room left in Ma for anger. "You're just making it worse."

"But, Elsie. Eddie didn't go. I'm trying to tell you. He's in his car, right across the street, right now. He's been there."

Wheeler looked at her sharply. Ma wasn't quite breathing.

Gram nodded. There were tears in her eyes now. "I knew we had to stop him," she said. "Those sleeping powders you have, Elsie. I put four of them in that sulfur 'n' molasses I gave him. I knew they'd work quick, and I watched out the window. He stumbled going across the street, and he got in his car, but he never started it. Go down and get him, Dickie Wheeler, and when you get him awake enough you do like I told you to."

Detective Fiction Weekly, August 2, 1941

Good Night, Good Knight

THE BAR in front of him was wet and sloppy; Sir Charles Hanover Gresham carefully rested his forearms on the raised dry rim of it and held the folded copy of *Stage-craft* that he was reading up out of the puddles. His forearms, not his elbows; when you have but one suit and it is getting threadbare you remember not to rest your elbows on a bar or a table. Just as, when you sit, you always pull up the trouser legs an inch or two to keep the knees from becoming baggy. When you are an actor you remember those things. Even if you're a has-been who never really was and who certainly never will be, living—barely—off blackmail, drinking beer in a Bowery bar, hung over and miserable, at two o'clock on a cool fall afternoon, you remember.

But you always read *Stagecraft*.

He was reading it now. "Gambler Angels Meller," a one-column headline told him; he read even that, casually. Then he came to a name in the second paragraph, the name of the playwright. One of his eyebrows rose a full millimeter at that name. Wayne Campbell, his *patron,* had written another play. The first in three full years. Not that that mattered to Wayne, for his last play and his second last had both sold to Hollywood for very substantial sums. New plays or no, Wayne Campbell would keep on eating caviar and drinking champagne. And new plays or no, he, Sir Charles Hanover Gresham, would keep on eating hamburger sandwiches and drinking beer. It was the only thing he was ashamed of—not the hamburgers and the beer, but the means by which he was forced to obtain them. Blackmail is a nasty word; he hated it.

But now, possibly, just possibly— Even that chance was worth celebrating. He looked at the bar in front of him; fifteen cents lay there. He took his last dollar bill from his pocket and put it down on the one dry spot on the bar.

"Mac!" he said.

Mac, the bartender, who had been gazing into space through the wall, came over. He asked, "The same, Charlie?"

"Not the same, Mac. This time the amber fluid."

"You mean whiskey?"

"I do indeed. One for you and one for me. *Ah, with the Grape my fading life provide. . .*"

Mac poured two shots and refilled Sir Charles's beer glass. "Chaser's on me." He rang up fifty cents.

Sir Charles raised his shot glass and looked past it, not at Mac the bartender but at his own reflection in the smeary back-bar mirror. A quite distinguished-looking gentleman stared back at him. They smiled at one another; then they both looked at Mac, one of them from the front, the other from the back.

"To your excellent health, Mac," they said—Sir Charles aloud and his reflection silently. The raw, cheap whiskey burned a warm and grateful path.

Mac looked over and said, "You're a screwy guy, Charlie, but I like you. Sometimes I think you really *are* a knight. I dunno."

"*A Hair perhaps divides the False and True,*" said Sir Charles. "Do you by any chance know Omar, Mac?"

"Omar who?"

"The tentmaker. A great old boy, Mac; he's got me down to a T. Listen to this:

> *After a momentary silence spake*
> *Some Vessel of a more ungainly Make:*
> *'They sneer at me from leaning all awry:*
> *What! did the Hand then of the Potter shake?'*"

Mac said, "I don't get it."

Sir Charles sighed. "Am I all awry, Mac? Seriously, I'm going to phone and make an important appointment, maybe. Do I look all right or am I leaning all awry? Oh, Lord, Mac, I just thought what that would make me. Hamawry."

"You look all right, Charlie."

"But, Mac, you missed that horrible pun. Ham awry. Ham on rye."

"You mean you want a sandwich?"

Sir Charles smiled gently. He said, "I'll change my mind, Mac; I'm not hungry after all. But perhaps the exchequer will stand another drink."

It stood another drink. Mac went to another customer.

The haze was coming, the gentle haze. The figure in the back-bar mirror smiled at him as though they had a secret in common. And they had, but the drinks were helping them to forget it—at least to shove it to the back of the mind. Now, through the gentle haze that was not really drunkenness, that figure in the mirror did not say, "You're a fraud and a failure, Sir Charles, living on blackmail," as it so often and so accusingly had said. No, now it said, "You're a fine fellow, Sir Charles; a little down on your luck for these last few—let us not say how many—years. Things are going to change. You'll walk the boards; you'll hold audiences in the palm of your hand. You're an *actor*, man."

He downed his second shot to that, and then, sipping his beer slowly, he read again the article in *Stagecraft*, the actor's Bible.

GAMBLER ANGELS MELLER

There wasn't much detail, but there was enough. The name of the melodrama was *The Perfect Crime*, which didn't matter; the author was Wayne Campbell, which did matter. Wayne could try to get him into the cast; Wayne would try. And not because of threat of blackmail; quite the converse.

And, although this didn't matter either, the play was being backed by Nick Corianos. Maybe, come to think of it, that did matter. Nick Corianos was a plunger, a real big shot. *The Perfect Crime* wouldn't lack for funds, not if Nick was backing it. You've heard of Nick Corianos. Legend has it that he once dropped half a million dollars in a single forty-hour session of poker, and laughed about it. Legend says many unpleasant things about him, too, but the police have never proved them.

Sir Charles smiled at the thought—Nick Corianos getting away with *The Perfect Crime*. He wondered if that thought had come to Corianos, if it was part of his reason for backing this particular play. One of life's little pleasures, thinking such things. Posing, posturing, knowing you were ridiculous, knowing you were a cheat and a failure, you lived on the little pleasures—and the big dreams. Still smiling gently, he picked up his change and went to the phone booth at the front of the tavern near the door. He dialed Wayne Campbell's number. He said, "Wayne? This is Charles Gresham."

"Yes?"

"May I see you, at your office?"

"Now listen, Gresham, if it's more money, no. You've got some coming in three days and you agreed, definitely agreed, that if I gave you that amount regularly, you'd—"

"Wayne, it's not money. The opposite, my dear boy. It can save you money."

"How?" He was cold, suspicious.

"You'll be casting for your new play. Oh, I know you don't do the actual casting yourself, but a word from you—a word from you, Wayne, would get me a part. Even, a walk-on, Wayne, anything, and I won't bother you again."

"While the play runs, you mean?"

Sir Charles cleared his throat. He said, regretfully, "Of course, while the play runs. But if it's a play of yours, Wayne, it may run a long time."

"You'd get drunk and get fired before it got out of rehearsal."

"No. I don't drink when I'm working, Wayne. What have you to lose? I won't disgrace you. You know I can act. Don't you?"

"Yes." It was grudging, but it was a yes. "All right—you've got a point if it'll save me money. And it's a cast of fourteen; I suppose I could—"

"I'll be right over, Wayne. And thanks, thanks a lot."

He left the booth and went outside, quickly, into the cool, crisp air, before he'd be tempted to take another drink to celebrate the fact that he would be on the boards again. *Might be,* he corrected himself quickly. Even with help from Wayne Campbell, it was no certainty.

He shivered a little, walking to the subway. He'd have to buy himself a coat out of his next—allowance. It was turning colder; he shivered more as he walked from the subway to Wayne's office. But Wayne's office was warm, if Wayne wasn't. Wayne sat there staring at him.

Finally he said, "You don't look the part, Gresham. Damn it all, you don't look it. And that's funny."

Sir Charles said, "I don't know why it's funny, Wayne. But looking the part means nothing. There is such a thing as makeup, such a thing as acting. A true actor can look any part."

Surprisingly, Wayne was chuckling with amusement.

He said, "You don't know it's funny, Gresham, but it is. I've got two possibilities you can try for. One of them is practically a walk-on; you'd get three short speeches. The other—"

"Yes?"

"It is funny, Gresham. There's a blackmailer in my play. And damn it all, you are one; you've been living off me for five years now."

Sir Charles said, "Very reasonably, Wayne. You must admit my demands are modest, and that I've never increased them."

"You are a very paragon of blackmailers, Gresham. I assure you it's a pleasure—practically. But the cream of the jest would be letting you play the blackmailer in my play so that for the duration of it I wouldn't be paying you blackmail. And it's a fairly strong supporting role; it'd pay you a lot more than you ask from me. But—"

"But what?"

"Damned if you look it. I don't think you'd be convincing, as a blackmailer. You're always so apologetic and ashamed about it—and yes, I know, you wouldn't be doing it if you could earn your eats—and drinks—any other way. But the blackmailer in my play is a fairly hard-boiled mug. Has to be. People wouldn't believe in anybody like you, Gresham."

"Give me a chance at it, Wayne. Let me read the part."

"I think we'd better settle for the smaller role. You said you'd settle for a walk-on, and this other part is a little better than that. You wouldn't be convincing in the fat role. You're just not a heavy, Gresham."

"Let me read it. At least let me read it."

Wayne Campbell shrugged. He pointed to a bound manuscript on a corner of his desk, nearer to Sir Charles than to him. He said, "Okay, the role is Richter. Your biggest scene, your longest and most dramatic speech is about two pages back of the first-act curtain. Go ahead and read it to me."

Sir Charles's fingers trembled just slightly with eagerness as he found the first-act curtain and thumbed back. He said, "Let me read it to myself first, Wayne, to get the sense of it." It was a longish speech, but he read it rapidly twice and he had it; memorizing had always been easy for him. He put down the manuscript and thought an instant to put himself in the mood.

His face grew cold and hard, his eyes hooded. He stood up and leaned his hands on the desk, caught Wayne's eyes with his own, and poured on the speech, his voice cold and precise and deadly.

And it was a balm to his actor's soul that Wayne's eyes widened as he listened to it. He said, "I'll be damned. You *can* act. Okay, I'll try to get you the role. I didn't think you had it in you, but you have. Only if you cross me up by drinking—"

"I won't." Sir Charles sat down; he'd been calm and cold during the speech. Now he was trembling a little again and he didn't want it to show. Wayne might think it was drink or poor health, and not know that it was eagerness and excitement. This might be the start of it, the comeback he'd hoped for—he hated to think how long it had been that he'd been hoping. But one good supporting role, and in a Wayne Campbell play that might have a long run, and he'd be on his way. Producers would notice him and there'd be another and slightly better role when this play folded, and a better one after that.

He knew he was kidding himself, but the excitement, the *hope* was there. It went to his head like stronger drink than any tavern served.

Maybe he'd even have a chance to play again in a Shakespeare revival, and there are always Shakespeare revivals. He knew most of every major Shakespearean role, although he'd played only minor ones. Macbeth, that great speech of Macbeth's—

He said, "I wish you were Shakespeare, Wayne. I wish you were just writing *Macbeth*. Beautiful stuff in there, Wayne. Listen:

> *Tomorrow, and tomorrow, and tomorrow,*
> *Creeps in this petty pace from day to day,*
> *To the last syllable of recorded time;*
> *And all our yesterdays have lighted fools*
> *The way to dusty death. Out, out—"*

"Brief candle, et cetera. Sure, it's beautiful and I wish, too, that I were Shakespeare, Gresham. But I haven't got all day to listen."

Sir Charles sighed and stood up. Macbeth had stood him in good stead; he wasn't trembling any more. He said, "Nobody ever has time to listen. Well, Wayne, thanks tremendously."

"Wait a minute. You sound as though I'm doing the casting and have already signed you. I'm only the first hurdle. We're going to let the director do the actual casting, with Corianos's and my advice and consent, but we haven't hired a director yet. I think it's going to be Dixon, but it isn't a hundred per cent sure yet."

"Shall I go talk to him? I know him slightly."

"Ummm—not till it's definite. If I send you to him, he'll be sure we are hiring him, and maybe he'll want more money. Not that it won't take plenty to get him anyway. But you can talk to Nick; he's putting up the money and he'll have a say in the casting."

"Sure, I'll do that, Wayne."

Wayne reached for his wallet. "Here's twenty bucks," he said. "Straighten out a little; get a shave and a haircut and a clean shirt. Your suit's all right. Maybe you should have it pressed. And listen—"

"Yes?"

"That twenty's no gift. It comes out of your next."

"More than fair. How shall I handle Corianos? Sell him on the idea that I can handle the part, as I did you?"

Wayne Campbell grinned. He said, *"Speak the speech, I pray you, as you have pronounced it to me, trippingly on the tongue; but if you mouth it, as many of your players do, I had as lief the towncrier spoke my lines. Nor do not saw the air—* I can recite Shakespeare, too."

"We'll not mention how." Sir Charles smiled. "Thanks a million, Wayne. Good-bye."

He got the haircut, which he needed, and the shave, which he didn't really need—he'd shaved this morning. He bought a new white shirt and had his shoes shined and his suit pressed. He had his soul lifted with three Manhattans in a respectable bar—three, sipped slowly, and no more. And he ate—the three cherries from the Manhattans.

The back-bar mirror wasn't smeary. It was blue glass, though, and it made him look sinister. He smiled a sinister smile at his reflection. He thought, *Blackmailer. The role; play it to the hilt, throw yourself into it. And someday you'll play Macbeth.*

Should he try it on the bartender? No. He'd tried it on bartenders before.

The blue reflection in the back-bar mirror smiled at him. He looked from it to the front windows and the front windows, too, were faintly blue with dusk. And that meant it was time. Corianos might be in his office above his club by now.

He went out into the blue dusk. He took a cab. Not for practical reasons; it was only ten blocks and he could easily have walked. But, psychologically, a cab was important. As important as was an oversize tip to the driver.

The Blue Flamingo, Nick Corianos' current club, was still closed, of course, but the service entrance was open. Sir Charles went in. One waiter was working, putting cloths on tables. Sir Charles asked, "Will you direct me to Mr. Corianos' office, please?"

"Third floor. There's a self-service elevator over there." He pointed, and, looking again at Sir Charles, he added, "Sir."

"Thank you," said Sir Charles.

He took the elevator to the third floor. It let him off in a dimly lighted corridor, from which opened several doors. Only one door had a light behind it showing through the ground glass. It was marked "Private." He tapped on it gently; a voice called out, "Come in." He went in. Two big men were playing gin rummy across a desk.

One of them asked him, "Yeah?"

"Is either of you Mr. Corianos?"

"What do you want to see him about?"

"My card, sir." Sir Charles handed it to the one who had spoken; he felt sure by looking at them that neither one of them was Nick Corianos. "Will you tell Mr. Corianos that I wish to speak to him about a matter in connection with the play he is backing?"

The man who had spoken looked at the card. He said, "Okay," and put down his hand of cards; he walked to the door of an inner office and through it. After a moment he appeared at the door again; he said, "Okay." Sir Charles went in.

Nick Corianos looked up from the card lying on the ornate mahogany desk before him. He asked, "Is it a gag?"

"Is what a gag?"

"Sit down. Is it a gag, or are you really Sir Charles Hanover Gresham? I mean, are you really a—that would be a knight, wouldn't it? Are you really a knight?"

Sir Charles smiled. "I have never yet admitted, in so many words, that I am not. Would it not be foolish to start now? At any rate, it gets me in to see people much more easily."

Nick Corianos laughed. He said, "I see what you mean. And I'm beginning to guess what you want. You're a ham, aren't you?"

"I am an actor. I have been informed that you are backing a play; in fact, I have seen a script of the play. I am interested in playing the role of Richter."

Nick Corianos frowned. "Richter—that's the name of the blackmailer in the play?"

"It is." Sir Charles held up a hand. "Please do not tell me offhand that I do not look the part. A true actor can look, and can be, anything. I can be a blackmailer."

Nick Corianos said, "Possibly. But I'm not handling the casting."

Sir Charles smiled, and then let the smile fade. He stood up and leaned forward, his hands resting on Nick's mahogany desk. He smiled again, but the smile was different. His voice was cold, precise, perfect. He said, *"Listen, pal, you can't shove me off. I know too much. Maybe I can't prove it myself, but the police can, once I tell them where to look. Walter Donovan. Does that name mean anything to you, pal? Or the date September first? Or a spot a hundred yards off the road to Bridgeport, halfway between Stamford and there. Do you think you can—?"*

"That's enough," Nick said. There was an ugly black automatic in his right hand. His left was pushing a buzzer on his desk.

Sir Charles Hanover Gresham stared at the automatic, and he saw it—not only the automatic, but everything. He saw death, and for just a second there was panic.

And then all the panic was gone, and there was left a vast amusement.

It had been perfect, all down the line. *The Perfect Crime*—advertised as such, and he hadn't guessed it. He hadn't even suspected it.

And yet, he thought, why wouldn't—why shouldn't—Wayne Campbell be tired enough of a blackmailer who had bled him, however mildly, for so many years? And why wouldn't one of the best playwrights in the world be clever enough to do it this way?

So clever, and so simple, however Wayne had come across the information against Nick Corianos which he had written on a special page, especially inserted in his copy of the script. *Speak the speech, I pray you*— And he had even known that he, Charles, wouldn't give him away. Even now, before the trigger was pulled, he could blurt: "Wayne Campbell knows this, too. He did it, not I."

But even to say that now couldn't save him, for that black automatic had turned fiction into fact, and although he might manage Campbell's death along with his own, it wouldn't save his own life. Wayne had even known him well enough to know, to be sure, that he wouldn't do that—at no advantage to himself.

He stood up straight, taking his hands off the desk but carefully keeping them at his sides, as the two big men came through the wide doorway that led to the outer office.

Nick said, "Pete, get that canvas mail sack out of the drawer out there. And is the car in front of the service entrance?"

"Sure, chief." One of the men ducked back through the door.

Nick hadn't taken his eyes—or the cold muzzle of the gun—off Sir Charles.

Sir Charles smiled at him. He said, "May I ask a boon?"

"What?"

"A favor. Besides the one you already intend to do for me. I ask thirty-five seconds."

"Huh?"

"I've timed it; it should take that long. Most actors do it in thirty—they push the pace. I refer, of course, to the immortal lines from *Macbeth*. Have I your permission to die thirty-five seconds from now, rather than right at this exact instant?"

Nick's eyes got even narrower. He said, "I don't get it, but what's thirty-five seconds, if you really keep your hands in sight?"

Sir Charles said, "*Tomorrow, and tomorrow, and tomorrow—*"

One of the big men was back in the doorway, something made of canvas rolled up under his arm. He asked, "Is the guy screwy?"

"Shut up," Nick said.

And then no one was interrupting him. No one was even impatient. And thirty-five seconds were ample.

> "... *Out, out, brief candle!*
> *Life's but a walking shadow, a poor player*
> *That struts and frets his hour upon the stage*
> *And then is heard no more; it is a tale*
> *Told by an idiot, full of sound and fury,*
> *Signifying nothing.*"

He paused, and the quiet pause lengthened.

He bowed slightly and straightened so the audience would know that there was no more. And then Nick's finger tightened on the trigger.

The applause was deafening.

Originally published as "Last Curtain" in New Detective, July 1949

A Matter of Death

THE BUS PULLED into the union depot on Vine Street and the driver called out:

"Dinner stop, folks, half-hour."

I had to step out into the aisle to let the plumbing supplies salesman who'd been sitting next to the window get out. But then I sat back down again.

I'm not hungry, I thought. *I'll sit this one out.* Cincinnati—I hate the town. The town I was never going back to.

Sure and I was back there now, but if I didn't get off the bus it didn't count. I leaned back in the seat and tilted my hat over my eyes.

And everything would have been all right if it hadn't been for that glass of beer I'd had at the last rest stop. If it hadn't been for that one glass of beer, I'd have made it. One glass of beer.

The humor of it didn't strike me until I was on my way back to the bus from the washroom.

You're in Cincinnati, Jack, I told myself. *You got off the bus, so you're in Cincinnati again. And drinking did it. Drink made you leave this town six years ago, and now—solely because of one glass of beer—you're back here again.*

Then don't be so grim about it. It's childish to go back and sit in that bus, like a kid with the sulks. You're twenty-eight now, and you're not a kid anymore.

So I went through the waiting room and stood on the sidewalk of Vine Street, and I was home again.

It looked just the same. It looked like Vine Street always looked at five forty-five in the evening. Some of the stores had different signs on them and there was a haberdashery across the street where the cigar store used to be, but everything in general looked pretty much the same. The same yellow street cars with the same familiar names. Colerain. College Hill. Spring Grove.

I wonder if Charlie's place is still around the corner, I thought. *There's time for a beer.*

It was still there, but Charlie wasn't behind the bar. I asked, and was told he came on about seven o'clock.

That's good, I thought. *Then you won't see him. At seven you'll be an hour's ride to the east. You'll get through here without seeing a soul you know. You won't have to talk to any of them. Let them keep on thinking you're dead, or whatever they do think.*

So I sipped my beer slowly and when I looked up at the clock, it was a quarter after six, and the bus was gone. And I knew then that I'd intended, all along, to stop over for the night.

~§~

I knew that I wanted to see some of the people I didn't want to see at all.

It occurred to me I'd better get myself a hotel room while there were still some open. I walked two blocks north to the Clinton and registered for a two-dollar room.

A little pudgy man in shell-rimmed glasses who was sitting in the lobby looked at me curiously as I walked past him. As though he knew me. But I'd never seen him before. I was pretty sure of that.

It occurred to me as I signed the register that I should have bought a change of linen on my way there, so I could bathe and change. You get pretty dirty riding on a bus, and my suitcase was on its way east ahead of me.

I told them I wouldn't go up to my room just yet, and went out to look for a men's furnishings store that would still be open. As I crossed the lobby I saw the pudgy little man get up and stroll toward the desk. Probably, I thought, he'd mistaken me for someone else and would find out his mistake when he read my name on the register.

I found a store, finally, and bought what I needed. But I'd walked back past Charlie's place searching, and it was seven-fifteen when I started past it again, back toward the Clinton. Charlie would be behind the bar now, so I stopped in. The bath could wait a few minutes.

He was behind the bar and I walked up and stuck out my hand. He looked at me a minute before he took it. Something was wrong with the way he looked at me and something was wrong with the way he shook my hand.

"Hello, Jack," he said.

"Six years, Charlie," I said. "I've been gone six years and you say hello like I'd been gone six hours."

He grinned, but it wasn't a whole-hearted grin. It was—well, it looked wary, cautious.

"Back for good?" he asked, and looked relieved when I said I'd be gone by tomorrow noon.

"Where's all the gang?" I wanted to know.

"In the Army, a lot of them. Most of the rest are around. Some of 'em will be in later. You look—a little not so good, Jack. Still hitting the bottle too hard?"

I laughed. "Hit one too hard this afternoon. That's why I stopped here overnight. If I hadn't—"

A customer down at the other end of the counter rapped a coin on the wood.

"Stick around a minute," Charlie said, and went down to take the order.

Something was wrong. "Stick around a minute," from Charlie. Guys don't change that much in six years.

"*I shouldn't have stopped over,*" I thought. "*I hate this town. I'll always hate it.*"

I'd have got off the stool and walked out, but I didn't want to act childish. I waited until Charlie came back. I asked for a beer and he drew it.

"What's been happening," I asked.

He started to say something, hesitated.

"You know that your father—uh—"

"Died five years ago," I said. "Yes, I heard it. A month too late for me to come back. I was in Mexico then." I thought a minute and then said, "I wish I'd heard it sooner and been closer. I'd have come back, even if it wouldn't have done any good. I mean, he wouldn't have known it. I wish—"

I didn't go on with it, because I didn't want to sound mushy. What I really wished was that I'd come back during that first year, before Dad had died, and squared myself with him. He'd been pretty much right in kicking me out. I'd been a pretty dissolute young pup.

But it was too late to think about that now.

"Your uncle, Ray Stillwell," Charlie said. "You heard he's married?"

I shook my head.

"Three years ago."

Good, I thought. *Uncle Ray's a good guy. I hope he got the right woman.*

Charlie must have been a mind reader.

"Crazy about her," he said. "A society gal, but not one of the stuck-up ones. They drop in once in a long while. They get along."

"Good," I said.

There was a silence. I hadn't asked the question I wanted to ask. I mean, about Margie.

Six years is a long time. But I found out then how badly I wanted to know.

"Charlie," I said, "have you seen—"

And then the guy at the other end of the bar rapped his coin again. I didn't want a quick yes-or-no answer so I said:

"Go ahead, Charlie. I'll ask when you get back."

I sipped at my beer. Six years is a long time. *You shouldn't ask,* I thought. *You've forgotten. You've got over it. Let it go. You don't really want to know.*

I heard the outer door opening and turned around.

It would have been the devil of a coincidence—if it had been a coincidence.

She came in with a fellow who looked familiar to me, but it took me a few seconds to place him. His name was Gerald Breese and he was a clerk in the law office of John Garry, who had been my Dad's attorney.

But I hardly noticed him. I was looking at Margie Delaney.

Six years wasn't so long. At first I thought she looked just the same, and then I saw that there were changes, and that they were all for the better. She was more beautiful, more poised and mature. She wasn't a pretty girl—she was a beautiful woman now.

"Margie," I said, and she turned and saw me. Her eyes went wide and there was a sudden flush of color in her face.

She opened her mouth to speak, and then Breese had stepped in between us. He said something to Margie that I couldn't hear, but his voice sounded urgent, insistent. Margie hesitated, then she turned and walked out.

Walked out without having spoken to me at all.

Gerald Breese turned, then, to me and cursed me. Quietly. No one else in the place could have heard him.

I think that if he'd said anything even less than that, I'd have killed him. His stepping in between Margie and me had been enough.

But that was too much. For some reason, instead of intensifying the sudden red mist of anger, it drove it away. It left me sitting there not angry at all, but cold and hard and curious.

Something, I knew, was more than met the eye. Charlie hadn't been cordial, exactly. Margie had cut me. And now this bozo whom I barely remembered...

I let go of my glass of beer on the bar and put my hands in my pockets. *They'd be safer there,* I thought.

Breese's face went pale and he stepped back quickly. It took me a second to realize he had thought I was going for a gun.

That tore it. I laughed, and turned away from him, back to the bar. He stood there a minute—I could see him in the mirror—then turned and went out.

Charlie came back.

"You were going to ask—" he said.

"Never mind," I told him.

He had been busy down at the other end and maybe he hadn't seen what happened.

"You don't look so good, Jack," he said. "Maybe you've had too much already. Shall I fix you a mountain oyster?"

And then again, maybe he had seen what happened. A bartender generally glances toward the door when it opens, even if he's mixing a drink.

Anyway, I realized suddenly that I wasn't enjoying Charlie's place, or his company. I told him I didn't want the mountain oyster and I got up and walked out.

I should have waited a little longer. Margie and Breese were talking just outside. Margie looked angry and so did Breese. I turned the other way so I wouldn't have to go past them, and I walked rapidly.

It was dark now.

I found myself looking into the window of a novelty shop on Fountain Square. It was full of bright practical jokes to play on people. Artificial bugs. Exploding matches. A cushion that *miaouwed* when sat upon.

I hate this town, I thought.

I should have stayed on the bus. I shouldn't have stopped over. I should never have drunk that glass of beer, which was the cause of my getting off the bus.

~§~

I walked back to the Clinton. I said "Six-fourteen" to the clerk behind the desk. He turned and started to reach for the key. Then he turned back.

"Oh, six-fourteen," he said. "You're Mr. Trent. A friend of yours has been waiting for you to return and he borrowed the key so he could wait in your room. Mr. Zimmerman."

"Lovely," I said. "Who is Mr. Zimmerman?"

He looked surprised. "You mean you don't know him? But he said it would be all right and showed me his card. And I knew you hadn't been up to your room as yet and could have left nothing there, and—uh—I'm sorry if I shouldn't have let him up."

"What did the card he showed you say, besides Zimmerman?"

"Cincinnati *Herald.* Uh—I think the first name was Walter. Yes, Walter Zimmerman, Cincinnati *Herald.* But—uh—from the way he spoke, I gathered that he was a friend of yours, not that he wanted to see you as a reporter."

I had to laugh at that. You don't expect naiveté in a hotel clerk. But this one looked pretty young. He'd probably been at the job all of a week or two.

I told him it was all right, and I rode the elevator up to the sixth floor.

The hallways at the Clinton are well-carpeted. I had no reason for trying to walk silently, but my footsteps along the corridor didn't make much noise.

Because, just as I reached out my hand for the knob of Six-fourteen, I heard a voice say:

"Lajoie?"

Were there two men in my room?

"Zimmerman calling, Lajoie," the voice went on, and I realized then that he was talking over the phone. Not loudly, but the transom was wide open and I could hear distinctly. I stood there without moving.

"Yeah, I'm onto something that may be big, but I want you to know where I am, just in case. . . No, I don't know in case what. Maybe in case the guy throws me out the window when he finds out what I've got on him . . . Yeah, Jack Trent. Took Room Six-fourteen at the Clinton and I'm waiting for him. Yeah, in his room. Look up the morgue on him and have it ready. Yeah, might be a big story. I can't tell till I talk to him. Jerry says he's a killer, and. . . No, don't send cops over. He's not wanted that I know of. . . Sure, you might check with Headquarters. Just say you heard a rumor he's back in town, but don't tip our hand. I want an exclusive. . . No, I won't take any chances. I'll just ask him why he—"

The clang and rattle of the elevator door drowned out the rest of that sentence and two elderly women got off the elevator and turned down the corridor toward me.

I couldn't just stand there listening. I had to go on into the room or move on, quick.

I moved on. I didn't want to go in till I'd had time to sort out in my mind what I'd just heard. Zimmerman was waiting for me and wouldn't run off.

So I walked on. Toward, I realized, the blank end of the corridor. But a door at my right said "Shower" and I turned in there.

I bolted the door and leaned against it to think.

Not that it did any good. Something was rotten in the State of Ohio—that far I could get, but no farther.

It just didn't make sense. Five minutes later it still didn't and I realized that I might just as well have gone into Six-fourteen right away instead of stalling.

So I went out into the hall and down to Six-fourteen and this time I opened the door and walked in.

The room was empty.

The light was on and the key was inside the door, but the room was empty.

Lovely, I thought. *He's maybe hiding in the closet to surprise me. After telling the clerk he'd be waiting here and leaving the light on, the key in the door, he wants to surprise me.*

Sure it was a screwy thought, but everything that had happened since I got off the bus had been screwy.

I went over and opened the closet door, and I was right, dead right.

He surprised me.

He surprised me by falling out of the closet with a thud that seemed to shake the whole hotel. He was as dead as a salted mackerel, and he hadn't got into that closet and died of heart failure waiting for me. There was blood matted in his hair. That meant he hadn't committed suicide, either, because suicides don't generally hit themselves over the head.

He had been murdered.

I sat down on the bed for a moment, and then I got up and rolled him over for a better look.

He didn't look any better rolled over.

~§~

It was the pudgy little man who had looked at me curiously when I'd walked through the lobby an hour or two ago to register. He still wore the shell-rimmed glasses and neither being murdered nor falling out of a closet had knocked them off.

I took his wallet out of his pocket and looked at the cards in it. A press pass made out to Walter B. Zimmerman, Cincinnati *Herald.* Other identification to match, and twenty-two dollars in bills. I put the wallet back in his pocket.

Lovely, I thought. *Oh, lovely.*

Because it wasn't just finding a corpse in my room. It was an airtight frame for murder. Motive—Lajoie would prove a motive after that phone call he had just heard from Zimmerman, who had said he was waiting for me and "had something" on me.

Had Zimmerman actually made that phone call and then been murdered? Or had he been dead then, and had I stood outside my own door listening, to the murderer frame me? Well, the frame was just as tight in either case.

I got up and walked to the window and stood looking out, thinking.

The hotel clerk's evidence. Lajoie's evidence. Oh, it was beautiful. Perfect.

I could call the police right now, wait for them to come, and go to jail with them when they left, to await my trial.

Or I could blow town.

Or I could get myself in deeper.

I decided to get myself in deeper. I turned out the light and left my room.

I tossed my key on the desk and scowled at the clerk. "Nobody was in my room," I told the clerk, "but the key was in the door. Fine system. Did you see him go by the desk on his way out?"

"Why no, but. . . Well, I might not have noticed him if I'd been talking to another guest or. . . I was back in the washroom once for a few minutes, but—"

"Haven't been in the hotel business long, have you, sonny?"

"N-no. But I wouldn't have given him your key, Mr. Trent, if you'd been up to your room at all or had a chance to leave any of your property there. But as you hadn't, I thought—"

"Okay," I said. "No harm done, but don't do it again?"

I left him slightly flustered and apologetic, which was what I wanted to accomplish. If I'd walked out alone, without bawling him out, he might have started wondering what had happened to my guest, and might have sent a bellboy up to investigate. But now I'd spiked his guns and given him something else to worry about. I'd given myself time before the body would be found.

And, of course, tightened the noose around my own neck.

I went over to Central Avenue, where the hock shops grow. I bought myself a pistol. I didn't know yet what I was going to do with it, but its weight in my pocket was slightly comforting.

I went to the *Herald* office, and leaned against the information desk to talk to the little blonde who turned around from the switchboard to ask what she could do for me.

"Zimmerman in?" I asked.

She shook her head. "Day shift."

"Doesn't he ever drop in evenings?"

"He'd have come by here. I'd have seen him."

"Oh," I said. "Then you know him by sight. I'm not quite sure he's the guy I want anyway. Is he about five feet five, sort of pudgy, wears shell-rimmed glasses, black hair?"

"That's him, yes. Anyone else you'd want to talk to?"

"Who's in charge of the editorial room flow?"

"Mr. Lajoie. Night city editor."

"N-no," I said. "That isn't the name. Who's city ed, days?"

"Mr. Monahan."

"That's the guy. I remember now. Well, I'll drop in tomorrow and see either him or Zimmerman. Thanks, sister."

Not so good, I thought. *If the corpse in my room had been a phony, it might have been something to work on. But he was a bona fide newshawk, and Lajoie was a real person, too. A city editor, whose testimony would do me no good.*

Maybe, I thought, *I should kill Lajoie. And the hotel clerk. And the elevator operator. And dump the corpse out the window and let the police guess which floor it came from.*

And burn down the hotel so my name wouldn't be on the register.

And failing that, I thought, *maybe the next best thing would be to see Charlie again. And this time make him open up as to what made the cool breeze across the bar.*

I headed for Charlie's place. I just might get something to start on.

~§~

I wasn't expecting anything pleasant, and that's where I got fooled again. The minute I stepped in the door.

Margie Delaney, sitting alone in a booth, had been watching the door. She came up to me.

"Jack," she said, "I'm sorry. I didn't mean to be rude. I—"

"It's all right, Margie," I said. "Let's sit down."

I led her back to the booth and sat across from her. There weren't many people in the place and the booths on either side were empty, so it would be a good place to talk.

"Gerald told me to go outside and wait—that it was important," she said. "I thought he was going to bring you out with him. Then he came out alone and—we quarreled. I left him and came back in to see you, but you were gone. I waited here, hoping you'd come back. I didn't know any other way to find you."

"And I did come back," I said. "So everything's all right."

"Everything's all right," she said. Her hand, on the table, moved nearer, and I put mine over it.

Everything's all right, I thought. *Everything except a little matter of a murder rap.*

"I came back here," I said aloud, "to ask Charlie some questions. But maybe I won't have to. Maybe you know the answers. What happened here since I left?"

"Why, what do you mean?"

"I mean that when I came in here tonight I didn't get a rousing welcome, even from Charlie. And your friend Breese—he wasn't exactly enthusiastic about renewing our slight acquaintance. Has somebody been telling tales out of school about me since I've been gone? Or what?"

Her eyes dropped. She didn't pull her hand back, but I took mine off it. I didn't want any sentiment mixed in with this. I wanted it cold.

"Weren't you arrested for killing a man in New Orleans two years ago?"

"Go on," I said.

"And released for lack of evidence? And there was a man here who said he knew you in El Paso, and. . . Well, were the things he said about you true?"

"Such as?"

"That you were a puller-in, whatever that is, for a gambling place there and—and had other jobs like that, but couldn't hold them because you were drinking too heavily again. And. . . Oh, other stories of that sort."

"Where did you meet this gentleman from El Paso?" I asked.

"In here, one night. I stopped in alone on my way home from working late, and he was talking to Charlie. I heard most of what he said."

"Had he been to New Orleans, too?"

"No, that was in the newspaper. It—it wasn't a big story, but somebody showed it in here. A little reporter from the *Herald* showed it to Charlie and asked if it was the Jack Trent who used to come here. Of course, it might not have been."

"Jack Trent's a common name," I said. "Was the reporter named Zimmerman?"

"I believe that was his name. Charlie said it must be some other

Jack Trent. But then when the man from El Paso—"

"I see," I said. "Anything else?"

"It seems trivial beside the other things, but you didn't come back when your father was dying. His attorney, Mr. Garry, wrote you three weeks before your father actually died. He had an address then in El Paso, and the letter never came back, so you must have got it. Or did you?"

"I got it," I told her.

~§~

Margie and I were silent a moment. She hadn't moved her hand, and I put mine back upon it.

"I got the letter," I said, "three weeks too late. I was working for a mining company deep in Mexico then, and our mail came in by burro, once a month. In the same mail was a newspaper three weeks old, with an account of Dad's death."

Her hand turned, under mine, palm upward and her fingers gripped mine.

"I knew it must have been something like that," she said.

"I had a good job with the mining company," I went on. "I stayed there until the radio got excited one Sunday in December. Took me two weeks to get back and enlist. I was in Australia when some guy named Jack Trent got in trouble in New Orleans. And I was on Makin Island about the time the gentleman from El Paso was here in Cincinnati. I got a medical discharge a month ago and was heading—"

"Jack, were you wounded?"

"Only by a mosquito. I'll be completely okay in six months or so, and I'm going to reenlist then if they'll take me back. That is, if it looks then like they'll still need me."

"Jack, I'm so glad! Then *none* of it was true! I don't understand about the man from El Paso. You've explained about the letter Mr. Garry sent, and it must have been another Jack Trent in New Orleans, but this man from El Paso said it was *you*. Charlie showed him that snapshot of you and him the time the two of you went hunting up on the Little Miami River and he said yes that was the Trent he'd known in El Paso. It must have been a deliberate lie. But why?"

"I don't know," I told her.

"But. . . oh, it doesn't matter now. You're back, and everything's all right."

Her hand tightened on mine. And that reminded me. Everything was not all right. There was the little matter of a murder.

"Margie, listen—" I said.

And then I realized I couldn't tell her. Not without making her an accessory after the fact, if the case against me held.

"Wait a minute, Margie," I said, and went to the telephone booth back at the end of the room.

I couldn't remember the first name of Garry, the lawyer who had handled my father's affairs, but I remembered he lived in Walnut Hills and found his phone number.

I called it, and he was home. I told him who I was, then asked:

"How much of an estate did my father leave?"

"It'll be about eighty thousand, after all fees and taxes."

"Will be?" I said. "Why the future tense? Mean it hasn't been settled yet?"

"No. I've been trying to get in touch with you, Trent. It's rather a complicated situation."

"He disinherited me, didn't he? I understood Uncle Ray was to get the estate."

"Well—yes and no. Where are you calling from?"

I told him.

"Can you come out here to my place this evening?" he wanted to know.

I hesitated. "Maybe. But can't you tell me, roughly anyway, what it's all about? Now, over the phone."

"Well—"

"Look, then," I said. "Can you possibly grab a taxi and come down here? Someone's with me, and I'd rather not leave now."

"All right. I'll be down in twenty minutes."

I stepped out of the phone booth, and the first thing I noticed was that the other customers besides myself and Margie—there had been three or four of them—were gone.

Charlie was just closing the outer door. He walked back to me and stuck out his hand.

"Margie just told me, Jack," he said. "Forgive me?"

"Sure." I shook his hand and almost got the bones of mine crushed. Charlie has a grip.

"Jack, I should have known those stories were phonies. I don't know why I gave them a thought."

"Skip it," I told them. "I don't blame you."

"Look," he said. "The place is yours tonight. I shooed out the riff-raff, and the drinks are all on the house for you and everybody you want to invite down. It's a welcome-home party for the rest of the night."

Somehow, *now*, in the jam that I was in, that hurt worse than the cold shoulder I'd got from everybody earlier in the evening.

"Thanks, Charlie," I said. "Thanks a thundering lot, but I'm afraid it's not my night to howl."

"What do you mean?"

I saw I had to tell at least part of it.

"Come on and sit down," I said.

I sat next to Margie and Charlie sat across from us. And I talked, wording it as carefully as I could. When I'd finished, they knew what the score was, but they didn't know anything specific enough to make them accessories.

"You should have called a copper, Jack, the minute you found him," Charlie said. "You'd've been cleared."

"Would I? Don't forget that call he—or the guy who killed him—made to Lajoie at the *Herald.*"

"It would have looked black. But you made it look blacker. Gosh, what a mess!"

There was a minute's silence, then Margie said:

"That man who said he was from El Paso, Jack. He might be a lead."

"I never saw him before or after," Charlie said. "But lemme describe him to you."

"Let me try," I said. "Middle-aged and just beginning to show it, but he'd been good-looking once. Wore good clothes, well-kept, but a long way from new. Maybe even a patch or two, but his shoes were shined and he was freshly shaved. Looked and talked more like New York than El Paso. Good voice, but slightly overdramatized everything he said."

"You know him, then?" Charlie cut in.

I shook my head. "Guessing. Giving you a sketch of an actor out of work. The kind of out-of-work actor who'd slipped just far enough he could be hired to pull a con like that. For twenty bucks."

Charlie nodded slowly, "Now I think of it, he probably was an actor. Listen, Lajoie was here that night."

"He comes here?"

"Sure. He and Zimmerman. And your—"

Somebody tried the doorknob, then rapped on the glass. Charlie went to the door and it was Garry, the lawyer, so he opened up and then locked the door again when Garry had come in.

I sat him down with the rest of us.

"I—I really shouldn't give you this information for six more days, Trent," he said. "But six days isn't much out of five years and such minor matters were left to my discretion as executor. In fact, your father told me that—"

I'd glanced at the calendar the minute he mentioned six days and I interrupted.

"You mean, Mr. Garry, that in six days Dad will have been dead exactly five years?"

"Yes. As you know, he made a will completely disinheriting you. But after you'd left, he made another will. It provided that, after specific bequests, the bulk of his estate was to go into a trust fund for five years. At the end of five years, you were to receive it, under certain conditions. The conditions were that you had—ah—shall we say, reformed?—ah—found yourself, overcome your youthful wayward tendencies and—ah—"

"And what?" I demanded.

He coughed deprecatingly. "And kept out of jail. Your father felt it deeply that time seven years ago when you were arrested for disorderly conduct and for resisting an officer. About that point the will is specific and incontestable. If you have been in jail, on any charge, you forfeit the inheritance. Ah—have you been?"

I shook my head.

I was beginning to see light, although I didn't yet see where it came from.

"I haven't been," I said. "But there are six days to go?"

"Yes, six days. And of course, if you are wanted by police authorities anywhere—or, to be technical, if you are wanted six days from now, you would also forfeit the inheritance. But that, of course, is unimportant."

"Of course," I agreed.

"Because certainly, now that you know the conditions of the will, you will take no chances for the short time remaining. But—ah—you can prove your whereabouts during the time you have been gone? Of course, it will be my duty, as executor, to check up. There have been rumors which have led me to believe, until now, that the check-up would be superfluous, that if we *did* find you, you would not even claim the estate under the will."

"Ask him the sixty-four-dollar question, Jack." Charlie said. I realized then that I'd been stalling on doing just that.

"Who inherits if I do go to jail?" I asked.

"Your uncle, Mr. Stillwell."

"The devil you say," said Charlie, and saved me saying it.

The light had gone out, the light I'd begun to see when I heard the terms of that will. Because Uncle Ray was a swell guy. He couldn't want money badly enough to frame a murder charge on me to get it. Let alone commit a murder himself to do it.

Not that Ray Stillwell didn't have his wild moments. But murder wasn't in him.

Charlie stood up. "Just the same," he said, "I'm going to get him down here. Might as well make it a party"

I didn't object and Charlie went back to the phone booth. He came back and said:

"He was working late at his office. Union Trust Building. He'll be here in a few minutes. He's blame glad to know you're back."

And Uncle Ray was glad. I could tell that by the way he shook hands when he came in a few minutes later. But he looked different. He had aged plenty in the six years since I'd last seen him. There were lines in his face that hadn't been there before, and crows-feet of worry around his eyes. He wasn't dapper any more, either.

There was something wrong, but not in the way he greeted me.

Charlie had gone over behind the bar. Now he came back with a freshly opened bottle of White Horse, some soda and a tray of glasses, and put them on the table.

It should have been a party, but it was a wake.

I could tell by Garry's manner and Uncle Ray's that they could feel something was wrong.

There wasn't any use holding out, but I didn't want to have to do the telling. And I wanted, suddenly some fresh air and to be alone for just a minute.

"Charlie, tell them," I said, "I'll be back in a minute."

I went to the front door and stepped outside, throwing the catch so I could get in again. I stood there a minute and then I turned and looked through the glass at the four of them, inside. Charlie talking. Margie. Uncle Ray Garry.

"They're swell people," I thought.

Why did I hate this town, just because I made a fool of myself here once, a long time ago when I wasn't much more than a kid? They were real people, and so were all the other friends I had here. It was I who was wrong, not the town.

Does one always find out things too late, I wondered.

And then it was Margie alone I was looking at, and I realized that there again was something I'd found out maybe too late.

I didn't want to go in again until I saw Charlie was through talking, and I turned around to face the street again, leaning back against the door.

All right, I told myself, *you were so smart, and now what? You were going to clear yourself. You still haven't the faintest idea who killed Zimmerman.*

The sudden squeal of hastily-applied brakes made me look up. A car had stopped suddenly in the middle of the Street. There was a big man in it. I thought I recognized him but I wasn't sure.

He swung the car into the curb, got out and came back, walking fast until he saw that I wasn't moving, then he slowed down. Yes, it was Moran. He had been a beat copper six years ago. Now he was out of harness, but he was still a cop. You could tell that just by looking at him.

"Hello, Moran," I said. "They find Zimmerman?"

He nodded. "There's a pick-up order out for you. Sorry Jack, but I'll have to take you in."

"I'll go," I told him. "I'll go, but I didn't do it. I didn't kill him."

"I wouldn't know about that," he said. "But I hope you're right. I wasn't on the case. I don't know what they've got on you."

"Plenty," I told him. I tried to laugh, but it didn't quite jell. "The only hope I see is that there may be too much," I said. "Look, I've got friends inside here. I'll have to tell 'em I'm going."

~§~

When I walked back through the door, Moran came right behind me. There was a dead silence from the group in Charlie's.

A wake, I thought. *It's really like a wake.*

I tried to speak lightly. "A little matter has come up. I'm going down to Headquarters with Moran. Be gone only a few minutes."

It didn't go over.

"Sure, Jack," Charlie said. He came over and put his hand on Moran's arm. "Listen, Irish," he said, "I want to talk to you. Come on over by the bar."

"Won't do any good, Charlie," I told him. "Moran's not on the case—don't know anything about it except the pick-up order."

"Just the same," said Charlie, "I want at least one copper to have your side of it. Won't hurt you to have a friend down there."

"I'm already Jack's friend," Moran said. "But I gotta take him in."

Charlie propelled him to the bar. "Then we'll have a drink on that, and you'll listen. He won't run away and there's no hurry."

I was almost sorry Charlie had done that. Now I'd have to face the others again. I didn't want to look at Margie. So instead I turned to Garry, the lawyer.

"May I ask you a question, sir?"

"Of course, my boy."

"Who, besides my uncle, would benefit by my going to jail? Benefit financially, I mean."

"Why, no one."

"Not even you?"

"Not even me." He smiled wryly. "In fact, I'd probably be better off the other way, a little. For if you should inherit, I could at least hope you'd let me continue management of the estate. Your uncle's a lawyer and a C.P.A. himself. He won't need me. And for the same reason—"

"Yes," I prompted.

"That's on the assumption, which happens to be truth, that I've managed the estate honestly. If I hadn't, my motive for wanting you to inherit would be even stronger. You can see that."

"Sure," I said glumly, "I can see that." Obviously, he could fool me to cover up any irregularities, a thousand times easier than my uncle.

A blank wall. Nothing but blank walls.

I strolled over to the bar, wishing Charlie and Moran would hurry up and get it over with. Then I thought of something I'd wanted to ask Charlie.

"Charlie," I said, "who—besides this Lajoie—might Zimmerman have called to tell I was in town? He must have called someone *before* he called Lajoie. Someone had to know he was there waiting for me, in order to go there and kill him."

Charlie shrugged. "Dunno. Jerry, maybe. Zimmerman and Lajoie and Jerry hung out together a lot and were all pretty close. And he knew Jerry knew you and might have phoned him to tell him you were back."

Jerry! That phone call I'd overheard. I'd forgotten. "Jerry says he's a killer."

"Who the devil is Jerry?" I asked.

"Why, you know him. Gerald Breese."

Gerald Breese, I thought. *Gerald Breese! The guy who had cursed me at thirty-two minutes after seven o'clock. Who had come in here with Margie, maybe because he's heard from Zimmerman I was in town, and knew where to find me.*

But there wasn't any motive, *any* reason!

Then I turned around again and saw my uncle's face. It was dead-white and had that shocked look I'd seen on the faces of men who have been hit by a bullet in a vital spot, whose minds know they're dead before their bodies find it out.

I saw that he knew the answer now, and that gave it to me.

It was an answer I didn't want, because it meant that to make a case against Gerald Breese, Uncle Ray would have to be ruined, somehow. Uncle Ray, recently married to a woman he loved deeply and who loved him.

"Jack," he was saying in a curiously flat voice, "I'd better tell you that—"

"Shut up," I said.

I whirled back to Moran. "Listen, Irish," I said, "I know who killed

Zimmerman. Breese did. I know why, and how. But it would be the devil and all to prove."

"So?" Moran said. "Well, give us the dope and we'll try. I'll try. But first I got to take you down to Headquarters."

"No," I said. "You'll never prove it, then. Neither can I, after tonight. But you let me talk to Breese now, right now, while the iron is hot and. . . Well, if it doesn't work, then we go down to the station and that's that."

"But, man, I can't wait," Moran said.

Charlie put a hand on his shoulder. "Listen, Irish—" he said.

"All right, all right," Moran said. "But I got to go along." I nodded. "Just so he doesn't know you're along. He's got to think I'm alone."

"Why?"

"It's bluff, all bluff. Maybe it's a wild idea, but I think I may put it over. Come on! What are we waiting for?"

And then we were getting into Moran's car. Charlie and Margie and Uncle Ray were getting into the back seat, over my protests and Moran's.

"Shut up," Charlie said, slamming the back door of the sedan. "This is a party, ain't it? You can't kick us out yet."

Charlie directed us to the apartment building where Breese lived.

"First floor back," he said. "And there's a light on. He's there."

"Good," I said. "The ground floor's a break. Moran, you got skeleton keys?"

"Sure, but I don't know about using them."

"I'll go in the front way, back the hall to his door and knock. He'll let me in. You go to the back, take off your shoes and let yourself in the back way. Just come to the door of the front room, and listen."

"Me go around to the back? How do I know you won't lam?"

"You don't," I said.

"All right, all right. I'm a sucker."

I got out of the car and went into the front door of the apartment building. I took my time walking the length of the hallway, to think out just what I was going to say, and to give Moran time to get around to the back.

I knocked on the door.

It started to open, and I lunged through it. With my left hand I shoved Gerald Breese back across the room, and with my right I yanked out the gun I'd bought on Central Avenue and aimed it at him. I kicked the door shut behind me.

"I'm going to kill you, Breese," I said.

I heard a faint noise from the back of the apartment and knew Moran was coming in. Breese didn't hear it. All his attention was on me and the gun aimed at the middle button of his shirt.

I tried my best to look desperate and kill-crazy. From the way Breese stared back at me across the room, it went over. He was scared stiff. He licked his lips.

"Trent, what's the idea?" he said. "I'm sorry I said what I did to you in Charlie's, but. . . Lord, that's nothing to kill a man for, if he'll apologize."

"The devil with that," I said. "I'm talking about framing me for Zimmerman's murder."

"You're crazy! I mean, why would I do that?"

"For money," I said. "You've been blackmailing my uncle. You've got something on him. I don't know what, and don't want to know. But you've not only been bleeding him, you've figured to cash in big when he inherited that estate.

"And you meant to see he got it. You planted rumors about me, even hired an actor to spread them. But tonight when I checked in at the Clinton your reporter pal happened to be in the lobby and recognized me. He knew you worked for the firm that handled Dad's estate and phoned you the news. That's why you pulled that stunt at Charlie's."

He licked his lips again. "I don't see why I'd do that."

"It was a first feeble attempt. You got Margie and brought her around to Charlie's, and used her and then that clever little remark of yours to try to get me to attack you. You wanted me to go to jail on an assault charge before I could find out what it was all about," I laughed. "If it hadn't been so blasted obvious you *wanted* me to slug you, I would have. You overplayed. And the whole stunt was childish.

"You saw me start off away from the Clinton, so you went there, with a better idea. You knew, from Zimmerman's call, he'd be waiting in my room. Bump him off there, and let me take a real rap. I don't know whether you got him, at the point of a gun, to make that call to Lajoie and then killed him, or whether you killed him first and made that call yourself impersonating him. I don't give a hoot which it was."

"That's silly, Trent. Curse it, you can't—"

"Can't prove it? No. I know I can't. I'm framed tight. That's why I'm going to make this a little personal matter. I'm going to lam, but first, I'm cashing you in."

I clamped my lips tight, like a man who's through talking. I raised the gun higher and sighted along the barrel. He was looking right into the muzzle. I started to tense my finger on the trigger.

"Wait!"

He almost yelled it. He was chalky white now. He had his hand out in front of him as if to ward off the bullet.

"Wait," he yelled. "Don't! Listen!" His voice was hoarse with fear. "I'll cut you in. Don't shoot me, and I'll make it worth your while. Ten thousand—"

"Nuts," I said. "I should wait around for it? Do I look as crazy as that?"

"I've got it! I've got ten thousand, out of what I've already got from your uncle. It's all the cash I got, but now I can get more. Look, you said yourself the frame is air-tight, so you've got to lam out anyway. But with ten grand you could go a long way."

I let the gun waver just a little.

"Okay, but first," I said, and took a step toward him. The toe of my shoe caught the edge of the rug and I fell like a ton of bricks.

The pistol flew out of my hand and slid across the rug, right to his feet. He stooped to pick it up.

He was straightening up with it in his hand when Moran yelled from the doorway:

"Hey, drop that!"

Breese whirled around. He must have realized, in that second, how he had been trapped. He must have been desperate. Because he whirled with the gun pointing toward Moran and his finger was tightening on the trigger when Moran's Police Positive cut him down.

I got up slowly. I felt weak.

Moran, his shoes in one hand and the pistol still in the other, was glaring at me. Coming up behind him, as though they'd been in the room but farther from the doorway, were Charlie and Margie and my uncle.

"You fool!" Moran said. "You didn't tell me you had a gun."

"You didn't ask," I reminded him.

"And then you practically throw it at him! Of all the dumb—"

"Dumb, your grandmother," I said. "That was beautifully timed and executed. I fell on purpose. Don't you see?"

"See what?"

"I had to play it that way, so you'd have to shoot him to take him. Otherwise, at a trial, he'd have spilled whatever he had on Uncle Ray. If I'd've killed him, it would have been murder, but if you shot him for resisting arrest that was something else again."

Moran looked stunned. "But, you dope," he said, "what if I hadn't been quick enough on my draw? What if he'd shot first?"

I grinned at him. "The gun not only didn't have bullets, but there wasn't even a firing pin. That's the only reason the guy on Central Avenue would sell it to me without a permit."

"So you made a sap outa me, then, just to put your trick over."

Charlie put a hand on Moran's shoulder.

"Listen, Irish—" he said.

Moran started to laugh, and I knew everything was all right.

More than all right, for I saw the look that was on my uncle's face.

And the look on Margie's.

Everything was going to be better than all right.

Thrilling Detective, November 1944

Get Out of Town

IT WAS A DULL EVENING, but even so there were quite a few people in my place, mostly regulars. I was alone behind the bar. I had told George, my bartender, to go home and catch himself some sleep. I knew me and Mary could handle it all right. Mary to wait on the table trade and me for the bar.

There was one party there I didn't like, but I couldn't do anything about it. "King" Costello with his latest pickup from the Gayety chorus, him and "Chub" Moberly and Moberly's moll at the table back in the corner. The molls were all diked out, and maybe Costello thought he was, too, in his plus-fours like he wanted everybody to know he knew what a golf stick was.

So I was mixing a sidecar for somebody and Mary was back kidding with some printers just off the lobster shift at the *Herald,* and, like I said, it was a dull evening.

That was when this guy Barry walked in.

I didn't know that was his name then, of course. I looked him over when he pushed in the door, just like I look over anybody comes in my place. And with him I didn't know much more after I'd looked than before. He might have been anywhere between twenty and thirty-five for all you could tell.

He was tall and thin and his hair was dark and rumpled. He didn't wear a hat. His clothes was good quality but not pressed lately and he could have used a shave, though he didn't need one real bad. He had one of these heavy blue-black beards that makes a guy's face look bluish around the jowls even when he's shaved to the quick. And his face was what I've heard people who sling fancy words call saturnine.

He came up to the bar and asked for a short beer and I gave it to him. "This one's on the house," he said.

I thought he was kidding around like a lot of guys do and he would throw down a dime sooner or later. So I didn't say nothing, and he nursed the beer along and looked about him a bit. He never did pay for that beer, come to think about it.

When he got to the bottom of the glass, he turned back to me and grinned.

"Someone told me your ivory pounder quit last night," he said.

I nodded. "Got himself a job with an orchestra. We'll get another one." Then I happened to notice his hands, and I asked, "You play?"

"Some people think so and some don't," he told me.

He put down his glass and turned around and walked across to where the piano is. He sat down on the stool and ran one hand along the length of the keyboard in a long arpeggio. He was good; just from the way he ran that chord you could tell.

He turned around on the stool and said, "It's in tune," like he hadn't expected it would be.

"Once a month it gets it," I told him. "I'm finicky that way."

He swiveled back to the ivories and, just with his left hand, began to tickle the basses. Not playing anything but chords and stuff, but they were chords that weren't in the books, mostly. But, brother, they *were* chords. He took a cigarette out of his pocket with his free hand, got it lighted without stopping, and then he put it down on the ledge and reached in with his right hand, too.

Joe Rogers down at the end of the bar called out to me for another shot. "In a minute," I said. "Shut up."

And I stood there listening until the lightning quit playing across the keyboard and there was a lull in the storm.

Then, after I gave Joe his drink, I poured another shot and drew a beer and went around the end of the bar and set them on top of the piano. I looked him over from the side while he was still playing, and I still couldn't figure him out. He might have had ten times as much money as I got or he might have been down and out and broke, or he might have been in between.

But I took a chance. "Do you want the job?" I asked him.

"I got the job," he told me, without turning around. "Unless—you know anything about music?"

"Took up violin when I was a kid. Why?"

"Got any ideas on how Moszkowski should be interpreted?"

"Who?" I asked.

"Swell," he said. "I'll keep the job."

Maybe he was crazy, I thought, but he could play. I asked him what that first thing he'd played was, the one that sounded like lightning hitting the Black Maria. He grinned around at me.

"A pot-boiler of Brahms as Tchaikovsky would have written it if he'd had a nightmare and thought he was Wagner with the Valkyrie after him."

I shrugged and went back to behind the bar. As long as it sounded like that, I didn't care if he was playing flyspecks instead of notes.

Others were beginning to listen, too, I noticed. One of the printers wanted "My Wild Irish Rose," and he got it. At least, my new pianist used that melody for a starting-off point and where he went from there I don't know, but there was a lump in my throat when he pulled out the stops—and I've always thought those "Take-me-back-to-Erin" things are the corniest of all corn. Maybe because I'm Scotch.

And then he got into Gershwin's Concerto—I recognized that one—and I mentally doubled the salary I'd paid our previous player and had had in mind to pay this one.

I took some drinks back to the King Costello party and then went over to the piano again. I asked him what his name was.

"Barry," he said. "Barry Stowe."

"Okay, Barry. Listen, one of the customers just now asked if you'd play 'Traumerei'."

He hit a discord, and then turned it into something that had wings.

"Nix," he said. "It smells. I don't like it."

I was still dumb. It hadn't dawned on me that there might be trouble.

Mary came over and wanted "Night and Day" and he played it and she sat down by the piano, and he turned around and watched her while he played it. Then he cut from Cole Porter into something else and she stayed sitting there and he kept watching her while he played, instead of the keys.

I walked back to King Costello, and I grinned at him. I thought it was a joke. That's how dense I was.

"He won't play Traumerei," I told him. Yeah, just like that. I didn't have sense enough to lie to him and say Barry didn't know the number.

"Why won't he?" King wanted to know, and he didn't grin back at me, and I felt my own grin slipping and propped it up. I didn't want any trouble with King.

"He says it smells," I told him, and tried to make it sound funny. It didn't. It fell flat on its face in the middle of the table and lay there.

King Costello's face got ugly suddenly.

"Did you tell him who wanted it?" he said.

I walked back to the piano. "Listen, Barry, you better play it," I said. "King Costello put in the request for it, see?"

He looked up, and his face showed interest.

"Costello? Isn't that the chap who put another chap in the bay last week with his feet in a chunk of cement?"

I looked around quick, because he had said it fairly loud.

"*Shhh!*" I said. "Listen—don't mention that if you want to stay healthy. Nobody proved the King done it."

"Or anything else," he said. "But, according to what I read and heard, everybody knows he did it, don't they? He runs a protective association racket, I heard, and this guy was a sucker who wouldn't kick in to him, and he—"

"*Shhh*, kid—for gosh sake shut up," I said. "And you better play this Traumerei. Costello might make trouble. He don't like to be crossed."

"You belong to this protective association?"

I looked at him, and then I nodded. No use denying it. The Costello-Moberly mob cost me fifty a week, and they thought they were letting me get by light.

He turned back to the piano and swung into something new. For a minute I didn't get what it was, and then I remembered the tune and hoped like sin no one else in the place remembered the name of it. It was the "Yellow Dog Blues," and it wasn't the right time or place to play it. Not with Costello looking our way, and with this guy Barry turning his head around to look smack at Costello while he played it.

I ankled quick over to the table in the corner.

I said what I should have said in the first place.

"He don't know Traumerei, Mr. Costello," I said.

It didn't jell. I saw that right away. I'd have got away with it if I'd had sense enough to spring it the first time, but not now.

Chub Moberly started to get up, and the King put a hand on his arm and motioned him to sit down again. He had straightened out his face now, and acted like he was enjoying it, and I think in a way he was. He was getting a chance to show off in front of the pony from the Gayety chorus.

"Tell the guy to play it or fire him," he said.

I went back to the piano. I hated to do it but I said:

"Listen, Barry, you're fired. I'm sorry, but—"

He kept right on playing, but he turned and looked up at me.

"Listen, Pop," he said, "I don't want to be fired. I like this dump of yours. If I play Traumerei for him, do I keep the job?"

I gave a sigh of relief. "Sure," I said.

I nodded to Costello, and then I strolled back toward the bar. That was that, I thought. Somehow I was a little disappointed.

But that wasn't that. This guy Barry started in playing Traumerei all right, but he was playing it with one finger only, and he made that finger stumble and he gave a perfect imitation of somebody who can't play trying to pick out a tune and almost making it—like when a stew sits down at the piano and picks out "My Country 'tis of Thee" with his wobbly forefinger.

No basses, no rhythm, no nothing. Just the least possible minimum that could be called "Traumerei" if you wanted to cuss at it.

~§~

By that time everybody in the room got it that something was going on. Me, I had cold shivers running up and down my spine.

I saw King Costello stand up, and instinct made me reach for the bung-starter, but I pulled my hand away quick like I'd reached for something red-hot. The King and Chub Moberly would be heeled and you can't match lead with bung-starters, even if you're sap enough to try it.

And that gosh-awful melody went on, and each note seemed to hang in the air like a dead body hanging by its neck from one of a row of gibbets.

I saw Mary put her hand on Barry's arm and say something to him I couldn't hear to try to stop him, but he wasn't having any. He was going all the way through that piece. I'd promised him I wouldn't fire him if he played it, and I hadn't specified how.

"Hey, Mary, come here!" I called out sharply.

She turned around and when she caught the look in my eye she came on over and stood behind the bar with me.

"Stay away from there," I told her. "That fool's trying to get himself killed."

"Pop, stop them!" she said. "Oh—"

King Costello had shoved his chair back and he was crossing the room to the piano. Before he got there, this guy Barry had finished the request number and he was playing something again. I mean playing.

King put his hand on this guy Barry's shoulder and swung him around.

"Pop—" Mary said, and turned around again to me like she was afraid to watch.

I whispered to her. "Listen, King will kayo the guy and that'll satisfy him. He won't pull a rod in here. But listen—you go back and powder your schnozzle until this is over with."

This guy Barry's face was expressionless when he got swung around, and it was right smack in the middle of that face that the King's hand landed, flat, hard. It wasn't a try for a knockout; just hard enough, Costello was figuring, to make a guy mad or to make him crawl.

I imagine you could have heard the crack that flat-handed wallop made halfway down the block.

This guy Barry rocked back with it until his head almost hit the hammers of the frontless piano. Then he got his balance, and he grinned and stood up. It wasn't exactly a good-natured grin, but it wasn't any more saturnine than the one he had given me when I'd asked him that first time what he'd been playing.

That was what Costello had been hoping for—that Barry would stand up. Costello was as tall as this guy Barry and maybe fifty pounds heavier. And as soon as Barry stood up, Costello cocked a right that was meant to push Barry right through that piano. And while the right was cocked, his left flicked out in a short hook to the jaw to keep the ivory pounder off balance. Costello had been a boxer once.

Barry didn't try to duck that left hook, which was all that saved him from being a sucker for the murderous right. He took the left hook on the side of his jaw and he rode with it, limber as a steel spring, and let it carry his head way over to one side. And he kept it going that way and the heavy artillery whistled over his shoulder when Costello crossed.

All this is taking a long time to tell about but it happened while you could maybe count up to two if you counted pretty fast. This guy Barry's right fist was lashing out meanwhile, a short low blow with hardly any arc to it that caught King right above the belt buckle and made him grunt. Because that's always the weak spot of any ex-boxer that doesn't stay in training.

And he gave ground a step with the grunt, and that's when Barry's right found room to swing. It came up to the King's jaw like an airmail special delivery. It didn't need any signed receipt. Costello went back from his heels.

That was when I really started to worry. This thing had ended in a kayo all right, but it had been the wrong kayo to really end it, if you know what I mean. The King would never let it go that way. He couldn't, for purely business reasons, if no others. This was more than a fight now. It was going to be a murder, unless Barry got out of town in time, and it would have to be pretty quick time at that.

I quick swung around to see how Chub Moberly was taking this. Barry was looking at him too. Chub wasn't taking it one way or the other, from his face. He was sitting there smoking his cigarette like nothing was happening. But the two girls at the table were white and the rouge on their cheeks stood out like round red smears the size of silver dollars.

All this while, Costello was falling, falling as a tree falls. Two women rushed to him; one the pony from the Gayety. She got his head in her lap and then glared at Mary. Yes, Mary was the other one. But all she did was slide a hand quick inside his coat to make sure the ticker was still pumping, and when she found it was, she took her hand away like she had been touching a snake, and stood up.

Chub Moberly's girl was still at the table, and for some reason she started to cry. Chub said something to her out of the corner of his mouth and then got up and strolled over to where things had been happening. He had his hands thrust into his trousers pockets, and that was good as far as it went, because he wouldn't be packing a gun there.

He walked up to this guy Barry, who was leaning against the piano and rubbing his knuckles a little.

"That wasn't smart," he said. His face was strictly deadpan and so was his voice. You couldn't tell whether he was going to make trouble or not.

Barry didn't say anything, and Chub said:

"Guy, you get out of town, tonight. He ain't gonna forget this, see?"

Barry looked at him level. "Is that a threat?" he said.

"Pal," Moberly told him, "it's a friendly tip. A plenty friendly tip. No matter what the King says when he comes around, you play it that way. Get out of town."

So it was going to be all right, maybe.

The King was coming around. I noticed that he opened his eyes once and moved his head a trifle, and then snapped his eyes back shut, and I knew what was going on under his hair.

He was going to play he was still out until he figured what he was going to do when he opened his peepers for keeps.

I gave a little sigh of relief then, because it would probably be okay, for now. If Costello hadn't stopped to think, he might have come up shooting, but he wouldn't now. Having time to think it over, he wouldn't stick his head into a murder rap he couldn't beat.

He might come up wanting more fight, or he might come up trying to laugh it off. And that would give this ivory pounder of mine time to hop a train if he hopped fast.

Then the King sat up, slowly, and I saw I'd guessed right. Without looking at anybody in particular he dusted himself off. Then he turned to my ivory pounder.

"Guy, you got a mean left," he said. "Want a job?"

"I got a job."

"If Pop here don't treat you right, come up and see me," Costello said.

"I'll keep it in mind," Barry said.

Then he sat down at the piano, swiveled around with his back to all of us and began to play again. I don't know what it was he played. But little bouncy notes seemed to ricochet off the walls, and in a way they got in your hair, too. It wasn't the right time to play a tune like that. Not in a room that smelled of murder.

Costello talked to Chub and the two girls, but with the piano going, I couldn't tell what they were saying. They started for the door and went on out without saying "So long" or anything.

Then the door opened again, and Chub Moberly came in alone. He walked up to me at the bar and asked for cigarettes and I gave him a pack.

"From now on, Pop, it's double," he said.

I hoped I didn't get him. "What is?" I asked.

"The dues, Pop, the dues. You're a Class-A member now, and you're getting off lucky. A hundred a week, the King said to tell you."

"But listen, Mr. Moberly. The place hardly makes that. I'll have to go out of business. Listen, this wasn't my fault; I didn't—"

His eyes didn't even flicker.

"Let us know when you're closing up," he said. "We'll throw a farewell party."

He turned on his heel and walked out. I heard him call out something to the others in his party as he went through the door, and the girls laughed.

Mary came over to where I was.

"What did he say?" she asked.

I looked at her, and her face was so pale I was sure now what I had always guessed. She didn't wear any makeup and that usual color of hers was the real McCoy. A swell kid, Mary. If I was twenty years younger and still had hair on my head . . .

"Nothing, kid," I told her. "He was outa cigarettes."

"He didn't say anything about—" She moved her head in the direction of the piano.

"No. Not this time. You heard what he said before."

"Listen, Pop, he was right on that. This Barry—you *got* to get him out of town. Quick, tonight. Listen, if he's broke give him money. You can take it out of—"

"Hey," I said, "who told you I didn't have money myself? Listen, go tell the guy to come here, and then take a powder."

She crossed over and put her hand on this guy Barry's shoulder and said something to him and he stopped playing right in the middle of a phrase and turned around.

She went back and started to clear off the table where the Costello-Moberly party had been, and this guy Barry came over and leaned against the front of the bar. I drew him a beer and set it in front of him. I'd have given him a shot, too, but I saw he hadn't touched the one I'd set on top of the piano for him.

"Listen, you're fired and I mean it," I said to him. "If you're still in town tomorrow, it ain't going to be so good. There's a train at three, but I wouldn't go to the station to get on it if I was you. You can swing aboard when it slows down for the curve at the top of the grade, pulling out. How you fixed for money?"

"Listen, Pop," he said. "I like it here. I'm staying."

"You can't. Blast it, those boys are killers. You're on the list. The King didn't mean it when he acted like he was laughing off that kayo. He just don't kill out in the open, see?"

"Pop, no two-bit gangster is going to make me—"

"You sap, he isn't a two-bit gangster. He's a killer. Anyway, you're fired flat. Your piano-playing is lousy."

He grinned at me. "You're a liar, Pop, but you mean all right. Okay, so I'm fired. I'll play your piano for fun on my own time till you change your mind."

He downed the last of his beer, put the glass down on the bar, and started back for the piano.

"Wait a minute," I said, in a different tone of voice, because I'd just thought of something, and he came back.

"Listen," I said, being darned sure I spoke softly enough that nobody else could hear me. "There's something I got a right to know. Was this by any chance on purpose?"

He looked puzzled. "I don't get you."

"I mean, are you a cop, or a Fed or anything? Or maybe got a personal or a business reason for starting something with the King?"

"Nope, Pop. Honest. Cross my heart."

"How long you been in town here?"

"Month, about."

"And you never crossed the King's trail? Or got hired by anybody working against him? Or maybe had somebody you liked get the dirty end of a protective deal? Or—"

"Honest Injun, Pop. I just don't like Traumerei, and I don't like a mug like that telling me what I've got to do. I've read about this racket bunch in the papers, and I've heard stories about them, and that's all."

"That's straight?"

"Straight."

He went back and started to play "Nola." Mary looked at me questioningly across the room, and I shrugged. She started over toward me and I thought, "What am I going to tell her?" You could see that she liked this guy Barry—and, for that matter, so did I.

And here he was on the list, and trying to get himself murdered, and what could I do about it? He was sitting there calmly playing the piano and he might be alive tomorrow morning, but I doubted pretty much if he'd be alive much longer, unless he got out of town. And you can tell a guy to get out of town, but you can't push him on a train—not a guy like that.

Mary was at the bar now.

"He won't go?" she said.

"He won't go," I admitted.

"Pop, you got to do something."

I looked at her face and there was moisture in the corner of those big brown eyes of hers.

"It's that way?" I said.

She talked like there was a lump in her throat.

"How do I know, Pop?" she said. "I—I just met him tonight, but I guess maybe, it is that way. Or would be."

I took a deep breath, and there was only one thing, and I might as well try it.

"I'll do something," I said. "You tell those printers we're closing up early, and give 'em a last one on the house if they'll drink it quick. Then put your coat on and go, the front way, see?"

"You're... What are you going to do, Pop?"

"I'll phone you tomorrow and tell you about it. Listen, don't worry. I'm not going to do anything heroic or anything. When the rest of you are out of here, I'll talk him out of being a sap. That's all. Now run along."

~§~

I sat down on the stool back of the bar because I felt too punk to even help Mary get the printers out of there, because of what I was going to do.

No, like I told her, it wasn't anything heroic. But it was going to hurt. It would work, though, if anything would work. Maybe I'd have done it to keep this guy Barry from getting murdered and maybe not, but if Mary felt that way about him, then there wasn't anything else to do.

Don't get me wrong. I'm not sloppy about Mary. I'm forty-eight and I'm bald and I got a paunch coming on and I been happily married once, and I like Mary more like a daughter than anything else. But you don't want your daughter to run into anything like this was going to be if Barry stuck around.

So, when the door closed, I walked over to where this Barry was still playing and said:

"Okay, feller, we're through. You can stop now, unless you want to play to the cockroaches."

"I've played to worse than that," he said, but he let whatever he was playing die out slow, and he closed down the lid over the keys and got up. "What time tomorrow?"

"Not any. We're through. I'm closing."

He whistled softly. "How come, Pop? Looks like a nice business you do here."

He turned and looked around him. The place, I'll admit, didn't look poverty-struck.

"We did," I said. "But the protective racket jacked up the take tonight. From fifty to a flat C. And that's just about my margin and there's no use my working for nothing, is there? And I guess I got enough to get myself a farm somewhere and—"

"Nuts," he said. "You don't want a farm. You like running this place. I could tell."

"Well, yeah," I admitted. "I liked it here. So what? I'm getting old and I'm going to die peaceful and not—"

The way he was grinning at me made me realize how silly I must have sounded.

"All right," I said. "So I'm only forty-eight, but I feel old."

"What's the matter with the cops in this town?" he wanted to know.

"Nothing," I said. "It's my fault, see? Me, and guys like me. We're afraid to squawk, let alone testify. I mean we're each afraid to be the first one, because the first one gets the chopper, and the second and maybe the third, and— Well, if a few of us wanted to stick our necks out and get killed maybe by that time the cops would get a case on one of the killings and be able to prove that—"

"Don't talk so much, Pop. You'll sprain a tonsil. Listen, why'd they raise the ante on you that high? It's cutting their own take if they drive you out of business . . . Say—when was this?"

"When Chub Moberly came back in just as they were leaving."

"Chub is King Costello's second in command, isn't he?"

I nodded. I still didn't get what he was driving at.

"Say," he said, "I'll, bet tonight's the night he'll . . . Say, I'll bet there's a chance I could—"

"There's a chance you could do nothing," I said. "Listen, dang you. You're going to get out of town. Tonight. Or—"

"Pipe down, Pop. What's this place worth?"

I scratched where my hair used to be.

"A thousand, maybe, on forced sale of stock and fixtures. And right now, that's all there is."

He pulled out a worn billfold and opened it, and there was a solitary bill in it, all alone by itself, and he pulled it out and it was a single. He held it out to me.

"We'll make out the papers tomorrow. You're selling me a one-thousandth interest. You retain the privilege of buying it back at the same price any time. Fair enough?"

"What for?" I said.

"To deal me in," he said. "Pop, I'm a fool but not a nitwit. It was *after* I'd laid out that four-bit gangster that they raised the ante on you. I stuck out your neck too. And I want an excuse to do something about it."

I gawked at him. "Do you think you can lick Costello and Moberly and the whole gang? Those boys play rough. You'll get yourself killed as sure as little green apples."

There was that saturnine look in his face again that wasn't exactly a grin or anything else.

"Pop," he said, "I got an interest now and I got a right to try. Look, that hundred-dollar blackmail we're paying weekly is costing me a dime a week personally on my one-thousandth interest, and I won't pay."

I guess he was right about the interest, because somehow I found that I was holding that dollar bill instead of him holding it, but I don't remember taking it. Anyway, it was in my hand and I guess that meant the place was part his.

"And, Pop," he said, "this is the night."

"Why?" I'm dumb sometimes. I'd still missed the boat.

Instead of answering right away, he asked:

"Do you know where either of those girls who were here with them live?"

"The one with King—her name's Estelle Devorell—is a chorine at the Gayety. They all stay at the Strober House."

"I want to find out if the girls got ditched," he said. "You phone the Strober House and see if the dame is there."

I didn't know why, but I went across to the phone and dropped in a nickel and dialed the Strober. I asked for the pony and pretty soon a voice says, "Hello." And I said, "Estelle?" and she said, "Yeah, who is it?" I said, "I want the King. It's important. Where is he?"

"Who is this?" she asked. I said, "Chub." My voice is low pitched and a lot like Chub's and I thought I could get away with it and I did.

"What the devil, Chub?" she said. "Did he duck out on you too? I thought you and him was giving Mae and me the run-around together. She's here with me."

"Stick around Baby," I said, "I'll be up." I hung up the receiver.

I turned back to Barry. "The two dames are together," I told him. "Chub and the King ditched them and they don't like it much. So what?"

"I think it means Chub's moving in," he said. "Didn't you get that picture, Pop? He comes back *alone* to do that ante-raising. And why tonight? Well, look what happened to the King. And what always happens when a throne totters?"

"I'll be blowed," I said, because I saw he was right.

He had never seen these mobsters before tonight and I had seen 'em too often, but he'd got a part of the picture I had clear missed. I remembered now how Chub had sat there when the King had taken it on the chin and gone down for ten, and how he had acted afterwards, and it all fitted.

And I had known all along, too, that Chub Moberly was ambitious and that he would have liked to be on top if he dared. But he had been afraid of the King. Yes, and I'd seen his whole attitude different when the King had been taken down. Yet it took an outsider to tell me what it added up to. An outsider who knew about the gang only from the newspapers and what not.

"Pop," Barry said, "what's the best way to figure out who might be out front or out back right now?"

I thought a minute. "Second floor's vacant," I said. "I got the key so I could show people around. I'll run up there and see what I can see out of the windows without turning on a light. From the side front windows I can look both ways at the street."

"Is there a gun here, Pop?"

"No," I told him, and I went into the side hall and up to the flat above my tavern. I took a long look out the front windows on both sides, then tried the kitchen and went down again.

"It's too dark to see anything out the back way," I said, "but there's a car halfway down the block in front. I watched it till another car went by and the headlights showed it up, and there's just Chuck Willis in it."

I realized that he wouldn't get what I meant by the "just" so I explained. "Chuck" Willis was merely a punk and a hanger-on of the mob. If they meant business he wouldn't be in it—anyway not alone. I figured they had put him there merely to trail Barry when he left and report where he was staying. All Barry would have to do, now he knew, was give Chuck Willis the slip before he went wherever he was going.

"You don't think he's even packing a gun?"

"Huh-uh, not Chuck."

"Then, Pop, if there's a real torpedo around, he's out back." He sighed. "And I have to have a gun. Yes, there'll be somebody in back. That's the way they figure I'll leave. The guy in the car in front is just a check, and anyway maybe we were supposed to see him and play safe out the back."

He held out his hand. "Give me the key to the flat."

I did. "What you going to do?"

"Take him from behind, if I can. Building next door's a one-story garage, isn't it?"

I nodded.

"I'm going back along that roof," this guy Barry said, "till I find out where he's waiting. How I go about it after that depends."

"But—"

"I'll be back, Pop. But if you hear a shot, and I don't come back, you go on home, front way."

He went out into the side hall and took the steps toward the second floor three steps at a time.

Slowly, I started to clean up the place ready to leave for the night. That gave me something to do, because there was something I didn't exactly want to think about.

I had just about finished cleaning up when there was a soft knock on the back door. I walked back and heard:

"It's me, Pop. Open up."

I opened the door and he came in. He pulled something partly out of his coat pocket and I saw it was a thirty-two automatic.

"A guy with a little mustache gave me this. Medium height, stocky, about twenty-five. Know him, Pop?"

"Jimmy," I said, and I shuddered. "Jimmy Terrill. Did you—"

"He's in the garage next door sleeping it off. I didn't take time to tie him up, but he's good for a few hours. It's swell about that car out front. I'll need one. So long, Pop."

"Let me in on this, Barry," I said. "What you going to do? How do you think you can—"

"Pop, I can call the play, I think. Crooks always work according to a pattern. The guys these mobsters take for rides get taken out in the bay, don't they? Well, that's what Chub will do to King Costello. It's anyway a five-to-one shot he will. And he'll use the King's own sloop, and that docks down by the bend. Someone pointed it out to me when I was fishing last week. And they've got to take that sloop through the channel to get out on the bay, and . . . heck, maybe it's too late now. Bye, Pop."

He started for the front door.

"Wait!" I called.

He turned around.

"Listen, Barry, I want to know—what you doing this for? It ain't your fight, is it? Dang it, you can't take the whole—"

"What you mean it isn't my fight?" I could see from his face that he was dead serious. "I do this, or run, don't I?"

"But what do you get out of it?"

He grinned, and pointed at the piano.

"A chance to play that, and to respect myself because I wouldn't let myself be pushed around."

He turned again. . . and again I said, "Wait," and this time there was a tightness in my chest that I hadn't known for a long time. And he turned and because of what I was going to say the tightness went away and—well, let's skip that part. I can't tell you just how I felt.

"I'm going with you," I told him.

"Pop," he said, "don't be a fool. One man can have as good a chance on a fool stunt like this as two can, and anyway, you're—"

I yanked a bottle from the shelf next to the register and I didn't care if it was one of the most expensive bottles in the place because of what I was taking it for. I put a couple shot glasses in front of us and filled them and pushed one toward him.

"Drink to us, kid," I told him.

"Pop, you couldn't—"

"Kid," I said, "this stuff is cognac. I used to drink it in France when you were in diapers and I was going over the top at St. Mihiel. I—I guess I lost something since then, but I got it back now. I—"

I ran out of words and couldn't say it, but he looked at me and guessed what I meant and he picked up his glass and I picked up mine and we clinked them together solemnly and drank.

Maybe, I was thinking, this was the last time I would ever drink anything and cognac is just the stuff for a drink like that. It puts a warm spot where you need it when you're afraid the water of the bay is going to be cold.

Afraid? Sure, I was scared stiff, but I was happy in a dizzy sort of way because if I saw the sun come up I was going to be able to look myself in the face by the light of it. I hadn't done that—not right, I mean—since a year or so ago when the Costello mob had moved in.

~§~

Finally I turned out the lights and we went out and walked toward where Chuck Willis was parked. "Let me do this," I said.

"Better let me, Pop. He might—"

"Dang it, kid, don't be a hog. If you take the torpedoes, at least let me have the punks."

He laughed and said, "Okay, Pop."

When we got near the car, Chuck Willis must have known something was up that wasn't in the instructions he had, because he quick started the motor, but before he could pull away from the curb I took the last three steps running and yanked the door next to him open.

"Hi, Chuck," I said. "Move over. You got company."

He growled something and hauled off to take a poke at me, but I shoved the heel of my palm against his cheek and knocked him off balance.

"Move over," I said again, like I meant it, and he moved.

Barry got into the back seat of the car. I reached over and frisked the punk to be sure he wasn't packing steel, and he wasn't, and then I started the car.

"What you gonna—" he whined, and I said, "Shut up," and he shut.

I drove to the edge of town and a little past it I swung in the driveway of a filling station that was closed for the night.

I turned around to this guy Barry.

"We'll tie up the big-shot here and leave him in the station," I said. "He'll get found early in the morning."

Chuck tried to get his nerve back when he found out he wasn't going to get any worse than that.

"It's going to be tough on you guys when the King finds out you swiped one of his cars," he said. "He'll—"

Barry, who'd got out first, opened the door by Chuck and yanked him out and cuffed him one and he shut up. We tied Chuck up and left him there, and when we got back in the car, Barry got in front with me.

"Narrowest point in the channel," he suggested, and I nodded. Five minutes later I drove off the river road into a clump of trees and parked the car there with the lights off. It was so dark that at first we couldn't see our hands in front of our faces, but our eyes got used to it and we groped out of the trees and down to the river shore.

I took Barry's arm and turned him around to point out a couple of lights to our left.

"The bay's out there," I told him. "They'll grope through here sight-ing on those lights, and the channel's only thirty feet here so it'll be like threading a needle. They won't be making over half a knot, whether they use the engine or canvas."

We sat down there to wait, and the wind was off the water and it was cold, and I found myself shivering and cussing myself for going in for something dumb like this. I didn't see how we would stand a chance. And I began to wonder why we hadn't got the cops in on it and there didn't seem to be any real reason, except that it would probably have taken too long and anyway it was too late now.

We took off our shoes and unbuttoned our clothes ready to strip down quick and get out there. We would have time, because everything was so darned quiet that we would hear the sloop a long way off, even under sail.

Time went by and I began to hope it wouldn't come.

"Anyway," I thought, "if it doesn't, we're safe out here for tonight. If there are more torpedoes out hunting for this guy Barry—and maybe for me too by now—they sure won't think to come here after us."

We didn't talk very much, but once Barry said:

"This girl you called Mary at your—our—place. She doesn't look like she ought to be working in a place like that, Pop."

"Why not?" I wanted to know. "It's a respectable place, or I wouldn't let her. And she needed a job. She's worked for me a year now. I knew her father. He died a year or so ago."

"Looks like a nice kid, Pop."

"She is a nice kid. And listen, it's strictly hands off, understand, unless of course—"

There was light enough I could see him nod.

"I get you, Pop," he said. "That's what I thought. Anyway, I want to see some more of her. Maybe it'll turn out to be 'unless'."

Then there was just the soft lapping of the water for a while and some frogs croaking a long way off and a tree rustling in the breeze.

"Wind's blowing toward us," Barry said. "Mean's she'll be heeling over this way and easiest to board from this side. We can grab—"

"*Shhh*—listen!" I cut in.

We listened a minute, hardly breathing. I found myself whispering when we compared notes even though our voices couldn't possibly have carried out there.

It was hard to tell directions, but the distance was about right. And it was the sounds you would hear from a sloop running under canvas, creak of the boom and a flap of the jib as the wind slackened a minute and then hit back. And she was running without lights, because the sounds meant she was near enough for us to have seen her if she'd had them. It was her, all right.

We quickly slid our clothes off down to our shorts and walked out into the water. I had shivered at the thought of it while I had been waiting, but it was warmer than the air, once we were in it.

The bottom sloped down quick on our side of the river, and the middle of the channel wasn't more than thirty feet from shore. Which was a good thing because I'm not much of a swimmer. I hadn't told Barry that.

Pretty soon we were in up to our shoulders. Up to my shoulders anyway, and Barry ducked down so just his head showed. He had been holding the gun he had taken away from Jimmy Terrill up out of the water in his hand, and now he put it between his teeth and got ready to shove off.

We could see her now, or a faint shadow that we knew must be her coming. We watched a minute to get our directions, and then took our feet off bottom and swam toward where we'd meet her.

Barry shoved off first, using a breast stroke, so he could keep his head well up and the gun dry. I shoved off after him and swam as quiet as I could, keeping my feet down so they wouldn't break water and make a splash.

Then she was sliding up to meet us, easy, like a wraith in the night or a Flying Dutchman, and so quiet on board you would have thought she was a ghost for sure.

The mud-hook was hanging just to our side of the prow, and we both grabbed it and hung there for a minute, letting the boat pull us through the water. Then Barry pulled himself up and got his hands on the gunwales and began to work his way back toward the middle of the sloop and I did the same. I saw he wasn't going to pull himself up aboard until he got back opposite the cabin, where there would be the least chance of our being seen as we went aboard her.

When we got back there, he pulled himself up quietly and reached down and helped me up after him, and we lay there a minute on the deck alongside the cabin wall, and rested. Then he began to work his way forward along the cabin wall so as to make room for me. The cabin roof was about two and a half feet above the deck, and the deck itself was about that wide alongside the cabin. Lying there close to the cabin wall, we couldn't be seen from the tiller.

And low voices told us that at least two men were back aft. The bow, we knew, was clear. We had seen that as we had pulled ourselves from the anchor up to the gunwales.

Barry started to inch his way forward around the corner to the front of the cabin, but I lay where I was for a moment first and listened to those voices. I couldn't hear what they were saying, but it sounded like King Costello and "Muggsy" Roberts.

And that meant—if we had read aright the signs of what was due to happen tonight—that Chub's putsch had failed. That Chub was the one being taken out for planting in the bay. Or maybe we had been wrong altogether. Maybe this trip was for some completely different purpose.

I crawled after this guy Barry, and my flesh crawled a little too. Not because the wind was cold and I didn't have anything on but a pair of shorts, either. It was because we were bucking the King, instead of Chub. I don't know why I should have been more afraid of one than the other—a bullet does you just as much no good whoever fires it—but I was.

The moon was coming out a little bit from behind the clouds now, just peeping around the edge of one, and I was glad to get around the corner of the cabin where there wasn't a chance of being seen from the stern.

Barry was waiting for me there, and waited until I crawled up alongside him where he could put his lips right against my ear to whisper to me.

"Cabin window open there," he whispered. "Our best bet is get in cabin, jump him when he comes in."

"It's Costello back at the tiller," I whispered back. "And a guy named Muggsy."

He nodded and turned around to worm his way through the open window in the front wall of the cabin. I grasped his shoulder and held him back, then put my lips close to his ear again.

"Me first," I told him. "I'll be a tight fit there. You can pull me out if I stick."

He hesitated a moment, and then agreed.

It was a tight fit, all right, but I didn't stick. When I got most of myself through, Barry hung on to me and let me lower myself until I had hold of an iron rod that I figured would be the edge of a bunk. And bunks in a sloop are fastened to the walls and are good and solid. So I trusted my weight to it and was able to get down into the cabin.

I took Barry's hand as he came through and guided it to the same place and he got in, too. It was blacker there than the inside of your hat, and we just stood still for a moment holding on to the edge of the bunk and getting the feel of standing up on the sloop so we wouldn't fall when we took a step.

Then I moved my right foot and it hit something that felt like it was covered with a serge suit. Still hanging on to the edge of the bunk I bent over and felt with my hand. I felt a necktie, and then a face and the face was cold, so I pulled my hand away quick.

Here in the cabin I figured we could whisper without being heard way outside and back at the stern so I told Barry so he wouldn't fall over the stiff.

"There's another, in this other bunk, Pop," he said. "But I don't think he's dead. Wait." Then he said, "No, but I guess he's close to it. He's unconscious. Blood on his face."

I wondered which was Chub. I could guess who the other guy would be. Harry Blake. Harry was closer to Chub than any of the others of the gang, and if Chub had been trying to take over, Harry would have been with him, I thought.

"We must be getting out there now, kid," I whispered. "Pretty soon—"

"Whoever comes in to get these guys and dump 'em over will have a light, Pop. You go back and stay flat along the wall alongside the door to the companionway, out of range. I'll stay here with the gun and get the drop on him. You'll be in reserve."

"Suppose he comes in with a gun in his hand. The light'll be on you, not him, and—"

"But I'll hear when he's coming, and he don't know we're here. Odds are with us, Pop. If he douses the light, you grab him. But if there's shooting, stay to one side."

It didn't sound good to me. I would have played it with one of us on either side of the door so he might come all the way in without seeing us. But there wasn't much time to argue, so I found this guy Barry's hand in the dark and shook it.

"Well, kid," I said, "so long if it don't work."

"We'll make it work, Pop," he came back, and from the tone of his voice I got the idea that he was grinning in the dark even if I couldn't see the grin.

~§~

Groping my way carefully with my feet along the floor and my hands along one wall, I got back, felt where the door was, and got set. And I was scared stiff, and kind of—well, it sounds crazy to say it—but I felt kind of happy too.

I knew that, even as far as we'd got, the chances of our pulling it off were maybe one out of three, and that meant it was two-to-one I'd never see the sun come up. And standing there I felt some sort of a lump come up in my throat, and it wasn't because I was sorry for myself if I was going to die. And I was scared, but it wasn't because of that.

It was—well, dang it all, it sounds like I'm trying to be heroic or something, and I'm not, but I was glad I had played along with this guy Barry, even if it didn't work. Win, lose or draw, it was better this way, than the way things had been with me for a couple years now.

It got awful quiet and I could hear Costello's voice, and Muggsy's, again. They were talking louder now, and I could almost make out the words but not quite. And I heard the scratch of a match and that meant that they weren't worrying about a light being seen and figured they could smoke.

I knew that Barry wasn't more than eight feet from me, but we had taken our posts and we couldn't talk, and I felt almost as alone as though . . . Well, let's skip how I felt. The time did pass, and we heard one of the two men at the stern get up and come toward the cabin.

Then there was a streak of light at the crack at the bottom of the door and footsteps down the companionway, and the door opened.

In that first flash of light—I wasn't blinded by it because it wasn't aimed right my way—I saw a lot of things.

The dead guy on the floor was Harry Blake, just like I'd figured. And the unconscious guy on the bunk was Chub Moberly all right. His face was so bloody it looked like he had been through a sausage grinder. And the light must have roused him from being out because I saw his eyes open and blink, and he groaned.

Barry was standing there alongside Chub's bunk, with the gun steady in his hand, aimed square at the guy in the doorway. And the guy at the door—he had taken a step into the cabin before he saw what was up—was the King.

His hand flashed up toward a shoulder holster, but Barry's voice cut in sharp:

"Hold it! And if you drop that flashlight, I'll shoot. Don't kid yourself you can duck quick enough."

King hadn't seen me yet, but I was ready to grab at him, or at the flashlight if he dropped it or tried to click the switch. For just a fraction of a second the tableau held. None of us moved.

Then something happened that wasn't supposed to be in the script. I hadn't kept on watching Chub Moberly after that first quick look, but apparently he had kept on coming to, but he had done it suddenly and probably in delirium from the pain of his working over. He saw King standing there, the guy who had made hash out of his face and who was going to kill him, and he saw the gun in Barry's hand, not more than a foot away from him.

He didn't stop to think or figure out the play and I doubt if he saw me or realized who Barry was.

He gave a hoarse yell and grabbed the gun in Barry's hand. It went off, sounding like the firing of a cannon in that little cabin. But Chub's wild grab had knocked the gun out of line with the King, and had knocked it up. The bullet probably hit somewhere in the cabin roof.

Costello's hand flashed again toward his shoulder holster, while Barry struggled for control of the gun. The King didn't drop the flashlight. Now the edge was all with him. He would have time to draw and fire twice and there would be nobody behind that gun instead of two men.

His draw was fast, so fast that his gun was out of his holster and streaking downward before the momentum of my lunge hit him from the side. My arms closed around him and pinned down his arms so he couldn't aim. But the flashlight went down, too, and the darkness was sudden and complete.

But not silent. That other gun—the one Chub and this guy Barry were struggling for—kept going off. Chub had got a finger inside the trigger guard. I counted eight shots quick and I felt one of them burn the calf of my leg. But I was wrestling around with the King and didn't have time to worry about a little thing like that. Anyway, I knew eight shots meant that gun was empty.

I had switched and got both hands around Costello's right wrist, and was holding the gun down. That was all I could manage to do, and it was costing me plenty. With his free hand he was knocking the stuffing out of me.

Funny how you can think out a whole sequence of thoughts in a split second. Between a couple of the wallops I was taking I thought of Muggsy outside, and wondered if he was going to lash the tiller and be on our necks with another gun. Or maybe even just let go of the tiller and let the sloop yaw over into the wind, and come back here.

And like I say, between one wallop and the next, I saw he wouldn't. He knew Chub and Harry Blake were in here and he probably knew Chub wasn't dead yet and maybe he wasn't sure whether Harry was or was not, if King had taken care of that end of it.

And not knowing we had come aboard he would think this ruckus meant that Chub had got a gun somewhere and was shooting it out with the King. And I could follow his mind. With all those shots one or the other of 'em would be dead by now. If it was the King, he'd better switch over quick and be on Chub's side. And if Chub was dead, there wasn't any use coming and—

A mean blow grazed the side of my neck and then I heard a noise that was something between a thud and a crack like when a fist lands hard and square on a jaw, and the King went limp and fell down and me with him.

I found out afterwards that Barry had let go that other gun after the eighth shot and had got a sudden glimpse of the King's profile against the faint gray square of the doorway. And he had waded in and made good use of the target.

I hit hard, but that was because I didn't use my hands to break my fall. I kept one of them on Costello's wrist and grabbed farther out with the other and got the gun just as it was falling from his hand.

I didn't wait to grope for the flashlight. I figured now was the time to play my hunch on Muggsy before he realized that maybe this wasn't something between Chub and Costello, but something else again, and get set for it.

I scrambled to my feet and up the companionway, with the King's gun in my hand. And my guess was right and I caught Muggsy flat-footed. Standing there trying to look like he was starting out to help in the cabin in case the King came out, and like he was playing neutral in case it was Chub came out.

He didn't even have his hand on his gun. And instead of either the King or Chub, it was me that popped up out of that companionway—probably in my skin and white shorts looking like a ghost or something—and with the drop on him so cold that he never reached. And that was that.

We didn't mess around with sailing the sloop back. We found a flare and sent it up, and the Coast Guard sent out a cutter and took over sloop and all. Chub talked plenty, and the protective racket was a dead duck.

But I did find out a little more about this guy Barry a month or so later. It's a busy night at our place, with Barry spreading jam on the piano and spreading it thick. And the door opens and in pops a little guy with bushy gray hair that looks like it's been bobbed except that it sticks in funny angles, and his eyes look wild.

I know him, sure, because you and I and everybody has seen pictures of Waldemar Durri, who is two of the three greatest living pianists. And he looks around my place like he smelled something he didn't like.

Then he sees Barry and what he's doing to my piano. He puts his hands into his hair like he's going to tear out a couple handfuls, and rushes over to the piano and screeches, "*Stop* that!" with the word "stop" about two octaves above high C.

Barry stops in the middle of a hot lick and looks up, and darned if he doesn't look frightened half to death. Then he grins and says, "Maestro!" and gets up and takes Durri's arm and brings him over to the bar.

I'm busy throwing together a Martini for an alderman, and while I'm doing it they're both talking at once and neither of them listening to the other, only Barry is grinning and Durri is frowning.

When I move over to them, I catch Barry saying:

"But I won't play to stuffed shirts, Maestro, and I like it here and I like the people and I like playing anything I please, any way *I* happen to want to play it, and—"

And the little guy with all the hair is talking at the same time and twice as fast and I gather that Barry Stowe was on the verge of a brilliant career as a concert pianist and was a genius and had a duty to humanity and stuff.

Then Barry shuts up both himself and Durri and introduces me. While I'm shaking hands with Durri, Barry sneaks back to the piano. Mary has been watching this and she goes over and sits down on the bench beside him, and he goes into something so sentimental it's positively sloppy, even the marvelous way he plays it, and he talks to her while he plays.

"He's doing swell here, Mr. Durri," I says to Durri. "He owns a one-third interest now, and his playing has doubled business. He likes it swell and he's going to be married next week to that girl sitting next to him."

He looks around and sees that Mary has an apron on.

"A *barmaid?*" he says, shocked-like.

I almost reach for the bung-starter, in spite of who he is, but instead I just says: "Look at her."

He turns around and studies her face for a while, and then he turns back and says, "Hmmmm." And I pour us each a drink, although I drink only with very special customers, and we down them and he says, "Hmmmm," again and then, "Maybe he is not—ain't so—how do you say it?"

" 'Ain't so dumb?' " I asks and grins at him, and he nods.

"He ain't, Maestro," I tells him. "Take it from me, he ain't. Listen, will you do me a favor? Go over and ask him to play a certain number—Traumerei."

Thrilling Detective, September 1942

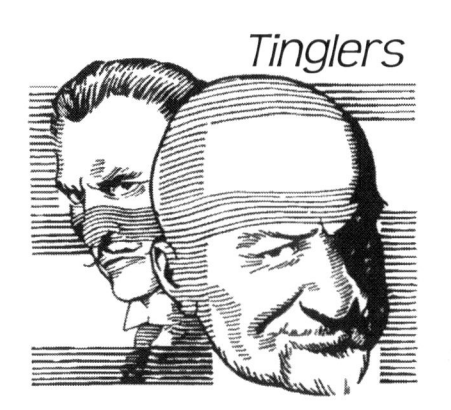

Tinglers

Granny's Birthday

THE HALPERINS were a very close-knit family. Wade Smith, one of the only two non-Halperins present, envied them that, since he had no family—but the envy was tempered into a mellow glow by the glass in his hand.

It was Granny Halperin's birthday party, her eightieth birthday; everyone present except Smith and one other man was a Halperin, and was named Halperin. Granny had three sons and a daughter; all were present, and the three sons were married and had their wives with them. That made eight Halperins, counting Granny. And there were four members of the second generation, grandchildren, one with his wife, and that made thirteen Halperins. Thirteen Halperins, Smith counted; with himself and the other non-Halperin, a man named Cross, that made fifteen adults. And there had been, earlier, three more Halperins on hand, great-grandchildren, but they had been put to bed earlier in the evening, at various hours according to their respective ages.

And he liked them all, Smith thought mellowly, although now that the children had been abed a while, liquor was flowing freely, and the party was getting a bit too loud and boisterous for his taste. Everyone was drinking; even Granny, seated on a chair not unlike a throne, had a glass of sherry in her hand, her third for the evening.

She was a wonderfully sweet and vivacious little old lady, Smith thought. Definitely, though, a matriarch; sweet as she was, Smith was thinking, she ruled her family with a rod of iron in a velvet glove. He was just inebriated enough to get his metaphors mixed.

He, Smith, was here because he'd been invited by Bill Halperin, who was one of Granny's sons; he was Bill's attorney and also his friend. The other outsider, a Gene or Jean Cross, seemed to be a friend of several of the grandson-generation Halperins.

Across the room he saw that Cross was talking to Hank Halperin and noticed that whatever they were saying had suddenly led to raised and angry voices. Smith hoped there wouldn't be trouble; the party was much too pleasant to be broken up now by a fight or even an argument.

But suddenly Hank Halperin's fist lashed out and caught Cross's jaw, and Cross went backward and fell. His head hit on the stone edge of the fireplace with a loud *thunk* and he lay still. Hank quickly ran and knelt beside Cross and touched him, and then Hank was pale as he looked up and then stood up. "Dead," he said thickly. "God, I didn't mean to— But he said—"

Granny wasn't smiling now. Her voice rose sharp and querulously.

"He tried to hit you first, Henry. *I* saw it. We *all* saw it, didn't we?"

She had turned, with the last sentence, to frown at Smith, the surviving outsider.

Smith moved uncomfortably. "I—I didn't see the start of it, Mrs. Halperin."

"You did," she snapped. "You were looking right at them, Mr. Smith."

Before Smith could answer, Hank Halperin was saying, "Lord, Granny, I'm sorry—but even that's no answer. This is *real* trouble. Remember I fought seven years in the ring as a pro. And the fists of a boxer or ex-boxer are legally considered lethal weapons. That makes it second degree murder even if he did hit first. You know that, Mr. Smith; you're a lawyer. And with the other trouble I've been in, the cops will throw the book at me."

"I—I'm afraid you're probably right," Smith said uneasily. "But hadn't somebody better phone a doctor or the police, or both?"

"In a minute, Smith," Bill Halperin, Smith's friend, said. "We got to get this straightened out among ourselves first. It *was* self-defense, wasn't it?"

"I—I guess. I don't—"

"Wait, everybody," Granny's sharp voice cut in. "Even if it was self-defense, Henry's in trouble. And do you think we can *trust* this man Smith once he's out of here and in court?"

Bill Halperin said, "But, Granny, we'll *have* to—"

"Nonsense, William. *I* saw what happened. We all did. They got in a fight, Cross and Smith, and killed each other. Cross killed Smith, and then, dizzy from the blows he'd taken himself, fell and hit his head. We're not going to let Henry go to jail, are we, children? Not a Halperin, *one of us.* Henry, muss that body up a little, so it'll look like he was in a fight, not just a one-punch business. And the rest of you—"

The male Halperins, except Henry, were in a circle around Smith now; the women, except Granny, were right behind them—and the circle closed in.

The last thing Smith saw clearly was Granny in her throne-like chair, her eyes beady with excitement and determination. And he was also aware of the sudden silence, which he could no longer make his voice penetrate. Then the first blow rocked him.

Alfred Hitchcock's Mystery Magazine, June 1960

Nightmare in Yellow

HE AWOKE when the alarm clock rang, but lay in bed a while after he'd shut it off, going a final time over the plans he'd made for embezzlement that day and for murder that evening.

Every little detail had been worked out, but this was the final check. Tonight at forty-six minutes after eight he'd be free, in every way. He'd picked that moment because this was his fortieth birthday and that was the exact time of day, of the evening rather, when he had been born. His mother had been a bug on astrology, which was why the moment of his birth had been impressed on him so exactly.

He wasn't superstitious himself but it had struck his sense of humor to have his new life begin at forty, to the minute.

Time was running out on him, in any case. As a lawyer who specialized in handling estates, a lot of money passed through his hands—and some of it had passed into them. A year ago he'd 'borrowed' five thousand dollars to put into something that looked like a surefire way to double or triple the money, but he'd lost it instead. Then he'd 'borrowed' more to gamble with, in one way or another, to try to recoup the first loss. Now he was behind to the tune of over thirty thousand; the shortage couldn't be hidden more than another few months and there wasn't a hope that he could replace the missing money by that time. So he had been raising all the cash he could without arousing suspicion, by carefully liquidating assets, and by this afternoon he'd have running-away money to the tune of well over a hundred thousand dollars, enough to last him the rest of his life.

And they'd never catch him. He'd planned every detail of his trip, his destination, his new identity, and it was foolproof. He'd been working on it for months.

His decision to kill his wife had been relatively an afterthought. The motive was simple: he hated her. But it was only after he'd come to the decision that he'd never go to jail, that he'd kill himself if he was ever apprehended, that it came to him that—since he'd die anyway if caught—he had nothing to lose in leaving a dead wife behind him instead of a living one.

He'd hardly been able to keep from laughing at the appropriateness of the birthday present she'd given him (yesterday, a day ahead of time); it had been a new suitcase. She'd also talked him into celebrating in his birthday by letting her meet him downtown for dinner at seven. Little did she guess how the celebration would go after that.

He planned to have her home by eight forty-six and satisfy his sense of the fitness of things by making himself a widower at that exact moment. There was a practical advantage, too, in leaving her dead. If he left her alive but asleep she'd guess what had happened and call police when she found him gone in the morning. If he left her dead her body would not be found that soon, possibly not for two or three days, and he'd have a much better start.

Things went smoothly at his office; by the time he went to meet his wife everything was ready. But she dawdled over drinks and dinner and he began to worry whether he could get her home by eight forty-six. It was ridiculous, he knew, but it had become important that his moment of freedom should come then and not a minute earlier or a minute later. He watched his watch.

He would have missed it by half a minute if he'd waited till they were inside the house. But the dark of the porch of their house was perfectly safe, as safe as inside. He swung the blackjack viciously once, as she stood at the front door, waiting for him to open it. He caught her before she fell and managed to hold her upright with one arm while he got the door open and then got it closed from the inside.

Then he flicked the switch and yellow light leaped to fill the room, and, before they could see that his wife was dead and that he was holding her up, all the assembled birthday party guests shouted *"Surprise!"*

Dude, May 1961

Cry Silence

IT WAS THAT OLD SILLY ARGUMENT about sound. If a tree falls deep in the forest where there is no ear to hear, is its fall silent? Is there sound where there is no ear to hear it? I've heard it—argued by college professors and by street sweepers.

This time it was being argued by the agent at the little railroad station and a beefy man in coveralls. It was a warm summer evening at dusk, and the station agent's window opening onto the back platform of the station was open; his elbows rested on the ledge of it. The beefy man leaned against the red brick of the building. The argument between them droned in circles like a bumblebee.

I sat on a wooden bench on the platform about ten feet away. I was a stranger in town, waiting for a train that was late. There was one other man present; he sat on the bench beside me, between me and the window. He was a tall, heavy man with an uncompromising kind of face, and huge, rough hands. He looked like a farmer in his town clothes.

I wasn't interested in either the argument or the man beside me. I was wondering only how late that damned train would be.

I didn't have my watch; it was being repaired in the city. And from where I sat I couldn't see the clock inside the station. The tall man beside me was wearing a wrist watch and I asked him what time it was.

He didn't answer.

You've got the picture, haven't you? Four of us; three on the platform and the agent leaning out of the window. The argument between the agent and the beefy man. On the bench, the silent man and I.

I got up off the bench and looked into the open door of the station. It was seven-forty; the train was twelve minutes overdue. I sighed, and lighted a cigarette. I decided to stick my nose into the argument. It wasn't any of my business, but I knew the answer and they didn't.

"Pardon me for butting in," I said, "but you're not arguing about sound at all; you're arguing semantics."

I expected one of them to ask me what semantics was, but the station agent fooled me. He said, "That's the study of words, isn't it? In a way, you're right, I guess."

"All the way," I insisted. "If you look up 'sound' in the dictionary, you'll find two meanings listed. One of them is 'the vibration of a medium, usually air, within a certain range,' and the other is 'the effect of such vibrations on the ear.' That isn't the exact wording, but the general idea. Now by one of those definitions, the sound—the vibration—exists whether there's an ear around to hear it or not. By the other, the vibrations aren't sound unless there is an ear to hear them. So you're both right; it's just a matter of which meaning you use for the word 'sound'."

The beefy man said, "Maybe you got something there." He looked back at the agent. "Let's call it a draw then, Joe. I got to get home. So long."

He stepped down off the platform and went around the station.

I asked the agent, "Any report on the train?"

"Nope," he said. He leaned a little farther out the window and looked to his right and I saw a clock in a steeple about a block away that I hadn't noticed before. "Ought to be along soon though."

He grinned at me. "Expert on sound, huh?"

"Well," I said, "I wouldn't say that. But I did happen to look it up in the dictionary. I know what the word means."

"Uh-huh. Well, let's take that second definition and say sound is sound only if there's an ear to hear it. A tree crashes in the forest and there's only a deaf man there. Is there any sound?"

"I guess not," I said. "Not if you consider sound as subjective. Not if it's got to be heard."

I happened to glance to my right, at the tall man who hadn't answered my question about the time. He was still staring straight ahead. Lowering my voice a bit, I asked the station agent, "Is he deaf?"

"Him? Bill Meyers?" He chuckled; there was something odd in the sound of that chuckle. "Mister, nobody knows. That's what I was going to ask you next. If that tree falls down and there's a man near, but nobody knows if he's deaf or not, is there any sound?"

His voice had gone up in volume. I stared at him, puzzled, wondering if he was a little crazy, or if he was just trying to keep up the argument by thinking up screwy loopholes.

I said, "Then if nobody knows if he's deaf, nobody knows if there was any sound."

He said, "You're wrong, mister. That man would know whether he heard it or not. Maybe the tree would know, wouldn't it? And maybe other people would know, too."

"I don't get your point," I told him. "What are you trying to prove?"

"*Murder,* mister. You just got up from sitting next to a murderer."

I stared at him again, but he didn't look crazy. Far off, a train whistled, faintly. I said, "I don't understand you."

"The guy sitting on the bench," he said. "Bill Meyers. He murdered his wife. Her and his hired man."

His voice was quite loud. I felt uncomfortable; I wished that far train was a lot nearer. I didn't know what went on here, but I knew I'd rather be on the train. Out of the corner of my eye I looked at the tall man with the granite face and the big hands. He was still staring out across the tracks. Not a muscle in his face had moved.

The station agent said, "I'll tell you about it, mister. I *like* to tell people about it. His wife was a cousin of mine, a fine woman. Mandy Eppert, her name was, before she married that skunk. He was mean to her, dirt mean. Know how mean a man can be to a woman who's helpless?

"She was seventeen when she was fool enough to marry him seven years ago. She was twenty-four when she died last spring. She'd done more work than most women do in a lifetime, out on that farm of his. He worked her like a horse and treated her like a slave. And her religion wouldn't let her divorce him or even leave him. See what I mean, mister?"

I cleared my throat, but there didn't seem to be anything to say. He didn't need prodding or comment. He went on.

"So how can you blame her, mister, for loving a decent guy, a clean, young fellow her own age when he fell in love with her? Just *loving* him, that's all. I'd bet my life on that because I knew Mandy. Oh, they talked, and they looked at each other—I wouldn't gamble too much there wasn't a stolen kiss now and then. But nothing to kill them for, mister."

I felt uneasy; I wished the train would come and get me out of this. I had to say something, though; the agent was waiting. I said, "Even if there had been, the unwritten law is out of date."

"Right, mister." I'd said the right thing. "But you know what that bastard sitting over there did? He went deaf."

"Huh?" I said.

"He went deaf. He came in town to see the doc and said he'd been having earaches and couldn't hear any more. Was afraid he was going deaf. Doc gave him some stuff to try, and you know where he went from the doc's office?"

I didn't try to guess.

"Sheriff's office," he said. "Told the sheriff he wanted to report his wife and his hired man were missing, see? Smart of him. Wasn't it? Swore out a complaint and said he'd prosecute if they were found. But he had an awful lot of trouble getting any of the questions the sheriff asked. Sheriff got tired of yelling and wrote 'em down on paper. Smart. See what I mean?"

"Not exactly," I said. "Hadn't his wife run away?"

"He'd murdered her. And him. Or rather, he was *murdering* them. Must have taken a couple of weeks, about. Found 'em a month later."

He glowered, his face black with anger.

"In the smokehouse," he said. "A new smokehouse made out of concrete and not used yet. With a padlock on the outside of the door. He'd walked through the farmyard one day about a month before—he said after their bodies were found—and noticed the padlock wasn't locked, just hanging in the hook and not even through the hasp.

"See? Just to keep the padlock from being lost or swiped, he slips it through the hasp and snaps it."

"My God," I said. "And they were in there? They starved to death?"

"Thirst kills you quicker, if you haven't either water or food. Oh, they'd tried hard to get out, all right. Scraped halfway through the door with a piece of concrete he'd worked loose. It was a thick door. I figure they hammered on that door plenty. Was there sound, mister, with only a *deaf* man living near that door, passing it twenty times a day?"

Again he chuckled humorlessly. He said: "Your train'll be along soon. That was it you heard whistle. It stops by the water tower. It'll be here in ten minutes." And without changing his tone of voice, except that it got louder again, he said: "It was a bad way to die. Even if he was right in killing them, only a black-hearted son of a bitch would have done it that way. Don't you think so?"

I said: "But are you sure he is—"

"Deaf? Sure, he's deaf. Can't you picture him standing there in front of that padlocked door, listening with his deaf ears to the hammering inside? And the yelling?

"Sure, he's deaf. That's why I can say all this to him, yell it in his ear. If I'm wrong, he can't hear me. But he can hear me. He comes here to hear me."

I had to ask it. "Why? Why would he—if you're right."

"I'm helping him, that's why. I'm helping him to make up his black mind to hang a rope from the grating in the top of that smokehouse, and dangle from it. He hasn't got the guts to, yet. So every time he's in town, he sits on the platform a while to rest. And I tell him what a murdering son of a bitch he is."

He spat toward the tracks. He said, "There are a few of us know the score. Not the sheriff he wouldn't believe us, said it would be hard to prove."

The scrape of feet behind me made me turn. The tall man with the huge hands and the granite face was standing up now. He didn't look toward us. He started for the steps.

The agent said, "He'll hang himself, pretty soon now. He wouldn't come here and sit like that for any other reason, would he, mister?"

"Unless," I said, "he *is* deaf."

"Sure. He could be. See what I meant? If a tree falls and the only man there to hear it is maybe deaf and maybe not, is it silent or isn't it? Well, I got to get the mail pouch ready."

I turned and looked at the tall figure walking away from the station. He walked slowly and his shoulders, big as they were, seemed a little stooped.

The clock in the steeple a block away began to strike for seven o'clock.

The tall man lifted his wrist to look at the watch on it.

I shuddered a little. It could have been coincidence, sure, and yet a little chill went down my spine.

The train pulled in, and I got aboard.

Black Mask, November 1948

I'll Cut Your Throat Again, Kathleen

I HEARD THE FOOTSTEPS coming down the hall and I was watching the door—the door that had no knob on my side of it—when it opened.

I thought I'd recognized the step, and I'd been right. It was the young, nice one, the one whose bright hair made so brilliant a contrast with his white uniform coat.

I said, "Hello, Red," and he said, "Hello, Mr. Marlin. I—I'll take you down to the office. The doctors are there now." He sounded more nervous than I felt.

"How much time have I got, Red?"

"How much— Oh, I see what you mean. They're examining a couple of others ahead of you. You've got time."

So I didn't get up off the edge of the bed. I held my hands out in front of me, backs up and the fingers rigid. They didn't tremble any more. My fingers were steady as those of a statue, and about as useful. Oh, I could move them. I could clench them into fists slowly. But for playing sax and clarinet they were about as good as hands of bananas. I turned them over—and there on my wrists were the two ugly scars where, a little less than a year ago, I'd slashed them with a straight razor. Deeply enough to have cut some of the tendons that moved the fingers.

I moved my fingers now, curling them inward toward the palm, slowly. The interne was watching.

"They'll come back, Mr. Marlin," he said. "Exercise—that's all they need." It wasn't true. He knew that I knew he knew it, for when I didn't bother to answer, he went on, almost defensively: "Anyway, you can still arrange and conduct. You can hold a baton all right. And—I got an idea for you, Mr. Marlin."

"Yes, Red?"

"Trombone. Why don't you take up trombone? You could learn it fast, and you don't need finger action to play trombone."

Slowly I shook my head. I didn't try to explain. It was something you couldn't explain, anyway. It wasn't only the physical ability to play an instrument that was gone. It was more than that.

I looked at my hands once more and then I put them carefully away in my pockets where I wouldn't have to look at them.

I looked up at the intern's face again. There was a look on it that I recognized and remembered—the look I'd seen on thousands of young faces across footlights—hero worship. Out of the past it came to me, that look.

He could still look at me that way, even after—

"Red," I asked him, "don't you think I'm insane?"

"Of course not, Mr. Marlin. I don't think you were ever—" He bogged down on that.

I needled him. Maybe it was cruel, but it was crueler to me. I said, "You don't think I was ever crazy? You think I was sane when I tried to kill my wife?"

"Well—it was just temporary. You had a breakdown. You'd been working too hard—twenty hours a day, about. You were near the top with your band. Me, Mr. Marlin, *I* think you were at the top. You had it on all of them, only most of the public hadn't found out yet. They would have, if—"

"If I hadn't slipped a cog," I said. I thought, what a way to express going crazy, trying to kill your wife, trying to kill yourself, and losing your memory.

Red looked at his wrist watch, then pulled up a chair and sat down facing me. He talked fast.

"We haven't got too long, Mr. Marlin," he said. "And I want you to pass those doctors and get out of here. You'll be all right once you get out of this joint. Your memory will come back, a little at a time—when you're in the right surroundings."

I shrugged. It didn't seem to matter much. I said, "Okay, brief me. It didn't work last time, but—I'll try."

"You're Johnny Marlin," he said. "*The* Johnny Marlin. You play a mean clarinet, but that's sideline. You're the best alto sax in the business, *I* think. You were fourth in the Down Beat poll a year ago, but—"

I interrupted him. "You mean I *did* play clarinet and sax. Not any more, Red. Can't you get that through your head?" I hadn't meant to sound so rough about it, but my voice got out of control.

Red didn't seem to hear me. His eyes went to his wrist watch again and then came back to me. He started talking again.

"We got ten minutes, maybe. I wish I knew what you remember and what you don't about all I've been telling you the last month. What's your right name—I mean, before you took a professional name?"

"John Dettman," I said. "Born June first, nineteen-twenty, on the wrong side of the tracks. Orphaned at five. Released from orphanage at sixteen. Worked as bus boy in Cleveland and saved up enough money to buy a clarinet, and took lessons. Bought a sax a year later, and got my first job with a band at eighteen."

"What band?"

"Heinie Wills'—local band in Cleveland, playing at Danceland there. Played third alto a while, then first alto. Next worked for a six-man combo called—What was it, Red? I don't remember."

"The Basin Streeters, Mr. Marlin. Look, do you really remember any of this, or is it just from what I've told you?"

"Mostly from what you've told me, Red. Sometimes, I get kind of vague pictures, but it's pretty foggy. Let's get on with it. So the Basin Streeters did a lot of traveling for a while and I left them in Chi for my first stretch with a name band— Look, I think I've got that list of bands pretty well memorized. There isn't much time. Let's skip it.

"I joined the army in forty-two—I'd have been twenty-two then. A year at Fort Billings, and then England. Kayoed by a bomb in London before I ever got to pull a trigger except on rifle range. A month in a hospital there, shipped back, six months in a mental hospital here, and let out on a P.N." He knew as well as I did what P.N. meant, but I translated it for us. "Psycho-neurotic. Nuts. Crazy."

He opened his mouth to argue the point, and then decided there wasn't time.

"So I'd saved my money," I said, "before and during the army, and I started my own band. That would have been—late forty-four?"

Red nodded. "Remember the list of places you've played, the names of your sidemen, what I told you about them?"

"Pretty well," I said. There wouldn't be time to go into that, anyway. I said, "And early in forty-seven, while I was still getting started, I got married. To Kathy Courteen. *The* Kathy Courteen, who owns a slice of Chicago, who's got more money than sense. She must have, if she married me. We were married June tenth, nineteen forty-seven. Why *did* she marry me, Red?"

"Why shouldn't she?" he said. "You're *Johnny Marlin!*"

The funny part of it is he wasn't kidding. I could tell by his voice he meant it. He thought being Johnny Marlin had really been something. I looked down at my hands. They'd got loose out of my pockets again.

I think I knew, suddenly, why I wanted to get out of this gilt-lined nuthouse that was costing Kathy Courteen—Kathy Marlin, I mean—the price of a fur coat every week to keep me in. It wasn't because I wanted *out,* really. It was because I wanted to get away from the hero worship of this redheaded kid who'd gone nuts about Johnny Marlin's band, and Johnny Marlin's saxophone.

"Have you ever seen Kathy, Red?" I asked.

He shook his head. "I've seen pictures of her, newspaper pictures of her. She's beautiful."

"Even with a scar across her throat?" I asked.

His eyes avoided mine. They went to his watch again, and he stood up quickly. "We'd better get down there," he said.

He went to the knobless door, opened it with a key, and politely held it open for me to precede him out into the hallway.

That look in his eyes made me feel foolish, as always. I don't know how he did it, but Red always managed to look *up* at me, from a height a good three inches taller than mine.

Then, side by side, we went down the great stairway of that lush, plush madhouse that had once been a million-dollar mansion and was now a million-dollar sanitarium with more employees than inmates.

We went into the office and the gray-haired nurse behind the desk nodded and said, "They're ready for you."

"Luck, Mr. Marlin," Red said. "I'm pulling for you."

So I went through the door. There were three of them, as last time.

"Sit down please, Mr. Marlin," Dr. Glasspiegel, the head one, said.

They sat each at one side of the square table, leaving the fourth side and the fourth chair for me. I slid into it. I put my hands in my pockets again. I knew if I looked at them or thought about them, I might say something foolish, and then I'd be here a while again.

Then they were asking me questions, taking turns at it. Some about my past—and Red's coaching had been good. Once or twice, but not often, I had to stall and admit my memory was hazy on a point or two. And some of the questions were about the present, and they were easy. I mean, it was easy to see what answers they wanted to those questions, and to give them.

But it had been like this the last time, I remembered, over a month ago. And I'd missed somewhere. They hadn't let me go. Maybe, I thought, because they got too much money out of keeping me here. I didn't really think that. These men were the best in their profession.

There was a lull in the questioning. They seemed to be waiting for something. For what? I wondered, and it came to me that the last interview had been like this, too.

The door behind me opened, quietly, but I heard it. And I remembered—that had happened last time, too. Just as they told me I could go back to my room and they'd talk it over, someone else had come in. I'd passed him as I'd left the room.

And, suddenly, I knew what I'd missed up on. It had been someone I'd been supposed to recognize, and I hadn't. And here was the same test again. Before I turned, I tried to remember what Red had told me about people I'd known—but there was so little physical description to it. It seemed hopeless.

"You may return to your room now, Mr. Marlin," Dr. Glasspiegel was saying. "We—ah—wish to discuss your case."

"Thanks," I said, and stood up.

I saw that he'd taken off his shell-rimmed glasses and was tapping them nervously on the back of his hand, which lay on the table before him. I thought, okay, so now I know the catch and next time I'll make the grade. I'll have Red get me pictures of my band and other bands I've played with and as many newspaper pictures as he can find of people I knew.

I turned. The man in the doorway, standing there as though waiting for me to leave, was short and fat. There was a tense look in his face, even though his eyes were avoiding mine. He was looking past me, at the doctors. I tried to think fast. Who did I know that was short and—

I took a chance. I'd had a trumpet player named Tubby Hayes.

"Tubby!" I said.

And hit the jackpot. His face lit up like a neon sign and he grinned a yard wide and stuck out his hand.

"Johnny! Johnny, it's good to see you." He was making like a pump handle with my arm.

"Tubby Hayes!" I said, to let them know I knew his last name, too. "Don't tell me you're nuts, too. That why you're here?"

He laughed, nervously. "I came to get you, Johnny. That is, uh, if—" He looked past me.

Dr. Glasspiegel was clearing his throat. He and the other doctors were standing now.

"Yes," he said, "I believe it will be all right for Mr. Marlin to leave."

He put his hand on my shoulder. They were all standing about me now.

"Your reactions are normal, Mr. Marlin," he said. "Your memory is still a bit impaired but—ah—it will improve gradually. More rapidly, I believe, amid familiar surroundings than here. You—ah—have plans?"

"No," I said, frankly.

"Don't overwork again. Take things easy for a while. And. . ."

There was a lot more advice. And then signing things, and getting ready. It was almost an hour before we got into a cab, Tubby and I.

He gave the address, and I recognized it. The Carleton. That was where I'd lived, that last year. Where Kathy still lived.

"How's Kathy?" I asked.

"Fine, Johnny. I guess she is. I mean—"

"You mean what?"

He looked a bit embarrassed. "Well—I mean I haven't seen her. She never liked us boys, Johnny. You know that. But she was square with us. You know we decided we couldn't hold together without you, Johnny, and might as well break up. Well, she paid us what we had coming—the three weeks you were on the cuff, I mean—and doubled it, a three-weeks' bonus to tide us over."

"The boys doing okay, Tubby?"

"Yep, Johnny. All of them. Well—except Harry. He kind of got lost in the snow if you know what I mean."

"That's tough," I said, and didn't elaborate. I didn't know whether I was supposed to know that Harry had been taking cocaine or not. And there had been two Harrys with the band, at that.

So the band was busted up. In a way I was glad. If someone had taken over and held it together maybe there'd have been an argument about trying to get me to come back.

"A month ago, Tubby," I said, "they examined me at the sanitarium, and I flunked. I think it was because I didn't recognize somebody. Was it you? Were you there then?"

"You walked right by me, through the door, Johnny. You never saw me."

"You were there—for that purpose? Both times?"

"Yes, Johnny. That Doc Glasspiegel suggested it. He got to know me, and to think of me, I guess, because I dropped around so often to ask about you. Why wouldn't they let me see you?"

"Rules," I said. "That's Glasspiegel's system, part of it. Complete isolation during the period of cure. I haven't even seen Kathy."

"No!" said Tubby. "They told me you couldn't have visitors, but I didn't know it went that far." He sighed. "She sure must be head over heels for you, Johnny. What I hear, she's carried the torch."

"God knows why," I said. "After I cut—"

"Shut up," Tubby said sharply. "You aren't to think or talk about that. Glasspiegel told me that while you were getting ready."

"Okay," I said. It didn't matter. "Does Kathy know we're coming?"

"We? I'm not going in, Johnny. I'm just riding to the door with you. No, she doesn't know. You asked the doc not to tell her, didn't you?"

"I didn't want a reception. I just want to walk in quietly. Sure, I asked the doctor, but I thought maybe he'd warn her anyway. So she could hide the knives."

"Now, Johnny—"

"Okay," I said.

I looked out of the window of the cab. I knew where we were and just how far from the Carleton. Funny my topography hadn't gone the way the rest of my memory had. I still knew the streets and their names, even though I couldn't recognize my best friend or my wife. The mind is a funny thing, I thought.

"One worry you won't have," Tubby Hayes said. "That lush brother of hers, Myron Courteen, the one that was always in your hair."

The red-headed interne had mentioned that Kathy had a brother. Apparently I wasn't supposed to like him.

So I said, "Did someone drop him down a well?"

"Headed west. He's a Los Angeles playboy now. Guess he finally quarreled with Kathy and she settled an allowance on him and let him go."

We were getting close to the Carleton—only a half-dozen blocks to go—and suddenly I realized there was a lot that I didn't know, and should know.

"Let's have a drink, Tubby," I said. "I—I'm not quite ready to go home yet."

"Sure, Johnny," he said, and then spoke to the cab driver.

We swung in to the curb in front of a swanky neon-plated tavern. It didn't look familiar, like the rest of the street did. Tubby saw me looking.

"Yeah, it's new," he said. "Been here only a few months."

We went in and sat at a dimly lighted bar. Tubby ordered two Scotch-and-sodas—without asking me, so I guess that's what I used to drink. I didn't remember. Anyway, it tasted all right, and I hadn't had a drink for eleven months, so even the first sip of it hit me a little.

And when I'd drunk it all, it tasted better than all right. I looked at myself in the blue mirror back of the bar. I thought, there's always this. I can always drink myself to death—on Kathy's money. I knew I didn't have any myself because Tubby had said I was three weeks on the cuff with the band.

We ordered a second round and I asked Tubby, "How come this Myron hasn't money of his own, if he's Kathy's brother?" He looked at me strangely. I'd been doing all right up to now. I said, "Yeah, there are things I'm still hazy about."

"Oh," he said. "Well, that one's easy. Myron is worse than a black sheep for the Courteens. He's a no-good louse and an all-around stinker. He was disinherited, and Kathy got it all. But she takes care of him."

He took a sip of his drink and put it down again. "You know, Johnny," he said, "none of us liked Kathy much because she was against you having the band and wanted you to herself. But we were wrong about her. She's swell. The way she sticks to her menfolk no matter what they do. Even Myron."

"Even me," I said.

"Well—she saved your life, Johnny. With blood—" He stopped abruptly. "Forget it, Johnny."

I finished my second drink. I said, "I'll tell you the truth, Tubby. I can't forget it—because I don't remember it. But I've got to know, before I face her. What did happen that night?"

"Johnny, I—"

"Tell me," I said. "Straight."

He sighed. "Okay, Johnny. You'd been working close to twenty-four hours a day trying to put us over, and we'd tried to get you to slow down and so did Kathy."

"Skip the buildup."

"That night, after we played at the hotel, we rehearsed some new stuff. You acted funny, then, Johnny. You forgot stuff, and you had a headache. We made you go home early, in spite of yourself. And when you got home—well you slipped a cog, Johnny. You picked a quarrel with your wife—I don't know what you accused her of. And you went nuts. You got your razor—you always used to shave with a straight edge—and, well you tried to kill her. And then yourself."

"You're skipping the details," I said. "How did she save my life?"

"Well, Johnny, you hadn't killed her like you thought. The cut went deep on one side of her throat but—she must have been pulling away—it went light across the center and didn't get the jugular or anything. But there was a lot of blood and she fainted, and you thought she was dead, I guess, and slashed your own wrists. But she came to, and found you bleeding to death fast. Bleeding like she was, she got tourniquets on both your arms and held 'em and kept yelling until one of the servants woke up and got the Carleton house doctor. That's all, Johnny."

"It's enough, isn't it?" I thought a while and then I added, "Thanks, Tubby. Look, you run along and leave me. I want to think it out and sweat it out alone, and then I'll walk the rest of the way. Okay?"

"Okay, Johnny," he said. "You'll call me up soon?"

"Sure," I said. "Thanks for everything."

"You'll be all right, Johnny?"

"Sure. I'm all right."

After he left I ordered another drink. My third, and it would have to be my last, because I was really feeling them. I didn't want to go home drunk to face Kathy.

I sat there, sipping it slowly, looking at myself in that blue mirror back of the bar. I wasn't a bad-looking guy, in a blue mirror. Only I should be dead instead of sitting there. I should have died that night eleven months ago. I'd tried to die.

I was almost alone at the bar. There was one couple drinking martinis at the far end of it. The girl was a blonde who looked like a chorus girl. I wondered idly if Kathy was a blonde. I hadn't thought to ask anyone. If Kathy walked in here now, I thought, I wouldn't know her.

The blonde down there picked up some change off the bar and walked over to the juke box. She put in a coin and punched some buttons, and then swayed her hips back to the bar. The juke box started playing and it was an old record and a good one—the Harry James version of the *Memphis Blues*. Blue and brassy stuff from the days back before Harry went commercial.

I sat there listening, and feeling like the devil. I thought, I've got to get over it. Every time I hear stuff like that I can't go on wanting to kill myself just because I can't play anymore. I'm not the only guy in the world who can't play music. And the others get by.

My hands were lying on the bar in front of me and I tried them again, while I listened, and they wouldn't work. They wouldn't ever work again. My thumbs were okay, but the four fingers on each hand opened and closed together and not separately, as though they were webbed together.

Maybe the Scotch was making me feel better, but—maybe, I decided—maybe it wouldn't be too bad—

Then the Harry James ended and another record slid onto the turntable and started, and it was going to be blue, too. *Mood Indigo*. I recognized the opening bar of the introduction. I wondered idly if all the records were blues, chosen to match the blue back-bar mirrors.

Deep blue stuff, anyway, and well-handled and arranged, whoever was doing it. A few Scotches and a blue mood, and that *Mood Indigo* can take hold of your insides and wring them. And this waxing of it was solid, pretty solid. The brasses tossed it to the reeds and then the piano took it for a moment, backed by wire-brush stuff on the skins, and modulated it into a higher key and built it up and you knew something was coming.

And then something came, and it was an alto sax, a sax with a tone like blue velvet, swinging high, wide and off the beat, and tossing in little arabesques of counterpoint so casually that it never seemed to leave the melody to do it. An alto sax riding high and riding hot, pouring notes like molten gold.

I unwound my fingers from around the Scotch-and-soda glass and got up and walked across the room to the juke box. I knew already but I looked. The record playing was Number 9, and Number 9 was *Mood Indigo*—Johnny Marlin.

For a black second I felt that I had to stop it, that I had to smash my fist through the glass and jerk the tone arm off the record. I had to because it was doing things to me. That sound out of the past was making me remember, and I knew suddenly that the only way I could keep on wanting to live at all was *not* to remember.

Maybe I would have smashed the glass. I don't know. But instead I saw the cord and plug where the juke box plugged into the wall outlet beside it. I jerked on the cord and the box went dark and silent. Then I walked out into the dusk, with the three of them staring at me—the blonde and her escort and the bartender.

The bartender called out "Hey!" but didn't go on with it when I went on out without turning. I saw them in the mirror on the inside of the door as I opened it, a frozen tableau that slid sidewise off the mirror as the door swung open.

I must have walked the six blocks to the Carleton, through the gathering twilight. I crossed the wide mahogany-paneled lobby to the elevator. The uniformed operator looked familiar to me—more familiar than Tubby had. At least there was an impression that I'd seen him before.

"Good evening, Mr. Marlin," he said, and didn't ask me what floor I wanted. But his voice sounded strange, tense, and he waited a moment, stuck his head out of the elevator and looked around before he closed the door. I got the impression that he was hoping for another passenger, that he hated to shut himself and me in that tiny closed room.

But no one else came into the lobby and he slid the door shut and moved the handle. The building slid downward past us and came to rest at the eleventh floor. I stepped out into another mahogany-paneled hall and the elevator door slid shut behind me.

It was a short hallway, on this floor, with only four doors leading to what must be quite large suites. I knew which door was mine—or I should say Kathy's. My money never paid for a suite like that.

It wasn't Kathy who opened the door. I knew that because it was a girl wearing a maid's uniform. And she must, I thought, be new. She looked at me blankly.

"Mrs. Marlin in?" I asked.

"No sir. She'll be back soon, sir."

I went on in. "I'll wait," I said. I followed her until she opened the door of a room that looked like a library.

"In here, please," she said. "And may I have your name?"

"Marlin," I said, as I walked past her. "Johnny Marlin."

She caught her breath a little, audibly. Then she said, "Yes, sir," and hurried away.

Her heels didn't click on the thick carpeting of the hall, but I could tell she was hurrying. Hurrying away from a homicidal maniac, back to the farthest reaches of the apartment, probably to the protective company of a cook who would keep a cleaver handy, once she heard the news that the mad master of the manse was back. And likely there'd be new servants, if any, tomorrow.

I walked up and down a while, and then decided I wanted to go to my room. I thought, if I don't think about it I can go there. My subconscious will know the way. And it worked; I went to my room.

I sat on the edge of the bed a while, with my head in my hands, wondering why I'd come here. Then I looked around. It was a big room, paneled like the rest of the joint, beautifully and tastefully furnished. Little Johnny Dettman of the Cleveland slums had come a long way to have a room like that, all to himself. There was a Capehart radio-phonograph across the room from me, and a big cabinet of albums. Most of the pictures on the walls were framed photographs of bands. In a silver frame on the dresser was the picture of a woman.

That would be Kathy, of course. I crossed over and looked at it. She was beautiful, all right, a big-eyed brunette with pouting, kissable lips. And the fog was getting thinner. I almost knew and remembered her.

I looked a long time at that photograph, and then I put it down and went to the closet door. I opened it and there were a lot of suits in that closet, and a lot of pairs of shoes and a choice of hats. I remembered; John Dettman had worn a sweater to high school one year because he didn't have a suit coat.

But there was something missing in that closet. The instrument cases. On the floor, there at the right, should have been two combination cases for sax and clarinet. Inside them should have been two gold-plated alto saxes and two sleek black Selmer clarinets. At the back of the closet should have been a bigger case that held a baritone sax I sometimes fooled around with at home.

They were all gone, and I was grateful to Kathy for that. She must have understood how it would make me feel to have them around.

I closed the door gently and opened the door next to it, the bathroom. I went in and stood looking at myself in the mirror over the wash bowl. It wasn't a blue mirror. I studied my face, and it was an ordinary face. There wasn't any reason in that mirror why anyone should love me the way my wife must. I wasn't tall and I wasn't handsome. I was just a mug who had played a lot of sax—once.

The mirror was the door of a built-in medicine cabinet sunk into the tile wall and I opened it. Yes, all my toilet stuff was neatly laid out on the shelves of the cabinet, as though I'd never been away, or as though I'd been expected back daily. Even—and I almost took a step backwards—both of my straight razors—the kind of a razor a barber uses—lay there on the bottom shelf beside the shaving mug and brush.

Was Kathy crazy to leave them there, after what I'd used such a thing for? Had it even been one of these very razors? I could, of course, have had three of them, but— No, I remembered, there were only two, a matched pair.

In the sanitarium I'd used an electric razor, naturally. All of them there did, even ones there for less deadly reasons than mine. And I was going to keep on using one. I'd take these and drop them down the incinerator, right now. If my wife was foolhardy enough to leave those things in a madman's room, I wasn't. How could I be sure I'd never go off the beam again?

My hand shook a little as I picked them up and closed the mirrored door. I'd take them right now and get rid of them. I went out of the bathroom and was crossing my own room, out in the middle of it, when there was a soft tap on the door—the connecting door from Kathy's room. "Johnny—" her voice said.

I thrust the razors out of sight into my coat pocket, and answered —I don't remember exactly what. My heart seemed to be in my throat, blocking my voice. And the door opened and Kathy came in—came in like the wind in a headlong rush that brought her into my arms. And with her face buried in my shoulder.

"Johnny, Johnny," she was saying, "I'm so glad you're back."

Then we kissed, and it lasted a long time, that kiss. But it didn't do anything to me. If I'd been in love with Kathy once, I'd have to start all over again, now. Oh, it was nice kissing her, as it would be nice kissing any beautiful woman. It wouldn't be hard to fall again. But so much easier and better, I thought, if I could push away all of the fog, if I could remember.

"I'm glad to be back, Kathy," I said.

Her arms tightened about me, almost convulsively. There was a big lounge chair next to the Capehart. I picked her up bodily, since she didn't want to let go of me, and crossed to the chair. I sat in it with her on my lap. After a minute she straightened up and her eyes met mine, questioningly.

The question was, "Do you love me, Johnny?"

But I couldn't meet it just then. I'd pretend, of course, when I got my bearings, and after a while my memory would come the rest of the way back—or I'd manage to love her again, instead. But just then, I ducked the question and her eyes.

Instead, I looked at her throat and saw the scar. It wasn't as bad as I'd feared. It was a thin, long line that wouldn't have been visible much over a yard away.

"Plastic surgery, Johnny," she said. "It can do wonders. Another year and it won't show at all. It—it doesn't matter." Then, as though to forestall my saying anything more about it, she said quickly, "I gave away your saxophones, Johnny. I—I figured you wouldn't want them around. The doctors said you'll never be able to—to play again."

I nodded. I said, "I guess it's best not to have them around."

"It's going to be so wonderful, Johnny. Maybe you'll hate me for saying it, but I'm—almost—glad. You know that was what came between us, your band and your playing. And it won't now, will it? You won't want to try another band—just directing and not playing—or anything foolish like that, will you, Johnny?"

"No, Kathy," I said.

Nothing, I thought, would mean anything without playing. I'd been trying to forget that. I closed my eyes and tried, for a moment, not to think.

"It'll be so wonderful, Johnny. You can do all the things I wanted you to do, and that you wouldn't. We can travel, spend our winters in Florida, and entertain. We can live on the Riviera part of the time, and we can ski in the Tyrol and play the wheels at Monte Carlo and—and everything I've wanted to do, Johnny."

"It's nice to have a few million," I said.

She pulled back a little and looked at me. "Johnny, you're not going to start *that* again, are you? Oh, Johnny, you can't—now."

No, I thought, I can't. Heaven knows why she wants him to be one, but little Johnny Dettman is a kept man, now, a rich girl's darling. He can't make money the only way he knows how now. He couldn't even hold a job as a bus boy or dig ditches. But he'll learn to balance teacups on his knee and smile at dowagers. He'll have to. It was coming back to me now, that endless argument.

But the argument was over now. There wasn't any longer anything to argue about.

"Kiss me, Johnny," Kathy said, and when I had, she said, "Let's have some music, huh? And maybe a dance—you haven't forgotten how to dance, have you, Johnny?"

She jumped up from my lap and went to the record album cabinet.

"Some of mine, will you, Kathy?" I asked. I thought I might as well get used to it now, all at once. So I won't feel again, ever, as I had when I'd almost put my fist through that juke box window.

"Of course, Johnny."

She took them from one of the albums, half a dozen of them, and put them on the Capehart. The first one started, and it was a silly gay tune we'd once *waxed—Chickery chick, cha la, cha la. . .* And she came back, holding out her hands to me to get up and dance, and I did, and I still knew how to dance.

And we danced over to the French doors that led to the balcony and opened them, and out onto the marble floor of the little railed balcony, into the cool darkness of the evening, with a full moon riding high in the sky overhead.

Chickery chick—a nice tune, if a silly tune. No vocal, of course. We'd never gone for them. Not gut-bucket stuff, either, but smooth rhythm, with a beat. And a high-riding alto sax, smooth as silk.

And I was remembering the argument. It had been one, a vicious one. Musician versus playboy as my career. I was remembering *Kathy* now, and suddenly tried not to. Maybe it would be better to forget all that bitterness, the quarreling and the overwork and everything that led up to the blankness of the breakdown.

But our feet moved smoothly on the marble. Kathy danced well. And the record ended.

"It's going to be wonderful, Johnny," she whispered, "having you all to myself... You're *mine* now, Johnny."

"Yes," I said. I thought, I've *got* to be.

The second record started, and was a contrast. A number as blue as *Mood Indigo,* and dirtier. *St. James Infirmary,* as waxed by Johnny Marlin and his orchestra. And I remembered the hot day in the studio when we'd waxed it. Again no vocal, but as we started dancing again, the words ran through my mind with the liquid gold of the alto sax I'd once played.

"I went down to St. James Infirmary... Saw my *baby* there... Stretched on a long white table... so sweet, so cold, so—"

I jerked away from her, ran inside and shut off the phonograph. I caught sight of my face in the mirror over the dresser as I passed. It was white as a corpse's face. I went back to the balcony. Kathy still stood there—she hadn't moved.

"Johnny, what—?"

"That tune," I said. "Those words. I *remember,* Kathy. I remember that night. *I didn't do it.*"

I felt weak. I leaned back against the wall behind me. Kathy came closer.

"Johnny—what do you mean?"

"I remember," I said. "I walked in, and you were lying there—with blood all over your throat and your dress—when *I came in the room.* I don't remember after that—but that's what must have knocked me off my base, after everything else. That's when I went crazy, not before."

"Johnny—you're wrong—"

The weakness was gone now. I stood straighter.

"Your brother," I said. "He hated you because you ran his life, like you wanted to run mine, because you had the money he thought should be his, and you doled it out to him and *ran* him. Sure, he hated you. I remember him now. Kathy, I remember. That was about the time he got past liquor and was playing with dope. Heroin, wasn't it? And that night he must have come in, sky-high and murderous, before I did. And tried to kill you, and must have thought he did, and ran. It must have been just before I came in."

"Johnny, please—you're wrong—"

"You came to, after I keeled over," I said. "It—it sounds incredible, Kathy, but it had to be that way. And, Kathy, that cold mind of yours saw a way to get everything it wanted. To protect your brother, and to get me, the way you wanted me. It was perfect, Kathy. Fix me so I'd never play again, and at the same time put me in a spot where I'd be tied to you forever because I'd think I tried to kill you."

I said, "You get your way, don't you, Kathy? At any cost. But you didn't want me to die. I'll bet you had those tourniquets ready *before you slashed my wrists.*"

She was beautiful, standing there in the moonlight. She stood tall and straight, and she came the step between us and put her soft arms around me.

"I don't see, though," I said, "how you could have known I wouldn't remember what really— Wait, I can see how you thought that. I had a drink or two on the way home. You smelled the liquor on me and thought I'd come home drunk, dead drunk. And I always drew a blank when I got drunk. That night I wasn't but the shock and the breakdown did even more to me. Damn you, Kathy."

"But, Johnny, don't I win?"

She was beautiful, smiling, leaning back to look up into my face. Yes, she'd won. *So sweet, so cold, so bare.* So bare her throat that in the moonlight I could see the faint scar, the dotted line. And one of my crippled hands, in my pocket, fumbled open one of the razors, brought it out of my pocket and up and across.

Mystery Book Magazine, winter 1948

A Little White Lye

DIRK came into their hotel room with excitement shining in his eyes. He grabbed Ginny and kissed her.

After the kiss, she pulled back a little to look at him.

"Dirk, have you—"

"Yes, Angel. Found just exactly the place we've been hoping for. In fact, better than we hoped to find, really. The house is smallish but not too small. Five rooms. But a big yard and no near neighbors, all the privacy and quiet in the world. On the edge of town, almost out in the country."

"It sounds—but can we afford it, Dirk? How much?"

"Believe it or not, only seven thousand. And one thousand down. Come on and give your okay so we can grab it before the agent finds out he's being gypped!"

It sounded to Ginny as though all their troubles were over, if only she liked the house.

Dirk's car was being repaired at the garage and they took the bus. The agent, Dirk told her, was to meet them there.

Ginny held her thumbs all the way out, hoping that she'd like it. A hotel is fine for a honeymoon, she thought, but it gets awful once you're back and want a place of your own. They'd been back a week now from their brief but ecstatic trip. Brief because Dirk had wanted to save his money for a down payment on a place of their own. The honeymoon had been as short but wonderful as the courtship that had preceded it. It seemed almost impossible to believe that she'd known Dirk only a month. It seemed impossible to believe that so much had happened in only four weeks.

Then they were off the bus, and walking, and after a few blocks Dirk said, "That's it, Angel!"

It *was* a nice house, or seemed to be from the outside. A bit lonely with the nearest other residence a full block away and screened by trees.

But that didn't matter much.

There was a little picket fence around the front yard, and the lawn was in excellent condition. The house had green shutters and plenty of windows.

A friendly agent met them on the porch and showed them through Ginny's eyes brightened as she planned just what furniture she would need to put in each room.

The agent seemed to be ignoring Dirk; he concentrated on Ginny as though Dirk was already in the bag, and he did a shrewd job of selling her. They came, finally, to the kitchen. This was the agent's hole card, this was the clincher.

It had windows over the sink, low windows, the kind that swing open. It had a nook for a refrigerator, and cabinets. Cabinets enough for anybody.

Ginny looked around once more, and took a deep breath. It *did* seem impossible that a place like this would go for such a price. She looked fearfully at the agent, wondering if Dirk could have misunderstood. She asked, "And—how much?"

"Seven thousand, Madam. And excellent terms, of course—"

They'd seen places for ten thousand, even twelve, that were worse.

The agent was hemming and hawing now. He said, "It's only fair, of course, to tell you—" He cleared his throat again. "Uh—you'll remember that it has an unfortunate history. That is the reason it's being sold so reasonably. The former tenant rented it, and—uh— you've heard about it, undoubtedly."

Ginny didn't seem to have anything to say at the moment, and Dirk said, "I don't believe we understand. What happened here?"

"The—uh—the newspapers called it the Love Nest Murder, Mr. Rogers. Undoubtedly you read about it, just a few months ago."

"I think I remember the headlines," said Dirk. "I never read that kind of story unless— You say it happened right here?"

The agent nodded, his eyes troubled. He said, "I never met Mr. Cartwright, the—murderer. I was working for another agency then. But I've read about the case. And I can assure you that the bathtub you just saw is a brand-new one."

"The bathtub?" echoed Ginny a bit blankly. And then suddenly, "*I* remember now, reading about it. After he strangled her he tried to—he put her in the bathtub and filled it with lye—"

Dirk shuddered a little.

He said, "The Love Nest Murder. It sounds—ugh!"

There was a curiously stubborn look on Ginny's oval face. She said, "Dirk, let's take it."

There was a strange twist to Dirk's lips. He said again, "The Love Nest Murder. Angel, I wish they'd *named* it something else. But I suppose we can forget about it. If you say so, we'll take it."

And they did. They moved in just five days later, and in the chaos of buying as much furniture as they could—on the installment plan—they almost succeeded in forgetting about "it."

But there were neighbors, even though they were a block away. They were neighborly neighbors, and Ginny got to know them. She told Dirk at dinner one evening: "That Mrs. Platt in the next house—the widow—told me all about this house today."

Dirk merely grunted, and Ginny looked at him suspiciously. "Aren't you interested?"

He shook his head. "Look," he said, "we're here, but the less we think about whatever happened—"

"Sissy," Ginny interrupted. Then her face became serious. "I think it's wrong to—to ignore it. To think about 'whatever' happened instead of knowing the whole thing. It's the unknown that gets people down. Just thinking of it as the Love Nest Murder instead of—"

"Don't," said Dirk, putting down his knife and fork, "use that awful phrase. All right, go ahead and tell me about it and get it off your mind."

"Well," Ginny began, "this woman had some money. At least, that's what everybody thought. Well-to-do and a bit eccentric because she didn't believe in keeping whatever money she had in banks and people said she hid it. She was thirty-six."

Dirk grunted. "Trust the neighbors to know that."

"Why shouldn't they know it? The marriage license applications in the papers show people's ages, don't they? And this Cartwright man was younger, and handsome in a way, and—"

"And he married her for her money," Dirk supplied wearily.

Ginny nodded. "And then he tired of her, I suppose, or maybe he couldn't *get* her money, so he strangled her in—"

"You told me about that part," Dirk said quickly.

"But her bones wouldn't dissolve," Ginny went on. "And he hadn't even finished getting rid of—uh—the rest of her, when some of her friends got suspicious and—called the police."

"What made them suspicious?"

Ginny said, "I don't know exactly. But he got scared, and got away in time. When the police came they found—they found the mess in the bathtub."

"Well," Dirk said. "Now I know. Now let's not talk about it anymore." He picked up his knife and fork, and then put them down again."

"This Cartwright," Ginny said ominously, "hasn't been caught—yet."

"He will be," Dirk said. He looked at Ginny thoughtfully. "Do you really feel better now that you've talked about all the sorry details?"

Ginny's lower lip was trembling. "I thought, maybe, I would; maybe if I said it all out loud I could forget it." There was moisture, suddenly, in her eyes. "Oh, Dirk—"

Swiftly he rose and came around the table. Tenderly he tilted her chin and kissed her. "Now *quit* thinking about it," he said. "Or bargain or no bargain, we move out of here quick."

Ginny wiped her eyes with an absurdly little handkerchief. She said, "All right, Dirk. But honestly, I'm *not* sorry we bought it. But—I'll feel better when that man is caught."

"And don't let that Mrs. Pratt next door talk to you about it. You—you just tell anybody that wants to talk to you about it that you don't."

Ginny nodded dutifully. Of course Dirk was right. He'd been right all along and she'd been a dumb-bunny to think the way to forget something was to talk about it. She felt so humble she didn't even correct him on his mispronunciation of Mrs. Platt's name. And that was quite something for Ginny, because she loved to correct people who made mistakes.

That had been Tuesday, at dinner, and it had spoiled the dinner.

There'd been a bad moment Tuesday night, around midnight. Ginny, who was usually a very heavy sleeper, chanced to wake up then. She rolled over—and found she was alone in the bed. Dirk was gone.

For an instant she was startled, then she remembered that Dirk often got up around that time to raid the icebox. He was a restless sleeper, and seldom slept soundly for more than an hour or two at a stretch.

She listened for sounds that would indicate that he was out there—the scrape of a chair or the opening or closing of the icebox door. Or—

But the sound she heard was a muffled tapping. It kept on a moment and then changed tone, as though Dirk—if it *was* Dirk—had quit tapping on something and started tapping on something else.

Tap—tap—tap. Tap—tap—tap. Not a familiar sound. It wasn't the noise Dirk's pipe made being knocked out, because that was a succession of more rapid taps. Faster and sharper.

Wide awake now, and a bit afraid without knowing what she was afraid of, Ginny slid her feet out of bed and into the slippers on the floor beside it. She slipped a bathrobe over her shoulders and went through the bedroom door, which led into the dining room.

Yes, the kitchen light was on. The kitchen door squeaked when she opened it, and Dirk, standing in front of the built-in cabinet over the sink, looked over his shoulder and then turned.

His voice was casual. "Did I wake you, Angel?"

"N-no. I just woke up. But what was that funny tapping noise?"

Dirk grinned a bit shamefacedly. "I imagined something. It looked to me as though this cupboard wasn't as deep on one side as on the other, and I just got curious. But I was wrong."

Ginny said, "Oh," a bit blankly. What if the cupboard *were* deeper on one side than the other?

"Something to eat, now that you're up?" Dirk asked. "I was just getting the crackers out of the cupboard, and there's some swell cheese. Just the thing for a little mouse like you."

She *was* hungry, a little. Neither of them had eaten much dinner, she remembered now, because— But no, don't think of what they'd been talking about, she told herself, or it would spoil her appetite now, too.

And Dirk, with a sharp knife in his hand, but smiling, was already slicing the cheese. . .

~§~

She didn't see the widow until late afternoon of the next day, when she walked by on the way to the grocery. The widow was working at the flowerbed just inside the fence, and Ginny said, "Hello, Mrs. Platt."

"Pratt," corrected the widow, smiling. "How are you my dear?"

"I'm fine," Ginny told her. "Sorry I got your name wrong. And my husband had it right, then. I didn't know he'd met you."

"He hasn't," said Mrs. Pratt. "These Zinnias are going to be beautiful here, I think. No, I've seen your husband only at a distance, when he's driven by. You must bring him over sometime."

"I will," Ginny said. "But I wonder how he knew your name when I told it to him wrong. I—" And then realizing that by implication she sounded as though she were doubting Dirk and Mrs. Pratt both, she said quickly, "Yes, zinnias will go nicely there. What have you planted in that other bed, back by the porch?"

"Gladioli. But about your husband—I'll bet the agent he bought the house from talked about me to him. I rent from him, too. And he probably said, 'Mr. Rogers, you want to be careful of that awful widow, Mrs. Pratt, who lives in the next house'."

Ginny laughed heartily at the very thought of anyone saying that. But undoubtedly it was—in a way—the explanation. The agent had brought Dirk here first and had talked to Dirk alone. He might easily have mentioned the name of the nearest neighbor, since he knew her.

Mrs. Pratt was taking off the cotton gloves she'd been wearing. She said, "Well, that's enough gardening for today. Will you have a cup of tea with me?"

"I really haven't time—" said Ginny hesitantly. But she did.

She wasn't, of course, going to talk about "it." That is, she thought she wasn't, until all of a sudden there was the subject, big as life, being talked about. And Ginny listening with both ears.

"My dear," Mrs. Pratt asked her. "Have you *searched* the place since you lived there? The police did, of course, and they didn't find anything, but I've often wondered—"

"Searched it?" Ginny wanted to know. "For what?"

"Why, for the *money*, of course. Everybody says it was hidden there, somewhere, and nobody knows whether *he* got it or not. He left in an awful hurry, you know, after—after he found the police were coming."

Ginny said hesitantly, "But he—he wouldn't have killed her, would he, unless he knew that he could get the money?"

Mrs. Pratt shrugged complacently. "Don't forget, my dear, he tried to dispose of the body. If he'd succeeded, he could have had time to take the house apart, practically, afterwards. I'd say he knew it was in the house all right, but he *may* not have found it."

"You say the police searched, though?" Ginny asked. (Why, Dirk had known about this and hadn't told her. That was why he had been searching in the kitchen last night. That was why she'd seen him wandering about the house so much, and with that curious, inquisitive expression on his face. Why hadn't Dirk told her?)

"Oh, they went through the place," said Mrs. Pratt, her manner clearly indicating that she didn't think much of either the police or their methods. "But I think they sort of assumed *he* had it already."

"Oh," said Ginny, feeling vaguely uneasy at the mere possibility of money, big money, being hidden in the house over there. It seemed almost worse, more dangerous, than—than the other. That was past. Maybe the money was *still there*.

She said, "But if he didn't get it wouldn't he have come back while the house was empty?"

Mrs. Pratt shrugged again. "He might have, of course, but if he did it was taking an awful chance. He's *wanted* now for murder. And all the while it was empty the policemen on the beat kept an eye on it, and the squad cars went by. And I told the police if I ever saw a light there at night I'd phone them."

"And there was no sign that he ever came back?"

"Nary a sign," said Mrs. Pratt. "What *I* think is that he ran far when he ran. That he's *miles* away from here and will stay away until it's all blown over, and then some day when he thinks it's safe he'll— Oh, I shouldn't say this, my dear"

Ginny found that her lips were tightly pressed together. She relaxed them with an effort and forced herself to smile. She said, "I'm afraid you've already said it. And I won't lie to you, I am a bit frightened. But I won't let it scare me out. It's our house now, and I'm going to live there no matter what."

"Does your husband have a revolver?"

"Yes," said Ginny. Dirk didn't have one, but she made up her mind then and there that he would buy one the next day, so she might as well answer in the affirmative now, hadn't she? (Oh, Dirk, you should have thought of that yourself. You knew about the possibility of the money being there, or you wouldn't have been hunting for it. Why didn't you tell me?)

Mrs. Pratt said, "And if I were you I'd be very, very careful about agents, and vacuum cleaner salesmen and people like that. You know he was an actor, I suppose?"

"No, I didn't," said Ginny, faintly.

"Well, he was. He could probably disguise himself so you wouldn't know him at all. I wouldn't let anybody in the house, unless he was short and fat, maybe. Even an actor couldn't do that with makeup."

"He was tall and thin, then?" Ginny asked.

"Not really tall," said Mrs. Pratt. "But an inch or two above average. Five foot eleven, about. Slender, but not thin. You have a telephone, of course, haven't you?"

"Of course," said Ginny, and then resolutely changed the subject and, ten minutes later, got away.

It was too late now to go to the grocery after all, and Dirk would have to be satisfied with eating something that was already in the house. But Dirk was good about such things; he seldom complained.

(Dirk, dearest, were you trying to spare my feelings by not telling me what you were searching for? *I'd rather know. I'd rather know the worst, any day.*)

Dirk was sitting in the Morris chair, reading, when she came in. Had he been sitting there all along, or had he been searching again, while she was out, and run for the chair and the book when he heard her coming?

He said, "Hi, Angel. What's for grub?"

"Dirk, I'm so sorry. I didn't get to the store at all. Mrs. Pratt asked me in for a cup of tea and we talked so much I looked up at the clock and—"

"Ummm-hmmm," Dirk drawled. "Baked beans, I suppose."

"No, I can make a salad except that it won't have any celery in it, and we've got some boiled ham left, enough for a sandwich apiece."

"Swell," said Dirk. "A loaf of bread, a slice of ham, and thou beside me sitting in the wilderness"

"Dirk, do you—don't you think it would be a good idea for you to get a revolver? Tomorrow?"

"Why—I've been arranging to get one, Angel." He looked at her, and the laughter was out of his eyes. "Matter of fact, I'm going to get it this evening, from a friend of mine who has a spare one."

He put the book down on the arm of the chair, shutting it without marking his place. "Have you been talking to this widow-woman about—you know what?"

"N-no," said Ginny.

Dirk smiled, surprisingly, and said "Tsk, tsk. Never stutter when you tell a lie. But I'm glad to know you're not a good liar, Angel. First time you ever tried it, and it sticks out like a sore thumb. Now I can trust you."

He reached out and caught her wrist, pulled her into his lap and kissed her soundly.

(And this, Ginny thought, is the time I should take him to task for lying to *me*. About the cupboard last night and— But he didn't really lie, did he? No, he just didn't tell all the truth, and that's not quite as bad. But— Dirk, can't we be frank with one another?)

But she didn't say any of it. Dirk had stopped kissing her and his voice was very serious.

He said, "Ginny"—and it was seldom he called her that instead of Angel—"you *do* know the whole story about this house now. That Mrs. Pratt told you. Are you still sure you want to live here?"

"Yes," said Ginny, and again a bit fiercely, *"yes.* It's our house, Dirk, *ours!* If we'd rented it, it might be different. But we're going to stay here, forever."

And she jumped up from his lap and ran out into the kitchen to get supper ready for them.

It was getting dark out, and she turned on the kitchen light and scurried about getting the salad put together.

Dirk was an awful dear not to complain when she treated him like this, and from now on she'd keep things on hand so he could have a real meal, even if she didn't have time to go to the store.

When they had eaten, Dirk yawned and stood up. He said, "Well, Angel, guess I'll pop over to see Walter Mills and get that pistol. He's letting me have it for twenty bucks."

"Could—could you teach me how to shoot?"

"Why not? We can set up a little range in the basement. I'd like a spot of practice myself. I'll take the car and be back in—oh, an hour and a half at most."

Ginny washed the dishes and straightened up the kitchen as soon as he'd left, and that still gave her an hour to wait before he'd return. Or maybe he'd be later than he said, if he stopped to talk. Who was this Walter Mills? She hadn't heard his name mentioned before.

She went into the living room and sat down in the Morris chair. It was becoming Dirk's favorite chair, and she'd resolved to sit in it only when he wasn't there. Giving it up to him when he was there gave her a comfortable feeling of being a dutiful wife. After all, a man should have a chair all his own.

The book—a mystery novel—was still on the arm where Dirk had left it. She opened it to the first page and tried to read, but found that the words didn't mean anything to her.

She sighed, put the book down again, and let herself think.

Was there money hidden in the house? If so, it wasn't hers or Dirk's, and it wouldn't do them any good to find it, because they'd have to turn it over to the police, so why was Dirk so interested?

But wait—it *would* do good to find it.

Of course—that was why Dirk was hunting for it! There wouldn't be any danger, then. They'd give it to the police, and be sure that the story got in the papers, all the papers. And that *man* would read it, and he'd know the money wasn't here and there wouldn't be any reason for his coming back, ever.

Of course! The end of danger, the end of worry and fear, if the money was found. (Dirk, now I understand. You knew that, but you didn't talk about it because you didn't want to scare me about the danger while the money might still be here.)

But where would it be hidden? Could she find it, where the police and Dirk had failed? Well, she had one edge on them; she was a woman, and the money had been hidden by a woman. She said, "Let's see, let's pretend I've got some money *I* want to hide."

And she closed her eyes. A compartment in a cupboard, or something built into a wall? No, because I'd have to have someone build it for me and then I wouldn't be the only one who knew. I can't use tools, so probably poor Mrs. Cartwright couldn't.

But I wouldn't just put it in a drawer. I wouldn't put it in a mattress or anything like that because that's where somebody would look first. I think I'd hide it down in the cellar somewhere. I don't know just why, but a cellar seems somehow *permanent*. There seems more security in something hidden in a cellar, doesn't there?

Ginny got up out of the Morris chair and went through the kitchen to the head of the stairs leading down to the basement, and turned on the lights down there. And slowly, thoughtfully, went down the steep steps, looking around.

In or around the furnace? Oh, no, there's *heat* there. I wouldn't want my money to burn or to char from heat. Well away from the furnace.

Those dusty shelves? There were some old cans standing on them, things left there that hadn't been thrown out yet. In one of these cans, maybe? No, *I* wouldn't put it there, she thought. Because a can might get thrown out by mistake when I wasn't around.

But just the same, Ginny went over and looked at the shelf. There was a paint can, with the lid stuck on so tightly that she couldn't get it off, and it wouldn't be in there anyway. There was a little paint sloshing around in it, and *she* wouldn't put money in a messy paint can anyway.

The next can had some nails in it, rusty second-hand nails that had been salvaged and saved.

The next can—why, that was a new one! Dirk must have put it there. The label was turned the other way, and in idle curiosity she picked it up. The lid was loose and fell off as she took it down off the shelf.

And then, with horrid fascination, she was staring into the white powder that filled the can three-fourths of the way up, and she knew somehow what it was even before she turned it around to read the label. *Lye.*

What on earth had Dirk been doing with lye?

And then, because it was important that she have an answer to that at once, she stood there until she found it. Of course—he'd been here alone the second day, while she'd been downtown buying curtains. And he'd cleaned out the basement here with a hose.

And he must have had trouble with the drain, and got some lye from the store and fixed it. Of course.

And he hadn't mentioned it to her because of the horrible connotation that *lye* had, in that house they lived in. Probably he'd intended to throw out the rest of it, and that was why he hadn't bothered to put the lid on tightly again.

Her hand shook a little as she put the can back on the shelf.

And besides, it would take more than one can of lye to—

But she caught herself up quickly before her mind could complete that hideous thought.

(Dirk, why don't you hurry? Come back quickly, my dear, so I won't think the things I'm thinking. So I won't keep remembering now that I've known you only a month, and that I've never known much about your affairs, and that *you* found this house and brought me to it. And that you knew better when I called Mrs. Pratt by the wrong name, and that you've avoided meeting her, and that the agent you bought the house from hadn't known *him.*

(And, Dirk, that you're slender and within half an inch of being five feet eleven, and that you didn't mention buying lye, and you didn't tell me why you were searching the house.

(Come back quickly, Dirk, so I can *look* at you and know how silly all of that is.)

That was part of Ginny's mind, and the rest of it was frantically following her eyes around the cellar, looking for a hiding place for money, a hiding place a woman might have used, that she, Ginny, would use.

Concentrate on that to keep from thinking about the other.

The meter box, there on the wall. Why not? It was metal, and it had a permanent look, and it was something a man wouldn't think about because it belonged to the electric company and not to the house, and it had a hinged front. *If* inside it there was a place where—

Ginny crossed to the box and opened it, and the money, of course, wasn't there. A silly place, come to think of it; any meter reader might find it.

But between the box and the wall? It didn't look flush on one side, room even for the tips of Ginny's fingers to reach in. They touched paper, but couldn't pull it out.

Up higher, and she found the top corner of whatever it was, pushed down gently, and it came out. A dirty white envelope, with something in it. And the something proved to be banknotes, about twenty or twenty-five of them, new, and in denominations Ginny had never seen before.

And then suddenly she was aware that she was alone in the house, and with fingers that trembled she pushed the envelope back where it had been and hurried up the stairs to the living room.

The clock showed her she'd been down there longer than she'd thought. It was time for Dirk to be back. (Dirk, please hurry. Why, tonight of all nights, did you stay to talk to your friend?)

Maybe she could see his car coming now. Quickly she crossed over to the window that opened off the hall, the window that showed the vista toward town, the direction Dirk had gone.

Up there past the first corner, opposite that patch of trees, there was a car parked at the curb. Half a block past Mrs. Pratt's place. Odd that a car should stand there; there wasn't a house within half a block of it. And it looked like Dirk's car.

But it couldn't be. Why would he have parked it there?

Moonlight shone brightly on the front of the car, but the back end of it was in the shadow of the trees. At that distance almost any sedan, she told herself, would look like Dirk's. But—

Dirk's field glasses! She ran and got them, and peered at the car through them. Yes, it was Dirk's car.

And Ginny, feeling cold all over, knew the terrible truth. Not the details yet. But the main point. Her wild guesses hadn't been so wild. Dirk *was—the man!* The murderer. It all fitted now, almost.

And there was only one thing to do. Feeling as though she were commanding somebody else's body instead of her own, Ginny walked—she couldn't run—to the telephone. She'd have to call the police, tell them she'd found the money and—to hurry.

The receiver to her ear, she jiggled the hook nervously, waiting for the "Number, please," that would let her ask for the police, quickly. But the Number, please," didn't come, and it came to her slowly that there wasn't the familiar buzzing sound of a live telephone connection.

He'd cut the phone wire.

Stunned, Ginny sat there by the phone for seconds before the hand holding the receiver dropped from her ear, and the receiver itself clattered to the floor.

The noise it made frightened her. It reminded her that she was utterly alone. Or was she?

Alone—or *worse*.

Because she heard the footsteps now on the walk outside. Heavy footsteps of someone who made no effort to walk silently.

Coming here. There wasn't any house beyond this. Coming here. For the money? For her? For—

The footsteps turned in at the walk, came up the wooden steps and resounded across the wooden porch, and the doorbell rang.

Should she run, out the back door and across the backyard, across the field behind it, *run*—?

But her feet were taking her, instead, to the side window of the porch, whence she could see without being seen. She peered through the curtain, and then sobbing with relief ran to open the door.

It wasn't Dirk. It was a policeman, and never before had she been so glad to see a blue uniform.

He took off his hat a bit awkwardly and said, "You're Mrs. Rogers? The chief told me to stop in. Is your husband—"

She didn't let him finish. "*I've found the money!* The money Mrs.— Mrs. Cartwright hid." And in breathless haste, her words were tumbling over one another in their eagerness to get it out, because now she was safe.

". . . down in the cellar. Come on and I'll show you, and then—you can go with me to headquarters and we can turn it in, and—"

Her heels clicked down the cellar stairs, and heavier footsteps followed and the envelope with the money in it was in her hand and she gave it to him. And caught her breath—and lost it.

Because the man in the uniform looked less and less like a policeman as she stared at him. He was just under six feet tall, and he'd looked heavy, but she could see now in the light that that was because the shoulders of his coat were thickly padded.

He stood there right under the light, looking into the envelope with greedy eyes, and she could see that there was make-up on his face. He stuffed the envelope in his pocket and turned to her.

Ginny screamed, because there was murder in his eyes.

There was a service revolver holstered at his belt, but he didn't reach for it. His hands were reaching for her throat, and he was between her and the stairway.

She backed away, and he came on. In a moment now, she'd be

backed into a corner and it would be over with. She backed away, and then she couldn't back any farther because something was against her shoulder blades.

The shelf. And with desperate hope, her hand closed around the can. The lye.

His hands were almost on her throat when she threw it, can and all, with the white powder flaring out of the open can into his face. Into his eyes.

And it was his turn to scream, then, a scream of agony as he backed away. Too blinded with pain now to think of anything else, and unresisting as Ginny's trembling hands got the gun from his holster...

~§~

Dawn was different. She was sitting beside Dirk's bed in the hospital and he was conscious now, and even cheerful, although he was careful how he moved his head.

His story had been told now. On his way back from Walter's house, and a block and a half from home, a policeman had waved him to the curb. He'd obeyed and the policeman had come up and slugged him with a blackjack before he could even raise a hand to defend himself.

And Ginny and the real police finished the story for him from there. Dirk had been tied and gagged, shoved down out of sight in the back of the car and Cartwright had come on to the house. Probably his original intention had been to overcome Ginny and tie her up, then have a full night to search the place at his leisure. He'd known that the house, unoccupied, had been watched. But he'd waited his first opportunity once they'd moved in and the police surveillance was lessened...

"But, Angel," Dirk said, wincing as he moved his head to look up at her again. "I know you did swell, and you're a heroine and I was a washout. But aren't you getting your story confused? You said once that you knew right away he wasn't really a policeman and you figured your only chance was down there—where you could get at the lye while he was opening the envelope. And then something about being so glad to see him that—"

Ginny put her fingers across his lips. "Doctor said you mustn't talk too much, Dirk."

Yes, she realized she *had* got a bit mixed up in telling it. But there was one part Dirk must never know. She must never let him know what she had suspected and then actually thought during those awful moments before the killer came. She'd have to get her story straight so he'd never catch her out on that.

"Of course I knew right away, Dirk. I mean, when I went to the door. But first I looked out the window, and I didn't know then and that was when I thought he was a real policeman and I'd just found the money so I was glad. And out the window I saw—"

"My car? Didn't you see it parked down there?"

"I saw *a* car," said Ginny, "but I didn't guess it was yours." And she resolved to put the field glasses away quickly, the moment she got home, before he could find she'd used them.

And then, because he was going to ask another question, she bent down and kissed him, and there were tears of penitence in her eyes.

She said, "Oh, Dirk, let's not talk about it anymore. It's all over, and it's *our* place now, and I'll never be afraid again."

And she thought, *I'll have to be such a good wife to him to make up for those suspicions I had. And he'll never know.* And she smiled, because a rather silly pun had just popped into her head: a little white lye had saved her life last night; and from now on a little white lie would help keep her marriage happy. Dirk would never, never know.

10 Detective Aces, September 1942

The Joke

THE BIG MAN in the flashy green suit stuck his big hand across the cigar counter. "Jim Greeley," he said. "Ace Novelty Company." The cigar dealer took the offered hand and then jerked convulsively as something inside it buzzed painfully against his own palm.

The big man's cheerful laughter boomed. "Our Joy Buzzer," he said, turning over his hand to expose the little metal contraption in his palm. "Changes a shake to a shock; one of the best numbers we got. A dilly, ain't it? Gimme four of those perfectos, the two-for-a-quarters. Thanks."

He put a half-dollar on the counter and then, concealing a grin, lighted one of the cigars while the dealer tried vainly to pick up the coin. Then, laughing, the big man put another—and an ungimmicked—coin on the counter and pried up the first one with a tricky little knife on one end of his watch chain. He put it back in a special little box that went into his vest pocket. He said, "A new number—but a pretty good one. It's a good laugh, and—well, 'Anything for a Gag' is Ace's motto and me, I'm Ace's salesman."

The cigar dealer said, "I couldn't handle—"

"Not trying to sell you anything," the big man said. "I just sell wholesale. But I get a kick out of showing off our merchandise. You ought to see some of it."

He blew a ring of cigar smoke and strolled on past the cigar counter to the hotel desk. "Double with bath," he told the clerk. "Got a reservation—Jim Greeley. Stuff's being sent over from the station, and my wife'll be here later."

He took a fountain pen from his pocket, ignoring the one the clerk offered him, and signed the card. The ink was bright blue, but it was going to be a good joke on the clerk when, a little later, he tried to file that card and found it completely blank. And when he explained and wrote a new card it would be both a good laugh and good advertising for Ace Novelty.

"Leave the key in the box," he said. "I won't go up now. Where are the phones?"

He strolled to the row of phone booths to which the desk clerk directed him and dialed a number. A feminine voice answered.

"This is the police," he said gruffly. "We've had reports that you've been renting rooms to crooked boarders. Or were those only false roomers?"

"Jim! Oh, I'm so glad you're in town!"

"So'm I, sweetie. Is the coast clear, your husband away? Wait, don't tell me; you wouldn't have said what you just said if he'd been there, would you? What time does he get home?"

"Nine o'clock, Jim. You'll pick me up before then? I'll leave him a note saying I'm staying with my sister because she's sick."

"Swell, honey. What I hoped you'd say. Let's see; it's half-past five. I'll be right around."

"Not that soon, Jim. I've got things to do, and I'm not dressed. Make it—not before eight o'clock. Between then and half-past eight."

"Okay, honey. Eight it is. That'll give us time for a big evening, and I've already registered double."

"How'd you know I'd be able to get away?"

The big man laughed. "Then I'd have called one of the others in my little black book. Now don't get mad; I was only kidding. I'm calling from the hotel, but I haven't actually registered yet; I was only kidding. One thing I like about you, Marie, you got a sense of humor; you can take it. Anybody I like's got to have a sense of humor like I have."

"Anybody you *like?*"

"And anybody I love. To pieces. What's your husband like, Marie? Has *he* got a sense of humor?"

"A little. A crazy kind of one; not like yours. Got any new numbers in your line?"

"Some dillies. I'll show you. One of 'em's a trick camera that—well, I'll show you. And don't worry, honey. I remember you told me you got a tricky ticker and I won't pull any scary tricks on you. Won't scare you, honey; just the opposite."

"You big goof. Okay, Jim, not before eight o'clock now. But plenty before nine."

"With bells on, honey. Be seeing you."

He went out of the telephone booth singing "Tonight's My Night with Baby," and straightened his snazzy necktie at a mirror in front of a pillar in the lobby. He ran an exploring palm across his face. Yes, needed a shave; it felt rough even if it didn't show. Well, plenty of time for that in two and a half hours.

He strolled over to where a bellboy sat. "How late you on duty, son?" he asked.

"Till two-thirty, nine hours. I just came on."

"Good. How are rules here on likker? Get it any time?"

"Can't get bottle goods after nine o'clock. That is, well, sometimes you can, but it's taking a chance. Can't I get it for you sooner if you're going to want it?"

"Might as well." The big man took some bills out of his wallet. "Room 603. Put in a fifth of rye and two bottles of soda sometime before nine. I'll phone down for ice cubes when we want 'em. And listen, I want you to help me with a gag. Got any bedbugs or cockroaches?"

"Huh?"

The big man grinned. "Maybe you have and maybe you haven't, but look at these artificial ones. Ain't they beauties?" He took a pillbox from his pocket and opened it.

"Want to play a joke on my wife," he said. "And I won't be up in the room till she gets here. You take these and put 'em where they'll do the most good, see? I mean, peel back the covers and fill the bed with these little beauties. Don't they look like real ones? She'll really squeal when she sees 'em. Do you like gags, son?"

"Sure."

"I'll show you some good ones when you bring up the ice cubes later. I got a sample case full. Well, do a good job with those bedbugs."

He winked solemnly at the bellboy and sauntered across the lobby and out to the sidewalk.

He strolled into a tavern and ordered rye with a chaser. While the bartender was getting it he went over to the juke box and put a dime in, pushing two buttons. He came back grinning, and whistling "Got a Date with an Angel." The juke box joined in—in the wrong key—with his whistling.

"You look happy," said the bartender. "Most guys come in here to tell their troubles."

"Haven't got any troubles," said the big man. "Happier because I found an oldie on your juke box and it fits. Only the angel I got a date with's got a little devil in her too, thank God. Real she-devil, too."

He put his hand across the bar. "Shake the hand of a happy man," he said.

The buzzer in his palm buzzed and the bartender jumped.

The big man laughed. "Have a drink with me, pal," he said, "and don't get mad. I like practical jokes. I sell 'em."

The bartender grinned, but not too enthusiastically. He said, "You got the build for it all right. Okay, I'll have a drink with you. Only just a second; there's a hair in that chaser I gave you." He emptied the glass and put it among the dirties, coming back with another one, this one of cut glass of intricate design.

"Nice try," said the big man, "but I told you I *sell the* stuff; I know a dribble glass when I see one. Besides, that's an old model. Just one hole on a side and if you get your finger over it, it don't dribble. See, like this. Happy days."

The dribble glass didn't dribble. The big man said, "I'll buy us both another; I like a guy who can dish a job out as well as take one." He chuckled. "*Try* to dish one out, anyway. Pour us another and lemme tell you about some of the new stuff we're gonna put out. New plastic called Skintex that—hey, I got a sample with me. Lookit."

He took from his pocket a rolled-up object that unrolled itself, as he put it on the bar, into a startlingly lifelike false face. The big man said, "Got it all over every kind of mask or false face on the market, even the expensive rubber ones. Fits so close it stays on practically of its own accord. But what's really different about it is by gosh it looks so real you have to look twice and look close to see it ain't the real McCoy. Gonna be an all-year-round seller for costume balls and stuff, and make a fortune every Halloween."

"Sure looks real," said the bartender.

"Bet your boots it does. Comes in all kinds, it will. Got only a few actually in production now, though. This one's the Fancy Dan model, good looking. Pour us two more, huh?"

He rolled up the mask and put it back into his pocket. The juke box had just ended the second number and he fed a quarter into it, again punching "Got a Date with an Angel," but this time waiting to whistle until the record had started, so he'd be in tune with it.

He changed it to patter when he got back to the bar. He said, "Got a date with an angel, all right. Little blonde, Marie Rhymer. A beauty. Purtiest gal in town. Here's to 'er."

This time he forgot to put his finger over the hole in the dribble glass and got spots of water on his snazzy necktie. He looked down at them and roared with laughter. He ordered drinks for the house—not too expensive a procedure, as there was only one other customer and the bartender.

The other customer bought back and the big man bought another round. He showed them two new coin tricks—in one of which he balanced a quarter on the edge of a shot glass after he'd let them examine both the glass and the coin, and he wouldn't tell the bartender how that one was done until the bartender stood a round.

It was after seven when he left the tavern. He wasn't drunk, but he was feeling the drinks. He was really happy now. Ought to grab a bite to eat, he thought.

He looked around for a restaurant, a good one, and then decided no, maybe Marie would be expecting him to take her to dinner; he'd wait to eat until he was with her.

And so what if he got there early? He could wait, he could talk to her while she got ready.

He looked around for a taxi and saw none; he started walking briskly, again whistling "Tonight's My Night with Baby," which hadn't, unfortunately, been on the juke box.

He walked briskly, whistling happily, into the gathering dusk. He was going to be early, but he didn't want to stop for another drink; there'd be plenty of drinking later, and right now he felt just right.

It wasn't until he was a block away that he remembered the shave he'd meant to get. He stopped and felt his face, and yes, he really needed one. Luck was with him, too, because only a few doors back he'd passed a little hole-in-the-wall barber shop. He retraced his steps and found it open. There was one barber and no customers.

He started in, then changed his mind and, grinning happily, went on to the areaway between that building and the next. He took the Skintex mask from his pocket and slipped it over his face; be a good gag to see what the barber would do if he sat down in the chair for a shave with that mask on. He was grinning so broadly he had trouble getting the mask on smoothly, until he straightened out his face.

He walked into the barber shop, hung his hat on the rack and sat down in the chair. His voice only a bit muffled by the flexible mask, he said, "Shave, please."

As the barber, who had taken his stand by the side of the chair, bent closer in incredulous amazement, the big man in the green suit couldn't hold in his laughter any longer. The mask slipped as his laughter boomed out. He took it off and held it out for examination. "Purty lifelike, ain't it?" he asked when he could quit laughing.

"Sure is," said the little barber admiringly. "Say, who makes those?"

"My company. Ace Novelty."

"I'm with a group that puts on amateur theatricals," the barber said. "Say, we could use some of those—for comic roles mainly, if they come in comic faces. Do they?"

"They do. We're manufacturers and wholesalers, of course. But you'll be able to get them at Brachman & Minton's, here in town. I call on 'em tomorrow, and I'll load them up. How's about that shave, meanwhile. Got a date with an angel."

"Sure," said the little man. "Brachman & Minton. We buy most of our make-up and costumes there already. That's fine." He rinsed a towel under the hot-water faucet, wrung it out. He put it over the big man's face and made lather in his shaving cup.

Under the hot towel the man in the green suit was humming "Got a Date with an Angel." The barber took off the towel and applied the lather with deft strokes.

"Yep," said the big man, "got a date with an angel and I'm too damn early. Gimme the works—massage, anything you got. Wish I could look as handsome with my real face as with that there mask—that's our Fancy Dan model, by the way. Y'oughta see some of the others. Well, you will if you go to Brachman & Minton's about a week from now. Take about that long before they get the merchandise after I take their order tomorrow."

"Yes, sir," said the barber. "You said the works? Massage *and* facial?" He stropped the razor, started its neat clean strokes.

"Why not? Got time. And tonight's my night with baby. *Some* number, pal. Pageboy blonde, built like you-know-what. Runs a rooming house not far from—Say, I got an idea. Good gag."

"What?"

"I'll fool 'er. I'll wear that Fancy Dan mask when I knock on the door and I'll make her think somebody *really* good-looking is calling on her. Maybe it'll be a letdown when she sees my homely mug when I take it off, but the gag'll be good. And I'll bet she won't be *too* disappointed when she sees it's good old Jim. Yep. I'll do that."

The big man chuckled in anticipation. "What time's it?" he asked.

He was getting a little sleepy. The shave was over, and the kneading motion of the massage was soporific.

"Ten of eight."

"Good. Lots of time. Just so I get there well before nine. That's when— Say, did that mask really fool you when I walked in with it?"

"Sure did," the barber told him. "Until I bent over you after you sat down."

"Good. Then it'll fool Marie Rhymer when I go up to the door. Say, what's the name of your amatcher theatrical outfit? I'll tell Brachman you'll want some of the Skintex numbers."

"Just the Grove Avenue Social Center group. My name's Dane. Brachman knows me. Sure, tell him we'll take some."

Hot towels, cool creams, kneading fingers. The man in green dozed.

"Okay, mister," the barber said. "You're all set. Be a dollar sixty-five." He chuckled. "I even put your mask on so you're all set. Good luck."

The big man sat up and glanced in the mirror. "Swell," he said. He stood up and took two singles out of his wallet. "That's even now. G'night."

He put on his hat and went out. It was getting dark now and a glance at his wrist watch showed him it was almost eight-thirty, perfect timing.

He started humming again, back this time to "Tonight's My Night with Baby."

He wanted to whistle, but he couldn't do that with the false face on. He stopped in front of the house and looked around before he went up the steps to the door. He chuckled a little as he took the VACANCY sign off the nail beside the door and held it as he pressed the button and heard the bell sound.

Only seconds passed before he heard her footsteps clicking to the door. It opened, and he bowed slightly. His voice muffled by the mask so she wouldn't recognize it, he said, "You haff—a rrrooom, blease?"

She was beautiful, all right, as beautiful as he remembered her from the last time he'd been in town a month before. She said hesitantly, "Why, yes, but I'm afraid I can't show it to you tonight. I'm expecting a friend and I'm late getting ready."

He made a jerky little bow. He said, "Vee, moddomm, I viii rrre-turrrn."

And then, jerking his chin forward to loosen the mask and pinching it loose at the forehead so it would come loose with his hat, he lifted hat and mask.

He grinned and started to say—well, it didn't matter what he'd started to say, because Marie Rhymer screamed and then dropped into a crumpled heap of purple silk and cream-colored flesh and blond hair just inside the door.

Stunned, the big man dropped the sign he'd been holding and bent over her. He said, "Marie, honey, what—" and quickly stepped inside and closed the door. He bent down and—remembering her "tricky ticker"—put his hand over where her heart should be beating. *Should* be, but wasn't.

He got out of there quickly. With a wife and kid of his own back in Minneapolis, he couldn't be— Well, he got out.

Still stunned, he walked quickly out.

He came to the barber shop, and it was dark. He stopped in front of the door. The dark glass of the door, with a street light shining against it from across the way, was both transparent and a mirror. In it, he saw three things.

He saw, in the mirror part of the door, the face of horror that was his own face. Bright green, with careful expert shadowing that made it the face of a walking corpse, a ghoul with sunken eyes and cheeks and blue lips. The bright-green face mirrored above the green suit and the snazzy red tie—the face that the make-up expert barber must have put on him while he'd dozed—

And the note, stuck against the inside of the glass of the barber shop door, written on white paper in green pencil:

CLOSED
DANE RHYMER

Marie Rhymer, Dane Rhymer, he thought dully. While *through* the glass, inside the dark barber shop, he could see it dimly—the white-clad figure of the little barber as it dangled from the chandelier and turned slowly, left to right, right to left, left to right. . .

Published as "If Looks Could Kill", Detective Tales, October 1948

Little Apple Hard To Peel

THE APPEL FAMILY moved to our part of the county when John Appel was ten or eleven years old. He was the only kid.

New kids didn't move in very often and, naturally, some of us took considerable interest in finding out whether we could lick him. He liked to fight, we found, and he was good at it.

His name being John Appel, Jonathan Apple was the nickname we picked at first. For some reason, it made him mad, and there wasn't any trouble getting him to fight. He fought with a cold calmness that was unusual for a boy. He never seemed to see red, like the rest of us.

He was small for his age, but tough and muscular. He could lick, we soon learned, any kid his own size. And he could lick most kids who were bigger. He licked me twice, and Les Willis three or four times.

Les Willis, my best pal, was a little slow on the uptake. It took him that many lickings to find out that the Appel kid was too much for him.

It was one of the bigger kids, a few grades above us in school, that first called him "Little Apple Hard to Peel." Appel liked that nickname. He used to brag about it, in fact. Of course nobody called him that much, because it was too long.

The first incident occurred when he'd been around only a week. He knocked a chip off Nick Burton's shoulder. Nick was only a few months older than Appel, but Nick was big for his age. Appel fought like a devil but he just couldn't handle Nick. After the fight was over, he got up and we dusted him off and he wanted to shake hands with Nick. That shaking hands after a fight was new to us; usually we kids stayed mad a few hours and tapered off, sort of.

It was the next day at school that Nick sat on the nail and had to go home. He was in bed three days, and limped quite a while. Somebody'd driven a long, thin nail up through the bottom of his seat, so it stuck out almost two inches.

We kids had often played tricks like that with thumb tacks, but this was something else again. It wasn't any joke. It was obviously meant to hurt badly, and it succeeded. There was quite an inquisition about it, but no one ever found out who had put it there. Somebody, though, had made a secret trip to the schoolhouse at night. Nick sat on it first thing in the morning after the bell rang.

Those of us who knew about the fight Nick had had with Appel wondered a little, but that was all. It didn't seem possible a kid would do something as cruel as that.

Then there was that dirty drawing on the blackboard. Not the usual comic caricature of a teacher that kids draw, but something pretty smutty. There wasn't any name signed to it, but it was done in yellow chalk, and Les Willis was the only one in the class who had any yellow chalk. The teacher believed Les' denial, finally, or at least she said she did.

But Les failed that year in school and it put him a year behind the rest of us. He'd been sort of on the borderline of keeping up before; he might have made it, if it hadn't been for that. The drawing on the board happened a couple days after Les beat Appel in the tryouts for pitcher for our class team. Appel played second base. But next term he pitched, because Les was still back in the same grade and the rest of us had moved on.

There was another thing. Appel never liked dogs, and dogs didn't take to him at all. There was the time Bud Sperry's little fox terrier, Sport, bit Appel in the leg. Two weeks later Sport died. He died in one of the most painful ways a dog can die. Someone had fed him, not poison, but a sponge pressed tight and coated with meat grease to make a dog gobble it quick. Then that sponge swells up inside the dog. Bud Sperry's uncle was a vet, and when Sport's agony started, Bud took him to his uncle. His uncle chloroformed the dog, and then cut him open— on a hunch—and found the sponge.

Bud Sperry would have killed whoever gave Sport that sponge, if he'd *known* for sure. But there wasn't ever any proof. Not then, or later.

I think it would have been a good thing if Bud Sperry had killed Appel then, proof or no proof. That's a hell of a thing for a sheriff to say. But other things happened, after that, and not always to dogs.

Appel was a good-looking kid about the time we graduated from high school. He was still small, but he was stocky. Despite his size, he'd made a good football player, and he had curly hair, and the girls were crazy about him.

Les Willis had quit high school in his second year and was helping his folks on their farm, just outside of town. The Appel place was just down the road. John Appel wasn't doing anything then, just living with his folks and "looking around." You got the idea, from the way he put it, that there wasn't anything in town good enough for him to do, but that he was looking anyway.

And I was running errands for the sheriff's office, as sort of quasi-deputy with the promise of a deputy's badge when I got a "couple years older and a little less fat in the head."

We were all about eighteen then. Les Willis and John Appel were both in love with Lucinda Howard. She seemed to prefer Les at first, although I wouldn't go so far as to say that she was ever really in love with him.

But Les was starry-eyed about Lucinda. It was serious with Les all right, the kind of love that happens only once in a lifetime and then only to someone who is as fine and clean a fellow as Les. He was the best friend I ever had, and he was a prince of a chap. But he didn't have any glamor. He didn't have curly hair and he wasn't a football player, and he worked pretty hard and didn't have as much time off to take her places.

And besides, after the accident to his foot, he limped. And that meant he couldn't dance, and Lucinda loved to dance. Appel took her out after that and had the field pretty much to himself. Lucinda fell in love with him.

Les' foot—well, it could have been an accident. He was in the habit of taking a morning plunge in good weather, in a creek half a mile back of the Willis farmhouse. He always ran along the path, both ways, barefoot and in just his swimming trunks, and one morning he stepped into a trap along the path. Just a small trap, but barefoot as he was, it cost him two toes and laid him up for quite a while. It was during that time that John Appel made the most progress with Lucinda.

Lucinda fell for him hard. I know that she thought of herself as being engaged to him, although the engagement was never announced.

Then, suddenly, John Appel wasn't around anymore, and we learned that he'd taken the night train and bought a ticket for Chicago, and had taken all his clothes and things with him. All but Lucinda; he hadn't even said good-bye to her. And he hadn't left a forwarding address, even with his folks. We didn't know that till later, though.

It didn't make a splash. Nobody thought much about it except maybe to wonder whether Lucinda was telling the truth. She said, with her head up and her chin firm, that she'd heard from him by mail and he'd been offered a job that was too good to turn down. Bud Sperry's father was postmaster then and he didn't remember that Lucinda Howard had got any letter from Chicago. And he'd have noticed.

A week later they fished Lucinda Howard's body out of the river. Yes, she'd been going to have a child. She didn't leave a note or anything blaming anybody. There still wasn't any provable charge against Appel.

Les took it hard. Seemed to break him all up inside. He was just back from the hospital then; an infection had set in after his toes were amputated and almost healed. He'd been waiting a decent time for Lucinda to get over John and for him to be able to get around again, before he called on her. Yes, Les would have wanted to marry her anyway. He was that kind of guy. And Lucinda had meant the whole world to him, and now there wasn't any world left. If he hadn't had a good strong religion, he might have followed Lucinda.

Nobody in town heard of John Appel for a long time after that. Twelve years, in fact. I was sheriff then; at thirty I was about the youngest sheriff in the state. Couple of plainclothes men were down from Chicago, checking up on a pennyweighter who'd been down our way and gypped old Angstrom, our jeweler, out of some rings.

I said to them, "Ever hear of a guy named Appel, John Appel? Local boy moved up your way. I was wondering if he made good in the big city."

One of them whistled and shoved his hat back on his head. "Don't tell me Appel came from this freckle on the map."

"I've watched the circulars," I told him. "Never saw his name or his mug. Tell me about him."

"Runs a chunk of the north side of Chi, if it's the same Appel. Short, stocky, about your age?"

I nodded.

The Chicago detective grinned. "They call him Little Apple Hard to Peel."

"Harry Weston gave him that nickname," I told him. "Nearly twenty years ago. He liked it, and I reckon he started it himself where he is now. Used to kind of brag about it."

The Chicago man's eyes narrowed. "Ain't no charge from back here we could make stick, is there? My God, if there is—"

I shook my head slowly.

He sighed. "That was hoping for too much. Listen, there ain't a charge on the blotter against him. Just if there's somebody he don't like or that double-crosses him, something happens to them, that's all. Something not nice. They don't even die clean, mostly, if you understand what I mean."

"That's the guy," I assured him.

"He's too smart. Even makes out his income tax returns right. Or right enough so they can't prove otherwise. He's a legitimate business man. Runs a chain of laundries!" He snorted.

"Officially," I said. "Outside of that?"

His face wasn't nice to look at. There are square cops even from Chicago.

"When someone thinks of something dirtier than peddling dope to school kids," he said, "John Appel will back them. But if there's trouble they'll take the rap, not him."

"That his line?"

"I couldn't prove it, but I'd say it was one of them."

The Chi men left town an hour or so later. I didn't say anything about that conversation to Les because it would have opened an old wound.

One thing did occur to me though. Lucinda Howard might have been worse off than she was. Appel might have taken her with him.

Les Willis had, in a way, gathered up the pieces of his life. He'd been pretty no-count for a couple of years, and then he had the full responsibility of the farm put on his shoulders when his pa got sick, and he plunged in and worked like a horse and the work seemed to do him good.

He got to looking all right again, and he acted and thought all right, too, except there was a sort of blank in one part of his mind, as though he'd built up a wall there to shut off one corner. His love for Lucinda Howard was still there, I guess, in that walled-off corner.

I think Mary Burton understood that part of him better than any of the rest of us. Mary was Nick Burton's kid sister, and she'd loved Les in a quiet sort of way, all through school. He'd dated her a few times when Lucinda had turned him down, but he'd never taken her seriously.

But after his parents died, I guess it was lonesomeness made Les turn to her again. As a friend, at first. But Mary was wise, and she understood him.

For a couple of years she was just a good pal to him. Then Les discovered that she was more than that, and they were married. He was twenty-five, by then, and Lucinda had been dead six years. Mary was twenty-two.

After their honeymoon Les fixed up the old farmhouse until you wouldn't have known it was the same place, and pretty soon he was painting one room light blue for a nursery. They had twins a year after they were married. A boy and a girl, Dottie and Bill. For Les and Mary the sun rose and set in those kids.

The years rolled along, and the twins were in school, then in high school. No one here thought of John Appel much, except when his parents died, almost at the same time, and our local lawyer sent a routine advertisement for him to the Chicago papers.

A lawyer from Chicago came down, then, with a power of attorney from John, and took over the farm. It wasn't put up for sale, nor was it used. A check for taxes came each year, and the fields lay fallow and the yard was choked with weeds. Plow and harrow rusted in a rotting barn.

Occasionally a bit of news would reach us from Chicago Appel was tangling in this racket or that. Then there was a rumor that he was dipping into politics; another that he'd sold out all but his gambling interests and was concentrating on that and extending his territory.

Then, utterly without warning, John Appel returned. He dropped off the afternoon train, alone, as casually as though he were returning after a weekend trip. It had been twenty years.

He walked over to where I was standing talking to the station master and said, "Hello, Barney," just as casually as that.

He still had the same curly blond hair, and he looked scarcely any older than when I'd seen him last. He was heavier, but he hadn't picked up a paunch. His skin was tanned, and he looked as fit as an athlete.

Then he noticed the badge I was wearing and grinned. "Glad to see you've made good," he said. He was wearing a suit that had cost at least two hundred dollars, and there was a three-carat diamond ring on his left hand.

"Coming back to show off to the home folks?" I asked casually. "Or hiding out from someone?"

"You name it."

"For long?" I asked. "And if you feel that way about it, consider the question official."

But I'd noticed that the boys were unloading several trunks from the baggage car, and Appel was the only passenger who'd got off the train, so I didn't need the answer to my question.

He took out a platinum cigarette case. I refused, but he lighted one himself. He blew a long exhalation of smoke through his nostrils before he answered, if one could call it an answer. He said, "Do you always welcome people so enthusiastically? Don't tell me you've been hearing stories about me."

"We don't want you here," I told him.

He grinned again, apparently genuinely amused this time.

"Don't tell me *that's* official, Barney. If it is, I'd be curious to know the charge."

He turned away before I could reply. Which was just as well, because there wasn't any answer. He was a property-holder, and there wasn't a legal reason I could think of for taking official action. There wasn't a proven charge against him here; probably none in Chicago or elsewhere. But I'd let him know where he stood with me, and I wasn't sorry.

Then I heard footsteps coming around the wooden platform from the other side of the station, and for a moment my heart slowed. For those footsteps limped; they were made by Lea Willis.

I thought for a moment he knew that Appel was here and that this was why he had come. Then I saw his clear eyes as he walked toward me and I realized he'd come to the station on some other errand.

I put my hand on his arm and said, "Take it easy, Les."

He looked at me, puzzled, and then before I could explain he turned and flashed a glance up and down the platform as though he'd guessed. And he saw John Appel.

I was holding tightly to his arm and I felt him start to tremble. I didn't look at his face; I thought it best not to, just then. That tremble wasn't because of fear.

I spoke softly. "Take it easy, Les, I know how you feel, but there's nothing we can do. Nothing. There's not a scrap of evidence against him on any charge."

He didn't answer. I don't know whether he heard me or not. I said, "Go home, Les. Keep away from him. He won't stay long. Keep clear of him—for Dottie and Bill's sake! He's a killer now, Les!"

I guess it was the mention of the twins that brought him back. But he said, "He was a killer even when he was a kid, Barney."

I knew what Les meant. To me, too, those things that had happened more than twenty years ago seemed worse to us than the real murders Appel had undoubtedly committed since. Possibly because we were closer to them. Those things had happened to people we knew and loved. They weren't gangster stuff.

I heard Appel crossing toward where we stood. I could tell by Les' face that he was coming too. I said, "Les, for God's sake, go—"

He said, quietly, "I'm all right, Barney. Don't worry."

His voice was so calm that I took my hand off his arm.

Appel said smoothly, "If it isn't Willis. You look older, Les. Golly, you look twenty years older'n Barney here. Been misbehaving?"

Les Willis showed better sense than I'd dared to hope he would show. He didn't answer, but turned on his heel and started off.

Appel's face got ugly at that. I think if Les had gotten mad and cussed him out, it would have amused him, but not speaking at all managed to get under his hide. He said, loud enough so Les would hear it, "Barney, there's gratitude for you. I go off and leave him a clear field to get that little tramp he was in love with—what was her name? Lucinda something—and here he—"

Thinking it over afterward, I guess Appel had never heard what had happened to Lucinda Howard. He was merely trying to bait Les into an argument. Otherwise he would have been prepared for what happened.

Les was a few steps beyond me. He whirled and was back past me almost in a single leap, so suddenly that I wasn't able to stop him. His fist caught Appel flush on the mouth, and Appel went down—not knocked out, but simply carried over backward by the momentum of the blow.

He started to scramble to his feet. Les, his face twisted with cold fury, stood over him, fists clenched. I got between them.

"Les," I said sharply, and took him by the arm and shook him. "Get out of here. Remember Dottie and Bill—your kids. You can't start trouble! For their sakes!"

I shook him harder. He didn't answer, but he turned and walked off like a man in a daze. His footsteps limped across the platform toward the steps.

I whirled on Appel. And I had my hand on the butt of the gun in my pocket as I whirled. He'd just got to his feet. His face was a gargoyle mask. He took a step as though to push past me, but I stopped him. I said, "Cut it out. This isn't Chicago."

His face returned to normal so suddenly that I thought I had misread the expression that had been on it before. His fists unclenched. He said, "That's right. This isn't Chicago."

I said, "You had that coming; you know it. The matter's over, unless you want to bring an assault charge. If you do—"

He grinned. "Maybe I had it coming. Nope, I won't bring any charge, sheriff. I won't hurt your little boy, Les, if he stays away from me from now on."

Yes, I was fool enough to believe him. I sighed with relief. I knew I could talk Les out of ever going near him again, and I thought I'd avoided trouble. Sure, I remembered the way Appel had held grudges before, but that was when he was younger. He'd grown up now, he was interested in bigger game and bigger money. Besides he'd admitted he was in the wrong.

I even relented enough to walk with him to the hotel, although I refused a drink. I heard him order the best room they had.

The next day a dozen workmen went out to the old Appel place. Carpenters, painters, decorators, gardeners. They worked three days putting the place in shape. His orders, I learned, had been to repair and restore—not to change anything. To make it as nearly as possible like the place it had been twenty years ago when he'd known it last. I've never understood that. A strange sentimental streak in a man who hadn't come back for the funerals of his own parents.

But he insisted that same furniture be retained, placed just as it was, except that it should be refinished and repaired.

No, I never understood that about John Appel, any more than I understood why he came back at all or for how long he had originally intended to stay.

I was fool enough to think that maybe it meant that he was tired of crime, that he was coming back to try to find himself. I gave him the benefit of the doubt. Having no legal excuse for ordering him out of the county, I made a virtue of a necessity by telling myself that possibly it was for the best.

I saw him but a few times—and then only casually—before the end of the week when the work on the old Appel farm was done, and he moved his trunks out there from the hotel. He took no servants to live with him, and said he was going to do his own cooking, but he made arrangements with a woman to come in three times a week to do cleaning and laundering.

Meanwhile, of course, I'd talked to Les Willis. He'd listened to all I had to say, and had answered, "All right, Barney." But I could see that he'd changed, almost overnight. That wall across one section of his mind had broken down again. He was remembering. I don't mean that he'd ever forgotten, actually, but he'd managed not to think about certain things. Now those memories were back with him.

It was two weeks and four days after Appel had stepped off the train that Les Willis' house burned down.

The fire must have started about midnight. Les had driven Mary over to her mother's to spend the evening. The twins were in high school then and they'd been left at home to study, as they had final exams the next day.

As it happened, the Burtons' mare was foaling that evening. Les was a good hand with animals and knew quite a bit about vetting. He'd stayed to help, and that was why he and Mary didn't leave until after twelve o'clock.

It was a bright moonlit night. As they drove their car out of the Burtons' driveway they saw the red glow against the sky.

Right away they knew it was a fire somewhere near their place, and for a minute they were going back in to the Burton house to phone town for the fire apparatus. Then, through the still night, they heard its clanging bell and knew that someone else had phoned already.

Les put the accelerator to the floor and held it there. When they got home the fire department was already on the scene. And there wasn't much left of the house.

It had been an old, weathered frame building that had gone up like tinder. The twins, Dottie and Bill, slept in bedrooms that had been partitioned off in the attic. Apparently smoke had smothered them in their sleep and they'd never awakened.

I got there rather late.

Chet Harrington, the fire chief, called me over. He said, "Barney, maybe this is a case for you. Looks like this fire was *set.*"

He pointed toward where a shapeless piece of candle-stub lay in a puddle of water alongside one corner of the house.

"My guess," he said, "is that that could be the joker. Someone could'a splashed some gasoline on this side of the house—it went first—and stuck that piece of candle against the house and lit it. Look, what's left of that candle is gutted along one side like it burned horizontally, and then dropped off. It rolled out from the house then when it hit, and—"

"Where's Les?" I interrupted.

"Mary sorta collapsed. They took her into town. Guess Les went along."

"Les see that candle? Did you tell him about it, Chet?"

He nodded. "I didn't show him, but I saw him looking queerly at it once."

I ran over to the people by the gate. "Did Les go into town with Mary?"

There were conflicting answers at first. Then it was decided Les hadn't gone in that car. But Les' own car was gone. . . No, there it was, still on the road. Who'd seen Les last?

While they were arguing about that, I started running across the fields to the Appel farm.

From some distance away I could see that there was a light on downstairs, and I tried to run faster.

Then I saw Les Willis coming across the porch, from inside the house. It was dark in the shadows of the porch, but I knew him by his slight figure, and by the limp. I knew, of course, that he'd killed Appel, and that was bad enough, but I'd figured it would be the other way. That Appel would have had another self-defense killing to his credit.

No, I hadn't expected to see Les Willis alive again. He came down the porch steps into the bright moonlight, holding onto the rail. And I saw that he wasn't alive, really. He stood there holding onto the post of the railing to keep from falling. I saw that he was covered with blood. I could see where at least two bullets had hit him. And with bullets in those places, he had no reason to be alive. But all that blood couldn't have come from those wounds.

I said, "Les?"

I wouldn't have known his voice. I had to strain my ears to catch the words. He said, "He wasn't too hard to peel. But he died. . . too soon."

His knees buckled, and as he crumpled slowly something fell from his hand. It was a knife—the kind used for skinning game.

It was minutes before I got up the nerve to enter the house, to see what was in that lighted room.

Les' funeral was one of the biggest our town had ever seen, but only the coroner and I attended the other one. I imagine, though, that we could have had a tremendous gate for the funeral of Little Apple Hard to Peel if I hadn't announced that the coffin was nailed shut and would stay that way.

Detective Tales, February 1942

Don't Look Behind You

JUST SIT BACK and relax, now. Try to enjoy this; it's going to be the last story you ever read, or nearly the last. After you finish it you can sit there and stall a while, you can find excuses to hang around your house, or your room, or your office, wherever you're reading this; but sooner or later you're going to have to get up and go out. That's where I'm waiting for you: outside. Or maybe closer than that. Maybe in this room.

You think that's a joke of course. You think this is just a story in a book, and that I don't really mean you. Keep right on thinking so. But be fair; admit that I'm giving you fair warning.

Harley bet me I couldn't do it. He bet me a diamond he's told me about, a diamond as big as his head. So you see why I've got to kill you. And why I've got to tell you how and why and all about it first. That's part of the bet. It's just the kind of idea Harley would have.

I'll tell you about Harley first. He's tall and handsome, and suave and cosmopolitan. He looks something like Ronald Colman, only he's taller. He dresses like a million dollars, but it wouldn't matter if he didn't; I mean that he'd look distinguished in overalls. There's a sort of magic about Harley, a mocking magic in the way he looks at you; it makes you think of palaces and far-off countries and bright music.

It was in Springfield, Ohio, that he met Justin Dean. Justin was a funny-looking little runt who was just a printer. He worked for the Atlas Printing & Engraving Company. He was a very ordinary little guy, just about as different as possible from Harley; you couldn't pick two men more different. He was only thirty-five, but he was mostly bald already, and he had to wear thick glasses because he'd worn out his eyes doing fine printing and engraving. He was a good printer and engraver; I'll say that for him.

I never asked Harley how he happened to come to Springfield, but the day he got there, after he'd checked in at the Castle Hotel, he stopped in at Atlas to have some calling cards made. It happened that

Justin Dean was alone in the shop at the time, and he took Harley's order for the cards; Harley wanted engraved ones, the best. Harley always wants the best of everything.

Harley probably didn't even notice Justin; there was no reason why he should have. But Justin noticed Harley all right, and in him he saw everything that he himself would like to be, and never would be, because most of the things Harley has, you have to be born with.

And Justin made the plates for the cards himself and printed them himself, and he did a wonderful job—something he thought would be worthy of a man like Harley Prentice. That was the name engraved on the card, just that and nothing else, as all really important people have their cards engraved.

He did fine-line work on it, freehand cursive style, and used all the skill he had. It wasn't wasted, because the next day when Harley called to get the cards he held one and stared at it for a while, and then he looked at Justin, seeing him for the first time. He asked, "Who did this?"

And little Justin told him proudly who had done it, and Harley smiled at him and told him it was the work of an artist, and he asked Justin to have dinner with him that evening after work, in the Blue Room of the Castle Hotel.

That's how Harley and Justin got together, but Harley was careful. He waited until he'd known Justin a while before he asked him whether or not he could make plates for five and ten dollar bills. Harley had the contacts; he could market the bills in quantity with men who specialized in passing them, and—most important—he knew where he could get paper with the silk threads in it, paper that wasn't quite the genuine thing but was close enough to pass inspection by anyone but an expert.

So Justin quit his job at Atlas and he and Harley went to New York, and they set up a little printing shop as a blind, on Amsterdam Avenue south of Sherman Square, and they worked at the bills. Justin worked hard, harder than he had ever worked in his life, because besides working on the plates for the bills, he helped meet expenses by handling what legitimate printing work came into the shop.

He worked day and night for almost a year, making plate after plate, and each one was a little better than the last, and finally he had plates that Harley said were good enough. That night they had dinner at the Waldorf-Astoria to celebrate and after dinner they went the rounds of the best night clubs, and it cost Harley a small fortune, but that didn't matter because they were going to get rich.

They drank champagne, and it was the first time Justin ever drank champagne and he got disgustingly drunk and must have made quite a fool of himself. Harley told him about it afterwards, but Harley wasn't mad at him. He took him back to his room at the hotel and put him to bed, and Justin was pretty sick for a couple of days. But that didn't matter, either, because they were going to get rich.

Then Justin started printing bills from the plates, and they got rich. After that, Justin didn't have to work so hard, either, because he turned down most jobs that came into the print shop, told them he was behind schedule and couldn't handle any more. He took just a little work, to keep up a front. And behind the front, he made five and ten dollar bills, and he and Harley got rich.

He got to know other people whom Harley knew. He met Bull Mallon, who handled the distribution end. Bull Mallon was built like a bull; that was why they called him that. He had a face that never smiled or changed expression at all except when he was holding burning matches to the soles of Justin's bare feet. But that wasn't then; that was later, when he wanted Justin to tell him where the plates were.

And he got to know Captain John Willys of the Police Department, who was a friend of Harley's, to whom Harley gave quite a bit of the money they made, but that didn't matter either, because there was plenty left and they all got rich. He met a friend of Harley's who was a big star of the stage, and one who owned a big New York newspaper. He got to know other people equally important, but in less respectable ways.

Harley, Justin knew, had a hand in lots of other enterprises besides the little mint on Amsterdam Avenue. Some of these ventures took him out of town, usually over weekends. And the weekend that Harley was murdered Justin never found out what really happened, except that Harley went away and didn't come back. Oh, he knew that he was murdered, all right, because the police found his body—with three bullet holes in his chest—in the most expensive suite of the best hotel in Albany. Even for a place to be found dead in Harley Prentice had chosen the best.

All Justin ever knew about it was that a long distance call came to him at the hotel where he was staying, the night that Harley was murdered—it must have been a matter of minutes, in fact, before the time the newspapers said Harley was killed.

It was Harley's voice on the phone, and his voice was debonair and unexcited as ever. But he said, "Justin? Get to the shop and get rid of the plates, the paper, everything. Right away. I'll explain when I see you." He waited only until Justin said, "Sure, Harley," and then he said, "Attaboy" and hung up.

Justin hurried around to the printing shop and got the plates and the paper and a few thousand dollars' worth of counterfeit bills that were on hand. He made the paper and bills into one bundle and the copper plates into another, smaller one, and he left the shop with no evidence that it had ever been a mint in miniature.

He was very careful and very clever in disposing of both bundles.

He got rid of the big one first by checking in at a big hotel, not one he or Harley ever stayed at, under a false name, just to have a chance to put the big bundle in the incinerator there. It was paper and it would burn. And he made sure there was a fire in the incinerator before he dropped it down the chute.

The plates were different. They wouldn't burn, he knew, so he took a trip to Staten Island and back on the ferry and, somewhere out in the middle of the bay, he dropped the bundle over the side into the water.

Then, having done what Harley had told him to do, and having done it well and thoroughly, he went back to the hotel—his own hotel, not the one where he had dumped the paper and the bills—and went to sleep.

In the morning he read in the newspapers that Harley had been killed, and he was stunned. It didn't seem possible. He couldn't believe it; it was a joke someone was playing on him. Harley would come back to him, he knew. And he was right; Harley did, but that was later, in the swamp.

But anyway, Justin had to know, so he took the very next train to Albany. He must have been on the train when the police went to his hotel, and at the hotel they must have learned he'd asked at the desk about trains for Albany, because they were waiting for him when he got off the train there.

They took him to a station and they kept him there a long time, days and days, asking him questions. They found out, after a while, that he couldn't have killed Harley because he'd been in New York City at the time Harley was killed in Albany, but they knew also that he and Harley had been operating the little mint, and they thought that might be a lead to who killed Harley, and they were interested in the counterfeiting, too, maybe even more than in the murder. They asked Justin Dean questions, over and over and over, and he couldn't answer them, so he didn't. They kept him awake for days at a time, asking him questions over and over. Most of all they wanted to know where the plates were. He wished he could tell them that the plates were safe where nobody could ever get them again, but he couldn't tell them that without admitting that he and Harley had been counterfeiting, so he couldn't tell them.

They located the Amsterdam shop, but they didn't find any evidence there, and they really had no evidence to hold Justin on at all, but he didn't know that, and it never occurred to him to get a lawyer.

He kept wanting to see Harley, and they wouldn't let him; then when they learned he didn't really believe Harley could be dead, they made him look at a dead man they said was Harley, and he guessed it was, although Harley looked different dead. He didn't look magnificent, dead. And Justin believed, then, but still didn't believe. And after that he just went silent and wouldn't say a word, even when they kept him awake for days and days with a bright light in his eyes, and kept slapping him to keep him awake. They didn't use clubs or rubber hoses, but they slapped him a million times and wouldn't let him sleep. And after a while he lost track of things and couldn't have answered their questions even if he'd wanted to.

For a while after that, he was in a bed in a white room, and all he remembers about that are nightmares he had, and calling for Harley and an awful confusion as to whether Harley was dead or not, and then things came back to him gradually and he knew he didn't want to stay in the white room; he wanted to get out so he could hunt for Harley. And if Harley was dead, he wanted to kill whoever had killed Harley, because Harley would have done the same for him.

So he began pretending, and acting, very cleverly, the way the doctors and nurses seemed to want him to act, and after a while they gave him his clothes and let him go.

He was becoming cleverer now. He thought, what would Harley

tell me to do? And he knew they'd try to follow him because they'd think he might lead them to the plates, which they didn't know were at the bottom of the bay, and he gave them the slip before he left Albany, and he went first to Boston, and from there by boat to New York, instead of going direct.

He went first to the print shop, and went in the back way after watching the alley for a long time to be sure the place wasn't guarded. It was a mess; they must have searched it very thoroughly for the plates.

Harley wasn't there, of course. Justin left and from a phone booth in a drugstore, he telephoned their hotel and asked for Harley and was told Harley no longer lived there; and to be clever and not let them guess who he was, he asked for Justin Dean, and they said Justin Dean didn't live there any more either.

Then he moved to a different drugstore and from there he decided to call up some friends of Harley's, and he phoned Bull Mallon first and because Bull was a friend, he told him who he was and asked if he knew where Harley was.

Bull Mallon didn't pay any attention to that; he sounded excited, a little, and he asked, "Did the cops get the plates, Dean?" and Justin said they didn't, that he wouldn't tell them, and he asked again about Harley.

Bull asked, "Are you nuts, or kidding?" And Justin just asked him again, and Bull's voice changed and he said, "Where are you?" and Justin told him. Bull said, "Harley's here. He's staying under cover, but it's all right if you know, Dean. You wait right there at the drugstore, and we'll come and get you."

They came and got Justin, Bull Mallon and two other men in a car, and they told him Harley was hiding out way deep in New Jersey and that they were going to drive there now. So he went along and sat in the back seat between two men he didn't know, while Bull Mallon drove.

It was late afternoon then, when they picked him up, and Bull drove all evening and most of the night and he drove fast, so he must have gone farther than New Jersey, at least into Virginia or maybe farther, into the Carolinas.

The sky was getting faintly gray with first dawn when they stopped at a rustic cabin that looked like it had been used as a hunting lodge. It was miles from anywhere, there wasn't even a road leading to it, just a trail that was level enough for the car to be able to make it.

They took Justin into the cabin and tied him to a chair, and they told him Harley wasn't there, but Harley had told them that Justin would tell them where the plates were, and he couldn't leave until he did tell.

Justin didn't believe them; he knew then that they'd tricked him about Harley, but it didn't matter, as far as the plates were concerned. It didn't matter if he told them what he'd done with the plates, because they couldn't get them again, and they wouldn't tell the police. So he told them, quite willingly.

But they didn't believe him. They said he'd hidden the plates and was lying. They tortured him to make him tell. They beat him. And they cut him with knives, and they held burning matches and lighted cigars to the soles of his feet, and they pushed needles under his fingernails. Then they'd rest and ask him questions and if he could talk, he'd tell them the truth, and after a while they'd start to torture him again.

It went on for days and weeks—Justin doesn't know how long, but it was a long time. Once they went away for several days and left him tied up with nothing to eat or drink. They came back and started in all over again. And all the time he hoped Harley would come to help him, but Harley didn't come, not then.

After a while what was happening in the cabin ended, or anyway he didn't know any more about it. They must have thought he was dead; maybe they were right, or anyway not far from wrong.

The next thing he knows was the swamp. He was lying in shallow water at the edge of deeper water. His face was out of the water; it woke him when he turned a little and his face went under. They must have thought him dead and thrown him into the water, but he had floated into the shallow part before he had drowned, and a last flicker of consciousness had turned him over on his back with his face out.

~§~

I don't remember much about Justin in the swamp; it was a long time, but I just remember flashes of it. I couldn't move at first; I just lay there in the shallow water with my face out. It got dark and it got cold, I remember, and finally my arms would move a little and I got farther out of the water, lying in the mud with only my feet in the water. I slept or was unconscious again and when I woke up it was getting gray dawn, and that was when Harley came. I think I'd been calling him, and he must have heard.

He stood there, dressed as immaculately and perfectly as ever, right in the swamp, and he was laughing at me for being so weak and lying there like a log, half in the dirty water and half in the mud, and I got up and nothing hurt any more.

We shook hands and he said, "Come on, Justin, let's get you out of here," and I was so glad he'd come that I cried a little. He laughed at me for that and said I should lean on him and he'd help me walk, but I wouldn't do that, because I was coated with mud and filth of the swamp and he was so clean and perfect in a white linen suit, like an ad in a magazine. And all the way out of that swamp, all the days and nights we spent there, he never even got mud on his trouser cuffs, nor his hair mussed.

I told him just to lead the way, and he did, walking just ahead of me, sometimes turning around, laughing and talking to me and cheering me up. Sometimes I'd fall but I wouldn't let him come back and help me. But he'd wait patiently until I could get up. Sometimes I'd crawl instead when I couldn't stand up any more. Sometimes I'd have to swim streams that he'd leap lightly across.

And it was day and night and day and night, and sometimes I'd sleep, and things would crawl across me. And some of them I caught and ate, or maybe I dreamed that. I remember other things, in that swamp, like an organ that played a lot of the time, and sometimes angels in the air and devils in the water, but those were delirium, I guess.

Harley would say, "A little farther, Justin; we'll make it. And we'll get back at them, at all of them."

And we made it. We came to dry fields, cultivated fields with waist-high corn, but there weren't ears on the corn for me to eat. And then there was a stream, a clear stream that wasn't stinking water like the swamp, and Harley told me to wash myself and my clothes and I did, although I wanted to hurry on to where I could get food.

I still looked pretty bad; my clothes were clean of mud and filth but they were mere rags and wet, because I wouldn't wait for them to dry, and I had a ragged beard and I was barefoot.

But we went on and came to a little farm building, just a two-room shack, and there was a smell of fresh bread just out of an oven, and I ran the last few yards to knock on the door. A woman, an ugly woman, opened the door and when she saw me she slammed it again before I could say a word.

Strength came to me from somewhere, maybe from Harley, although I can't remember him being there just then. There was a pile of kindling logs beside the door. I picked one of them up as though it were no heavier than a broomstick, and I broke down the door and killed the woman. She screamed a lot, but I killed her. Then I ate the hot fresh bread.

I watched from the window as I ate, and saw a man running across the field toward the house. I found a knife, and I killed him as he came in at the door. It was much better, killing with the knife; I liked it that way.

I ate more bread, and kept watching from all the windows, but no one else came. Then my stomach hurt from the hot bread I'd eaten and I had to lie down, doubled up, and when the hurting quit, I slept.

Harley woke me up, and it was dark. He said, "Let's get going; you should be far away from here before it's daylight."

I knew he was right, but I didn't hurry away. I was becoming, as you see, very clever now. I knew there were things to do first. I found matches and a lamp, and lighted the lamp. Then I hunted through the shack for everything I could use. I found clothes of the man, and they fitted me not too badly except that I had to turn up the cuffs of the trousers and the shirt. His shoes were big, but that was good because my feet were so swollen.

I found a razor and shaved; it took a long time because my hand wasn't steady, but I was very careful and didn't cut myself much.

I had to hunt hardest for their money, but I found it finally. It was sixty dollars.

And I took the knife, after I had sharpened it. It isn't fancy; just a bone-handled carving knife, but it's good steel. I'll show it to you, pretty soon now. It's had a lot of use.

Then we left and it was Harley who told me to stay away from the roads, and find railroad tracks. That was easy because we heard a train whistle far off in the night and knew which direction the tracks lay. From then on, with Harley helping, it's been easy.

You won't need the details from here. I mean, about the brakeman, and about the tramp we found asleep in the empty reefer, and about the near thing I had with the police in Richmond. I learned from that; I learned I mustn't talk to Harley when anybody else was around to hear. He hides himself from them; he's got a trick and they don't know he's there, and they think I'm funny in the head if I talk to him. But in Richmond I bought better clothes and got a haircut and a man I killed in an alley had forty dollars on him, so I had money again. I've done a lot of traveling since then. If you stop to think you'll know where I am right now.

I'm looking for Bull Mallon and the two men who helped him. Their names are Harry and Carl. I'm going to kill them when I find them. Harley keeps telling me that those fellows are big time and that I'm not ready for them yet. But I can be looking while I'm getting ready so I keep moving around. Sometimes I stay in one place long enough to hold a job as a printer for a while. I've learned a lot of things. I can hold a job and people don't think I'm too strange; they don't get scared when I look at them like they sometimes did a few months ago. And I've learned not to talk to Harley except in our own room and then only very quietly so people in the next room won't think I'm talking to myself.

And I've kept in practice with the knife. I've killed lots of people with it, mostly on the streets at night. Sometimes because they look like they might have money on them, but mostly just for practice and because I've come to like doing it. I'm really good with the knife by now. You'll hardly feel it.

But Harley tells me that kind of killing is easy and that it's something else to kill a person who's on guard, as Bull and Harry and Carl will be.

And that's the conversation that led to the bet I mentioned. I told I Harley that I'd bet him that, right now, I could warn a man I was going to use the knife on him and even tell him why and approximately when, and that I could still kill him. And he bet me that I couldn't and he's going to lose that bet.

He's going to lose it because I'm warning you right now and you're not going to believe me. I'm betting that you're going to believe that this is just another story in a book. That you won't believe that this is the *only* copy of this book that contains this story and that this story is true. Even when I tell you how it was done, I don't think you'll really believe me. You see I'm putting it over on Harley, winning the bet, by putting it over on you. He never thought, and you won't realize, how easy it is for a good printer, who's been a counterfeiter too, to counterfeit one story in a book. Nothing like as hard as counterfeiting a five dollar bill.

I had to pick a book of short stories and I picked this one because I happened to notice that the last story in the book was titled *Don't Look Behind You* and that was going to be a good title for this. You'll see what I mean in a few minutes.

I'm lucky that the printing shop I'm working for now does book work and had a type face that matches the rest of this book. I had a little trouble matching the paper exactly, but I finally did and I've got it ready while I'm writing this. I'm writing this directly on a linotype, late at night in the shop where I'm working days. I even have the boss' permission, told him I was going to set up and print a story that a friend of mine had written, as a surprise for him, and that I'd melt the type metal back as soon as I'd printed one good copy.

When I finish writing this I'll make up the type in pages to match the rest of the book and I'll print it on the matching paper I have ready. I'll cut the new pages to fit and bind them in; you won't be able to tell the difference, even if a faint suspicion may cause you to look at it. Don't forget I made five and ten dollar bills you couldn't have told from the original, and this is kindergarten stuff compared to that job. And I've done enough bookbinding that I'll be able to take the last story out of the book and bind this one in instead of it and you won't be able to tell the difference no matter how closely you look. I'm going to do a perfect job of it if it takes me all night.

And tomorrow I'll go to some bookstore, or maybe a newsstand or even a drug store that sells books and has other copies of this book, ordinary copies, and I'll plant this one there. I'll find myself a good place to watch from, and I'll be watching when you buy it.

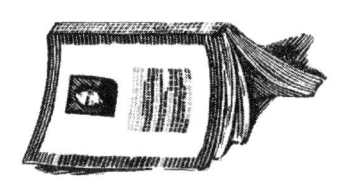

The rest I can't tell you yet because it depends a lot on circumstances, whether you went right home with the book or what you did. I won't know till I follow you and keep watch till you read it—and I see that you're reading the last story in the book.

If you're home while you're reading this, maybe I'm in the house with you right now. Maybe I'm in this very room, hidden, waiting for you to finish the story. Maybe I'm watching through a window. Or maybe I'm sitting near you on the streetcar or train, if you're reading it there. Maybe I'm on the fire escape outside your hotel room. But wherever you're reading it, I'm near you, watching and waiting for you to finish. You can count on that.

You're pretty near the end now. You'll be finished in seconds and you'll close the book, still not believing. Or, if you haven't read the stories in order, maybe you'll turn to start another story. If you do, you'll never finish it.

But don't look around; you'll be happier if you don't know, if you don't see the knife coming. When I kill people from behind they don't seem to mind so much.

Go on, just a few seconds or minutes, thinking this is just another story. Don't look behind you. Don't believe this—*until you feel the knife.*

Ellery Queen's Mystery Magazine, May 1947

Shaggy Dogs

Life and Fire

MR. HENRY SMITH rang the doorbell. Then he stood looking at his reflection in the glass pane of the front door. A green shade was drawn down behind the glass and the reflection was quite clear.

It showed him a little man with gold-rimmed spectacles of the pince-nez variety, wearing a conservatively cut suit of banker's gray.

Mr. Smith smiled genially at the reflection and the reflection smiled back at him. He noticed that the necktie knot of the little man in the glass was a quarter of an inch askew; he straightened his own tie and the reflection in the glass did the same thing.

Mr. Smith rang the bell a second time. Then he decided he would count up to fifty and that if no one answered by then, it would mean that no one was home. He'd counted up to seventeen when he heard footsteps on the porch steps behind him, and turned his head.

A loudly checkered suit was coming up the steps of the porch. The man inside the suit, Mr. Smith decided, must have walked around from beside or behind the house. For the house was out in the open, almost a mile from its nearest neighbor, and there was nowhere else that Checkered Suit could have come from.

Mr. Smith lifted his hat, revealing a bald spot only medium in size but very shiny. "Good afternoon," he said. "My name is Smith. I—"

"Lift 'em," commanded Checkered Suit grimly. He had a hand jammed into his right coat pocket.

"Huh?" There was utter blankness in the little man's voice. "Lift what? I'm sorry, really, but I don't—"

"Don't stall," said Checkered Suit. "Put up your mitts and then march on into the house."

The little man with the gold pince-nez glasses smiled. He raised his hands shoulder-high, and gravely replaced his hat. Checkered Suit had removed his hand halfway from his coat pocket and the heavy automatic it contained looked—from Mr. Smith's present point of view—like a small cannon.

"I'm sure there must be some mistake," said Mr. Smith brightly, smiling doubtfully this time. "I am not a burglar, nor am I—"

"Shut up," Checkered Suit said. "Lower one hand enough to turn the knob and go on in. It ain't locked. But move slow."

He followed Mr. Smith into the hallway.

A stocky man with unkempt black hair and a greasy face had been waiting just inside. He glowered at the little man and then spoke over the little man's shoulder to Checkered Suit. "What's the idea bringing this guy in here?" he wanted to know.

"I think it's the shamus we been watching out for, Boss. It says its name's Smith."

Greasy Face frowned, staring first at the little man with the pince-nez glasses and then at Checkered Suit.

"Hell," he said. "That ain't a dick. Lots of people named Smith. And would he use his right name?"

Mr. Smith cleared his throat. "You gentlemen," he said, with only the slightest emphasis on the second word, "seem to be laboring under some misapprehension. I am Henry Smith, agent for the Phalanx Life and Fire Insurance Company. I have just been transferred to this territory and am making a routine canvass.

"We sell both major types of insurance, gentlemen, life *and* fire. And for the owner of the home, we have a combination policy that is a genuine innovation. If you will permit me the use of my hands, so I can take my rate book from my pocket, I should be very pleased to show you what we have to offer."

Greasy Face's glance was again wavering between the insurance agent and Checkered Suit. He said "Nuts" quite disgustedly.

Then his gaze fixed on the man with the gun, and his voice got louder. "You half-witted ape," he said. "Ain't you got eyes? Does this guy look like—?"

Checkered Suit's voice was defensive. "How'd I know, Eddie?" he whined, and the insurance agent felt the pressure of the automatic against his back relax. "You told me we were on the lookout for this shamus Smith, and that he was a little guy. And he coulda disguised himself, couldn't he? And if he did come, he wouldn't be wearing his badge in sight or anything."

Greasy Face grunted. "Okay, okay, you done it now. We'll have to wait until Joe gets back to be sure. Joe's seen the Smith we got tipped was coming up here."

The little man in the gold-rimmed glasses smiled more confidently now. "May I lower my arms?" he asked. "It's quite uncomfortable to hold them this way"

The stocky man nodded. He spoke to Checkered Suit, "Run him over, though, just to make sure."

Mr. Smith felt a hand reach around and tap his pockets lightly and expertly, first on one side of him and then on the other. He noticed wonderingly that the touch was so light he probably wouldn't have noticed it at all if the stocky man's remark had not led him to expect it.

"Okay," said Checkered Suit's voice behind him. "He's clean, Boss. Guess I did pull a boner."

The little man lowered his hands, and then took a black leather-bound notebook from the inside pocket of his banker's-gray coat. It was a dog-eared rate book.

He thumbed over a few pages, and then looked up smiling. "I would deduce," he said, "that the occupation in which you gentlemen engage—whatever it may be—is a hazardous one. I fear our company would not be interested in selling you the life insurance policies for that reason.

"But we sell both kinds of insurance, life and fire. Does one of you gentlemen own this house?"

Greasy Face looked at him incredulously. "Are you trying to kid us?" he asked.

Mr. Smith shook his head and the motion made his pince-nez glasses fall off and dangle on their black silk cord. He put them back on and adjusted them carefully before he spoke.

"Of course," he said earnestly, "it is true that the manner of my reception here was a bit unusual. But that is no reason why—if this house belongs to one of you and is not insured against fire—I should not try to interest you in a policy. Your occupation, unless I should try to sell you life insurance, is none of my business and has nothing to do with insuring a house. Indeed, I understand that at one time our company had a large policy covering fire loss on a Florida mansion owned by a certain Mr. Capone who, a few years ago, was quite well known as—"

Greasy Face said, "It ain't our house."

Mr. Smith replaced his rate book in his pocket regretfully. "I'm sorry, gentlemen," he said.

He was interrupted by a series of loud but dull thuds, coming from somewhere upstairs, as though someone was pounding frantically against a wall.

Checkered Suit stepped past Mr. Smith and started for the staircase. "Kessler's got a hand or a foot loose," he growled as he went past Greasy Face. "I'll go—"

He caught the glare in Greasy Face's eyes and was on the defensive again. "So what?" he asked. "We can't let this guy go anyway, can we? Sure, it was my fault, but now he knows we're watching for cops and that *something's* up. And if we can't let him go, what for should we be careful what we say?"

The little man's eyes had snapped open wide behind the spectacles. The name Kessler had struck a responsive chord, and for the first time the little man realized that he himself was in grave danger. The newspapers had been full of the kidnaping of millionaire Jerome Kessler, who was being held for ransom. Mr. Smith had noted the accounts particularly, because his company, he knew, had a large policy on Mr. Kessler's life.

But the face of Mr. Smith was impassive as Greasy Face swung round to look at him. He stepped quite close to him to peer into his face, the gesture of a nearsighted man.

Mr. Smith smiled at him. "I hope you'll pardon me," he said mildly, "but I can tell that you are in need of glasses. I know, because I used to be quite nearsighted myself. Until I got these glasses, I couldn't tell a horse from an auto at twenty yards, although I could read quite well. I can recommend a good optometrist in Springfield who can—"

"Brother," said Greasy Face, "if you're putting on an act, don't overdo it. If you ain't—" He shook his head.

Mr. Smith smiled. He said deprecatingly, "You mustn't mind me. I know I'm talkative by nature, but one has to be to sell insurance. If one isn't that way by nature, he becomes that way, if you get what I mean. So I hope you won't mind my—"

"Shut up."

"Certainly. Do you mind if I sit down? I canvassed all the way out here from Springfield today, and I'm tired. Of course, I have a car, but—"

As he talked, he had seated himself in a chair at the side of the hall; now, before crossing his legs, he carefully adjusted a trouser leg so as not to spoil the crease.

Checkered Suit was coming down the stairs again. "He was kicking a wall," he said. "I tied up his foot again." He looked at Mr. Smith and then grinned at Greasy Face. "He sold you an insurance policy yet?"

The stocky man glowered back. "The next time you bring in—"

There were footsteps coming up the drive, and the stocky man whirled and put his eye to the crack between the shade of the door and the edge of its pane of glass. His right hand jerked a revolver from his hip pocket.

Then he relaxed and replaced the revolver. "It's Joe," he said over his shoulder to Checkered Suit. He opened the door as the footsteps sounded on the porch.

A tall man with dark eyes set deep into a cadaverous face came in. Almost at once those eyes fell on the little insurance agent, and he looked startled. "Who the hell—?"

Greasy Face closed the door and locked it. "It's an insurance agent, Joe. Wanta buy a policy? Well, he won't sell you one, because you're in a hazardous occupation."

Joe whistled. "Does he know—?"

"He knows too much." The stocky man jerked a thumb at the man in the checkered suit. "Bright Boy here even pops out with the name of the guy upstairs. But listen, Joe, his name's Smith—this guy here, I mean. Look at him close. Could he be this Smith of the Feds, that we had a tip was in Springfield?"

The cadaverous-faced man glanced again at the insurance agent and grinned. "Not unless he shaved off twenty pounds weight and whittled his nose down an inch, it ain't."

"Thank you," said the little man gravely. He stood up. "And now that you have learned I am not who you thought I was, do you mind if I leave? I have a certain amount of this territory which I intend to cover by quitting time this evening."

Checkered Suit put a hand against Mr. Smith's chest and pushed him back into the chair. He turned to the stocky man. "Boss," he said,

"I think this little guy's razzing us. Can I slug him one?"

"Hold it," said the stocky man. He turned to Joe. "How's about—what you were seeing about? Everything going okay?"

The tall man nodded. "Payoff's tomorrow. It's airtight." He shot a sidewise glance at the insurance agent. "We gonna have this guy on our hands until then? Let's bump him off now."

Mr. Smith's eyes opened wide. "Bump?" he asked. "You mean murder me? But what on earth would you have to gain by killing me?"

Checkered Suit took the automatic out of his coat pocket. "Now or tomorrow, Boss," he asked. "What's the cliff?"

Greasy Face shook his head. "Keep your shirt on," he replied. "We don't want to have a stiff around, just in case."

Mr. Smith cleared his throat. "The question," he said, "seems to be whether you kill me now or tomorrow. But why should the necessity of killing me arise at all? I may as well admit that I recognized Mr. Kessler's name and have deduced that you are holding him here. But if you collect the ransom tomorrow for him, you can just move on and leave me tied up here. Or release me when you release him. Or—"

"Listen," said Greasy Face, "you're a nervy little guy and I'd let you go if I could, but you can identify us, see? The bulls would show you galleries and you'd spot our mugs and they'd know who we are. We've been photographed, see? We ain't amateurs. But we'll let you stick around till tomorrow if you'll only shut up and—"

"But hasn't Mr. Kessler seen you also?"

The stocky man nodded. "He gets it, too," he said calmly. "As soon as we've collected."

Mr. Smith's eyes were wide. "But that's hardly fair, is it? To collect a ransom with the agreement that you will release him, and then fail to keep your part of the contract? To say the least, it's poor business. I thought that there was honor among—er—it will make people distrust you."

Checkered Suit raised a clubbed revolver. "Boss," he pleaded, "at least let me conk him one."

Greasy Face shook his head. "You and Joe take him down to the cellar. Cuff him to that iron cot and he'll be all right. Yeah, tap him one if he argues about it, but don't kill him, yet."

The little man rose with alacrity. "I assure you I shall not argue about it. I have no desire to be—"

Checkered Suit grabbed him by an arm and hustled him toward the cellar steps. Joe followed.

At the foot of the steps, Mr. Smith stopped so suddenly that Joe almost stepped on him. Mr. Smith pointed accusingly at a pile of red cans.

"Is that gasoline?" He peered closer. "Yes, I can see that it is, and smell that it is. Keeping cans of it like that in a place like that is a fire hazard, especially when one of the cans is leaking. Just look at the floor, will you? Wet with it."

Checkered Suit yanked at his arm. Mr. Smith gave ground, still protesting. "A wooden floor, too! In all the houses I've examined when I've issued fire policies, I've never seen—"

"Joe," said Checkered Suit, "I'll kill him if I sock him, and the boss'll get mad. Got your sap?"

"Sap?" asked the little man. "That's a new term, isn't it? What is a—?"

Joe's blackjack punctuated the sentence.

It was very dark when Mr. Smith opened his eyes. At first, it was a swirling, confused, and thunderous darkness. But after a while it resolved itself into the everyday damp darkness of a cellar, and there was a little square of moonlight coming in at a window over his head. The thunder, too, resolved itself into nothing more startling than the sound of footsteps on the floor above.

His head ached badly, and Mr. Smith tried to raise his hands to it. One of them moved only an inch or two before there was a metallic clank, and the hand couldn't be moved any farther. He explored with the hand that was free and found that his right hand was cuffed to the side of the metal cot with a heavy handcuff.

He found, too, that there was no mattress on the bed and that the bare metal springs were cold as well as uncomfortable.

Slowly and painfully at first, Mr. Smith raised himself to a sitting position on the edge of the bed and began to examine the possibilities of his situation.

His eyes were by now accustomed to the dimness. The metal cot was a very heavy one. Another one just like it stood on end against the wall at the head of the cot to which Mr. Smith was handcuffed. At first glance it appeared ready to crash down on Mr. Smith's head, but he reached out his left hand and found that it stood there quite solidly.

He heard the cellar door open and footsteps starting down. A light flashed
on back by the steps and another at a work bench on the opposite side of the cellar. Checkered Suit appeared, and crossed to the work bench. He glanced over toward the dark corner where Mr. Smith was, but Mr. Smith was lying quietly on the cot.

After a moment at the bench he went back up the stairs. The two lights remained on.

Mr. Smith rose to a sitting position again, this time slowly so the springs of the cot would make no noise. Once erect, however, he went to work rapidly. What he was about to attempt was, he knew, a long-shot chance, but he had nothing to lose.

With his free hand he pushed and pulled at the iron cot leaning against the wall, first grasping the frame as high as he could reach, then as low. It was heavy and hard to shift, but finally he got it off balance, ready to topple over on his head if he had not held it back. Then he got it back on balance again, by a hair. He moved his hand away experimentally. The cot stood, a sword of Damocles over his head.

Then lifting a foot up to the edge of the cot on which he sat, he took out the lace of one of his shoes. It wasn't easy, with one hand, to tie an end of the shoelace to the frame of the upended cot, but he managed. Holding the other end of the shoelace, he lay down again.

He had worked more rapidly than had been necessary. It was a full ten minutes before Checkered Suit returned to the cellar.

Through slitted eyes, the insurance agent saw that he carried several objects—a cigar box, a clock, dry-cell batteries. He put them down on the bench and started to work.

"Making a bomb?" Mr. Smith asked pleasantly.

Checkered Suit turned around and glowered. "You talking again? Keep your lip buttoned, or I'll—"

Mr. Smith did not seem to hear. "I take it you intend to plant the bomb near that pile of gasoline cans tomorrow?" he asked. "Yes, I can see now that I was hasty in criticizing it as a fire hazard. It's all in the point of view, of course. You want it to be a fire hazard. Seeing things from the point of view of an insurance man, I can hardly approve. But from your point of view, I can quite appreciate—"

"Shut up!" Checkered Suit's voice was exasperated.

"I take it you intend to wait until you have collected the ransom money for Mr. Kessler, and then, leaving him and me in the house—probably already dead—you will set the little bomb and take your departure."

"That sock Joe gave you should have lasted longer," said Checkered Suit. "Want another?"

"Not particularly," Mr. Smith replied. "In fact, my head still aches from the last one I had from that—did you call it a 'sap'?" He sighed. "I fear my knowledge of the slang of the underworld to which you gentlemen belong is sadly lacking—"

Checkered Suit slammed the cigar box back on the bench and took the automatic from his pocket. Holding it by the barrel, he stalked across the cellar toward Mr. Smith.

The little man's eyes appeared to be closed, but he rambled on, "It is rather a coincidence, isn't it, that I should call here to sell insurance—life and fire—and that you should be so sadly ill-qualified to receive either one? Your occupation is definitely hazardous. And—"

Checkered Suit had reached the bed. He bent over and raised the clubbed pistol. But apparently the little man's eyes hadn't been closed. He jerked up his free hand to ward off the threatened blow, and the hand held the shoestring. The heavy metal cot, balanced on end, toppled and fell.

It had gained momentum by the time a corner of it struck the head of Checkered Suit. Quite sufficient momentum. Mr. Smith's long-shot chance had come off. He said *"Oof"* as Checkered Suit fell across him and the cot came on down atop Checkered Suit.

But his left hand caught the automatic and kept it from clattering to the floor. As soon as he caught his breath, he wormed his hand, not without difficulty, between his own body and that of the gangster. In a vest pocket, he found a key that unlocked the handcuff.

He wriggled his way out, trying to do so quietly. But the upper of the two cots slipped and there was a clang of metal against metal.

There were footsteps overhead and Mr. Smith darted around behind the furnace as the cellar door opened. A voice—it seemed to be the voice of the man they had called Joe—called out, "Larry!" Then the footsteps started down the stairs.

Mr. Smith leaned around the furnace and pointed Checkered Suit's automatic at the descending gangster. "You will please raise your hands," he said. Then he noticed that smoke curled upward from a lighted cigarette in Joe's right hand. "And be very careful of that—"

With an oath, the cadaverous-faced man reached for a shoulder holster. As he did so, the cigarette dropped from his hand.

Mr. Smith's eyes didn't follow the cigarette to the floor, for Joe's revolver had leaped from its holster almost as though by magic and was spitting noise and fire at him. A bullet nicked the furnace near Mr. Smith's head.

Mr. Smith pulled at the trigger of the automatic, but nothing happened. Desperately, he pulled harder. Still nothing—

At the foot of the staircase a sheet of bright flame, started by Joe's dropped cigarette, flared upward from the wooden floor, saturated with gasoline from the leaky can.

The sheet of flame leaped for the stack of cans, found the hole in the leaky one. Mr. Smith had barely time to jerk his head back behind the furnace before the explosion came.

Even though he was shielded from its force, the concussion sent him sprawling back against the steps that led to the outer door of the cellar. Behind him, as he got to his feet, half the cellar was an inferno of flames. He couldn't see Joe—or Checkered Suit.

He ran up the steps and tried the slanting outside cellar door. It seemed to be padlocked from the outside. But he could see where the hasp of the padlock was. He put the muzzle of the automatic against the door there, and tried the trigger again. He brought up his other hand and tried the gun with both hands.

It wouldn't fire.

He glanced behind him again. Flames filled almost the entire cellar. At first he thought he was hopelessly trapped. Then through the smoke and flame he saw that there was an outside window only a few yards away, and a chair that would give him access to it.

Still clinging to the gun that wouldn't shoot, he got the window open and climbed out. A sheet of flame, drawn by the draft of the opened window, followed him out into the night.

He paused only an instant for some cool air and a quick look, to be sure his clothing wasn't afire, and then ran around the house and up onto the front porch. Already the fire was licking upward. Through the first-floor windows he could see its red glare.

He ran up onto the front porch. The gun that wouldn't shoot came in handy to knock the glass, already cracked by explosion, out of the front door so he could reach in and turn the key.

As he went into the hallway, Mr. Smith heard the back door of the house slam, and surmised that Greasy Face was making his getaway. But Mr. Smith's interests lay upstairs; he didn't believe that the fleeing criminal would have untied his captive.

The staircase was ablaze, but still intact. Mr. Smith took a handkerchief from his pocket, held it tightly over his mouth and nose, and darted up through the flames.

The hallway on the second floor was swirling with smoke, but not yet afire. He stopped only long enough to beat out the little flame that was licking upward from one of his trouser cuffs, and then began to throw open the doors that led from the hallway.

In the center room on the left, just down the hallway from the stairs, a bound and gagged man was lying on a bed. Hurriedly Mr. Smith took off the gag and began to work on the ropes that were knotted tightly about his feet and ankles.

"You're Mr. Kessler?" he asked.

The gray-haired man took a deep breath and then nodded weakly. "Are you the police or—?"

Mr. Smith shook his head. "I'm an agent for the Phalanx Life and Fire Insurance Company, Mr. Kessler. I've got to get you out of here, because the house is burning down and we've got a big policy on your life. Two hundred thousand, isn't it?"

The ropes at the wrists of the prisoner gave way. "You rub your wrists, Mr. Kessler," said Mr. Smith, "to get back your circulation, while I untie your ankles. We'll have to work fast to get out of here. I hope we haven't a policy on this house, because there isn't going to be a house here in another fifteen or twenty minutes."

The final knots parted. Over the crackling of flames, Mr. Smith heard the cough of an automobile's engine. He ran to the open window and looked out, while Mr. Kessler stood up.

Through the windshield of the car nosing out of the garage behind the house, he could see the face of the leader of the trio of kidnapers. The driveway ran under the window.

"The last survivor of your three acquaintances is leaving us," said Mr. Smith over his shoulder. "I think the police would appreciate it if we slowed down his departure."

He picked up a heavy metal-based lamp from the bureau beside the window and jerked it loose from its cord.

As he leaned out of the window, the car, gathering speed, was almost directly below him. Mr. Smith poised the lamp and slammed it downward.

It struck the hood just in front of the windshield. There was the sound of breaking glass, and the car swerved into the side of the house and jammed tightly against it. One wheel kept on rolling, but the car itself didn't.

Greasy Face came out of the car door, and there was a long red gash across his forehead from the broken glass. He squinted up at the window as he stepped back, then raised a revolver and fired. Mr. Smith ducked back as a bullet thudded into the house beside the window.

"Mr. Kessler," he said, "I'm afraid I made a mistake. I should have permitted him to depart. We'll have to leave by the other side of the house."

Kessler was stamping his foot to help bring his cramped leg muscles back to normal. Mr. Smith ran past him and opened the door to the hallway. He staggered back and slammed it shut again as a sheet of flame burst in.

The room was thick with smoke now, and on the inside edge, flames were beginning to lick through the floorboards.

"The hallway is quite impassable," said the insurance agent. "And I fear the stairs are gone by now, anyway. I fear we shall have to—" He coughed from the smoke and looked around. There was no other door.

"Well," he said cheerfully, "perhaps our friend has—" Two shots, as he appeared at the window, told him that Greasy Face was still there. One of them went through the upper pane of the window, near the top.

Mr. Smith leaped to one side, then peered cautiously out again. The leader of the kidnapers stood, revolver in hand, twenty feet back from the house, beyond the wrecked car under the window. His face was twisted with anger.

"Come out and get it, damn you," he yelled. "Or stay in there and sizzle."

The gray-haired man was coughing violently now. "What can we—?"

Mr. Smith took the automatic from his pocket and glanced at it regretfully. "If only this thing— Mr. Kessler, do you know how many bullets a revolver holds? He's shot three times. And he's nearsighted. Maybe—"

"Six, most of them, I think. But—" The gray-haired man was gasping now.

Mr. Smith took a deep breath and stepped to the window, started to climb through it. If he could get the kidnaper to empty his revolver, probably he could bluff him with the automatic that wouldn't shoot.

The gun below him barked and a bullet thudded into the window sill. Another; he didn't know where it landed. The third shot went just over his head as he let go and dropped to the top of the wrecked car.

He whirled, jumped to the grass. It was farther than he thought and he fell, but still clung to the automatic. He was flat on his face in the grass only a few steps from the kidnaper.

Greasy Face didn't wait to reload. He clubbed the revolver and stepped in. Mr. Smith rolled over hastily, bringing the automatic up, held in both hands. "Raise your—" His grip on the weapon was tight with desperation and one thumb chanced to touch and move the safety lever. The automatic roared so loudly and suddenly that the unexpected recoil knocked it out of the insurance agent's hands.

But there was a look of surprise on the face of the stocky man, and there was a hole in his chest. He turned slowly as he fell, and Mr. Smith felt slightly ill to see that there was a hole, much larger, in the middle of the kidnaper's back.

Mr. Smith rose a bit unsteadily and hurried back to the car to help Mr. Kessler down to the ground. Over the crackling roar of the flames they could now hear the wail of approaching sirens.

The gray-haired man glanced apprehensively at the fallen kidnaper. "Is he—?"

Mr. Smith nodded. "I didn't mean to shoot—but I *told* them they were in a hazardous occupation. Someone must have seen the blaze and reported it. Some of those sirens sound like police cars. They'll be glad to know you're safe, Mr. Kessler. They've been—"

Five minutes later, the gray-haired man was surrounded by a ring of excited policemen. "Yes," he was saying, "three of them. The insurance chap says the other two are dead in the cellar. Yes, he did it all. No, I don't know his name yet but that reward—"

The police chief turned and crossed the grass toward the little man in the rumpled banker's-gray suit and the gold-rimmed glasses. Outlined in the red glare of the blazing house, he was talking volubly to the fireman on the front end of the biggest hose.

"And because we sell both life *and* fire insurance, we have special consideration for firemen. So instead of charging higher rates for them, as most companies do, we offer a very special policy, with low premiums and double indemnities, and—"

The chief waited politely. At long last he turned to a grinning sergeant. "If that little guy *ever* gets through talking," he said, "tell him about the reward and get his name. I've got to get back to town before morning."

Detection Fiction Weekly, March 22, 1941

The Shaggy Dog Murders

PETER KIDD should have suspected the shaggy dog of something, right away. He got into trouble the first time he saw the animal. It was the first hour of the first day of Peter Kidd's debut as a private investigator. Specifically, ten minutes after nine in the morning.

It had taken will power on the part of Peter Kidd to make himself show up a dignified ten minutes late at his own office that morning instead of displaying an unprofessional overenthusiasm by getting there an hour early. By now, he knew, the decorative secretary he had engaged would have the office open. He could make his entrance with quiet and decorum. The meeting with the dog occurred in the downstairs hallway of the Wheeler Building, halfway between the street door and the elevator. It was entirely the fault of the shaggy dog, who tried to pass to Peter Kidd's right, while the man who held the dog's leash—a chubby little man with a bulbous red nose—tried to walk to the left. It didn't work.

"Sorry," said the man with the leash, as Peter Kidd stood still, then tried to step over the leash. That didn't work, either, because the dog jumped up to try to lick Peter Kidd's ear, raising the leash too high to be straddled, even by Peter's long legs.

Peter raised a hand to rescue his shell-rimmed glasses, in imminent danger of being knocked off by the shaggy dog's display of affection.

"Perhaps," he said to the man with the leash, "you had better circumambulate me."

"Huh?"

"Walk around me, I mean," said Peter. "From the Latin, you know. *Circum*, around—*ambulare*, to walk. Parallel to *circumnavigate*, which means to sail around. From *ambulare* also comes the word *ambulance*— although an ambulance has nothing to do with walking. But that is because it came through the French *hôpital ambulant*, which actually means—"

"Sorry," said the man with the leash. He had already circumambulated Peter Kidd, having started the procedure even before the meaning of the word had been explained to him.

"Quite all right," said Peter.

"Down, Rover," said the man with the leash. Regretfully, the shaggy dog desisted in its efforts to reach Peter's ear and permitted him to move on to the elevator.

"Morning, Mr. Kidd," said the elevator operator, with the deference due a new tenant who has been introduced as a personal friend of the owner of the building.

"Good morning," said Peter. The elevator took him to the fifth, and top floor. The door clanged shut behind him and he walked with firm stride to the office door whereupon—with chaste circumspection—golden letters spelled out:

PETER KIDD
PRIVATE INVESTIGATIONS

He opened the door and went in. Everything in the office looked shiny new, including the blonde stenographer behind the typewriter desk. She said, "Good morning, Mr. Kidd. Did you forget the letterheads you were going to pick up on the floor below?"

He shook his head. "Thought I'd look in first to see if there were any—ah—"

"Clients? Yes, there were two. But they didn't wait. They'll be back in fifteen or twenty minutes."

Peter Kidd's eyebrows lifted above the rims of his glasses. "Two? Already?"

"Yes. One was a pudgy-looking little man. Wouldn't leave his name."

"And the other?" asked Peter.

"A big shaggy dog," said the blonde. "I got *his* name, though. It's Rover. The man called him that. He tried to kiss me."

"Eh?" said Peter Kidd.

"The dog, not the man. The man said 'Down, Rover,' so that's how I know his name. The dog's, not the man's."

Peter looked at her reprovingly. He said, "I'll be back in five minutes," and went down the stairs to the floor below. The door of the Henderson Printery was open, and he walked in and stopped in surprise just inside the doorway. The pudgy man and the shaggy dog were standing at the counter. The man was talking to Mr. Henderson, the proprietor.

"—will be all right," he was saying. "I'll pick them up Wednesday afternoon, then. And the price is two-fifty?" He took a wallet from his pocket and opened it. There seemed to be about a dozen bills in it. He put one on the counter. "Afraid I have nothing smaller than a ten."

"Quite all right, Mr. Asbury," said Henderson, taking change from the register. "Your cards will be ready for you."

Meanwhile, Peter walked to the counter also, a safe distance from the shaggy dog. From the opposite side of the barrier Peter was approached by a female employee of Mr. Henderson. She smiled at him and said, "Your order is ready. I'll get it for you."

She went to the back room and Peter edged along the counter, read, upside down, the name and address written on the order blank lying there: Robert Asbury, 633 Kenmore Street. The telephone number was BEacon 3-3434. The man and the dog, without noticing Peter Kidd this time, went on their way out of the door.

Henderson said, "Hullo, Mr. Kidd. The girl taking care of you?"

Peter nodded, and the girl came from the back room with his package. A sample letterhead was pasted on the outside. He looked at it and said, "Nice work. Thanks."

Back upstairs, Peter found the pudgy man sitting in the waiting room, still holding the shaggy dog's leash.

The blonde said, "Mr. Kidd, this is Mr. Smith, the gentleman who wishes to see you. And Rover."

The shaggy dog ran to the end of the leash, and Peter Kidd patted its head and allowed it to lick his hand. He said, "Glad to know you, Mr.—ah—Smith?"

"Aloysius Smith," said the little man. "I have a case I'd like you to handle for me."

"Come into my private office, then, please, Mr. Smith. Ah—you don't mind if my secretary takes notes of our conversation?"

"Not at all," said Mr. Smith, trotting along at the end of the leash after the dog, which was following Peter Kidd into the inner office. Everyone but the shaggy dog took chairs.

The shaggy dog tried to climb up onto the desk, but was dissuaded.

"I understand," said Mr. Smith, "that private detectives always ask a retainer. I—" He took the wallet from his pocket and began to take ten-dollar bills out of it. He took out ten of them and put them on the desk. "I—I hope a hundred dollars will be sufficient."

"Ample," said Peter Kidd. "What is it you wish me to do?"

The little man smiled deprecatingly. He said, "I'm not exactly sure. But I'm scared. Somebody has tried to kill me—twice. I want you to find the owner of this dog. I can't just let it go, because it follows me now. I suppose I could—ah—take it to the pound or something, but maybe these people would keep on trying to kill me. And anyway, I'm curious."

Peter Kidd took a deep breath. He said, "So am I. Can you put it a bit more succinctly?"

"Huh?"

"Succinctly," said Peter Kidd patiently, "comes from the Latin word, *succinctus,* which is the past participle of *succiugere,* the literal meaning of which is *to gird* up—but in this sense, it—"

"I knew I'd seen you before," said the pudgy man. "You're the circumabulate guy. I didn't get a good look at you then, but—"

"Circumambulate," corrected Peter Kidd.

The blonde quit drawing pothooks and looked from one to another of them. "What was that word?" she asked.

Peter Kidd grinned. "Never mind, Miss Latham. I'll explain later. Ah—Mr. Smith, I take it you are referring to the dog which is now with you. When and where did you acquire it—and how?"

"Yesterday, early afternoon. I found it on Vine Street near Eighth. It looked and acted lost and hungry. I took it home with me. Or rather, it followed me home once I'd spoken to it. It wasn't until I'd fed it at home that I found the note tied to its collar."

"You have the note with you?"

Mr. Smith grimaced. "Unfortunately, I threw it into the stove. It sounded so utterly silly, but I was afraid my wife would find it and get some ridiculous notion. You know how women are. It was just a little poem, and I remember every word of it. It was—kind of silly, but—"

"What was it?"

The pudgy man cleared his throat.

"It went like this:

> *I am the dog*
> *Of a murdered man.*
> *Escape his fate, Sir,*
> *If you can."*

"Alexander Pope," said Peter Kidd.

"Eh? Oh, you mean Pope, the poet. You mean that's something of his?"

"A parody on a bit of doggerel Alexander Pope wrote about two hundred years ago, to be engraved on the collar of the King's favorite dog. Ah—if I recall correctly, it was:

> *I am the dog*
> *Of the King at Kew.*
> *Pray tell me, Sir,*
> *Whose dog are you?"*

The little man nodded. "I'd never heard it, but— Yes, it would be a parody all right. The original's clever. '*Whose dog are you?*'" He chuckled, then sobered abruptly. "I thought my verse was funny, too, but last night—"

"Yes."

"Somebody tried to kill me, twice. At least, I think so. I took a walk downtown, leaving the dog at home, incidentally, and when I was crossing the street only a few blocks from home, and auto *tried* to hit me."

"Sure it wasn't accidental?"

"Well, the car actually swerved out of its way to get me, when I was only a step off the curb. I was able to jump back, by a split second, and the car's tires actually scraped the curb where I'd been standing. There was no other traffic, no reason for the car to swerve, except—"

"Could you identify the car? Did you get the license number?"

"I was too startled. It was going too fast. By the time I got a look at it, it was almost a block away. All I know is that it was a sedan, dark blue or black. I don't even know how many people were in it, if there was more than one. Of course, it might have just been a drunken driver. I thought so until, on my way home, somebody took a shot at me.

"I was walking past the mouth of a dark alley. I heard a noise and turned just in time to see the flash of the gun, about twenty or thirty yards down the alley. I don't know by how much the bullet missed me—but it did. I ran the rest of the way home."

"Couldn't have been a backfire?"

"Absolutely not. The flash was at shoulder level above the ground, for one thing. Besides— No, I'm sure it was a shot."

"There have never been any other attempts on your life, before this? You have no enemies?"

"No, to both questions, Mr. Kidd."

Peter Kidd interlocked his long fingers and looked at them. "And just what do you want me to do?"

"Find out where the dog came from and take him back there. To—uh—take the dog off my hands meanwhile. To find out what it's all about."

Peter Kidd nodded. "Very well, Mr. Smith. You gave my secretary your address and phone number?"

"My address, yes. But please don't call me or write me. I don't want my wife to know anything about this. She is very nervous, you know. I'd rather drop in after a few days to see you for a report. If you find it impossible to keep the dog, you can board it with a veterinary for some length of time."

When the pudgy man had left, the blonde asked, "Shall I transcribe these notes I took, right away?"

Peter Kidd snapped his fingers at the shaggy dog. He said, "Never mind, Miss Latham. Won't need them."

"Aren't you going to work on the case?"

"I *have* worked on the case," said Peter. "It's finished."

The blonde's eyes were big as saucers. "You mean—"

"Exactly," said Peter Kidd. He rubbed the backs of the shaggy dog's ears and the dog seemed to love it. "Our client's right name is Robert Asbury, of six-thirty-three Kenmore Street, telephone Beacon three, three-four-three-four. He is an actor by profession, and out of work. He did not find the dog, for the dog was given to him by one Sidney Wheeler, who purchased the dog for that very purpose, undoubtedly—who also provided the hundred-dollar fee. There's no question of murder."

Peter Kidd tried to look modest, but succeeded only in looking smug. After all, he'd solved his first case—such as it was—without leaving his office.

He was dead right, too, on all counts except one:

The shaggy dog murders had hardly started.

~§~

The little man with the bulbous nose went home—not to the address he had given Peter Kidd, but to the one he had given the printer to put on the cards he'd had engraved.

His name, of course, *was* Robert Asbury and not Aloysius Smith. For all practical purposes, that is, his name was Robert Asbury. He had been born under the name of Herman Gilg. But a long time ago he'd changed it in the interests of euphony the first time he had trodden the boards; 633 Kenmore Street was a theatrical boardinghouse.

Robert Asbury entered, whistling. A little pile of mail on the hall table yielded two bills and a theatrical trade paper for him. He pocketed the bills unopened and was looking at the want ads in the trade paper when the door at the back of the hall opened.

Mr. Asbury closed the magazine hastily, smiled his most winning smile. He said, "Ah, Mrs. Drake."

It was Hatchet-face herself, but she wasn't frowning. Must be in a good mood. Swell! The five-dollar bill he could give her on account would really tide him over. He took it from his wallet with a flourish.

"Permit me," he said, "to make a slight payment on last week's room and board, Mrs. Drake. Within a few days I shall—"

"Yes, yes," she interrupted. "Same old story, Mr. Asbury, but maybe this time it's true even if you don't know it yet. Gentleman here to see you, and says it's about a role."

"Here? You mean he's waiting in the—?"

"No, I had the parlor all tore up, cleaning. I told him he could wait in your room."

He bowed. "Thank you, Mrs. Drake."

He managed to walk, not run, to the stairway, and start the ascent with dignity. But who the devil would call to see him about a role? There were dozens of producers any one of whom might phone him, but it couldn't be a producer calling in person. More likely some friend telling him where there was a spot he could try out for.

Even that would be a break. He'd felt it in his bones that having all that money in his wallet this morning had meant luck. A hundred and ten dollars! True, only ten of it was his own, and Lord, how it had hurt to hand out that hundred! But the ten meant five for his landlady and two and a half for the cards he absolutely *had* to have—you can't send in your card to producers and agents unless you have cards to send in— and cigarette money for the balance.

Funny job that was. The length some people will go to play a practical joke. But it was just a joke and nothing crooked, because this Sidney Wheeler was supposed to be a right guy, and after all, he owned that office building and a couple of others; probably a hundred bucks was like a dime to him. Maybe he'd want a follow-up on the hoax, another call at this Kidd's office. That would be another easy ten bucks.

Funny guy, that Peter Kidd. Sure didn't look like a detective; looked more like a college professor. But a good detective *ought* to be part actor and not look like a shamus. This Kidd sure talked the part, too. Circum—am—Circumambulate, and—uh—succinctly. "Perhaps you had better circumambulate me succinctly." Goofy! And that "from the Latin" stuff!

The door of his room was an inch ajar, and Mr. Asbury pushed it open, started through the doorway. Then he tried to stop and back out again.

There was a man sitting in the chair facing the doorway and only a few feet from it—the opening door had just cleared the man's knees. Mr. Asbury didn't know the man, didn't *want* to know him. He disliked the man's face at sight and disliked still more the fact that the man held a pistol with a long silencer on the barrel. The muzzle was aimed toward Mr. Asbury's third vest button.

Mr. Asbury tried to stop too fast. He stumbled, which, under the circumstances, was particularly unfortunate. He threw out his hands to save himself. It must have looked to the man in the chair as though Mr. Asbury was attacking him, making a diving grab for the gun.

The man pulled the trigger.

~§~

"'I am the dog of a murdered man,'" said the blonde. "'Escape his fate, Sir, if you can.'" She looked up from her shorthand notebook. "I don't get it."

Peter Kidd smiled and looked at the shaggy dog, which had gone to sleep in the comfortable warmth of a patch of sunlight under the window.

"Purely a hoax," said Peter Kidd. "I had a hunch Sid Wheeler would try to pull something of the sort. The hundred dollars is what makes me certain. That's the amount Sid thinks he owes me."

"Thinks he *owes* you?"

"Sid Wheeler and I went to college together. He was full of ideas for making money, even then. He worked out a scheme of printing special souvenir programs for intramural activities and selling advertising in them. He talked me into investing a hundred dollars with the understanding that we'd split the profits. That particular idea of his didn't work and the money was lost.

"He insisted, though, that it was a debt, and after he began to be successful in real estate, he tried to persuade me to accept it. I refused, of course. I'd invested the money and I'd have shared the profits if there'd been any. It was *my* loss, not his."

"And you think he hired this Mr. Smith—or Asbury—"

"Of course. Didn't you see that the whole story was silly? Why would anyone put a note like that on a dog's collar and then try to kill the man who found the dog?"

"A maniac might, mightn't he?"

"No. A homicidal maniac isn't so devious. He just kills. Besides, it was quite obvious that Mr. Asbury's story was untrue. For one thing, the fact that he gave a false name is pretty fair proof in itself. For another he put the hundred dollars on the desk before he even explained what he wanted. If it was his own hundred dollars, he wouldn't have been so eager to part with it. He'd have asked me how much of a retainer I'd need.

"I'm only surprised Sid didn't think of something more believable. He underrated me. Of all things—a lost shaggy dog."

The blonde said, "Why not a shag— Oh, I think I know what you mean. There's a shaggy dog *story,* isn't there? Or something?"

Peter Kidd nodded. "*The* shaggy dog story, the archetype of all the esoteric jokes whose humor values lie in sheer nonsensicality. A New Yorker, who has just found a large white shaggy dog, reads in a New York paper an advertisement offering five hundred pounds sterling for the return of such a dog, giving an address in London. The New Yorker compares the markings given in the advertisement with those of the dog he has found and immediately takes the next boat to England. Arrived in London, he goes to the address given and knocks on the door. A man opens it. 'You advertised for a lost dog,' says the American, 'a shaggy dog.' 'Oh,' says the Englishman coldly, 'not so damn shaggy'. . . and he slams the door in the American's face."

The blonde giggled, then looked thoughtful. "Say, how did you know that fellow's right name?"

Peter Kidd told her about the episode in the printing shop. He said, "Probably didn't intend to go there when he left here, or he wouldn't have taken the elevator downstairs first. Undoubtedly he saw Henderson's listing on the board in the lobby, remembered he needed cards, and took the elevator back up."

The blonde sighed. "I suppose you're right. What are you going to do about it?"

He looked thoughtful. "Return the money, of course. But maybe I can think of some way of turning the joke. After all, if I'd fallen for it, it *would* have been funny."

~§~

The man who had just killed Robert Asbury didn't think it was funny. He was scared and he was annoyed. He stood at the washstand in a corner of Asbury's dingy little room, sponging away at the front of his coat with a soiled towel. The little guy had fallen right into his lap. Lucky, in one way, because he hadn't thudded on the floor. Unlucky, in another way, because of the blood that had stained his coat. Blood on one's clothes is to be deplored at any time. It is especially deplorable when one has just committed a murder.

He threw the towel down in disgust, then picked it up and began very systematically to wipe off the faucets, the bowl, the chair, and anything else upon which he might have left fingerprints.

A bit of cautious listening at the door convinced him that the hallway was empty. He let himself out, wiping first the inside knob and then the outside one, and tossing the dirty towel back into the room through the open transom.

He paused at the top of the stairs and looked down at his coat again. Not too bad—looked as though he'd spilled a drink down the front of it. The towel had taken out the color of blood, at least.

And the pistol, a fresh cartridge in it, was ready if needed, thrust through his belt, under his coat. The landlady—well, if he didn't see her on the way out, he'd take a chance on her being able to identify him. He'd talked to her only a moment.

He went down the steps quietly and got through the front door without being heard. He walked rapidly, turning several corners, and then went into a drugstore which had an enclosed phone booth. He dialed a number.

He recognized the voice that answered. He said, "This is—me. I saw the guy. He didn't have it. . . Uh, no, couldn't ask him. I—well, he won't talk to anyone about it now, if you get what I mean."

He listened, frowning. "Couldn't help it," he said. "Had to. He—uh—well, I had to. That's all. . . See Whee—the other guy? Yeah, guess that's all we can do now. Unless we can find out what happened to—it. . . Yeah, nothing to lose now. I'll go see him right away."

Outside the drugstore, the killer looked himself over again. The sun was drying his coat and the stain hardly showed. Better not worry about it, he thought, until he was through with this business. Then he'd change clothes and throw this suit away.

He took an unnecessarily deep breath, like a man nerving himself up to something, and then started walking rapidly again. He went to an office in a building about ten blocks away.

"Mr. Wheeler?" the receptionist asked. "Yes, he's in. Who shall I say is calling?"

"He doesn't know my name. But I want to see him about renting a property of his, an office."

The receptionist nodded. "Go right in. He's on the phone right now, but he'll talk to you as soon as he's finished."

"Thanks, sister," said the man with the stain on his coat. He walked to the door marked PRIVATE—SIDNEY WHEELER, went through it, and closed it behind him.

~§~

Stretched out in the patch of sunlight by the window, the white shaggy dog slept peacefully. "Looks well fed," said the blonde. "What are you going to do with him?"

Peter Kidd said, "Give him back to Sid Wheeler, I suppose. And the hundred dollars, too, of course."

He put the bills into an envelope, stuck the envelope into his pocket. He picked up the phone and gave the number of Sid Wheeler's office. He asked for Sid.

He said, "Sid?"

"Speaking— Just a minute—"

He heard a noise like the receiver being put down on the desk, and waited. After a few minutes Peter said, "Hello," tried again two minutes later, and then hung up his own receiver.

"What's the matter?" asked the blonde.

"He forgot to come back to the phone." Peter Kidd tapped his fingers on the desk. "Maybe it's just as well," he added thoughtfully.

"Why?"

"It would be letting him off too easily, merely to tell him that I've seen through the hoax. Somehow, I ought to be able to turn the tables, so to speak."

"Ummm," said the blonde. "Nice, but how?"

"Something in connection with the dog, of course. I'll have to find out more about the dog's antecedents, I fear."

The blonde looked at the dog. "Are you sure it *has* antecedents?

And if so, hadn't you better call in a veterinary right away?"

Kidd frowned at her. "I must know whether he bought the dog at a pet shop, found it, got it from the pound, or whatever. Then I'll have something to work on."

"But how can you find that out without—? Oh, you're going to see Mr. Asbury and ask him. Is that it?"

"That will be the easiest way, if he knows. And he probably does. Besides, I'll need his help in reversing the hoax. He'll know, too, whether Sid had planned a follow-up of his original visit."

He stood up. "I'll go there now. I'll take the dog along. He might need— He might have to—ah—a bit of fresh air and exercise may do him good. Here, Rover, old boy."

He clipped the leash to the dog's collar, started to the door. He turned. "Did you make a note of that number on Kenmore Street? It was six hundred something, but I've forgotten the rest of it."

The blonde shook her head. "I made notes of the interview, but you told me that afterward. I didn't write it down."

"No matter. I'll get it from the printer." Henderson, the printer, wasn't busy. His assistant was talking to Captain Burgoyne of the police, who was ordering tickets for a policemen's benefit dance. Henderson came over to the other end of the railing to Peter Kidd. He looked down at the dog with a puzzled frown.

"Say," he said, "didn't I see that pooch about an hour ago, with someone else?"

Kidd nodded. "With a man named Asbury, who gave you an order for some cards. I wanted to ask you what his address is."

"Sure, I'll look it up. But what's it all about? He lose the dog and you find it, or what?"

Kidd hesitated, remembered that Henderson knew Sid Wheeler. He told him the main details of the story, and the printer grinned appreciatively.

"And you want to make the gag backfire," he chuckled. "Swell. If I can help you, let me know. Just a minute and I'll give you this Asbury's address."

He leafed a few sheets down from the top on the order spike. "Six-thirty-three Kenmore."

Peter Kidd thanked him and left.

A number of telephone poles later, he came to the corner of Sixth and Kenmore. The minute he turned that corner, he knew something was wrong. Nothing psychic about it—there was a crowd gathered in front of a brownstone house halfway down the block. A uniformed policeman at the bottom of the steps was keeping the crowd back. A police ambulance and other cars were at the curb in front.

Peter Kidd lengthened his stride until he reached the edge of the crowd. By that time he could see that the building was numbered 633. By that time the stretcher was coming out of the door. The body on the stretcher—and the fact that the blanket was pulled over the face showed that it was a dead body—was that of a short, pudgy person.

The beginning of a shiver started down the back of Peter Kidd's neck. But it was a coincidence, of course. It had to be, he told himself, even if the dead man *was* Robert Asbury.

A dapper man with a baby face and cold eyes was running down the steps and pushing his way out through the crowd. Kidd recognized him as Wesley Powell of the *Tribune*. He reached for Powell's arm, asked, "What happened in there?"

Powell didn't stop. He said, "Hi, Kidd. Drugstore—phone!"

He hurried off, but Peter Kidd turned and fell in step with him. He repeated his question.

"Guy named Asbury, shot. Dead."

"Who was it?"

"Dunno. Cops got description from landlady, though. Guy was waiting for him in his room when he came home less'n hour ago. Musta burned him down, lammed quick. Landlady found corpse. Heard other guy leave and went up to ask Asbury about job—guy was supposed to see him about a job. Asbury an actor, Robert Asbury. Know him?"

"Met him once," Kidd said. "Anything about a dog?"

Powell walked faster. "What you mean," he demanded, "anything about a dog?"

"Uh—did Asbury have a dog?"

"Hello, no. You can't keep a dog in a rooming house. Nothing was said about a dog. Damn it, where's a store or a tavern or *any* place with a phone in it?"

Kidd said, "I believe I remember a tavern being around the next corner."

"Good." Powell looked back, before turning the corner, to see if the police cars were still there, and then walked even faster. He dived into the tavern and Kidd followed him.

Powell said, "Two beers," and hurried to the telephone on the wall.

Peter Kidd listened closely while the reporter gave the story to a rewrite man. He learned nothing new of any importance. The landlady's name was Mrs. Belle Drake. The place was a theatrical boardinghouse. Asbury had been "at liberty" for several months.

Powell came back to the bar. He said, "What was that about a dog?" He wasn't looking at Kidd, he was looking out into the street, over the low curtains in the window of the tavern.

Peter Kidd said, "Dog? Oh, this Asbury used to have a dog when I knew him. Just wondered if he still had it."

Powell shook his head. He said, "That guy across the street—is he following you or me?"

Peter Kidd looked out the window. A tall, thin man stood well back in a doorway. He didn't appear to be watching the tavern. Kidd said, "He's no acquaintance of mine. What makes you think he's following either of us?"

"He was standing in a doorway across the street from the house where the murder was. Noticed him when I came out of the door. Now he's in a doorway over there. Maybe he's just sightseeing. Where'd you get the pooch?"

Peter Kidd glanced down at the shaggy dog. "Man gave him to me," he said. "Rover, Mr. Powell. Powell, Rover."

"I don't believe it," Powell said. "No dog is actually named Rover anymore."

"I know," Peter Kidd agreed solemnly, "but the man who *named* him didn't know. What about the fellow across the street?"

"We'll find out. We go out and head in opposite directions. I head downtown, you head for the river. We'll see which one of us he follows."

When they left, Peter Kidd didn't look around behind him for two blocks. Then he stopped, cupping his hands to light a cigarette and half turning as though to shield it from the wind.

The man wasn't across the street. Kidd turned a little farther and saw why the tall man wasn't across the street. He was directly behind, only a dozen steps away. He hadn't stopped when Kidd stopped. He kept coming.

As the match burned his fingers, Peter Kidd remembered that these two blocks had been between warehouses. There was no traffic, pedestrian or otherwise. He saw that the man had already unbuttoned his coat—which had a stain down one side of it. He was pulling a pistol out of his belt.

The pistol had a long silencer on it, obviously the reason why he'd carried it that way instead of in the holster or in a pocket. The pistol was already half out of the belt.

Kidd did the only thing that occurred to him. He let go the leash and said, "Sic him, Rover!"

The shaggy dog bounded forward and jumped up just as the tall man pulled the trigger. The gun pinged dully but the shot went wild. Peter Kidd had himself set by then, jumped forward after the dog. A silenced gun, he knew, fires only one shot. Between him and the dog, they should be able.

Only it didn't work that way. The shaggy dog had bounded up indeed, but was now trying to lick the tall man's face. The tall man, his nerve apparently having departed with the single cartridge in his gun, gave the dog a push and took to his heels. Peter Kidd fell over the dog.

That was that. By the time Kidd untangled himself from dog and leash, the tall man was down an alley and out of sight.

Peter Kidd stood up. The dog was running in circles around him, barking joyously. It wanted to play some more. Peter Kidd recovered the loop end of the leash and spoke bitterly. The shaggy dog wagged its tail.

They'd walked several blocks before it occurred to Kidd that he didn't know where he was going. For that matter, he told himself, he didn't really know where he'd been. It had been such a beautifully simple matter, before he'd left his office.

Except that if the shaggy dog *hadn't* been the dog of a murdered man, it was one now. Except for that bullet having gone wild, his present custodian, one Peter Kidd, might be in a position to ask Mr. Aloysius Smith Robert Asbury just exactly what the devil it was all about.

It had been so beautifully simple, as a *hoax*. For a moment he tried to think that— But no, that was silly. The police department didn't go in for hoaxes. Asbury had really been murdered.

"I am the dog of a murdered man. . . . Escape his fate, Sir, if you can. . . ."

Had Asbury actually found such a note and then been murdered? Had the man with the silenced gun been following Kidd because he'd recognized the dog? A nut, maybe, out to kill each successive possessor of the shaggy dog?

Had Asbury's entire story been true—except for the phony name he'd given—and had he given a wrong name and address only because he'd been afraid?

But how to—? Of course. Ask Sid Wheeler. If Sid had originated the hoax and hired Asbury, then the murder was a coincidence—one hell of a whopping coincidence.

Yes, they were bound for Sid Wheeler's office. He knew that now, but they'd been walking in the wrong direction. He turned and started back, gradually lengthening his strides. A block later, it occurred to him it would be quicker to phone. At least to make certain Sid was in, not out collecting rents or something.

He stopped in the nearest drugstore and: "Mr. Wheeler," said the feminine voice, "is not here. He was taken to the hospital an hour ago. This is his secretary speaking. If there is anything I can—"

"What's the matter with Sid?" he demanded. There was a slight hesitation and he went on: "This is Peter Kidd, Miss Ames. You know me. What's wrong?"

"He—he was shot. The police just left. They told me not to g-give out the story, but you're a detective and a friend of his, so I guess it's all ri—"

"How badly was he hurt?"

"They—they say he'll get better, Mr. Kidd. The bullet went through his chest, but on the right side and didn't touch his heart. He's at Bethesda Hospital. You can find out more there than I can tell you. Except that he's still unconscious—you won't be able to see him yet."

"How did it happen, Miss Ames?"

"A man I'd never seen before said he wanted to see Mr. Wheeler on business and I sent him into the inner office. Mr. Wheeler was talking on the phone to someone who'd just called— What was that, Mr. Kidd?"

Peter Kidd didn't care to repeat it. He said, "Never mind. Go on."

"He was in there only a few seconds and came out and left, fast. I couldn't figure out why he'd changed his mind so quick, and after he left I looked in and— Well, I thought Mr. Wheeler was dead. I guess the man thought so too, that is, if he meant to kill Mr. Wheeler, he could have easily—uh—"

"A silenced gun?"

"The police say it must have been, when I told them I hadn't heard the shot."

"What did the man look like?"

"Tall and thin, with a kind of sharp face. He had a light suit on. There was a slight stain of some kind on the front of the coat."

"Miss Ames," said Peter Kidd, "did Sid Wheeler buy or find a dog recently?"

"Why, yes, this morning. A big white shaggy one. He came in at eight o'clock and had the dog with him on a leash. He said he'd bought it. He said it was to play a *joke* on somebody."

"What happened next—about the dog?"

"He turned it over to a man who had an appointment with him at eight-thirty. A fat, funny-looking little man. He didn't give his name. But he must have been in on the joke, whatever it was, because they were chuckling together when Mr. Wheeler walked to the door with him."

"You know where he bought the dog? Anything more about it?"

"No, Mr. Kidd. He just said he bought it. And that it was for a joke."

Looking dazed, Peter Kidd hung up the receiver.

Sid Wheeler, shot.

Outside the booth, the shaggy dog stood on its hind legs and pawed at the glass. Kidd stared at it. Sid Wheeler had bought a dog. Sid Wheeler had been shot with intent to kill. Sid had given the dog to actor Asbury. Asbury had been murdered. Asbury had given the dog to him, Peter Kidd. And less than half an hour ago, an attempt had been made on *his* life.

The dog of a murdered man.

Well, there wasn't any question now of telling the police. Sid might have started this as a hoax, but a wheel had come off somewhere, and suddenly

He'd phone the police right here and now. He dropped the dime and then—on a sudden hunch—dialed his own office number instead of that of Headquarters. When the blonde's voice answered, he started talking fast: "Peter Kidd, Miss Latham. I want you to close the office at once and go home. Right away, but be sure you're not followed before you go there. If anyone seems to be following you, go to the police. Stay on busy streets meanwhile. Watch out particularly for a tall, thin man who has a stain on the front of his coat. Got that?"

"Yes, but—but the police are here, Mr. Kidd. There's a Lieutenant West of Homicide here now, just came into the office asking for you. Do you still want me to—?"

Kidd sighed with relief. "No, it's all right then. Tell him to wait. I'm only a few blocks away and will come there at once."

He dropped another coin and called Bethesda Hospital. Sid Wheeler was in serious, but not critical, condition. He was still unconscious and wouldn't be able to have visitors for at least twenty-four hours.

He walked back to the Wheeler Building, slowly. The first faint glimmering of an idea was coming. But there were still a great many things that didn't make any sense at all.

~§~

"Lieutenant West, Mr. Kidd," said the blonde. The big man nodded. "About a Robert Asbury, who was killed this morning. You knew him?"

"Not before this morning," Kidd told him. "He came here—ostensibly—to offer me a case. The circumstances were very peculiar."

"We found your name and the address of this office on a slip of paper in his pocket," said West. "It wasn't in his handwriting. Was it yours?"

"Probably it's Sidney Wheeler's handwriting, Lieutenant. Sid sent him here, I have cause to believe. And you know that an attempt was made to kill Wheeler this morning?"

"The devil! Had a report on that, but we hadn't connected it with the Asbury murder as yet."

"And there was another murder attempt," said Kidd.

"Upon me. That was why I phoned. Perhaps I'd better tell you the whole story from the beginning."

The lieutenant's eyes widened as he listened. From time to time he turned to look at the dog.

"And you say," he said, when Kidd had finished, "that you have the money in an envelope in your pocket? May I see it?"

Peter Kidd handed over the envelope.

West glanced inside it and then put it in his pocket. "Better take this along," he said. "Give you a receipt if you want, but you've got a witness." He glanced at the blonde.

"Give it to Wheeler," Kidd told him. "Unless—maybe you've got the same idea I have. You must have, or you wouldn't have wanted the money."

"What idea's that?"

"The dog," said Peter Kidd, "might not have anything to do with all this at all. Today the dog was in the hands of three persons—Wheeler, Asbury, and myself. An attempt was made—successfully, I am glad to say, in only one case out of the three—to kill each of us. But the dog was merely the—ah—*deus ex machina* of a hoax that didn't come off, or else came off too well. There's something else involved—the money."

"How do you mean, Mr. Kidd?"

"That the money was the object of the crimes, not the dog. That money was in the hands of Wheeler, Asbury, and myself, just as was the dog. The killer's been trying to get that money back."

"Back? How do you mean, *back?* I don't get what you're driving at, Mr. Kidd."

"Not because it's a hundred dollars. Because it isn't."

"You mean counterfeit? We can check that easy enough, but what makes you think so?"

"The fact," said Peter Kidd, "that I can think of no other motive at all. No reasonable one, I mean. But postulate, for the sake of argument, that the money *is* counterfeit. That would, or could, explain everything. Suppose one of Sid Wheeler's tenants is a counterfeiter."

West frowned. "All right, suppose it."

"Sid could have picked up the rent on his way to his office this morning. That's how he makes most of his collections. Say the rent is a hundred dollars. Might have been slightly more or less—but by mistake, sheer mistake, he gets paid in counterfeit money instead of genuine.

"No counterfeiter—it is obvious—would ever dare give out his own product in such a manner that it would directly trace back to him. It's—uh—"

"Shoved," said West. "I know how they work."

"But as it happened, Sid wasn't banking the money. He needed a hundred to give to Asbury along with the dog. And—"

He broke off abruptly and his eyes got wider. "Lord," he said, "it's obvious!"

"What's obvious?" West growled.

"Everything. It all spells *Henderson.*"

"Huh?"

"Henderson, the job printer on the floor below this. He's the only printer-engraver among Wheeler's tenants, to begin with. And Asbury stopped in there this morning, on his way *here*. Asbury paid him for some cards out of a ten-dollar bill he got from Wheeler! Henderson saw the other tens in Asbury's wallet when he opened it, knew that Asbury had the money he'd given Wheeler for the rent.

"So he sent his torpedo—the tall thin man—to see Asbury, and the torpedo kills Asbury and then finds the money is gone—he's given it to me. So he goes and kills Sid Wheeler—or thinks he does—so the money can't be traced back to him from wherever Asbury spent it.

"And then—" Peter Kidd grinned wryly— "I put myself on the spot by dropping into Henderson's office to get Asbury's address, and *explaining* to him what it's all about, letting him know *I* have the money and know Asbury got it from Wheeler. I even tell him where I'm going—to Asbury's. So the torpedo waits for me there. It fits like a glo—*Wait,* I've got something that proves even better. This—"

As he spoke he was bending over and opening the second drawer of his desk. His hand went into it and came out with a short-barreled Police Positive.

"You will please raise your hands," he said, hardly changing his voice. "And, Miss Latham, you will please phone for the police. . ."

~§~

"But how," demanded the blonde, when the police had left, "did you guess that he wasn't a *real* detective?"

"I didn't," said Peter Kidd, "until I was explaining things to him, and to myself at the same time. Then it occurred to me that the counterfeiting gang wouldn't simply drop the whole thing because they'd missed me once, and—well, as it happens, I was right. If he'd been a real detective, I'd have been making a fool out of myself, of course, but if he wasn't, I'd have been making a corpse out of myself, and that would be worse."

"And me, too," said the blonde. She shivered a little. "He'd have had to kill both of us!"

Peter Kidd nodded gravely. "I think the police will find that Henderson is just the printer for the gang and the tall thin fellow is just a minion. The man who came here, I'd judge, was the real entrepreneur."

"The what?"

"The manager of the business. From the Old French *entreprendre*, to undertake, which comes from the Latin *inter* plus *pren*—"

"You mean the big shot," said the blonde. She was opening a brand-new ledger. "Our first case. Credit entry—one hundred dollars counterfeit. Debit—given to police—one hundred dollars counterfeit. And—oh, yes, one shaggy dog. Is that a debit or a credit entry?"

"Debit," said Peter Kidd.

The blonde wrote and then looked up. "How about the credit entry to balance it off? What'll I put in the credit column?"

Peter Kidd looked at the dog and grinned. He said, "Just write in 'Not so *damn* shaggy!'"

Detective Tales, September 1944, as "To Slay a Man About A Dog"

The Spherical Ghoul

I HAD NO PREMONITION of the horror to come. When I reported to work that evening I had not the faintest inkling that I faced anything more startling than another quiet night on a snap job.

It was seven o'clock, just getting dark outside, when I went into the coroner's office. I stood looking out the window into the gray dusk for a few minutes.

Out there, I could see all the tall buildings of the college, and right across the way was Kane Dormitory, where Jerry Grant was supposed to sleep. The same Grant being myself.

Yes, "supposed to" is right. I was working my way through the last year of an ethnology course by holding down a night job for the city, and I hadn't slept more than a five-hour stretch for weeks.

But that night shift in the coroner's department *was* a snap, all right. A few hours' easy work, and the rest of the time left over for study and work on my thesis. I owed my chance to finish out that final year and get my doctor's degree despite the fact that Dad had died, to the fact that I'd been able to get that job.

Behind me, I could hear Dr. Dwight Skibbine, the coroner, opening and closing drawers of his desk, getting ready to leave. I heard his swivel chair squeak as he shoved it back to stand up.

"Don't forget you're going to straighten out that card file tonight, Jerry," he said. "It's in a mess."

I turned away from the window and nodded. "Any customers around tonight?" I asked.

"Just one. In the display case, but I don't think you'll have anybody coming in to look at him. Keep an eye on that refrigeration unit, though. It's been acting up a bit."

"Thirty-two?" I asked just to make conversation, I guess, because we always keep the case at thirty-two degrees.

He nodded. "I'm going to be back later, for a little while. If Paton gets here before I get back tell him to wait."

He went out, and I went over to the card file and started to straighten it out. It was a simple enough file—just a record of possessions found on bodies that were brought into the morgue, and their disposal after the body was either identified and claimed, or buried in potter's field—but the clerks on the day shift managed to get the file tangled up periodically.

It took me a little while to dope out what had gummed it up this time. Before I finished it, I decided to go downstairs to the basement—the morgue proper—and be sure the refrigerating unit was still holding down Old Man Fahrenheit.

It was. The thermometer in the showcase read thirty-two degrees on the head. The body in the case was that of a man of about forty, a heavyset, ugly-looking customer. Even as dead as a doornail and under glass, he looked mean.

Maybe you don't know exactly how morgues are run. It's simple, if they are all handled the way the Springdale one was. We had accommodations for seven customers, and six of them were compartments built back into the walls, for all the world like the sliding drawers of a file cabinet. Those compartments were arranged for refrigeration.

But the showcase was where we put unidentified bodies, so they could be shown easily and quickly to anybody who came in to look at them for identification purposes. It was like a big coffin mounted on a bier, except that it was made of glass on all sides except the bottom.

That made it easy to show the body to prospective identifiers, especially as we could click a switch that threw on lights right inside the display case itself, focused on the face of the corpse.

Everything was okay, so I went back upstairs. I decided I would study a while before I resumed work on the file. The night went more quickly and I got more studying done if I alternated the two. I could have had all my routine work over within three hours and had the rest of the night to study, but it had never worked as well that way.

I used the coroner's secretary's desk for studying and had just got some books and papers spread out when Mr. Paton came in. Harold Paton is superintendent of the zoological gardens, although you would never guess it to look at him. He looked like a man who would be unemployed eleven months of the year because department store Santa

Clauses were hired for only one month out of twelve. True, he would need a little padding and a beard, but not a spot of make-up otherwise.

"Hello, Jerry" he said. "Dwight say when he was coming back?"

"Not exactly, Mr. Paton. Just said for you to wait."

The zoo director sighed and sat down.

"We're playing off the tie tonight," he said, "and I'm going to take him."

He was talking about chess, of course. Dr. Skibbine and Mr. Paton were both chess addicts of the first water, and about twice a week the coroner phoned his wife that he was going to be held up at the office and the two men would play a game that sometimes lasted until well after midnight.

I picked up a volume of *The Golden Bough* and started to open it to my bookmark. I was interested in it because *The Golden Bough* is the most complete account of the superstitions and early customs of mankind that has ever been compiled.

Mr. Paton's eyes twinkled a little as they took in the title of the volume in my hand.

"That part of the course you're taking?" he asked.

I shook my head. "I'm picking up data for my thesis from it. But I do think it ought to be in a course on ethnology."

"Jerry, Jerry," he said, "you take that thesis too seriously. Ghosts, ghouls, vampires, werewolves. If you ever find any, bring them around, and I'll have special cages built for them at the zoo. Or could you keep a werewolf in a cage?"

You couldn't get mad at Mr. Paton, no matter how he kidded you. That thesis was a bit of a sore point with me. I had taken considerable kidding because I had chosen as my subject, "The Origin and Partial Justification of Superstitions." When some people razzed me about it, I wanted to take a poke at them. But I grinned at Mr. Paton.

"You shouldn't have mentioned vampires in that category," I told him. "You've got them already. I saw a cageful the last time I was there."

"What? Oh, you mean the vampire bats."

"Sure, and you've got a unicorn too, or didn't you know that a rhinoceros is really a unicorn? Except that the medieval artists who drew pictures of it had never seen one and were guessing what it looked like."

"Of course, but—"

There were footsteps in the hallway, and he stopped talking as Dr. Skibbine came in.

"Hullo, Harold," he said to Mr. Paton, and to me: "Heard part of what you were saying, Jerry, and you're right. Don't let Paton kid you out of that thesis of yours."

He went over to his desk and got the chessmen out of the bottom drawer.

"I can't outtalk the two of you," Mr. Paton said. "But say, Jerry, how about ghouls? This ought to be a good place to catch them if there are any running loose around Springdale. Or is that one superstition you're not justifying?"

"Superstition?" I said. "What makes you think that's —"

Then the phone rang, and I went to answer it without finishing what I was going to say.

When I came away from the phone, the two men had the chess pieces set up. Dr. Skibbine had the whites and moved the pawn to king's fourth opening.

"Who was it, Jerry?" he asked.

"Just a man who wanted to know if he could come in to look at the body that was brought in this afternoon. His brother's late getting home."

Dr. Skibbine nodded and moved his king's knight in answer to Mr. Paton's opening move. Already both of them were completely lost in the game. Obviously, Mr. Paton had forgotten what he had asked me about ghouls, so I didn't butt in to finish what I had started to say.

I let *The Golden Bough* go, too, and went to look up the file folder on the unidentified body downstairs. If somebody was coming in to look at it, I wanted to have all the facts about it in mind.

There wasn't much in the folder. The man had been a tramp, judging from his clothes and the lack of money in his pockets and from the nature of the things he did have with him. There wasn't anything at all to indicate identification.

He had been killed on the Mill Road, presumably by a hit-and-run driver. A Mr. George Considine had found the body and he had also seen another car driving away. The other car had been too distant for him to get the license number or any description worth mentioning.

Of course, I thought, that car might or might not have been the car that had hit the man. Possibly the driver had seen and deliberately passed up the body, thinking it was a drunk.

But the former theory seemed more likely, because there was little traffic on the Mill Road. One end of it was blocked off for repairs, so the only people who used it were the few who lived along there, and there were not many of them. Probably only a few cars a day came along that particular stretch of the road.

Mr. Considine had got out of his car and found that the man was dead. He had driven on to the next house, half a mile beyond, and phoned the police from there, at four o'clock.

That's all there was in the files.

I had just finished reading it when Bill Drager came in. Bill is a lieutenant on the police force, and he and I had become pretty friendly during the time I had worked for the coroner. He was a pretty good friend of Dr. Skibbine too.

"Sorry to interrupt your game, Doc," he said, "but I just wanted to ask something."

"What, Bill?"

"Look—the stiff you got in today. You've examined it already?"

"Of course, why?"

"Just wondering. I don't know what makes me think so, but—well, I'm not satisfied all the way. *Was* it just an auto accident?"

~§~

Dr. Skibbine had a bishop in his hand, ready to move it, but he put it down on the side of the board instead.

"Just a minute, Harold," he said to Mr. Paton, then turned his chair around to stare at Bill Drager. "Not an auto accident?" he inquired. "The car wheels ran across the man's neck, Bill. What more do you want?"

"I don't know. Was that the sole cause of death, or were there some other marks?"

Dr. Skibbine leaned back in the swivel chair.

"I don't think being hit was the cause of death, exactly. His forehead struck the road when he fell, and he was probably dead when the wheels ran over him. It could have been, for that matter, that he fell when there wasn't even a car around and the car ran over him later."

"In broad daylight?"

"Um—yes, that does sound unlikely. But he could have fallen into the path of the car. He had been drinking plenty. He reeked of liquor."

"Suppose he was hit by a car," Bill said. "How would you reconstruct it? How he fell, I mean, and stuff like that."

"Let's see. I'd say he fell first and was down when the car first touched him. Say he started across the road in front of the car. Horn honked and he tried to turn around and fell flat instead, and the motorist couldn't stop in time and ran over him."

I had not said anything yet, but I put in a protest at that.

"If the man was as obviously drunk as that," I said, "why would the motorist have kept on going? He couldn't have thought he would be blamed if a drunk staggered in front of his car and fell, even before he was hit."

Drager shrugged. "That could happen, Jerry," he said. "For one thing, he may not have any witnesses to prove that it happened that way. And some guys get panicky when they hit a pedestrian, even if the pedestrian is to blame. And then again, the driver of the car might have had a drink or two himself and been afraid to stop because of that."

Dr. Skibbine's swivel chair creaked.

"Sure," he said, "or he might have been afraid because he had a reckless driving count against him already. But, Bill, the cause of death was the blow he got on the forehead when he hit the road. Not that the tires going over his neck wouldn't have finished him if the fall hadn't."

"We had a case like that here five years ago. Remember?"

Dr. Skibbine grunted. "I wasn't here five years ago. Remember?"

"Yes, I forgot that," said Bill Drager.

I had forgotten it, too. Dr. Skibbine was a Springdale man, but he had spent several years in South American countries doing research work on tropical diseases. Then he had come back and had been elected coroner. Coroner was an easy job in Springdale and gave a man more time for things like research and chess than a private practice would.

"Go on down and look at him, if you want," Dr. Skibbine told Bill. "Jerry'll take you down. It will get his mind off ghouls and goblins."

I took Bill Drager downstairs and flicked on the lights in the display case.

"I can take off the end and slide him out of there if you want me to," I said.

"I guess not," Drager said and leaned on the glass top to look closer at the body. The face was all you could see, of course, because a sheet covered the body up to the neck, and this time the sheet had been pulled a little higher than usual, probably to hide the unpleasant damage to the neck.

The face was bad enough. There was a big, ugly bruise on the forehead, and the lower part of the face was cut up a bit.

"The car ran over the back of his neck after he fell on his face, apparently," Bill Drager said. "Ground his face into the road a bit and took off skin. But—"

"But what?" I prompted when he lapsed into silence.

"I don't know," he said. "I was mostly wondering why he would have tried to cross the road at all out there. Right at that place there's nothing on one side of the road that isn't on the other."

He straightened up, and I switched off the showcase lights.

"Maybe you're just imagining things, Bill," I said. "How do you know he tried to cross at all? Doc said he'd been drinking, and maybe he just staggered from the edge of the road out toward the middle without any idea of crossing over."

"Yeah, there's that, of course. Come to think of it, you're probably right. When I got to wondering, I didn't know about the drinking part. Well, let's go back up."

We did, and I shut and locked the door at the head of the stairs. It is the only entrance to the morgue, and I don't know why it has to be kept locked, because it opens right into the coroner's office where I sit all night, and the key stays in the lock.

Anybody who could get past me could unlock it himself. But it's just one of those rules. Those stairs, incidentally, are absolutely the only way you can get down into the morgue which is walled off from the rest of the basement of the Municipal Building.

"Satisfied?" Dr. Skibbine asked Bill Drager, as we walked into the office.

"Guess so," said Drager. "Say, the guy looks vaguely familiar. I can't place him, but I think I've seen him somewhere. Nobody identified him yet?"

"Nope," said Doc. "But if he's a local resident, somebody will. We'll have a lot of curiosity seekers in here tomorrow. Always get them after a violent death."

Bill Drager said he was going home and went out. His shift was over. He had just dropped in on his own time.

I stood around and watched the chess game for a few minutes. Mr. Patton was getting licked this time. He was two pieces down and on the defensive. Only a miracle could save him.

Then Doc moved a knight and said, "Check," and it was all over but the shouting. Mr. Paton could move out of check all right, but the knight had forked his king and queen, and with the queen gone, as it would be after the next move, the situation was hopeless.

"You got me, Dwight," he said. "I'll resign. My mind must be fuzzy tonight. Didn't see that knight coming."

"Shall we start another game? It's early."

"You'd beat me. Let's bowl a quick game, instead, and get home early."

After they left, I finished up my work on the card file and then did my trigonometry. It was almost midnight then. I remembered the man who had phoned that he was coming in and decided he had changed his mind. Probably his brother had arrived home safely, after all.

I went downstairs to be sure the refrigerating unit was okay. Finding that it was, I came back up and locked the door again. Then I went out into the hall and locked the outer door. It's supposed to be kept locked, too, and I really should have locked it earlier.

After that, I read *The Golden Bough,* with a notebook in front of me so I could jot down anything I found that would fit into my thesis.

I must have become deeply engrossed in my reading because when the night bell rang, I jumped inches out of my chair. I looked at the clock and saw it was two in the morning.

Ordinarily, I don't mind the place where I work at all. Being near dead bodies gives some people the willies, but not me. There isn't any nicer, quieter place for studying and reading than a morgue at night.

But I had a touch of the creeps then. I do get them once in a while. This time it was the result of being startled by the sudden ringing of that bell when I was so interested in something that I had forgotten where I was and why I was there.

I put down the book and went out into the long dark hallway. When I had put on the hall light, I felt a little better. I could see somebody standing outside the glass-paned door at the end of the hall. A tall thin man whom I didn't know. He wore glasses and was carrying a gold-headed cane.

"My name is Burke, Roger Burke," he said when I opened the door. "I phoned early this evening about my brother being missing. Uh—may I—"

"Of course," I told him. "Come this way. When you didn't come for so long, I thought you had located your brother."

"I thought I had," he said hesitantly. "A friend said he had seen him this evening, and I quit worrying for a while. But when it got after one o'clock and he wasn't home, I—"

We had reached the coroner's office by then, but I stopped and turned.

"There's only one unidentified body here," I told him, "and that was brought in this afternoon. If your brother was seen this evening, it couldn't be him."

The tall man said, "Oh," rather blankly and looked at me a moment. Then he said, "I hope that's right. But this friend said he saw him at a distance, on a crowded street. He could have been mistaken. So as long as I'm here—"

"I guess you might as well," I said, "now that you're here. Then you'll be sure."

I led the way through the office and unlocked the door.

I was glad, as we started down the stairs, that there seemed little likelihood of identification. I hate to be around when one is made. You always seem to share, vicariously, the emotion of the person who recognizes a friend or relative.

At the top of the stairs I pushed the button that put on the overhead lights downstairs in the morgue. The switch for the showcase was down below. I stopped to flick it as I reached the bottom of the stairs, and the tall man went on past me toward the case. Apparently he had been a visitor here before.

I had taken only a step or two after him when I heard him gasp. He stopped suddenly and took a step backward so quickly that I bumped into him and grabbed his arm to steady myself.

He turned around, and his face was a dull pasty gray that one seldom sees on the face of a living person.

"My God!" he said. "Why didn't you warn me that—" It didn't make sense for him to say a thing like that. I've been with people before when they have identified relatives, but none of them had ever reacted just that way. Or bad it been merely identification? He certainly looked as though he had seen something horrible.

I stepped a little to one side so that I could see past him. When I saw, it was as though a wave of cold started at the base of my spine and ran up along my body. I had never seen anything like it—and you get toughened when you work in a morgue.

The glass top of the display case had been broken in at the head end, and the body inside the case was—well, I'll try to be as objective about it as I can. The best way to be objective is to put it bluntly. The flesh of the face had been eaten away, eaten away as though acid had been poured on it, or as though—

I got hold of myself and stepped up to the edge of the display case and looked down.

It had not been acid. Acid does not leave the marks of teeth.

Nauseated, I closed my eyes for an instant until I got over it. Behind me, I heard sounds as though the tall man, who had been the first to see it, was being sick. I didn't blame him.

"I don't—" I said, and stepped back. "Something's happened here."

Silly remark, but you can't think of the right thing to say in a spot like that.

"Come on," I told him. "I'll have to get the police."

The thought of the police steadied me. When the police got here, it would be all right. They would find out what had happened.

~§~

As I reached the bottom of the stairs my mind started to work logically again. I could picture Bill Drager up in the office firing questions at me, asking me, "When did it happen? You can judge by the temperature, can't you?"

The tall man stumbled up the stairs past me as I paused. Most decidedly I didn't want to be down there alone, but I yelled to him:

"Wait up there. I'll be with you in a minute."

He would have to wait, of course, because I would have to unlock the outer door to let him out.

I turned back and looked at the thermometer in the broken case, trying not to look at anything else. It read sixty-three degrees, and that was only about ten degrees under the temperature of the rest of the room.

The glass had been broken, then, for some time. An hour, I'd say offhand or maybe a little less. Upstairs, with the heavy door closed, I wouldn't have heard it break. Anyway, I hadn't heard it break.

I left the lights on in the morgue, all of them, when I ran up the stairs.

The tall man was standing in the middle of the office, looking around as though he were in a daze. His face still had that grayish tinge, and I was just as glad that I didn't have to look in a mirror just then, because my own face was likely as bad.

I picked up the telephone and found myself giving Bill Drager's home telephone number instead of asking for the police. I don't know why my thoughts ran so strongly to Bill Drager, except that he had been the one who had suspected that something more than met the eye had been behind the hit-and-run case from the Mill Road.

"Can—will you let me out of here?" the tall man said. "I—I—that wasn't my—"

"I'm afraid not," I told him. "Until the police get here. You—uh—witnessed."

It sounded screwy, even to me. Certainly he could not have had anything to do with whatever had happened down there. He had preceded me into the morgue only by a second and hadn't even reached the case when I was beside him. But I knew what the police would say if I let him go before they had a chance to get his story.

Then Drager's voice was saying a sleepy, "Hullo," into my ear. "Bill," I said, "you got to come down here. That corpse downstairs—it's—I—"

The sleepiness went out of Drager's voice.

"Calm down, Jerry," he said. "It can't be that bad. Now, what happened?"

I finally got it across.

"You phoned the department first, of course?" Drager asked.

"N-no. I thought of you first because—"

"Sit tight," he said. "I'll phone them and then come down. I'll have to dress first, so they'll get there ahead of me. Don't go down to the morgue again and don't touch anything."

He put the receiver on the hook, and I felt a little better. Somehow the worst seemed to be over, now that it was off my chest. Drager's offering to phone the police saved me from having to tell it again, over the phone.

The tall man—I remembered now that he had given the name Roger Burke—was leaning against the wall, weakly.

"Did—did I get from what you said on the phone that the body wasn't that way when—when they brought it in?" he asked.

I nodded. "It must have happened within the last hour," I said. "I was down there at midnight, and everything was all right then."

"But what—what happened?"

I opened my mouth and closed it again. Something had happened down there, but what? There wasn't any entrance to the morgue other than the ventilator and the door that opened at the top of the stairs. And nobody—nothing—had gone through that door since my trip of inspection.

I thought back and thought hard. No, I hadn't left this office for even a minute between midnight and the time the night bell had rung at two o'clock. I had left the office then, of course, to answer the door. But whatever had happened had not happened then. The thermometer downstairs proved that.

Burke was fumbling cigarettes out of his pocket. He held out the package with a shaky hand, and I took one and managed to strike a match and light both cigarettes.

The first drag made me feel nearly human. Apparently he felt better too, because he said:

"I—I'm afraid I didn't make identification one way or the other. You couldn't—with—" He shuddered. "Say, my brother had a small anchor tattooed on his left forearm. I forgot it or I could have asked you over the phone. Was there—"

I thought back to the file and shook my head.

"No," I said definitely. "It would have been on the record, and there wasn't anything about it. They make a special point of noting down things like that."

"That's swell," Burke said. "I mean— Say, if I'm going to have to wait, I'm going to sit down. I still feel awful."

Then I remembered that I had better phone Dr. Skibbine, too, and give him the story firsthand before the police got here and called him. I went over to the phone.

The police got there first—Captain Quenlin and Sergeant Wilson and two other men I knew by sight but not by name. Bill Drager was only a few minutes later getting there, and around three o'clock Dr. Skibbine came.

By that time the police had questioned Burke and let him go, although one of them left to go home with him. They told him it was because they wanted to check on whether his brother had shown up yet, so the Missing Persons Bureau could handle it if he hadn't. But I guessed the real reason was that they wanted to check on his identity and place of residence.

Not that there seemed to be any way Burke could be involved in whatever had happened to the body, but when you don't know what has happened, you can't overlook any angle. After all, he was a material witness.

Bill Drager had spent most of the time since he had been there downstairs, but he came up now.

"The place is tighter than a drum down there, except for that ventilator," he said. "And I noticed something about it. One of the vanes in it is a little bent."

"How about rats?" Captain Quenlin asked.

Drager snorted. "Ever see rats break a sheet of glass?"

"The glass might have been broken some other way." Quenlin looked at me. "You're around here nights, Jerry Grant. Ever see any signs of rats or mice?"

I shook my head, and Bill Drager backed me up.

"I went over the whole place down there," he said. "There isn't a hole anywhere. Floor's tile set in cement. The walls are tile, in big close-set slabs, without a break. I went over them."

Dr. Skibbine was starting down the steps.

"Come on, Jerry," he said to me. "Show me where you and this Burke fellow were standing when he let out a yip."

I didn't much want to, but I followed him down. I showed him where I had been and where Burke had been and told him that Burke had not gone closer to the case than about five feet at any time. Also, I told him what I had already told the police about my looking at the thermometer in the case.

Dr. Skibbine went over and looked at it.

"Seventy-one now," he said. "I imagine that's as high as it's going. You say it was sixty-three when you saw it at two? Yes, I'd say the glass was broken between twelve-thirty and one-thirty."

Quenlin had followed us down the stairs. "When did you get home tonight, Dr. Skibbine?" he asked.

The coroner looked at him in surprise. "Around midnight. Good Lord, you don't think *I* had anything to do with this, do you, Quenlin?"

The captain shook his head. "Routine question. Look, Doc, why would anybody or anything do that?"

"I wouldn't know," Skibbine said slowly, "unless it was to prevent identification of the corpse. That's possible. The body will never be identified now unless the man has a criminal record and his prints are on file. But making that 'anything' instead of 'anybody' makes it easier, Cap. I'd say 'anything' was hungry, plenty hungry."

I leaned back against the wall at the bottom of the stairs, again fighting nausea that was almost worse than before.

Rats? Besides the fact that there weren't any rats, it would have taken a lot of them to do what had been done.

"Jerry," said Bill Drager, "you're sure you weren't out of the office up there for even a minute between midnight and two o'clock? Think hard. Didn't you maybe go to the washroom or something?"

"I'm positive," I told him.

Drager turned to the captain and pointed up to the ventilator.

"There are only two ways into this morgue, Cap," he said. "One's through the door Jerry says he sat in front of, and the other's up there."

My eyes followed his pointing finger, and I studied the ventilator and its position. It was a round opening in the wall, twelve or maybe thirteen inches across, and there was a wheel-like arrangement of vanes that revolved in it. It was turning slowly. It was set in the wall just under the high ceiling, maybe sixteen feet above the floor, and it was directly over the display case.

"Where's that open into?" Quenlin asked.

"Goes right through the wall," Dr. Skibbine told him. "Opens on the alley, just a foot or two above the ground. There's another wheel just like that one on the outside. A little electric motor turns them."

"Could the thing be dismantled from the outside?"

Dr. Skibbine shrugged. "Easiest way to find that out is to go out in the alley and try it. But nobody could get through there, even if you got the thing off. It's too narrow."

"A thin man might—"

"No, even a thin man is wider than twelve inches across the shoulders, and that's my guess on the width of that hole."

Quenlin shrugged.

"Got a flashlight, Drager?" he asked. "Go on out in the alley and take a look. Although if somebody did get that thing off, I don't see how the devil they could have—"

Then he looked down at the case and winced. "If everybody's through looking at this for the moment," he said, "for crying out loud put a sheet over it. It's giving me the willies. I'll dream about ghouls tonight."

The word hit me like a ton of bricks. Because it was then I remembered that we had talked about ghouls early that very evening. About—how had Mr. Paton put it?—"ghosts, ghouls, vampires, werewolves," and about a morgue being a good place for ghouls to hang around; and about—

Some of the others were looking at me, and I knew that Dr. Skibbine, at least, was remembering that conversation. Had he mentioned it to any of the least, was remembering that conversation. Had he mentioned it to any of the others?

Sergeant Wilson was standing behind the other men and probably didn't know I could see him from where I stood, for he surreptitiously crossed himself.

"Ghouls, nuts!" he said in a voice a bit louder than necessary. "There ain't any such thing. Or is there?"

It was a weak but dramatic ending. Nobody answered him.

Me, I had had enough of that morgue for the moment. Nobody

had put a sheet over the case because there was not one available downstairs.

"I'll get a sheet," I said and started up for the office. I stumbled on the bottom step.

"What's eating—" I heard Quenlin say, and then as though he regretted his choice of words, he started over again. "Something's wrong with the kid. Maybe you better send him home, Doc."

He probably didn't realize I could hear him. But by that time I was most of the way up, so I didn't hear the coroner's answer.

~§~

From the cabinet I got a sheet, and the others were coming up the steps when I got back with it. Quenlin handed it to Wilson.

"You put it on, Sarge," he said.

Wilson took it, and hesitated. I had seen his gesture downstairs and I knew he was scared stiff to go back down there alone. I was scared, too, but I did my Boy Scout act for the day and said:

"I'll go down with you, Sergeant. I want to take a look at that ventilator."

While he put the sheet over the broken case, I stared up at the ventilator and saw the bent vane. As I watched, a hand reached through the slit between that vane and the next and bent it some more.

Then the hand, Bill Drager's hand, reached through the widened slit and groped for the nut on the center of the shaft on which the ventilator wheel revolved. Yes, the ventilator could be removed and replaced from the outside. The bent vane made it look as though that had been done.

But why? After the ventilator had been taken off, what then? The opening was too small for a man to get through and besides it was twelve feet above the glass display case.

Sergeant Wilson went past me up the stairs, and I followed him up. The conversation died abruptly as I went through the door, and I suspected that I had been the subject of the talk.

Dr. Skibbine was looking at me.

"The cap's right, Jerry," he said. "You don't look so well. We're going to be around here from now on, so you take the rest of the night off. Get some sleep."

Sleep, I thought. What's that? How could I sleep now? I felt dopy, I'll admit, from lack of it. But the mere thought of turning out a light and lying down alone in a dark room—huh-uh! I must have been a little lightheaded just then, for a goofy parody was running through my brain:

A ghoul hath murdered sleep, the innocent sleep, sleep that knits.

"Thanks, Dr. Skibbine," I said. "I—I guess it will do me good, at that."

It would get me out of here, somewhere where I could think without a lot of people talking. If I could get the unicorns and rhinoceros out of my mind, maybe I had the key. Maybe, but it didn't make sense yet.

I put on my hat and went outside and walked around the building into the dark alley.

Bill Drager's face was a dim patch in the light that came through the circular hole in the wall where the ventilator had been.

He saw me coming and called out sharply, "Who's that?" and stood up. When he stood, he seemed to vanish, because it put him back in the darkness.

"It's me—Jerry Grant," I said. "Find out anything, Bill?"

"Just what you see. The ventilator comes out, from the outside. But it isn't a big enough hole for a man." He laughed a little off-key. "A ghoul, I don't know. How big is a ghoul, Jerry?"

"Can it, Bill," I said. "Did you do that in the dark? Didn't you bring a flashlight?"

"No. Look, whoever did it earlier in the night, if somebody did, wouldn't have dared use a light. They'd be too easy to see from either end of the alley. I wanted to see if it could be done in the dark."

"Yes," I said thoughtfully. "But the light from the inside shows."

"Was it on between midnight and two?"

"Um—no. I hadn't thought of that."

I stared at the hole in the wall. It was just about a foot in diameter. Large enough for a man to stick his head into, but not to crawl through.

Bill Drager was still standing back in the dark, but now that my eyes were used to the alley, I could make out the shadowy outline of his body.

"Jerry," he said, "you've been studying this superstition stuff. Just what is a ghoul?"

"Something in Eastern mythology, Bill. An imaginary creature that robs graves and feeds on corpses. The modern use of the word is confined to someone who robs graves, usually for jewelry that is sometimes interred with the bodies. Back in the early days of medicine, bodies were stolen and sold to the anatomists for purposes of dissection, too."

"The modern ones don't—uh—"

"There have been psychopathic cases, a few of them. One happened in Paris, in modern times. A man named Bertrand. Charles Fort tells about him in his book *Wild Talents.*"

"*Wild Talents,* huh?" said Bill. "What happened?"

"Graves in a Paris cemetery were being dug up by something or someone who—" there in the dark alley, I couldn't say it plainly— "who—uh—acted like a ghoul. They couldn't catch him but they set a blunderbuss trap. It got this man Bertrand, and he confessed."

Bill Drager didn't say anything, just stood there. Then, just as though I could read his mind, I got scared because I knew what he was thinking. If anything like that had happened here tonight, there was only one person it could possibly have been.

Me.

Bill Drager was standing there silently, staring at me, and wondering whether I —

Then I knew why the others had stopped talking when I had come up the stairs just a few minutes before, back at the morgue. No, there was not a shred of proof, unless you can call process of elimination proof. But there had been a faint unspoken suspicion that somehow seemed a thousand times worse than an accusation I could deny.

I knew, then, that unless this case was solved suspicion would follow me the rest of my life. Something too absurd for open accusation. But people would look at me and wonder, and the mere possibility would make them shudder. Every word I spoke would be weighed to see whether it might indicate an unbalanced mind.

Even Bill Drager, one of my best friends, was wondering about me now.

"Bill," I said, "for God's sake, you don't think—"

"Of course not, Jerry."

But the fact that he knew what I meant before I had finished the sentence, proved I had been right about what he had been thinking.

There was something else in his voice, too, although he had tried to keep it out. Fear. He was alone with me in a dark alley, and I realized now why he had stepped back out of the light so quickly. Bill Drager was a little afraid of me.

But this was no time or place to talk about it. The atmosphere was wrong. Anything I could say would make things worse.

So I merely said, "Well, so long, Bill," as I turned and walked toward the street.

Half a block up the street on the other side was an all-night restaurant, and I headed for it. Not to eat, for I felt as though I would never want to eat again. The very thought of food was sickening. But a cup of coffee might take away some of the numbness in my mind.

Hank Perry was on duty behind the counter, and he was alone.

"Hi, Jerry," he said, as I sat down on a stool at the counter. "Off early tonight?"

I nodded and let it go at that.

"Just a cup of black coffee, Hank," I told him, and forestalled any sales-talk by adding, "I'm not hungry. Just ate."

Silly thing to say, I realized the minute I had said it. Suppose someone asked Hank later what I had said when I came in. They all knew, back there, that I had not brought a lunch to work and hadn't eaten. Would I, from now on, have to watch every word I said to avoid slips like that?

But whatever significance Hank or others might read into my words later, there was nothing odd about them now, as long as Hank didn't know what had happened at the morgue.

He brought my coffee. I stirred in sugar and waited for it to cool enough to drink.

"Nice night out," Hank said.

I hadn't noticed, but I said, "Yeah."

To me it was one terrible night out, but I couldn't tell him that without spilling the rest of the story.

"How was business tonight, Hank?" I asked.

"Pretty slow."

"How many customers," I asked, "did you have between midnight and two o'clock?"

"Hardly any. Why?"

"Hank," I said, "something happened then. Look, I can't tell you about it now, honestly. I don't know whether or not it's going to be given out to the newspapers. If it isn't, it would lose me my job even to mention it. But will you think hard if you saw anybody or anything out of the ordinary between twelve and two?"

"Um," said Hank, leaning against the counter thoughtfully. "That's a couple of hours ago. Must have had several customers in here during that time. But all I can remember are regulars. People on night shifts that come in regularly."

"When you're standing at that grill in the window frying something, you can see out across the street," I said. "You ought to be able to see down as far as the alley, because this is a pretty wide street—"

"Yeah, I can—"

"Did you see anyone walk or drive in there?"

"Golly," said Hank. "Yeah, I did. I think it was around one o'clock. I happened to notice the guy on account of what he was carrying."

I felt my heart hammering with sudden excitement.

"What was he carrying? And what did he look like?"

"I didn't notice what he looked like," said Hank. "He was in shadow most of the time. But he was carrying a bowling ball—"

"A bowling ball?"

Hank nodded. "That's what made me notice him. There aren't any alleys—I mean bowling alleys—right around here. I bowl myself so I wondered where this guy had been rolling."

"You mean he was carrying a bowling ball under his arm?"

I was still incredulous, even though Hank's voice showed me he was not kidding.

He looked at me contemptuously.

"No. Bowlers never carry 'em like that on the street. There's a sort of bag that's made for the purpose. A little bigger than the ball, some of them, so a guy can put in his bowling shoes and stuff—"

I closed my eyes a moment to try to make sense out of it. Of all the things on this mad night it seemed the maddest that a bowling ball had been carried into the alley by the morgue—or something the shape of a bowling ball. At just the right time, too. One o'clock.

It would be a devil of a coincidence if the man Hank had seen hadn't been the one.

"You're sure it was a bowling ball case?"

"Positive. I got one like it myself. And the way he carried it, it was just heavy enough to have the ball in it." He looked at me curiously. "Say, Jerry, I never thought of it before, but a case like that would be a handy thing to carry a bomb in. Did someone try to plant a bomb at the morgue?"

"No."

"Then if it wasn't a bowling ball—and you act like you think it wasn't—what would it have been?"

"I wish I knew," I told him. "I wish to high heaven I knew—"

I downed the rest of my coffee and stood up.

"Thanks a lot, Hank," I said. "Listen, you think it over and see if you can remember anything else about that case or the man who carried it. I'll see you later."

~§~

What I needed was some fresh air, so I started walking. I didn't pay any attention to where I was going; I just walked.

My feet didn't take me in circles, but my mind did. A bowling ball! Why would a bowling ball, or something shaped like it, be carried into the alley back of the morgue? A bowling ball would fit into that ventilator hole, all right, and a dropped bowling ball would have broken the glass of the case.

But a bowling ball wouldn't have done—the rest of it.

I vaguely remembered some mention of bowling earlier in the evening and thought back to what it was. Oh yes. Dr. Skibbine and Mr. Paton had been going to bowl a game instead of playing a second game of chess. But neither of them had bowling balls along. Anyway, if Dr. Skibbine had told the truth, they had both been home by midnight.

If not a bowling ball, then what? A ghoul? A spherical ghoul?

The thought was so incongruously horrible that I wanted to stop, right there in the middle of the sidewalk and laugh like a maniac. Maybe I was near hysteria.

I thought of going back to the morgue and telling them about it, and laughing. Watching Quenlin's face and Wilson's when I told them that our guest had been a man-eating bowling ball. A spherical—

Then I stopped walking, because all of a sudden I knew what the bowling ball had been, and I had the most important part of the answer.

Somewhere a clock was striking half-past three, and I looked around to see where I was. Oak Street, only a few doors from Grant Parkway. That meant I had come fifteen or sixteen blocks from the morgue and that I was only a block and a half from the zoo. At the zoo, I could find out if I was right.

So I started walking again. A block and a half later I was across the street from the zoo right in front of Mr. Paton's house. Strangely, there was a light in one of the downstairs rooms.

I went up onto the porch and rang the bell. Mr. Paton came to answer it. He was wearing a dressing gown, but I could see shoes and the bottoms of his trouser legs under it.

He didn't look surprised at all when he opened the door.

"Yes, Jerry?" he said, almost as though he had been expecting me.

"I'm glad you're still up, Mr. Paton," I said. "Could you walk across with me and get me past the guard at the gate? I'd like to look at one of the cages and verify—something."

"You guessed then, Jerry?"

"Yes, Mr. Paton," I told him. Then I had a sudden thought that scared me a little. "You were seen going into the alley," I added quickly, "and the man who saw you knows I came here. He saw you carrying—"

He held up his hand and smiled.

"You needn't worry, Jerry," he said. "I know it's over—the minute anybody is smart enough to guess. And—well, I murdered a man all right, but I'm not the type to murder another to try to cover up, because I can see where that would lead. The man I did kill deserved it, and I gambled on— Well never mind all that."

"Who was he?" I asked.

"His name was Mark Leedom. He was my assistant four years ago. I was foolish at that time—I'd lost money speculating and I stole some zoo funds. They were supposed to be used for the purchase of— Never mind the details. Mark Leedom found out and got proof.

"He made me turn over most of the money to him, and he— retired, and moved out of town. But he's been coming back periodically to keep shaking me down. He was a rat, Jerry, a worse crook than I ever thought of being. This time I couldn't pay so I killed him."

"You were going to make it look like an accident on the Mill Road?" I said. "You killed him here and took him—"

"Yes, I was going to have the car run over his head, so he wouldn't be identified. I missed by inches, but I couldn't try again because another car was coming, and I had to keep on driving away.

"Luckily, Doc Skibbine didn't know him. It was while Doc was in South America that Leedom worked for me. But there are lots of people around who did know him. Some curiosity seeker would have identified him in the week they hold an unidentified body and—well, once they knew who he was and traced things back, they'd have got to me eventually for the old business four years ago if not the fact that I killed him."

"So that's why you had to make him unidentifiable," I said. "I see. He looked familiar to Bill Drager, but Bill couldn't place him."

He nodded. "Bill was just a patrolman then. He probably had seen Leedom only a few times, but someone else— Well, Jerry, you go back and tell them about it. Tell them I'll be here."

"Gee, Mr. Paton, I'm sorry I got to," I said. "Isn't there anything—"

"No. Go and get them. I won't run away, I promise you. And tell Doc he wouldn't have beat me that chess game tonight if I hadn't let him. With what I had to do, I wanted to get out of there early. Good night, Jerry."

He eased me out onto the porch again before I quite realized why he had never had a chance to tell Dr. Skibbine himself. Yes, he meant for them to find him here when they came, but not alive.

I almost turned to the door again, to break my way in and stop him. Then I realized that everything would be easier for him if he did it his way.

Yes, he was dead by the time they sent men out to bring him in. Even though I had expected it, I guess I had a case of the jitters when they phoned in the news, and I must have showed it, because Bill Drager threw an arm across my shoulders.

"Jerry," he said, "this has been the devil of a night for you. You need a drink. Come on."

The drink made me feel better and so did the frank admiration in

Drager's eyes. It was so completely different from what I had seen there back in the alley.

"Jerry," he told me, "you ought to get on the Force. Figuring out that—of all things—he had used an armadillo."

"But what else was possible? Look! All those ghoul legends trace back to beasts that are eaters of carrion. Like hyenas. A hyena could have done what was done back there in the morgue. But no one could have handled a hyena—pushed it through that ventilator hole with a rope on it to pull it up again.

"But an armadillo is an eater of corpses, too. It gets frightened when handled and curls up into a ball, like a bowling ball. It doesn't make any noise, and you could carry it in a bag like the one Hank described. It has an armored shell that would break the glass of the display case if Paton lowered it to within a few feet and let it drop the rest of the way. And of course he looked down with a flashlight to see—"

Bill Drager shuddered a little.

"Learning is a great thing if you like it," he said. "Studying origins of superstitions, I mean. But me, I want another drink. How about you?"

Thrilling Mystery, January 1943

Moon Over Murder

PETE HOLM stared out past the wharf a long time. Out there over the silver-dappled water of Cape Cod hung an unbelievable iridescent disc of moon. Something, he thought, that you couldn't put on canvas unless you had pigments with cold and hot fire in them, pigments that would freeze on the brush or burn smoldering holes in the canvas. The Provincetown moon which, with the color-mad sunsets and the Rand-McNally-blue water of the cape, drew artists from all over the continent every summer.

And Pete Holm said a word and kicked at an inoffensive piling of the wharf, then turned away down Commercial Street. He went past the Colony House and the Neptune, and turned in at the White Horse Bar. "Shorty" Wellman, looking like a white-aproned beer keg, called out.

"Hi, Pete. Howzit?"

"Swell," Pete Holm lied.

Shorty was already drawing an ale, without waiting for him to order. Plunking it down on the bar, Shorty turned back to the man standing at the other end of the bar. Pete Holm noticed the man then.

Anywhere else the man's rakish buff beret and more than rakish moustache and the brilliance of his blazer would have attracted attention, but not here. Provincetown, in season, takes berets in its stride; and the season was almost, if not quite, on. But the man's nose was, to Holm, the attention-compelling feature.

He knew at once that he didn't like that nose, and couldn't possibly like the man who wore it. It was a long, thin, pale nose. Pale almost to translucence, as though no blood flowed through the tissue under the thin, almost bluish skin. And it was curved like a scimitar.

The man was looking at him, and there was a stiff smile under the nose and the rakish moustache.

"Hullo," he said.

Holm nodded. He wished the guy had not spoken because now he would have to be polite, and Provincetown in season was supposed to have the easy camaraderie which permitted everybody to talk to everybody else, no matter what. Tradition. Even when; you wanted to brain people with a codfish, you couldn't snub them.

So he said, "Beautiful night out."

And the man with the nose slid his drink along the bar until he was within casual conversational distance of Holm.

"Art student?" he asked.

"Yeah," Pete Holm said, and took a long draught of his ale. It annoyed him a bit that the man had guessed correctly, for Holm rather had prided himself on not dressing or looking like the transient members of the colony. That beret, for instance—Holm wouldn't be caught dead in a beret. Or a blazer.

"Like it here?"

"So-so," Holm said, and wished the guy would shut up.

Funny part was, he did want to talk. Wanted, he guessed, to cry on somebody's shoulder, because in a few days he would be leaving all this, and for good, taking an office job in New York. The wrong way around, completely. New Yorkers came to Provincetown.

Then he noticed that his glass was being refilled, at the instructions of Scimitar-nose. If he had noticed in time, he would have made the excuse that he had to run along and didn't have time for another ale, but it was too late now. So he picked up the glass.

"Thanks," he said, and because it seemed rude to say nothing more, he asked, "you a painter?"

There seemed to be an amused glint in the eyes above the repellent nose. The man shook his head.

"Sculptor."

"Oh," Holm said. "A chiseler, huh?"

He put his glass back down on the bar and turned, with a grin.

It was a stock gag, of course. Sculptors were used to it; rather missed it when it didn't come. But even before he had finished turning around, Pete Holm sensed that there was something wrong. There was an electric tension in the room. The grin was still on Holm's face as his head finished the turn, but that was just because he hadn't had time to take the grin off.

Scimitar-nose had not moved, but his eyes had changed. Suddenly they were as friendly as ball-bearings, and as soft. He started to say something, and got as far as "You—"

And automatically, without even thinking about it, Pete Holm was pulling back his right hand, the fingers clenching into a fist, and starting to bring up his left.

But Shorty was there. He was on the wrong side of the bar, but he had been wiping the top of it with a damp towel, and suddenly that damp towel hit Holm's glass of ale. The glass tipped. It hit the bar without breaking, but its contents splashed on Pete Holm. On the front of his corduroy jacket and on his cocked right fist, level with the top of the bar. And he jerked back involuntarily, and the fingers of the fist unclenched.

Shorty was coming around the end of the bar.

"Gosh, Pete," he was saying, "I'm sorry. Here, take that jacket off quick before it soaks through. And here's a towel for your hands."

He was bustling in between Pete and Scimitar-nose, apparently unconscious of the tension that was fading now as quickly as it had started. For Shorty was fat enough to be an immovable object.

He turned Holm around to help him off with the splattered jacket.

Anything after that would have been anticlimactic. The man with the thin nose must have felt that, because he downed the last of his drink and strode out. Pete Holm's eyes followed him, through the pane of the front window, as he crossed the street.

"You fool," Shorty said. "He might have shot you if you hit him. He had a gun. I'll send your jacket to the cleaners. I saw the gun once when he leaned over the bar. Shoulder-holster."

"Well, he sure wasn't a sculptor," said Holm. "He didn't even get the gag, or anyway not in time. But why—"

Shorty went back of the bar.

"Snow," he said. "I've seen 'em before, but not many, up here. He was loaded. Makes 'em jumpy. Mid-Western accent. I'd say, Chicago."

"Give me a drier towel," Holm said. "My hands are still sticky. He met someone outside, across the street. Wonder if—"

"Drink more and wonder less," Shorty cut in. "You live longer. Like your Uncle Jacks. Full as usual tonight, maybe fuller. I shoved him out while he could still walk. You'll be a rich man when he dies—if you live that long. He said so."

Shorty grinned, and Holm grinned back.

"Been moon-cussing again has he, huh?" asked Holm. "Once a week, about, for twenty years now he does that. What washed up this time? Chest of pearls, as usual?"

"He was kinda mysterious about it for a while," said Shorty. "Finally broke down and admitted it was gold bullion. S'pose they'll ever lock him up, Pete?"

Pete Holm shook his head. "I've talked with the police about it, Shorty. Finally convinced them he's better off as is. He's harmless enough, heaven knows. Someday he'll go on a bat and won't come out of it, I guess—but then he's eighty-one and he can't live forever."

Shorty nodded. "And if they put him in an institution, he'd die quick. He's the kind that would. Let 'im live out there in his shack and dig his clams and be happy, I say. Someday. . . But why go into that? Say, Pete, somebody told me you were leaving."

"One more ale, Shorty," Holm said. "Yeah. I'm taking a job in New York. It's a good opportunity."

"I thought you were going to be a painter. I thought you were going good. I thought we were going to have one local boy to match the Mike Angelos that come here only for the season."

"I—" Pete Holm began, and then discovered that he didn't want to talk about it. Not even to Shorty. "Aw, probably I'd never amount to anything as a painter anyway."

"Didn't you place second in—"

"Skip it, Shorty. I—I'd just rather not talk about it. Say—" He glanced up at the clock." I got to beat it. Ellen's off at twelve, and I—" He started toward the door.

"Oh," said Shorty, with a world of cognizance packed into that one syllable, "So that's—"

But Holm didn't stay to listen to the rest. He knew it already, and he was out on the sidewalk, walking rapidly. As soon as he was out of sight of Shorty's window, he slowed down. He had plenty of time to get there. But he had discovered he didn't want to have to justify what he was doing to Shorty, or to anybody else.

Ellen was taking off her apron when he got to the all-night restaurant where she waited counter until midnight. She smiled at him.

"Your uncle was in tonight," she told him. "He—"

"Yeah," said Holm. "I know about it."

He realized he had been abrupt, and his voice was contrite as they went out.

"Sorry, dear. Didn't mean to bite your head off—although it's so pretty I'd like to. Tired?"

"A bit. But let's walk a while. Over the dunes maybe. I want to talk to you."

He tucked her arm into his.

"Sure," he said. "We got lots of planning to do, before Saturday. Golly, look at that moon. I'd like—"

"What?"

He laughed. "Nothing, Ellen. I got everything in the world I want—or will have in a month, when I send for you."

They crossed Bradford Street, turned into a footpath that led back among the dunes and toward the outside shore of the cape two miles away.

They walked mostly in silence, broken by occasional attempts by one or the other of them to talk lightly about nothing. They were almost to the last row of dunes. Behind it in the distance they could already hear the soft swish of the breakers.

Something's on her mind, thought Holm. *When we get to the shore there, I'll make her tell me what it is.*

But he didn't have to wait. It came abruptly. Out of a silence, she said:

"Pete, it's off. I—I've changed my mind."

He stopped, and turned her around to face him.

"Ellen," he said, "you can't—" Then he saw the tears in her eyes. And he understood, and smiled down at her. "Oh, I get it. You think I'm ruining a career by taking that job, huh? And you're being noble. Listen, you little mutt, there are painting classes in New York, night classes. As soon as we're married and settled down, I'll—"

"No." Despite that wetness of her eyes, her chin was firmly set. "You're getting a real start here. And you belong here. Not in an office, keeping books. New York, and that kind of work, would do something to you, Pete. After a while, you'd hate me."

"I'd— But that's silly. And, Ellen, we can't go on this way." Then, fiercely, but not quite convincingly: "I'm tired of being poor, of selling a few paintings a year for a few dollars each, and scrimping over every penny. And having you work in a place like—"

"It's a perfectly respectable place, and you know it. And I'd be perfectly happy to marry you and keep on working there until—"

"Until when? It might be years. That's out."

"It won't be years. A year, or maybe two. And then you'll be making at least as much as you'd be making in an office. Dravinski said—"

"Dravinski?" Holm was really angry now. "So that's where you got these ideas. Wait till I see that dimwitted goof. I'll wrap his easel—"

"Pete." She put her hand on his arm. "Let's not talk until we get to the beach. By then you'll have cooled down. We can talk sensibly. Fair enough?"

"I'll—Oh, all right."

He looked down at her as they walked on. She was tiny, delicate, fragile-looking. But he knew well how stubborn she could be, once she'd made up her mind about something. It was going to be tough going now, to convince her. But it was too much to wait, when waiting might be a matter of years. Particularly with Ellen working at a job that was just a bit too hard for her.

Then, walking around the curve in the path where it wound between the dunes, they saw the body. A dozen paces ahead.

"Good Lord!" said Holm, startled out of his moodiness. "Looks like Uncle Jacques. He did get too much tonight. We'll have to get him—"

And then they were close enough to see, in the bright moonlight, the pool of blood in which the head lay. Holm heard Ellen's gasp, and put out an arm to steady her. But she was standing straight and still.

"Pete," she said, "he's been murdered!"

"He might have—"

But Pete Holm didn't finish the sentence. It was all too obvious that she was right. There was nothing nearby on which he could have struck his head in a fall which would have made a wound like that. Nor could he have possibly fallen hard enough to have killed himself.

"Don't look, Ellen," Holm said. "I'll make sure."

But he knew, of course, even before he put his hand to the cold flesh, that Jacques Holm was dead.

Pete Holm stood up slowly.

"Yes, Ellen," he said, "it was—murder. I can guess why. Somebody who didn't know him heard him talking tonight about that washed-up treasure chest he always finds. Somebody who didn't know he was—a little off. Are you game to go back alone, Ellen, to tell the police? I'm going on to—"

"Pete. I was going to tell you before. He—your uncle—was in at the restaurant tonight. He was only a little under the weather then. And he said to tell you he'd really found it. That he wanted you to come out tomorrow and—"

He shook his head slowly. "That's what he always says—said. He was just talking, honey. Naturally he believed his delusion. Listen, I'd like to run ahead and see if anybody's at his shack, hunting around. You go back to town and tell—"

"But, Pete! There might be several of them. Or if there's only one, he might be armed!"

"I'm not going to try to take him, or them. I'll stay in the background, honey, and see which way they go. Now run along." He patted her shoulder gently, turned her around.

And, hearing her sharp intake of breath, Pete Holm turned too, and saw the man with the thin nose, the beret, and the blazer walking toward them. There was an automatic in his hand.

"Hey, Baldy, come on!" he called out, "It's only a kid and a girl."

"Sure—coming," a voice from around the bend in the path said.

Ellen didn't seem to be scared. "You murdered—" she began hotly.

Scimitar-nose was grinning. "Sure, girlie," he cut in. "You and your boyfriend know the guy?"

Pete Holm nudged her, but before she caught the signal, she had said, "Sure, we—" and then stopped.

"Swell," said the man with the gun. "Then at least one of you'll know where his shack is. Baldy, go ahead and drag that stiff out of sight behind a sand-hill, and scatter sand over that blood."

"Okay, Boss," said the voice behind them.

"Glad you came along," Scimitar-nose said to them. "The old guy fought and we had to slug him, harder than we meant. He didn't like it when he found we were following him." He smiled coldly.

Pete squeezed Ellen's arm to keep her from talking. He kept his own voice flat and expressionless.

"We can show you the shack," he said, "but there's nothing there. You made a mistake. He was a little—well, touched. He always talked that way, like he did tonight."

Scimitar-nose grinned again. "We'll decide that."

"But one thing," said Pete Holm. "One point first. What happens to us? No use pretending we—I—couldn't identify you."

"Well—" Scimitar-nose hesitated. "We can tie you up in the shack. Getaway'll take us only a few hours. You won't be found for that long."

"We might not be found for weeks."

"Everything fixed, Boss," the voice behind them said. "There ain't a mark left."

"Get going," the man with the gun said to Holm.

"It might be days," Pete Holm protested, "before somebody'd go to that shack. Or even weeks."

A metallic click was the only answer—the sound of the safety of the automatic being thrown off.

"Don't be a fool, Pete," Ellen said. Then to the man, "We'll show you."

She was right, of course, and Holm nodded. There wasn't any use getting themselves shot for nothing. He wondered, as he turned to lead the way to the isolated little shack among the dunes, whether even the promise to tie them up in the shack would be kept.

Now that these crooks had committed one murder, wouldn't they consider it safer not to leave anyone alive behind them who could give evidence against them? Quite likely. But Holm knew that he and Ellen would have to take that chance unless an opportunity for a break presented itself. And against two armed men he didn't see how it could.

He had a look now at the man who had been called "Baldy." Big and stupid-looking he was, with a flat, pasty face. But he looked as if he would be a formidable opponent in a fight, even if he didn't have a gun.

There didn't even seem to be a path where they turned off among the dunes. And there was the shack, down between two of the sand hills and ahead of it, a hundred yards away, the beach and the sea. It was a rickety little wooden hut that looked as though a bad storm would blow it flat.

Outside the padlocked door, Scimitar-nose said:

"Tie their hands, Baldy. Then we won't have to watch 'em so close while we look around."

"Sure," Baldy said, and walked around behind them.

Pete Holm felt a hand reach into his pocket and take out his handkerchief, and because a gun was aimed at his belt buckle and there wasn't anything else to do, he stuck out his wrists behind him and felt them being tied firmly and efficiently.

When Ellen's wrists were tied, too, Scimitar-nose clubbed his automatic and knocked off the padlock of the small house's door. Baldy kicked in the door.

"I'll turn on the light, Boss," he said. "Gosh, what a smell in here. Where's the light switch?"

In spite of the spot they were in, Pete Holm grinned.

"You won't find one," he said. "Try the lamp. Probably it's on the table."

There was the scratching of a match and then, a moment later, a steady light in the cabin.

"Go on in," the man in the blazer order Holm and Ellen. He followed them and closed the door. "Stand in the corner there, and just keep out of the way. We'll tend to you later."

The words could have meant anything, and the tone was nothing out of the ordinary, but Holm knew now, for sure, what "tending to them" would mean. These two men had already committed a murder, had admitted the fact, and they wouldn't leave anyone alive who had heard that admission. They wouldn't count that strongly on never being traced after their getaway.

"Here's what smells, Boss," Baldy's disgusted voice said. "This lard bucket's gone rancid. Here it goes out."

"Not so fast. Take something and probe it first."

Baldy grunted, but picked up a table-knife and obeyed orders.

"Nope," he said. "Nothing in it."

He opened a window, and threw out the knife and the bucket.

Scimitar-nose had put his automatic back into its holster, and was going through the sea-chest back of the table.

"Take the cupboard there, or whatever it is," he told Baldy. "Look into everything. Stuff like sugar or salt, probe down through it. These old boys are cagy about where they hide stuff."

"Maybe this one was batty," Baldy grumbled. "He'd have to be to live in a place that smells like this one. Whew!"

"Won't take long to find out, a place this size."

The man in the blazer stood up, his cold eyes making a slow circuit of the plain board walls, the ceiling that held only spider webs, the wood boards of the floor that showed no marks of being recently disturbed.

"Could be buried somewhere around," suggested Baldy. "But- Heck, Boss, if he was alive, we coulda made him tell us. You shouldn't a slugged him."

"Shut up."

Scimitar-nose looked at Pete Holm and Ellen.

"Move," he said, and jerked his head at the corner of the shack on the opposite side of the door.

Holm and Ellen moved across. They tied Ellen to a chair, but left Holm standing. Ellen's being so near Holm gave him an idea, a long-shot idea. He had been trying to loosen that knotted handkerchief ever since they had entered the shack, but it hadn't budged. He couldn't reach the knot with his fingers. But maybe Ellen—As soon as the two men moved away from Ellen he edged over back of her chair.

He nudged against her, and then reached his bound wrists as far to the side as he could without distorting his shoulders and making it obvious what he was trying to do. She caught on. There was no change of expression on her face, but he felt her fingertips, behind her, touch his wrist, then start to pick at the tight double knot.

"Ain't no use, Boss," Baldy was saying. "This guy and jane must've been telling it straight. The old geezer didn't find anything. He was loco. Huh! I thought at the time it was goofy that he'd—"

The man in the blazer kicked a chair viciously.

"Okay, okay, you were right," he said. "So what? We were going to leave here tonight anyway, so what'd we lose?"

He turned toward Holm. The knot was not loose yet, but Holm tensed, strained to pull his wrists apart, knowing what was coming. Baldy had his gun in his hand.

"Shall I—"

"Wait," Scimitar-nose told him. "This bright young lad was going to pop me one back in town. He gets that back with interest before we. . . Step aside, sister."

His hand pushed Ellen's shoulder, shoved her roughly away from

Pete Holm's side, and his right fist clenched and went back for a blow. His lips drew tightly across his teeth, and the swing started.

The knot was slipping. Ellen had untied the outer of the two knots, and pulling the other loose was a matter of seconds. But there were no seconds to spare.

The blow was coming now. Holm jerked his head aside and the fist scraped against his ear as it went by. And, inside the blow, he threw himself against Scimitar-nose, and sent him staggering backward from the impact.

"Stand back, Boss!" he heard Baldy yell, and caught a glimpse of Baldy's gun.

But he didn't have time to worry about that. His own wrists were loose now, and he was bringing his hands around front where he could use them. Scimitar-nose was going for the gun in his shoulder holster, not trusting anymore to his fists. The hand that gripped the gun butt was coming into sight.

Pete Holm grabbed the wrist of that hand, and closed in, getting his other arm around the man's shoulders, trying to swing him around as a shield against Baldy's pistol. But he wouldn't be in time. Baldy's gun was coming up. For a frozen instant he thought he could see right into the muzzle of it.

Then there was another noise, a skittering, clattering noise, and out of the corner of his eye Holm could see that Ellen, even though she was still tied, had tumbled herself, chair and all, falling across the floor toward Baldy. Ellen and the chair struck his ankles just as his gun roared, and the gun jerked up. The bullet went through the tarpaper roof.

Baldy cursed, but before he could bring his gun down for a second shot, Holm had swung his opponent around and thrown him into Baldy, plowing in himself so that their combined weight hit the man with the gun. All three went down in a struggling heap, and the walls of the shack trembled.

But Holm was on top and with both hands free, he got Scimitar-nose's automatic away from him with a quick jerk and clubbed it flatwise on Baldy's head. Baldy's revolver hit the floor. Then it was all over, except untying Ellen and tying up the two killers.

And the moonlight was even brighter as Pete Holm and Ellen walked to the Coast Guard Station, a bit nearer than anything else, to phone for police.

"Poor Uncle Jacques," Ellen said softly, holding Holm's right hand. "But—well, he had a long life and, I guess, a pretty full one. You're his nearest relative, aren't you? You'll have to postpone your trip to take care of the funeral and things."

Holm nodded. "Longer than that, honey. I'm not going now. Now I can stick it out here, until I make good. And we can get married as soon as we should after the funeral."

Her eyes, round with wonder, looked up at him.

"Oh, Pete! Then you'll keep on studying, and let me keep on working, and—"

He smiled down at her and shook his head.

"Nope. You won't be working, either. Didn't you recognize—? No, you wouldn't. You've been here less than a year and you're a landlubber, as those two crooks are. But a lovely little landlubber. You see, Uncle Jacques did have his treasure, this time."

She stopped walking. "Pete, you're fooling!"

"Ambergris," Pete Holm said. "That smelly stuff from whales that washes on shore once in a blue moon. Sells for around five hundred bucks a pound, as a base for expensive perfumes and what not.

"And Uncle Jacques must have found it last night or today. This time he wasn't off. That lard bucket—I buried it in the sand before we left—was what he put it in. And those two fools were probing for hidden trinkets in about ten-thousand dollars' worth of ambergris. And then they threw it out the window!"

The Masked Detective, Spring 1942

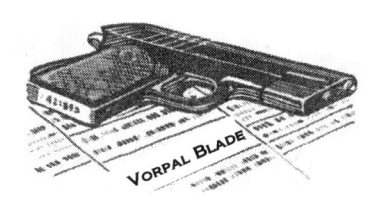

Saturday Matinees

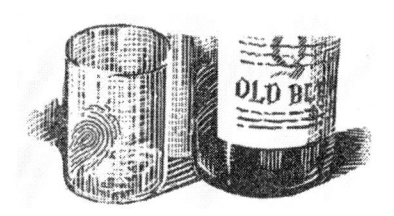

The Djinn Murder

A YEAR AGO, Prof. John E. Trent's class in Psychology IV (Abnormal) wasn't abnormal in the least. The way they'd rushed through the door of the classroom almost before the bell had stopped ringing was proof of that.

Professor Trent grinned, watching them. Again that bell had caught him in the middle of a sentence and the sentence had never been finished. A suspended sentence, one might say. Someday, he'd manage to time his peroration so as to finish under the bell.

"You wished to talk to me, Professor?"

Trent turned his head, startled. He'd completely forgotten telling his one graduate student to remain after class. But there she was. She'd pushed the papers aside from one corner of his desk and was sitting there. A window bright with sunlight was behind her, and the light made a shining golden aura of her blonde hair.

It was a beautiful, a breathtaking, effect. Had he not been a psychology instructor, Professor Trent might have known enough about psychology to realize that she had chosen that pose with deliberate intent.

Not realizing, he tried to frown severely. He said, "Um, Miss Standish—"

"Liz, pliz," said the girl. Her voice was demure, but her eyes were devilish.

"That," said Professor Trent, "is exactly the mental attitude which I have been trying, in your case, to correct ever since you entered my class. Psychology is not a study to be taken lightly, to be joked about; not if one wishes to master it and to—uh—be given a passing grade. Now, Miss Standish, I—"

"Will you settle for Elizabeth, then?"

Professor Trent sighed helplessly. "Elizabeth, then. Now, I Elizabeth, I—" He paused, not quite knowing how to go on without repeating himself.

Somehow, it was deucedly distracting to have her sitting there, like that, on the corner of his desk. None of his other students affected him that way. Most of them, of course, were Josephine Colleges, making a fetish of sartorial and mental sloppiness.

Miss Standish, being a graduate student, was a bit older, She was different in other ways, too. She was brilliant, when she chose to study, but she just *wouldn't* take Psychology IV (Abnormal) seriously. And she was more feminine than the others. *Very* feminine. But he, Professor John E. Trent, had no time for interest in femininity.

And besides, she was only mocking him. She couldn't really be interested in an uninteresting scholar like himself, easily ten years her senior and— He broke off that line of thought and started in again.

"Miss Standish—uh—I mean, Elizabeth—I—" A dry cough from the direction of the doorway interrupted him. A bit relieved at the interruption, he turned.

"You are Professor Trent?" The voice was sepulchral in tone, and matched, thereby, the figure standing in the doorway. A tall, thin man with a cadaverous face, dressed in black like an undertaker—or at any rate as undertakers used to dress before they became morticians.

"Yes," said Trent. "I—uh— What can I do for you?"

The tall man advanced farther into the classroom.

"They told me I'd find you here; that you'd just finished your last class for the day, and— My name is Glosterman. Harvey Glosterman. I've heard that you specialize in the occult."

"Not exactly, Mr. Glosterman," said Trent, judiciously. "My researches in psychology have led me into borderline territory, and I have investigated alleged psychic phenomena, but—"

The tall man nodded. "Yes. I—I need help and advice, Professor Trent. My brother has disappeared, very strangely. I think it was the djinn."

"Eh?" said Professor Trent.

"I may be wrong, of course. But he had opened the bottle—the—uh—container."

"But that's a matter for the police, Mr. Glosterman. There is no indication, is there, that any psychic forces are involved? And what can a bottle of gin have to do with a disappearance?"

"Not gin," said the tall man, very earnestly. "Djinn."

"I beg your pardon?"

"D-j-i-n-n," spelled out Mr. Glosterman. "Djinn. He brought it back from South Africa, sealed in a sort of jug or demijohn or—uh—earthenware bottle, with the Seal of Solomon on the wax. And last night he broke the jug, and— Well, he's gone."

Professor Trent closed his eyes and opened them again. He counted, silently, to three. Then he said, "Mr. Glosterman, there is a difference between psychic research and sheer superstition. There is no such thing as a djinn, and never was. It's a legend of the East, anyway, and not of South Africa. And if your brother has disappeared, djinn bottle or no djinn bottle, I'd suggest you go to the police."

"He wouldn't like it, if I did. I think he's trying to communicate with me, and—Well, I'd like help getting the message so I'll *know* what he wants me to do."

"How?" It was the blonde's voice, and it sounded very interested. "*How* is he trying to communicate?"

"By spirit rappings, Miss. But I can't make them spell out anything. The messages just don't make sense. That's what I want the Professor to help me on. I understand he's investigated spirit rappings and—uh—things like that."

He looked appealingly at Trent. "I can offer you any reasonable fee, Professor. I am not poor, and my brother is—was—quite wealthy. I hope you will not refuse to help me—us."

Professor Trent sighed. He turned to the girl. "Miss Standish, you may go. The matter we were discussing can be taken up at some other time."

Her eyes were very wide open as she looked at him. "But Professor, I don't *want* to go. I have no other plans for today, and I'm sure Mr. Glosterman won't mind if—" She turned to the tall man and gave him a dazzling smile. "Mr. Glosterman, you won't mind if I help, too, will you? I'm a graduate student, and I've been studying psychic phenomena *very* intensively. In fact, some people say I'm psychic myself, and I've had some strange experiences."

Professor Trent frowned at her. She was lying outrageously.

But Glosterman, under the influence of that smile, was looking almost human. "Of course, of course," he said, "I shall be most happy.

Most happy."

"In fact," said Elizabeth Standish, "even if Professor Trent is too busy to help you, I'll be glad to see if I can get in communication with your brother."

But Professor Trent was taking his hat out of the bottom drawer of his desk, and was rather surprised to find himself slamming the drawer shut. He'd intended to say something else entirely, but the childish slamming of the drawer made him feel foolish, so he said instead, "I'll be glad to try to help you, Mr. Glosterman."

Glosterman's car, parked near the campus entrance, matched the appearance of its owner. It was a huge black sedan of the type undertakers use in driving funeral guests to the cemetery.

"We're bound for the house my brother rented," said Glosterman, as he started the engine. "He disappeared from there, and the—uh—phenomena occur there. It's at 6530 North Wayne Boulevard."

"Quite a way out," Trent said. "Suppose you tell us something about your brother."

"Name's John—John Glosterman, of course. My first name's Harvey, as I told you. We're twins, but don't look much alike. He's shorter than I, and heavier. We're both retired from business. He was an importer, mostly precious and semiprecious stones. Had a couple of hobbies—entomology, for one. Collecting was the other one."

"Collecting what?" Elizabeth added. "Old djinn bottles?"

"Uh—something like that. Collecting objects connected with primitive superstitions. Old idols, spirit gongs, juju masks, voodoo drums—all that sort of thing. He traveled a lot."

"You say he returned recently from South Africa?"

"Just a few days ago, in fact. He rented the house on Wayne Boulevard because his own home's being remodeled—and enlarged, to make room for more collector's items. He planned to camp out in the Wayne Boulevard place until he could get back in his own home, you see. It was already furnished and ready for immediate occupancy."

"I see," said Trent. "But wouldn't a hotel have been more convenient for a short while?"

"John hates hotels. He's—well, he's a bit eccentric, Professor Trent. Prefers to be alone. He has servants come in during the day, of course, but insists they don't live there."

"Um," said Trent. "Gives us a pretty good picture of him. Is he still in business, at all?"

"Not actively. Has a flock of investments, of course. But his lawyer handles most of that for him, and leaves him free to follow his hobbies."

Trent nodded. He asked, "Would you say your brother is superstitious? Is that his reason for collecting the sort of objects he collects?"

"Superstitious? Not at all, not at all. He's no more superstitious than I am."

"Oh," said Professor Trent. "But—uh—what's this business about the bottle djinn?"

"It was an earthenware receptacle—ancient, very ancient. The Arabic inscriptions said it contained an imprisoned djinn. And the stopper was sealed on with the inscription called the Seal of Solomon on the wax."

"The superimposed equilateral triangles. Yes. But what was an Arabian artifact doing in South Africa?"

Glosterman shrugged. "The earliest slavers were Arabs. Possibly one of them brought it. Here's the house."

He swung the big sedan into the driveway and stopped it just past the sidewalk. Another car was already parked there, just ahead, with two men sitting in it.

They got out, and one of them—the fat one—said, "Hello, Mr. Glosterman. You're just on time."

"Yes," said Glosterman. "Miss Standish, Professor Trent, this is Mr. Wolters. My brother's attorney—mine, too, incidentally. And his clerk, Mr. Johnson. I asked them to come here, too; we're going to look over my brother's papers, if he has any here, to see whether there is—uh—anything that—uh—"

The lawyer smiled. "Mr. Glosterman is doubtful whether his brother's disappearance is voluntary or—otherwise. In the former case, he wishes to avoid going to the police, of course. In the latter—"

"Exactly," said Glosterman. "Of course, I could have looked myself, but it would have been hardly legal. But Mr. Wolters has my brother's power of attorney."

Wolters nodded. "You brought the key, Johnson?" he asked of his assistant, a slim young man with patent-leather hair and a cigarette dangling, gangster-fashion, from the corner of his mouth.

Professor Trent looked at Mr. Johnson curiously and wondered whether to believe the cigarette or the neat gray business suit and the shell-rimmed glasses. The effect of movies on the young, he reflected, led to strange combinations. He'd noticed that fact in his own students.

"Yes," said Johnson, and quickly added "Sir." He went ahead to open the door with a key tied to a large cardboard tag.

The front hallway proved to be spacious, well-lighted, and much more cheerful looking than the exterior of the house.

Glosterman gestured to a doorway on the right. "He was using this room as a study," he told them. "Whatever we're looking for would—uh—most likely be here. Anyway, we'll start here."

Elizabeth Standish caught Trent's arm as they followed the others through the doorway. She whispered, "Do you *really* think— *Oooh*, look, that must be the djinn thing."

For there, in plain sight on the top of the desk, was— Well, *he'd* call it a vase, Professor Trent decided. Glosterman had called it a jug or bottle, but it was really more the shape of a vase than either of those, although there was a jug-like handle on one side.

It was about a foot tall, almost globular at the base and tapering into a narrow neck at the top. It looked very, very old and the most obvious thing about it was that it had been broken. Apparently quite recently, and glued back together. A bottle of liquid cement and a small brush lay on a folded newspaper beside the vase.

"You see the seal?" Glosterman pointed out. "The two triangles. John told me it *was* the Seal of Solomon. He said he wasn't going to open it. I don't think he really thought it contained an imprisoned djinn, of course, but—"

"But what?" demanded Elizabeth.

"But what was the *use* of breaking the Seal? It was—well, the vase was pretty light, so it contained either nothing at all, or—Well, why take a chance? And ruin the Seal, too."

"Um," said Professor Trent. "The Arabic characters. Could he read Arabic, or did he have them translated?"

"Yes. They told that a powerful djinn named Eydhebhe was inside and—uh—was a dangerous being. It warned against breaking the Seal."

"I guess breaking the bottle would be just as bad," said Elizabeth helpfully. "Do you think he did it on purpose?"

"I'm pretty sure not, Miss Standish. He'd have taken out the sealing-wax stopper instead."

"A nice point in logic," said the lawyer. "Either it was empty, or it wasn't. If it was, he broke the Seal or the vase for nothing. If it wasn't—well, it would have been, of course. The only djinn these days goes into Tom Collinses. Johnson, let's start with this desk. You take the drawers on that side—"

Glosterman turned back to Trent with a deprecatory shrug.

"Sorry," he said, "but I suppose we'd better wait until they've finished their business here before we start—uh—ours. We'll want quiet and—uh—privacy for that."

Outside the study, in which they left the lawyer and his clerk searching, Trent asked, "When did you last see your brother, Mr. Glosterman? And when did you decide that he might be—ah—missing?"

"I helped him move in here day before yesterday, and haven't seen him since. He'd just arrived in town, then, and this place had been rented for his temporary use. The earthenware container was *not* broken then. I noticed he handled it carefully, and asked him what it was. I gathered that while he scoffed at the djinn story, he was going to be careful just the same. And as Mr. Wolters pointed out, he had nothing to gain by—uh—testing the theory. As to when I found he was missing—that was yesterday afternoon. I rang the bell and there was no answer."

"You didn't come inside?"

"Not then. I returned again late in the evening, and there was no light on, and still no answer to the bell. This morning I borrowed the key from Mr. Wolters and let myself in. I looked around and saw—uh—the broken container. And then I heard the spirit rappings, and that was when I became really worried."

"What kind of—" Elizabeth started to ask, but Trent interrupted.

"Then you returned to Wolters' office and arranged to meet him here this afternoon, and brought us along?"

"Exactly. For a quite different purpose, of course. About the rappings—I was in the study, and I happened to tap on the desk, a nervous habit of mine when I'm concentrating. And there was an answer."

"It couldn't have been an echo?"

"Positively not. I'd tap once and it would tap once, or if I tapped twice, it would tap twice. But too late for an echo. It seemed to come from the closet."

"Did you search there?"

"Very thoroughly. And then the raps came from somewhere else in the room—I couldn't just decide where. But when I tried asking questions—suggesting one rap for yes and two for no—I couldn't get an answer. The phenomena had ceased. If you'll pardon me a moment, I'll see if they've found anything."

When Glosterman had left the hallway, Elizabeth whispered, "Professor, do you think his brother is playing a trick of some kind? It—it doesn't make sense otherwise. Or maybe one brother or the other is a bit touched, huh?"

Trent shook his head slowly. "I'm afraid not. I might be wrong. But I think John Glosterman is dead."

Her eyes widened. "Then you *do* believe in spirit rappings?"

Harvey Glosterman returned before Trent could answer. He said, "They're making a good job of it. I hope you're not in a hurry?"

"Not at all," said Trent. "Meanwhile, there are two questions I'd like to ask. First, did your brother have a sense of humor?"

"Very much so, Professor. A peculiar, dry sense of humor. But you don't think this is—"

"No, I don't," said Trent. "The other question is personal. Was your brother—well, was he strictly honest in all his business dealings, or did he cut corners when there was a chance?"

Glosterman hesitated. He said, "But my brother is retired. He hasn't had any business dealings for some time. So—uh—"

"Thanks," said Trent. "Do you mind if I wander about a bit? I'd like to look at the house, if I may."

When Glosterman nodded, Trent strode off. Apparently, he'd intended to go alone, but Elizabeth caught up with him in the kitchen.

"Professor, why on earth did you ask such silly questions? What can honesty and a sense of humor have to do with—with whatever happened? Unless this John *is* playing a practical joke of some—"

"He isn't. I think he's dead. I wouldn't be surprised if the body is somewhere in the house. No, I think you'd better go back and wait near the study while I—"

"I will *not*," said Elizabeth firmly. Her eyes were wide with excitement. "Mama goes where papa goes."

"You don't mind—uh—corpses?"

"I love them!"

But ten minutes later, when they found John Glosterman in the cellar, she gasped almost loudly enough to be heard upstairs, and clung very tightly to Trent's arm. So tightly that he winced as he stepped back.

The body was that of a short, heavyset elderly man whose features somewhat resembled those of Harvey Glosterman—enough so that Trent had no doubt of the identity of the corpse.

He said, quietly, "Must have been dragged down here, and put there behind the furnace, but there wasn't any effort to hide it."

"But why would anyone bring the body down here?"

Trent shrugged. "A play for time, that's all. If the body had been left upstairs—in the hall, or the study—it would have been found yesterday morning. Here it would be found only if a search of the house was made. Matter of a day or so difference."

"How was he—killed? Can you tell?"

"Shot. There. Very little external bleeding but you can see if you look close that—"

The girl was shivering. "I don't *want* to look close. Let's get out of here. I don't like corpses as much as I thought I would. I'll even wait to make you tell me why you were so sure that—"

"*Shhh,*" said Trent.

"You down there?" called Glosterman's voice from the top of the cellar stairs.

"Coming right up," Trent called back. And as they walked toward the stairs: "Awful lot of junk down here, Mr. Glosterman."

"Find anything interesting?"

"Not a thing," said Trent, cheerfully. "Wolters and his man through in the study?"

"Almost," said Glosterman, as they joined him. "I came to tell you they said they'd be out in five minutes."

Trent nodded. "Good, let's go there now. I'd like to see whether—" He let the sentence trail off into nothingness as he led the way back to the study. He hoped Elizabeth Standish had got that look of horror off her face sufficiently so that Glosterman and the others wouldn't notice.

Wolters was zipping shut his brief case as they entered the study.

The clerk with the patent-leather hair was leaning against the wall lighting a cigarette with bored concentration.

"Find anything?" Trent inquired.

"Nothing, I'm afraid, that throws any light on where he may have gone, or why. We're going to take a look in the room he slept in upstairs, but—" The lawyer's tone of voice showed that he expected to find nothing there.

There was a big morris chair in one corner of the room. Trent dropped into it with the languid air of a man who has all day to do nothing in. He stretched his lanky legs out in front of him and dropped his arms along the wooden arms of the chair.

He said, "We were planning a sort of—ah—séance. At Mr. Glosterman's suggestion. I don't know whether you're interested in the occult, but you may stay if you wish, Mr. Wolters. You too, Mr. Johnson."

The lawyer shook his head. "Afraid I don't give much credence to the supernatural, Professor. I'd be a disturbing influence. How about you, Johnson? If you want to stay here while I look upstairs—"

The clerk was grinning. "I don't go for spirits, either. Not that kind. Now if you had some good Scotch or Bourbon—"

"Or djinn?" Elizabeth suggested. Johnson's grin widened, as he looked at her appreciatively—and, Trent thought, a bit appraisingly. He said, "Well, that all depends on—"

"*Shhh!*"

Trent's sudden sibilant cut him off in mid-sentence. The professor was sitting bolt upright in the chair now, and his hands gripped the arms so tightly his knuckles were white. There was an expression of strained listening on his face.

Glosterman was looking at him expectantly; the other curiously. But none of them moved or spoke.

The tableau held a few seconds, and then Trent's face relaxed. He said, "Sorry, I thought I heard—"

He paused, as though groping for the right word, and in that pause they all heard the sharp rap that came from the direction of the desk.

Professor Trent's eyes lighted up, almost ecstatically, as he put a finger to his lips for the others to keep silence.

Then, speaking slowly and framing each word distinctly, he asked, "Are you—John Glosterman?"

Unmistakably, the single rap that gave affirmative answer came from the direction of the desk. They were staring at the desk now. Wolters and Johnson, who had just searched it, were staring almost hypnotically.

Glosterman's eyes were gleaming as he turned back to face Trent. He whispered, "Ask him—" But Trent motioned him to silence.

Again Trent's question was slow and distinct. "Then you are dead?"

A single rap.

"Did you die a natural death?"

And this time, two raps. A negative.

Elizabeth Standish's lips were slightly parted and the expression on her face was that of utter incredulity.

There were sudden beads of sweat on the lawyer's forehead. Johnson, the clerk, happened to be the nearest of them to the desk. He took a step away from it, turned and looked at Trent, and then took two steps closer to the desk, until he was within reach of it.

Trent asked, "Did you break the vase accidentally?"

Two raps.

"On purpose?"

One.

Glosterman whispered, "Ask him whether the—" A violent shake of Trent's head stopped him again.

"Because there was something inside it? Something valuable?"

One rap. "Papers?"

Two raps.

"Money?"

Again, two.

Trent hesitated, as though wondering what to ask next. He wetted his lips with the tip of his tongue. and asked, "Diamonds?"

Johnson was staring at Trent. His face had gone pasty white, and one hand came up slowly and took the cigarette from between his lips.

There was a single affirmative rap.

"You were murdered for the diamonds?"

One rap.

"You left them—in Wolters' safe?"

One rap.

"With Mr. Wolters personally?"

One rap, and with it a sharp gasp of fear, as Johnson whirled and made a break for the doorway.

He shoved Wolters aside. Elizabeth was standing almost in the open doorway, but one look at the panic-filled eyes of the clerk—and she hastily stepped out of his way. Not quite enough, however, to give him clear passage.

Her hand gave the door a push and Johnson ran full into the edge of it as it was swinging shut. Then Trent, who had started moving as soon as Johnson, had the clerk's right arm pinned and twisted behind his back, and the break was over.

Trent said quietly, "Your brother's body is in the basement, Mr. Glosterman. You'd better phone for the police."

~§~

"Yes," Professor Trent was explaining, after Johnson had been taken away, "Mr. Glosterman—Mr. John Glosterman—had been an importer. And apparently, while he was in Africa, he couldn't resist bringing in a few illicit diamonds. Possibly he bought the djinn container first and that made him think of using it to smuggle in gems, or maybe he had a chance to buy diamonds cheaply, and bought the vase specially for the purpose of smuggling them."

"But how," Wolters was asking, "did you know he'd left the diamonds in my safe?"

"I didn't. I played a hunch it was one of the three of you, and watched your faces while I questioned the 'ghost.' Your clerk was the only one who reacted when I mentioned diamonds, so I shot the other questions already knowing the answers.

"You see, after John Glosterman took the diamonds out of the vase, he wanted a safe place to put them. There wasn't any safe here, so he dropped in your office to ask you to leave a package in your safe for him. You weren't there—and he made the mistake of trusting your clerk. But Johnson opened the package. He guessed, of course, that the diamonds had been smuggled in and that no one else knew about them. If he killed Glosterman, they'd be his."

"Um," said the lawyer. "But why *diamonds?* Of course, coming from Africa, that's the logical thing to smuggle, but—"

Trent smiled. "He told his brother what was in the vase. Anyway, it would have been an enormous coincidence that the djinn was named *Eydhebhe—Ey—dhe—bhe—*if it wasn't a pun on I.D.B. Illicit Diamond Buyer, of course. Those initials are known all over the world. That's why I asked Mr. Glosterman if his brother had a sense of humor, of course. . ."

There was more, and there was still more at police headquarters, with a stenographer taking it down. And there was Elizabeth Standish looking at him in bright-eyed admiration.

Even in the taxi in which he took her home from the station after their deposition had been signed.

"Professor," she said, is there *anything* you don't know? Arabic and logic and psychology and entomology—Tell me some more about that beetle. The one that made the spirit rappings. What did you call it?"

"The *tock-tockie* beetle," said Trent. "Indigenous to South Africa. With Glosterman an entomologist, of course he'd have been interested. They don't live in this country; not long, anyway. But I thought of it when Glosterman—the living one—told me about tapping in the study and getting an answer. The *tock-tockiebeetle* does that.

"And its ability to perceive faint vibrations is phenomenal. Maeterlinck—you should read his *Life of the White Ant,* if you haven't—experimented with them. He found if he barely touched his finger to the ground in tapping, the male beetle, many yards away, would feel the vibration, and respond by tapping back. My taps on the underside of the chair arm were inaudible. Even to me. But the beetle—"

"You said the male beetle," interrupted Elizabeth. "Has it something to do with mating?"

"Entirely. The female—when she is in a mood for—uh—romance, taps, usually twice. Out in the open, it has a *tock-tock* sound. The male hears her—I use 'hear' in the broad sense of perceiving vibrations—and responds and they locate one another through—"

"A double tap?" asked Elizabeth. "Like this?" Her fingernail tapped lightly twice against the patent leather handbag lying in her lap.

"Yes, like that."

"But it didn't work," she said plaintively. "Shall I try again?"

"Didn't work? What on earth do you—?" He turned to look at her. And her eyes were laughing at him, but there was more than laughter in them.

"Oh," said Professor Trent. And, after all, he merely *taught* Psychology IV (Abnormal); he was not a specimen of abnormality himself. His hand trembled just a trifle as he leaned forward and rapped twice on the glass partition of the taxi.

The driver half-turned in his seat and lowered the glass. "Don't take us straight there," said Trent. "Just drive around a while."

Ellery Queen's Mystery Magazine. January 1944

Handbook for Homicide

IT WAS RAINING like the very devil, and I couldn't see more than twenty feet ahead. The road was a winding mountain road, full of unexpected turns and dips apparently laid out by someone with more experience constructing roller coasters than highways.

Worse, it was soft gooey mud. I had to drive fast to keep from sinking in, and I had to drive slow to keep from going off the outer edge into whatever depth lay beyond.

They'd told me, forty miles back in Scardale, that I'd better not try to reach the Einar Observatory until the storm was over. And I was discovering now that they'd known what they were talking about.

Then, abruptly and with a remark I won't record, I slammed on the brakes. The car slithered to a stop and started to sink.

Dead ahead in the middle of the narrow road, right at the twenty-foot limit of my range of vision, was a twin apparition that resolved itself, as I slid to a stop five feet from it, into a man leading a donkey toward me.

There was a big wooden box on each side of the donkey, and there definitely wasn't going to be room for one of us to pass the other.

About twenty yards back behind me, I remembered, was a wider place in the road. But backward was uphill. I put the car into reverse and gunned the engine. The wheels spun around in the slippery mud, and sank deeper.

I cranked down the glass of the window and over the beat of the storm I yelled, "I can't back. How far behind you is a wider place in the road?"

The man shook his head without answering. I saw that he was an Indian, young and rather handsome. And he was magnificently wet.

Apparently he hadn't understood me, for a shake of the head wasn't any answer to my question. I repeated it.

"Two mile," he yelled back.

I groaned. If I had to wait while he led that donkey two miles back the way he had come, there went my chances of reaching Einar before dark. But he wasn't making any move to turn the beast around. Instead, he was untying the rope that held the wooden boxes in place.

"Hey, what's—" And then I realized that he was being smart, not dumb. The donkey, unencumbered by the load, could easily pass my car and could be reloaded on the other side.

He got one of the boxes off and came toward me with it. Alongside my car, he reached up and put it on the roof over my head.

I opened my mouth to object, and thought better. The box seemed light and probably wouldn't scratch the top enough to bother about.

Instead, I asked him what was in the boxes.

"Rattlesnakes."

"Good Lord," I said. "What for?"

"Sell 'em tourists—rattles, skins. Sell 'em venom drugstore."

"Oh." I said. And hoped the boxes wouldn't break or leak while they were on my car. A few loose rattlers in the back seat would be all I needed.

"Want buy big rattler? Diamondback? Cheap?"

"No thanks," I told him.

He nodded, and led the donkey along the edge of nowhere past the car. Then he came back and got the boxes to reload on the donkey.

I yelled back, "Thanks!" and threw the shift into low. Downhill, it ought to start all right. But it didn't.

I opened the door and leaned out to look down at the wheels. They had sunk in up to the hubs.

The donkey, the rattlesnakes, and the Vanishing American were just starting off. I yelled.

The Indian came back. "Change 'em mind? Buy rattler?"

"Sorry, no. But could that creature of yours give this car a pull?"

He stared down at the wheels. "Plenty deep?"

"It's headed downhill, though. And if I started the engine while he pulled, it ought to do it."

"Got 'em tow rope?"

"No, but you got the rope those boxes are tied with."

"Weak. No pull 'em."

"Five bucks," I said.

He nodded, went back to the donkey and untied the boxes. He put them down in the mud this time and tied the rope to my front bumper, looping it several thicknesses. Then he led the donkey back front and hitched it.

We tried for ten minutes—but the car was still stuck. I leaned out and yelled a suggestion: "Let the donkey pull while you rock the car."

We tried that. The wheels spun again, madly, and then caught hold. The car lurched forward suddenly—too suddenly—and what I should have foreseen happened. I slammed the brakes on, too late.

The donkey had stopped dead the minute the pull relaxed. The radiator of the car struck the creature's rump a glancing blow, and the donkey went over the edge. The car jerked sidewise toward the edge of the road, and there was a crackling sound as the rope broke.

Regardless of the knee-deep mud, I got out and ran to the edge.

The Indian was already there, looking down. He said, "It isn't deep here. But damn it, I haven't got my gun along. Lend me your crank or a heavy wrench."

I hardly noticed the change in his English diction. I said, "I've got a revolver. Can you get down and up again?"

"Sure," he said. I got the revolver and handed it to him, and he went down. I could see him for the first few yards and then he was lost in the driving rain. There wasn't any shot, and in about ten minutes he reappeared.

"Didn't need it," he said, handing me back the pistol. "He was dead, poor fellow."

"What are you going to do now?" I asked him.

"I don't know. I suppose I'll have to stash those boxes and hike out."

"Look," I said, "I'm bound for the Einar Observatory. Come on with me, and you can get a lift from there back to town the first time a car makes the trip. How much was that donkey worth?"

"I'll take the lift," he said, "and thanks. But losing Archimedes was my own damn fault. I should have seen that was going to happen. Say, better get that car moving before it gets stuck again?"

It was good advice and just in time. The car barely started. I kept it inching along while he tied the boxes on back and then got in beside me.

"Those boxes," I said. "Are they really rattlers, or was that off the same loaf as the Big Chief Wahoo accent?"

He smiled. "They're rattlesnakes. Sixty of them. Chap in Scardale starting a snake farm to supply venom to pharmaceutical labs hired me to round him up a batch."

"I hope the boxes are good and tight."

"Sure. They're nailed shut. Say, my name's Charlie Lightfoot."

"Glad to know you," I told him. "I'm Bill Wunderly. Going to take a job up at Einar."

"The hell," he said. "You an astronomer, or going on as an assistant?"

"Neither. Sort of an accountant-clerk. Wish I did know astronomy."

Yes, I'd been wishing that for several years now, ever since I'd fallen for Annabel Burke. That had been while Annabel was taking her master's degree in math, and writing her thesis on probability factors in quantum mechanics.

Heaven only knows how a girl with a face like Annabel's and a figure like Annabel's can possibly be a mathematics shark, but Annabel is.

Worse, she had the astronomy bug. She loved both telescopes and me, but I came out on the losing end when she chose between us. She'd taken a job as an assistant at Einar, probably the most isolated and inaccessible observatory in the country

Then a month ago Annabel had written me that there was to be an opening at the observatory which would be within the scope of my talents.

I wrote a fervid letter of application, and now I was on my way to take the job. Nor storm nor mud nor dark of night nor boxes of rattlesnakes could stop me from getting there.

"Got a drink?" Charlie asked.

"In the glove compartment," I told him. "Sorry I didn't think to offer it. You're soaked to the skin."

He laughed. "I've been wet before and it hasn't hurt me. But I've been sober, and it has."

"You go to Haskell, Charlie?"

"No. Oxford. Hit hisn't the 'unting that 'urts the 'orse; hit's the 'ammer 'ammer—"

"You're kidding me."

"No such luck." I heard the gurgle of liquid as he tilted the bottle

Then he added, "Oil. Pop's land."

I risked an unbelieving look out of the corner of my eye. Charlie's face was serious.

He said, "You wonder why I hunt rattlesnakes. For one reason, I like it, and for another— Well, if this was a quart instead of a pint, I could show you."

"But what happened to the oil money?"

"Pop's still got it. But the third time I went to jail, I stopped getting any of it. Not that I blame him. Say, take it easy down this hill. The bridge at the bottom was washed out four years ago, last time there was a big storm like this one."

But the bridge was still there, with the turbid waters of a swollen stream swirling almost level with the plank flooring. I held my breath as we went across it.

"It'll be gone in an hour," Charlie said, "if it keeps raining this hard. You haven't another bottle of that rye, have you?"

"No, I haven't. How do you catch rattlers, Charlie?"

"Pole with a loop of thin rope running through a hole in the end. Throw the loop over a snake and pull the loop tight. Then you can ease the pole in and grab him by the back of the neck."

"How about the ones you don't see?"

"They strike. But I wear thick shoes and I've got heavy leather leggings under my trousers. They never strike high, so I'm safe as long as I stay upright on level ground." He chuckled. "You ought to hear the sound of them striking those puttees. When you step in a nest of them, it sounds like rain on a tin roof."

I shivered a little, and wished I hadn't asked him.

Then, ahead of us, there were lights.

Charlie said, "Take the left turn here. You might as well drive right up to the garage."

I turned left, around the big dome on the north end of the building. Apparently, someone had heard us coming or seen our headlights, for the garage doors were opening.

I said, "You know the place, Charlie?"

"Know it?" His voice sounded surprised. "Hell, Bill, I designed it."

~§~

Annabel was more beautiful than I had remembered her. I wanted to put my arms around her then and there, despite the presence—in the hallway with us—of Charlie Lightfoot and a morose-looking man in overalls, who'd let me in the garage and then led us into the main building.

But I had a hunch I wouldn't get away with it, besides I was standing in the middle of a puddle of water and was as wet as though I'd been swimming instead of driving.

Annabel looked fresh and cool and dry in a white smock. She said, "You should have waited in Scardale, Bill. I'm surprised you made it. Hello, Charlie."

Charlie said, "Hi, Annabel. I guess Bill's in safe hands now, so I'm going to borrow some dry clothes. See you later."

He left us, managing somehow to walk as silently as a shadow despite the heavy, wet shoes he was wearing.

Annabel turned to the man in overalls. "Otto, will you take Mr. Wunderly to his room?"

He nodded and started off, and I after him. But Annabel said, "Just a minute, Bill. Here's Mr. Fillmore."

A tall, saturnine man who had just come in one of the doorways held out his hand. "Glad to know you, Wunderly. Annabel's been talking about you a lot. I'm sure you're just the man we need."

I said, "Thanks. Thanks a lot." I guess I was thanking him mostly for telling me that Annabel had talked a lot about me.

I remembered, now, having heard of him. Fergus Fillmore, the lunar authority.

A minute later I followed the janitor up a flight of stairs and was shown to the room which was henceforth to be mine. I lost no time getting rid of my wet clothes and into dry ones. Then I hurried back downstairs.

A bridge game was in progress in the living room. Annabel and Fergus Fillmore were partners. Their opponents were a handsome young man and a rather serious-looking young woman who wore shell-rimmed glasses.

Annabel introduced them.

"Zoe, this is Mr. Wunderly. Bill, Miss Fillmore . . . And Eric Andressen. He's an assistant, as I am."

Andressen grinned. "This is an experiment, Wunderly. Annabel thinks she can apply Planck's constant h to a tenace finesse."

There was a cheerful crackling fire in the fireplace. I stood with my back to it, behind Annabel's chair. But I didn't watch the play of the hand; I was too interested in studying the people I had just met.

Eric Andressen had a young, eager face and was darkly handsome. He could not have been more than a few years out of college. Something in his voice—although his English was perfect—made me think that college had been across the pond. Scandinavian, probably, as his name would indicate.

Zoe Fillmore, playing opposite Andressen, looked quite a bit like her father. She was attractive without being pretty. She seemed much less interested in the game than the others.

She caught me looking at her and smiled. "Would you care to take my hand after this deal, Mr. Wunderly? I'm awfully poor at cards. I don't know why they make me play."

While I was trying to decide whether to accept her offer a man I had not yet met came into the room. He said, "You were right, Fillmore. I blink-miked that corner of the plates again and—"

Fergus Fillmore interrupted him. "You found it, then? Well, never mind the details. Paul, this is Bill Wunderly, our new office man. Wunderly, Paul Bailey, our other assistant."

Bailey shook hands. "Glad to know you, Wunderly. I've heard a lot about you from Annabel. If you're as good as she says you are—"

Annabel looked flustered. She said, "Bill, this sounds like a conspiracy. Really, I haven't talked about you quite as much as these people would lead you to think."

Fillmore said, "Zoe has just offered Wunderly her hand, Paul. Would you care to take mine?"

Bailey's voice was hesitant. As though groping for an excuse, he said, "I'd like to—but—"

He paused, and, in the silence of that pause, there was a dull thud overhead.

We looked at one another across the bridge table. Bailey said, "Sounds like someone—uh—fell. I'll run up and see." He ran out the door that led to the hallway and we heard his swift footsteps thumping up the stairs.

There was an odd, expectant silence in the room. Eric Andressen had a card in his hand ready to play but held it.

We heard Bailey's footsteps overhead, heard him try a door and then rap on it lightly. Then he came down the stairs two steps at a time. Andressen and Fillmore were on their feet by now, crossing the room toward the doorway when Bailey appeared there.

His face was pale and in it there was a conflict of emotions that was difficult to read. Consternation seemed to predominate.

He said breathlessly, "My door's bolted from the inside. And it sounded as though what we heard came from there. I'm afraid we'll have to—"

"You mean somebody's *in* your room?" Zoe's voice was incredulous.

Her father turned and spoke to her commandingly. "You remain here Zoe. And will you stay with her, Annabel?"

Obviously, he was taking command. He said to me, "You'd better come along, Wunderly. You're the huskiest of us and we might need you. But we'll try a hammer first, to avoid splintering the door. Will you get one, Eric?"

All of us, except Eric —who went into the kitchen for a hammer— went up the stairs together. Almost as soon as we'd reached Bailey's door, Andressen came running up with a heavy hammer.

Fergus Fillmore turned the knob and held it so the latch of the door was open. He showed Andressen where to hit with the hammer to break the bolt. On Eric's third try, the door swung open.

Bailey and Fillmore went into the room together. I heard Bailey gasp. He hurried toward a corner of the room. Then Andressen and I went through the doorway.

The body of a young woman with coppery red hair lay on the floor.

Bailey was bending over her. He looked up at Fillmore. "She's *dead!* But I don't understand how—?"

Fillmore knelt, looked closely at the dead girl's face, gently lifted one of her eyelids and studied the pupil of the eye. He ran exploratory fingers around the girl's temples and into her hair. Turning her head slightly to one side, he felt the back of the skull.

Then he stood up, his eyes puzzled. "A hard blow. The bone is cracked and a portion of it pressed into the brain. It seems hard to believe that a fall—"

Bailey's voice was harsh. "But she *must* have fallen. What else could have happened? That window's locked and the door was bolted from the inside."

Eric Andressen said slowly, "Paul, the floor's carpeted. Even if she fell rigidly and took all her weight on the back of the head, it would hardly crack the skull."

Paul Bailey closed his eyes and stood stiffly, as though with a physical effort he was gathering himself together. He said, "Well—I suppose we'd better leave her as she is for the moment. Except—" He crossed to the bed on the other side of the room and pulled off the spread, returned and placed it over the body.

Andressen was staring at the inside of the door. "That bolt could be pulled shut from the outside, easily, with a piece of looped string. Look here, Fillmore."

He went out into the hall and the rest of us followed him. At the second door beyond Bailey's room, he turned in. In a moment he returned with a piece of string.

He folded it in half and put the fold over the handle of the small bolt, then with the two ends in his hand he came around the door. He said, "Will you go inside, Wunderly? So you can open the door again, if this works. No use having to break my bolt, too."

I went inside and the door closed. I saw the looped string pull the bolt into place. Then, as Andressen let go one end of it and pulled on the other, the string slid through the crack of the door.

I rejoined the others in the hallway. Bailey's face was white and strained. He said, "But *why* would anyone want to kill Elsie?"

Andressen put his hand on Bailey's shoulder. He said, "Come on, Paul. Let's go find Lecky. It'll be up to him, then, whether to notify the police."

When they'd left, I asked Fergus Fillmore, "Who is—was—Elsie?"

"The maid, serving-girl. Lord, I hope I'm wrong about that head-wound being too severe to be accounted for by a fall. There's going to be a bad scandal for the observatory, if it's murder."

"Were she and Paul Bailey—?"

"I'm afraid so. And it's pretty obvious Paul knew she was waiting for him in his room. When he heard that thud downstairs, you remember how Paul acted."

I nodded, recalling how Bailey had hurried upstairs before anyone else could offer to investigate. And how he'd gone directly to his own room, not looking into any of the adjacent ones.

Fillmore said, "Mind holding the fort here till Lecky comes? I'm going down to send Zoe home."

"Home?" I asked. "Doesn't she live here?"

"Our house is a hundred yards down the slope, next to Lecky's. There are three houses outside the main building, for the three staff members. Everyone else lives in the main building."

When Fillmore had left I walked to the window at the end of the hallway. The storm outside had stopped—but the one inside was just starting.

Bailey and Andressen returned with a short, bald-headed, middle-aged man. Abel Lecky, the director. He and the others turned into Bailey's room and I went back downstairs.

Annabel was alone in the room in which the bridge game had been going on. She stood up as I came in. "Bill, Fergus tells me that Elsie's dead. He took his daughter on home. But how—?"

I told her what little I knew.

"Bill," she said, "I'm afraid. Something's been wrong here. I've felt it."

I put my hands on her shoulders.

She said, "I'm—I'm glad you're here, Bill." She didn't resist or push me away when I kissed her but her lips were cool and passive.

~§~

There were heavy footsteps. Annabel and I stepped apart just as the door opened. A short, very fat man wearing a lugubrious expression came into the room. Pince-nez spectacles seemed grotesquely out of place on his completely round face.

He said, "Hullo, Annabel. And I suppose this is your wonderful Wunderly." Without giving either of us a chance to speak, he held out his hand to me and kept on talking. "Glad to know you, Wunderly. I'm

Hill. Darius Hill. Annabel, what's wrong with Zoe? I passed her and Fillmore out in the hall. She looked as though she'd seen ghillies and ghosties."

Annabel said, "Elsie Willis is dead, Darius."

"Elsie *dead?* You're fooling me, Annabel. Why, I saw her only a few hours ago, and—Could it have been *murder?*"

The italics were his. He took off his pince-nez glasses and his eyes went as round as his face.

I said, "Nobody knows, Mr. Hill. It might have been accidental. Probably she fainted and fell."

"Fainted? A buxom wench like Elsie?" He shook his head vigorously. "But —you say fell? That would imply a head injury, would it not? Of course.

"But what a banal method of murder—with a garage full of rattlesnakes at hand. And with Bailey a chemist, too. Or would Zoe have done it? I fear she would be inclined to direct and unimaginative methods but I didn't think she harbored any animosity—"

"Please, Mr. Hill." Annabel's voice was sharp and I noticed she addressed him by his last name this time, not his first. "If it was murder, neither Paul nor Zoe could have done it. They were both in this room, right here, when she died. We all heard her fall."

"Ah—then the scene of the crime was upstairs? And right over this room. Let's see—of course. She was in Bailey's room, waiting for him."

"Apparently. Paul had been sent to check plates on the blink-mike and he was passing through here on his way to his room when—when it happened. If you'll both pardon me, I think I'd better go tell the housekeeper about it. She should know right away."

Hill and I both nodded. Hill said, "I'd like to talk to you, Wunderly. Come on up to my room and have a drink.

"This way—" He was taking my acceptance for granted, so I could do nothing but follow.

Hill's room was just like the one that had been assigned to me, save that one entire side of it was made up of shelves of books.

While he hunted for the bottle and glasses, I strolled to the shelves and looked them over. The books were in haphazard order and they concerned, as far as I could see, only three subjects; one of which didn't fit at all with the other two. Astronomy, mathematics—and criminology.

When I turned around, Hill had poured drinks for us. He waved me to a chair, saying:

"And now you will tell me about the murder."

He listened closely, interrupting several times with pertinent questions.

When I had finished, he chuckled. "You are a close observer Wunderly. If I am to solve this case, I shall let you be my Watson."

"Or your Archie?"

He laughed aloud. "*Touché!* I grant more resemblance, physically at least, to Nero Wolfe than to the slender Holmes."

He sipped his drink thoughtfully for a moment, then said, "I'm quite serious, though, about solving it. As you've undoubtedly deduced from your examination of my library, murder is my hobby. Not committing murder, I assure you, but studying it. I consider murder—the toss of a monkey-wrench into the wheels of the infinite—the most fascinating of all fields of research.

"Yes, I shall most certainly take full advantage of the fact that someone has, figuratively, left a corpse conveniently in my very back yard."

I said, "But if you're serious about investigating shouldn't you—"

"Study the scene of the crime and the *corpus delicti?* Not at all, my dear boy. I assure you that I am much more likely to reach the truth listening to the sound of my own voice than by looking at dead young women."

"Why do you think that?"

"Isn't it obvious? *A* kills *B*—or rather, in this case, X kills *Elsie.* One could pun with the formula X kills *LG,* but that is irrelevant, not to say irreverent. My point is—would he leave her body in such a manner that looking at it would inform the looker who killed her? Of course not, and if a calling card is found under the body, it might or might not be that of the murderer... What do you think of Andressen?"

"Eric?" The sudden question surprised me. "Why, I hardly know him. Seems likable enough. He's Norwegian, isn't he?"

"Yes. He plays cello, too. Not badly. A brilliant, if erratic chap. How do you like Fergus Fillmore?"

"I like him well enough. His main interest is the moon, isn't it?"

"Right. Good old Luna, goddess of the sky. Thinks the others of us waste our time with distant galaxies and nebulae. How about another drink, Wunderly?"

"Thanks, no," I told him. "I think I'd better look up Annabel. She—"

"Nonsense. You're going to see plenty of Annabel from now on. Right now we're talking about murder, or had we digressed? Are you interested in murder, by the way?"

"Not personally. Oh, I like to read a good murder mystery but—"

"Murder mysteries? Bah, there's no mystery in them. A clever reader can always guess the murderer. I ought to know; I read them by the dozens. One simply ignores the clues and analyzes the author's manner of presenting the characters.

"No, Wunderly, I'm talking about real murder. It's fascinating. I'm writing a book on the subject. Call it 'The Murderer's Guide'. If I say so myself— it is excellent. Superb, in fact."

"I'd like to read it."

"Oh, you shall, you shall. It will be difficult for you to avoid reading it, I assure you. Here is the manuscript to date—first fifteen chapters and there are two more to be written. Take it along with you."

I took the thick sheaf of typed manuscript hesitantly. "But do you want to part with it for a day or two? I doubt if I'll have time to read it tonight, so may I not borrow it later instead?"

"Take it along. No hurry about returning it. Leave it in your room and go seek your Annabel. Later, if you're not sleepy, you might want to read a chapter or two before you turn in. Possibly you'll read something that will come in handy within the next few days."

"Thanks," I said and stood up, glad to be dismissed. "But what do you mean about the next few days?"

"The next murder, of course. You don't think Elsie is going into the great unknown all by herself, do you? Think it over, and you'll see what I mean. Who is Elsie to deserve being murdered? A scullery maid with red hair and willing disposition. Nobody would want to kill Elsie!"

"But unless it was an accidental death after all," I said, a bit bewildered by this point of view, "somebody *did* kill her."

"Exactly. That proves my point. The death of a scullery maid would scarcely be the real desideratum of the murderer, would it?"

In my room, I put the manuscript down on the desk and leafed it open to a random paragraph. I was curious merely to see whether Darius Hill's style of writing matched his brand of conversation.

"*The murderer,*" I read, "*who is completely ruthless has the best chance of evading detection. By ruthless I mean willing to kill without strong motive which can be traced back to him, or, better still, without motive at all other than the desire to confuse.*

"*Adequate motive is the murderer's* bête noire. *The mass murderers who lacks in each crime adequate motive therefor, is less vulnerable to suspicion than the murderer of a single victim through whose death he benefits.*

"*It is for this reason that the clever murderer, rather than the stupid one, is led from crime to crime . . .*"

There was a rap on my door. I said, "Come in."

Eric Andressen opened the door. "Annabel's looking for you. Thought you'd want to know."

"Thanks," I told him. "I'll be right down. Hill just loaned me the manuscript of his book, by the way. Have you read it?"

He grinned wryly. "Everybody here who can read has read it. And those who can't read have had it read *to* them."

I flicked off my light and joined him in the hallway. I asked, "Have the police arrived?"

"The police won't be here," said Andressen grimly. "The bridge is gone. Phone wires are down, too, but we notified them by shortwave. There's a two-way set here."

I whistled softly. "Are we completely cut off, or is there another way around?"

"Yes, over the mountains, but it would take days. Be quicker to wait till they send men out from Scardale to replace the bridge. The stream will be down by tomorrow night."

~§~

Fergus Fillmore was just leaving the main room downstairs when I entered. Lecky, the director, looking austere and thoughtful, was standing in front of the fireplace.

I heard Fillmore say, "Here's Eric back. He and I can manage Elsie between us. And if you can think of something for Paul Bailey to do, he'll be better off out of the way."

Lecky nodded. "Tell him I said to go to my office and wait for me there."

"Come on, Eric," Fillmore said to Andressen. "Get your flashbulbs and camera. We'll take pictures before we move the body."

"All right. Where are we—uh—going to put her?"

"We'll use the crate that the cylinder of the star-camera came in. We can turn it into a makeshift sort of refrigerator with some tubing and Rex's help. We'll borrow this refrigerating unit out of the—"

Their conversation faded as they went up the steps.

Director Lecky said, "An unfortunate evening, Wunderly. I'm afraid you're not getting much of a welcome but we're glad you're here."

"When shall I start on my duties, sir?"

"Don't worry about that. Take a day or two to familiarize yourself with the place and get to know the people you'll work with. Work is light here anyway, in bad weather."

"Shall I help Fillmore and Andressen?" I suggested.

"They'll do all right. Andressen's a bug on photography; got enough equipment to set up as a professional. And Rex Parker will have the refrigeration ready for them when they're ready for it. Have you met Rex?"

"No. Is he another of the assistants?"

"He's our electrician-mechanic. But— Lord, I nearly forgot to tell you. Annabel went up on the roof and you're to join her there. In fact, I've delegated her to show you around."

I found Annabel looking out over the parapet at the edge of the roof. Following her gaze, I saw a jagged, rocky landscape. Here and there one could catch glimpses of the tortuous turnings of the swollen stream.

She asked, "Did Darius talk an arm off you, Bill?"

"It was dangling by a shred," I told her. "He gave me the manuscript of his book to read."

"That book!" Annabel said. "It's horrible; let's not talk about it. Darius is a bit of a bore, but he really isn't as bad as that book would lead you to believe."

"It's hardly bedtime reading," I admitted. "But I've a hunch I'm going to find it interesting. Annabel—"

"Now, Bifi, don't start talking in *that* tone of voice. Not tonight, anyway. Look, there's the dome down at that end of the building. Tomorrow I'll show you around inside it. It's—"

"Sixty feet high," I said, "and houses the thirty-inch telescope, which is forty-six feet long. The dome is movable and the floor is a great elevator whose motion enables the observer to follow the eyepiece of the telescope without climbing ladders. I've read all about it, so let's talk about us."

"Not tonight, Bill, please."

"All right," I sighed. "But I'm more interested in people than telescopes. Have I met everyone? Or let's put it this way: I've heard about a few people I haven't met; a housekeeper, a cook, and an electrician named Rex something. Are there any others?"

"Parker is Rex's last name. I guess that's all of us except a handy man who helps Otto the janitor. You met Otto. And—oh, yes, there's Mrs. Fillmore and Mrs. Lecky; you haven't met either of them. Neither were over at the main building tonight. And there's a stenographer who'll help you, but she's away on sick leave."

"The three astronomers live in separate houses?"

"Lecky and Fillmore do. There's another house for the third staff member, but it's vacant because Darius Hill is a bachelor and doesn't want to live in it alone. So he rooms in, like the rest of us."

I counted on my fingers. "Three astronomers; Lecky, Fillmore, Hill. Three assistants; Paul Bailey, Eric Andressen, and you. Rex Parker, Otto the janitor, and a handy man. Housekeeper, cook, wives of two astronomers and daughter of one. Fifteen of us here, if I counted right."

"And Charlie Lightfoot. Not a resident but he drops in often."

"Sixteen people," I said, "and sixty rattlesnakes. I hope *they* don't drop in often. Say, about Paul Bailey. Is he—"

I never finished that question, for from somewhere below us, and outside the building, came the sound of a scream.

There is something more frightening in the scream of a man than that of a woman. Possibly it is because men, in general, scream less often and, in most cases, only with greater cause.

At any rate, I felt a tingling sensation on my scalp—as though my hair were rising on end. Annabel and I ran to the parapet on the south end of the building and looked down.

A man was running from the garage, screaming as he ran.

We heard a door of the main building jerk open and slam shut. Then Annabel and I were hurrying for the stairs that led down from the roof.

"It was Otto," she gasped. "Do you suppose that a snake—?"

That was just what I did suppose and I didn't like to think about it. Because it was very unlikely that *one* snake had got loose—and there were thirty in each box.

We pounded down the stairs and ran along the hallway. A man in dungarees and a blue denim shirt almost collided with me. I guessed him to be Parker, the electrician.

He hurried past us. "Stay out of there, Miss Burke. Charlie's ripping Otto's clothes off. I'm getting ammonia." Then he was past us.

I said, "Wait in the living room, Annabel. I'll see if I can help Charlie."

I shoved her firmly through the door of the living room. Not because I shared Parker's prudishness but because I had in mind doing something Annabel would probably object to my doing.

From the roof I had seen that Otto had left the garage door open. That door wouldn't be visible from the windows here and the others wouldn't know about it. That door should be closed.

I pushed through into the kitchen.

Otto was stretched out on the floor there. Fergus Fillmore and the cook held him down, while Charlie Lightfoot worked on him.

About each of Otto's legs, high on the thigh, Charlie had tied a makeshift tourniquet.

Now he was busy with a sharp knife, using it with the cool precision of a surgeon. I could see that there were several gashes from that knife in each leg.

No one paid any attention to me as I sidled past. I looked out through the pane of the door, and there was moonlight enough in the yard for me to see something I didn't like at all—high grass.

But I opened the door and slipped out, closing it quickly behind me. If I hurried, maybe I could get that garage door shut in time.

I held my breath as I headed for the garage building. My eyes strained against the dimness and my ears against the silence of the night, my muscles alert to leap back at the first sound of a rattle.

I'd almost made the garage before I heard it. A five-foot rattler had been coming through the open doorway. He coiled and rattled.

I froze where I stood, six feet from him. I knew he wouldn't be able to reach me from where he was; no rattlesnake can strike farther than two-thirds of his own length.

Keeping a good distance from him, I began to circle around to put the open door between us. Now I was in double danger, for my course took me off the path and into the high grass. If other snakes had already come out of the garage, I'd probably step on one without seeing it.

But I didn't; I got behind the door and I threw myself forward against it and slammed it shut.

I'd have been safer walking back to the main building but I ran instead. Even running, it seemed as though it took me thirty minutes to cover the thirty steps to the kitchen door.

Then I was safe inside.

"Couldn't do a thing," Charlie was saying. "Seven bites—and one of them—*that* one—hit a vein. They die in three minutes, when the fangs hit a vein."

Otto was lying very still now.

Rex Parker burst in the door, a glass in one hand and a bottle in the other. "The ammonia. One teaspoonful in—Oh! Too late?"

Charlie Lightfoot stood up slowly. He saw me and his eyes widened.

"Bill, you look as though—Good Lord! I remember now I heard that door closing. Did you go out in the yard?"

I nodded and leaned back against the door behind me. Reaction had left me weak as a kitten.

"He left the garage door open," I told them. "We saw that from the roof. I closed it."

"You didn't get bit?"

"No." I saw a bottle of whiskey on the table and crossed unsteadily toward it to pour myself a drink. But my hand shook and Charlie took the bottle from me. He poured a stiff shot and handed it to me.

He said, "You got guts, Wunderly."

I shook my head. "Other way around. Too damn afraid of snakes to have slept if I'd known there were a lot of them around loose."

I felt better when I'd downed the shot.

Charlie Lightfoot said, "I'll have to go out there and count noses, as soon as I get my puttees back on."

Parker said, "Are you sure it isn't too—"

"I'll be safe enough, Rex. Get me a flashlight or a lantern, though."

Fillmore's voice sounded wobbly. "We'll have to take care of Otto's body like we took care of Elsie's. Wunderly, will you tell Andressen to come help me?"

"Sure. Is he in his room?"

Fillmore nodded. "Listen. That's his cello."

I listened and realized now, as one can realize and remember afterwards, that I had heard it all along—from the moment Annabel and I had come through the doorway passage from the roof.

I asked, "Shall I look up Dr. Lecky, too?"

"He went over to his house," Fillmore said. "I'll call him on the house phone. It's still working, isn't it, Rex?"

Parker nodded. "Sure. But look, Mr. Fillmore, better tell Lecky not to try to come over here. There may be rattlers loose around outside, even if the door did get shut before most of them got out."

Charlie Lightfoot put down the whiskey bottle. "Hell, yes. Tell him within half an hour I'll know how many are at large, if any. And Fillmore, how about your wife and daughter? Is there any chance either of them would go out of the house tonight? If so, you better warn them."

"I'll do that, Charlie. They're both in for the night. But I'll phone and make sure."

I went to the living room first, told Annabel what had happened and told her I was going up to get Andressen.

She said, "I'm going upstairs, too. I think I'll turn in."

"Excellent idea," I told her.

I left Annabel at the turn of the corridor, with a kiss that made my lips tingle and my head spin.

"Be sure," I whispered, "that you lock and bolt your door tonight. And don't ask me why. I don't know."

Andressen was playing Rimsky-Korsakoffs *Coq D'Or*. A pagan hymn to the sun that seemed a strange choice for an astronomer.

My knock broke off the eerie melody. The bow was still in his hand when he opened the door.

"Otto Schley is dead, Eric," I told him. "Fillmore wants your help."

Without asking any questions, he tossed the bow down on the bed and flicked off the light switch.

"About Mr. Hill and Paul Bailey," I asked. "Do you know where they are?"

"Bailey's probably asleep. He had a spell of the jitters, so Darius and I gave him a sedative—and we made it strong. Darius is probably in his room."

He hurried downstairs, and I went on along the corridor to Darius Hill's room and knocked on the door.

He called out, "Come in, Wunderly."

~§~

I closed the door behind me, and asked curiously, "How did you know who it was?" Hill's chuckle shook his huge body. He snapped shut the book he had been reading and put it down on the floor beside his morris chair. Then he looked up at me.

"Simple, my dear Wunderly. I heard your voice and that of Eric. One of you goes downstairs, the other comes here. It would hardly be Eric; he dislikes me cordially. Besides, he has been in his room playing that miserable descendant of the huntsman's bow. So I take it that you came to tell him, and then me, about the second murder."

I stared at him, quite likely with my mouth agape.

Darius Hill's eyes twinkled. "Come, surely you can see how I know that. My ears are excellent, I assure you. I heard that scream—even over the wail of the violin cello. It was a man's voice. I'm not sure, but I'd say it was Otto Schley. Was it?"

I nodded.

"And it came from the approximate direction of the garage. There are rattlesnakes in the garage. Or there were."

"There are," I said. "Probably fewer of them." I wished I knew that. "But why did you say it was murder?" I asked him. "Loose rattlesnakes are no respecters of persons."

"Under the circumstances, Wunderly, do *you* think it was an accident?"

"Under what circumstances?"

Darius Hill sighed. "You are being deliberately obtuse, my young friend. It is beyond probability that two accidental deaths should occur so closely spaced, among a group of seventeen people living in non-hazardous circumstances."

"Sixteen people," I corrected.

"No, seventeen. I see you made a tabulation but that it was made after Elsie's death so you didn't count her. But if you figure it that way, you'll have to deduct one for Otto and call it fifteen. There are now fifteen living, two dead."

"If you heard that scream, why didn't you go downstairs? Or did you?"

"I did not. There were able bodied men down there to do anything that needed doing. More able-bodied, I might say, than I. I preferred to sit here in quiet thought, knowing that sooner or later someone would come to tell me what happened. As you have done."

The man puzzled me. Professing an interest in crime, he could sit placidly in his room while murders were being done, lacking the curiosity to investigate at first hand.

He pursed his lips. "You countered my question with another, so I'll ask it again. Do you think Schley's death was accidental?"

I answered honestly. "I don't know what to think. There hasn't been time to think. Things happened so—"

His dry chuckle interrupted me. "Does not that answer your question as to why I stayed in this room? You rushed downstairs and have been rushing about ever since, without time to think. I sat here quietly and thought. There was nothing I could learn downstairs that I cannot learn now, from you. Have a drink and tell all."

I grinned, and reached for the bottle and glass. The more I saw of Darius Hill, the less I knew whether I liked him or not I believed that I could like him well enough if I took him in sufficiently small doses.

"Shall I pour one for you?" I asked him.

"You may. An excellent precaution, Wunderly."

"Precaution?" I asked. "I don't understand."

"Did I underestimate you? Too bad. I thought you suspected the possibility of my having poisoned the whiskey in your absence. It is quite possible—as far as you know—that I am the murderer. And that you are the next victim."

He picked up the glass I handed to him and held it to the light.

"Caution, in a situation like this, is the essence of survival. Will you trade glasses with me, Wunderly?"

I looked at him closely to see whether or not he was serious. He was.

He said, "You turned to the bureau to pour this. Your back was toward me. It is possible— You see what I mean?"

Yes, he was dead serious. And, staring at his face, I saw something else that I had not suspected until now. The man was frightened. Desperately frightened.

And, suddenly, I realized what was wrong with Darius Hill.

I brought a clean glass and the whiskey bottle from the bureau and handed it to him. I said, "I'll drink both the ones I poured, if I may. And you may pour yourself a double one to match these two."

Gravely, Darius Hill filled the glass from the bottle.

"A toast," I said and clinked my glass to his. "To necrophobia."

Glass half upraised to his lips, he stared at me. He said, "Now I *am* afraid of you. You're clever. You're the first one that's guessed."

I hadn't been clever, really. It was obvious, when one put the facts together. Darius Hill's refusal to go near the scene of a crime, despite his specialization in the study of murder—in theory.

Necrophobia; fear of death, fear of the dead. The very depth of that fear would make murder—on paper—a subject of morbid and abnormal fascination for him.

To some extent, his phobia accounted for his garrulity; he talked incessantly to cover fear. And he made himself deliberately eccentric in other directions so that the underlying cause of his true eccentricity would be concealed from his colleagues.

We drank. Darius Hill, very subdued for the first time since I'd met him, suggested another. But the double one had been enough for me. I declined, and left him.

In the corridor I heard the bolt of his door slide noisily home into its socket.

I headed for my own room but heard footsteps coming up the stairs. It was Charlie coming down the hallway toward me. His face looked gaunt and terrible. What would have been pallor in a white man made his face a grayish tan.

He saw me and held out his right hand, palm upward. Something lay in it, something I could not identify at first. Then, as he came closer, I saw that it was the rattle from a rattlesnake's tail.

He smiled mirthlessly. "Bill," he said, "Lord help the astronomers on a night like this. Somebody's got a rattlesnake that won't give warning before it strikes. Better take your bed apart tonight before you get into it."

"Come in and talk a while," I suggested, opening my door.

Charlie Lightfoot shook his head. "Be glad to talk, but let's go up on the roof. I need fresh air. I feel as though I'd been pulled through a keyhole."

"Sure," I said, "but first shall we—"

"Have a drink?" he finished for me. "We shall not. Or rather, I shall not. That's what's wrong with me at the moment, Bill. Sobering up."

We were climbing the steps to the roof now. Charlie opened the door at the top and said, "This breeze feels good. May blow the alky fumes out of my brain. Look at that dome in the moonlight, will you? Looks like a blasted mosque. Well, why not? An observatory is a sort of mosque on the cosmic scale, where the devotees worship Betelgeuse and Antares, burning parsecs for incense and chanting litanies from an ephemeris."

"Sure you're sober?" I asked him.

"I've got to be sober; that's what's wrong. I was two-thirds pie-eyed when Otto— Say, thanks for closing that garage door. You kept most of them in. I didn't dare take time to go out, because of Otto."

I asked, "Was it murder, Charlie? Or could the box have come apart accidentally if Otto moved it?"

"Those boxes were nailed shut, Bill. Someone took the four nails out of the lid of one of them, with a nail-puller. Then the box was stood on end leaning against the door, with the lid on the underside and the weight of the box holding the lid on. Otto must have heard it fall when he went in but must not have guessed what it was."

"How many of the snakes did you find?"

"You kept seventeen of them in the garage when you slammed the door. I got two more in the grass near the door. That leaves eleven that got away, and I'll have to hunt for them as soon as it's light. That's why I've got to sober up. And, dammit, sobering up from the point I'd reached does things to you that a hangover can't touch."

I said, "Well, at last there's definite proof of murder, anyway. Do you think the trap was set for Otto Schley, or could it have been for someone else? Is he the only one who would normally have gone to the garage?"

Charlie nodded. "Yes. He always makes a round of the buildings before he turns in. Nobody else would be likely to, at night."

"You know everybody around here pretty well," I said. "Tell me something about—Well, about Lecky."

"Brilliant astronomer, but rather narrow-minded and intolerant."

"That's bad for Paul Bailey," I said. "I mean, now that the cat's out of the bag about his affair with Elsie. You think Lecky will fire him?"

"Oh, no. Lecky will overlook that. He doesn't expect his assistants to be saints. I meant that he's intolerant of people who disagree with him on astronomical matters. Tell him you think there isn't sufficient proof of the period-luminosity law for Cepheid variables—and you'd better duck. And he's touchy as hell about personal remarks. Very little sense of humor."

"He and Fillmore get along all right?"

"Fairly well. Fillmore's a solar system man, and Lecky doesn't know there's anything closer than a parsec away. They ignore each other's work. Fillmore's always grousing because he doesn't get much time with the scope."

I strolled over to the parapet and leaned my elbows on it, looking down into the shadow of the building on the ground below. Somewhere down there, eleven rattlesnakes were at large. Eleven? Or was it ten? Had the murderer brought the silent one, the de-rattled one, into the building with him?

And if so, for whom?

"For you, maybe," said Charlie.

Startled, I turned to look at him.

He was grinning. "Simple, my dear Wunderly—as my friend Darius Hill would say. I could almost hear you taking a mental census of rattlesnakes when you looked down there. And the next thing you'd wonder about was obvious. No, I haven't a detective complex like Darius has. How do you like Darius, by the way?"

"He could be taken in too large doses," I admitted. "Charlie, what do you know about Eric Andressen?"

"Not much. He's rather a puzzle. Smart all right but I think he missed his bent. He should have been an artist or a musician instead of a scientist. Just the opposite of Paul Bailey."

"Is Bailey good?"

"Good? He's a wiz in his field. He can think circles around the other assistants—even your Annabel."

"What's Bailey's specialty?"

"He's going to be an astrochemist. After university, he worked five years as research man in a commercial chem lab before he got into astronomy. I guess it was Zoe and her father who got him interested in chemistry on the cosmic scale. He knew Zoe at university. They were engaged."

I whistled. "Then this Elsie business must have hit Zoe pretty hard, didn't it?"

"Not at all. Bailey came here about eight months ago, and his engagement with Zoe lasted only a month after he came. And it was mutual; they just decided they'd made a mistake. And I guess they had at that. Their temperaments weren't suited to one another at all."

"And they're still on friendly terms?"

"Completely. What animosity there is seems to be between Bailey and Fillmore, instead of between Bailey and Zoe. Fillmore didn't like their decision to break the engagement and he seemed to blame Paul for it, although I'm pretty sure the original decision was Zoe's. They're still cool toward one another—Paul and Fillmore, I mean. But for other reasons."

"What kind of reasons?" I asked.

"Well—professional ones, in a way. I don't know the whole story but Fillmore was very friendly toward Paul when Paul and Zoe were engaged. He is really the one who persuaded Paul to come here as an assistant. And talked the board of regents, back in Los Angeles, into hiring Paul.

"Then he had a reaction when the engagement was broken. I think he tried to undermine Paul then and to get him fired. At any rate, he threatened to do it."

"Hmm," I said. "Sounds as though Fillmore isn't quite the disinterested scientist at heart."

"There may be something on his side," said Charlie. "Fillmore himself isn't too popular with Lecky and with the regents. And he thinks, rightly or wrongly, that Paul Bailey is shooting for his, Fillmore's, job. If so, it's quite possible Paul will succeed. He's got an ingratiating personality and he knows how to rub Lecky the right way."

"Who has the say-so on hiring and firing— the director or the regents?"

"The regents, really. But under ordinary circumstances, they'd take Lecky's advice."

I glanced at the luminous dial of my wrist watch. "Getting late," I said. "If you're going to hunt those rattlesnakes at dawn, hadn't you better get some sleep?"

"Don't think I'll sleep tonight. It's too late, now, to turn in. And anyway— Oh, hell, I just don't want to sleep. I'm too jittery."

~§~

Back in my room, I picked up the manuscript of the book Hill had given me. I was beginning to get a bit sleepy and "The Murderer's Guide" ought to affect that, one way or the other. I didn't care which way. If it made me sleepy, I'd sleep.

It started out slowly, dully. I was surprised, because the random paragraphs I had read previously had been far from dull. In fact, they'd been uneasy reading in a place where murder had just been done.

But, before I became really sleepy, I reached the second chapter. It was entitled "The Thrill of Killing; a Study in Atavism."

And here Darius really started to ride his hobby and to become eloquent about it. Man, he said, survived his early and precarious days by being a specialist in the art of killing. He killed to live, to eat, to obtain clothing in the form of furs. Killing was a necessary and natural function.

"Man," Darius wrote, *"has a gruesomely long heritage of murder. Nationalities, government, and progress are based upon it. The first inventions that raised man above the lesser beasts who were stronger than he, were means of murder— the club, the spear, the missile...*

"Is it any wonder, then, that in most of us survives an atavistic tendency to kill? In many it is rationalized as a desire to indulge in the murder-sports of hunting and

fishing.

"But occasionally this atavistic impulse breaks through to the surface in its original, primitive violence. Often the first step is an unintended slaying. The murderer, without really intending to do so, or forced to do so by circumstances beyond his control, has tasted blood. And blood, to a creature with man's heritage, can be more heady than wine. . ."

And his third chapter was "The Mass Murderer; Artist of Crime."

A clever man who kills many, Hill wrote, is less likely to be caught and punished than one who commits a single crime. He gave a host of instances—uncaught and unpunished Jack-the-Rippers.

A single crime, he said, is almost always a strongly motivated one, and motivation gives it away. If a killer kills only for deep-lying cause, the motive can almost invariably be traced back to him and proved. On the contrary, a man who kills for the most casual and light of reasons is far less likely to be suspected of his crimes.

"The indigent heir who kills for a fortune, the betrayed husband who slays, the victim who kills his blackmailer—all these act from the most obvious of motives and are therefore doomed from the start, no matter how subtle the actual methods they use. The man who puts nicotine in another man's coffee merely because the latter is a bore, is far more likely to remain free.

"Taking advantage of this, the clever killer will often extend his crime from a single one to a series, one or more of which are, by design, completely without motive. Confronted with such a series, the police are helpless to use their usual effective methods."

There was more, much more, in this vein. Case after case quoted, most of them solved, if at all, only by a voluntary confession years after the crimes. Case after case of *series* of crimes which have never been solved to this day.

And suddenly, as I read something came to my mind with a shock.

Undoubtedly the murderer; the man or woman who had killed Elsie Willis and Otto Schley had read this very book. Was using it, in fact, as a blueprint for murder.

There was a soft rap on my door. I said "Come in," and Charlie Lightfoot stuck his head in the doorway.

He said, "Come on down to the kitchen for coffee, Bill."

"Huh? At this time of night?"

Charlie grinned. "Night is day in an observatory, Bill. These guys never go to bed till later than this in seeing weather. Even in bad weather they stay up late out of habit. They always have coffee around this time."

Coffee sounded good, now that Hill's book had made me wakeful again. I said, "Sure, I'll be down in a minute," and Charlie went on.

I put on slippers instead of replacing my shoes, and put the manuscript away in a drawer of the bureau.

As I neared the bottom of the staircase, I noticed Fergus Fillmore writing at a desk in a niche off the hallway. I wondered for a moment why he didn't find it more convenient to work in his room—then I remembered he didn't have a room here, and was cut off from his own house until Charlie gathered in the rest of the rattlesnakes in the morning.

He looked up at me and nodded a greeting. "Hullo, Wunderly. I see you're turning nocturnal like the rest of us."

"Having coffee?" I asked him.

"In a few minutes. The police will be here tomorrow or the next day; they'll get through somehow. They'll want our testimony, and I'm making notes while things are fresh in my mind. I'm almost through."

"Good idea," I said. "I'll do the same when I get back upstairs."

I went on into the kitchen.

"It's cafeteria, Wunderly," Darius Hill told me. "Pour yourself a cup and sit down."

He, Charlie Lightfoot, Eric Andressen and Rex Parker were seated around the square table in the center of the big kitchen. Charlie slid his chair to make room for me. He said, "I guess Paul Bailey's asleep. I rapped lightly on his door and he didn't answer."

Andressen said, "He should sleep through all right; we gave him a pretty strong dose. Where's Fergus?"

"Right here," said Fillmore from the doorway. "Darius, what's this about your twisting the tails of spectroscopic binaries?"

"Haven't made them holler yet," said Darius slowly, "but maybe I've got something. Look, Fergus, on an eclipsing binary the maximum separation of the spectral lines when they are double determines the relative velocity of the stars in their orbits."

"Obviously."

"Therefore—" said Darius, and went on with it. At the fourth cosine, I quit listening and reached for a ham sandwich.

As I ate, I looked at the faces of the men around me. Charlie Lightfoot, Eric Andressen, Rex Parker, Fergus Fillmore, Darius Hill. . . . Was one of these men, I wondered, a murderer? Was one of these men even now planning further murders?

It seemed impossible, as I studied their faces. The Indian's haggard and worried, Hill and Fillmore eager on their abstruse discussion with Andressen listening intently and Rex looking bored.

Charlie was the first to leave, then Parker and Andressen together. When I stood up, Darius Hill stood also. He asked:

"Play chess, Wunderly?"

"A little," I admitted.

"Let's play a game before we turn in."

When we reached his room, he produced a beautiful set of ivory chessmen. He said apologetically, "Don't judge my game by these men, Wunderly. They were given to me. I'm just a dub."

He wasn't, by a long shot. But I managed to hold him to a close game that resolved itself finally into a draw when I traded my last piece for his final pawn.

"Good game," he said. "Another?"

But I excused myself and left.

My slippers made no sound along the carpeted hallway. Possibly if I'd been noisy I'd have never seen that crack of faint light under the edge of Paul Bailey's door. Maybe it would have been turned off, in time.

But I saw it and stood there outside the door wondering whether it meant anything. If Bailey had awakened and turned on a lamp, certainly I'd make a fool of myself turning in an alarm.

~§~

Yet if an intruder—the murderer—was in there, I'd warn him if I knocked on the door. There seemed only one way of finding out. I stooped down and looked into the keyhole.

All I could see was the desk at the far side of the room. The lamp on the desk wasn't on and the light that shone on the desk came from the right and couldn't be from the overhead bulb.

A flashlight? Someone standing still on the right side of the room, holding a flashlight pointing at the desk. But why would anyone be standing there?

Something else caught my eye; there was a lot of chemical equipment shoved back under the desk itself. Bottles, a rack of test tubes, a retort—and a DeWar flask.

I'm no chemist, but I do know what a DeWar flask is. And the moment I saw it, I knew how Elsie Willis had been killed. Knew, rather, why we had heard the sound of her fall downstairs *when* we heard it, just after Paul Bailey had walked into the living room.

As I straightened up from the keyhole I lost my balance. Instinctively my hand grasped the doorknob to regain my equilibrium. And the doorknob rattled!

That ended the advantage of secrecy, and I hurled myself through the doorway.

The flashlight was there, but it was not being held. It was lying flat on the bureau.

There was no one in sight. The killer, then, was *behind* me on the same side of the room as the bed! I tried to turn around—too late. I didn't even feel the blow that felled me.

Charlie Lightfoot was bending over me, and past him I could see a blur of other faces. Then my eyes came more nearly to focus and I could make out Annabel among them.

Charlie was saying, "Bill, are you all right?"

I sat up and put my hand back of my head. It hurt like hell. I took my hand away again.

"Bill!" It was Annabel's voice this time. "Are you all right?"

"I—I guess so," I said. And then, quite unnecessarily, "Somebody conked me. I—"

"You don't know who it was, Wunderly?" It was Darius Hill's voice.

I started to shake my head, but that hurt, so I answered verbally instead. Then, because I was beginning to wonder how long I'd been out, I asked Darius:

"How—how long has it been since I left your room?"

"About half an hour. Did this happen right after that?"

"Yes, only a minute or two after. I saw a light under Bailey's door.

I busted in and turned the wrong way."

I tried to stand up. Charlie gave me a hand on one side and Annabel on the other. I made it, all right, but leaned back against the wall for a moment until I got over the slight dizziness.

Other people were talking excitedly and I had time to take inventory. Eric Andressen and Fergus Fillmore were both still fully dressed. Darius had a lounging robe and slippers on but still wore trousers and shirt under the robe. Paul Bailey, looking sleepy and as though he was suffering from a bad hangover was sitting on the edge of the bed, a bathrobe thrown across his shoulders over pajamas. Annabel wore a dressing gown.

Charlie Lightfoot and Rex Parker, who was standing in the doorway, were both fully dressed.

I said, "Charlie, who found me?"

"I did, on my way down from the roof. You groaned as I was going by the door. I thought it was Paul groaning but I came in."

Fillmore asked, "What was the yell that brought us all running? I heard it downstairs."

Charlie grunted. "That was Paul. He must've been having a nightmare. When I shook him he let out a yowl like a steam engine before he woke up."

Bailey said, "I thought —

"Hell, I don't know *what* I thought. I don't remember yelling—but if Charlie says I did, I guess I did."

"Lecky," said Darius Hill. "We'll have to let Lecky know."

"He can't get over here before dawn," Fillmore pointed out, "unless he wants to run the gauntlet of rattlesnakes. We'd just wake him up."

Charlie said, "Darius is right. Something else has happened. We ought to let Lecky know. What time is it?"

"Four-thirty," Hill said.

"Then it'll be light in less than an hour. I'll go find those other snakes. But if I don't find them all right away, I'll escort Lecky over here—beat trail for him. I can take Fergus too, if he wants to get back home."

Darius Hill had walked over to the window and looked out. "There's a light over at Lecky's house. I'm going to phone now. Let's all go downstairs to the living room."

We went down in more or less of a group, Darius going ahead. He went into the room where the house telephone was, and the rest of us herded into the living room. All of us were quiet and subdued; none seemed able or willing to offer much comment on the situation we were in.

Darius would probably have been verbose enough, if he'd been there, but Darius wasn't there. He was taking an unconscionably long time at the telephone. For some reason, it worried me.

I strolled to the door of the hall without attracting attention and went down the hall and into the room which Darius had entered.

He was at the phone, listening, and I could see from the whiteness of his face that something was wrong.

"...Yes, Mrs. Lecky," he said. Then a long pause. "You're *sure* you don't want one of us to come over right away? I know it's almost dawn but—"

He talked a minute longer, then put down the phone and looked at me.

He said, slowly, "Lecky's dead, Wunderly. Good old Lecky. She found him at his desk just now with a knife in his back."

Then suddenly the words were tumbling out of him so fast that they were hardly coherent. "Good Lord! I thought I knew something about criminology and detection. What a damn fool I was! This is my fault, Wunderly, for pretending to be so damn smart about something.

"My fault. That book. I don't know who's doing these murders—I can't even guess—but he got the idea out of that damned book of mine. Just to be clever, I started something that—"

I said, "But it isn't your fault, Hill. What you wrote in that book is true, in a way."

"I'm going to burn that manuscript, Wunderly. What business has a fat old fool like me to give advice that—that gets people killed? Somebody's committing murder by the book—and the worst of it is that *the book's right*. That's why I should never have written it..."

There wasn't any use arguing with him.

"When was Lecky killed?" I asked.

"Just now. Less than fifteen minutes ago. While you were unconscious upstairs, probably."

"The hell," I said. "How do you know it was *then?* You said his wife just found him."

"She was talking to him fifteen minutes before. He was in his study typing. She'd been in bed but waked up. She told him to come on to bed and he answered.

"Then just now—fifteen minutes after that—she heard the phone ring . . . my call. And it wasn't answered, so she came downstairs and—found him dead."

"Lord," I said, "and she had wits enough to answer the phone right away and give you the details without getting hysterical?"

"You haven't met Mrs. Lecky, or you'd understand. Damn! One of us ought to go over there, though. It's almost light enough. Charlie could put his leggings on and—"

"Wait!" I said. "I've got—"

I thought it over a second and the more I thought about it the better it looked. It might work.

"Darius," I said, "look, if whoever killed Lecky is among the group in the living room—and it *must* be one of them—then he just got back into this building five or ten minutes ago."

"Of course. But how—?"

"Murderers aren't any braver than anyone else. He wouldn't have crossed an area where there were rattlesnakes loose without taking precautions. See what I mean? Whoever went over there and back would have put on puttees or leggings under his trousers."

"I—I suppose he would. And—you think he wouldn't have had a chance to take them off again?"

"I doubt it," I told him. "He must have been just getting into the building when Paul Bailey let out that yell. And everybody converged on Bailey's room. He'd have to go along to avoid suspicion; he'd be the last one to want to give himself away by being late getting there!"

"And since then, he certainly hasn't had a chance to be alone."

Darius' eyes gleamed. He said, "Wunderly, it's a chance! A good chance."

He grabbed my arm, but I held back.

"Wait," I said, "this has got to be your idea—not mine."

"Why?"

"Your position here, your seniority. Your work. Look some people may figure as you did just now—blame that book of yours for a share of what happened. But if you solve the murders, you'll be exonerated. The credit for that idea doesn't mean anything to me. I'd rather you took it."

He stared at me hopefully but almost unbelievingly. "You mean, knowing I'm a bag of wind, you'd—"

"You're not," I said. "You're one of the best astronomers living. And it was that phobia of yours—not your fault—that led you to write what you did. I agree you should never have it published. But in writing it—you stuck your neck out, as far as your colleagues are concerned. It means everything to you to solve the murders. It means nothing to me."

His hand gripped my upper arm and squeezed hard. "I—I don't know how to thank—"

"Don't try," I said. "Let's go."

We went into the other room and I walked over and stood beside Annabel while Hill announced the death of the director. He told them, quite simply, quite unemotionally, what had happened.

And then while they were still shocked by the news, he sprang the suggestion that each man in the group immediately prove he was not wearing protection of any sort on his lower legs.

"I'll lead off," he said.

He lifted the cuffs of his trousers up as high as the bottom of the lounging robe he was wearing over them, exposing neatly-clocked black socks.

Paul Bailey chuckled nervously. He had seated himself cross-legged in the morris chair, and his rather short pajama trousers were already twisted halfway up the calves of his bare legs. He said, "I believe I can join the white sheep without even moving."

~§~

None of us quite knew what had happened, at first. The sound of a shot, unexpected in the confined space of a room, can be paralyzing as well as deafening.

We heard the thud of the falling body before any of us—unless it was Darius—knew who had been shot. For Darius was the only one who had been facing Fergus Fillmore, who had been standing at the back of the group in a corner of the room.

Charlie Lightfoot and I were the first ones to reach him. The revolver—a small pearl-handled one—was still in his right hand, and the shot had been fired with its muzzle pressed to his temple.

Charlie's gesture of feeling for the beat of Fillmore's heart was perfunctory. He said wonderingly, "I suppose this means that *he*— But in heaven's name, *why?*"

I nodded toward Fillmore's ankles, exposed where his fall had hiked up the cuffs of his trouser-legs above the tops of his high shoes. Under the trousers a pair of heavy leggings were laced on.

"Mine," said Charlie.

Hill said, "Isn't—isn't that the corner of an envelope sticking just past the lapel of his coat?"

Surprised, I looked up at Darius Hill. He was standing very rigidly, his hands clenched. But he was looking at the corpse; he had, to that extent at least, overcome his necrophobia.

Charlie took the envelope from Fillmore's inside coat pocket. It was addressed to Darius.

And Hill, his face pale and waxen, but his voice steady, read to us the letter it contained:

"Dear Darius: Are you really a criminologist, or are you a monumental bluff? I have a hunch it's hot air, my dear Darius, but if you ever read this letter, I apologize. It will mean that you were more clever that I—or perhaps I should say you are more clever than the book you wrote. To meet that contingency, I carry a pistol—for a purpose you have already discovered. It would be quite absurd for a man of my position to stand trial for murder. You will understand that.

"I am writing this at the desk in the hallway. As soon as I finish writing, I shall join you for coffee and a sandwich in the kitchen. Then I shall carry out the third step in the program which has been forced upon me by the necessity of keeping my neck out of a noose.

"I remembered your book, Darius, as soon as I discovered, early this evening, that Elsie was dead. She walked into Paul Bailey's room early this evening while I was searching that room to get back the letter which Paul had held as a threat over my head—"

Darius Hill looked up from the letter and said to Bailey, "What letter is that, Paul?"

The bewilderment on Bailey's face seemed genuine enough.

Then, suddenly, "*That* letter! Good grief, he thought I still had it. Why, I'd destroyed it months ago."

"What *was* it?"

"One Fergus wrote me about ten months ago, while he was trying to get me to take the job here. He talked too freely—or rather—wrote too freely, in that letter."

"What do you mean, Paul?" Darius demanded.

"He criticized Dr. Lecky—pretty viciously. And said some things Lecky would never have forgiven, if he'd ever seen the letter. And he took some swipes at the regents in Los Angeles, too. From what I've learned since about how touchy Lecky was, I have a hunch that letter would have cost Fillmore his job—if either Lecky or the regents had ever seen it. But I didn't keep it. I threw it away before I packed my stuff to come here."

"But you threatened Fillmore with it, later?"

Bailey shifted uneasily in his chair. "Well—not exactly, no. But when Zoe broke our engagement—and it *was* Zoe who broke it—Fillmore had the crust to tell me that unless I managed to patch things up between Zoe and me, he'd see that I lost my job. We had some words and I told him his own job wasn't any too secure if Lecky and the regents knew what he'd written about them. I didn't threaten him with the letter but he may have got the impression I still had it."

Darius turned back to the letter and resumed reading:

"I happened to be to the left of the door, and Elsie walked in without seeing me. But in a moment, I knew, she would turn. I acted involuntarily, although I swear my intention was merely to stun her so I could leave the room without being identified.

"I was standing beside the bureau and I picked up the first convenient object—a hairbrush. I struck with the back of it.

"Then I found—as I caught her and lowered her to the floor so there would be no sound of a fall—that I was a murderer. A man after your own heart, Darius.

"And it was then that I recalled those lessons in your book, about how to get away with murder. Recalled them after I was already, inadvertently, a murderer. And some of the things in your manuscript make sense, Darius. As you say, a killer of several suffers no worse penalty than a killer of one.

"I forced myself, very deliberately, to sit down for a few minutes and think out a course of action. First, an alibi. I could not prove I was elsewhere when Elsie was killed but I could make her seem to be killed when I was elsewhere—playing bridge.

"A DeWar flask was the answer to that. I went downstairs, found Bailey and set him a task with the blink-mike which would keep him busy for an hour. Then I went to the lab and liquefied some air, taking it upstairs in the flask.

"Extreme cold applied to the leg joints of the body froze them, and I propped the corpse erect in a corner. By the time the flesh thawed and she fell, I was playing bridge downstairs with several of you. Was that not simple, Darius? Is this news to you, or had you solved the method?

"Even the coroner's examination of the body will not show what happened, because I'll see to it there is a leak in the tubing of the makeshift refrigerator we rigged up to preserve the body."

Rex Parker's voice cut in. "I'd better check that right away, Mr. Hill."

Hill nodded and read on, as Parker left the room. "But Otto Schley saw me leaving Bailey's room. It meant nothing to him then and he mentioned it to no one. But he will be a source of danger if the police ferret out—or you ferret out—the fact that Elsie's death did not occur during the bridge game but at about the time Otto saw me.

"So I remembered your book, Darius. And my method of dealing with Otto needs no explaining.

"A fortunate accident added to the confusion. I refer to the rattlesnake with the missing rattle—or the rattle from the missing rattlesnake. I had nothing to do with that. Wunderly says he slammed the door on a snake, and it is probable that the closing of the door knocked off or pinched off the rattle."

I said, "Damn," softly to myself.

"But now all is quiet again," Darius Hill continued reading. "Bailey is asleep under a mild drug. After coffee, I shall go to complete my search of his room. I am almost convinced, by now, that he does not have the letter any longer and that his tacit threat was a bluff.

"And then, whether or not I find it, a third and final murder.

"You see, Darius, I have taken your lessons to heart. No one will suspect that I would kill Lecky merely because—whether you or I receive the directorship—I shall be freer to concentrate on lunar and planetary observations and no longer will take orders from a doddering fool.

"No, I would *not* kill him if I had a stronger motive than that. I shall not kill Bailey, for that very reason. If I succeed to the directorship, however, he would be taken care of. Of course, I would not kill Lecky for so slight a motive, as motives go, save that the doing of two murders has made a third a matter of slight moment.

"Adieu, then, Darius. Coffee, then Bailey's room, then I shall steal Charlie Lightfoot's leather leggings from the closet, lace them on, and visit friend Lecky. Then—but if you ever read this, you'll know the rest."

Darius looked up. He said, in a curiously flat voice, "That's all."

~§~

A month later, Annabel and I were married at the observatory Darius Hill, the director, had insisted on giving the bride away. Charlie Lightfoot was my best man.

Darius spoke, copiously, at the dinner afterwards. He'd been at it for what seemed like hours

". . .and it is most fitting that Einar should be the setting for this sacred ceremony," said Darius, "wherein are joined the most beautiful woman who ever graced a problem in differential calculus, and a young man who, although he came to us in an hour of tribulation, has proved. . ."

"Ugh," said Charlie Lightfoot. "Paleface talk too much."

He reached for his glass—and I reached, under the table, for Annabel's hand.

Detective Tales, March 1942

The Jabberwocky Murders

Chapter 1

Looking-Glass Shadow

'Twas 'brilli, and the slithy toves
  Did gyre and gimble in the wabe:
All mimsy were the borogoves,
  And the mome raths outgrabe.

I TOOK ANOTHER DRINK out of the bottle on my desk and then typed the last take and handed it to Jerry Kiosterman to take over to his linotype. He looked it over.

"About one sentence strong, Doc," he said. "There were fourteen lines to fill."

"Then cut out the part about sullying the fair name of Carmel City," I told him.

He nodded and went over to the machine. I took the last drink and dropped the bottle into the wastebasket. Then I walked over to the window and looked out into the dusk while the mats clicked down the channels of the linotype. Smoothly and evenly. Jerry rarely poked a wrong key.

The lights of Oak Street flashed on while I stood there.

Across on the other sidewalk Miles Harrison hesitated in front of Smiley's Inn, as though the thought of a cool glass of beer tempted him. I could almost see his mind work.

"No, I'm a deputy sheriff of Carmel County and I have a job to do yet tonight. The beer can wait."

His conscience won. He walked on. I wonder now whether, if he had known he'd be dead before midnight, he wouldn't have taken that beer. I think he would have. I'd have done it, but that doesn't prove anything, because I'd have taken it anyway. I never had a New England conscience like Miles Harrison.

But of course I wasn't thinking that then, because I didn't know any more than Miles did what was going to happen. I found mild amusement in his hesitation, and that was all.

Jerry called to me from the stone, where he had just dropped in the newly set lines at the bottom of the column.

"She's a line short now, Doc. But I can card it out."

"Lock it up and pull a stone proof," I said. "I'll be in Smiley's. I'll buy you a drink when you bring it over."

I put on my hat and went out.

That's the way it always was on Thursday evenings. The Carmel City Courier is a weekly, and we put it to bed all ready to run on Thursday night. Friday morning the presses roll—or to be more accurate the press, singular, which is a Miehie Vertical, shuttles up and down. And about Friday noon we start to distribute.

Big Smiley Wessen grinned when I came in.

"How's the editing business, Doc?" he said, and laughed as though he'd said something excruciating. Smiley has as much sense of humor as a horse.

"Smiley, you give me a pain," I said. It's safe to tell Smiley the truth. He always thinks you're joking anyway.

He grinned appreciatively. "Old Henderson?"

"Old Henderson it is," I said, and he poured it and I drank it.

He went down to the other end of the bar and I stood there, not thinking about anything. This time Thursday evening always was a letdown. So I just stood there and tried not to see myself in the mirror and didn't succeed.

I could see myself Doc Bagden, a small man getting gray around the temples and thin on top. Editor of a small-town weekly and, thank goodness, not much chance of ever getting any higher than that. Another twenty—thirty years of that is bleak to look forward to, but anything else is bleaker. Nor a harp at the end of it. I envy some of my fellow townsmen their confidence in harps, for it might be something to wait around for.

I heard a car swing in to the curb out front and, for no reason, blow its klaxon.

"Al Carey," I told myself.

He came in, which was a treat for Smiley's Inn, for Alvin Carey usually went to swankier places in the nearby larger towns. Not that I blamed him for that. He had a spot to fill as the nephew of the town's richest man and naturally he spent as much of his uncle's money as he could get his hands on. Which was pretty much for Carmel City, although it wouldn't have made a splash in New York.

Of course I'd called him a wastrel—not by name—in editorials, because people expected me to. But I liked him, and had a hunch I'd make a worse scion of wealth than Alvin did.

Besides, he read a lot of the right things and had more of an idea of what it was all about than the rest of town.

"Hi, Doc," he said. "Have a drink, and when are we going to have another game of chess?"

"Old Henderson," I told Smiley. "Alvin, my son, I am playing chess now, and so are you. The White Knight is sliding down the poker. He balances very badly."

He grinned. "Then you're still in the second square. Have another drink."

"And there," I said, "it takes all the drinking I can do to stay in the same place. But that won't be for long. From the second square to the fourth, I travel by train, remember?"

"Then don't keep it waiting, Doc. The smoke alone is worth a thousand pounds a puff."

"Old Henderson," I said to Smiley.

Then Al left—he'd just come in for a short snort.

"What the devil were you guys talking about?" asked Smiley.

There wasn't any use trying to explain. "Crawling at your feet you may observe a bread-and-butter-fly," I said. "Its wings are thin slices of bread—and—butter, its body a crust, and its head is a lump of sugar."

"Where?" said Smiley. I don't think he was kidding.

Then Jerry Klosterman appeared with the rolled-up stone proof of the final page. I don't think I ever did get around to telling Smiley what Al and I had been talking about.

It was getting too much trouble to keep track of individual drinks, so I bought the rest of the bottle from Smiley, and got another glass for Jerry.

Then we took the page proof over to a table and spread it out, and I gave it a rapid reading. I marked a few minor errors and one major one—a line in an ad upside down. The ads, if you don't know, are the most important part of a newspaper. And I circled, for my own convenience, all the filler items that could be pulled out in case anything worth mentioning happened in Carmel City during the night. Not that it ever did or that it would tonight. Or so I thought.

"We can catch these in the morning," I told Jerry. "Won't have to go back tonight. Did you lock up?"

He nodded and poured himself another drink.

"There was a phone call for you just after you left," he said.

"Who?"

"Wouldn't give a name. Said it wasn't important."

"That," I said firmly, "is the fallacy of civilized life, so—called, Jerry. Why should things be arbitrarily divided into things that are important and that aren't? How can anyone tell? What is important and what is unimportant?"

Jerry is a printer. "Well, Doc, it's important that we get the paper up, isn't it?" he said. "And unimportant what we do afterward."

"Not at all," I told him. "Just the opposite, in fact. We get the blamed paper out of the way solely so we can do what we please afterward. That's what's important—if anything is."

Jerry shook his head slowly. "You're really not sure anything is, are you, Doc?" He picked up his drink and stared at it. "How's about death? Isn't that?"

"Somebody you like," I said. "His death can be important to you. But not your own. Jerry, there's one thing sure. If you were to die right now, you'd never live to regret it."

"Poor Doc," he said, downed his drink and stood up. "Well, I'm going home. I suppose you'll get tight, as usual."

"Unless I think of a better idea," I agreed. "And I haven't yet. So long, Jerry."

"So long, Doc."

I stared for a while at the calendar over the bar. It had the kind of picture on it that you usually see on calendars over bars. It was just a bit of bother to keep my eyes focused properly, although I hadn't had enough to drink to affect my mind at all.

One corner of my mind persisted in wondering if I could get Beal Brothers Store to continue running a half-column ad instead of going back to six inches. I tried to squelch the thought by telling myself I didn't care whether anybody advertised in the Courier or not. Or whether the Courier kept on being published. I didn't, much.

The picture on the calendar got on my nerves. "Smiley, there aren't any women like that," I said. "It's a lie. You ought to take it down."

"Women like what? Take what down?"

"Never mind, Smiley," I said. After all, the picture was a dream. Somebody's dream of what something ought to be like.

The air was hot and close, and Smiley was rattling glasses, washing them, back of the bar.

I turned around and looked out the window, and a car with two dead men in it went by. But I didn't know that, although I had a feeling of wide-awareness that should have told me, if there's anything in prescience.

"There goes Barnaby Jones to the bank," I told Smiley. That was all it meant to me.

"The bank?" Smiley answered. "Ain't it closed?"

I looked at him to see whether he was kidding, and then remembered he hadn't any sense of humor. But I thought everyone in town knew about the Barnaby Jones Company payroll. Old man Barnaby's shoe factory was in the next town, but he banked in Carmel City, where he lived, and every first and fifteenth he took the payroll over himself. Two trips, one for the day shift and one for the night shift. Miles Harrison had to strap on a gun and go with Barnaby over to the bank for the money and then guard him on the way.

"The bank opens up any time Barnaby Jones wants it to, Smiley," I explained. "Tonight's payroll."

"Oh," Smiley said, and laughed. I wanted to choke him.

Maybe there was something important, after all, I decided—a sense of humor.

Maybe there was something important, after all, I decided—a sense of humor. That was why I never stayed at Smiley's on Thursday evenings. I always bought a bottle and went home where my bookcase gives me the best company there is.

I bought a bottle and started home with it. It was still fairly early evening, but the streets were dark.

Darker than I thought.

Chapter 2

Smell of Blood

Beware of Jabberwock, my son!
The jaws that bite, the claws that catch!
Beware the Jubjub bird, and shun
The frumious Bandersnatch!

MAYBE I WEAVED just a little along the sidewalk, for at this stage I'm never quite as sober as I am later on. But the mind—ah, it was a combination of crystal clarity with fuzziness around the edges. It's hard to explain or define, but that's a state of mind which makes even Carmel City tolerable.

Down Oak Street past the corner drugstore, Pop Hinkle's place, where I used to drink Cokes as a youngster, past Gorham's Feed Store, where I'd worked summers while I was going to college, past the bank, with Barnaby Jones' Packard still standing in front of it, past the Bijou, past Hank Greeber's undertaking parlor—beg pardon—H. Greeber, Mortician, past Bing Crosby-Dorothy Lamour at the Aihambra, with a lot of cars parked in front, and I recognized Alvin Carey's even with the klaxon silent—a big contrast from the sedate black Packard his uncle used, back at the bank—past Deek's music store, where I'd once bought a violin, past the courthouse, with a light still burning in the room I knew was the office of Pete Lane, the sheriff.

I almost turned in there, from force of habit, to see if there was any news. Then I remembered it was Thursday night, and kept on walking.

Out of the store district no past the house Elsie had lived in and died in, while we were engaged, past the house Elmer Conlin had lived in when I bought the Courier from him—past my whole blasted life, on the way home.

But with a bottle in my pocket and good company waiting for me there, my old tried-and-true friends in the bookcase. Reading a book is almost like listening to the man who wrote it talk. Except that you don't have to be polite. You can take your shoes off and put your feet up on the table and drink and forget who you are.

And forget the newspaper that hung around your neck like a millstone every day and night of the week except this one.

So to the corner of Campbell Street and my turning.

My house ahead, with no lights waiting. But on the porch a shadow moved.

And came forward as I mounted the steps. The dim light from the street lamp back on the corner showed me a strange, pudgy little man. My own height, perhaps, but seeming shorter because of his girth. Light, insufficient to show his features clearly, nevertheless reflected glowing pinpoints in his eyes, a cat-like gleam. Yet there was nothing sinister about him. A small, pudgy man is never sinister, no matter where nor when, nor how his eyes look.

"You are Doctor Bagden?" he inquired.

"Doc Bagden," I corrected him. "But not a doctor—of medicine. If you are looking for a doctor, you've got the wrong place."

"No I am aware that you are not a medico, Doctor. PhD, Harvard, 1913, I believe. Author of 'Lewis Carroll Through the Looking-Glass,' and 'Red Queen and White Queen'."

It almost sobered me. Not that he had the right year of my magna cum laude, but the rest of it. The Lewis Carroll thing had been a brochure of a dozen pages, printed eighteen years ago, and not over five hundred copies run off. If one existed anywhere outside my own library, it was a surprise to me. And the "Red Queen and White Queen" article had appeared at least ten years ago in an obscure magazine long discontinued and forgotten.

"Why, yes," I said. "What can I do for you, Mr.—?"

"Smith," he said gravely, and then chuckled. "And the first name is Yehudi."

"No!" I said.

"Yes. You see, Doctor Bagden, I was named forty years ago when the name Yehudi, although uncommon, did not connote what it connotes today. My parents were not psychic, you see. Had they guessed the difficulty I might have in convincing people that I am not spoofing them when I tell them my given name—" He laughed ruefully. "I always carry cards."

He handed me one. It read: *Yehudi Smith*

There was no address. Absently, I stuck it in my pocket.

"There's Yehudi Menuhin, the violist, you know" he said. "And then there's—"

"Stop, please," I said, "you're making it plausible. I liked it better the other way"

He smiled. "I have not misjudged you then. Have you ever heard of the Vorpal Blades?"

"Plural? No. Of course in Jabberwocky—in *'Alice Through the Looking-Glass,'* there's a line about a— Great Scott! Why are we talking about vorpal blades on my front porch? Come on in. I have a bottle, and I presume it would be superfluous to ask a man who talks about vorpal blades whether he drinks."

~§~

I unlocked the front door and stepped in first to light the hall light. Then I ushered him back to my den. I swept the litter off the table—it's the one room my housekeeper, who comes in for a few hours every day—is forbidden to clean, and I brought glasses and filled them.

"Take that chair," I said. "This is the one I drink in. And now; Mr. Smith—to Lewis Carroll."

He raised his glass.

"To Charles Lutwidge Dodgson, known as Lewis Carroll when in Wonderland," he said.

We put down our glasses empty, and I filled them. I was more than glad I'd brought home a quart. There was a warm glow in my body—the glow I'd lost on the long walk home.

"And now," I said, "what of vorpal blades?"

"It's an organization, Doctor. A very small one, but just possibly a very important one. The Vorpal Blades."

"Admirers of Lewis Carroll, I take it?"

"Well, yes, but—" His voice became cautious. "—much more than that. I feel that I should tell you something. It's dangerous. I mean, really dangerous."

"That," I said, "is marvelous. Wonderful. Go on."

He didn't. He sat there and toyed with his glass a while and didn't look at me. I studied his face. It was an interesting face, and there were deep laughter-lines, around his eyes and his mouth. He wasn't quite as young as I thought he was. One would have to laugh a long time to etch lines like those.

But he wasn't laughing now. He looked dead serious, and if he was faking, he was good. He looked serious, and he didn't look crazy. But he said something strange.

"You've studied Dodgson's fantasies thoroughly, Doctor. I've read your articles on them. Has it ever occurred to you that—that maybe they aren't fantasies?"

I nodded. "You mean symbolically, of course. Yes, fantasy is often closer to fundamental truth than fact."

"I don't mean that, Doctor I mean—we think that Charles Dodgson had knowledge of another world and creatures of that world, and had entry into it, somehow we think—"

The phone rang. Impatiently, I went out into the hall and answered it.

"Bagden speaking," I said.

"This is Evers, Doc. You sober?"

"Why?" I asked.

"You offered to sell me the Courier last week. I've been thinking it over. Seriously."

"I'll talk it over with you tomorrow, Evers," I told him. "Tonight I'm busy. I have a guest, and anyway if I talked to you tonight, I'd be tempted to sell the Courier for fifteen cents."

"And tomorrow?"

"At least twenty cents. Providing you take over the debts. But I can't talk now, honestly. I got to see a man about a Jabberwock."

"You are drunk, Doc."

"Not yet, and you're keeping me from it. 'Night."

I put the receiver back on the hook and went back to the den. I poured two more drinks before I sat down.

"Let's get one thing straight," I said. "Is this a roundabout way of selling me an insurance policy or something?"

"I assure you I have nothing to sell. Nor am I crazy, I hope. If I am, I have company. There are several of us, and we have checked our findings very thoroughly. One of us—" He paused with dramatic effect. "—checked them too thoroughly, without taking proper precautions. That is why there is a vacancy in our small group."

"You mean—what?"

He pulled a wallet from his pocket and from an inner compartment took a newspaper clipping, a short one of about four paragraphs. He handed it to me. I read it, and I recognized the type and the set-up, a clipping from the Bridgeport Argus. And I remembered now having read it, a few days ago. I'd considered clipping it as an exchange item, and then decided not to. The heading read as follows:

MAN SLAIN BY UNKNOWN BEAST

It had caught my eye and interest. The rest of the article brought matters down to prosaic facts.

A man named Cohn Hawks, a recluse, had been found dead along a path through the woods. The man's throat had been torn, and police opinion was that a large and vicious dog had attacked him. But the reporter who wrote the article suggested the possibility that only a wolf or possibly even a lion or panther escaped from a circus, could have caused the wounds.

I folded the article up again and handed it back to Smith. It didn't mean or prove anything, of course. Anybody could have clipped that article from a newspaper and used it to help substantiate a wild yarn. Undoubtedly somebody's vicious police dog, on the loose, had done the killing.

But something prickled at the back of my neck.

Funny what the word "unknown" and the thought back of it can do to you. If that story had told of a man killed by a dog or by a lion, either one, there's nothing more than ordinarily frightening about it. But if the man who writes the article doesn't know what it was did the killing and calls it an "unknown beast"—well, if you've got imagination, you'll see what I mean.

"You mean this man who was killed was one of your members?" I said.

"Yes. Are you willing to take his place?"

Silly, but there was that darned chill down my spine again. Was I alone here in the house with a madman?

He didn't look mad.

Funny, I thought, here I don't like life particularly. But now suddenly pops up danger, and I'm afraid. Afraid of what? A madman—or a Jabberwock?

And the absurdity of that brought me back to sanity and I wanted to laugh. I didn't, of course. I was host and even if fear of his slitting my throat wouldn't keep me from laughing at a possible madman, then politeness would.

Besides, hadn't I been bored stiff for years? With Carmel City and with myself and with everything in it? Now something screwball was happening and was I going to funk out before I got to first base?

I picked up my glass.

"If I say yes?" I asked.

"There is a meeting tonight, later. We will go to it. There you will learn what we are doing. The results, thus far, of our research."

"Where is the meeting to be held?"

"Near here. I came up from New York to attend it. I have directions to guide me to a house on a road called the Dartown Pike. About six miles out from Carmel City. My car will get us there, or get me there alone, if you do not care to come."

The Dartown Pike, I thought, about six miles out from here.

"You wouldn't by any chance be referring to the Wentworth Place?"

"That's the name. Wentworth. You know it?"

Right then and there, if it hadn't been for the drinks I'd taken, I should have seen that this was all too good to be true. I should have smelled blood.

"We'll have to take candles," I said. "Or flashlights. That house has been empty since I was a kid. We used to call it a haunted house. Would that be why you chose it?"

"Of course, Doctor. You are not afraid to go?"

Afraid to go? Gosh, yes, I was afraid to go.

"Gosh, no," I said.

Chapter 3

Appointment with Death

He took his vorpal sword in hand:
  Long time the manxome foe he sought—
So rested he by the Tumtum tree,
  And stood awhile in thought.

PERHAPS I WAS A BIT MORE DRUNK than I thought. I remember how utterly crystal clear my mind was, and that's always a sign. There's nothing more crystal clear than a prism that makes you see around corners.

It was three drinks later. I was interested particularly in the way Smith took those drinks. A little tilt to the glass and it was gone. Like a conjuring trick. He could take a drink of whisky neat with hardly a pause in his talking.

I can't do that, myself Maybe because I don't really like the taste of whisky.

"Look at the dates," he was saying. "Charles Dodgson published 'Alice in Wonderland' in eighteen sixty-five and 'Through the Looking Glass' in Seventy-one, six years later. He was only thirty-two or thereabouts when he wrote the Wonderland book, but he was already on the trail of something. You know what he had published previously?"

"I'm afraid I don't remember," I told him.

"In Eighteen Sixty, five years before, he'd written and published 'A Syllabus of Plane Algebraic Geometry' and only a year later his 'Formulae of Plane Trigonometry.' I don't suppose you have ever read them?"

I shook my head. "Math has always been beyond me."

"Then you haven't read his 'Elementary Treatise on Determinants,' either, I suppose. Nor his 'Curiosa Mathematica'? Well, you shall read the latter. It's nontechnical, and most of the clues to the fantasies are contained in it. There are further references in his 'Symbolic Logic,' published in Eighteen Ninety-six, just two years before his death, but they are less direct."

"Now, wait a minute," I said, "if I understand you correctly, your thesis is that Lewis Caroll—I can't seem to think of him as Dodgson—worked out through mathematics and symbolic logic the fact that there is another—uh—plane of existence. A through-the-looking-glass plane of fantasy, a dream plane—is that it?"

"Exactly, Doctor. A dream plane. That is about as near as it can be expressed in our language. Consider dreams. Aren't they the almost-perfect parallel of the Alice adventures? The wool-and-water sequence where everything Alice looks at changes. Remember in the shop, with the sheep knitting, how whenever Alice looked hard at any shelf to make sure what was on it, that shelf was always empty although the others around it were crowded full?"

"Things flow about so here, was her comment," I said. "And the sheep asks if she can row and hands her a pair of knitting needles, and they turn into oars in her hands, and she's in a boat."

"Exactly, Doctor. A perfect dream sequence. And the poem Jabberwocky, the high point of the second book in my estimation, is in the very language of dreams. 'Frumious,' 'manxome,' 'tulgey'—words that give you a vague picture, in context, but that you can't put your finger on. Like something you hear in a dream, and understand, but which is meaningless when you awaken."

~§~

Between "manxome" and "tulgey" he'd downed his latest drink. I replenished his glass and mine.

"But why postulate the reality of such a world?" I asked him. "I see the parallel, of course. The Jabberwock itself is the epitome of dream—creatures of nightmare. With eyes of flame, jaws that bite and claws that catch, it whiffles and burbles—Freud and James Joyce, in tandem, couldn't do any better than that. But why isn't a dream a dream? Why talk of getting through to it, except in the sense that we invade that world nightly in our dreams? Why assume it's more real than that?"

"You'll hear evidence of that tonight, Doctor. Mathematical evidence—and, I hope, further actual proof. The calculations are there, the methods, in *'Curiosa Mathematica'*. Dodgson was a century ahead of his time, Dr. Bagden. Have you read of the recent experiments with the subconscious of Liebnitz and Winton? They're putting forth feelers in the right direction—the mathematical approach.

"You see, only recently, aside from a rare exception like Dodgson, has science realized the possibility of parallel planes of existence, existences like nested Chinese boxes, one inside the other. With gaps between that consciousness, the mind can bridge in sleep under the influence of drugs. Why do the Chinese use opium except to bridge that gap? If the mind can bridge it, why not the body?"

"Down a rabbit-hole," I suggested. "Or through a looking-glass."

He waved a pudgy hand. "Both symbolic. But both suggestive of formulae you'll find in his Syllabus, formulae that have puzzled mathematicians."

I won't try to repeat the rest of what he told me. Partly, if not mainly, because I don't remember it. It was over my head and sounded like Einstein on a binge.

This must have been partly because I was getting drunker. At times there was a mistiness about the room and the man across the table from me seemed to come closer and then recede, his face to become clear and then to blur. And at times his voice was a blur of sines and cosines.

I gave up trying to follow.

He was a screwball, and so was I, and we were going to a haunted house to meet other screwballs and to try something crazy. I'm not certain whether we were going to try to fish a Bandersnatch out of limbo or to break through a looking-glass veil ourselves and go hunting one in its native element. Among the slithy toves in the wabe.

I didn't care which. It was crazy, of course, but I was having the best time I'd had since the Halloween almost forty years ago when we—but never mind that. It's a sign of old age to reminisce about one's youth, and I'm not old yet.

But part of the mistiness in the room was smoke. I hadn't opened the window and I looked across at it now and wondered if I wanted it opened badly enough to get up and cross the room.

A black square, that window in the wall of this lighted room. A square of glass against which pressed murder and the monstrous night. As I watched it, I heard the town clock strike ten times. I reached for my glass and then pulled back my hand. I'd had enough, or too much, already for ten o'clock in the evening.

The window. A black square!

We are not clairvoyant.

Out there in the night a man, a man I knew, lay dead with his skull bashed in and blood and brains mixing with his matted hair. The pistol butt was raised to strike the other man's head.

A third murder was planned, already committed in a warped brain.

Ten o'clock, the hour they would ask an alibi.

"I was with Yehudi," I would say.

Who's Yehudi?

Oh, if murder was ever funny, this set-up was funny. Some day when I'm as drunk again as I was at ten o'clock that evening, I'll be able to laugh at it.

Murder and the monstrous night.

But I merely decided that the smoke was too thick after all, and I got up and opened the window. I could still walk straight.

Men were being murdered, and Smith spoke. "We'll have to leave soon," he said.

"Have another drink," I asked him. "I'm ahead of you. I drank at Smiley's."

He shook his head. "I've got to drive."

I stood at the window and the cool air made me feel a bit less fuzzy. I took in deep draughts of it. Then, because if I left it wide open the room would be too cool when I returned, I pushed it down again to within an inch or two of the sill.

And there was my reflection again. An insignificant little man with graying hair, and glasses, and a necktie badly askew.

~§~

I grinned at my reflection. *You blasted fool, you,* I thought to myself. *Going out with a madman to hunt Jabberwocks. At your age.*

The reflection straightened its necktie, and grinned back. It was probably thinking:

> *"You are old, Father William," the young man said.*
> *"And your hair has become very white.*
> *And yet you incessantly stand on your head.*
> *Do you think, at your age, it is right?"*

Well, maybe it wasn't, but I hadn't stood on my head for a long time and maybe this was the last chance I'd ever have.

Over my shoulder, in the mirror of the window glass, I could see Smith getting to his feet. "Ready to go?" he asked.

I turned around and looked at him, at his bland, round face, at the laughter tracks in the corners of his eyes, at the rotund absurdity of his body.

And an impulse made me walk over and hold out my hand to him and shake his hand when he put it in mine rather wonderingly. We hadn't shaken hands when we'd introduced ourselves on the porch, and something made me do it now.

Just an impulse, but one I'm very glad I followed.

"Mr. Smith, frankly I don't follow or swallow your theory about Lewis Carroll," I said. "I'm going with you, although I don't expect any Jabberwocks. But even so, you've given me the most enjoyable evening I've had in a good many years. I want to thank you for it, in case I forget later. I'm taking the bottle along."

Yes, I'm glad I said that. Often after people are dead, you think of things you'd like to have said to them while you had the chance. For once, I said it in time.

He looked pleased as could be.

"Thanks, Doc," he said, shortening the title into a nickname for the first time. But also, for the first time, his eyes didn't quite meet mine.

We went out to his car, and got in.

It's odd how clearly you remember some things and how vague other things are. I remember that there was a green bulb on the speedometer on the dashboard of that car, and that the gearshift knob was brightly polished onyx. But I don't remember what make of car it was, nor even whether it was a coupe or a sedan.

I remember directing him across town to the Dartown Pike, but I can't for the life of me recall which of several possible routes we took.

But then we were out of town on the pike, purring along through the night with the yellow headlight beams cutting long spreading swaths through the black dark.

"We've clocked five and a half miles from the town limits," Smith said. "You know the place? Must be almost there."

"Next driveway on your right," I told him.

Gosh, but the place must be old, I thought. It was an old house forty years ago when I was a boy of twelve. It had been empty then. My dad's farm had been a mile closer to town, and Johnny Haskins, who lived on the next farm, and I had explored it several times. In daylight. Johnny had been killed in France in 1917. In daytime, I hope, because he'd always been afraid of the dark. I'd picked up a little of that fear from him, and had kept it for quite a few years after I grew up.

But not anymore. Older people never stay afraid. By the time you pass the fifty mark, you've known so many people who are now dead that ghosts, if there were such things, aren't such strangers. You'd find too many friends among them.

"This it?" Smith asked.

"Yes," I said.

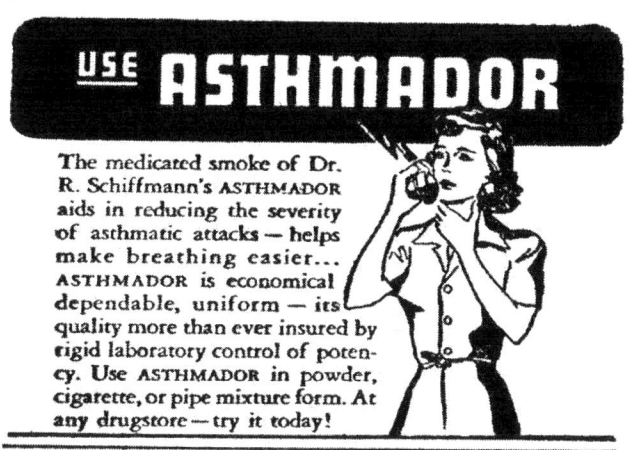

USE ASTHMADOR

The medicated smoke of Dr. R. Schiffmann's ASTHMADOR aids in reducing the severity of asthmatic attacks — helps make breathing easier... ASTHMADOR is economical, dependable, uniform — its quality more than ever insured by rigid laboratory control of potency. Use ASTHMADOR in powder, cigarette, or pipe mixture form. At any drugstore — try it today!

Chapter 4

Bottle from Wonderland

And as in uffish thought he stood,
The Jabberwock, with eyes of flame,
Came whiffling through the tulgey wood
And burbled as it came!

WE STOOD in front of the house that had been the bugaboo of my childhood, and it looked just about as it had looked then.

I ran the beam of my flashlight up on the porch, and it seemed that not a board had changed.

Just imagination, of course. It had been lived in for twenty years since then. Colonel Wentworth had bought it in about 1915 and had lived there until he died eight years ago. But during those eight years it had stood empty and again it had gone to rack and ruin.

"The others aren't here yet," Smith said. "But let's go in."

We went up on the creaking porch and found the door was not locked. The beams of our flashlights danced ahead of us down the long dimness of the hallway.

Was someone else really coming here tonight? I wondered. Again that prickle of danger roughed the hair on the back of my neck. Undoubtedly I was a fool to have come here with a man I didn't know. But there was nothing dangerous about Smith, I felt sure. Crackpot he might be, but not a homicidal one.

We turned into a huge living room on the left of the hallway. There was furniture there, white-sheeted. But the sheets were not too dirty nor was there much dust anywhere. Apparently the inside of the place, at least, was being cared for.

Furniture under white muslin has a ghostly look.

I took the bottle out of my pocket and held it out to Smith, but he shook his head silently.

But I took a drink from it. The warm feeling began to drive the cold one from the pit of my stomach.

I didn't dare get sober now, I told myself, or I'd start wondering what I was doing there.

I heard the sound of a car turning in the driveway.

Or so it seemed. For we stood quiet a long time and nothing happened. No footsteps on the porch, no more car-sound. I began to wonder if I'd been mistaken.

Maybe a minute passed, maybe an hour. I took another drink.

Smith had laid his flashlight on top of the bureau, with the switch turned on, pointed diagonally across the room. The furniture made huge black shadows on the wall. He stood in the middle of the room and when he turned to face me the flashlight was full in his face.

He looked a bit scared himself, until he smiled.

"They'll be here soon, I'm sure," he said.

"How many are coming?" For some reason we were both talking softly, almost in whispers.

I was finding it hard, deucedly hard, to keep my eyes in focus on his face. It was an effort to stand up straight, and I took a step backward so I could lean against the wall. Somehow, I didn't want to sit down in one of those sheeted chairs.

I didn't feel any too good, now. I wished I was back home, so I could lie down for a while and let the bed go around in soothing circles.

Smith didn't seem to hear my question about how many were coming. Again I thought the engine of a car was running, but Smith turned and walked to the window, and the sound of his footsteps drowned the noise, if there was any noise,

When he reached the window he stopped and I heard it again, distinctly. A car, if my ears told me aright, was driving away from the house. Had someone come, and gone? Finally the sound died away.

It didn't make sense, but then what did?

I was tired of listening to nothing and looking at Smith's back. He kept staring at the blank, black pane of window as though he could see out of it. I was sure he couldn't.

For no particular reason, I took another look around the room.

In the shadows of one corner there was a single article of furniture that was not covered by a dust sheet. It was a glass-topped table. A small, round three-legged affair; like a magician's table. There was something on it that I couldn't make out.

I looked away, and then, because something about it haunted me, I looked back. Where had I seen a table like that before? Somewhere.

No, a picture of one. I remembered now.

In the John Tenniel illustrations of Alice in Wonderland, of course. The glass-topped table Alice had found in the hall at the bottom of the rabbit hole. The table on which stood a little bottle with a label tied around the neck.

I walked over and, yes, there were two things on the table, as there should have been. A bottle and a key. The key was a small Yale key, and the bottle was really a vial, about two inches high, just as in the Tenniel picture.

The label, of course, said "DRINK ME." I picked the bottle up and looked at it unbelievingly, and I became aware that Smith was standing at my elbow. He must have heard me walking across the room and left the window.

He reached out, took the bottle from my hand and looked at it. He nodded.

"They've been here, then," he said.

"Who? You mean this—the table and the key and all—is part of—uh—what we came here for?"

He nodded again. "They brought this, and left it."

He loosened the cork in the bottle as he spoke.

"I'm sorry, Doc," he said. "I can't let you have the honor. But you're not really a member yet and—well—I am!"

He put the bottle to his lips and drank it off with the same quick motion he'd used in polishing off the whiskeys I'd given him back in my room.

Don't ask me what I expected to happen. Whether I expected him to shut up like a telescope and shrink to about ten inches high, just the right height to go through the little door into the garden, I can't say. Only, like Alice, he'd neglected to take the key off the table first.

I don't know what I expected to happen. But nothing happened. He put the bottle back down on the table and went right on with what he'd been saying.

"When you have met the others and have been accepted, you may, if you wish, try out our—"

And then he died.

What the poison was, I don't know, but its action was sudden despite the fact that it had not paralyzed his lips or mouth. He died before he even started to fall. I could tell it by the sudden utter blankness of his face.

The thud of his fall actually shook the floor.

I bent over and shoved my hand inside his coat and shirt and his heart wasn't beating. I waited a while to be sure.

I stood up again, and my knees were wobbly.

If he'd tried to poison me! But he hadn't. He drunk it himself and his death had been murder and not suicide. Nobody, no matter how mad he might be, would ever commit suicide in the offhand manner in which he'd tossed off the contents of that bottle.

The empty bottle had jarred off the table and was lying on the floor beside him and my eyes went from it back to the glass table and the key. I picked the key up and looked at it.

It was a false note, that key. It should have been a gold key, and small as it was, it should have been smaller. And not a Yale key. But maybe it opened something. What good is a key without a lock? I stuck it absently into my pocket and looked down again at Smith.

He was still dead.

And it was then that I got scared and ran. I'd seen dead men before, plenty of them, and it wasn't Smith I was afraid of.

It was the utter complete screwiness of everything that had been happening this mad night.

That, and the fact that I was alone. In a haunted house, too! Like all cynics who don't believe in haunted houses, I have a good deal of respect for them.

I stumbled and fell in the darkness of the hallway, and then remembered the flashlight in my hip pocket, and put it into action. I got out the door and off the porch before I even wondered where I was going, or why.

The police, of course. I'd have to get word to Sheriff Pete Lane as soon as I possibly could. I considered knocking someone awake in a nearby farmhouse and telephoning, but it would be quicker, in the long run, to take Smith's car and drive the six miles back to town. I could do that in fifteen minutes and it might take twice that long to find a telephone.

Beyond this, beyond notifying the sheriff, I wasn't thinking yet.

I had a hunch that if I thought about what had happened and tried to figure out what it all meant and why that "DRINK ME" bottle had been poison, I'd have gone off my rocker.

The less thinking I did before I talked to Pete Lane, the better off I'd be.

So I flashlighted my way around the corner of the house to where we'd left the car, and I got another jolt.

The car was there, or a car was there. But it was my own car, not the one Smith had driven me out in. My own Plymouth coupe, which up to that afternoon, had been out in my garage on blocks, with the air let out of the tires. There'd been only a few miles left in those tires anyway and I'd decided to save those few miles for something important, if anything important ever came up.

~§~

Well, something important had come up, and here was my Car. There was air in the tires, too. And gas in the tank, probably, unless somebody had towed it there.

I walked around it warily, almost expecting to see it vanish in a puff of smoke or to find the March Hare or the Mock Turtle seated behind the steering wheel. Those drinks were still with me.

But there wasn't anyone behind the steering wheel, and I got in. I flicked on the dashboard lights and looked at the gas gauge, and there were three gallons in the tank.

Could I have been driven here in my own car without realizing it? No, I remembered that onyx gearshift knob, and the green light on the dashboard of the other car. And the instrument panel had been different. I was sure of that.

I took a deep breath and started the engine. It purred smoothly, and I eased the coupe out to the road and aimed it south for town.

I think I might have driven wide open if it hadn't been my own car. But the familiar feel of it sobered me a little more and that was just enough to realize how drunk I still was. The road ahead seemed like a weaving ribbon at times. And one of those tires might give way any minute.

I parked in front of the courthouse, and there was still a light on in the sheriff's office.

I started in, but stopped in the doorway long enough to take another drink. This wasn't going to be easy.

Pete Lane was talking on the telephone when I went into his office.

"You're blamed right, we're trying," he said into the mouthpiece. "I got two of my own men on it, and I've just notified the state police. Huh? No, we ain't told anybody else yet. No use doing that till we find 'em."

He hung up the receiver and looked at me. He looked angry and harassed. "What the devil do you want, Doc?" he said.

"I got to report a murder," I said. I closed the door and leaned against it. Then I was catapulted nearly off my feet and onto the sheriff's desk as the door opened violently from the outside. Harry Bates came in. He had his clothes on over his pajamas, for the bottoms of them showed below his trouser cuffs. His shoes weren't tied.

"Walter just phoned from Burlington," Bates said. "Your line was busy so I took it on the switchboard. He didn't find much."

Pete interrupted him. "Just a minute, Harry. What's this about a murder, Doc?"

"Out at the old Wentworth place on the road to Burlington. There's a man dead there."

"Is it Jones?"

"Jones?" The name didn't register with me. "No. His name was Smith, not Jones. Or that's what he told me. His first name was a funny one."

I didn't quite dare. There was the card Smith had given me, in my pocket. I handed it to Pete.

He looked at it and let out a howl.

"Yehudi?" he yelled. "Doc, if this is a rib, I'm going to smack you."

I sat down on the corner of the desk because I felt safer sitting down.

"It's no rib, darn it," I told him. "He got me out there with him, and then he took poison out of a bottle that we found."

Pete wasn't even listening to me. He was staring at the card I'd handed him. Suddenly he looked up.

"Doc, what's your bug number?" he asked me.

"My bug number?" For an awful instant I thought he was crazy too. Then I remembered that some people call the union label—that tiny device which, with the number of the shop, must appear on every job printed in a union print shop—the "bug."

"Seventeen," I told him, and he cursed.

"Doc, you printed this yourself," he said. He cursed again. "Yehudi! Doc, if you weren't drunk, I'd ram your teeth down your throat for barging in here like this. We got trouble, and I mean trouble. Barnaby Jones started for Burlington with his payroll, taking Miles Harrison along, three hours ago, and didn't show up there. Three hours, and it's only twenty miles. Get the devil out of here."

I didn't move.

"Pete, sure I'm drunk," I said. "But blast your hide, you've known me all your life, and would I pull a gag about something like this? I tell you there's a dead man at the Wentworth place. I went there with him. I'd never seen him before tonight."

"What'd you go there for?"

Although the incredulity had left his voice, I knew it wasn't the time to say why we went there. I could imagine his face if I told him a tenth of it.

"That's not important, now," I said. "Man, this is a murder. Come out there with me and I'll show you the body."

"Just a minute, Doc. Harry, is Walter still on the line?"

"He's waiting for us to call him back with instructions. Here's the number." He put a slip of paper on Pete's desk.

"Walter's got to drive past the Wentworth house anyway. I'll have him look in. What room?"

"Living room," I said. "Middle room on the north side, downstairs. He'll find a body on the floor, and he'll find a glass table, and a bottle lying by the body, with label."

But I stopped just in time. Whew! Pete Lane picked up the phone and asked for Burlington.

Chapter 5

Head on a Platter

One, two! One, two! And through and through
The vorpal blade went snicker-snack!
He left it dead, and with its head
He went galumphing back.

NO, I DIDN'T FEEL GOOD. In fact, I felt goofy.

But I sat in a chair back in the corner of Pete's office, with Pete barking orders to half a dozen people, in person and over the phone, and I felt glad that he was paying no attention to me.

He was holding my case in abeyance as being less important than the disappearance of Barnaby Jones and Miles Harrison. Maybe he had it down as a figment of my drunken imagination.

I kept wishing that he was right, but I knew better.

As soon as he got the report from Walter that the body was really there, he'd swarm all over me with questions. But I was only too glad to wait because then—with a body in hand, so to speak—the answers I'd have to give him would sound a lot more plausible.

The office was taking on a fuzzy look, and my tongue was starting to feel like an angora kitten. It was easier to keep my eyes shut than try to make them see straight. All I really wanted was to get this over with, go home and slide into bed.

But I heard Pete walking out of the office and opened my eyes and stood up. There was one thing I felt curious about and now was the time to find out. I walked over to his desk and picked up the Yehudi Smith calling card. I held it close to my eyes, and—yes, there was the little union label in the corner and the number seventeen under it. Either it had been printed in my own shop, or someone had gone to a little trouble to make it seem that it had. The type was ten-point Garamond. I had Garamond in stock.

I was putting the card down thoughtfully when Pete came back and saw me.

"What's the idea of that card?" he asked.

"I was just wondering," I told him. "I didn't print it, and Jerry Klosterman didn't either, or I'd have seen the order for it. I'd remember a name like that."

He laughed without humor. "Who wouldn't. Listen, Doc. I've done everything I can do at the moment about the Jones and Harrison business. The search is organized, and we'll find them. But until then—well, let's get back to this Wentworth place business. You say a man you don't know took you out there?"

I nodded.

"Anyone see him with you? What I mean is—can you prove it?"

"No, Pete. You'll have to take my word for it. That and the fact that he's still out there, dead."

"We'll skip that till I get the report. This card?" He looked at it and scowled. "Any other souvenirs?"

I shook my head, and then remembered.

"This," I said, and took the key from my pocket and handed it to him. Again, somehow it looked familiar. But all Yale keys look alike. Still, the minute I'd given it to him, I wished I hadn't. It would probably turn out to open something at the Courier office. It might be as phony as that calling card.

"He gave you this key?" Pete asked.

"No, not exactly. I found it at the Wentworth house, but it may not be important."

Walter Hanswert came in without knocking. Walter is the man who does most of the work for the sheriff's office, but Pete Lane has the job and draws the pay. You'll find some hardworking horse like Walter back of every politically-elected sheriff or else the mechanism of law and order goes to pot.

"Anything?" Pete said.

"Not a lead, Pete. I drove slow all the way back from Burlington, looking for any place a car might have skidded off the road or any sign of something to help us. No dice."

"How about the Wentworth house, Walter?"

"I stopped there. Not a thing. I went through it fast, from attic to cellar."

Maybe you stop being surprised after a while. This didn't really jar me.

"Walter, were you in the living room?" I said. "Didn't you find a glass table and a bottle on the floor?"

"Nope. That's the room Pete said to search. I even looked under all the dust covers. Couple of tables there, cloth—covered, but neither of them glass, and no bottle. Front door of the house was open."

"I left it open, I guess," I said.

My knees were getting that way again. I didn't want to argue, but I had to.

"Cuss it, Pete!" I cried. "There was a body there. Somebody took it away. Heaven knows why. Heaven knows what any of this is all about, but I didn't imagine they'd clean up things so quick."

He put a gentle hand on my shoulder. "Doc, Walter will drive you home. Sleep it off."

~§~

The word "sleep" got me. Oh, I knew quite well that I wasn't going to sleep off what had happened. But I could, and wanted to, sleep off this fuzziness. Tomorrow, in the clear light of day, maybe I could add things up and make sense out of them.

A few hours' sleep, I told myself, just two or three hours, and everything might look different.

"Okay, Pete," I said. "Perhaps you're right."

"Got your car here?"

"In front." I should have left it go at that, but my tongue was loose. "We took Smith's car out to the Wentworth's place, but mine was out there after he was killed. I don't know how that happened."

"Just a minute," said Pete. His face looked different. "Your car's really downstairs? I thought you had it blocked up? You had it out tonight?"

"Yes and no, Pete. I didn't take it out of the garage but it's out just the same."

"It's in front," Walter said. "I saw it."

Pete Lane looked at his assistant, and then back at me. "And you had it out on the Dartown Pike tonight, Doc?"

"I told you that," I said impatiently. I didn't know what he was getting at, but I didn't like the way he was doing it.

"Doc, you never liked Barnaby Jones, did you?"

"Barnaby?" I was surprised. "He's a stuffed shirt and a miser and a prig. No, I don't like him. Why?"

He didn't answer. He leaned back against the desk and stared into the far corner of the room, with his lips pursed as though he was whistling, but no sound coming out of them.

When he spoke, he didn't look at me this time. And his voice was soft. Almost soothing.

"Doc, we're going to take a look at that car of yours," he said. "You can wait up. No, you come along with us, and then I'll drive you home."

I didn't get the idea, but I didn't care particularly. Just so I got home, and the sooner the better.

We went outside, Pete, Walter and I, and I noticed that they worked it so I walked between them.

My car was parked right outside the door, and the sheriff's car, which Walter had used to drive to Burlington and back, was in front of it. An open roadster with the top down.

Pete opened the door of my coupe and looked in. He pulled a flashlight out of his pocket and flashed it around inside, and looked carefully at the seat cushions and the floorboards. He looked carefully, but didn't seem to find anything.

He fished through an assortment of junk in the glove compartment, and then reached into the door pocket. His face changed and he pulled his hand out slowly with a revolver in it. He held it by the cylinder between his thumb and forefinger, just the way he'd first got hold of it.

"This yours, Doc?"

"No," I said.

He looked at me, hard, for a second or two and then sniffed at the end of the muzzle.

"Either hasn't been fired," he said, "or it's been cleaned." He was talking to Walter, not to me. "Let's look further."

He turned the gun over and held the lens of his flashlight close to the end of the butt. Even from where I stood back on the sidewalk I could see there was a smear there. A smear that might have been blood.

Pete Lane took a clean handkerchief from his pocket. It was folded and he shook it open and put it down on the running board of the coupe and laid the pistol gently on top of it.

"Where's the key to the rumble, Doc?" Pete asked me. "I'm afraid we'll have to look in there."

I shook my head. "Haven't got it. With me, I mean. When I blocked up the car I took the keys off my ring and left them in the drawer of my desk. The one at home."

He turned and looked back in the car aiming his flashlight at the instrument panel. The ignition key was in the lock there, but there were no other keys with it.

"That one isn't in your desk at home," said Pete. He walked around to the back of the car and stared at the lock in the handle of the rumble seat.

He looked at it a minute, then reached into his pocket and took out a key. The key I'd handed him. The key that had been on the glass table beside the "DRINK ME" bottle. The key that should have been the key to the little door into the garden where Alice had found the Two, Seven and Five of Hearts painting white roses red so the Queen wouldn't order their heads chopped off.

Pete put the key into the lock of the rumble seat and it fitted, and turned. He lifted the lid.

From where I stood, all I could see was a small brown leather grip, but I recognized it. It was the grip that Barnaby Jones used to carry the payroll money in, from Carmel City to Burlington.

But the grip wasn't resting on the seat. It was resting on something that was lying on the seat or it wouldn't have stuck up that way. I heard the hissing sound of Pete Lane sucking in his breath, and Walter Hanswert took a quick step to look down into the rumble seat, too.

I didn't. I didn't have to be sober to guess what was in there, and I'd already seen one murdered man tonight.

Somebody had done a beautiful job of something. I'd come galumphing back from my date with a Jabberwock carrying, not its head, but my own, on a silver platter to the police.

And shades of Old Henderson, what a story I had to go with the bodies of Barnaby Jones and Miles Harrison! A story based on a little man named Yehudli—the little man who wasn't there! Yehudi whom no one but myself had ever seen. I'd given the sheriff my two souvenirs of the evening and one had been printed in my own shop and the other was the key to my own car and the incriminating evidence in it.

I don't know whether I was suddenly very drunk or very sober to do what I did. But like a flash of lightning I had a picture of myself in court or an alienist's office telling him about a glass-topped table and a bottle labeled "DRINK ME" and the death of Yehudi the vanishing corpse.

I lunged for the running board of my coupe and got the pistol Pete had left there and forgotten for the moment in the excitement of his find in the rumble seat.

Pete yelled at Walter and Walter dived for me, but too late. I had straightened up with the pistol in my hand before he got within grabbing distance and he stepped back.

"Now, Doc," said Pete, in a wheedling voice, as one would use to a child. But there was fear in his eyes, plenty of it, although Walter's a brave man. He thought he was facing a homicidal maniac.

I didn't try to disillusion him. I didn't even have my finger inside the trigger guard. If he'd reached out and grasped the gun, I'd have let him take it.

"Step out from behind there, Pete," I said. "Both of you back into the courthouse."

I groped behind me and took the ignition key out of my own car and pocketed it. I wasn't going to take that car, with its ghastly burden. But I didn't want them to use it either.

I moved toward the sheriff's car while they sidled cautiously across the sidewalk toward the courthouse. I was gambling that Walter hadn't bothered to take the keys out when he'd come upstairs to report. And I was right.

They stepped through the doorway and the instant they were out of sight I heard running footsteps. Pete was sprinting for his office for his own gun, if I guessed correctly, and Walter would be taking the switchboard to block all the roads out of town.

That was all right by me. I wasn't going out of town. I put the murder gun down on the curb—I didn't want it any more than I wanted my own car—and got in Pete's car and drove off.

Chapter 6

Hidden Foe

"And hast thou slain the Jabberwock?
Come to my arms, my beamish boy!
O frabjous day! Callooh! Callay!"
He chortled in his joy.

SWINGING AROUND THE CORNER, I gunned the engine to get up speed, and then shut it off. On momentum, I swung it into the alley back of the courthouse and let it coast to a stop.

Looking up, I could see the lighted window of Pete's room, and could imagine the frantic telephoning going on right now to stop and hold a car that would stand, probably unnoticed, for the rest of the night, right under his window

I got out quietly by stepping over the door instead of opening it, and walked up the alley, going on tiptoe until I was out of earshot of the courthouse.

They'd be looking for me, I knew, at the outskirts of town, not in the middle of it. The place I had in mind ought to be safe for a couple of hours, at least. And I didn't care, beyond that. I wasn't making a getaway. I just wanted a chance to do a few chores and think out a few things before I gave myself up. Gave myself up, that is, unless I could work out my plans.

I went along the alley two blocks and turned in at the back door of Smiley's. Pete and his men, I felt sure, would be too busy to do any drinking for a while.

"Hi, Doc," Smiley said. "Thought you'd be asleep long ago." He laughed his meaningless laugh.

"Old Henderson, double," I said. "I've been asleep ever since I left here, Smiley. Maybe I can wake up. Leave that bottle on the bar."

There was a pinochle game in the back corner. Outside of that I had the place to myself.

I downed the double Henderson and felt a little better. I gave it time to get home and took another. There's a second-wind stage of inebriation, and hitting that was my only chance to get my mind hitting on six cylinders. Sobriety's good for thinking, too, but I hadn't a chance of getting sober for hours yet. The other way was quicker.

I looked at the calendar a while, but that didn't help. Things went in dizzying circles inside my head. Who's Yehudi? Where is what's left of him? Why did he drink the "DRINK ME"? Was he really expecting other members of some nitwit organization to show up there?

Had he been kidding me, or was he being kidded?

Jabberwocks. Glass tables with "DRINK ME" bottles and keys that should have been gold and led into a garden, but which were Yale and led into the nuthouse by way of a rumble seat. And of all names, Yehudi Smith!

Oh, it would have been funny, it would have been a wow of a practical joke, if there hadn't been three corpses cluttering up the scenery, and the fact that this meant the end of my freedom, whether I ended up in a bughouse or a hoosegow. Or at the end of a rope.

No, looking at the calendar didn't help.

"Give me a deck, Smiley," I said.

I took another drink while he got it, and deliberately I didn't think at all while I counted out the stacks for solitaire. Then, as I started the game, I let go. I mean, I didn't try to think, but I didn't try not to. I just relaxed.

Red queen on a black king. Wasn't the Red Queen the one who met Alice in the second square, and told her about the six squares she'd have to go through before she could be a queen herself?

And a black jack for the red queen.

But that was a red chess queen, not a card queen. The one who ran so fast. "A slow sort of country," she'd told Alice. "Now here, you see, it takes all the running you can do to keep in the same place."

An ace up on top, and then I took another drink before I put the red six on the black seven. The cards looked different now—sharp of outline, crystal clear.

Like my mind felt. Ten on the jack.

Yehudi had been a pawn. A sucker, like me. Somebody had moved him. Somebody had hired him to come there and pull a razzle-dazzle on me. To give me a story that nobody'd believe in ten lifetimes, a story whose only proof was a card some friend of mine had printed in my own shop. Yehudi had been made as incredible as possible, from Christian name to "DRINK ME."

There was only one answer to Yehudi. A character actor at liberty, probably hired in New York and brought here for the purpose of framing me. And he framed himself. Given a set of instructions for the evening that included the planted drink-me bottle, and went beyond it, because he hadn't been told what was in that bottle.

So Yehudi wasn't in on the real play. Somebody had hired Yehudi to play what he thought was an elaborate practical joke.

Nine on the ten, and bring up a deuce for my ace on top.

~§~

Somebody who knew me intimately, and who knew how I felt Thursday evenings and my predilection for Lewis Carroll and nonsense in general, and that I'd be sure to fall for a gag like Yehudi's. Someone who came to see me at the print shop and at home, once in a while, at least. Maybe to play chess with me?

Anyway, there was the other red queen.

"How you coming?" Smiley asked.

"I'm in the fifth square," I told him. "I crossed the third by railroad, with the Gnat. And I think I just crossed the brook into the fifth."

"Squares? There ain't any squares in solitaire."

"Cards are rectangles," I said. "And what's a square but a rectangle somebody sat on? You're a swell guy, Smiley, but shut up."

He laughed and moved off down the bar.

I took another drink, but just a short one. The edges of the cards and the outlines of the pips on them were very sharp and clear now. No fuzziness, no mussiness.

Another ace for the top row.

Because, if the money was still in that bag that was planted in my car, there was only one person who benefited by what had happened tonight. The man who'd inherit Barnaby Jones' factory and his fortune. The one man who'd need a scapegoat, because of his a priori motive.

That was the sixth brook. I had a hunch I was entering the seventh square now But I took a look back to be sure.

Alvin Carey would inherit his uncle's fortune. Al knew me pretty well. We played chess, and somebody who played chess had engineered the set—up tonight. Al Carey knew my screwy literary tastes, and my Thursday night habits. He'd dropped in here, in Smiley's, early. And that would have been to check up that I was running true to form.

Al Carey had enough money to have hired a character actor to lead me to the slaughter. Al Carey was smart enough to have made a dupe of the actor instead of an accomplice who could blackmail him afterwards.

Al Carey had everything.

Al Carey had me in a cleft stick. He'd finagled me into a situation so utterly preposterous that the more of the truth I told, the crazier I'd look. Nuttier than peanut brittle I'd look.

"Smiley," I said. "Come here. I want to ask you something."

He moved along the bar toward me, and grinned. He always acted that way when he was puzzled.

"One more brook to cross," I told him. "But it's wider than the Mississippi. What good does it do to know something if you can't prove it?"

"Well," he said, "what good does it do you if you can prove it?"

"Smiley," I said, "I reach the king-row, and I'm crowned. But this side of that last brook, I'm still a pawn, in pawn. What do you know about Alvin Carey?"

"Huh? He's a crackpot like you, Doc, but I don't like him. I think he's a sneak. But he's smart."

"Smiley," I said, "you surprise me. And for once I mean what I say. Someday I'll write an editorial about you, if I ever get a chance to write another editorial. What else do you know about Alvin, to his detriment? To his disadvantage, I mean."

"Well, he's yellow."

"I'm not sure of that," I said. "The draft board turned him down, if that's what you mean. Something about a trick knee. And—well, I know one stunt he pulled recently that took a lot of cool nerve."

"But don't you remember the time last year when a little chimney fire broke out at his place?" said Smiley, quickly. "A little smoke, that's all. But he ran out in his pajamas without waking anybody else up to tell 'em. He didn't stop till he reached the fire station, because he was too excited and scared to think there was a thing as a telephone."

"Smiley," I answered, "I bow before you. It's an outside chance. Pete's got his hands full right now, and is working like a Trojan to find somebody. Probably he hasn't called Alvin Carey yet. Shut up, sage, and let me think fast."

I closed my eyes and opened them again.

"I need three things, and I need them quick," I said. "I need a gun, and I need a candle stub, and I need a bottle of some kind of a cleaning fluid that smells like gasoline but is non-inflammable."

"Carbozol. I got a bottle of it, sure. And a candle, because once in a while the lights here go on the blink. But no gun."

"Smiley, this is in a desperate hurry; and I can't explain," I said. "But take a plain pint bottle, no label, and fill it with Carbozol for me. And get me a candle. Cut it off short, to half an inch or so. A quarter of an inch, if you can cut it that fine. And have you got anything that looks like a gun?"

For a moment Smiley rubbed his chin thoughtfully. Then he grinned.

"I got an old thirty-two pistol I took away from a drunk in here one night when he got waving it around. But there ain't no bullets. I had the firing pin filed off so I could give it to my kid."

"That's the gun I want," I told him. "Quick, Smiley, get it and the other things for me. And I'll let you finish this game of solitaire for me. And it's going to play out, too."

I sat back in the chair and waited for him to return.

And then, with the stuff he gave me safely stowed in my pockets, I went out the back door and cut through alleys as fast as I could travel without getting out of breath. Pretty soon I got there.

There wasn't any lights on, which was a good sign. It meant that maybe Pete Lane hadn't got around yet to notifying the nearest of kin. If I knew Pete, he'd try to get me first, so he'd have crime and criminal all in the same report and make a good impression on Carey. For, as Barnaby's heir Al was going to be the richest guy in town. Unless my wild idea worked.

It was a warm evening and some of the downstairs windows were open, and that was good, too. The screens were put on with turnbolts from the outside and I took one off without making any noise.

I got inside, and I was quiet about it. I didn't kid myself that Al Carey might be asleep after the night's work he'd done. But he'd be in bed, playing possum, waiting for a telephone call.

Inside the window, I took off my shoes and left them. I sneaked into the hallway and up the stairs. Outside Al's door, which was an inch ajar I took a deep breath.

Then I stepped inside and flicked on the light switch. I had the gun ready in my hand and I pointed it at Al Carey.

"Be quiet," I warned him.

The flick of the light switch had brought him bolt upright in bed. He was in pajamas, all right, and his hair was tousled. But his eyes showed he hadn't been asleep.

I didn't give him a chance to think it over. I walked right up to the edge of the bed, keeping that broken pistol aimed smack between his eyes, and then before he could guess what I was going to do, I raised it and brought the butt down on top of his head.

Chapter 7

Test by Fire

'Twas brilli', and the slithy toves
* Did gyre and gimble in the wabe:*
All mimsy were the borogoves,
* And the morne raths outgrabe.*

THAT WAS THE TRICKIEST THING I had to do—to gauge that blow just right. I'd never hit a man over the head before.

And if this stunt I had in mind was going to work, it all depended on conking him out, not for too long, and without killing him. Just long enough for me to tie him up, because I couldn't have done that and held the gun on him at the same time.

If the blow killed him it wouldn't have hurt my conscience too much. Miles Harrison had been a nice guy. So had Yehudi Smith, whatever his real name was. But if the blow killed Carey, well, there'd be one more evidence of my homicidal mania for the police.

Al went out like a light, but his heart was still beating. And I worked fast at tying him. I used everything I could find, bathrobe cords, belts, neckties—he had almost a hundred of them—and I tore one sheet into strips.

He was swathed like a mummy when I got through, tied with his head and shoulders braced up against the head of the bed so he could see the bed itself. And a handkerchief inside his mouth held in by a scarf around the outside made a good gag. I used the strips of sheeting to tie him so he couldn't roll off the bed.

But I left his right arm free from the elbow down.

Then I slapped his face until his eyes opened. They looked groggy, at first, so I wet a washrag in the bathroom and sloshed him a few times with that. When he tried to get loose, I knew he knew what was going on.

I grinned at him. "Hello, Al," I said.

I took the pint bottle of non-inflammable cleaning fluid out of my pocket and took out the cork. Smiley had given me the right stuff.

It smelled like gasoline, all right.

I poured it over Al and over the bed, all around him.

Then, down by his knees, on a spot where the mattress was pretty wet with it, I put the half-inch stub of candle. I struck a match and held it to the wick.

"Better stop struggling, Al," I said. "You'll knock this over."

He stopped, all right. He lay as still as though he were dead, and his horrified eyes stared at that burning wick. Stared at it with the terrible fear of a pyrophobiac. For that's what Smiley's story of Al Carey and the chimney fire had reminded me of Al had an abnormal, psychopathic fear of fire.

I took out of my pocket the notebook I always carry, and a stub of pencil, and put them down within reach of his free right hand.

"Any time you want to write, Al," I told him. Turning my back on him, I walked over to the window. I waited a minute and then looked back. I had to avoid looking at his eyes.

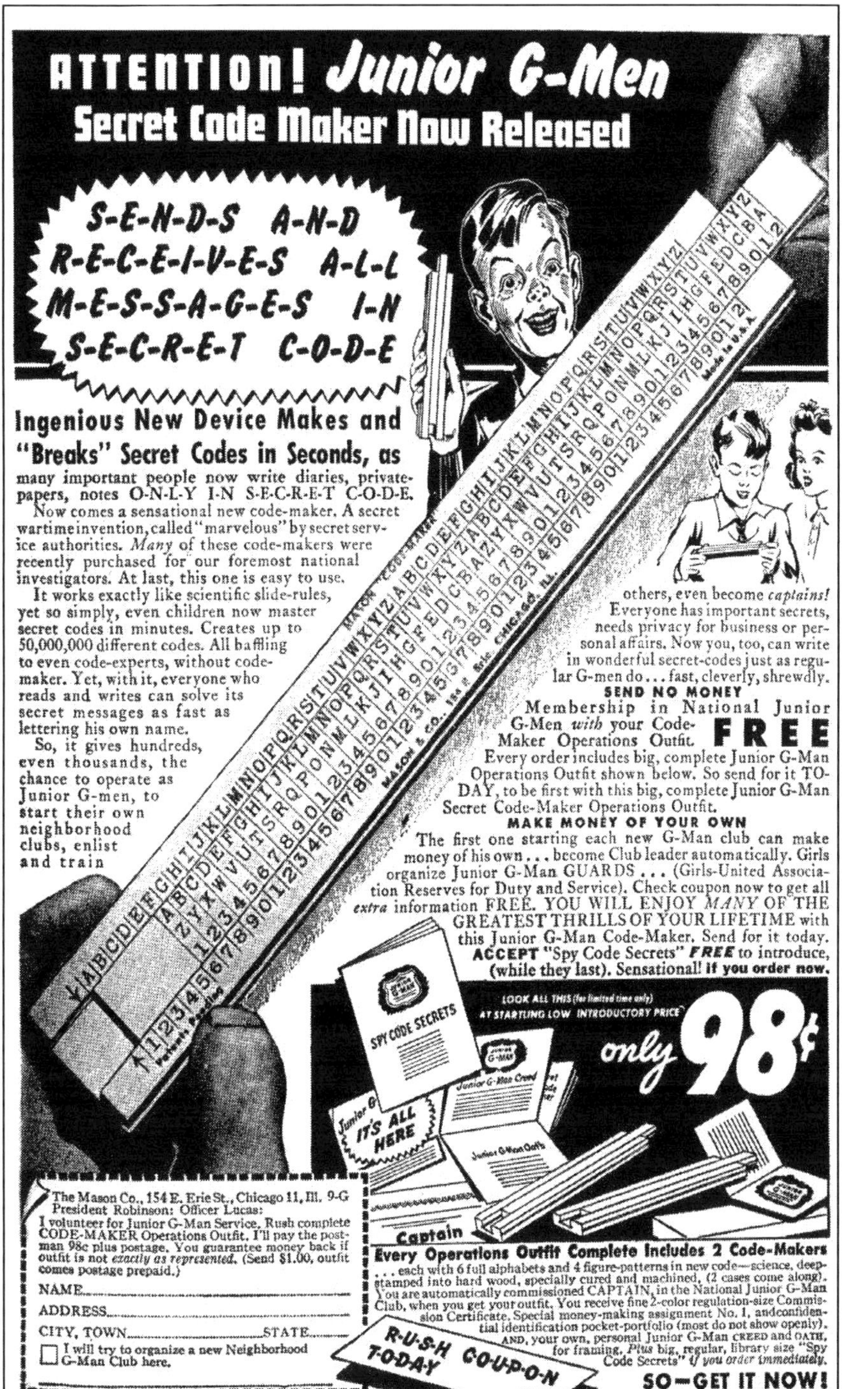
ATTENTION! Junior G-Men
Secret Code Maker Now Released
S-E-N-D-S A-N-D R-E-C-E-I-V-E-S A-L-L M-E-S-S-A-G-E-S I-N S-E-C-R-E-T C-O-D-E
Ingenious New Device Makes and "Breaks" Secret Codes in Seconds, as many important people now write diaries, private-papers, notes O-N-L-Y I-N S-E-C-R-E-T C-O-D-E.
Now comes a sensational new code-maker. A secret wartime invention, called "marvelous" by secret service authorities. Many of these code-makers were recently purchased for our foremost national investigators. At last, this one is easy to use.
It works exactly like scientific slide-rules, yet so simply, even children now master secret codes in minutes. Creates up to 50,000,000 different codes. All baffling to even code-experts, without code-maker. Yet, with it, everyone who reads and writes can solve its secret messages as fast as lettering his own name.
So, it gives hundreds, even thousands, the chance to operate as Junior G-men, to start their own neighborhood clubs, enlist and train others, even become captains! Everyone has important secrets, needs privacy for business or personal affairs. Now you, too, can write in wonderful secret-codes just as regular G-men do . . . fast, cleverly, shrewdly.
SEND NO MONEY
Membership in National Junior G-Men with your Code-Maker Operations Outfit. FREE
Every order includes big, complete Junior G-Man Operations Outfit shown below. So send for it TODAY, to be first with this big, complete Junior G-Man Secret Code-Maker Operations Outfit.
MAKE MONEY OF YOUR OWN
The first one starting each new G-Man club can make money of his own . . . become Club leader automatically. Girls organize Junior G-Man GUARDS . . . (Girls-United Association Reserves for Duty and Service). Check coupon now to get all extra information FREE. YOU WILL ENJOY MANY OF THE GREATEST THRILLS OF YOUR LIFETIME with this Junior G-Man Code-Maker. Send for it today.
ACCEPT "Spy Code Secrets" FREE to introduce, (while they last). Sensational! If you order now.
LOOK ALL THIS (for limited time only) AT STARTLING LOW INTRODUCTORY PRICE
only 98¢
SPY CODE SECRETS
IT'S ALL HERE
Captain
Every Operations Outfit Complete Includes 2 Code-Makers
. . . each with 6 full alphabets and 4 figure-patterns in new code—science, deep-stamped into hard wood, specially cured and machined, (2 cases come along). You are automatically commissioned CAPTAIN, in the National Junior G-Man Club, when you get your outfit. You receive fine 2-color regulation-size Commission Certificate. Special money-making assignment No. 1, andconfidential identification pocket-portfolio (most do not show openly). AND, your own, personal Junior G-Man CREED and OATH, for framing. Plus big, regular, library size "Spy Code Secrets" if you order immediately.
The Mason Co., 154 E. Erie St., Chicago 11, Ill. 9-G
President Robinson: Officer Lucas:
I volunteer for Junior G-Man Service. Rush complete CODE-MAKER Operations Outfit. I'll pay the postman 98c plus postage. You guarantee money back if outfit is not exactly as represented. (Send $1.00, outfit comes postage prepaid.)
NAME
ADDRESS
CITY, TOWN STATE
I will try to organize a new Neighborhood G-Man Club here.
R-U-S-H COUPON T-O-D-A-Y
SO—GET IT NOW!

"It'll burn down in ten minutes," I said. "You'll just about have time if you start writing. I want it in full, the main details, anyway, addressed to Pete Lane. And tell him where to find the body you hid or buried. The actor. Tell him where to look for the glass-topped table, and the bottle that had the poison in it. You'll have to write fast. If you finish in time, I'll pick up the candle."

I said it calmly, as though it didn't matter.

Then I turned away again. Only seconds later, I heard the scratch of the pencil. . .

It was nine o'clock when Jerry and I finished remaking the paper. We'd had to rip it wide open to make room. For three murders in one evening was the biggest thing that had ever happened in Carmel City.

It rushed us more than we had been rushed in years, but we didn't mind that. Nor the extra trouble. Hot news never seems like work.

The phone rang, and I answered it, and it was Jay Evers.

Jerry was staring at me in utter amazement when I put the receiver back after I finished talking.

"Who the devil were you talking to like that?" he asked me.

"Evers," I told him. "He wanted to buy the Courier, and I said no."

"But couldn't you have said no without that embroidery on it? Why insult him like you did? He'll never speak to you again."

"That was the idea," I told him. I grinned cheerfully. "Look, Jerry, if I didn't insult him, he might ask me again tomorrow"

"But what's that got to do with what you're telling me?"

"And tomorrow, Jerry, I'm going to have the ancestor of all hangovers, and I'd sell the paper to him, and I don't want to sell it. I like the Courier, I like Carmel City. And I enjoy being free and not in the boobyhatch and the hoosegow. So let the presses roll!"

"Doc, you better sit down before you fall down!"

But he was too late. Seconds too late.

Thrilling Mystery, Summer 1944
Later expanded into the novel, Night of the Jabberwock, 1950

The Cat from Siam

WE WERE in the middle of our third game of chess when it happened.

It was late in the evening—eleven thirty-five, to be exact. Jack Sebastian and I were in the living room of my two-room bachelor apartment. We had the chess game set up on the card table in front of the fireplace, in which the gas grate burned cheerfully.

Jack looked cheerful too. He was wreathed in smoke from his smelliest pipe and he had me a pawn down and held a positional edge. I'd taken the first two games, but this one looked like his. It didn't look any less so when he moved his knight and said, "Check." My rook was forked along with the king. There didn't seem to be anything I could do about it except give up the rook for the knight.

I looked up at the Siamese cat who was sleepily watching us from her place of vantage on the mantel.

"Looks like he's got us, Beautiful," I said. "One should never play with a policeman."

"I wish you wouldn't do that, dammit," Jack said. *"You* give me the willies."

"Anything's fair in love and chess," I told him. "If it gives you the willies to have me talk to a cat, that's fine. Besides, Beautiful doesn't kibitz. If you see her give me any signals, I'll concede."

"Go ahead and move," he said, irritably. "You've got only one move that takes you out of check, so make it. I take your rook, and then—"

There was a noise, then, that I didn't identify for a second because it was made up of a *crack* and a *ping* and a *thud.* It wasn't until I turned to where part of the sound came from that I realized what it had been. There was a little round hole in the glass of the window.

The *crack* had been a shot, the *ping* had been the bullet coming through the glass—and the *thud* had been the bullet going into the wall behind me!

But by the time I had that figured out, the chessmen were spilling into my lap.

"Down, quick!" Jack Sebastian was saying sharply.

Whether I got there myself, or Jack pushed me there, I was on the floor. And by that time I was thinking.

Grabbing the cord of the lamp, I jerked the plug out of the wall and we were in darkness except for the reddish-yellow glow of the gas grate in the fireplace. The handle of that was on Jack's side, and I saw him, on his knees, reach out and turn it.

Then there was complete darkness. I looked toward where the window should be, but it was a moonless night and I couldn't see even the faintest outline of the window. I slid sideways until I bumped against the sofa. Jack Sebastian's voice came to me out of the darkness.

"Have you got a gun, Brian?" he asked.

I shook my head and then realized he couldn't see me. "No," I said. "What would I be doing with a gun?"

My voice, even to me, sounded hoarse and strained. I heard Jack moving.

"The question is," he said, "what's the guy outside doing with one? Anybody after you, pal?"

"N-no," I said. "At least, not—"

I heard a click that told me Jack had found the telephone. He gave a number and added, "Urgent, sister. This is the police." Then his voice changed tone and he said, "Brian, what's the score? Don't you know anything about who or why—"

He got his connection before he could finish the question and his voice changed pitch again.

"Jack Sebastian, Cap," he said. "Forty-five University Lane. Forty-five University Lane. Somebody just took a potshot in the window here. Head the squad cars this way from all directions they can come from. Especially the campus—that's the logical way for him to lose himself if he's on foot. Start 'em. I'll hold the line."

Then he was asking me again, "Brian, what can I add? Quick."

"Tell 'em to watch for a tall, slender, young man," I said. "Twenty-one years old, thin face, blond hair."

"The hell," he said. "*Alistair Cole?*"

"Could be," I told him. "It's the only guess I can make. I can be wrong, but—"

"Hold it." Whoever he'd been talking to at the police station was back on the line. Without mentioning the name, Jack gave the description I'd just given to him. He said, "Put that on the radio and come back in."

Again to me, "Anything else?"

"Yes," I said. "Tell 'em to converge those squad cars on Doc Roth's place, Two-ten University Lane. Forget sending them here. Get them *there*. Quick!"

"Why? You think if it's Alistair Cole, he's going for Doc Roth, too?"

"Don't argue. Tell 'em. Hurry!"

I was on my feet by now, trying to grope my way across the pitch black room to the telephone to join him. I stepped on a chessman and it rolled and nearly threw me. I swore and got my lighter out of my pocket and flicked the wheel.

The tiny flame lighted part of the room dimly. The faint wavering light threw long dancing shadows. On the mantel, the Siamese was standing, her back arched and her tail thick. Her blue eyes caught and held the light like blue jewels.

"Put that out, you fool," Jack snapped.

"He isn't standing there at the window," I said impatiently. "He wouldn't stay there after we doused the light. Tell them what I said about Roth's, quick."

"Hello, Cap. Listen, get some of the cars to Two-ten University Lane instead. Two-one-oh. Fast. No, I don't know what this is about either. Just do it. We can find out later. The guy who took a shot here might go there. That's all I know. So long."

He put the receiver back on the hook to end argument. I was there by that time, and had the receiver in my hand.

"Sorry, Jack," I said, and shoved him out of the way. I gave Dr. Roth's number and added, "Keep ringing till they answer."

I held the receiver tight against my ear and waited. I realized I was still holding up the tiny torch of the cigarette lighter and I snapped it shut. The room snapped again into utter darkness.

"You stay in here," Jack said. "I'm going out."

"Don't be a fool. He's got a gun."

There was a sharp knock on the door, and we neither of us moved until the knock came again, louder. Then we heard Professor Winton's high, nervous voice.

"Brian, was that a shot a minute ago? Are you all right?"

Jack muttered something under his breath and groped for the door handle. In the receiver against my ear I could hear Dr. Roth's phone still ringing. He hadn't answered yet. I put my hand over the mouthpiece.

"I'm all right, Dr. Winton," I called out.

By that time, Jack had found the knob and opened the door. Light streamed into the room from the hallway outside, and he stepped through the door quickly and closed it behind him.

"Someone shot through the window, Doctor," I heard him say, "but everything's under control. We've called the police. Better get back inside your room, though, till they get here."

Dr. Winton's voice said something, excitedly, but I didn't hear what, because Jeanette Roth's voice, husky and beautiful, but definitely sleepy, was saying "Hello," in my ear. I forgot Jack and Winton and concentrated my attention on the phone.

I talked fast. "This is Brian Carter, Jeanette," I said. "Listen, this is important. It's maybe life and death. Just do what I say and don't argue. First, be sure all the lights in your house are out, all doors and windows locked tight— bolted, if they've got bolts. Then don't answer the door, unless you're sure it's the police—or me. I'm coming over, too, but the police may get there first."

"Brian, what on earth—?"

"Don't argue, darling," I said. "Do those things, fast. Lights out. Everything locked. And don't answer the door unless it's me or the police!"

I hung up on her. I knew she'd do it faster that way than if I stayed on the line.

I groped my way through the dark room and out into the lighted hallway. The door to Dr. Winton's room, just across from my apartment, was closed, and there was nobody in the hallway. I ran to the front door and out onto the porch.

Out front on the sidewalk, Jack Sebastian was turning around, looking. He had something in his hand. When he turned so light from the street lamp down on the corner shone on it, I could see that it was a long-barreled pistol. I ran out to join him.

"From Winton. It's a target pistol, a twenty-two. But it's better than throwing stones. Look, you sap, get back in there. You got no business out in the open."

I told him I was going to Roth's place, and started down the sidewalk at a trot.

"What's the score?" he called after me. "What makes you think it was that Cole kid and why the excitement about Roth?"

I saved my breath by not answering him. There'd be plenty of time for all that later. I could hear him running behind me. We pounded up the steps onto the porch of Dr. Roth's place.

"It's Brian Carter—and the police!" I called out while I rang the bell.

Maybe Jack Sebastian wasn't exactly the police, in the collective sense, but he was a detective, the youngest full-fledged detective on the force. Anyway, it wasn't the time for nice distinctions. I quit leaning on the bell and hammered on the door, and then yelled again.

The key turned in the lock and I stepped back. The door opened on the chain and Jeanette's white face appeared in the crack. She wasn't taking any chances. Then, when she saw us, she slid back the chain and opened the door.

"Brian, what," she began.

"Your father, Jeanette. Is he all right?"

"I—I knocked on his door after you phoned, Brian, and he didn't answer! The door's locked. Brian, what's *wrong?*"

~§~

Out front a car swung into the curb with a squealing of brakes and two big men got out of it. They came running up the walk toward us and Jack stepped to the edge of the porch, where light from a street lamp would fall on his face and identify him to the two men. It also gleamed on the gun dangling from his hand.

Jeanette swayed against me and I put my arm around her shoulders. She was trembling.

"Maybe everything's okay, Jeanette," I said. "Maybe your father's just sleeping soundly. Anyway, these are the police coming now, so *you're* safe."

I heard Jack talking to the two detectives who'd come in the squad car, and then one of them started around the house, on the outside, using a flashlight. Jack and the other one joined us in the doorway.

"Let's go," Jack said. "Where's your father's room, Miss Roth?"

"Just a second, Jack," I said. I snapped on the hall lights and then went into the library and turned on the lights there and looked around to be sure nobody was there.

"You wait in here, Jeanette," I said then. "We'll go up and try your father's door again, and if he still doesn't answer, we'll have to break—"

Footsteps pounded across the porch again and the other detective, the one who'd started around the house, stood in the doorway.

"There's a ladder up the side of the house to a window on the second floor—northwest corner room," he said. "Nobody around unless he's upstairs, in there. Shall I go up the ladder, Sebastian?"

Jack looked at me, and I knew that he and I were thinking the same thing. The killer had come here first, and there wasn't any hurry now.

"I'll go up the ladder," he said. "We won't have to break the door now. Will you two guys search the house from attic to cellar and turn all the lights on and leave them on? And, Brian, you stay here with Miss Roth. Can I borrow your flashlight, Wheeler?"

I noticed that, by tacit consent, Jack was taking charge of the case and of the older detectives. Because, I presumed, he was the first one on the scene and had a better idea what it was all about.

One of the men handed over a flashlight and Jack went outside. I led Jeanette into the library

"Brian," she asked, "do you think Dad is—that something has happened to Dad?"

"We'll know for sure in a minute, darling. Why make guesses meanwhile? I don't know."

"But—what happened that made you call me up?"

"Jack and I were playing chess at my place," I told her. "Someone took a shot through the window. At me, not at Jack. The bullet went into the wall behind me and just over my head. I—well, I had a sudden hunch who might have shot at me, and if my hunch was right, I thought he'd consider your father his enemy, too. I'm afraid he may be—mad."

"Alistair Cole?"

"Have you noticed anything strange about him?" I asked her.

"Yes. He's always scared me, Brian, the way he's acted. And just last night, Dad remarked that—"

She broke off, standing there rigidly. Footsteps were coming down the stairs. That would be Jack, of course. And the fact that he walked so slowly gave us the news in advance of his coming.

Anyway, when he stood in the doorway, Jeanette asked quietly, "Is he dead?" and Jack nodded.

Jeanette sat down on the sofa behind her and dropped her head into her hands, but she didn't cry.

"I'll phone headquarters," Jack said. "But first—you and he were alone in the house tonight, weren't you, Miss Roth?"

She looked up and her eyes were still dry. "Yes," she said. "Mother's staying overnight with my aunt—her sister—in town. This is going to hit her hard. Will you need me here? I—I think it would be best if I were the one to break it to her. I can dress and be there in half an hour. I can be back in an hour and a half. Will it be all right?"

Jack looked at me. "What do you think, Brian? You know this guy Cole and you know what this is all about. Would Miss Roth be in any danger if she left?"

"You could figure that yourself, Jack," I said. "Cole was here, alone in the house with her after he killed Dr. Roth, and he had all the time in the world because there hadn't been an alarm yet. But let me go with her, though, just to be sure."

He snorted. "Just to be sure—of *what?* He *is* after you, fine friend. Until we get Cole under lock and key—and throw away the key—you're not getting out from under my eye."

"All right," I said, "so I'm indispensable. But everybody isn't, and this place will be full of police in a few minutes. If I'm not mistaken, that sounds like another squad car coming now. Why not have one of the boys in it use it to drive Miss Roth over to her aunt's?"

He nodded. "Okay, Miss Roth. I'll stick my neck out—even though Headquarters may cut it off. And Wheeler and Brach have finished looking around upstairs, so it'll be okay for you to go to your room if you want to change that housecoat for a dress."

He went to the front door to let the new arrivals in.

"I'm awfully sorry, Jeanette," I said then. "I know that sounds meaningless, but—it's all I can think of to say."

She managed a faint smile. "You're a good egg, Brian. I'll be seeing you."

She held out her hand, and I took it. Then she ran up the stairs. Jack looked in at the doorway.

"I told the new arrivals to search the grounds," he said. "Not that they'll find anything, but it'll give 'em something to do. I got to phone Headquarters. You stay right here."

"Just a second, Jack," I said. "How was he killed?"

"A knife. Messy job. It was a psycho, all right."

"You say messy? Is there any chance Jeanette might go into—?"

He shook his head. "Wheeler's watching that door. He wouldn't let her go in. Well, I got to phone—"

"Listen, Jack. Tell me one thing. How long, about, has he been dead? I mean, is there any chance Cole could have come here after he shot at me? I might have thought of phoning here, or getting here a minute or two sooner. I'd feel responsible if my slowness in reacting, my dumbness—"

Jack was shaking his head. "I'm no M.E.," he said, "but Roth had been dead more than a few minutes when I found him. I'd say at least half an hour, maybe an hour."

He went to the phone and gave the Headquarters number. I heard his voice droning on, giving them the details of the murder and the attempted murder.

I sat there listening, with my eyes closed, taking in every word of it, but carefully keeping the elation off my face.

It had gone perfectly. Everything had worked out.

Whether or not they caught Alistair Cole—and they *would* catch him—nothing could go wrong now. It had come off perfectly.

I would never be suspected, and I stood to gain a million dollars—and Jeanette...

She came down the stairs slowly, as one approaching a reluctant errand. I waited for her at the foot of the staircase, my eyes on her beautiful face. There was shock there, but—as I had expected and was glad to see—not too much grief. Roth had been a cold, austere man. Not a man to be grieved for deeply, or long.

She stopped on the second step, her eyes level with mine and only inches away. I wanted to kiss her, but this was not the time. A little while and I would, I thought.

But I could look now, and I could dream. I could imagine my hand stroking that soft blonde hair. I could imagine those soft, misty blue eyes closed and my lips kissing the lids of them, kissing that soft white throat, her yielding lips. Then— My hand was on the newel post and she put hers over it. It almost seemed to burn.

"I wish I could go with you, darling," I said. "I wish there was something I could do to help you."

"I wish you could come with me too, Brian. But—your friend's right. And didn't you take an awful chance coming over here anyway—out in the open, with a madman out to kill you?"

"Jack was with me," I said.

Jack was calling to me from the library. "Coming," I said, and then I told Jeanette, "It's cool out, darling. Put a coat on over that thin dress."

She nodded absently. "I wish you could come with me, Brian. Mother likes you —"

I knew what she meant, what she was thinking. That things were going to be all right between us now. Her mother did like me. It was her stuffy, snobbish father who had stood in the way. Jack called again impatiently.

"Take care of yourself, Brian," Jeanette whispered quickly. "Don't take any chances, please."

She pressed my hand, then ran past me toward the coat closet. I saw that one of the detectives was waiting for her at the door. I went into the library. Jack was still sitting at the telephone table, jotting things into a notebook. He looked very intent and businesslike.

"Captain Murdock—he's head of Homicide—is on his way here," Jack said. "He'll be in charge of the case. That's why I wanted you to let the girl get out of here first. He might insist on her staying."

"What about you?" I asked him. "Aren't you staying on the case?"

He grinned a little. "I've got my orders. They're to keep you alive until Cole is caught. The Chief told me if anything happens to you, he'll take my badge away and shove it up my ear. From now on, pal, we're Siamese twins."

"Then how about finishing that chess game?" I said. "I think I can set up the men again."

He shook his head. "Life isn't that simple. Not for a while yet, anyway. We'll have to stick here until Cap Murdock gets here, and then I'm to take you into the Chiefs office. Yeah, the Chiefs going down there at this time of night."

It was after one when Jack took me into Chief Randall's office. Randall, a big, slow-moving man, yawned and shook hands with me across his desk.

"Sit down, Carter," he said, and yawned again.

I took the seat across from him. Jack Sebastian sat down in a chair at the end of the desk and started doodling with the little gold knife he wears on the end of a chain.

"This Roth is a big man," Chief Randall said. "The papers are going to give us plenty if we don't settle this quick."

"Right now, Chief," Jack said, "Alistair Cole is a bigger man. He's a homicidal maniac on the loose."

The Chief frowned. "We'll get him," he said. "We've got to. We've got him on the air. We've got his description to every railroad station and airport and bus depot. We're getting out fliers with his picture—as soon as we get one. The state patrolmen are watching for him. We'll have him in hours. We're doing everything."

"That's good," I told him. "But I don't think you'll find him on his way out of town. I think he'll stay here until he gets me—or until you get him."

"He'll know that you're under protection, Brian," Jack said. "Mightn't that make a difference? Wouldn't he figure the smartest thing to do would be to blow town and hide out for a few months, then come back for another try?"

I thought it over. "He might," I said, doubtfully. "But I don't think so. You see, he isn't thinking normally. He's under paranoiac compulsion, and the risks he takes aren't going to weight the balance too strongly on the safety side. He was out to kill Dr. Roth and then me. Now I'm no expert in abnormal psychology, but I think that if he'd missed on his first killing he might do as you suggested—go away and come back later when things had blown over. But he made his first kill. He stepped over the line. He's going to be under terrifically strong compulsion to finish the job right away—at any risk!"

Jack said, "One thing I don't get. Cole was probably standing right outside that window. We reacted quickly when that shot came, but not instantaneously. He should have had time for a second shot before we got the light out. Why didn't he take that second shot?"

"I can suggest a possibility," I told them. "I was in Alistair's room about a week ago. I've been there several times. He opened a drawer to take out his chess set for our game, and I happened to notice a pistol in the drawer. He slammed the drawer quickly when he saw me glancing that way, but I asked him about the pistol.

"He said it had been his brother's, and that he'd had it since his brother had died three years ago. He said it was a single-shot twenty-two caliber target pistol, the kind really fancy marksmen use in tournaments. I asked him if he went in for target shooting and he said no, he'd never shot it."

"Probably telling the truth about that," Chief Randall said, "since he missed your head a good six inches at—how far would it have been, Jack?"

"About twelve feet, if he'd been standing just outside the window. Farther, of course, if he'd been farther back." Jack turned to me. "Brian, how good a look did you get at the pistol? Was it a single-shot, the kind he described?"

"I think so," I said. "It wasn't either a revolver or an automatic. It had a big fancy walnut handle, silver trimmings, and a long, slender barrel. Yes, I'd say I'm reasonably sure it was a single-shot marksman's gun. And that would be why he didn't shoot a second time before we got the light and the gas-grate turned out. I think he could have shot by the light of that gas flame even after I pulled out the plug of the floor lamp."

"It would have been maybe ten seconds, not over fifteen," Jack said, "before we got both of them out. A pistol expert, used to that type of gun, could have reloaded and shot again, but an amateur probably couldn't have. Anyway, maybe he didn't even carry extra cartridges, although I wouldn't bet on that."

"Just a second," Randall said. He picked up the phone on his desk and said, "Laboratory." A few seconds later he said, "That bullet Wheeler gave you, the one out of the wall at Brian Carter's room. Got anything on it?" He listened a minute and then said, "Okay," and, hung up.

He said, "It was a twenty-two all right, a long rifle, but it was too flattened out to get any rifling marks. Say, Jack, do you know if they use long rifle cartridges in those target guns?"

"A single-shot will take any length—short, standard, or long rifle. But, Brian, why would he carry as—as inefficient a gun as that? Do you figure he planned this on the spur of the moment, and didn't have time to get himself a gun with bigger bullets and more of them?"

"I don't think it was on the spur of the moment," I said. "I think he must have been planning it. But he may have stuck the target gun in his pocket on the spur of the moment. I figure it this way: The knife was his weapon. He intended to kill us both with the knife. But he brought along the gun as a spare. And when he got to my place after killing Dr. Roth and found you there, Jack, instead of finding me asleep in bed, it spoiled his original idea of coming in my window and doing to me what he did to Roth. He didn't want to wait around until you left because he'd already made one kill, and maybe he remembered he'd left the ladder at the side of the house. There might be an alarm at anytime."

Randall nodded. "That makes sense, Carter. Once he'd killed Roth, he was in a hurry to get you."

Jack quit doodling with his penknife and put it in his vest pocket. "Anything from the M.E.?" he asked.

Randall nodded. "Says the stroke across the jugular was probably the first one, and was definitely fatal. The rest of the—uh—carving was just trimming. The ladder, by the way, belonged to a painting contractor who was going to start on the house the next day. He painted the garage first—finished that today. The ladder was lying on its side against a tree in the yard, not far from where Cole used it. Cole could have seen it there from the front walk, if he'd gone by during the day or during the early evening while it was still light."

"Did the medical examiner say about when he was killed?" I asked.

"Roughly half an hour to an hour before he was found," Randall said. He sighed. "Carter, have you told us everything about Cole that you think of?"

"Everything."

"Wish I could talk you into sleeping here, under protective custody. What are your plans for the next few days?"

"Nothing very startling," I told him. "This is Friday night—Saturday morning, now. I have to teach a class Monday afternoon at two. Nothing special to do until then, except some work of my own which I can do at home. As for the work I was doing with Dr. Roth, that's off for the time being. I'll have to see what the Board of Regents has to say about that."

"Then we'll worry about Monday when Monday comes," Randall said. "If as you think, Cole is going to stay around town, we'll probably have him before then. Do you mind Sebastian staying with you?"

"Not at all."

"And I'm going to assign two men to watch the outside of your place—at least for the next forty-eight hours. We won't plan beyond that until we see what happens. Right now, every policeman in town is looking for Cole, and every state policeman is getting his description. Tomorrow's newspapers and the Sunday papers will carry his photograph, and then the whole city will be on the lookout for him. You have your gun, Sebastian?"

Jack shook his head. "Just this twenty-two I borrowed from Winton."

"You better run home and get it, and whatever clothes and stuff you'll need for a couple of days."

"I'll go with him," I said.

"You'll wait here," Jack told me. "It's only a few blocks. I'll be right back." He went out.

"While he's gone, Carter," Randall said, "I want to ask a few things he already knows, but I don't. About the set-up at the university, the exact relationship between you and Roth and between Roth and Alistair Cole, what kind of work you do—things like that."

"Dr. Roth was head of the Department of Psychology," I said. "It's not a big department, here at Hudson U. He had only two full professors under him. Winton, who stays where I do, is one of them. Dr. Winton specializes in social psychology.

"Then there are two instructors. I'm one of them. An instructor is somewhere between a student and a professor. He's taking post-graduate courses leading to further degrees which will qualify him to be a professor. In my own case, I'm within weeks of getting my master's. After that, I start working for a doctorate. Meanwhile, I work my way by teaching and by helping in the research lab, grading papers, monitoring exams—well, you get the idea.

"Alistair Cole was—I suppose we can consider him fired now—a lab assistant. That isn't a job that leads to anything. It's just a job doing physical work. I don't think Cole had even completed high school."

"What sort of work did he do?"

"Any physical work around the laboratory. Feeding the menagerie—we work with rats and white mice mostly, but there are also Rhesus monkeys and guinea pigs—cleaning cages, sweeping—"

"Doesn't the university have regular cleaning women?"

"Yes, but not in the lab. With experiments going on there, we don't want people who don't know the apparatus working around it, possibly moving things that shouldn't be moved. The lab assistants know what can be touched and what can't."

"Then, in a way, Dr. Roth was over both of you?"

"More than in a way. He didn't exactly hire us—the Board of Regents does all the hiring—but we both worked under him. In different capacities, of course."

"I understand that," Randall said. "Then you could say Dr. Roth's job was something like mine, head of a department. Your relationship to him would be about that of your friend, Sebastian, to me, and Alistair Cole would be—umm—a mess attendant over on the jail side, or maybe a turnkey."

"That's a reasonably good comparison," I agreed. "Of course I was the only instructor who worked directly under Dr. Roth, so I was a lot closer to him than Jack would be to you. You have quite a few detectives under you, I'd guess."

He sighed. "Never quite enough, when anything important happens."

There was a knock on the door and he called out, "Yeah?"

The detective named Wheeler stuck his head in. "Miss Roth's here," he announced. "You said you wanted to talk to her. Shall I send her in?"

Chief Randall nodded, and I stood up. "You might as well stay, Carter," he told me.

Jeanette came in. I held the chair I'd been sitting in for her, and moved around to the one Jack had vacated. Wheeler had stayed outside, so I introduced Jeanette and Randall.

"I won't want to keep you long, Miss Roth," Randall said, "so I'll get right down to the few questions I want to ask. When did you see Alistair Cole last?"

"This afternoon, around three o'clock."

"At your house?"

"Yes. He came then and asked if Dad was home. I told him Dad was downtown, but that I expected him any minute. I asked him to come in and wait."

"Did he and you talk about anything?"

"Nothing much. As it happened, I'd been drinking some coffee, and I gave him a cup of it. But we talked only a few minutes—not over ten—before Dad came home."

"Do you know what he wanted to see your father about?"

"No. Dad took him into the library and I went out to the kitchen. Mr. Cole stayed only a few minutes, and then I heard him leaving."

"Did it sound as though he and your father were quarreling? Did you hear their voices?"

"No, I didn't hear. And Dad didn't say, afterwards, what Mr. Cole had wanted to see him about. But he did say something about Mr. Cole. He said he wondered if the boy was—how did he put it?—if he was all right. Said he wondered if maybe there wasn't a tendency toward schizophrenia, and that he was going to keep an eye on him for a while."

"Had you noticed anything strange about Cole's actions or manner when you talked to him before he saw your father?"

"He seemed a little excited about something and—well, trying to hide his excitement. And then there's one thing I'd always noticed about him—that he was unusually reticent and secretive about himself. He never volunteered any information about his—about anything concerning himself. He could talk all right about other things."

"Do you know if Cole knew your mother would not be there tonight?"

"I don't believe—Wait. Yes, he did. I forget just how it came into the conversation when I was talking with Mr. Cole, but I did mention my aunt's being sick. He'd met her. And I think I said Mother was staying with her a few nights."

"Was anything said about the ladder in your yard?"

"He asked if we were having the house painted, so I imagine he saw it lying there. It wasn't mentioned specifically."

"And tonight—what time did you last see your father?"

"When he said goodnight at about ten o'clock and went up to bed. I finished a book I was reading and went upstairs about an hour later. I must have gone right to sleep because it seemed as though I'd been asleep a long time when I heard the phone ringing and went to answer it."

"You heard nothing until—I mean, you heard nothing from the time your father went to sleep at ten until you were wakened by the phone—which would have been at a quarter to eleven?"

"Not a sound."

"Did your father usually lock the door of his room?"

"Never. There was a bolt on the door but he'd never used it that I know of."

Chief Randall nodded. "Then Cole must have bolted the door before he went back down the ladder," he said. "Is there anything you can add, Miss Roth?"

Jeanette hesitated. "No," she said. "Nothing that I can think of." She turned and smiled, faintly, at me. "Except that I want you to take good care of Brian."

"We'll do that," Randall told her. He raised his voice, "Wheeler!" The big detective opened the door and Randall said, "Take Miss Roth home now. Then take up duty at Forty-five University Lane—that's where Carter here lives. Outside. Jack Sebastian'll be inside with him. If the two of you let anything happen to him—God help you!"

~§~

Pulling the car to the curb half a block from my place, Jack said, "That looks like Wheeler in a car up ahead, but I'm not taking any chances. Wait here."

He got out and walked briskly to the car ahead. I noticed that he walked with his hand in his right coat pocket. He leaned into the car and talked a moment, then came back.

"It's Wheeler," he said, "and he's got a good spot there. He can watch both windows of your room, and he has a good view of the whole front of the place besides."

"How about the back?" I asked him.

"There's a bolt on the back door. Cole would have trouble getting in that way. Besides, we'll both be in your place and your door will be locked. If he could get into the house, he's got two more hurdles to take—your door and me."

"And don't forget me."

"That's the hurdle he wants to take. Come on. I'll leave you with Wheeler while I case the joint inside before I take you in."

We walked up to Wheeler's car and I got in beside him. "Besides looking around in my place," I told Jack, "you might take a look in the basement. If he got in while we were gone, and is hiding out anywhere but in my place, it would be there. Probably up at the front end."

"I'll check it. But why would he be there?"

"He knows that part of the place. Mr. Chandler, the owner, turned over the front section of the basement to me for some experiments that Dr. Roth and I were doing on our own time. We were working with rats down there—an extension of some experiments we started at the university lab, but wanted to keep separate. So Alistair Cole's been down there."

"And if he wanted to lay for you someplace, that might be it?"

"It's possible. He'd figure I'd be coming down there sooner or later."

"Okay, but I'll get you into your apartment first, then go down there."

He went inside and I saw the lights in my place go on. Five minutes later he came out to the car. "Clean as a whistle," he said.

"Wait till I get my stuff from my own car and we'll go in."

He went to his own car half a block back and returned with a suitcase. We went into the house and into my place.

"You're safe here," he said. "Lock me out now, and when I come back, don't let me in until you hear and recognize my voice."

"How about a complicated knock? Three shorts and a long."

He looked at me and saw I was grinning. He shook his finger at me. "Listen, pal," he said, "this is dead serious. There's a madman out to kill you, and he might be cleverer than you think. You can't take anything for granted until he's caught."

"I'll be good," I told him.

"I've got more at stake on this than you have," he said, "because if he kills you, you're only dead. But me, I'll be out of a job. Now let's hear that door lock when I go out in the hall."

I locked it after him, and started to pick up the chessmen from the floor. The Siamese blinked at me from her perch on the mantel. I tickled her under the chin.

"Hi, Beautiful," I said. "How'd you like all the excitement?"

She closed her eyes, as all cats do when they're having their chins chucked, and didn't answer me.

I leaned closer and whispered, "Cheer up, Beautiful. We're in the money, almost. You can have a silken cushion and only the best grades of calves' liver."

I finished picking up the chessmen and went over to the window. Looking out diagonally to the front, I could see the car that Wheeler was sitting in. I made a motion with my hand, and got an answering motion from the car.

I pulled down the shades in both rooms and was examining them to make sure that one couldn't see in from the outside when there was a tap at the door. I walked over and let Jack back in after he'd spoken to me.

"Nothing down there but some guinea pig cages and what look like mazes. The cages are all empty."

"They're rat cages," I told him. "And the things that look like mazes, strangely enough, are mazes. That's a sizable suitcase you brought. Planning to move in on me?"

He sat down in my most comfortable chair. "Only suitcase I had. It isn't very full. I brought an extra suit, by the way, but it's not for me. It's for Alistair Cole."

"Huh? A suit for—"

"Strait jacket. Picked it up at Headquarters, just in case. Listen, pal, you got any idea what it means to take a maniac? We'll take him alive, if we can, but we'll have to crease him or sap him, and I'll want some way of holding him down after he comes to." He shuddered a little. "I handled one of them once. Rather, I helped handle one. It took four of us, and the other three guys were huskier than I am. And it wasn't any picnic."

"You're making me very happy," I told him. "Did you by any

picnic."

"You're making me very happy," I told him. "Did you by any chance pick up an extra gun for me?"

"Can you shoot one? Ever handled one?"

I said, "You pull the trigger, don't you?"

"That's what I mean. That's why I didn't get you one. Look, if this loonie isn't caught, and he makes a clean getaway, I'll tell you what I'll do. I'll get you a permit for a gun, help you pick one out, and take you down to the police range and teach you how to use it. Because I won't be able to stay with you forever."

"Fine," I said. "I'd feel happier with one right away, though."

"Brian, people who don't know guns, who aren't expert with them, are better off without them. Safer. I'll bet if Alistair Cole hadn't had a gun tonight, he'd have got you."

"How do you figure that?"

"Simple. He looked in the window and saw, me playing chess with you. If he'd had only the shiv he'd have hidden somewhere until after I'd left and given you time to get to sleep. Then he'd have come in your window—and that would have been that. But since he had a gun, he took a chance with it. Not knowing how to squeeze a trigger without moving his sights, he overshoots. And, I hope, ends his chances of getting you."

I nodded, slowly. "You've got a point," I admitted. "All right, I'll wait and learn it right, if you don't get Alistair. Want to finish that game of chess?" I glanced toward Beautiful, now sound asleep, but still perched where she could overlook the game. "I promise you that Beautiful won't kibitz."

"Too late," Jack said. "It's after three. How long have you had that cat, Brian?"

"You should remember. You were with me when I bought her. Four years ago, wasn't it? Funny how a pet gets to mean so much to you. I wouldn't sell her for anything on earth."

Jack wrinkled his nose. "A dog, now, I could understand. They're some company to a guy."

Moving my hand in a deprecating gesture, I laughed at him. "That's because you're not used to such intelligent and aesthetic company. Next to women, cats are the most beautiful things on earth, and we rate women higher only because we're prejudiced. Besides, women talk back and cats don't. I'd have gone nuts the last few months if I hadn't had Beautiful to talk to. I've been working twelve to fourteen hours a day, and—that reminds me. I'd better get some sleep. How about you?"

"Not sleepy yet, but don't let me stop you. I'll go in the other room and read. What have you got that might give me some dope on Alistair Cole. Got any good books on abnormal psychology?"

"Not a lot. That's out of our line here. We don't have courses in the abnormal brand. We work with fundamentals, mostly. Oh, I've got a couple of general books. Try that *Outline of Abnormal Psychology* on the top shelf, the blue jacket. It's pretty elementary, I guess, but it's as far as you'll cover in a few hours reading anyway."

I started undressing while Jack got the book and skimmed the table of contents. "This looks okay," he said. "Chapters on dementia praecox, paranoia, waking hypnosis—never heard of that. Is it common?"

"Certainly," I told him. "We've tried it. It's not really part of abnormal psychology at all, although it can be used in treatment of mental troubles. We've subjected whole classes—with their consent, of course—to experiments in automatic writing while under suggestion in waking state amnesia. That's what I used for my senior thesis for my B.A. If you want to read up on what's probably wrong with Alistair Cole, read the chapter on paranoia and paranoid conditions, and maybe the chapter on schizophrenia—that's dementia praecox. I'd bet on straight paranoia in Cole's case, but it could be schiz."

I hung my clothes over the chair and started to pull on my pajamas.

"According to Jeanette," Jack said, "Dr. Roth thought Cole might have a touch of schizophrenia. But you bet on paranoia. What's the difference?"

I sighed. "All right, I'll tell you. Paranoia is the more uncommon of the two disorders, and it's harder to spot. Especially if a subject is tied up in knots and won't talk about himself. A man suffering from paranoia builds up an airtight system of reasoning about some false belief or peculiar set of ideas. He sticks to these delusions, and you can't convince him he's wrong in what he thinks. But if his particular delusion doesn't show, you can't spot him, because otherwise he seems normal.

"A schizophrenic, on the other hand, may have paranoid ideas, but they're poorly systematized, and he's likely to show other symptoms that rambling, untidiness, apathy—all sorts of symptoms. Cole didn't show any of them."

"A paranoiac, then, could pretty well hide what was wrong with him," Jack said, "as long as no one spotted the particular subject he was hipped on?"

"Some of them do. Though if we'd been specialists, I think we'd have spotted Cole quickly. But listen. Hadn't you better get some sleep too?"

"Go ahead and pound your ear. I'll take a nap if I get tired. Here goes the light."

He turned it out and went into the next room. He left the door ajar, but I found that if I turned over and faced the wall, the little light that came in didn't bother me.

Beautiful, the cat, jumped down from the mantel and came over to sleep on my feet, as she always does. I reached down and petted her soft warm fur a moment, then I lay back on the pillow and quit thinking. I slept.

A sound woke me—the sound of a window opening slowly.

~§~

With me, as with most people, dreams are forgotten within the first few seconds after waking. I remember the one I was just having, though, because of the tie-up it had with the sound that wakened me.

My dream had changed that slow upward scrape of the window into the scrape of claws on cement, the cement of the basement. There in the little front room of the basement, Dr. Roth was standing with his hand on the latch of a rat cage, and a monstrous cat with the markings of a Siamese was scraping her claws on the floor, gathering her feet under her to spring. It was Beautiful, my cat, and yet it wasn't. She was almost as large as a lion. Her eyes glowed like the headlights of a car.

Dr. Roth cowered back against the tier of rat cages, holding a hand in front of him to ward off the attack. I watched from the doorway, and I tried to open my mouth to scream at her to stop, not to jump. But I seemed paralyzed. I couldn't move a muscle or make a sound.

I saw the cat's tail grow larger. Her eyes seemed to shoot blue sparks. And then she leaped.

I saw the cat's tail grow larger. Her eyes seemed to shoot blue sparks. And then she leaped.

Dr. Roth's arm was knocked aside as though it had been a toothpick. Her claws sank into his shoulders and her white, sharp teeth found his throat. He screamed once, and then the scream became a gurgle and he lay on the cement floor, dead, in a puddle of his blood. And the cat, backing away from him, was shrinking to her real size, getting smaller, her claws still scraping the cement as she backed away.

And then, still frozen with the horror of that dream, I began to know that I was dreaming, that the sound I heard was the opening of a window.

I sat up in bed, fast. I opened my mouth to yell for Jack. Someone stood there, just inside the window!

And then, before I had yelled, I saw that it was Jack who stood there. Enough light came in from the other room that I could be sure of that. He'd raised the shade. He was crouched down now, and his eyes, level with the middle of the lower pane, stared through it into the night outside.

He must have heard the springs creak as I sat up. He turned. "*Shhh,*" he said. "It's all right—I think."

He put the window back down again then, and threw over the lock. He pulled down the shade and came over to the bed and sat down in a chair beside it.

"Sorry I woke you," he said, very quietly. "Can you go back to sleep, or do you want to talk a while?"

"What time is it?" I asked.

"Three-forty. You were asleep only half an hour. I'm sorry, but—"

"But what? What's been happening? Did you think you heard a sound outside?"

"Not outside the window, no. But a few minutes ago I thought I heard someone try the knob of the hall door. But when I got there and listened, I couldn't hear anything."

"It could have been Alistair Cole," I said, "if he got in the back way. Wheeler isn't watching the back door."

"That's what I thought, even though I didn't hear anything back there. So I went to the window. I thought if I could attract Wheeler's attention, he'd come in the front way. Then I'd take a chance opening the hall door—with my gun ready, of course. If Cole was there, we'd have him between us."

"Did you get Wheeler's attention?"

He shook his head slowly. "His car isn't where it was. You can't even see it from the window. Maybe he moved it to a different spot where he thought he'd be less conspicuous, or could watch better."

"That's probably it. Well, what are you going to do?"

"Nothing. Sit tight. If I stick my neck out into that hall, or go outside through the window, the edge is going to be with Cole. If I sit here and make him come to me, it's the other way round. Only I'm through reading for tonight. I'm sitting right here by the bed. If you can sleep, go ahead. I'll shut up and let you."

"Sure," I said. "I can sleep swell. Just like a lamb staked out in the jungle to draw a tiger for the hunters. That's how I can sleep."

He chuckled. "The lamb doesn't know what it's there for."

"Until it smells tiger. I smell tiger." That reminded me of my dream, and I told him about it.

"You're a psychologist," he said. "What does it mean?"

"Probably that I had a subconscious dislike for Dr. Roth," I told him. "Only I know that already. I don't need to interpret a dream to tell me that."

"What did you have against Roth, Brian? I've known there was something from the way you've talked about him."

"He was a prig, for one thing," I said. "You know me well enough, Jack, to know I'm not too bad a guy, but he thought I was miles away from being good enough for Jeanette. Well—maybe I am, but then again, so's everybody else who might fall in love with her."

"Does she love you?"

"I think so." I thought it over. "Sure, I practically know she does, from things she said tonight."

"Anything else? I mean, about Roth. Is that the only reason you didn't like him?"

I didn't say anything for a while. I was thinking. I thought, why not tell Jack now? Sooner or later he'll know it. The whole world will know it. Why not get it off my chest right now, while there was a good chance to get my side of it straight?

Something made me stop and listen first. There wasn't a sound from outside, nor from the hallway.

"Jack," I said, "I'm going to tell you something. I'm awfully glad that you were here tonight."

"Thanks, pal." He chuckled a little.

"I don't mean what you think I mean, Jack. Sure, maybe you saved my life from Alistair Cole. But more than that, you gave me an alibi."

"An alibi? For killing Roth? Sure, I was with you when he was killed."

"Exactly. Listen, Jack, I had a reason for killing Roth. That reason's coming out later anyway. I might as well tell you now."

He turned and stared at me. There was enough light in the room so that I could see the movement of his head, but, not enough so that he could watch my face. I don't know why he bothered turning.

"If you need an alibi," he said, "you've sure got one. We started playing chess at somewhere around eight. You haven't been out of my sight since then, except while you were in Chief Randall's office."

"Don't think I don't know that," I told him. "And don't think I'm not happy about it. Listen, Jack. Because Roth is dead, I'm going to be a millionaire. If he was alive, I still might be, but there'd have been a legal fight about it. I would have been right, but I could have lost just the same."

"You mean it would have been a case of your word against his?"

"Exactly. And he's—he was—department head, and I'm only a flunky, a little better on his social scale than Alistair Cole. And it's something big, Jack. Really big."

"What?"

"What kind of rat cages did you find in the basement when you looked down there?" I asked him.

"What kind? I don't get you. I don't know makes of rat cages."

"Don't worry about the make," I said. "You found only one kind. Empty ones. The rats were dead. And disposed of."

He turned to look at me again. "Go on," he said.

Now that I'd started to tell him, I knew I wouldn't even try to go back to sleep. I was too excited. I propped the pillow up against the head of the bed.

"Make a guess, Jack," I said. "How much food do rats eat a year in the United States alone?"

"I wouldn't know. A million dollars' worth?"

"A hundred million dollars' worth," I said, "at a conservative estimate. Probably more than a million dollars is spent fighting them, each year. In the world, their cost is probably a billion dollars a year. Not altogether—just for one year! How much do you think something would be worth that would actually completely eliminate rats—both *Mus Rattus* and *Mus Norvegicus*—completely and once and for all? Something that would put them with the hairy mammoth and the roc and the dinosaurs?"

"If your mathematics are okay," Jack said, "it'd be worth ten billion bucks in the first ten years?"

"Ten billion, on paper. A guy who could do it ought to be able to get one ten-thousandth that much, shouldn't he? A million?"

"Seems reasonable. And somebody ought to throw in a Nobel prize along with it. But can you do it?"

"I can do it," I said. "Right here in my basement I stumbled across it, accidentally, Jack, in the course of another experiment. But it works. It works! It kills rats!"

"So does Red Squill. So does strychnine. What's your stuff got that they haven't?"

"Communicability. Give it to *one* rat—and the whole colony dies! Like all the rats—thirty of them, to be exact—died when I injected one rat. Sure, you've got to catch one rat alive—but that's easy. Then just inject it and let it go, and all the rats in the neighborhood die."

"A bacillus?"

"No. Look, I'll be honest with you. I don't know exactly how it works, but it's not a germ. I have a hunch that it destroys a rat's immunity to some germ he carries around with him normally—just as you and I carry around a few million germs which don't harm us ordinarily because we also carry around the antibodies that keep them in check. But this injection probably destroys certain antibodies in the rat and the germs become—unchecked. The germs also become strong enough to overcome the antibodies in other rats, and they must be carried by the air because they spread from cage to cage with no direct contact. Thirty rats died within twenty-four hours after I inoculated the first one—some in cages as far away as six feet."

Jack Sebastian whistled. "Maybe you have got something," he said softly. "Where did Roth come in on it, though? Did he claim half, or what?"

"Half I wouldn't have minded giving him," I said. "But he insisted the whole thing belonged to the university, just because I was working on an experiment for the university—even though it was in my own place, on my own time. And the thing I hit upon was entirely outside the field of the experiment. I don't see that at all. Fortunately, he didn't bring it to an issue He said we should experiment further before we announced it."

"Do you agree with that?"

"Of course. Naturally, I'm not going off half-cocked. I'm going to be sure, plenty sure, before I announce it. But when I do, it's going to be after the thing has been patented in my name. I'm going to have that million bucks, Jack!"

"I hope you're right," he said. "And I can't say I blame you, if you made the discovery here at your own place on your own time. Anyone else know about it?"

"No."

"Did Alistair Cole?"

"No, he didn't. I think, Jack, that this thing is bigger even than you realize. Do you know how many human lives it's going to save? We don't have any bubonic here in this country—or much of any other rat-and-flea borne disease, but take the world as a whole."

"I see what you mean. Well, more power to you, keed. And if everything goes well, take me for a ride on your yacht sometime."

"You think I'm kidding?"

"Not at all. And I pretty well see what you mean by being glad you've got an alibi. Well, it's a solid one, if my word goes for anything. To have killed Dr. Roth—no matter how much motive you may have had—you'd have had to have had a knife on a pole a block and a half long. Besides—"

"What?"

"Nothing. Listen, I'm worried about Wheeler. Probably he moved that car to another spot, but I wish I knew for sure."

"It's a squad car, isn't it?" I asked.

"Yes

"With two-way radio?"

"Yes, but I haven't got a radio in here."

"We got a telephone. If you're worried about Wheeler—and you're getting me that way too—why don't you phone Headquarters and have them call Wheeler and phone you back?"

"Either you're a genius or I'm a dope," he said. "Don't tell me which."

He got up out of the chair and I could see he was still holding the gun in his hand. He went first to the door and listened carefully, then he went to the window. He listened carefully there. Finally, he pulled back the shade a crack to look out.

"Now you're giving me the willies, and I might as well get up," I said. "For some reason, I'd rather get killed with my pants on—if I'm going to get killed." I looked at my cat. "Sorry, Beautiful," I said as I pulled my feet out from under the Siamese.

I took off my pajamas and started putting on my shirt and trousers.

"Wheeler's car still isn't anywhere I can see," Jack said.

He went over to the telephone and lifted the receiver off the hook. I slipped my feet into a pair of loafers and looked over. He was still holding the receiver and hadn't spoken. He put it back gently. "Someone's cut the wires," he said. "The line is dead."

~§~

I said, "I don't believe this. It's out of a horror program on the radio. It's a gag."

Jack snorted. He was turning around, looking from the window to the door. "Got a flashlight?"

"Yes. In the drawer over there."

"Get it," he said. "Then sit back in that corner where you're not in direct range from the window or the door. If either opens, bracket it with your flash. I've got my flash but I'm using it left-handed. Anyway, two spots are better than one, and I want to see to shoot straight."

While I was getting the flashlight, he closed the door to the other room, leaving us in pitch darkness except for our flashes. I lighted my own way to the chair he'd pointed out.

"There's a window in that other room," I said. "Is it locked?"

"Yes," he answered. "He can't get in there without breaking that window. Okay, turn out that light and sit tight."

I heard him move across the room to another corner. His flashlight played briefly first on the door to the hallway, then swept across to the window. Then it went out.

"Wouldn't the advantage be with us if we kept the light on?" I asked.

"No. Listen, if he busts in the window, when you aim your flash at it, hold it out from your body, out over the arm of your chair. So if he shoots at the flash, he won't hit you. Our two lights should blind him. We should be able to see him, but he shouldn't be able to see us."

"Okay," I said.

I don't know how many minutes went by. Then there was a soft tapping at the window. I tensed in my chair and aimed the flashlight at the window without turning it on.

The tapping came again. An irregular series: *tap—tap—tap—tap*.

"That's Wheeler," Jack whispered. "It's the code tap. Cole couldn't possibly know it. Sit tight."

I could hear him moving across the room in the darkness. I could see the streak of grayness as he cautiously lifted one side of the shade, then peered through the crack between shade and window. As quietly as he could, he raised up the shade and unlocked and raised the window.

It was turning slightly gray outside, and a little light came from the street lamp a quarter of a block away. I could recognize the big body of Wheeler coming through the window. Wheeler, and not Alistair Cole.

I began breathing again. I got up out of the chair and went over to them. Wheeler was whispering.

". . . So don't put down the windows," he was saying. "I'll come in that way again."

"I'll leave it up to Brian," Jack whispered back. "If he wants to take that chance. Meanwhile, you watch that window."

He pulled me to one side then, away from the open window. "Listen," he said. "Wheeler saw somebody moving in back. He'd moved his car where he could watch part of the backyard. He got there in time to see a window going down. Alistair Cole's inside the building. Wheeler's got an idea now, only it's got a risk to it. I'll leave it up to you. If you don't like it, he'll go out again and get help, and we'll sit tight here, as we were until help comes."

"What's the idea?" I asked. If it wasn't too risky, I'd like it better than another vigil while Wheeler went for help.

"Wheeler," Jack said, "thinks he should walk right out of the door into the hall and out the front door. He thinks Cole will hear that, and will think I'm leaving you. Wheeler will circle around the house and come in the window again. Cole should figure you're here alone and come in that hallway door—and both Wheeler and I will be here to take him. You won't be taking any risk unless by some chance he gets both of us. That isn't likely. We're two to one, and we'll be ready for him."

I whispered back that it sounded good to me. He gripped my arm.

"Go back to your chair then. That's as good a place as any."

Groping my way back to the chair, I heard Jack and Wheeler whispering as they went toward the hallway door. They were leaving the window open and, since it was momentarily unguarded, I kept my eyes on it, ready to yell a warning if a figure appeared there. But none did.

The hallway door opened and closed quickly, letting a momentary shaft of light into the room. I heard Jack back away from the door and Wheeler's footsteps going along the hallway. I heard the front door open and close, Wheeler's steps cross the porch.

A moment later, there was the soft *tap—tap—tap—tap* on the upper pane of the open window, and then Wheeler's bulk came through it.

Very, very quietly, he closed the window and locked it. He pulled down the shade. Then I heard the shuffle of his footsteps as he moved into position to the right of the door.

I haven't any idea how long we waited after that. Probably five or ten minutes—but it seemed like hours. Then I heard, or thought I heard, the very faintest imaginable sound. It might have been the scrape of shoes on the carpet of the hall outside the door. But there wasn't any doubt about the next sound. It was the soft turning of the knob of the door. It turned and held. The door pushed open a crack, then a few inches. Light streamed over a slowly widening area.

Then one thing Jack hadn't counted on happened. A hand reached in, between the door and the jamb, and flicked on the light switch. Dazzling light from the bulks in the ceiling almost blinded me. And it was in that blinding second that the door swung back wide and Alistair Cole, knife in one hand and single-shot target pistol in the other, stood in the doorway. His eyes flashed around the room, taking in all three of us.

But then his eyes centered on me and the target pistol lifted.

Jack stepped in from the side and a blackjack was in his upraised hand. It swung down and there was a sound like someone makes thumping a melon. He and Wheeler caught Alistair Cole, one from each side, and eased his way down to the carpet.

Wheeler bent over him and got the gun and the knife first, then held his hand over Cole's heart.

"He'll be all right," he said.

He took a pair of handcuffs from his hip pocket, rolled Cole over and cuffed his hands together behind him. Then he straightened, picking up the gun he'd put down on the carpet while he worked on Cole.

I'd stood up, my knees still shaking a little. My forehead felt as though it was beaded with cold sweat. The flashlight was gripped so tightly in my right hand that my fingers ached.

I caught sight of Beautiful, again on the mantel, and she was standing up, her tail bushy and straight up, her fur back of the ears and along the back standing up in a ridge, her blue eyes blazing. "It's all right, Beautiful," I said to her soothingly. "All the excitement's over, and everything's—"

I was walking toward the mantel, raising my hand to pet her, when Wheeler's excited voice stopped me.

"Watch out," he yelled. "That cat's going to jump—"

And I saw the muzzle of his gun raising and pointing at the Siamese cat.

My right hand swung up with the flashlight and I leaped at Wheeler. Out of the corner of my eye I saw Jack stepping in as Wheeler ducked back. The corner of my eye caught the swing of his blackjack.

The overhead light was bright in my eyes when I opened them. I was lying flat on the bed and the first thing I saw was Beautiful, curled up on my chest looking at me. She was all right now, her fur sleek and her curled tail back to normal. Whatever else had happened, she was all right.

I turned my head, and it hurt to turn it, but I saw that Jack was sitting beside the bed. The door was closed and Wheeler and Cole were gone.

"What happened?" I asked.

"You tried to kill Wheeler," Jack said. There was something peculiar about his voice, but his eyes met mine levelly.

"Don't be silly," I said "I was going to knock his arm down before he could shoot. He was crazy. He must have a phobia against cats."

Jack shook his head. "You were going to kill him," he said. "You were going to kill him whether he shot or not."

"Don't be silly." I tried to move my hands and found they were fastened behind me. I looked at Jack angrily. "What's wrong with you?"

"Not with me, Brian," he said. "With you. I know—now that it was really you who killed Dr. Roth tonight. Yes, I know you've got an alibi. But you did it just the same. You used Alistair Cole as your instrument. My guess would be waking hypnosis."

"I suppose I got him to try to kill me, too!" I said.

"You told him he'd shoot *over your head* and then run away. It was a compulsion so strong he tried it again tonight, even after he saw Wheeler and me ready to slug him if he tried. And he was aiming high again. How long have you been working on him?"

"I don't know what you're talking about."

"You do, Brian. You don't know it all, but you know this part of it. You found out that Cole had schizophrenic tendencies. You found out, probably while playing chess with him, that you could put him under waking hypnosis without his knowing it. And you worked on him. What kind of a fantasy did you build in him? What kind of a conspiracy, did you plant in his mind, Dr. Roth was leading against him?"

"You're crazy."

"No, *you* are, Brian. Crazy, but clever. And you know that what I've just told you just now is right. You also know I'll never be able to prove it. I admit that. But there's something else you don't know. I don't have to prove it."

For the first time I felt a touch of fear. "What do you mean?" I asked.

"You gave Cole his fantasies, but you don't know your own. You don't know that—under the pressure, possibly, of working too hard and studying too hard—your own mind cracked. You don't know that your million-dollar rat-killer is *your* fantasy. You don't believe me, now that I'm telling you that it is a fantasy. You'll never believe it. The paranoiac builds up an airtight system of excuses and rationalization to support his insane delusions. You'll never believe me."

I tried to sit up and couldn't. I realized then that it wasn't a matter of my arms being tied. Jack had put the strait jacket on me. "You're part of it, then," I said. "You're one of those in the plot against me."

"Sure, sure. You know, Brian. I can guess what started it. Or rather what set it off, probably only a few days ago. It was when Dr. Roth killed your cat. That dream you told me about tonight—the cat killing Dr. Roth. Your mind wouldn't accept the truth. Even your subconscious mind reversed the facts for the dream. I wonder what really happened. Possibly your cat killed a rat that was an important part of an experiment and, in anger, Dr. Roth—"

"You're crazy," I shouted. "Crazy!"

"And ever since, Brian, you've been talking to a cat that wasn't there. I thought you were kidding, at first. When I figured out the truth, I told Wheeler what I figured. When you gave us a clue where the cat was supposed to be, on the mantel, he raised his gun and pretended—"

"Jack!" I begged him, to break off the silly things he was saying. "If you're going to help them railroad me, even if you're in on the plot—please get them to let me take Beautiful with me. Don't take her away too. Please!"

Cars were driving up outside. I could feel the comforting weight and warmth of the cat sleeping on my chest.

"Doth worry, Brian," Jack said quietly. "That cat'll go wherever you go. Nobody can take it away from you. Nobody."

Popular Detective, September 1949

Puzzles

Satan One-and-a-Half

MAYBE YOU KNOW how it is, when a man seeks solitude to do some creative work. As soon as he gets solitude, he finds it gives him the willies to be alone. Back in the middle of everything, he thought, "If I could only get away from everybody I know, I could get something done." But let him get away—and see what happens.

I know; I'd had solitude for almost a week, and it was giving me the screaming-meamies. I'd written hardly a note of the piano concerto I intended composing. I had the opening few bars, but they sounded suspiciously like Gershwin.

Here I was in a cottage out at the edge of town, and that cottage had seemed like what the doctor ordered when I rented it. I'd given my address to none of my pals, and so there were no parties, no jam sessions, no distractions.

That is, no distractions except loneliness. I was finding that loneliness is worse than all other distractions combined.

All I did was sit there at the piano with a pencil stuck behind my ear, wishing the doorbell would ring. Anybody. Anything. I wished I'd had a telephone put in and had given my friends the number. I wished the cottage would turn out to be haunted. Even that would be better.

The doorbell rang.

I jumped up from the piano and practically ran to answer it.

And there wasn't anybody there.

I could see that without opening the door, because the door is mostly glass. Unless someone had rung the bell and then run like hell to get out of sight.

I opened the door and saw the cat. I didn't pay any particular attention to it though. Instead, I stuck my head out and looked both ways. There wasn't anybody in sight except the man across the street mowing his lawn.

I turned to go back to the piano, and the doorbell rang again.

This time I wasn't more than a yard from the door. I swung around, opened it wide, and stepped outside.

There wasn't anybody there, and the nearest hiding place—around the corner of the house—was too far away for anybody to have got there without my seeing him.

Unless the cat.

I looked down for the cat and at first I thought it, too, had disappeared. But then I saw it again, walking with graceful dignity along the hallway, inside the house, toward the living room. It was paying no more attention to me than I had paid to it the first time I'd looked out the door.

I turned around again and looked up and down the street, and at the trees on my lawn, at the house next door on the north, and at the house next door on the south. Each of those houses was a good fifty yards from mine and no one could conceivably have rung my bell and run to either of them.

Even leaving out the question of *why* anyone should have done such a childish stunt, nobody could have.

I went back in the house, and there was the cat curled up sound asleep in the Morris chair in the living room. He was a big, black cat, a cat with character. Somehow, even asleep, he seemed to have a rakish look about him.

I said, "Hey," and he opened big yellowish-green eyes and looked at me. There wasn't any surprise or fear in those handsome eyes; only a touch of injured dignity.

I said, "Who rang that doorbell?"

Naturally, he didn't answer.

So I said, "Want something to eat, maybe?" And don't ask me why he answered that one when he wouldn't answer the others. My tone of voice, perhaps. He said, "*Miaourr . . .*" and stood up in the chair.

I said, "All right, come on," and went out into the kitchen to explore the refrigerator. There was most of a bottle of milk, but somehow my guest didn't look like a cat who drank much milk. But luckily there was plenty of ground meat, because hamburgers are my favorite food when I do my own cooking.

I put some hamburger in a bowl and some water in another bowl and put them both on the floor under the sink. He was busily working on the hamburger when I went back into the front hallway to look at the doorbell.

The bell was right over the front door, and it was the only bell in the house. I couldn't have mistaken a telephone bell because I didn't have a phone, and there was a knocker instead of a bell on the back door. I didn't know where the battery or the transformer that ran the bell was located, and there wasn't any way of tracing the wiring without tearing down the walls.

The push button outside the door was four feet up from the step. A cat, even one smart enough to stand on its hind legs, couldn't have reached it. Of course, a cat could have jumped for the button, but that would have caused a sharp, short ring. Both times, the doorbell had rung longer than that.

Nobody could have rung it from the outside and got away without my seeing him. And, granting that the bell could be short-circuited from somewhere inside the house, that didn't get me an answer. The cottage was so small and so quiet that it would have been impossible for a window or a door to have opened without my hearing it.

I went outside again and looked around, and this time I got an idea. This was an ideal opportunity for me to get acquainted with the girl next door—an opportunity I'd been waiting for since I'd first seen her a few days ago.

I cut across the lawn and knocked on the door.

Seeing her from a distance, I'd thought she was a knockout. Now, as she opened the door and I got a close look, I knew she was.

I said, "My name is Brian Murray. I live next door and I—"

"And you play with Russ Whitlow's orchestra." She smiled, and I saw I'd underestimated how pretty she was. Strictly tops. "I was hoping we'd get acquainted while you were here. Won't you come in?"

I didn't argue about that. I went in, and almost the first thing I noticed inside was a beautiful walnut grand piano. I asked, "Do you play, Miss—?"

"Carson. Ruth Carson. I give piano lessons to brats with sticky fingers who'd rather be outside playing ball or skipping rope. When I heard Whitlow on the radio a few nights ago, the piano sounded different. Aren't you still—?"

"I'm on leave," I explained. "I had rather good luck with a couple of compositions a year ago, and Russ gave me a month off to try my hand at some more."

"Have you written any?"

I said ruefully, "To date all I've set down is a pair of clef signs. Maybe now. . ." I was going to say that maybe now that I'd met her, things would be different. But that was working too fast, I decided.

She said, "Sit down, Mr. Murray. My uncle and aunt will be home soon, and I'd like you to meet them. Meanwhile, would you care for some tea?"

I said that I would, and it was only after she'd gone out into the kitchen that I realized I hadn't asked the question I'd come to ask. When she came back, I said:

"Miss Carson, I came to ask you about a black cat. It walked into my house a few minutes ago. Do you know if it belongs to anybody here in the neighborhood?"

"A black cat? That's odd. Mr. Lasky owned one, but outside of that one, I don't know of any around here."

"Who is Mr. Lasky?"

She looked surprised. "Why, didn't you know? He was the man who lived in that cottage before you did. He died only a few weeks ago. He—he committed suicide."

The faintest little shiver ran down my spine. Funny, in a city, how little one knows about the places one lives in. You rent a house or an apartment and never think to wonder who has lived there before you or what tragedies have been enacted there.

I said, "That might explain it. I mean, if it's his cat. Cats become attached to people. It would explain why the cat—"

"I'm afraid it doesn't," she said. "The cat is dead, too. I happened to see him bury it in your back yard, under the maple tree. It was run over by a car, I believe."

The phone rang, and she went to answer it. I started thinking about the cat again. The way it had walked in, as though it lived there—it was a bit eerie, somehow. If it were my predecessor's cat, that would explain its apparent familiarity with the place. But it couldn't be my predecessor's cat. Unless he'd had more than one. . .

Ruth Carson came back from the hallway. She said, "That was my aunt. They won't be home until late tonight, so probably you won't get to meet them until tomorrow. That means I'll have to get my own dinner, and I hate to eat alone. Will you share it with me, Mr. Murray?"

That was the easiest question I'd ever had to answer in my life.

We had an excellent meal in the breakfast nook in the kitchen. We talked about music for a while, and then I told her about the cat and the doorbell.

It puzzled her almost as much as it had puzzled me. She said, "Are you sure some child couldn't have rung it for a prank, and then ducked out of sight before you got there?"

"I don't see how," I said. "I was just inside the door the second time it rang. Tell me about this Mr. Lasky and about his cat."

She said, "I don't know how long he lived there. We moved here just a year ago, and he was there then. He was rather an eccentric chap, almost a hermit. He never had any guests, never spoke to anyone. He and the cat lived there alone. I think he was crazy about the cat."

"An old duck?" I asked.

"Not really old. Probably in his fifties. He had a gray beard that made him look older."

"And the cat. Could he possibly have had two black cats?"

"I'm almost positive he didn't. I never saw more than the big black tom he called Satan. And there was no cat around during the week after it was killed."

"You're positive it died?"

"Yes. I happened to see him burying it, and it wasn't in a box or anything. And it was almost the only time I ever heard him speak; he was talking to himself, cursing about careless auto drivers. He took it hard. Maybe—"

She stopped, and I tried to fill in the blank. "You mean that was why he committed suicide a week later?"

"Oh, he must have had other reasons, but I imagine that was a factor. He left a suicide note, I understand. It was in the papers, at the time. There was one particularly unhappy circumstance about it. He wrote the note and then took poison. But before the poison had taken effect, he regretted it or changed his mind; he telephoned the police and they rushed an ambulance and a doctor—but he was dead when they got there."

For an instant I wondered how he could have phoned the police from a house in which there was no telephone. Then I remembered that there had been one, taken out before I moved in. The rental agency had told me so, and that the wiring was already there in case I wanted one installed. For privacy's sake I'd decided against having it done.

We'd finished our meal, and I insisted on helping with the dishes. Then I said, "Would you like to meet the cat?"

"Of course," she said. "Are you going to let him stay?"

I grinned. "The question seems to be whether he's going to let me stay. You know how cats are. Come on; maybe you can give me a recommendation."

We were right by her kitchen door, so we cut across the back yards into my kitchen. All the hamburger I'd put under the sink was gone. The cat was back in the Morris chair, asleep again. He blinked at us as I turned on the light.

Ruth stood there staring at him. "He's a dead ringer for Mr. Lasky's Satan. I'd almost swear it's the same. But it *couldn't* be!"

I said, "A cat has nine lives, you know. Anyway, I'll call him Satan. And since the question arises whether he's Satan One or Satan Two, let's compromise. Satan One-and-a-Half. So, Satan One-and-a-Half, you've got the only comfortable chair in this room. Mind giving it up for a lady?"

Whether he minded or not, I picked him up and moved him to a straight chair. Satan One-and-a-Half promptly jumped down to the floor from his straight chair, went back to the Morris, and jumped up on Ruth's lap.

I said, "Shall I shut him in the kitchen?"

"No, don't. Really, I like cats." She was stroking his fur gently, and the cat promptly curled into a black ball of fur and went to sleep.

"Anyway," I said, "he's got good taste. But now you're stuck. You can't move without waking him, and that would be rude."

She smiled. "Will you play for me? Something of your own, I mean. Did you mean it literally when you said you'd composed nothing since you've been here, or were you being modest?"

I looked down at the staff paper on the piano. There were a few bars there, an opening. But it wasn't any good. I said, "I wasn't being modest. I can compose, when I have an idea. But I haven't had an idea since I've been here."

She said, "Play the 'Black Cat Nocturne'."

"Sorry, I don't know—"

"Of course not. It hasn't been written yet."

Then I got what she was talking about, and it began to click.

She said, "A doorbell rings, but nobody is there. The ghost of a dead black cat walks in and takes over your house. It—"

"Enough," I said, very rudely. I didn't want to hear any more. All I needed was the starting point.

I hit a weird arpeggio in the base, and it went on from there. Almost by itself, it went on from there. My fingers did it, not my mind. The melody was working up into the treble now, with a soft dissonant thump-thump in the accompaniment that was like a cat walking across the skin of a bass drum and—

The doorbell rang.

It startled me and I hit about the worst discord of my career. I'd been out of the world for maybe half a minute, and the sudden ring of that bell was as much of a jolt as if someone had thrown a bucket of ice water on me.

I saw Ruth's face; it, too, was startled looking. And the cat lying in her lap had raised its head. But its yellow-green eyes, slitted against the light, were inscrutable.

The bell rang again, and I shoved back the piano bench and stood up. Maybe, by playing, I'd hypnotized myself into a state of fright, but I was afraid to go to that door. Twice before, today, that doorbell had rung. Who, or what, would I find there this time?

I couldn't have told what I was afraid of. Or maybe I could, at that. Down deep inside, we're all afraid of the supernatural. The last time that doorbell had rung, maybe a dead cat had come back. And now—maybe its owner. . .

I tried to be casual as I went to the door, but I could tell from Ruth's face that she was feeling as I did about it. That damn music! I'd picked the wrong time to get myself into a mood. If I went to the door and nobody was there, I'd probably be in a state of jitters the rest of the night.

But there was someone there. I could see, the moment I stepped from the living room into the hallway, that there was a man standing there. It was too dark for me to make out his features, but, at any rate, he didn't have a gray beard.

I opened the door.

The man outside said, "Mr. Murray?"

He was a big man, tall and broad-shouldered, with a very round face. Right now it was split by an ingratiating smile. He looked familiar and I knew I'd seen him before, but I couldn't place him. I did know that I didn't like him; maybe I was being psychic or maybe I was being silly, but I felt fear and loathing at the sight of him.

I said, "Yes, my name is Murray."

"Mine's Haskins. Milo Haskins. I'm your neighbor across the street, Mr. Murray."

Of course, that was where I'd seen him. He'd been mowing the lawn over there this afternoon, when the cat came.

He said, "I'm in the insurance game, Mr. Murray. Sometime I'd like to talk insurance with you, but that isn't what I came to see you about tonight. It's about a cat, a black cat."

"Yes?"

"It's mine," he said. "I saw it go in your door today, just before I went in the house. I came over just as soon as I could to get it."

"Sorry, Mr. Haskins," I told him. "I fed it and then let it out the back door. Don't know where it went from here."

"Oh," he said. He looked as though he didn't know whether or not to believe me. "Are you sure it didn't come back in a window or something? Would you mind if I helped you look around?"

I said, "I'm afraid I would mind, Mr. Haskins. Good night."

I stepped back to close the door, and then something soft rubbed against my leg. At the same instant, I saw Haskins's eyes look down and then harden as they came up and met mine again.

He said, "So?" He bent and held out a hand to the cat. "Here, kitty. Come here, kitty."

Then it was my turn to grin, because the cat clawed his fingers.

"Your cat, eh?" I said. "I thought you were lying, too, Haskins. That's why I wouldn't give you the cat. I'll change my mind now; you can have him if he goes with you willingly. But lay a hand on him, and I'll knock your block off."

He said, "Damn you, I'll—"

"You'll do nothing but leave. I'll stand here, with the door open, till you're across the street. The cat's free to follow you, if he's yours."

"It's my cat! And damn it, I'll—"

"You can get a writ of replevin, tomorrow," I said. "That is, if you can prove ownership."

He glared a minute longer, opened his mouth to say something, then reconsidered and strode off down the walk. I closed the door, and the cat was still inside, in the hallway.

I turned, and Ruth Carson was in the hallway too, behind me. She said, "I heard him say who he was and what he wanted, and when the cat jumped down and went toward the door, I—"

"Did he see you?" I asked.

"Why, yes. Shouldn't I have let him?"

"I—I don't know," I said. I did know that I wished he hadn't seen her. Somehow, somewhere, I sensed danger in this. There was danger in the very air. But to whom, and why?

We went back into the living room, but I didn't sit on the piano bench this time; I took a chair instead. Music was out for tonight. That ringing doorbell and the episode that had followed had ended my inclination to improvise as effectively as though someone had chopped up the piano with an ax. Ruth must have sensed it; she didn't suggest that I play again.

I said, "What do you know about our pleasant neighbor, Milo Haskins?"

"Very little," she said. "Except that he's lived there since before we moved into the neighborhood last year. He has a wife—a rather unpleasant woman—but no children. He does sell insurance. Mostly fire insurance, I believe."

"Does he own a cat, that you know of?"

She shook her head. "I've never seen one. I've never seen any black cat in this neighborhood except Mr. Lasky's, and—" She turned to look at Satan One-and-a-Half, who was lying on his back on the rug, batting a forepaw, at nothing apparently.

I said, "Cat, if you could only talk. I wish I knew whether—" I stood up abruptly. "To what side of that maple tree and how far from it did Mr. Lasky bury that cat?"

"Are you going to. . . ?"

"Yes. There's a trowel and a flashlight in the kitchen, and I'm going to make sure of something, right now."

"I'll show you, then."

"No," I said. "Just tell me. It might not be pleasant. You wait here."

She sat down again. "All right. On the west side of the tree, about four feet from the trunk."

I found the trowel and the flashlight and went out into the yard.

Five minutes later I came in to report.

"It's there," I told her, without going into unpleasant details. "As soon as I wash up, I'd like to use your phone. May I?"

"Of course. Are you going to call the police?"

"No. Maybe I should—but what could I tell them?" I tried to laugh; it didn't quite go over. This wasn't funny. Whatever else it was, it wasn't funny. I said, "What time do you expect your aunt and uncle home?"

"No later than eleven."

I said, "For some reason, this Haskins is interested in that cat. Too interested. If he sees us leave here, he might come in and get it, or kill it, or do whatever he wants to do with it. I can't even guess. We'll sneak out the back way and get to your place without his seeing us, and we'll leave the lights on here so he won't know we've left."

"Do you really think something is—is going to happen?"

"I don't know. It's just a feeling. Maybe it's just because the things that have happened don't make sense that I have an idea it isn't over yet. And I want you out of it."

I washed my hands in the kitchen, and then we went outside. It was quite dark out there, and I was sure we couldn't be seen from the front as we cut across the lawn between the houses.

We'd left the light burning in her kitchen. I said, "I noticed before where your phone is. I'll use it without turning on the light. I just want to see if I can get any information that will clear this up."

I phoned the *News* and asked for Monty Billings who is on the city desk, evenings. I said, "This is Murray. Got time to look up something for me?"

"Sure. What?"

"Guy named Lasky. Committed suicide at 4923 Deverton Street, three or four weeks ago. Everything you can find out. Call me back at—"

I used my flashlight to take the number off the base of the phone— "at Saunders 4848."

He promised to call back within half an hour and I went out into the kitchen again. Ruth was making coffee for us.

"I'm going back home after that phone call comes," I told her. "And you'd better stay here. Your uncle has a key, of course?"

She nodded.

"Then lock all the doors and windows when I leave. If you hear anyone prowling around or anything, phone for the police, or yell loud enough so I can hear you."

"But why would anyone—?"

"I haven't the faintest idea, except that Haskins knows you were at my place. He might think the cat is here, or something. I haven't anything to work on except a hunch that something's coming. I don't want you in on it."

"But if you really think it's dangerous, *you* shouldn't. . ."

We'd argued our way through two cups of coffee apiece by the time the phone rang.

It was Monty. He said, "It was three weeks ago last Thursday, on the fourteenth at around midnight. Police got a frantic call from a man who said he'd taken morphine and changed his mind and would they rush an ambulance or a doctor or something. Gave his name as Cohn Lasky, and the address you mentioned. They got there within eight minutes, but it was too late."

"Left a suicide note, I understand. What was in it?"

"Just said he was tired of living and he'd lost his last friend the week before. The police figured out he meant his cat. It had been killed about that time, and nobody knew of him having any friend but that. He'd lived there over ten years and hadn't made any friends. Hermit type, maybe a little wacky. Oh, yeah—and the note said he preferred cremation and that there was enough money in a box in his bureau to cover it."

"Was there?"

"Yes. There was more than enough; five hundred and ten dollars, to be exact. There wasn't any will, and there wasn't any estate, except the money left over after the cremation, and some furniture. The landlord, the guy who owned the house and had rented it to Lasky, made the court an offer for the furniture and they accepted it. Said he was going to leave it in the house, and rent the place furnished."

I asked, "What happens to the money?"

"I dunno. Guess if no heir appears and no claims are made against the estate, the state keeps it. It wouldn't amount to very much."

"Did he have any source of income?"

"None that could be found. The police guess was that he'd been living on cash capital, and the fact that it had dwindled down to a few hundred bucks was part of why he gave himself that shot of morphine. Or maybe he was just crazy."

"Shot?" I asked. "Did he take it intravenously?"

"Yes. Say, the gang's been asking about you. Where are you hiding out?"

I almost told him, and then I remembered how close I had come this evening to getting a composition started. And I remembered that I wasn't lonesome any more, either.

I said, "Thanks, Monty. I'll be looking you up again some of these days. If anyone asks, tell 'em I'm rooming with an Eskimo in Labrador. So long."

I went back to Ruth and told her. "Everything's on the up and up. Lasky's dead, and the cat is dead. Only the cat is over in my living room."

I went across the back way, as I had come, and let myself in at the kitchen door. The cat was still there, asleep again in the Morris chair. He looked up as I came in, and damn if he didn't say "Miaourr?" again, with an interrogative accent.

I grinned at him. "I don't know," I admitted. "I only wish you could talk, so you could tell me."

Then I turned out the lights, so I could see out better than anyone outside could see in. I pulled a chair up to the window and watched Ruth's house.

Soon the downstairs light went out, and an upstairs one flashed on. Shortly after that I saw a man and woman who were undoubtedly Ruth's uncle and aunt let themselves in the front door with a key. Then, knowing she was no longer alone over there, I made the rounds of my own place.

Both front and back doors were locked, with the key on the inside of the front door, and a strong bolt in addition to the lock was on the back door. I locked all the windows that would lock; two of them wouldn't.

On the top ledge of the lower pane of each of those two windows, I set a milk bottle, balanced so it would fall off if anyone tried to raise the sash from the outside. Then I turned out the lights.

Yellow eyes shone at me from the seat of the Morris chair. I answered their plain, if unspoken, question. "Cat, I don't know why I'm doing this. Maybe I'm crazy. But I think you're bait, for someone, or something. I aim to find out."

I groped my way across the room and sat down on the arm of his chair. I rubbed my hand along his sleek fur until he purred, and then, while he was feeling communicative, I asked him, "Cat, how did you ring that doorbell?"

Somehow there in the quiet dark I would not have been too surprised if he had answered me.

I sat there until my eyes had become accustomed to the darkness and I could see the furniture, the dark plateau of the grand piano, the outlines of the doorways. Then I walked over to one of the windows and looked out. The moon was on the other side of the house; I could see into the yard, but no one outside would be able to see me standing there.

Over there, diagonally toward the alley, in the shadow of the group of three small linden trees— Was that a darker shadow? A shadow that moved slightly as though a man were standing there watching the house?

I couldn't be sure; maybe my eyes and my imagination were playing tricks on me. But it was just where a man would stand, if he wanted to keep an eye on both the front and back approaches of the cottage.

I stood there for what seemed to be a long time, but at last I decided that I'd been mistaken. I went back to the Morris chair. This time I put Satan One-and-a-Half down on the floor and used the chair myself. But I'd scarcely settled myself before he had jumped up in my lap. In the stillness of the room, his purring sounded like an outboard motor. Then it stopped and he slept.

For a while there were thoughts running through my mind. Then there were only sounds—notes. My fingers itched for the piano keys, and I wished that I hadn't started this damn fool vigil. I *had* something, and I wanted to turn on the lights and write it down. But I couldn't do that, so I tried memorizing it.

Then I let my thoughts drift free again, because I knew I had what I'd been trying to get. But my thoughts weren't free, exactly. They seemed to belong to the girl, Ruth Carson.

I must have been asleep, because she was sitting there in the room with me, but she wasn't paying any attention to me. We were both listening respectfully to the enormous black cat which was sitting on the piano while it told us how to ring doorbells by telekinesis.

Then the cat suggested that Ruth come over and sit on my lap. She did. A very intelligent cat. It stepped down from, the top of the piano onto the keyboard and began to play, by jumping back and forth among the keys. The cat led off with *"La Donna e Mobile"* and then—of all tunes to hear when the most beautiful girl in the world is sitting on your lap— he started to play *"The Star-Spangled Banner."*

Of course Ruth stood up. I tried to stand, too, but I couldn't move. I struggled, and the struggle woke me.

My lap *was* empty. Satan One-and-a-Half had just jumped off. It was so quiet that I could hear the soft pad of his feet as he ran for the window. And there was a sound at the window.

There was a face looking through the glass—the face of a man with a white beard!

My hunch had been right. Someone had come for the cat. Lasky, who was dead of morphine, had come back for his black cat which had been run over by an auto and was buried in the back yard. It didn't make sense, but there it was. I wasn't dreaming now.

For an instant I had an eerie feeling of unreality, and then I fought through it and jumped to my feet. The cat, at least, was real.

The window was sliding upward. The cat was on its hind feet, forepaws on the window sill. I could see its alert head with pointed black ears silhouetted against the gray face on the other side of the window.

Then the precariously balanced milk bottle fell from the upper ledge of the window. Not onto the cat, for it was in the center, and I'd made the bottle less conspicuous by putting it to one side. While the window was still open only a few inches, the milk bottle struck the floor inside. It shattered with a noise that sounded, there in the quiet room, like the explosion of a gigantic bomb.

I was running toward the window by now, and jerking the flashlight out of my pocket as I ran. By the time I got there, the man and the cat were both gone. His face had vanished at the sound of the crash, and the cat had wriggled itself through the partly open window and vanished after him.

I threw the window wide, hesitating for an instant whether or not to vault across the sill into the yard. The man was running diagonally toward the alley, and the cat was running with him. Their course would take them past the linden trees where I'd thought, earlier, I'd seen the darker shadow of a watcher.

Half in and half out of the window, still undecided whether this was my business or not, I flipped the switch of my flashlight and threw its beam after the fleeing figure.

Maybe it was my use of that flashlight that caused the death of a man. Maybe it wouldn't have happened otherwise. Maybe the man with the beard would have run past the watcher in the trees without seeing him. And certainly, as we learned afterward, the watcher had no good reason to have made his presense known.

But there he was, in the beam of my flashlight—the second man, the one who'd been hiding among the lindens. It was Milo Haskins.

The bearded man had been running away from the house; now at the sight of Haskins standing there between him and the alley, directly in his path, he pulled up short. His hand went into a pocket for a gun.

So did Haskins's hand, and Haskins fired first. The bearded man fell.

There was a black streak in the air, and the cat had launched itself full at the pasty moon-face of Milo Haskins.

He fired at the cat as it flew through the air at his face, but he shot high; the bullet shattered glass over my head.

The bearded man's gun was still in his hand, and he was down, but not unconscious. He raised himself up and carefully shot twice at Haskins.

I must have got out of the window and run toward them, for I was there by that time Haskins was falling. I made a flying grab at the bearded man's automatic, but the man with the beard was dead. He'd fired those last two shots, somehow, on borrowed time.

I scooped up Haskins's revolver. The cat had jumped clear as he had fallen; it crouched under the tree.

I bent over Haskins. He was still alive but badly hurt. Lights were flashing on in neighboring houses, and windows were flying up. I stepped clear of the trees and saw Ruth Carson's face, white and frightened, leaning out of an upper window of her house.

She called, "Brian, are you all right? What happened?"

I said, "I'm all right. Will you phone for a police ambulance?"

"Aunt Elsa's already phoning the police. I'll tell her."

~§~

We didn't learn the whole story until almost noon the next day, when Lieutenant Becker called. Of course we'd been making guesses, and some of them were fairly close.

I let Lieutenant Becker in and he sat down—not in the Morris chair—and told us about it. He said, "Milo Haskins isn't dying, but he thought he was, and he talked. Lasky was Walter Burke." He stopped as though that ought to make sense to us, but it didn't, so he went on:

"He was famous about fifteen years ago—Public Enemy Number Four. Then no one heard of him after that. He simply retired, and got away with it.

"He moved here and took the name of Lasky, and became an eccentric cuss. Not deliberately; he just naturally got that way, living alone and liking it."

"Except for the cat," I said.

"Yeah, except for the cat. He was nuts about that cat. Well, a year or so ago, this Haskins found out who his neighbor across the street was. He wrote a letter to the police about it, put the letter in a deposit box, and started in to blackmail Lasky, or Burke."

"Why a letter to the police?" Ruth asked. "I don't see—"

I explained that to her. "So Lasky couldn't kill him and get clear of the blackmail that way. If he killed Haskins, the letter would be found. Go on, Lieutenant."

"Burke had to pay. Even if he ran out, Haskins could put the police on his trail and they might get him. So he finally decided to fool Haskins—and everybody else—into thinking he was dead. He wanted to take the cat with him, of course, so the first thing he did was to fake its

death. He boarded it out to a cat farm or cat kennel or whatever it would be, and got another black cat, killed it, and buried it so people would notice. Also that gave color to the idea of his
committing suicide. Everybody knew he was crazy about the cat.

"Then, somewhere, maybe by advertising, he found a man about his age and build, and with a beard. He didn't have to resemble Lasky otherwise, the way Lasky worked it.

"I don't know on what kind of a story Lasky got the other guy here, but he did, and he killed him with morphine. Meanwhile, he'd written the suicide note, timed his phone call to the police telling them he'd taken morphine, and then ducked out—with, of course, the balance of his money. When the police got here, they found the corpse."

"But wouldn't they have got somebody to identify it?"

The lieutenant shrugged. "I suppose, technically, they should have. But there wasn't any relative or friend to call in. And there didn't seem to be any doubt. There was the suicide note in Lasky's handwriting, and he'd phoned them. I guess it simply never occurred to anyone that further identification was necessary.

"And none of his neighbors, except maybe Haskins, knew him very well. He'd probably trimmed the other guy's beard and hair to match his, and probably if any neighbor had been called down to the morgue, they might have made identification. A man always looks different anyway, when he's dead."

I said, "But last night why did Haskins—?"

"Coming to that," said the lieutenant. "Somehow the cat got lost from Lasky. I mean Burke. Maybe he just got around to calling for it where it'd been boarded, and found it had got away, or maybe he lost it himself, traveling, before it got used to a new home. Anyway, he figured it'd find its way back here, and that's why he took the risk of coming back to get it. See?"

"Sure. But what about Haskins?" I asked.

"Haskins must have seen the cat come back," said the lieutenant.

I nodded, remembering that Haskins had been mowing his lawn when I'd gone to the door.

"He realized it was Lasky's cat and that Lasky had tricked him. If the cat was alive, probably Lasky was too. He figured Lasky would come back for the cat, and he watched the house for that reason. First he tried to get you to give him the cat by saying it was his. He figured he'd have an ace in the hole if he had the cat himself.

"He didn't intend to kill Lasky; he had no reason to. He just wanted to follow him when he left, and find out where he was and under what identity, so he could resume the blackmail. But Lasky saw him there when you turned on the flashlight. Lasky went for a gun. Haskins had brought one because he knew he was dealing with a dangerous man. He beat Lasky, I mean Burke, to the draw. That's all."

That explained everything—except one thing. I said, "Haskins was too far away to have rung my doorbell. Burke wasn't there. Who rang it?"

"The cat," said Lieutenant Becker simply. "Huh? *How?* The button was too high for it to—" The lieutenant grinned. He said, "I told you Lasky was crazy about that cat. It had a doorbell of its own, down low on one side of the door frame, so when he let it out it wouldn't have to yowl to get back in. It could just ring the bell with its paw. He'd taught it to do that when it wanted in."

"I'll be damned," I said. "If I'd thought to look—"

"Black cats look pretty much alike," said the lieutenant, "but that was how Haskins knew this was Lasky's cat. From across the street he saw it ring that trick doorbell."

I looked at the cat and said, "Satan," and he opened his eyes. "Why didn't you explain that, damn you?"

He blinked once, and then went back to sleep.

I said, "The laziest animal I ever saw. Say, Lieutenant, I take it nobody's going to claim him."

"Guess not. You and your wife can buy a license for him if you want to keep him."

I looked at Ruth to see how she liked being mistaken for my wife. There was a slight flush in her cheeks that wasn't rouge.

But she smiled, and said, "Lieutenant, I'm not—"

I said, "Can't we get two licenses while we're at it?"

I wasn't kidding at all; I meant it. And Ruth looked at me and I read something besides surprise in her face—and then remembered the lieutenant was still around.

I turned to him. "Thanks for starting this, Lieutenant, but I don't need a policeman to help me the rest of the way—if you know what I mean."

He grinned, and left.

Dime Mystery, November 1942

The Case of the Dancing Sandwiches

I

IT WAS AN EVENING like any other evening—up to midnight, when the drinks began to sneak up on him. And Carl Dixon was a man like any other man, so he began to forget that he had a fiancée who was out of town for a few days, and he began to hold Dorothy more tightly when they danced.

He squeezed her hand and felt an answering pressure. She turned her head and looked at him, her face only inches from his, and her face was beautiful in the smoky dimness of the night club. Her body was beautiful, too, although he couldn't see that. It was too close to him.

She put her head back on his shoulder and he got a heady whiff of the perfume again. It was wonderful. By inversion it made him think of Susan because Susan didn't go in for perfume. And he was discovering now that he liked perfume. Maybe he should give some perfume to Susan. She'd probably use it if she were given some. Possibly the same—

"Dorothy," he said.

"Yes, Carl?" into his shoulder.

"What kind of perfume is that? It's wonderful."

She raised her head from his shoulder again, and again her face was inches from his. "Why do you want to know?" She was laughing at him.

"Just curious. Is it a secret?"

"*Le Secret?* No, I have some of that, too. But this is called *Une Nuit d'Amour.*"

Her dark eyes were laughing into his and her so-red tempting lips were laughing, too. But just for a second—and a second can be a long time—there was something in her eyes besides laughter. Then her face was turned from his again.

But it shook him so that he almost missed a step. The way she'd said *it—Une Nuit d'Amour—*and the way she'd looked at him, well, his French wasn't much but it was enough to translate *Une Nuit d'Amour* into a night of love. And his knowledge of women wasn't much but it was enough to translate that look she'd given him into the promise of a night of love, this very night, if he wished.

It almost sobered Carl Dixon because it proposed so many simultaneous questions—practical and moral—for his keen, accountant's mind to answer. There was Susan. He loved Susan—not fervently, not passionately, but, he thought, sincerely. He was going to marry her next spring. They'd be happy together. Was it worth risking *that,* however slight the risk might be? Part of him said no and part of him said yes, and his mind weighed the two and decided that the balance depended upon whether the risk was negligible or considerable.

He thought, *what about her brother? How would they get rid of him? But there must be an answer to that, else why her invitation?*

But what about his job, if he risked a scandal?

~§~

The dance ended and the clarinet tootled a little "That's all" to show that it was the end of a set. And Carl Dixon followed Dorothy back to the table where her brother waited. Walking three steps behind, he couldn't keep his eyes off her bare white shoulders and her almost-bare white back, the black sleekness of her hair (Susan's was a nondescript brown) and the black sleekness of the satin that molded her hips and thighs as smoothly as the white skin molded her back and shoulders.

Vic Tremaine grinned at them, showing the gold tooth that was the only thing about him Carl Dixon didn't like.

"Hi, kids," he said. "I had our drinks replenished while you were gone."

Carl held Dorothy's chair for her and then took his own and sipped moodily at his drink, wondering.

For one thing he wondered just what he knew about these people and decided he didn't really know a thing except what Vic had told him. He'd met Vic Tremaine quite casually in a bar about two weeks ago. They'd been standing next to each other and he couldn't remember now which of them had spoken first. He rather thought it had been he. He'd asked Vic for a match. Then they'd got to talking and had liked each other.

But neither of them had tried to follow up the acquaintance. Three days ago he'd run into Vic again, this time on the street, and they'd had lunch together. Over that lunch they'd exchanged addresses, quite casually, Vic explaining that he was still a stranger in Manhattan and didn't know many people—wouldn't Carl give him a ring sometime if he found himself at a loose end? And Vic had talked a little more about himself then. He'd run a roadhouse near Chicago, but things were dull there and he'd sold out and come to New York. Now he was looking for a place near New York, preferably on Long Island, but possibly in Jersey. A quiet little place, nothing big or pretentious with a floor show—but with a good pianist who could sing, to alternate with a three-piece combo for dancing.

He'd probably be in partnership with a man by the name of Richard Ancin—he'd known Ancin for many years and had shared other enterprises with him. Ancin was a great guy. Carl would like him. And Carl would also like his, Vic's, sister Dorothy, who'd be joining him in New York shortly.

And tonight, just as he'd got home from work, Vic had called. He'd said there were two things to celebrate. Dorothy had just arrived in town for one thing. For another, Dick Ancin had found a little place for them in Jersey and was already there, running it. The man they'd bought it from had turned it over right away.

Would Carl have dinner with him and Dorothy?

Carl Dixon had demurred at first, but not long. He was a bit lonesome, with Susan out of town visiting her parents in Philadelphia. And it was Friday night, so he didn't have to go to work the next day. And he did like Vic, in spite of the gold tooth. And, on the phone, Vic said it was his celebration and on him, that Carl wasn't even to bring his wallet along. Yes, it was an invitation that would have been hard to turn down.

And since then—until now—he'd been glad he'd accepted. Dorothy Tremaine had turned out to be a knockout. They'd had cocktails—several apiece—at a crowded bar at the Astor and Carl felt a mild, delightful glow even before they'd eaten dinner at Lindy's. Dorothy said she'd never been to Lindy's other times she'd been in New York and wanted to see all the celebrities. So they went to Lindy's (without Carl admitting that he'd never been there either) and had a fine dinner, although they didn't see—or at least they didn't recognize—any celebrities.

It had been almost ten o'clock when they'd got in Vic's car, all three of them in the front seat, and Carl had to put his arm up along the back of the seat so there'd be room. Dorothy had been very soft and warm against him and for the first time he'd been close enough to smell that perfume.

It had been almost more intoxicating than the Martinis. Not in just the same way, of course.

Dorothy had done quite a bit of talking and had, as women can, led him into doing quite a bit of talking, too. So he'd hardly noticed where or even what direction they went after the Holland Tunnel. He did remember the tunnel because there was so much of it and because he'd remarked to Dorothy how wonderful it was that a car could turn into a submarine and go right under a river.

Anyway, he didn't know Jersey. They had gone through several towns that might have been Jersey City, Hoboken, and Weehawken, or they might have been Jersey City, Newark, and Elizabeth. Or any other reasonable combination you can suggest.

Finally Vic had turned in a parking lot beside a brightly lighted place and Dorothy had asked eagerly, "Is this it, Vic?"

Vic had laughed and said no, his place wasn't anywhere near this big, although they were going to expand it a bit now that they had it.

"It's early yet," he said. "Not much after eleven, and you said you wanted to dance a bit. Let's spend an hour here and have a few more drinks and you and Carl can dance a couple of times."

Dorothy had said it was a good idea and then, as they were getting out of the car, she'd laughed and said to Carl, "You'll *have* to dance with me, Carl. Vic won't. He says it's practically incest for a man to dance with his own sister."

Carl had laughed, too, but down inside he'd been just a little shocked. Susan wouldn't have said that. Just maybe—and some other little things pointed that way—Dorothy wasn't quite as moral a girl as Susan. In fact, maybe—just maybe—

And now it was midnight and several dances and quite a few drinks later, and the maybe wasn't a maybe any more, and it worried him so that he almost wished that he hadn't come with them. He was a little drunk by now, but he could still think clearly enough to realize the problems involved.

Well, he didn't have to decide right away. Vic and Dorothy were talking about the new place and Carl felt that he should say something.

"What's the name of it, Vic?" he asked.

"We're going to call it Ancin and Vic's," Vic told him. "There are so many fancy names around, that's more likely to be remembered. And Dick likes to use his last name and I'd rather use my first, so we decided on that. Like it?"

"Sounds okay."

"Dick and Vic's would sound silly," Dorothy said. "And Ancin and Tremaine would be worse. Too—what's the word I want, Carl?"

He was still sober enough to think of it. "Pretentious, maybe?"

She patted his hand. And then let her hand remain on top of his.

Vic glanced at his wrist watch. He said, "One more drink and we'll go there."

Carl said, "Maybe I'd better skip this one."

Vic laughed at him, and ordered three drinks. And Carl didn't want to look like a sissy so he drank his, but he shouldn't have. He had to concentrate pretty hard after that not to give away how drunk he was. At any rate, he hoped he wasn't giving it away.

He could still follow what Vic was saying about the size of the new place. "It's about two-thirds the size it's going to be when we get the addition built for the bar," Vic said. "Right now the bar's in the main part of the building, right along with the dance floor and the tables. The dance floor's too small, that way, and the music they got is terrible. But we took over the combo and we let them play out their contract, ten more days. Anyway, that's why I let you kids dance here instead of there. It's a crummy band and a bad floor. Well, you ready?"

Vic settled the bill, just as he'd settled at the Astor and at Lindy's, over Carl's not too vociferous protests. At least Vic hadn't been exaggerating when he'd said the evening was on him.

They got back in Vic's car and drove some more. By this time Carl didn't know whether they were going north, south, or west—or, for that matter, up or down. But this time—although he still hadn't got his ledger balanced—he let his arm drop from the back of the seat across Dorothy's shoulders. She snuggled up against him and again there was *Une Nuit d'Amour* in his nostrils and on his mind, in more ways than one.

Then the car was slowing down and Vic said delightedly, "By golly, he's got the neon sign up already. We didn't think it would be here before tomorrow at the earliest. Look!" And Carl looked out of the window and saw a brightly-lighted little roadhouse with a fair-sized red neon sign that said ANCIN AND VIC in foot-high capital letters, and then Vic turned into the driveway and back to the parking lot.

They went in the side door and it was a nice place, although not large. There were about a dozen customers at tables or in booths and a few more at the bar. The dance floor was small, as Vic had said, and the combo was down to two pieces because no one was sitting at the trap drums. But the accordion and sax made plenty of noise.

Vic looked around and shook his head disgustedly. "Business looks rotten," he said. "Oh, well, we'll build it up when we get going. Take a booth, kids. I'll see where Dick is."

He walked over to the bar and talked to the bartender a moment while Dorothy slid into a booth and Carl sat down beside her. He felt pretty wobbly by now and was having trouble keeping his eyes in focus. But, he told himself, he was having a swell time.

II

IT WAS A JOB like any other job, but Tom Anders didn't like it. Not that there was anything hard about it. It was duck soup and a quick hundred bucks and he needed the hundred bucks. Besides, Jerry Trenholm had promised him another hundred if everything went smoothly. Not that he'd count on that second hundred until he saw the green of its eyes, but it was nice to think that he might get it.

He sat there back in the booth in the corner and didn't seem to pay attention when the three of them came in. That was the program. He waited until the girl and the mooch sat down with their backs to him and then he went out the side door and got the cloth back as Jerry had told him to. Nobody had spotted it. That part was all right.

He came back in and Jerry was still at the bar talking to the bartender. So he went back to the corner booth and sat there again waiting for Jerry to give him the high sign to go into his act. He went over the details in his mind so he wouldn't miss up on anything. Not that he would anyway. He'd been at short-con and long-con so long that he could talk in his sleep without breaking cover.

Anders looked at Jerry Trenholm and told himself that Jerry Trenholm was now Vic Tremaine, his partner in this measly little joint. Vic Tremaine—call him Vic. And he, Tom Anders, was Richard Ancin, and Jerry would call him Dick. They were supposed to have been in partnership before, out in Chicago. Good. That was easy. And the mooch's name was Carl Dixon, although he wasn't supposed to know that until they'd been introduced. But then he could say, "Oh sure, Vic has mentioned you to me."

And the dame was supposed to be named Dorothy Tremaine and to be Vic Tremaine's sister, just in from Chi. Anders had never seen her before, but the fact that he didn't know her real name made it easier to remember that she was Dorothy Tremaine. He didn't have to keep his mind on its toes about that, like he did about having to remember that he himself was Dick Ancin and Jerry was Vic Tremaine. Of course he would have to remember that he was supposed to have known Dorothy back in Chi, to greet her as an old friend.

And Jerry had said that he'd have the waiter fixed so the waiter wouldn't try to collect for the drinks—which would have been a giveaway, since they were supposed to own the joint.

Then Jerry turned around at the bar and gave him the high sign and he walked over to Jerry. He said, "Copacetic?" and Jerry nodded, but Jerry took him by the arm before they went to the table. They both glanced over and saw that the mooch wasn't looking toward them, but toward Dorothy, so there wasn't any hurry.

"One more drink," Jerry said, "and he'll be ready to pass out. He's up to the eyeballs now. Be sure he drinks it. Act hurt as the devil if he won't drink with you. Got that?"

"Sure, Jerry."

"And we watch him and get him outside just before he passes out. Don't want to attract attention having to get him out after he's out cold. He'll be wobbly, but we can get him out between us without anybody paying attention. But we don't want any big-eye stuff."

"Sure, Jerry, but—I don't like it."

"Don't like what?"

"Playing tag in the dark. I wish I knew what the score was, what you were shooting for, if for no other reason than so I won't make any bulls."

"You won't make any bulls. If you did, he's too drunk to notice. If you want that other hundred, just follow through."

"But if it's badger game, why do you want him to go—in my car instead of along with the dame? And if it isn't badger, what is it?"

Jerry took another quick look at the mooch and then looked back at Anders, and Anders saw that Jerry's eyes were cold.

"Look, Jerry," Anders said, "I'm not trying to chisel in. I don't care what the racket is, as long as it's not a bump-off. You say it's not, but how do I know, if I don't know what it really is? And you got to admit it looks funny, me getting him in my car—"

"The car I gave you money to rent."

"All right, the car you gave me money to rent. And God only knows why you wanted me to use the mooch's name to rent it under. That's one thing that's funny. And then, after he's passed out, to stop on that side road till you catch up. How do I know you're not figuring on bumping him off there? And I'd be the guy that left here with him and—"

"Use your brains, Anders." Jerry Trenholm's voice was getting ugly now. "If I wanted to bump him off, I could have done it a dozen times, a dozen places on the way here. And as for his leaving here with you, we're all four leaving together, and who's going to come outside to notice who gets in whose car? And why would I have come here and rung you into it at all?"

Tom Anders sighed. He'd thought of those angles too. It all didn't make sense. Must be some variation on the good old badger, but he couldn't see where the payoff was.

He tried once more. "But, Jerry—"

"All right," Jerry said. "Give me back the hundred. We'll skip it."

"All right, all right," Anders said. "If I got to work in the dark, I'll work in the dark. Just one thing, though. If I don't know what you're doing, how'll I know if it comes off or not—and whether you owe me the other hundred or not?"

"Do a good job on your part of it," Jerry said, "and you'll get your other hundred tomorrow, whether the deal comes off or not. Fair enough?"

"Okay," Anders said. Anyway, he'd got that much by arguing. And he couldn't have given the first hundred back anyway. There was only sixty of it left. "Do we go over now?"

"I will. You come in a minute, like you just turned up. And the waiter'll come right after you do, and he's fixed."

Anders ambled back to his corner booth. Might as well finish the drink he had back there. He drank it, watching Jerry Trenholm over the rim of his glass.

He still hated playing tag in the dark. Well, he'd hate it worse, he thought, if there was a chance that Jerry Trenholm could possibly know who it was had tipped off the coppers that time in Boston when Jerry was building up old Harrison to hang some paper on him. But hell, his own long-con on Harrison would have fallen through if the old man had been bitten by Jerry first. Anyway, that was eight years ago and Jerry hadn't found out.

He caught Jerry's eye and went over to their table. He slapped Jerry on the back.

"Hi, Vic," he said. "And Dorothy—swell to see you again. Vic phoned me you just got in. How're things in Chicago?"

She gave him her hand across the table and he had time to take a good look at her to see that she was quite a dish, and then Jerry was saying, "Dick, this is Carl Dixon. Carl—Dick Ancin, my partner."

And he was shaking hands with the mooch and saying, "Glad to know you, Dixon. Vic's mentioned you to me. How do you like the place here? Sure, I know it's a dump, but wait till we get through with it. You won't recognize—"

Then he broke off because the waiter was coming to the table, and they all ordered except Carl, who said he'd maybe better skip a round. But Anders gave him a frown and some good-natured mock indignation and they ordered a whisky and wash for him.

When you're trying to get anybody drunk, Anders knew, straight shots are the thing. Not so much because they're more potent, but because a mooch can't stall by sipping at one like he can on a highball or even a cocktail. Get him to down it, and then you can order another.

~§~

It might or might not, he decided, looking at the mooch, take another one. He was pretty well under. You could tell by his eyes and by the thickness of his voice. When a man's eyes looked that way, he was seeing double. And Dixon didn't look like someone who'd had much experience at drinking, so he'd go quick once he started to go.

They got him to drink that round easily. They waited until the waiter had left and then proposed a toast to the success of Ancin and Vic's, and it would have been boorish under the circumstances for the mooch not to have drunk to that. Anders studied him after that one and decided that one more would be just right, and plenty. They'd have to get him out quick after one more.

Jerry Trenholm must have figured the same way because he said he wanted to see how things were going back in the kitchen and excused himself from the table. Anders saw him talk to the waiter instead of going to the kitchen. Then, a minute after Jerry came back to the table, the waiter brought another full round of drinks and that put another shot of whisky in front of the mooch without his having had a chance to turn it down.

They sipped their own drinks without paying any attention to the mooch, and Anders pretended to be talking to Jerry about plans for the roadhouse.

But out of the corner of his eye Anders saw Dorothy squeeze the sucker's arm an instant. Then she picked up her own drink and glanced at his.

Anders heard her whisper, "Let's drink to *us,* Carl." And she smiled at the mooch, and he smiled back and downed his whisky like a good boy.

And that was enough. They all knew it. In a minute or three Jerry glanced at his watch.

"Say, it's getting late," he said. "Maybe we'd better get back to town. You coming, Dick?"

"Sure," Anders said. "I'm calling it a night. I'll let the boys close up. But I can't ride in with you, Vic. I'm stuck with my own car and I'll need it tomorrow morning, so I can't leave it here. How's about splitting two and two? One of you ride with me, so I won't have that long ride all alone?"

"Not Dorothy," Jerry said, "I've got something I haven't had a chance to talk to her about. Say, Carl, how'd you like to keep Dick Ancin company?"

The mooch frowned, and obviously started looking for a way out. Dorothy took care of that, neatly. Anders had to admire her technique. It would have worked on men less drunk than Dixon.

She squeezed his arm again and said, "You won't mind, will you, Carl? I haven't had a chance to talk to Vic yet, and I've got some things to tell him, too. Here's an idea. You and Dick come up to my place for a few minutes when we get into town. Vic took Suite 817 for me at the Ambassador."

"Deal me out, Sis," Vic said. "I'm going to drop you off and hit the hay. Got to see a man early tomorrow—about getting a decent combo for this place."

"'Fraid I can't come up, either, Dorothy," Anders said. "But I'll drop Carl off on your doorstep if he wants to have a nightcap with you."

And Dorothy said, "Will you, Carl? It's my first night in New York for years, and I feel like talking for hours yet."

It was as simple as that. The mooch was groggy when they stood up, but Jerry and Anders got him between them and outside to the car Anders had rented a few hours before in New York.

Their timing had been perfect, too. The mooch passed out cold the minute they got him comfortably settled in the front seat. And Anders got in behind the wheel and started driving along the route Jerry Trenholm had laid out for him when he'd given him the C-note, plus expenses, for the job.

He pulled out of the parking lot and Jerry's car pulled out after him, and then dropped back.

The only hard part of the job was over. That is, the part that could have been hard—getting the mooch into his car instead of the other one. Now he had about thirty miles to drive, then the turnoff into an unused side road where Jerry would catch up with him and they'd switch the mooch back to the other car. Then he had to drive to New York and turn his rented car in, and that was all. An easy hundred bucks for a few hours' simple work. Two hundred bucks, if Jerry kept his promise.

Just the same, he didn't like it. He'd be a lot happier if he knew what the score was.

III

Jerry Trenholm slowed down and let the car ahead pull out of sight. All the better not to keep a close tail as long as Anders was going to stop and wait for him anyway. Don't let the two cars be seen together. He leaned over and patted Claire's hand.

"You did a swell job, honey," he said. "Had him eating out of your hand. Another half hour and he'd have been eating your hand too."

"I kind of liked him," Claire said. "He was dumb, but nice. He didn't even try to paw me."

"Maybe we should change plans. Maybe we should take him up to your suite at the Ambassador. We'd have to rent you one first."

"Don't look now, Jerry, but your eyes are turning green." She laughed, and then stopped laughing. Her voice was different when she said, "Jerry, I'm a little scared."

"Nothing to be scared of, honey," he said. "I've figured the angles. There isn't any wheel going to come off. We're going to kill two birds with one stone. And it'll give us a racket, Baby, that will put us on top of the world. We'll roll in the green stuff. We'll wallow in it."

"But what if he goes to the cops when he wakes up?"

"He'll be scared to. But if he does, so what? He cooks his own goose. We lose out on the racket and I'll have spent two hundred bucks and some brain cells, but what the devil, the other part of it is worth that to me. I'll settle."

"I think you're wrong on one thing, Jerry. I think Carl will go to the cops. He's that kind of a guy."

Jerry Trenholm shrugged. "All right, so maybe he'll go to the cops. I told you I'd settle if he did. We're in the clear. And if he doesn't, we're in the bucks. That's the beauty of it."

"But what if this Tom Anders is heeled?"

"He isn't. I've got his gun. Picked it up when I went up to his room this afternoon to proposition him. And don't worry. Nobody saw me go up there. And he doesn't know I've got the heater. I got it when he went to the bathroom down the hall."

He laughed. "And I didn't even take a chance that maybe he'd go to the bathroom. I pretended I wanted to talk over old times and I brought a lot of beer with me and stayed a while. When a guy drinks a lot of beer—well, I was sure I could get his gun if he had one. And he did. That makes it perfect."

"But what if he missed it after you left?"

For the first time, Trenholm sounded annoyed. "If he had," he said, "he wouldn't have been here tonight. He'd have been scared off. Now shut up till we get there. I've got half an hour yet before our little rendezvous and I want to spend it thinking back over tonight. I want to be sure there isn't a single thing that could lead to us."

Claire was quiet. After a minute Jerry said, "One thing. Did you see anybody you knew tonight anywhere while we were with him? The Astor? Lindy's? The Golden Glow? The last place? Anywhere?"

"No, Jerry."

He grunted and then started thinking back again. He ran over the angles, all of them. He had time to check everything. Thus far he hadn't done a thing. If, in the next half hour, he could think of a single tangible that could lead the cops from Carl Dixon or from Tom Anders to him or to Claire, then there was still time. He could still call the whole thing off. He could tell Anders plans were changed and to drop the sucker off where he lived—or anywhere else for that matter. Thus far, he was out only a couple of hundred bucks.

Half an hour from now—

He began to sweat a little bit. He felt beads of perspiration on his forehead and he ran down the window on his side of the car and let a cool breeze blow in on his face. He'd killed before, twice, but both times had been back in the days when he was young and a gun punk during prohibition. This was different. This was like playing chess.

Only this was the *big* game. If you lost, you didn't play again.

But he couldn't lose, except the two hundred bucks. And since he'd found out six months ago that it had been Tom Anders who'd thrown him to the bulls that time in Boston, well it was worth two hundred bucks to do something about that. And if, in the process, he could set himself up to make money that might run into six figures, wasn't that a gamble worth taking?

Yes, it was. And he ran over the whole evening again, and then over everything that had happened in connection with Carl Dixon since the first time Dixon had been pointed out to him and he'd followed the guy into a bar and struck up an acquaintance, just in case, without as yet having any particular plan in mind.

Not a loophole. Nothing they could trace back to him.

Just the same, he began to sweat again. Despite the cold draft that came in the open window on his side of the car his forehead got wet again and he had to wipe it off with his handkerchief.

Then the side road where Anders would be waiting was only a mile ahead, two minutes ahead at the thirty-an-hour he was crawling along, and he had to make up his mind.

He made it up, and he wasn't scared any more. The coldness was in his mind now.

He turned into the side road and slowed down long enough to take Anders's gun out of the door pocket of the car and put it in his coat pocket. Then he kept going until he saw Anders's car parked off the road ahead of him.

He got out and walked up beside Anders. Anders turned the window down and leaned out.

"Hi, Jerry," he said. "He's out cold. You don't have to worry about talking, or about waking him, moving him."

"You sure?" Trenholm asked. It made a difference. If a man was really out, stiff, paralyzed, a gunshot near his ear wouldn't wake him. If Dixon was only asleep, then he'd have to use the butt of the gun on Anders. And it wouldn't be as good that way.

Anders laughed. "He's out like a light," he said. "I shook him good to make sure. Stuck a bottle in the glove compartment there, so I could give him another drink if he could use it. But nothing will wake him now. Listen to the way he's breathing."

"Good," Trenholm said. "Stay where you are, Tom, for a minute."

He walked around the car and opened the door on Dixon's side. He looked at Dixon and listened to him and then put his hand on Dixon's shoulder and shook him.

Okay, he thought, *a shot might wake him, but if it does, he can be slapped back to sleep.*

He took Tom Anders's short-barreled .38 revolver out of his pocket. He reached cross Carl Dixon's chest and jammed the muzzle of it into Anders' ribs.

He said, "For the favor you did me in Boston, Tom." He pulled the trigger.

And that was *that*. Even as he pulled the trigger, his eyes went from Anders's face to Dixon's. Dixon had jerked at the explosion of sound, but he hadn't awakened. It seemed impossible, but he hadn't. He moved in his sleep and his head slid down the other way, onto Anders's dead shoulder.

By the dim light of the bulb on the dashboard, Jerry Trenholm watched Dixon's face for a full thirty seconds before he was satisfied, and sure.

Then he went back to his own car and opened the door.

"It's okay, honey," he said. "Everything's swell. But come on. I want you to help me a few minutes. We got a few things to do." He reached into the glove compartment of his own car and took out another pistol. And a leather shoulder holster.

Claire got out of the car, shaking a little. "What, Jerry?" she asked. "What is there to do?"

"The thing I want you to help me with is to get Anders's coat off and put this shoulder holster on him. It's his. I swiped it with his gun. See, Baby, I want everything to fit. If he's got his shoulder holster on that fits the gun, the cops will know it's his gun even if they can't trace it to him otherwise. And if Dixon *is* fool enough to go to the cops with this, they'll figure he fought Anders for Anders's gun and shot him with it. So come on, Baby, it's going to be a job to get his coat off and on again, but we can do it between us."

He heard Claire grit her teeth a little. "All right, Jerry," she said. "For you, all right. And why the other gun?" She got out of the car.

"We got to fire another shot, honey—with Dixon's hand wrapped around the butt of a gun, so he'll have nitrate marks if they give him a paraffin test. And I can't use Anders's gun for that, because it should have only one bullet fired out of it. And everything will check for Sunday after I wipe my fingerprints off Anders's gun and put Dixon's on. And don't let me forget the door handles of the car. We're not missing *anything*, Baby."

They didn't. They didn't miss anything.

It took them fifteen minutes, but that didn't matter on a side road that nobody would use until morning. And when they were finished, Jerry Trenholm spent another five minutes just looking and thinking things over, making like he was a cop himself and looking for something, and there wasn't a thing he had missed.

Just the same, he sweated a little again as he drove away. He sweated a little now and then for two months, and then the trial was over and he knew he was safe—even though he'd missed the big gamble and the big money.

And that part of it was bad, but what the devil. He was safe, wasn't he? And he'd got Anders. And he was doing all right, even if he didn't have the six figures he'd hoped for.

Or maybe he did have six, one way you looked at it. Five figures in the bank. And then there was Claire's.

Even after the trial, he had a bad moment or two. But another month went by and finally he knew he was safe.

IV

HIS NAME WAS PETER COLE and he was a detective like any detective, and no smarter than the average. He was thirty-three. He'd graduated out of harness when he was twenty-eight and that meant he'd been a detective for five years. He had a good record, nothing brilliant, but no bad boners either.

He worked for the City of New York, and he worked out of the 24th Precinct Station on West 100th Street. There is a large proportion of Puerto Ricans in that precinct and Peter Cole got along well because he spoke fluent Spanish, having been born and raised in a Texas border town. New York's Puerto Ricans speak English, but they speak Spanish among themselves and they think in Spanish. If you can talk that language with them, you get along with them better. Peter Cole got along fine with them.

And now, at six o'clock of a November evening, he was heading for the door of the station, through for the day. Somebody yelled, "Hey, Pete," and he turned and said, "Yeah?"

"Phone."

He went back and picked up the phone and said, "Cole speaking."

"Mr. Cole, my name is Susan Bailey. You don't know me, but a mutual friend of ours, Mrs. Richmond, suggested that I ask your advice about—about a problem."

It was a nice voice. He liked it. "You're a friend of Grace Richmond's?" he said. "I haven't seen her for a couple of months. How is she?"

He'd gone to school with Grace in Texas twenty years ago. Now she was the only friend he had in New York who was from his home town. She and her husband had a little apartment in the Village and once in a while he was invited there to dinner and once in a while he took Grace and her husband, Harry Richmond, out to a restaurant, to reciprocate. He liked Harry too. Usually he saw them about once a month. This time it had been longer.

"Grace is fine," the voice on the phone assured him. "And so is Harry. But about my problem, Mr. Cole. It's awfully complicated to explain over the phone. Do you have any plans for this evening?"

"Well—" he said.

"I live in the apartment across the hall from the Richmonds'. If you're through work now—Grace told me you generally get off at six—I could rustle something to eat for us by the time you get here, and that would give us time to talk. And after that we could have Grace and Harry come over for some bridge."

Peter Cole liked bridge, and Grace and Harry were good players. "Do you ever trump your partner's ace?" he asked. "That's one thing I'd have to know."

"I did once. I had to, to get the lead, and we set a doubled contract by two tricks."

"Fine," he said. "In that case, I'll come. Will seven-thirty be all right?"

She said it was.

He went out, turning up the collar of his topcoat against the cold gray drizzle of rain, took the Columbus Avenue bus to 72nd Street, and went up to his hotel room to shave and change his clothes. He told himself that he was cleaning up, not because he'd liked the sound of Susan Bailey's voice, but because he was going to see Grace and Harry later in the evening.

He walked to the subway on Central Park West and rode to the 4th Street Station. At one minute after seven-thirty he pushed the buzzer of the apartment across the hall from the Richmonds'.

The door opened, and Peter Cole liked what he saw through it. Susan Bailey was a tall girl, almost as tall as he, and well built, not thin as so many tall girls are. She had a face that was pretty, if not beautiful, with a generous mouth and wide, clear brown eyes. Her hair was a nice shade of brown and she had a few well-arranged freckles on an otherwise clear, creamy skin. She wore no make-up, except some lip-colored lipstick, and he liked the fact that her fingernails were the color of fingernails instead of screaming scarlet or garish purple.

He liked the simple housedress she wore and the way she filled it. And he liked the unaffected naturalness of her smile and her voice when she said, "Come in, Mr. Cole."

He liked the efficient way in which she took care of his wet hat and topcoat, putting the latter on a hanger, but spreading a place for it in the closet so it wouldn't wet other things hanging there. And he liked the smell of frying chicken coming from the kitchenette. And he was ravenously hungry. This was an hour and a half, almost, after the time he usually ate.

~§~

The fried chicken tasted even better than it had smelled, and there was plenty of it and plenty of creamy mashed potatoes and chicken gravy—as rich and greasy as chicken gravy should be.

It was wonderful. Hungry as he was, it was too wonderful to interrupt by talking very much. Of course, they didn't eat in complete silence. But they talked about the horrible weather, about what nice people Grace and Harry Richmond were, and—from Cole—how wonderful the dinner was. And he wondered, aloud, why the Richmonds' hadn't invited her across the hall other times he'd been there and learned that she'd lived there only six weeks whereas the last time he'd been to see Grace and Harry had been two months ago, and that explained that.

Finally he put down his final cup of coffee, empty, and lighted cigarettes for both of them. He took a deep breath of satisfaction and managed, unobtrusively, to let out his belt a notch.

"And for that, Miss Bailey," he said, "I would slay dragons for you. If there are any around. Are there?" Banteringly, of course.

And then, all of a sudden, it looked as though she were going to cry. He didn't know what he'd said that was wrong, but he knew the light touch had been wrong.

He leaned across the table. "I'm sorry. Are you really in trouble, Susan?" He didn't even notice that he'd used her first name for the first time. "Is there anything I can do?"

But then her face was all right again. It was just the suddenness with which he'd veered the conversation from food to murder, not knowing that it was murder

"I'm not in any trouble myself," she said. "My fiancé is. Very bad trouble. He's in prison—for life—for murder. A murder he didn't commit."

Peter Cole stared at her. It was such a change of pace that he was thrown off base for a moment.

All he could think of to say was, "Tell me about it."

"His name is Carl Dixon. Does that tell you, or—?" She paused to see if the name meant anything to him.

It didn't, quite. "I seem to remember the name," he said, "but—"

"In New Jersey. Essex County. The trial was in Newark. The murder was three months ago. The trial was one month ago."

"I remember now. I read about it, but I didn't follow it closely. The man who was murdered was a crook, wasn't he? A conman, I believe. What was his name?"

"Tom Anders. Yes, he was a conman. But Carl didn't kill him. I *know* that."

"Want to run over the details for me?"

"Carl was taken out by a man who called himself Vic Tremaine and a woman he introduced as his sister, Dorothy. Cocktails at the Astor, dinner at Lindy's. Drinks and dancing at a place in Jersey. Then they drove to a little roadhouse called Ancin and Vic's—Carl saw the neon sign with that name on it—and they introduced him to this Tom Anders under the name of Dick Ancin. They got him drunk. About one-thirty or two o'clock they started back to New York and he was in Anders's car and he passed out, completely.

"He woke up—or came to—about five o'clock in the morning. He was in Anders's car, parked off the road. A little side road just inside Essex County, no houses nearby and no traffic late at night. Anders was behind the wheel, dead. He'd been shot in the side, the side toward Carl. The gun he'd been shot with was on the floor of the car between them, and Carl didn't touch it, of course.

"He got out of the car fast and started walking. You can imagine how he felt, physically, as well as mentally. He admits he seriously, very seriously, considered going home, not reporting it. If he went to the police, it might cost him his job. It never occurred to him it might cost him more than that."

"Why? I mean, why might he have lost his job?"

"He's an accountant for the New York State bank examiners. I mean he was. He isn't now, of course. With a job like that, you can't get into any scandals or associate with criminals. You've got to lean backward to be respectable. And he always had."

"I can see that," Cole said. "But honesty prevailed over interest and he went to the police."

"He phoned them from a farmhouse and waited for them."

"And they arrested him for the murder?"

"Not right away. They held him as a material witness for twenty-four hours, and by that time they had enough evidence against him to issue a warrant. And to convict him when it came to trial two months later. It was pretty bad evidence—bad for Carl, I mean."

Cole prompted her. "Such as?"

"His fingerprints were on the gun. And ballistics showed that it was the murder weapon. One shot had been fired out of it. And when they found that, they gave him a paraffin test and there were nitrate marks on his right hand, none on his left."

"That isn't conclusive. Nitrate marks can come from other things than firing a gun."

"That was admitted at the trial. But it was contributory evidence just the same. And the gun was Anders's, and he was wearing a shoulder holster that fitted it. That looked bad, too, with only the two of them in the car. The police figured he got the gun away from Anders and used it on him. They tried to get him to confess and plead self-defense, to say that Anders had pulled the gun to shoot or threaten Carl and that he'd fought for the gun and used it in self-defense."

"It would have been a good plea. It would probably have stood and he could have got a light sentence if any"

"But it wasn't true, Mr. Cole. At least it wasn't true as far as he knew. He was out cold at the time it happened."

"Then it could have happened that way. I mean, it could have been something that happened before he passed out, but while he was too drunk to know what he was doing or to remember afterward."

"I don't think so. He swears he remembers everything up to time he passed out. And Carl—well, he isn't a drinker, but he been drunk before, a few times, and he says he's never done anything he didn't remember. Some people are that way. Others aren't."

"I know," Cole said. "I'm that way myself. I've done some pretty silly things a few times, but I remembered them the next day. Was there any other evidence?"

"Plenty of it. There was *too much* of it, but the police just wouldn't recognize that. For one thing, they were unable to verify a single thing Carl told them about the early part of the evening. There are no such people as Vic Tremaine or Dorothy Tremaine as far as they've ever discovered. They haven't found the roadhouse where the three of them stopped on the way to what was supposed to be Vic's roadhouse, and as for that—well, there's no place called Ancin and Vic's within a hundred miles of New York."

"They check at the Astor bar and at Lindy's?"

"Yes, but they didn't get around to that for several days, and they didn't get anything. Carl gave them the location of the table at Lindy's and they found the waiter who'd been at that station on the night in question. He vaguely remembered having seen Carl, when they showed him Carl's picture, but he couldn't remember what evening it had been or who Carl was with."

Peter Cole nodded. "That's about all you could expect, after several days, unless he'd been a regular customer there or they'd given the waiter some reason to remember the party. How about the menu? Did they try that angle?"

"Carl told them what each of the three had ordered, and they were all things that had been on the menu that evening. But that didn't help. He could have found that out by eating there alone. Or even with Tom Anders. That's what they think. That he spent the evening with Tom Anders, and that he just made up Vic and Dorothy Tremaine."

"Nothing at the Astor?"

"Not a thing. They found all the bartenders who were on duty that evening, but none of them remembered Carl from his picture."

"Not surprising, of course. Anything else?"

"Two things on the positive side. Both very bad. One was that the car Anders had was a rented car and that he'd rented it earlier in the evening using the name of Carl Dixon. And you know what the prosecutor did with that?"

"No. Wait a minute, let me think. I can guess. He adds that fact to the fact that Anders was carrying a gun and comes up with the presumption that Anders rented the car for his meeting with Dixon, thought Dixon might possibly try to kill him and used Dixon's name so, if it did happen, it would leave a trail to Dixon when the cops traced the rented car."

"That's exactly it. And there was one thing worse. In the wastebasket in Tom Anders's room they found a crumpled sheet of stationery that he'd started to write a note on. He just got as far as 'Dear Carl—' and then crumpled it and threw it away. The police figured he'd started to write Carl—and they took that as a pretty strong indication that the two knew each other—and then had decided he would see him instead.

"See how it all seems to dovetail? Carl says Vic Tremaine phoned him that night about six, and the switchboard record shows he did get a call then. But the police think the call was from Anders, after Anders had started to write him a note and then changed his mind."

"But the note had just the first name Carl? Not the last name or address?"

"No, it could have been to any other Carl. But in connection with Anders renting the car under Carl's name, his full name, and—well, everything put together: fingerprints, nitrate test, their not being able to verify a single point of Carl's story—"

Peter Cole nodded slowly. He said, "I see what you mean. They had a case. It's a wonder they didn't give him the chair."

V

THE GIRL had an answer to that. "I think they would have, on Carl's testimony. I think his attorney saved him from the chair by making an about-face, more or less, in his final talk to the jury. He must have seen that he was licked, that there wasn't a chance on earth of an acquittal or even a split jury. So he managed, pretty cleverly, to get across the idea that even if Carl was lying, as they already thought anyway, he was probably lying out of having killed Anders in a fight over Anders's gun, or that maybe he really didn't remember doing it at all, that it had been in a drunken struggle after he was too far gone to know what he was doing.

"Anyway, they didn't see it as a cold-blooded, premeditated crime, so they gave him the benefit of that much doubt. They brought in a recommendation for mercy along with their verdict. And the judge gave him life. And that was fair enough, I guess. Nobody except me—and Carl—seemed to doubt he'd killed Anders, but some of them must have doubted that it was a premeditated crime. Some of the men who picked him up at the farmhouse after he'd phoned testified he was in bad physical shape and had obviously been pretty drunk."

"And did the prosecutor suggest a motive?"

"Yes, of course. Carl was a bank examiner. Anders was a conman. It would come in handy for a conman to know people's bank balances and transactions. The prosecutor suggested that Anders had some hold over Carl and was going to blackmail him into giving information that he could use."

"Pretty sound," Cole said. "But the one thing they wouldn't be able to understand is why Carl had called copper instead of going home after the murder. He wouldn't have known about the car being rented in his name or about the note in the wastebasket, so he wouldn't have known the crime could be traced to him."

She nodded solemnly. "And the fact that he didn't wipe his fingerprints off the gun. Those two things together made it look as though he really was pretty drunk and may actually not have known what he'd done. That was the doubt that got him life instead of—of the electric chair."

"Frankly," said Cole, "that's how it would look to me, I'm afraid. Are you sure that's not the way it was? Can you be sure?"

"I can be. I am. Because I know Carl. I know he isn't lying. I know he didn't know this Anders before that evening and that he'd met him as Dick Ancin and had no reason to kill him—drunk or sober. I know he didn't make up that story about Ancin and Vic's, or about Vic and Dorothy. And if all that is true, plus the fact that Carl isn't the type who does things when he's drunk and doesn't remember them, well, he didn't do it. Vic Tremaine must have. He was following them back to New York in his car. He must have done it while Carl was unconscious and put Carl's prints on the gun and left him there to take the blame."

Peter Cole stared at the girl across the table from him. "It could have been," he said. "It would be a devil of a thing to try to prove, now. Three months is a long time."

"I know it."

"What do you want me to do?"

"To do? Nothing. I couldn't ask you to do anything, of course. I want to ask your advice about a private detective. That is, I wanted the advice of some detective on the force as to who is a good private one, and Grace Richmond said I should ask you, that you'd probably know."

"Oh, I see." He thought of a few whom he knew, but he didn't mention them yet. Instead he asked, "Why now? If you were going to do that, why didn't you do it sooner? Even if you hoped for an acquittal until the trial was over, why didn't you think about a private detective right after the trial, a month ago?"

"I didn't have the money then. I did think of it. Wait, I'm going to make us some more coffee."

She went into the kitchenette to get it started and when she came back she said, "Carl had a little money saved up and so did I. When we saw how serious things were, how black it looked for him, I lent him what I had and we used it to get a really good lawyer. And I'm glad we did. With a poor one, even an average one, Carl might have—have got the chair. Stuart Willoughby—that's the lawyer we got—at least kept Carl alive. And that means there's still a chance."

A devil of a slim chance, Peter Cole thought. But he didn't say it.

"After the trial," she said, "we were both flat broke. I even lost my job." She smiled a little. "I'm a private secretary and my boss didn't see eye to eye with me on the necessity of my attending every day of the trial. He didn't exactly fire me, but he told me what a fool I was to stick by a murderer. Anyway, I quit. But I got another job two weeks ago.

"Meanwhile, early this week, an aunt of mine died and left me a small bequest. A thousand dollars. I ran into debt about a hundred during the trial, and while I was out of work, and I'll have to pay that off. That leaves me about nine hundred, clear. That may give Carl another chance, if I use it to hire a private detective."

The poor kid, he thought. *She really* does *believe he's innocent.*

"Maybe," he said, "it could better be spent for further legal steps."

"No. I asked Mr. Willoughby after the trial if there was anything at all that could be done. He said definitely not, unless there was new evidence." She smiled a bit wryly. "He said that in about ten years we could start working for a parole, that we wouldn't get one that soon, but we could start trying."

He said, "Let me think a minute."

"Of course. I'll get the coffee."

She came back with it and he'd been thinking. "There are the Pinkertons," he said, "if you could get them to handle it. But I doubt if they would unless they saw something they could do for you. I mean specific angles that they could investigate. I don't see offhand what those would be, but maybe we could think of some. They're pretty good, but they're good enough to be choosy about what they take, and this isn't exactly in their line. You could try them, and if they take it, you'll get your money's worth of time put in on the job, but I don't think they'll get anywhere. I don't see how they can, now."

"You think a small agency, a one or two man outfit, would do better?"

"No, and you'd be more likely to get gypped. But—"

He didn't know how to go on. What he really thought was that she shouldn't waste her money at all. It was too hopeless. It was like buying a part of a ticket on the Irish Sweepstakes. Now, after three months, even if her man was innocent, it must be hopeless. Surely the police had looked into every angle. And she'd gone broke for the guy once and now she was going to do it again. What it boiled down to was that he didn't think she should spend that nine hundred bucks at all.

"Thanks," she said gravely. "Then I'll try the Pinkerton Agency. I'll go there tomorrow."

"No, don't. Not yet." He said it irritably, not knowing that he was irritated or that he sounded that way. He was frowning at her. "Let me read up on the case in the papers. I'll get back numbers at the library. Let me think it over to see what angles there are that still *can* be investigated."

"But Mr. Cole, I'm not asking you to do all that. I merely asked you to recommend a private detective."

"And I'm not recommending one, not yet. Not even the Pinks. Look, I'm off work tomorrow. I want to go to the library and read up on the case. Then let me advise you."

"Well—if you want to do that. But you won't have to go to the library. I've got the newspapers. I kept them. I mean, I kept copies of the Newark *Star-Ledger* for the first few days after the murder and for all four days of the trial. It got better coverage there than in the New York papers because the murder was in Essex County and the trial was in Newark. And I've got a transcript of the trial itself."

"A transcript? What on earth for?"

"To study. I had Mr. Willoughby buy me a copy from the court reporter, at so much a page. It has all the testimony and cross-examination. You really want to read through it? It's long."

"Sure, and the newspapers you have, too. If I may take them along."

"Of course. But you won't have to carry all the newspapers if you look at them now while I do the dishes. Then you'll just have to take the trial transcript. That is, if you want to read them now."

"Why not? Except that I hate to see you stuck with all these dishes."

She didn't even answer that. She got the papers and put them and him on the sofa where he could stretch out and read comfortably, lying on his back as all sensible people like to read.

~§~

For a while he heard her working around in the kitchenette, then the sounds faded from his consciousness and he was completely absorbed in what he was reading. He was a moderately slow reader, but he had a retentive memory for details.

He was halfway through the trial when he became aware that she had finished and was standing in front of him. "Want to quit now and take the other papers along?"

"Don't bother me," he said. "Beat it. Take a walk around the block. Or sit down and shut up."

She laughed at that. She sat down and shut up, but she watched him. He knew she was watching him and it was harder to concentrate but he finished, through the last day of the trial, and the sentencing. Then he put the last paper down and frowned at her.

"It's going to be a tough job," he said. "Even if he's innocent, it's going to be a tough job. But wait till I've read that transcript of the trial before I stick my neck out any farther than that."

"But, Peter—" and she didn't notice that she'd used his first name for the first time—"I'm not asking you to stick your neck out at all. I just asked you—"

"How to waste your last nine hundred dollars?" he said. "Well, don't do anything until I've talked to you again. You work tomorrow?"

"Yes, tomorrow's Friday. Then I'm off two days, Saturday and Sunday. Why?"

"If I get any wild ideas while I'm reading that transcript tomorrow, can I phone you?"

"Of course." She gave him the number. "I haven't a phone here yet. But you can reach me through Grace across the hall. And that reminds me. I called you from her phone at six, and she heard the conversation, so she knows you're here and they're looking for us to go over for a rubber or two of bridge. Maybe we'd better. It's almost nine."

He didn't want to, but he said, "Sure," and they went across the hall.

He didn't play quite his usual game of bridge, because his mind was going in circles. But he didn't trump any of Susan's aces and they took two rubbers out of three.

And at eleven-thirty he went home, with a bulky envelope that contained the transcript under his topcoat to protect it from the drizzling rain. He didn't try to read it on the subway and he tried not to think about it after he was home and while he was going to sleep.

In the morning he slept late, as he always did on his day off, and when he went down for breakfast, he took the transcript with him. The rain had stopped and the weather was clear and cold. He read through three cups of coffee after his breakfast and then went back to his room and finished by midafternoon.

When he finished, he said, "Damn!" very fervently.

He didn't think Carl Dixon had killed Tom Anders. He didn't know whether it was anything he had read, either in the newspapers or in the transcript, or whether it was Susan Bailey's calm confidence that had infected him.

Maybe, more than anything else, it was the lack of motivation for Dixon's having acted as he did, having told the story he did, if he had been guilty, if the story wasn't true. And, blast it, there *was* a doubt. That's why he'd been given life instead of death. Neither juries nor judges are legally supposed to figure that way, but they do.

But it wasn't any of his business. He ought to go over things with Susan, figure some angles that could stand further checking, and then send her to the Pinks with those angles. Or to one of the best small operators if the Pinks didn't want it. That was the only sensible thing to do. It was even more than Susan had expected him to do.

So he picked up the phone and called Captain Blain. "This is Cole, Cap," he said. "I've got a couple of weeks of accumulated sick leave. Okay if I take part of it now, starting tomorrow? It's short notice, but if it isn't going to gum things too much—"

"I guess it will be all right. Not sick, are you?"

"No, I'm okay"

"Devil of a time of year to take a vacation. You must be crazy."

"That's it," Cole said. "I wondered what was wrong with me, Cap, and you hit it on the head. I must be crazy."

VI

HE CALLED Susan Bailey at the number she'd given him. "This is Peter Cole, Susan," he said. "I've finished the transcript and I'd like to talk it over with you. Are you free this evening?"

"Of course. Would you care to eat at my place again?"

"No, we're going out. We're going to have cocktails at one place and dinner at another."

"You sound very masterful, Peter. I don't seem to have any choice. But don't you like my cooking?"

"Sure I do. It's wonderful. But we're going to have cocktails at the Astor and dinner at Lindy's."

"Oh." Her voice sounded quite different. Softer. "Thank you, Peter. Thank you very much."

"Don't be silly," he said, and without knowing it his voice was quite irritated. "If you've got a pic of this Dixon guy, bring it along. There are pix in the papers, but you know how a newspaper picture is. Sometimes you wouldn't recognize your own brother. Can you be ready at six-thirty?"

"Easily, but why come all the way down to the Village? I can meet you uptown."

"Six-thirty, then. It's all right. I've got a car. Just wasn't using it last night."

"All right, then. And I have a photograph. Two, in fact."

"Only one thing, Susan. Understand that we probably won't get anything at either place. It was too long ago. But don't let that discourage you, because we won't expect to get anything."

He was right in one way, wrong in another. They didn't get anything that would help clear Carl Dixon, even though they were lucky enough to find the right waiter at Lindy's and two of the three bartenders who'd been on duty at the Astor bar on the night of August 16th. But they did get excellent Martinis at the bar and they had borscht, filet mignon, and pineapple cheese pie at Lindy's. So it wasn't a lost evening.

There was one question he remembered to ask her. "I was going to ask you this last night after I finished reading the Newark *Star-Ledgers*," he said. "In one of the papers during the trial there was a reference to their having tried to locate this place called Ancin and Vic's, and a box item they ran on it. Must have been in one of the papers in between the murder and the trial. Did you read it?"

"Yes, it was about a week after the murder, when the police were still trying to find something that might substantiate Carl's story. The *Star-Ledger* ran a boxed item on the front page headed 'Have You Been to Ancin and Vic's?' and asking anybody who might know where the place was to write in to them with the information."

"Get any answers at all?"

"Not that I know of. I presume if they had got anything, they'd have given it to the police, or at least printed it in the paper."

"A reasonable enough assumption. Susan, that place—Ancin and Vic's—is the key. We've got to find it, or we aren't going to get started. And that's going to be a sweet job, unless we get a lead. According to Carl's story, that place could be anywhere within a hundred miles of New York."

"Anywhere across the Hudson, that is. He didn't notice where they were driving, but he'd certainly have noticed if they'd recrossed the Hudson, either back through a tunnel or over a bridge. He'd surely have noticed that."

"At least, he might have. And for that reason, if they didn't want him to know where he was going, they wouldn't have crossed back. Okay, within a hundred miles of Manhattan, but west of the Hudson. That gives us most of New Jersey, a sizeable hunk of Pennsylvania, and a sizeable hunk of New York State if they turned north after they got into Jersey." He shook his head. "A semicircle with a radius of a hundred miles. If I remember my math, that would be—let's see, radius squared, ten thousand, times pi—which we'll call three even—thirty thousand for the whole circle. Fifteen thousand square miles, Susan. That's all we've got to cover to find Ancin and Vic's. Fifteen thousand square miles."

She smiled a bit wanly. "Sounds pretty bad when you put it that way."

"It isn't quite that bad. I hope. How about the neon sign angle? Did the police go into that?"

"Pretty thoroughly, they tell me. They checked with every maker of neon signs in the vicinity. It cost them plenty, because there were a lot of firms. But no one had sold a sign like that."

"It's bad they didn't get anything," he said, "but at least it saves us having to check on it. That would have been an awful job. It's going to be bad enough as it is."

"Peter, it isn't *your* job. I can't expect you to—"

"Be quiet," he said. "Look, I've got to go to Newark tomorrow, on business. While I'm up there I might drop in at the *Star-Ledger* and checkup on that question they ran about Ancin and Vic's, and I might drop in to talk to the prosecutor who handled the case. And tomorrow's Saturday. Want to come along?"

"Of course, if I won't be in the way."

"I won't let you. I'll be there at one o'clock, and I'll let you feed me before we start. And now—we can't sit here and take up a table at Lindy's forever. Want to go back to the Astor bar?"

"Let's go up to my place, Peter. We can talk better there, and I've got the wherewithal for some drinks."

So they went up to Susan's and talked, by mutual consent, about almost everything else but murder. Almost everything else. There was one other topic they avoided just as scrupulously.

For some reason, when he got home that night he was mad. He didn't know if he was mad at himself for being sucker enough to get himself roped into a business like this, a lost cause if he ever saw one, a case in which he was chasing shadows. But it must be that, because he wasn't mad at Susan. He had nothing against this Carl Dixon.

But just the same he stood a moment outside the door of his empty room, looking at the door and wanting to put his fist through it. But he used the key instead.

He slept late. It was almost eleven when he woke, and since he'd be eating at Susan's at one, he skipped breakfast except for a cup of coffee.

It was colder out and it was snowing. The fresh snow was clean and white on the streets and it was falling fast enough to stay that way except on very busy streets where the traffic outpaced its fall. It was the first really good snowfall of the year. He hated cold weather, but he liked snow. He'd take cold weather any time to get snow like that, falling in big soft flakes.

He drove east into Central Park and southward along its winding drives for as far south as it went, then he cut over to Fifth Avenue and kept on it south into the Village.

She had corned beef and cabbage ready and, particularly after no breakfast, it smelled like ambrosia to him. He wondered if she had guessed it was his favorite dish. He didn't see how she could have for he hadn't mentioned it in all the times he'd talked to her. That thought pulled him up short. All the times? He'd seen her for exactly two evenings.

They ate leisurely and talked a lot. It was after two when they started for Newark and it was three when they got there. He found the *Star-Ledger* building and parked in front of it.

They found the managing editor's office and asked him about the question he'd run boxed on the first page.

"That was an idea of one of our rewrite men," he said. "Anything that came in from it would have gone to him. But I don't think there was anything, or he'd have made something of it."

"Could I talk to him about it?" Cole asked.

The managing editor said into a phone, "Send Roy Green in here, please."

A minute later, a tall, stoop-shouldered man with iron gray hair came in.

"Roy," the editor said, "these people are interested in the Anders murder case. Did you get any replies at all to that question you ran on Ancin and Vic's?"

"Nothing that seemed important. One screwball letter from a man who offered to start a place and name it that if we'd lend him the money. The other was too vague to be taken seriously. It was from a man in Jersey City. He wrote that he vaguely remembered seeing a place called Ancin and Vic's, but he couldn't remember where or when. It didn't seem very helpful."

"Did you follow it up at all?"

"Yes, I did. I wrote and asked him to think it over and if he remembered anything more about it to let us know. We haven't heard from him, so I suppose he hasn't."

"Did it sound like a screwball letter to you?"

"No, I don't think it was. He sounded sane, and sincere. But possibly, even probably, he'd read the phrase Ancin and Vic's from a previous story on the case—then forgot where he'd read it and had a vague idea he really had seen a roadhouse with that name on it."

"Do you still have his name and address?" Cole asked.

"Not the address," Roy Green said, "but I remember the name because it was an unusual one. It was John Smith—John Smith, M.D. And it wasn't a gag signature because the letter was on his letterhead. So even without the street address, he should be findable. There won't be many Doctor John Smiths in Jersey City, and a doctor will certainly have a phone listing. Want me to get it for you?"

"Thanks, no. I can do that," Cole said. They thanked the editor, too, and left.

"Sounds like an awfully slim lead," Susan said.

"It does, but we may run it down. Next, I'm going to talk to the prosecutor who handled the case, if I can find him in. And I think you'd better sit that one out, Susan. If I talk to him as a New York cop who has a side interest in one angle of the case, he'll dig deeper than if he thinks I'm working with you to try to break down the case he built up. Understand?"

"Of course."

He left her in the car when he went up to see Roy Harlan, who, he knew from the newspapers and the trial transcript, had handled the case. Harlan was in his office and was willing to talk.

"I'm interested in Anders's record," Cole said. "Not much of that came out in the trial. No reason why it should have of course."

Harlan's eyebrows raised slightly. "You have that available in your files at New York. As much as we have."

"Of course," Cole said. "I mean recently, since the last pickup that would show on the books. Something must have come out on what he'd been doing recently."

Roy Harlan tented his fingers. "Nothing for six months or so. As I get it, he hadn't been doing very well. His room was in a cheap hotel and his wardrobe was only so-so, which is bad for a conman. I'd say he was pretty close to being on his uppers. He seemed to have money while he was in Boston, but not since he left there. He spent most of the last dozen years in Boston, but I guess it got too hot for him."

Cole nodded. "Maybe I'll run up there to check on him. Another thing, Mr. Harlan. According to the papers—anyway, according to the *Star-Ledger*—Anders rented a car that night under the name of Carl Dickson. D-i-c-k-s-o-n instead of D-i-x-o-n. Same sound, but different spelling. That wasn't brought up in the trial. Is it straight?"

"Yes, it's straight. No, we didn't bring it up at the trial because it didn't seem to matter. If it did, the implication would be that Anders had known Carl Dixon only through meeting him, whereas we contended he probably knew him pretty well. The defense knew about the variation in spelling, of course, but they didn't bring it up. Why should they? They contended Dixon didn't know Anders at all, at least at the time Anders rented the car. So it seemed to have no bearing and be no help to either side."

Cole overplayed his hand by snorting slightly. "Wasn't either side, by any chance, interested in what really did happen," he said, "instead of merely the point of getting an acquittal or a conviction for Carl Dixon?"

"I don't see the connection, Mr. Cole."

Peter Cole sighed. "I'm not sure I do, either," he said. "Well, thanks, Mr. Harlan."

He rejoined Susan in the car. "I didn't get much," he said, "but one thing sounds mildly encouraging."

"What?"

"Let's have a drink. We'll find a bar that's got a private phone booth and I'll call this Dr. John Smith of Jersey City. And then I'll tell you the mildly encouraging thing."

They found the bar and ordered the drinks, and then Cole got the Jersey City operator on the phone and she had no difficulty finding the listing of Dr. John Smith.

VII

MIRACULOUSLY, Dr. Smith was in, but, sadly, he confessed that he'd come no closer to remembering where he'd seen a place called Ancin and Vic's than he had been at the time he wrote the letter. He said that, afterward, he'd felt a little foolish about having written it, since it was all so vague.

Cole thanked him and went back to join Susan in the booth. "No dice with Doe Smith," he said. "He still doesn't remember where he saw that neon sign."

"I was almost beginning to hope. But what's the one thing that is encouraging—mildly encouraging?"

He told her about the Dixon-Dickson angle.

"I knew that," she said. "It was in the papers. Mr. Willoughby considered whether or not to bring it out at the trial, but decided it wouldn't help our case."

He frowned. "That's one thing wrong with this whole business. Every fact is looked at with the idea of whether it's going to help or hurt Carl Dixon. Well, maybe that was natural. But now we can stop doing it."

"What do you mean, Peter?" Susan asked, puzzled.

"He's past help, in a manner of speaking. He's convicted, so no fact can hurt him. And we'll never get him free by finding facts that help him. We've got to find who did kill Anders. In other words, we've got to find this Vic Tremaine. And Dorothy. If we can find them—and Ancin and Vic's roadhouse—we've got enough to get the police to question them. They'd certainly want to do that, even if only because they might suspect them of being accomplices of Carl's."

He stared moodily at his drink. "Anyway, I like that misspelling of the name Dixon."

"Why?"

"It makes the only positive motive I've been able to figure out make sense. Not the motive for the murder—Vic Tremaine may have had any kind of a motive for killing Anders. But what's puzzling is why he went to such lengths to frame Dixon."

"Yes."

"We can work it out one way, that I can see. Let's say Vic is a conman, forger, even a bank robber. I like forger best for this purpose. *If* such a man could get a bank examiner to give him inside dope on bank accounts all over the state, maybe get him photographic copies of signatures, give him inside information, he could make a fortune.

"Help from a clerk in any given bank would be invaluable to him, but if a lot of forgeries turned up on accounts at any one bank—well, the racket wouldn't hold up long. But a bank examiner could get him fresh data from lots of banks. Maybe he had in mind starting a ring to capitalize on it instead of working solo. He already has one accomplice, Dorothy. But, solo or otherwise, he could make a killing. Do you see, Susan?"

"Of course," Susan responded. "Carl thought of that and we talked it over with his lawyer, but we couldn't see how it was expected to work out. I mean, Carl's in jail now and can't help him. And the evidence was so strong, Vic couldn't have expected Carl to beat it. And—"

"Slow down. You're forgetting something. When he found himself in a jam, Carl went to the police. He wasn't supposed to do that. Vic figured him wrong, although he must have known there was a possibility that Carl would.

"But suppose it had been the other way, Susan. Carl wakes up in the car with a corpse and he's scared stiff of consequences and goes home and says nothing. The police find the car and the body, and the case is in the papers and they're looking for the killer. And *then* Vic goes to Carl and tells him his fingerprints are on the gun the police have, tells him all the evidence there is against him.

"Carl might or might not think the charge of murder against him would stand up, but he knows he'd be in plenty of trouble even if he told the truth and was believed. He'd walked out on a crime, instead of reporting it. If he was lucky, he might only lose his job. But on his own admission he could go to jail for walking away from the murder. At the worst, he could be convicted of it. Do you see the spot he'd have been in a week later, say, if he'd sneaked home that morning after he woke up? And that's what Vic must have figured he'd do."

Susan nodded. "But what's the spelling of the name Anders used in renting the car got to do with it?"

"I'm assuming Anders rented that car under Vic's orders and that Vic told him what name to use. Now suppose Vic had told him to rent it under the name 'Carl Dixon.' Police find the body and the car, trace the renting of the car, and—well, on the off chance that the name means something, they'd look up any Carl Dixons in New York, where the car came from. And if a policeman even walked in on Carl Dixon to ask him what time it was, he'd have given himself away. So Vic's trouble would have been for nothing."

"I see. It's—it's beginning to make sense, Peter. Rather horrible sense."

"Yes, having that car rented under the name 'Carl Dickson' was subtle. It wouldn't lead the police to Carl Dixon, but Carl would read it in the papers and shake in his shoes. He'd know it was a point against him if the police ever were aimed his way. He'd begin to see what he was up against."

"If we could only find that roadhouse!"

"It would help. But I'd rather find Vic Tremaine. I'm going to Boston."

"To Boston? Why?"

"Anders came from there, fairly recently. I'm going to check every point on his record, and talk to anybody in the department there who may have known him. I want to find out who might have wanted to kill him—and preferably someone he wouldn't know would want to kill him.

Apparently he trusted Vic. Want another drink?"

"No, thanks."

"Then let's go. I'll drop you home, and then I'm going to take a night train for Boston. I can get an early start in the morning."

"But tomorrow's Sunday. Can you get anything on Sunday?"

He laughed at that. "There aren't any Sundays for police departments. They'll be open."

"This is more than wonderful of you, Peter. But *why*—? When I asked you for advice, I didn't dream—"

"Forget it," he said, almost rudely. "I got interested, that's all. A busman's holiday, maybe, but if I want to, why shouldn't I?"

"But are you taking time off work? If you are, you've got to let me—"

"Don't say it. It's sick leave, and I'm getting paid for it. It's not costing me anything. If you insist, I'll keep track of expenses. Now come on, we might as well eat somewhere, and then I've got to find out about trains."

He caught the eight-thirty train and spent the whole trip thinking, not about what he was going to do in Boston—that was simple enough, whether it got him anywhere or not—but what other angles might be open. There was an idea at the back of his brain, but he couldn't get it front and center. It had something to do with Ancin and Vic's roadhouse. There ought to be *some* lead that would take him to it. Was there any way to jog the memory of the one man—Dr. John Smith of Jersey City—who remembered seeing it?

Was it worthwhile making a trip to Jersey City to talk to him? At least he could discover what parts of the state were familiar to the doctor and, unless the doctor were widely traveled, cut down the territory. But that seemed pretty futile.

And the incipient idea stayed incipient. He couldn't get any closer to it. Point by point he went over Carl Dixon's story, looking for a lead, something he could get his teeth into.

He couldn't.

Worse, he kept thinking about Susan Bailey.

He got to Boston in time to get a few hours sleep, but he slept restlessly. At nine o'clock he went to police headquarters and spent two hours there. Then he caught a fast train back to New York and went directly from Grand Central to New York police headquarters.

At five-thirty he phoned Susan. "Eaten yet?" he asked her. "If not, I'll pick you up. And I promise not to put it on your bill."

"Did you get anything, Peter?"

"Maybe. I don't know yet. I'll tell you about it."

"Come on around. We'll eat here, and you can tell me."

She was cooking dinner for them when he got there a little after six, but she stopped work long enough to sit down to listen to what he'd learned.

"I checked pretty far back and pretty thoroughly," he said. "I got names and descriptions of three men who might have disliked Anders enough to liquidate him. Only one of the three came anywhere close to Carl Dixon's description of Vic Tremaine. It's a guy named Jerry Trenholm and in a general way he fits the description. Eight years ago this Jerry Trenholm went to jail on a tip Anders gave the police. That isn't on the records, but I talked to a captain who remembered the case."

"What is he? What kind of criminal, I mean."

"A forger. He did five years in jail in Massachusetts. He's been out three years. They thought he'd come to New York—and he did. I checked that at Headquarters here. At least he was here six months ago. That was their last notation on him. But here's the real break, Susan. He's got a wife—or a woman—who's been with him a couple of years. Her name's Claire. Either Claire Evans or Claire Trenholm, if they're really married. And her description pretty well fits that of Dorothy Tremaine."

"Peter, wonderful!"

"I've got a photo of Jerry Trenholm. Couldn't get one of Claire because she's never been in jail, although she's been up for questioning a few times. Anyway, I'm going to Newark again tonight, to talk to Harlan, the prosecutor. I'm going to give him the Trenholm picture and ask him if he'll show it to Carl Dixon and see whether Dixon identifies Trenholm as Tremaine. They'll show it to him with a dozen other pictures, so if he picks out Trenholm, then we'll know we're on the right track.

"Now don't get your hopes too high. Even if we're right so far, and if he does identify Trenholm, then they aren't going to let him out on account of that. But they will pull in Trenholm for questioning—I'll promise that much."

That was all he had to tell her, so she finished getting dinner and they ate. Sitting across the table from her seemed natural by now. He wondered whether, if he got her man out of jail for her and they were married, did she have any wild idea that he, Peter Cole, was going to be a friend of the family, like he was a friend of Grace and Harry Richmond's? That was different.

He insisted on helping with the dishes afterward.

He wanted to have something to do besides sit and think.

~§~

It wasn't until they were driving through the tunnel that conversation got back to murder.

"Peter," she asked, "what if Mr. Harlan won't help us by showing the picture to Carl?"

"Then we'll have to wait for visiting day and you can show it to him. But Harlan will. Sure, he thinks Carl's guilty, but he'll play along with us in trying to clear him, Why shouldn't he? Policemen and prosecutors are human, Susan."

"I know *one* who is."

He let the remark go and concentrated on his driving. Then she was back on the subject of Carl again.

"Peter, suppose Carl can identify the picture of this Trenholm and that the police are willing to pick him up for questioning. Can they find him? Do they know where he is?"

"As I said, the last record is six months old. But unless he's hiding out, they'll be able to find him. And the one good thing about how bad this case is, is that he won't think he has any cause for hiding. If he's in New York, my guess is that he can be picked up in twenty-four hours if we really try"

VIII

WHEN they were driving into Newark, and not talking, suddenly that incipient idea that had been in the back of Peter Cole's mind on the train to Boston was back again, only it seemed closer. So close that he knew he could get it, if he kept trying.

He swung into the curb in front of a bar. "Let's have a drink, Susan," he said.

She looked a bit surprised at the sudden suggestion, but she didn't argue. They sat at the bar and ordered Martinis. He sipped his and the idea seemed closer, somehow. And then, quite suddenly, he slapped his hand on the bar.

"Susan," he said, "let's go to Jersey City. And from there—just maybe—to Ancin and Vic's. What do you say?"

"Are you—serious?"

"Why not? I can take this photo to Harlan tomorrow. He'll be less annoyed if I see him at his office instead of bothering him at home, and he won't get it to the prison tonight anyway."

"But *how?* I mean, how do we go to Ancin and Vic's, Peter?"

"We'll drive there." He felt so good now that he laughed out loud.

"After Dr. Smith tells us where it is, of course."

"But I thought he didn't remember."

"Susan, he doesn't *have* to remember. Look, there isn't any roadhouse called Ancin and Vic's. If there was, the investigation and the publicity would have turned it up. And yet Carl Dixon went there and saw the sign. So. That means the sign was put up temporarily for him to see. Anders, as Ancin, was already there and probably knew to the minute when Vic and Dorothy and Carl would arrive. He put up the sign just before they got there and took it down before he joined them at their booth. Probably Carl's mistaken in thinking it was a neon sign. That could be done, but it would have been a lot of expense and trouble."

Susan nodded. "That could be. But how does it help us find the place? I'd say it would be just that much harder to find."

"It would be if it weren't for Dr. Smith. Look, Susan, that sign would have been up only a few minutes. Still, some other cars must have gone by during those few minutes. Several people may have seen that sign while it was up, and one of them remembered it. Dr. Smith.

"So that changes the question. The doctor doesn't have to remember where he saw it. All he has to remember is *where he was at about half-past twelve on the night of August sixteenth!* If he was out on a call, as is probable at that time of night, he'd keep a record of the call and—Wait a minute, I'm going to phone him from here. Maybe we won't even have to go to see him."

He got a handful of change from the bartender and went to the phone booth. In ten minutes he came back, jubilant.

"Got it!" he said. "Within ten miles, which is closer than I hoped. It was a confinement case, out in the country, ten miles from Jersey City on Highway 106. He remembers the call for him to go there came about midnight, after he was in bed. He got dressed and drove there, and didn't get away until after three in the morning. So Ancin and Vic's is—was—on that ten mile stretch of Highway 106. He couldn't have passed it anywhere else!"

"Peter, let's go look right now."

"We're practically there now."

He could see how excited she was, her hands clenched to fists in her lap as she sat beside him in the car. He drove to Jersey City and found Highway 106. They followed it out of town.

"This must be about the edge of town," he said when the houses began to thin out. "Watch the reading on the speedometer and let me know when we've gone ten miles. We'll do the whole stretch first and stop to look over the likely places on our way back."

They passed three roadhouses before Susan said they'd gone a little over ten miles.

He kept on only until he came to a driveway and could turn the car around.

"The second one," Susan said, "looks like the best bet. The one called Brian's Inn. Let's go in and order a dancing sandwich."

"Huh?"

Susan laughed. "Didn't you notice the neon sign? It reads 'Brian's Inn, Dancing Sandwiches.' On three separate lines of course, but I still want to order a dancing sandwich."

Peter Cole grinned and started the car. "Okay," he said, "we'll have one if they've got them. But we're going to stop at all three. Even if Brian's is the best bet. And why, by the way, do you think it is?"

"Well—the distance back from the road. The size of the place. I guess that's all."

They stopped for a drink apiece at the nearest roadhouse and, once inside, agreed that it was eliminated. The arrangement of the place was completely different from Carl Dixon's description of Ancin and Vic's. If nothing else, there weren't any booths and obviously never had been. The place wasn't arranged for them.

They got back in the car and drove on to Brian's Inn. He slowed down to look at the sign before they turned into the parking lot.

Susan had been right. In big neon letters on a framework in the yard in front of the building it read:

BRIAN'S INN
DANCING
SANDWICHES

They went inside and there were booths. There were tables and a small dance floor. There was a platform about big enough to hold a three-piece combo although there weren't any musicians on it just then, possibly because it was not quite nine o'clock, very early evening for a roadhouse.

"Peter!" Susan said. "This is *it*. It's got to be."

He could hear the barely suppressed excitement in her voice and said, "Take it easy, Susan. Let's not go overboard. This could be it, but we haven't anything definite yet."

"That booth"—she pointed—"must be the one they sat at. Let's sit there."

"Okay." He followed her to the booth and they sat down, one on either side. She looked at him and her eyes were shining with excitement.

"Peter, this is *it*."

"I think you're right. But let's see if we can prove it. Let's not get excited unless we can."

A waiter was coming over to take their order, a tall thin man with a melancholy face like a bloodhound's. Before he reached them Peter grinned at Susan. "Shall we order dancing sandwiches?" he asked.

"No. Let's not be funny. This is it, Peter, and let's prove it."

The waiter was there by then and Peter Cole said, "Two Martinis, please," and then: "Just a minute," before the waiter could turn away. He flashed his buzzer quickly, not giving the man time to see that it was a New York and not a New Jersey badge.

"Don't worry," he said, "there's no trouble. Just want to see if you recognize a picture." He took the police photograph of Jerry Trenholm out of his pocket and handed it to the waiter.

The waiter studied it and shook his head slowly.

"He's never been here?" Cole asked, to make sure.

"Not that I remember, since I've been here. That ain't long."

"How long?"

"Month and a half, about."

"Oh. Who's here now that might have been here three months ago?"

"Joe, the bartender. The cook, I think. I'm not sure how long he's been here. And, of course, Powell, the owner."

"Is there a Brian?"

"Brian Powell. Brian's his first name."

"If he's here, would you ask him to drop over to talk to us?"

"Sure."

The waiter went into a back room before he went to the bar with their order. And, just as the Martinis came, a plump, cheerful-looking man with a fringe of gray hair around a very shiny bald spot came out of the back room and looked toward the waiter. The waiter nodded to their booth and the plump man came over

"I'm Brian Powell," he said. "You wanted to see me?"

"Won't you join us, Mr. Powell," Susan said, moving over to make room for him on her side of the booth. He smiled and sat down.

"We're interested in some people who may have been in here on the night of August sixteenth," Cole said. "About twelve-thirty to one-thirty in the morning. Do you by any chance recognize this man?"

Powell studied the picture of Trenholm. "Vaguely familiar," he said. "I may have seen him. I wouldn't know when. And August sixteenth—that's a long time ago. What day of the week was it?"

"A Friday"

"Then I was probably here. But if business was dull, I may have been back in my office, where I was tonight."

"How many people would have been working here that night?"

"Outside of the music? Well, Joe would have been behind the bar. Two waiters and the cook. And when things are busy, I help out myself wherever needed. Sometimes at the tables, sometimes behind the bar."

"It wasn't, I understand," Cole said, "a busy evening. One of the members of this party I'm talking about said there were only a few other customers."

"If it was that bad, there might have been only one waiter. I might have sent the other off duty early. I might be able to check my records, my employment records, if it's important. Is it?"

"Very," Susan told him.

"Excuse me a moment, then." He went to the back room again.

"Shall I show him a picture of Carl?" Susan asked. "I still have it in my purse."

"It won't hurt any. Give it to me now. While he's checking records, I'll show it and the Jerry Trenholm picture to the bartender. He might remember one of them, although the waiter's our best bet if they were served in a booth."

"And for another reason," Susan said.

"What's that?"

"They didn't pay for the drinks," Susan reminded him. "They were supposed to own the place, so they couldn't have. Either Anders or Vic Tremaine must have got the waiter aside and slipped him money, more than enough to cover whatever they expected to drink, and told him not to collect at the table, and to keep the change. They'd have to do it that way."

"Smart girl! I didn't think of that. Sure, the waiter would remember if they did that."

He went over to the bar and showed the pictures to Joe, talked to him awhile, and then went back into the kitchen.

When he came back to the table he told Susan, "Joe remembers seeing someone who looked like Trenholm in here once or twice, but doesn't remember when or any details. He doesn't remember Dixon. The cook never saw either of them. The waiter's going to be our best chance."

She nodded and he saw that she was trembling a little. He knew why. Ten minutes ago, things had looked wonderful. They had found the place. They had found Ancin and Vic's. And now it looked as though it might be useless for them to have found it. There wasn't going to be any proof.

"Chin up, Susan," he said. "If this is the place, we'll prove it."

"But how, Peter?"

Brian Powell was coming back. He sat down with them again.

"Yes," he said, "I sent one waiter home at midnight that night. There would have been only one on duty. Ray Wheeler."

"He still works for you?"

Powell shook his head. "He left a month and a half ago, in early September. Said he was going to Florida, and I haven't any address for him."

"Any way you know of that we could even try to reach him?"

"I'm afraid not. He's a drifter. Worked for me only three months."

Susan tried. "Does the name Ancin and Vic mean anything to you, Mr. Powell?" she asked.

"Ancin and Vic? It's vaguely familiar. Say, wasn't it in connection with that murder case near Newark a few months ago?"

"Yes. And we thought this place might— Well, never mind." Peter handed him the picture of Carl Dixon. "Ever seen this man?"

Powell studied the photograph. "Not in person, no. But I think I've seen his picture in the papers. Isn't he the one who was convicted in the Newark case?"

Peter Cole sighed. This had looked like their lucky day, until now.

Powell had a drink with them and then excused himself and went back to his office. Susan looked at Peter and there was a mist of tears in her eyes. He reached across the table and patted her hand.

"Buck up," he said. "We're not licked. We're just stuck for a moment. We've been at this only two days."

"I know, Peter. You've done wonderful. But right now it does seem pretty discouraging. So near, and yet so far."

"We'll get nearer."

He discovered that his hand was still lying on top of hers, and almost jerked it away.

She looked at him. "Should we go, Peter? You must be tired, after traveling to Boston last night and back today."

"No. I'm all right."

"Getting hungry? Want a dancing sandwich yet?"

"No. Shall I order you one?"

"No. I was just—trying to inject a light note into the gloom. Don't frown so, Peter. All right, maybe I started this, but now you look gloomier than I feel. But why didn't we kid Mr. Powell about those dancing sandwiches while he was here?"

"Susan, shut up. I want to think."

"I can't help?"

"By shutting up, yes. There must be some way—"

She must have realized he didn't want an answer, and she kept still. Peter Cole stared moodily into his drink and made wet circles on the wood with the bottom of the glass.

Suddenly the fingers that gripped the glass tightened, went white. "Susan!" he said. "I've got it!"

"What?"

"Wait!"

He got up, not even remembering to excuse himself, and went back into the room at the rear into which Powell had gone fifteen minutes before. He was in there two or three minutes and then came out. His eyes were shining and he looked across the room and caught Susan's eye. She'd been staring at the door.

He held up his right hand—thumb and forefinger making a circle.

Then he went into the phone booth.

He was in there longer, possibly ten minutes.

Then he was at the edge of the booth, his eyes still shining with excitement. "Come on, "he said. "Harlan's coming here. Right away."

"Harlan?"

"The prosecutor. I told him we'd found Ancin and Vic's. I told him I thought we had a picture of Vic Tremaine to show him. He's coming right away."

"But—" She got up, reached back for her purse. "But if he's coming here, why are we leaving?"

"We aren't. Come on. Don't bother with your purse. We're coming right back in."

He almost dragged her through the door and to his car parked in the parking lot.

He opened the back door instead of the front and instead of getting in, he reached in and pulled out a heavy auto robe. He said, "Hold this. By the corners."

"But Peter, what—"

"Shush. Do as you're told, woman."

She had hold of the robe and he got a pen knife out of the side pocket of his trousers.

He snapped open the knife and cut through the binding of the robe about a foot from the corner.

"Hold it tighter," he said, "so I can cut better. We can tear it, I think, once we get it started away."

"But why—?"

"It's an old robe. I don't like it anymore We're cutting and tearing it into strips. And no back talk."

While they worked, he said, "I've got Powell's permission to do this, so don't worry. And when Harlan sees it—"

Finally the robe was in strips and he cut some of the strips in half crosswise. "Come on" he said then, and with a double handful of the heavy strips, he was almost running around to the front of the roadhouse, to the big neon sign on the front lawn.

Susan's high heels had trouble keeping up with him.

"There ought to be a switch," he said, "tow switches, I mean, behind here. Powell says you can turn off— Here it is"

The top line of the sign, the eighteen inch blue letters that read BRIAN'S INN went dark. Only the two lines of red letters underneath, each line a foot high, remained.

They read:

DANCING

SANDWICHES

Peter Cole laughed.

"Watch, Susan, he said. "Here's to dancing sandwiches!"

He came around to the front of the sign and wrapped a strip of auto robe around the first and last letters of the top line. It read: ANCIN. He wrapped around the S of SANDWICHES and then folded one in half and covered only the first half of the letter W. Then he covered the last three letters of the word with one long strip wrapped around them. He stepped back to enjoy his handiwork and the sign read:

ANCIN

AND VIC

Susan, transfixed, was staring at it. Peter Cole reached out a hand toward her, remembered, and let the hand drop to his side.

For some reason his voice didn't sound cheerful.

"Come back inside," he said. "We'll let Harlan find it that way for himself when he drives up."

IX

IT WAS NOW MIDNIGHT, and Claire Evans was getting mad, plenty mad. An hour now she'd been stuck here in the hotel room, stood up. They'd left the Diamond Horseshoe before eleven, bored by fifty violins playing sweet music.

"Let's go to Eddie Condon's or Jimmy Ryan's and hear some real music, Baby," Jerry said.

She said it was a good idea, and then we they got outside it was snowing and colder and she wanted to drop in at the hotel to get her muskrat coat instead of the chubby she was wearing. Instead of keeping the cab, he'd paid it off and gone in with her. But at the elevator he'd touched her arm.

"Want to see a guy up on another floor for just a second, Baby," he'd said. "Wait in the room and I'll pick you up on my way down."

And that was all right except that it had been an hour ago, a darned long hour ago, and here she was alone and bored stiff right in the middle of the evening. Had he looked up another woman, or got in a floating crap game or what?

If only she knew was stood up, then it'd be all right. Sauce for the gander was sauce for the goose, and she could go out and finish the evening all right. Yes, and the night too, if he wanted things that way.

And it was after twelve now and the evening was being shot. But if she did go out, and she was wrong, and he stopped for her for a few minutes after she'd left—well, that would start something. And she got along pretty well with Jerry and didn't want to spoil it as long as he was on the level with her.

But she was getting plenty mad. The few drinks she'd had at the Horseshoe were wearing off and she'd be cold sober by the time they got going again—if they ever did. She started for the door, changed her mind and turned back. Instead she picked up the phone and got room service.

"Three-oh-four," she said. "Bottle of Scotch, bottle of sparkling, some ice cubes." All right, she'd wait another full hour, but she wouldn't have to do it dry. And if he wasn't back by one—She paced back and forth until there was a knock on the door, and then she called out, "Come in."

The door opened and a man came in, but he wasn't from room service and he wasn't bringing Scotch. He was a copper. No uniform, but a copper. And another one came in behind him.

"Claire Evans?" the first one said.

There wasn't any use denying it. If they were here, they knew who she was. "Mrs. Trenholm," she said. "Formerly Claire Evans."

"Jerry here?"

"No. I don't know where he is." She hoped Jerry wasn't in a bad jam, that this was just another pickup he could talk his way out of.

The coppers didn't take her word, of course. The first one nodded to the second one and the second went into the bedroom and she heard him open the bathroom door and look in there, too. He came back and shook his head.

"We'll get him later," the first said. "We'll take the dame in." To Claire he said, "Come on, Sister. Get your coat on. It's snowing."

"What's the charge, if I may ask?"

"A little matter to do with checks. Coming willingly?" She shrugged, and picked up the coat. They didn't have anything on her. They just wanted to pump her about Jerry, and a lot of good that would do them. Most she'd done for Jerry recently was play secretary a few times on the phone. They couldn't get an identification on that. Only she hoped Jerry wasn't going to be in bad trouble.

They drove her to Headquarters and took her to an office with *Captain J. C. Crandall* on the door. As she went in, one of the coppers said, "Claire Evans, Cap." Neither of them followed her in. They closed the door from the outside and went away.

The captain looked up at her briefly and then motioned to a chair at one side. "Sit down," he said. He went back to some paper work on his desk.

She waited fifteen minutes, beginning to fume. *What kind of a game was this?* "May I phone a lawyer?" she said finally.

"Not yet," he said, without even looking up.

Another fifteen minutes dragged by. It went so slowly that she thought her wrist watch had stopped and twice held it to her ear to be sure it was still ticking. "What's this all about?" she said when she couldn't stand it anymore.

The captain looked up again. "Cashed any checks recently?" he asked.

"No."

"Then you haven't a thing to worry about. A dame that fits your description passed one last Tuesday. The pen work could have been Jerry's. He's coming in. If he doesn't identify you, you can go home."

She breathed easier. She hadn't passed a check in months. She relaxed a little in the chair and lighted a cigarette. The captain smiled at her, "Sorry you have to wait, if it's a bum rap. He should have been here by now. Want something to look at?"

He took a couple of magazines out of a drawer of his desk and handed them to her. That should have warned her, but she said, "Thanks," and started leafing through one of them. There was a new Michael Shayne story in it, and she started reading it.

It was almost half an hour before there was a knock on the door and it opened. The captain said, "Come in," and a tall young man opened the door and stood in the doorway.

"I'm Pete Cole, Captain," the young man said. "We've got the guy here. Shall I send him in?"

Claire closed the magazine, but held the place with her finger. When this was over with, in a minute, she'd ask if she could take it along to finish the story.

Captain Crandall said, "Sure," and the man in the doorway—he was good looking, Claire thought, even if he was a copper—moved aside into the room and motioned to someone outside.

The someone outside came in—and Claire's mouth opened and the back of her hand flew up to push back the scream she felt coming.

Carl Dixon looked at her and smiled faintly. "Hello, Dorothy," he said.

~§~

It was a dawn like any other dawn, but it was the first one Susan Bailey had waited up for in a long time. She stood now at the window of her room and while she watched, the street lights, haloed by the falling snow, went out. The street grew whiter now as the air turned from dull gray to light gray. She'd been home since midnight, when Peter had sent her home in a cab, saying that he was going to stay and see things through. But he'd promised to come, no matter what the hour. So she hadn't gone to bed. She'd alternately tried to read and stood looking out the window.

She heard footsteps coming up the stairs. Twenty times since midnight, footsteps had come up the stairs and every time she had tensed. She felt herself go tense now, until there was a knock on the door. She hurried to it and threw it open.

Peter Cole stood there, snow on his hat and snow on the shoulders of his coat. He smiled at her, but it wasn't a convincing smile and for a moment she thought something had gone wrong.

"Everything's all right, Susan," he said then. "They're letting him out. He's completely cleared."

She pulled him into the room. He took off his hat, but held it, dripping, in his hand. He wouldn't give her his coat.

"I can stay only a minute," he said.

"Nonsense, Peter. Give me your coat."

"No, I'm leaving. There isn't much to tell. After I sent you home, I went with Harlan to the prison and Carl made a positive identification of the picture of Jerry Trenholm. Harlan phoned, right from the prison, to New York and asked them to pick up Trenholm and Claire Evans. They got Claire right away.

"Harlan got a release on Carl into his custody and we took him to New York. He identified Claire as Dorothy and she went to pieces. When we gave her a choice of a full share in a murder charge or a light term as accessory-after if she turned state's evidence, she sang beautifully.

"They got Trenholm a couple of hours later, and I watched them try to break him down, but they couldn't. He's sitting tight, but it doesn't matter. With Claire's testimony, they've got him cold. And even if he should beat the rap—not that he will—Carl is cleared."

"Where is Carl?"

"He's released by now. There were formalities, and they wanted him to help them with Jerry Trenholm and what not. But he'll be here any minute. I talked to him and told him you'd be up and to come here first, that you'd be waiting up for him. So I've got to go."

"Why? Wait, Peter. Don't run off. I haven't even—thanked you."

"Forget it. I don't want you to thank me. It's all right. It's all over. And I haven't slept for—"

"Peter, please be quiet."

"Huh?" He stared at her, puzzled.

"Peter, I'm awfully glad Carl is coming here right away, right now. So I can get it over with. I've got to break our engagement, and don't you see that this is the time to do it?—while he's so happy about being freed, about being cleared, getting his job back—for I'm sure he will—and everything.

"Carl is nice. I like him. But, Peter, I started falling out of love with him even before—three months ago. I might have broken the engagement within a week or two, then, but don't you see, I couldn't after he was in trouble. I had to stick by him, even though I didn't love him, when he was in trouble. Especially when I was sure that he was innocent, and I was just about the only one who was sure."

"Susan—"

"Don't say it yet, Peter. As long as Carl's coming here within minutes, let me tell him first. It won't hurt him, I'm sure. Not now. But will you wait? And we'll talk afterward. There's an all-night restaurant across the street. Will you wait there? When Carl has gone, I'll come down."

He started to put out a hand toward her, pulled it back. His face, through a twenty-four-hours' growth of beard, looked almost shining.

"No," he said. "I'll wait outside, across the street, until I see him come and go. I'll get covered with snow, but I love snow. Maybe I'll get cold, but—you'll thaw me out?"

She smiled, her eyes misty. And her eyes must have given enough answer, for he turned quite suddenly and went quickly down the stairs.

Mystery Book, Summer 1950

The Laughing Butcher

YESTERDAY must have been a dull day for news, because the Chicago *Sun* gave three inches to the funeral of a dwarf downstate, in Corbyville.

"Listen to this, Bill," Kathy said, and Wally—(that's my only in-law, Kathy's brother)—and I looked up from our game of cribbage.

"Yeah?" I said. Kathy read it to us.

Then she said, "Bill, wasn't that—" She let it trail off.

I looked at her warningly, because of her brother being there with us, and I said, "The dwarf that beat you at a game of chess five years ago? Yeah, that was the one."

Wally put down his last card, said, "Thirty-one for two," and pegged it. I scored my hand and he scored his and the crib, and it put him out and ended the game.

"Five years ago," he said. "And yesterday was your anniversary. That's put it on your honeymoon, if it was exactly five years ago, I mean. She play chess with dwarfs on your honeymoon?"

"One dwarf," I told him. "One game. In Corbyville. And she got beaten."

"Served her right," Wally said. "Look, Bill—wasn't it about that time, five years ago, they lynched a guy in Corbyville? The case they called 'The Corbyville Horror'?"

"A few weeks after that," I said.

"The guy was a butcher, and a black magician, or something. Or they thought he was. Killed somebody by magic, or. . . What was it about, anyway?"

I was looking at the window, and the window was a black, blank square of night, and I wanted to shiver, but with Wally watching me that way, I couldn't. I got up and walked over to the window instead, so I could look down on the lights and traffic of Division Street instead of at the black night above it.

"It was the butcher they lynched," I said. I turned around from the window. "We saw him, too."

Wally picked up his glass of beer and took a sip of it.

"Some of it's coming back to me," he said. "Corbyville's that circus town, isn't it? Town where a lot of ex-circus people live?"

I nodded.

"And this Corbyville Horror business. Wasn't a guy found out in the middle of a field of snow, dead, with two sets of footprints leading up to his body and none leading away from it?"

"That's right," I said.

"And one set of footprints was his own and the other set just led to the body and vanished as though the guy had flown?"

"Yes," I said.

"I remember now. And the town lynched this butcher-magician because he had a down on the guy who was killed, and—"

"Something like that."

"They never did find out what really happened?" Wally asked.

He took another sip of beer and shook his head.

"I remember now that it puzzled me. How could a set of tracks go halfway across a field of snow and then stop, and not either come back or go on?"

"One set's easy to explain," I said. "I mean those of the guy they found dead out there in the field."

"Sure, him. But what about the one who chased him? He did chase him, didn't he? I mean, if I remember rightly, his footprints were on top of the dead man's in the snow."

"That's right," I said. "I saw those footprints myself. Of course by the time I saw them there were a lot of other prints around and they'd taken the body away, but I talked to the men who found the body, and they were sure of their description of those prints, and of the fact that there weren't any other ones around, within a hundred yards."

"Didn't somebody suggest ropes?"

"No trees or telephone poles anywhere near. Nope."

Kathy went and got us some more beer. I asked Wally if he wanted another game of cribbage. "No," he said. "The story."

I poured his glass full and then mine.

"What do you want to know, Wally?" I asked.

"What killed him?"

"Heart failure," I said.

"But—what was chasing him?"

"Nothing was chasing him," I said slowly. "Nothing at all. He wasn't running away from anybody or anything. It was more horrible than that."

I went over and sat down in the big armchair. Kathy came over and curled up on my lap like a contented kitten. Over her shoulder I could see that black square of night that was the open window.

"It was much more horrible than that, Wally," I repeated slowly.

"He wasn't running away from something. He was running toward something. Something out in the middle of that field."

Wally laughed uneasily. "Bill," he said, "you don't talk like a Chicago copper. You talk like a fey Irishman. What was out in that field?"

"Death," I told him.

That held him for a minute. Then he asked, "What about the one-way tracks, the ones that led to the body and not away from it?"

~§~

It was warm and pleasant up there on top of the hill, I remember. I stopped the car at the side of the muddy road, put my arm around Kathy and kissed her, with the soundness that a second-day-of-honeymoon kiss deserves. We had been married the morning before, in Chicago, and were driving south. I had arranged a month off and we figured to get to New Orleans and back, driving leisurely, and stopping off wherever we wished. We had spent the first night of our honeymoon in Decatur, a town I'll never forget.

I won't forget Corbyville, either, although not for the same reason. But of course I didn't know that then. I pointed to the view through the windshield and down the hill into the valley, bright green and muddy brown from the recent rains. And with a little village at the bottom of it—three score or so of houses huddled together like frightened sheep.

"Ain't it purty?" I said.

"Beautiful," Kathy said. The valley, I mean. Is that Corbyville? Where are the elephants? Didn't I read they used elephants for the plowing outside Corbyville?"

I laughed at her. "One elephant, and it died years ago. I guess there are a lot of the circus people left there, though. Maybe we'll see some of them when we drive through."

"I forgot the story, Bill," Kathy said. "Why is it so many circus people live there? Some circus owner—"

"Old John Corby," I said. "He owned about the third biggest circus in the country and made a fortune from it. That was the town he came from—it had some other name then—and he put all his profits into the land there, got to own nearly the whole town and valley.

"And when he died, his will left houses and stores and farms to people in his circus, on the condition that they live there. A lot of 'em wouldn't, of course; weren't ready to settle down, and went with some other circus instead. But a lot of 'em did take what was left them and live there. Out of a population of a thousand or so, over a hundred, I think, are ex-circus people. . . . Did I ever tell you I love you, Kathy?"

"I seem to remem. . . Bill, not here! You—"

So after a minute I slid the car in gear and started down the slippery, winding road into the valley. We were off the main highway, coming in on a side road that wasn't used much, and it was pretty bad. The mud was inches deep in the ruts. It wasn't too bad until we were just a half-mile outside the village, and then suddenly the wheels were sliding and the back end of the car, despite my efforts with the wheel, slewed around and went off the road. I tried to start, and the back wheels spun in mud that was like soup.

I said appropriate words, suitably modified to fit Kathy's presence, and got out of the car, then looked around.

There was a little three-room frame farmhouse only a few dozen paces away, and a stocky, blond man of about thirty was already walking from the house toward the car.

He grinned at me.

"Nice roads we got here," he said. "You in very deep?"

"Not too bad," I told him. "If you can give me a hand, maybe two of us—"

"Wish I could," He said. "But anything heavy's against the rules. I've got a bum ticker. The doc won't let me pick up anything heavier than a potato, and I got to do that slow." He looked up and down the road. "We might get you out with some gunny sacks or boards, but it'd be hardly worth the trouble. Pete Hobbs is about due here. He's the mailman."

"Drive a truck?"

The blond man laughed. "Sure, but he won't need it. Pete used to be a strong man with Corby. He's getting old, but he can still pick up the back end of your car with one hand. You and the missus want to drop in the house till Pete gets here?"

Kathy had been listening, and she must have liked the man because she said sure, we'd be glad to.

So we went in, and it was half an hour before the mailman came along the road and we got to know the Wilsons fairly well, for half an hour. That was the blond man's name, Len Wilson. His wife, Dorothy, was a stunner. Almost as pretty as Kathy.

No, Len Wilson told us, he hadn't been with any circus. He had been born right here on this small farm and Dorothy had been born in Corbyville. They had been married four years, and you could see they were still in love. I noticed how considerate they were of each other; how, when he started up to get an ash tray from me, Dorothy almost spoke sharply to him to make him sit down again. The sort of sharpness one might use on a child.

I remember wondering how, since Len couldn't exert himself physically, he managed to run a farm, even a small one. Maybe he knew I'd be wondering that. Anyway, he told me the answer.

"I can work, all right," he told me, "as long as it isn't heavy, and I keep at a steady, dogged pace. I can lift a thousand pounds—about ten pounds at a time. I can walk a hundred miles, if I walk slowly and rest once in a while. And I can run a farm, a little one like this, the same way. Not that I get rich doing it." He grinned a little.

A honking out front brought us to our feet, and Dorothy Wilson said:

"That's Pete. I'll run ahead and be sure to catch him."

The rest of us followed more slowly, Kathy and I matching our pace to Len's. The ex-strongman got out of his mail truck and he and I easily lifted the car's back end around to where the wheels would find traction.

As I got under the wheel, Len waved.

"Might see you in town, if you're stopping there," he said. I'm riding in with Pete."

Anyway, that was how we met Len Wilson. We saw him only once more, in Corbyville, a little later.

I was going to drive on through, I remember, but Kathy wanted to stop and eat. I parked the car in front of a clean looking hamburger joint and we went in. That was where we met the dwarf.

I remember thinking, when we first went in and sat down at the counter, that there was something strange and out of proportion about the five-foot-tall little man who nodded to us from behind the counter and took our orders. But I didn't realize what it was until he walked back to the grill to put on the hamburgers we ordered. He wasn't five feet tall at all; he was about three feet. The area back of the counter was built up, about two feet higher than the floor in the rest of the room.

He saw me lean over the counter and look down, and grinned at me.

"My chin'd just about come to the level of the counter without that arrangement," he said.

"You ought to get a patent on it," Kathy said. "Say, isn't that a chess board down there at the end of the counter?"

He nodded. "I was working out a problem. You play?"

That was better than the smell of hamburgers to Kathy. Few women like chess, but she's one of the few, even if she doesn't look like it. To look at Kathy you'd think gin rummy would be her top intellectual entertainment, but you'd be fooled. She's got more brains and more education than I. Got a master's degree and would probably be teaching if she hadn't decided to marry me instead. Which, I'll admit, was a big waste of brains.

Kathy told him she played and how about a quick game? And she wasn't kidding on the quick part; she really does move fairly fast, and the dwarf—I noticed with relief—kept up with the pace she set. I know enough about chess, due to Kathy, to follow the moves, and when a game goes fairly quick, I can stay interested watching it.

Kathy had the men set up by the time he brought our hamburgers and coffee, and I watched until midgame while I ate. Then I strolled front to the doorway and stood leaning against the jamb, looking out across the street.

Directly across from me, in the doorway of the butcher shop, a butcher in a white apron was doing the same thing. My gaze passed him over lightly the first time, then went back to him and got stuck there. At first, I didn't even know why.

Then a child—a girl of about six or seven—came skipping along the street, noticed him when she was a dozen paces away, and stopped skipping. She circled widely, almost to the outer curb, to keep as much distance as possible between herself and the butcher. He didn't seem to notice her at all, and once she was safely behind his back, she started skipping again.

Definitely, I realized, she had been afraid of him.

It could have been nothing, of course; a child who'd been scolded for filching a wiener from the butcher shop, but—well, it didn't seem like that.

It didn't seem like that because what happened made me look at the butcher's face. It was calm, impassive. If he had noticed the child, he had neither frowned nor smiled at the wide circle she had made. And the face itself was handsome, but . . . I shivered a little.

A Chicago cop gets used to seeing faces that aren't nice to look at. He sees faces daily that might be Greek masks of hate or lust or avarice. He gets used to hopped-up torpedoes and crazy killers. He takes faces like that in his stride; they're his business.

But this wasn't that sort of face. It was an evil face, but subtly evil. The man's features were straight and regular and his eyes were clear. The evil was behind the face, behind the eyes. I couldn't even put my finger on how I knew it was there. It wasn't something I could see; it was something I felt.

The part of my brain that's trained to observe and remember was cataloguing the rest of him as well—I don't know why. Height, five eleven; weight, one eighty; age, about forty; black hair, brown eyes, olive complexion; distinguishing features—an aura of evil.

I wondered what the looie in charge of my precinct would say if I turned in a report like that.

I strolled back into the restaurant and looked at the chess game, mildly wishing Kathy would be through so she could leave with me while the butcher was still standing there. I wondered what her reaction to him would be.

There were still a lot of pieces on the board, though. Kathy looked up at me.

"Having trouble," she admitted. "This gentleman really knows how to play chess. Why aren't you smart like that, Bill?"

The dwarf grinned without looking up, and moved a pawn.

"She's played this game before, too," he said. "It's even so far."

"But not now," Kathy said.

I looked at the pieces and saw what she meant. The dwarf had left one of his knights unprotected. Kathy's hand hovered over the board a moment, then her bishop swooped to conquer.

"Attababy," I said to Kathy and patted her shoulder. "Take your time," I told her. "It's only our honeymoon."

I strolled back to the doorway. The white-aproned butcher was still there.

Out of the doorway of the store next door to the butcher shop came Len Wilson. He walked, as before, slowly. He walked toward the butcher shop. I started to hall him, to ask him to come over and have a cup of coffee with me while Kathy and the dwarf finished their game. I had my mouth open to call to him, but I didn't.

Len Wilson caught the butcher's eye, and stopped. There was something so peculiar about his way of stopping, as though he had run into a brick wall, that I didn't call. I watched, instead.

The butcher was smiling, but it wasn't a nice smile. He said something, but I couldn't hear it across the street, nor could I hear what Len answered. It was like watching a movie whose sound track had I stopped working.

I saw the butcher reach into his pocket and take something out, hold it casually in his hand. It looked like a tiny doll, about two inches long. It could have been made of wax. He did something, I couldn't see what, with the doll between his hands.

Then he said something again—several sentences—and laughed again. I could hear that laugh across the street, even though I hadn't heard the words. It wasn't loud, but it carried. And Len Wilson's fists clenched, and he started forward—not slowly at all—for the butcher.

I started, too, at the same time. There wasn't any mistaking the expression on Len's face. His intention wasn't any intention that a man with a bad ticker should have. He was going to take a poke at that butcher, a man bigger than he was and husky looking besides, and for a man in Len's shape it was going to be just too bad unless that I one poke did the work.

But Len had been only a few steps away, and I'd been across the street. I saw him swing wildly and miss, and then an auto horn and squealing brakes made me step back just in time to keep from getting killed in the middle of the street. When I looked again, the tableau had changed. The big butcher was standing behind Len, with Len's arm doubled in a hammerlock. Len's face was red with either pain or futile anger, or both.

I took a quick look for traffic both ways this time before I started across toward them. I don't mind telling you that I was afraid. Not physically afraid of that butcher, but—well, there was something about him that had made me want to hit him, even before Len had come along, but that made me afraid to do it, too.

Suddenly I noticed that Kathy and the dwarf were with me, Kathy abreast of me on one side, and the dwarf scuttling by me on the other side, his short legs going like piston rods as he passed me.

"Let go of him, Kramer, damn you!" he was yelling.

The butcher let go of Len and Len almost collapsed, leaning back against the building. The dwarf got to Len first, and reached into Len's vest pocket. He came out with a little box of pills. He handed them to me.

"Give him one, quick," he said. "I can't reach."

I got the box open—they were nitro pills, I noticed—and got Len to take one.

"Take him across to my place," the dwarf was saying. "Make him sit down and rest."

And Kathy was on Len's other side and we were helping him across the street.

The dwarf wasn't with us. I saw that Len seemed to be breathing normally and making it all right, then I glanced back over my shoulder.

Again it was a conversation I couldn't hear, but could see. The dwarf's face, on a level with the butcher's belt, was dark with fierce anger. There was smiling amusement on the butcher's face, and again I felt that impact of evil.

The butcher said something. The dwarf took a step forward and kicked viciously at the butcher's shin. He connected, too.

I almost stopped, thinking I'd have to let Kathy support Len while I ran back to rescue the foolhardy dwarf.

But the butcher didn't make a move. Instead, he leaned back against the door post of his shop and laughed. Great peals of loud laughter that must have been audible a full block away. He didn't even lean down to rub his kicked shin. He laughed.

He was still laughing when Kathy and I had taken Len through the open doorway of the restaurant. I turned around and the dwarf, his face almost purple with thwarted anger, was crossing the street after us, and the butcher still stood there laughing. It wasn't a nice laugh at all. It made me want to kill him, and I've got a pretty even disposition myself.

We let Len down into one of the seats at a booth, and the dwarf was beside us, his face calm again. I glanced out through the window and saw that the butcher was gone, probably back into his shop. And the silence, after that laughter, seemed blessed.

"Shall I get Doc?" the dwarf asked Len.

Len Wilson shook his head. "I'm all right. That nitro pill fixed me up. Just let me sit and rest a minute or two."

"Cup of coffee while you're resting?"

"Sure," Len said. "And make me a hamburger, will you, Joe? Haven't eaten much."

Kathy sat down across from Len in the booth and I went back with the dwarf named Joe. He went up the ramp that led to the raised area back of the counter and he again wasn't a dwarf any more. He was five feet tall and his eyes were higher than mine as I sat at one of the counter stools opposite the hamburger grill. He took a hamburger patty from the refrigerator and slapped it on the grill, and then I caught his eye.

"What," I asked, jerking my thumb in the direction of the butcher shop, "was that?"

"That," he said, "was Gerhard Kramer." He made it sound like profanity.

"And who is Gerhard Kramer?"

"A nice guy," he said, "if you listen to some people who think so. Most of us don't. Some of us are pretty close to thinking he's the devil himself."

"Outside of a butcher," I asked, "who is he? What was he?"

"Used to be with Corby's circus. Sideshow magician and mentalist.

He makes a better butcher. But he still keeps on with magic—only the black kind, the serious kind."

"He really believes in it? Wax dolls and that sort of stuff?"

"You saw that doll, then? Well, he makes people believe he believes in it. Got half the town scared stiff of him."

"Yet they buy in his store?"

He flipped over the hamburger frying on the grill. "They're afraid not to, I guess, if it comes to that. Oh, and some of the women aren't afraid of him. He's attractive to women. He does all right. He owns a good share of the town. Probably likes cutting up dead animals or he wouldn't have to run that shop. Yeah, he does all right."

Something in his tone of voice made me ask, "Except what?"

He slit a bun and put the hamburger in it, drew a cup of coffee, and started around the counter with them. I stayed still. I knew he'd answer my question when he got back.

He came back and said, "Len's wife, mister. That's the one thing he wants and can't have."

"Dorothy?" I asked, surprised. I don't know why I was surprised. He looked so puzzled that I realized he hadn't known that we had stopped at the Wilsons' place on our way into Corbyville. He had thought that our first sight of Len had been across the street. I told him about it.

"Yes, Dorothy," he said. "She was a town girl before she married Len Kramer wanted her and Len took her out from under his nose. Kramer's hated Len ever since. And, damn him, he'll probably get her if Len isn't more careful of himself. He'll keel over and leave a clear field."

"But won't Dorothy Wilson have something to say about that?" I asked. "Would she marry a—a guy like Kramer?"

He looked gloomy. "I told you women like him. She likes him—can't see anything wrong with him. Oh, I don't mean she'd cheat on Len, or anything like that. But if Len would die, why, after a year or so—"

"And that doll," I said. "That wax doll. Does that mean Kramer doesn't want to wait till Len dies naturally, if he does? Does Kramer really believe in that kind of magic?"

The dwarf looked at me cynically. "Sometimes that kind of magic can work, mister," he said. "You saw it blame near work just now, when he showed it to Len."

I saw what he meant. I got up and went back to the front of the store. Len looked better, and Kathy was talking to him animatedly.

"I've just learned that Len plays chess, Bill," she said. "He's a friend of Joe Laska—that's the man who runs the restaurant here—and says they play a lot. We could have played a game out at Len's house while we were there."

"Sure," I said, "only you didn't. How'd you come out on the game with Joe? You were a knight ahead, I remember, and I see he put the board back, so I guess you finished the game."

"Yes, we finished. We were coming out to join you just when—when the trouble started across the street."

With Len sitting there I didn't want to go into that; I'd tell Kathy later what it was all about. "Who won?" I asked quickly.

"Joe, darn him. That business of giving me the knight was a gambit. He checkmated me four moves later."

Len grinned, a little weakly. "Joe's a great guy for those gambits, lady. If you play with him again, watch out any time he offers you a piece for free."

The dwarf came back then and said that he was going to get a car to take Len home. But I wouldn't hear of that, of course. I made Len get into my car—he could walk all right by now—and Kathy and I drove him home.

Dorothy Wilson took a look at Len as he came through the door and took him off upstairs to put him to bed for the rest of the day. She had called back, asking us to wait, and we did.

But when she came down it turned out she had wanted us to wait so she could offer us something to eat, and we explained that we had just eaten in town. So Dorothy walked out to the car with us.

"Joe Laska phoned me," she said. "He said—well, I gathered that Len tried again to start a fight with Gerry Kramer. Oh, I wish Len wouldn't be so foolish. To hear Len—and Joe, too—talk, you'd think Gerry was a devil or something."

Something made me ask, "And isn't he?"

She laughed a little. "He's one of the nicest men in town. The men around here don't like him because he's handsome and polished and—well, you know how small-town people are."

"Oh," I said.

"But he's nice, really. Why, he holds a mortgage on this place of ours, overdue. He could put Len and me off any time he wanted, but he doesn't, in spite of the way Len acts about him."

I didn't want to hear any more of it. I wanted to say, "Sure, he'd rather let Len stay on a farm and work himself to death than maybe go to a city somewhere and get a softer job where he could last a longer time."

But I didn't say it. I had no business to, just because I hadn't liked the man's face and his laugh.

We said goodbye to Mrs. Wilson and drove off.

After a while, I said, "Women—" disgustedly, and then asked Kathy what she had thought of the butcher.

"I don't really know," she said. "He is good looking all right, and maybe Mrs. Wilson is right, but—well, I wouldn't trust him. There seemed to be something wrong about him, Bill. Something—uh—wicked, evil."

And since she was smart enough to have seen that for herself, I told her, as we drove along, everything that I had seen and what Joe, the dwarf, had told me.

We talked about it quite a while. There had been something about that scene in front of the butcher shop, and about the situation back of it, that wasn't going to be easy to forget. We wouldn't have forgotten it, I'm sure, even if it had ended there.

But after a while it slid into the back of our minds. We were, after all, on our honeymoon.

We drove to New Orleans and spent a wonderful two weeks in the marvelous fall weather they have there, and I remember the warmth was all the more wonderful when we read in the papers that Illinois and Indiana had been having freezing weather and early snows.

We started driving back then, leisurely. We didn't plan our route from day to day, and I don't know whether we would have driven through Corbyville at all, if we hadn't happened to buy a Centralia newspaper in Metropolis, just after we'd crossed the Ohio River from Paducah.

There was a headline:

BUTCHER LYNCHED
IN CORBYVILLE

And in that first story there wasn't any play-up at all of the "Corbyville Horror" angle that made Sunday supplements all over the country. The lynching—it was the first in a long time in the State of Illinois—was the angle of the Centralia paper.

Apparently the reporters hadn't actually been on the scene as yet, because there weren't many details. I read the story out loud to Kathy, then she took the paper away from me and read it again to herself, while I sat and thought, and finished my coffee.

It seemed, according to the Centralia paper, that one Len Wilson, a farmer living just outside Corbyville, had died under rather mysterious circumstances, and that the people of the town blamed the local butcher, Gerhard Kramer, for Wilson's death. The sheriff, summoned from Centralia, had refused, for lack of evidence, to arrest Kramer.

And while the sheriff was out at the farm a group of townsmen, who had already been out at the farm, yanked Gerhard Kramer out of his butcher shop and strung him up on the light pole right in front of the store. Sheriff's deputies had been unable to find out who—outside, I suppose, of Kramer himself—had been involved in the lynching.

I paid our check in the restaurant and we went out and got in the car.

"Are you going through Corbyville?" Kathy asked.

"Yes," I said. "I want to know what happened. Don't you?"

"I guess so, Bill," she said.

We got to Corbyville about two o'clock. It was a quiet town when we drove down the main street. It was unnaturally quiet.

I drove slowly. The butcher shop, I noticed, was closed, although there wasn't any wreath on the door. The hamburger stand across from it, the dwarf's place, was closed too. There, there was a sign on the door that read:

CLOSED TILL MONDAY

I drove on out to the Wilson farm.

There was still an inch of snow on the ground, and it was cold, unseasonably cold for early October. There were cars parked in front—four of them.

We got out and walked back where there was a little knot of men standing beside a fence, and beyond the fence was an open field. I could see the footprints—the two sets of footprints that the Sunday supplements and all the newspapers made so much of. Alongside of them were other prints now, of course, ones that would not have been there when the first ones were made.

I took a good look at those tracks, without climbing over the fence. You've read about them, and they were just what the papers said. Two sets of tracks led out across the snow-covered field; neither set came back. It put a little chill down your spine to look at them, to visualize how they had looked to the first men there, those who had discovered the body, when the rest of the field was virgin white.

Len Wilson's footprints were the smaller of the two sets. You could tell which they were easily enough. He had been running fast. The other set had been made after Len's. In places one of the bigger prints came on top of one of Len's.

Kathy stood staring at them, studying them.

I talked a few minutes to the men who were standing around. One was a deputy sheriff stationed there. He wanted to know who I was, and I showed him my Chicago credentials, and explained that I'd known Len slightly, and was interested for that reason. The other three men were reporters. One all the way from Chicago.

"Where is Mrs. Wilson?" I asked.

I didn't particularly want to talk to Dorothy Wilson, but I felt that if she was in the house, Kathy and I should go there, at least for a minute.

"With her folks in Corbyville," the Chicago reporter told me. "Say, those tracks: It's the damnedest thing." He turned and stared at them. Then he said, "I guess I can see why they lynched that butcher. If he hated Len Wilson, and if he went in for black magic—well, if this isn't what the hell is?"

The deputy sheriff spat over the fence. He started to say something, noticed Kathy, and changed his mind. He cleared his throat and said, "Black magic, phooey! But I'd still like to know how he did it. He was a circus sideshow magician, but even so—"

"Are those other footprints his?" I asked.

"His size. We haven't found the particular pair of shoes that made them. He probably ditched 'em."

"I—I guess I'm a little scared," Kathy said.

"I'm a lot scared," I told her.

We got in the car and drove away, north toward Chicago and home. "It—it's horrible, Bill," Kathy said, after a while. "What was he running from?"

"Nothing, Kathy," I told her. "He was running toward."

I told her how I figured it and why, and her eyes got wider and scareder. When I finished, she grabbed my arm. "Bill," she said. "You're a—a policeman. Does that mean you'll have to—to tell?"

I shook my head. "If I had any evidence, yes. But an opinion is my own, even if we know it's right."

Kathy relaxed, but we didn't talk much the rest of the way to Chicago.

~§~

Wally said, "All right, my beloved brother-in-law, I'm dumb and you're a big smart copper. I don't get it." He downed the last of his beer and put the empty glass down quietly. "What was he running toward?"

"Death," I said. "I told you that. Death, out in the middle of the field, standing there waiting for him. He was pretty sick, Wally. I'm guessing he knew he didn't have long to live anyway. Otherwise, it wouldn't have made too much sense. But he loved Dorothy, and he hated that laughing butcher, Kramer. He knew that he was going to die, anyway, and if he died in such a manner that the town would figure Kramer did it, either by black magic or by some trick of sleight of hand—"

"Sleight of foot," said Wally.

"All right, sleight of foot," I amended. "He'd have his revenge on Kramer. And the town knowing Kramer, knowing how Kramer hated Len and wanted him to die, would blame the butcher if there was any supernatural-looking angle to Len's death, anything unexplainable. Even if he wasn't arrested or lynched, the town would believe he had something to do with it. He'd have to leave. So by dying that way, a little sooner, Len got his revenge on a man he must have hated almost as much as he loved Dorothy—and he saved Dorothy from her blindness. If Len had waited to die naturally, she probably would have married

Kramer after a while, because for some reason she was blind to the evil in him. Don't you see?"

Kathy stirred in my lap.

"Like in chess, Wally," she said. "A gambit—where you make a sacrifice to win. Like Joe, the dwarf, gave me a knight, and then checkmated me. That's how Joe and Len, playing chess on the same side of the board for once, checkmated the butcher."

"Huh?" Wally said. "The dwarf was in on it?"

"He had to be," I said. "Who else could have made the footprints that led only one way from the body to the fence? Who besides the dwarf could have ridden on Len's back while he ran like mad out into the field until his heart gave way, and who but the dwarf could have fastened a pair of Kramer's shoes on, backward?"

Mystery Book Magazine, Spring (1948)

Slumming

Death is a Noise

I

SOMETHING was going by me as I lay there, and making a devil of a racket about it. There were cinders under my face, and as I lifted and turned it, I could see, even in the dark, that it was the wheels and cars of a freight train, rolling by within a yard of my nose.

Then I remembered; I had to catch that train, and I'd run smack into the post support of an overhead block signal. Fortunately I lay on the outside of the post; the other way and I'd have gone under those turning wheels.

I got up, holding on to the post, and shook my head to clear it. There was some reason that made it important that I catch that train before the rest of it went by.

Then I remembered that, too. I was going to Remmelton to get a job, a job that I was pretty sure of if I got there right away while they needed me.

I let go of the post and found I was all right, except that my head ached, and I was cold. The wind was bitter and it went through my thin suit like needles. And the rattler was sliding past me faster and faster as it gathered speed out of the division point. Gondola after gondola after gondola, and the empty boxcar I was looking for didn't come.

It was going to be murder to ride out in the open, dressed as I was, on a night like this. But way down the line and coming toward me fast, I could see the lights of the crummy-the caboose, if you've never hit the road.

So I was in for it all right, and I started to run alongside the train until I was going nearly enough as fast as it was to reach for the ladder rungs of a passing reefer and swing myself up.

I crawled up over the edge and sat straddling the catwalk, leaning forward into the wind to keep my balance. It would have been easier to humor the wind by lying flat, but this was my only suit and I wanted to reach Remmelton looking as nearly decent as possible.

The wind carried back a mournful wail from the whistle of the locomotive up ahead in the darkness, and when it had died down I heard the sound of voices from the car ahead.

Yes, I could see them now—or rather, I could see the darker shadows of their silhouettes. They were sitting on the edge of the car in front of mine, with their feet dangling over the edge between the cars, their backs to the wind.

I edged my way forward along the swaying catwalk to join them. I wouldn't be able to sleep up there on the car and it would make the trip faster if I had someone to talk to.

Then I was near enough to hear one of them say, "Here comes someone."

The words were short and quick as though it had been a warning, and then they were silent.

I called out "Hi" so they wouldn't take me for a brakie.

"What *you* want?"

It didn't sound like a bo's voice; the enunciation was careful. But the tone of voice made the implication plain, however it was worded.

"Nothing," I said. "Not a thing, if you feel that way about it."

"We do. Go on past if you want, but don't stop."

There was something about that voice I didn't like at all, but this wasn't the time and place to do anything about it.

Then the other voice, the one I'd heard first, cut in.

"We're talkin' business, buddy." The tone was more conciliating, as though he was trying to explain the other's attitude.

"Okay," I said, "put me down for a hundred shares of preferred." And I turned around and went back toward the tail end of the train. What they were talking about was none of my affair, and I didn't want to stop where they might think I was in listening range.

Probably a couple of hoods, I figured, on their uppers. You meet crooks on the road once in a while but not often. Mostly they ride the Pullmans. People you meet on the free trains are guys going somewhere to find work or guys going somewhere to get away from it.

A weak and sickly-looking moon slid out from behind the clouds and I could see well enough to walk easily. But I sat down again and took hold of the boards of the catwalk because the clank of couplings was coming back along the train as it slowed down to stop. If you're standing up when the jerk hits the car you're on, it can throw you for a loss.

We started to back into the yards again. Why, I didn't know and didn't care, but it would give me a chance to take another look for an empty boxcar up ahead and get in out of the wind.

So I went down over the side and stood there and let the train slide back past me. All the gondolas again, and then a string of boxes up near the engine, and luck was with me.

The third of the string was an empty, with the side door open. I ran alongside and got in.

The back end of a boxcar is the best place. You can sit facing forward with your back against the wall. I took a newspaper out of my pocket and unfolded it to sit on while I walked into the darkness of the back of the car. Walked slowly, feeling the way with my feet, so I wouldn't stumble over any bo who happened to be there.

I reached the back end without stepping on anyone, put down the paper and sat on it. I gave a contented grunt to be out of the wind, and shoved my hands into my pockets to get them warm again.

"Hullo," a voice alongside of me said. "Thought you had to get on back and I'd have to ride alone."

It was a girl's voice. She couldn't have seen the surprise on my face. I made my answer casual, so that I wouldn't frighten her.

"Afraid you got me mixed, sister. I'm not—"

Then the clank of couplings started again, at the back of the train this time, because it was going backward. You can't talk over that noise, so I kept still and leaned my head forward so the jerk wouldn't slam it against the end of the car. I had enough of a headache already.

Then, as the train stopped, there were voices outside the boxcar, as though a lot of men were running along both sides of the train.

I heard the girl start to stand up.

"Better sit tight," I said. "If anything's up, we're better off out of it."

"I guess you're—"

Then the voices were right outside the car we were in and three men, one with a lantern and two with flashlights, climbed up. I could hear footsteps of others going on past.

I stood up, then, and the flashlights bracketed me. All the men had guns, so I stood there while they walked back.

The girl was standing, too. Out of the corner of my eye I could see her backed tightly against the end of the car, as far away from them as she could get. I saw, too, that she was young and that she wore a pair of clean denim overalls and a scarf over her hair.

"Take it easy, guys," said one of the men. Then, in surprise, "One of 'em's a dame, Sheriff!"

I began to breathe a little easier. This was only a pinch, at worst.

The man addressed as "Sheriff" came in toward me. I expected to be frisked, but he didn't do that. Instead, he flashed the light around into the corners of the car. He kicked a crumpled newspaper with his foot, and then picked up the girl's suitcase and hefted it.

"Um—feels okay," he said, "but—"

He put it down flat and opened it. His deputy, who was wearing a star, too, came over and held the lantern beside him while he pawed quickly through the clothing in the suitcase. Then he grunted, and snapped it shut.

I saw that the third man had wandered to the front end of the boxcar, and was looking around up there. Someone had left an old cardboard carton in a corner, and he picked it up and then threw it down without looking inside it.

"All clear up here," he called back.

The sheriff was standing again. He looked at me and jerked his thumb toward the girl.

"Your wife?"

"Yes," I said.

"Stay right in this car till you're out of the state. I oughta pull you in, but—"

"Okay, Sheriff," I said, and tried to make it sound respectful.

He grunted, and without saying anything more, the three men got out of the car and I heard them moving on toward the back end of the train.

"Wait a minute, sister," I said to the girl. Then I walked quietly toward the center door of the car and peered out.

Moonlight was brighter out there now, but it shone on rolling fields and a ridge of mountains in the distance. Not even a building or a car. Nothing to account for the search they were making of the train.

I stuck my head out, and looked up toward the engine. Nothing up that way. But moving toward the other end of the train, at intervals, were a dozen lights.

I felt the presence of the girl standing behind me, although I hadn't heard her moving.

"Better—better not let them see you looking out," she said.

That was so silly I didn't answer. They'd seen me, when they'd searched the car, and they hadn't done anything about it. They weren't looking for hoboes. I stood there watching and trying to think it out. There'd been something funny about the way they'd searched the car.

They hadn't paid much attention to us at all. No frisk, no questioning. The sheriff had salved his official conscience by asking me one routine question, and he'd accepted my answer without question. Probably he'd guessed I was lying, but he didn't want to waste time picking us up.

He was looking for something else. He'd hefted that suitcase to find it, and one of the other men had picked up the cardboard carton. But he hadn't opened the carton when it felt empty, and the sheriff hadn't made a detailed search of the suitcase.

All that added up to one thing; they were looking for something that could fit into a suitcase or a carton, but too big to be carried in a pocket without showing. Something fairly heavy, too.

And then I remembered the tunnel up ahead. Our stop here was just a mile this side of the big tunnel, and that made sense. I thought of what I knew about that tunnel, and then I could see why they'd been looking for a bomb.

The S.R. & T. is the only route that runs into the mountains to the tungsten mines at Lassiter, and the S.R. & T. depends solely on that quarter-mile tunnel to get into the mountains and out again.

It had taken them two years to drill that tunnel, ten years ago. A bad cave-in now wouldn't take two years to fix, but it would take long enough, and while the road was out of operation, those scheelite mines would be just about as useful to the war program as rubber plantations in Malaya.

But I'd been through here before, and I knew they weren't stopping all trains here, before they went through the tunnel. There must be a tip-off that an attempt was to be made tonight. Then came the familiar jerk of couplings, and the train started to roll.

II

I WONDERED ABOUT THE GIRL, who she was, what she was doing here, and what she looked like. I'd had only a glimpse of her out of the corner of my eye when the flashlights had been in the car. But you don't ask people questions on the road. You don't even ask names. If a guy wants to tell you his name, he does; and until he does, you call him "Buddy" and let it go at that.

I knew how I could get another look at her without being rude, so I said:

"Want a cigarette? I've got makings."

"If you'll roll me one. 'Fraid I'm not good enough to do it in the dark."

I rolled one for her and one for myself and struck a match. As she leaned forward to light her cigarette, I was able to study her face, and I liked what I saw.

She was young. I don't mean schoolgirl age, but somewhere around twenty-five; ten years younger than I am. And good-looking without any of the baby-doll kind of prettiness that I've never cared for.

She had nice features with wide clear eyes. You couldn't see much of her hair because she had a scarf tied around it, but the part that showed was dark brown with that faint touch of titian that makes brown hair rich instead of drab. And there was a smudge of dirt on the end of her nose that seemed to somehow belong there, and to make her face more attractive.

As her cigarette glowed, her eyes lifted to mine over the flame of the match. And I thought, this is the girl I would like to marry.

Without knowing anything at all about her, I thought that, and I was as sure of it as I was ever sure of anything. No matter who or what she was. I wouldn't have called it love, exactly, although I knew it could grow to that. It was more a recognition of qualities I'd looked for in a woman and never found before.

I knew that this woman, if by any miracle she should ever feel the same about me as I felt about her, could make my life over into something that had meaning.

The match burned my fingers, and I dropped it. The stub of it lay there burning on the rough wood of the boxcar floor. I shifted my foot to stamp it out. Too late, for it flickered its last before my shoe reached it.

But in that brief last flare of the match's life, it lay beside the battered suitcase that the sheriff had searched, and it had illuminated the black scuffed leather and the celluloid-covered identification tag which was fastened to one of the straps on the side of the bag nearest me.

I thought I made out the name on that bag, and it just couldn't be what it seemed. No, I hadn't really read it, in that brief and flickering light. I'd just seen the capital letters and the length. I must have guessed incorrectly about the rest.

Deliberately, I struck another match and lighted my own cigarette and then I bent down casually with the match in my hand and took another look at the tag before I dropped the match and stepped on it. I needn't have been so careful, because the girl had turned away and was taking advantage of the brief light to locate the newspaper she'd been sitting on at the back of the car.

The tag read, "Mrs. George Scardale." There was an address, but it was printed in smaller letters and there hadn't been time or light enough for me to read it.

I stood there thinking, and then I went back and sat down beside her.

"I might as well introduce myself," I said. "My name's Joe Williams, and I'm heading for Remmelton to get a job at the Consolidated."

It was seconds before she answered. "Glad to know you, Joe." And for some reason it sounded as though there was a catch in her voice and it took me a moment to figure out why it had been there. "I'm—I'm stopping off at Remmelton, too."

That would have been wonderful news, a few minutes ago.

"Looking for work there?" I asked.

"Uh—yes. I was working as a waitress at Lassiter, but my place folded up."

"I thought Lassiter was booming," I said, "with the scheelite mines running full blast. They're digging the stuff out now regardless of percentage, just so there's tungsten in it."

"The place is going good, yes. I could probably have gotten another job but—well, there were reasons."

And those reasons were apparently none of my business, for she let it go at that. Hesitantly, she asked:

"You—you know anything about Remmelton, Mr.—Williams?"

"Make it Joe," I told her. "I've worked there at the nitro plant before. I know it pretty well."

Pretty soon, if I was right, she'd start pumping me. But there'd be a build-up first.

"My name is Beth, Joe," she said, "Beth Scardale."

I wanted to be able to watch her face, but I couldn't, of course. I had to be content with listening to every faint inflection of her voice.

"I knew a George Scardale," I said, "while I was working in the nitro plant. He was driving, and I worked inside. Any relation of yours?"

"My husband."

"Oh. I didn't know George was married, but then I haven't seen him since—" I broke off and asked, "Did he ever tell you why he quit?"

"Of course. He lost his nerve, got a phobia against nitroglycerine. But it wasn't cowardice; it was something he couldn't control. And he wasn't the only driver it ever happened to. It—it just hit him more suddenly than most."

I didn't say anything, and she went on, talking slowly.

"I can understand how he felt. It must be an awful job, driving one of those trucks. With the knowledge that if you hit the slightest bump, or—"

"It isn't so bad now," I cut in quickly. "They pack the stuff in sponge rubber and the trucks have special springs."

"But those mountain roads! George told me about them. Half the time hanging on the edge of nothing, and when you have to pass another car, knowing a few inches the wrong way means death."

There was perspiration on the inside of my palms, and I dried them with my handkerchief.

"It isn't that bad," I said. "And if it happens, it's clean. No pain or anything. Death is a noise, that's all, and I don't think you'd even hear it. That's the job I'm going to take this time. Driving a nitro truck."

"Oh. Then I shouldn't have said—"

It's all right. I know those things already. And the pay is good. Real money."

"Yes, but—"

"And the Army wouldn't take me, because of a broken metatarsus. But you don't need good arches to drive a nitro truck, and they need drivers, need them bad."

The train was slowing down a little, and I realized we must be near the tunnel. The engine highballed, and between the blasts the sound changed and I knew it was inside.

There was a rectangle of moonlight on the floor of the car opposite the center door, and I watched it.

I knew the sheriff had searched the girl's suitcase and this car, but I shifted a little toward her so my arm made light contact with hers and I could tell if she tried to move. If she did, I'd have to stop her.

I didn't see what she could do, here inside the boxcar, to endanger the tunnel, but then I knew she'd been lying to me. It was too big a thing to take chances on.

Then suddenly the rectangle of moonlight up ahead blacked out and the sounds of the moving train became hollow, reverberating sounds, and I knew we were inside.

Somehow, I found that I was holding my breath and holding my body rigid and ready. But the girl didn't move; it seemed that she leaned more closely against me in that utter darkness. Or perhaps it was I who had moved without knowing it.

We couldn't have been inside the tunnel more than half a minute, if the train was doing as much as thirty. But it seemed nearer half an hour before the moonlit square slid back into position on the floor up ahead and the sounds changed and were normal again. Another half minute and the back end of the train was through, and nothing had happened.

I turned toward the girl, and now that the echoes of the tunnel were gone, I could hear that she was sobbing quietly. I said nothing to her.

A long time, while the train rushed on into the night, that sobbing beside me continued, and then gradually it diminished and she was still. Her breathing was slow, and I knew that she slept.

III

OUTSIDE, the moon was high now. The square of moonlight on the floor had shrunk to a narrow slit just inside the doorway, and I knew we were almost due at Remmelton.

I hoped that the girl would continue to sleep and that I could leave her that way. It would make it easier to do what I had to.

The train was slowing down now, and it stopped without awakening her. I rose carefully and tiptoed to the door, and jumped down to the gravel path of the familiar Remmelton siding. No division point here, no yards. The train would stop for water and then go right on unless there were cars to uncouple.

Up ahead were the station lights. And out across the fields to my right, the bright lights of the Consolidated's nitrating plant where the vat-men were working night and day to keep the soup moving.

I walked up the steps of the station, and pushed through the door. The agent was alone in the room behind the ticket window.

He looked through into the waiting room, saw me and came to the inner door.

"George, old boy!" he said. "Just pull in on the red-ball? Say, something wrong? You look like you'd seen ghosts."

"I'm all right, Harry," I said. "Yes, I came back for a job again. But listen, I've got to use the phone. Give me a couple nickels for a dime."

He looked surprised, but gave me the nickels and I crossed the room to the phone booth and shut its door behind me. I asked the operator for the police, and wondered if Captain Craddock was still on nights.

He was; I recognized his voice when he said, "Police Department."

"This Craddock?"

"Yes."

"This is George Scardale, Cap," I said. "Just got in on the red-ball, and there's a—"

"Drop around, George. Nothing doing here tonight and we can play a game of cribbage."

"There'll be something doing, Cap," I said grimly. "And I don't want to be in on it. There's a girl on this train, asleep in Car Sixty-three eighty-nine hyphen six; the fifth one back from the locomotive. You'd better arrest her and hold her on suspicion until you can investigate."

"Huh? Well, if you say so. But it'll take me eight minutes to get around there and what if it pulls out before—"

"Then phone ahead and have her picked up at the next stop." That would be better anyway, I thought; then maybe I wouldn't have to confront her.

"Sure, but what—"

"I don't know, Cap. But it could be sabotage. She's traveling under a fake identity. Got my name somewhere, and she's coming here posing as my wife, probably because it would give her an in for a job here. And—well, maybe there's no connection, but I got a hunch there's something up tonight about the Wilmot Tunnel. Maybe she's in on that, and maybe—"

There was a click and the line went dead. Craddock would be running out the door to his car right now.

I dropped my other nickel into the phone box quickly, because I wanted to try to get away before Craddock arrived. I gave the Consolidated number, and asked for Roy Burke.

"Roy, this is George," I said. "George Scardale. How you set for drivers?"

"On the nitro trucks? We need 'em, but are you sure you got it licked, George? I mean, about—"

"I'm sure," I cut in.

"Start any time then."

"Swell. But won't I have to check in through the main office and fill out another application and all that?"

"No. We didn't let you quit, remember? Technically you're still on leave of absence and that leaves me free to put you on any time. How you set for sleep?"

"Fine," I lied. "Mean you got one going out tonight I can take?"

"One's just about loaded that Wescott is scheduled to drive. He's here ready, but he's got a bad tooth and he told me to raise a sub for him if I could. You'll be doing him a favor, if you can make it."

"I'll be right around," I told him.

I ducked into the station washroom and cleaned up as well as I could. A truck out tonight was fine, just what I wanted, to take my mind off what had happened back there on the train.

Then I started across the fields toward the highway. I heard a car driving up toward the station. It was probably Cap Craddock.

I tooled the truck carefully out the gate and turned into the road. The wheel felt good in my hands, and it took my mind off the other things.

Just a few hundred yards up the highway was the turnoff that would take me back across the tracks and on the long detour around Remmelton. You never drive a nitro truck through a town if there's any possible detour around it.

This one was a bad, dirt road, full of pits and hollows. The kind of holes that look like they go through to China when your headlights shine on them from an angle, and then level off when you're almost there.

I took it at the five miles an hour that's the maximum for that short chunk of road, with the roar of the engine in low gear so loud that I could hardly hear the sound of the freight-train that was pulling out.

And way off in the darkness, diagonally across the fields I could see an arc of light as the conductor leaned out from the crummy to swing the go-ahead with his lantern.

The first half of the train had gone by when I pulled to a stop at the tracks. I was glad of that; at least I wouldn't have to see the boxcar I'd ridden in. It would be deserted now, and I didn't like to think about that.

The rest of the train slid past, gathering speed. And then it was gone. I shifted the truck into low again and eased forward toward the tracks. There wasn't any other train due, but we always inched up to the tracks and looked both ways just to be sure. With a truckload of nitroglycerine behind him, a driver never cuts corners.

Just as my foot started to push in on the clutch, there was sudden movement on both sides of the truck, and both doors of the cab were jerked open simultaneously. A short-barreled revolver poked into my ribs.

"Take it easy, pal," a voice said softly.

I didn't recognize either of the men, but the voice was familiar. It was the voice of one of the two men I'd encountered on top of the freight train.

The one on my left got in and sat beside me. He slid his gun back into its shoulder holster for a moment and frisked me while the other held an automatic on me.

He searched thoroughly before he said, "Clean as a whistle."

"Look in the glove compartment," said the other.

It jerked open and slammed shut.

"Nothing. He isn't heeled."

The one on my right closed the cab door, came around and got in on the other side.

"Okay, start rolling," he said. "We're hooking a ride tonight, pal."

"Did you read the signs on this truck?" I asked. "Know what it's carrying? Not that *I* mind, understand, but it isn't what most people'd choose for a joy ride."

"Get rolling."

I still didn't get the play. My mind must have been slowed down, because all I could think of was that even if the law was close behind them, they could find a safer and faster way to travel. And if they meant to hijack the load, they'd have a sweet job finding a fence who'd handle anything as hot as nitro.

But I started the truck and eased it on across the tracks. My run was to Varnesville, and I hoped that direction was what they wanted, and that it was just a matter of a ride and they'd drop off somewhere en route.

We crossed the tracks and hit the Dartown road, and I let it out to twenty-five miles an hour. That road isn't too good, and the hoods started to act nervous.

"Take it easy, pal," the nearest one said, "we're not out for a speed record."

The uneasiness in his voice made me feel better. It made me realize that my phobia was licked. There wasn't even a trace, tonight, of the sudden awful fear that had hit me just before a run four months ago, and had made me a neurotic wreck.

Here tonight, I was tooling the truck along at the top safe speed for this kind of road and not worrying in the least about the load behind me.

"Where do I drop you off?"

"We'll tell you."

I drove on, and only slowly and unbelievingly at first did it come to me that maybe this tied in with what I'd figured out about the tunnel. These thugs had been on that train, and they'd been passed up, as I had, because they had no bomb around. But they had one now!

I'd thought, all too often, of a nitro truck as sudden death for the driver who made a slip, but I'd never before thought of one as a bomb that could be placed somewhere deliberately to destroy something.

Good Lord! If the truck would explode in the confined space of the tunnel it would nearly destroy that tunnel beyond all hope of repair. It would nearly blow the roof off the mountain. And there wouldn't be enough left of the train that hit the truck to make a key chain.

I thought ahead to figure out when I'd be sure about what they planned. It would be when we came to the side road off the highway just past Barney's Filling Station. That road ran up into the mountains, and crossed the S.R. & T. tracks only a few hundred yards from the end of the tunnel.

I kept quiet about that road, because it was a little-used one and it was just possible that they didn't know about it. I tried to keep outwardly calm, and to play the game as though I believed they were merely forcing their presence on me for the ride.

If my hunch was right and if they didn't know I'd guessed their purpose, it would give me an ace in the hole.

There seemed singularly little traffic on the roads that night. We passed hardly a car in the first thirty miles outside Remmelton. Then we began passing a long line of interstate trucks bound the other way.

The window on my side of the cab was down, and I waved at the driver of the first truck.

The revolver nudged my ribs.

"No signals, pal."

"Okay," I said, "but it'll look funnier to them if I won't wave. We generally do."

"Go ahead, then."

As a matter of fact, we generally didn't, because a nitro driver always keeps both hands on the wheel.

My waving wouldn't be enough out of the ordinary, though, to make the other drivers suspicious. But it would attract their attention to the nitro truck, and maybe one of them would notice that there were other men in the cab and report it in Remmelton.

I waved to the last of the string of trucks, and then we were on the short steep upgrade that led to Barney's Filling Station, and leveled off on top just before the side road branched off.

We went past the station, closed of course at this time of morning. I thought to myself, another minute and I'll know whether I'll ever see the sun come up again over those mountains.

If they told me to turn in that side road, I'd know for sure what was up, and I'd run this truckload of concentrated hell into the first tree or off the first ledge.

The Wilmot Tunnel was more important than I was, right then, to say nothing of the lives of everybody on the train that would crash into the truck.

No, not for all the tungsten in Lassiter were they going to run the truck up to the tunnel if I could help it. And helping it was pretty obviously going to cost me my life. But—well, this was a bigger chance to do a bigger thing than the Army could ever have given me if I'd passed their exam.

I happened to see my hands on the wheel, and they were white with the strain of my grip. I wondered if my face was like that, too, and I tried to make my muscles relax so they wouldn't notice.

Scared? Of course, I was scared stiff.

How had I said it to the girl, earlier tonight?—"Death is just a noise, and I don't think you even hear it." But death, this way, was going to be a pretty loud noise, whether I heard it or not, and it would be a noise that would splash me all over a mountainside. Something was wrong with the engine of the truck. It had stopped turning over, and we were slowing down to a stop.

I glanced at the dashboard and saw the ignition key wasn't there. It was in the hand of the man next to me; I'd been so busy thinking heroic thoughts that I hadn't seen him reach for it.

"Okay," he said. "Stop here."

I didn't have to; the truck had practically stopped itself by then, and it was too late to try to swerve into anything, or even off the road.

The other man was already getting out of the cab and walking around the front. He opened the door on my side and said, "Move over. I'll take it from here."

I slid over, glad that I was to be in the middle next to the wheel. If I didn't give away my intentions, I might still have a chance to reach over and send that truck off the road.

Even the gun in my ribs couldn't go off soon enough to keep me from giving one yank on the wheel, and one would be enough on any of half a dozen turns up there. I hadn't any doubt now, that we were going to turn into that side road.

And we did. The truck started up the long steep climb of rough gravel road off the highway. Going in low, too slow for me to be sure of getting away with a break here. But plenty of chances up ahead.

I sat quietly, trying not to look like a man who expects to kill himself within a matter of minutes.

IV

WE HAD GONE UP the long slow slope, and still were only crawling. I could see the reflection of the man who was driving, in the windshield, and there were little beads of sweat on his forehead. He was plenty scared, and he wasn't taking any chances with that load on the eight miles back to the crossing.

Then the truck was stopping again, here almost halfway between the highway and the tunnel, here four miles from nowhere. The stop had been too quick for me to make a play. The ignition key was out of the switch again, and the revolver muzzle tighter than ever against my ribs.

The thug who had been driving opened the door and stepped out, drawing his gun as he stepped down from the running board.

"End of the line, pal," he said. "This is where you get off."

I'd waited too long. Now, with the truck motionless and the ignition key gone, and with a gun aimed at me from either side, I was going to die and I was going to die without a chance to take things with me. I'd be shot down as soon as I got out of the cab and away from the truck.

I hesitated, trying to guess my chances if I dived out and tried to grab the gun in front of me, ignoring the one behind. But there was a way that gave me a little better chance, slight as it might be.

There was a steep slope down from the edge of the road, two yards from the outside of the truck. I slid under the wheel, put my foot on the running board. But I didn't step down from it normally as they would expect me to do. I left it in a running leap, and was over the edge before a gun roared, running diagonally downward as fast as I could.

Guns roared behind me now. But no bullet touched me as I made that mad dash, although half a dozen were fired before I reached the cover of trees at the bottom of the gully.

I slowed down, just enough to let me find my way through by the dim moonlight that filtered through the leaves. I had to get to the other side at once if my plan was to work. There was an inside hairpin turn ahead of the truck half a mile around the gully. My chance was that they didn't know that topography well enough to realize that I could make it faster than they.

I was halfway across the wooded bottom when I heard the doors of the truck slam, and the sound of the engine starting. I'd guessed right, at least, in thinking that they wouldn't try to follow me, once I'd gained cover.

I hurried, reached the bottom of the up-slope on the other side, and started to climb. It was so steep that I had to crawl on hands and knees part of the way, but I made it just ahead of them.

I stretched myself flat against the steep slope just at the far side of a slight curve in the road. And while I lay there, I found a couple of sizable chunks of rock to put in my pockets. Poor weapons against a gun, but better than bare hands.

Then the roaring of the engine in low gear came just above me. I scrambled up across the edge of the road, and ran after the red dangerlights on the back of the truck.

It was easy to catch up, at their speed. The back of the body wasn't designed to accommodate hitchhikers, but at ten miles an hour I was able to board it, hanging onto the locked handles of the double doors and standing with my feet on the bumper.

It was a precarious grip; I'd never have been able to hang on if the truck had been going fast. But I knew already that the man behind the wheel had plenty of respect for his cargo and he'd probably crawl the truck all the way there.

I was still hanging on when we reached the S.R. & T. tracks and turned off the road. And here, over the bumpy ties of the railroad, he went even slower.

My hands ached from their grip on the door handles, but now I could drop down, and I did. I kept up with the truck on foot easily, trotting along behind it and staying a little to the left so I wouldn't show up in the rear vision mirror.

We passed the switch that converted the double track to a single one for the length of the tunnel, and then were inside the tunnel itself.

The timing was perfect. Just as the moonlight blacked out, I heard the long, mournful wail of a distant train whistle.

The men in the cab must have heard it, too, because the truck ahead of me started to go faster despite the bumps, for a short distance into the tunnel, and then stopped. Probably they'd meant to drive in farther, but this was enough.

We were still near enough to the end of the tunnel that I could see dimly. As the truck stopped, I took the two pieces of rock from my coat pockets and held one in each hand.

A door of the cab opened, and I thought it sounded like the right side. I stood waiting at that corner of the truck. I knew they'd come around the back end of the truck, toward me, because the far end of the tunnel was too distant.

And as a shadow, darker than the surrounding darkness, came around the corner of the truck, I lashed out.

The rock and my fist together must have made a mess of his face. It did unpleasant things to my knuckles and fingers, too, but I didn't think about that just then.

The door on the other side had already opened, and I groped my way around the back of the truck toward the other side. This time I didn't see my opponent, nor he me. We collided in the dark.

I dropped my stones and grabbed at him, trying to pin his arms so he couldn't reach for his bolstered gun. The advantage of surprise was with me, for he hadn't suspected I was there and his first reaction was to think that his accomplice had blundered all the way around the truck and run into him.

He tried to push me off, rather than to fight, and said sharply, "Herman! It's—"

The sound of his voice located his face for me. I reached for it, and shoved sidewise suddenly with all my weight behind it. His head thudded against the rock wall of the tunnel, and he went down without a sound.

I stepped over him and got into the cab of the truck, flicked on the dashboard lights, and saw the ignition key was gone. With frantic haste I got out of the cab and searched the pockets of the man I'd just knocked down. The key wasn't on him.

And then I realized what had probably happened. Force of habit had made him pull out the key when he left the truck, then realizing he wouldn't want it found on him if he was ever picked up, he'd have thrown it down as he left the cab.

It took precious seconds to get the flashlight out of the glove compartment and throw its beam along the ground at the side of the tunnel. But I caught the gleam of metal, and picked up the key.

The train whistled again, nearer, and I knew from the sound that it was back of the truck, coming to enter the tunnel from the same end we'd gone in.

But I threw the gear shift lever into reverse. Chances were better the short way, even if I had to go toward the oncoming train.

I was just at the end of the tunnel when I heard the whistle again—a frantic warning blast this time. I knew the engineer had seen the truck and would be throwing on the air brakes.

I twisted the wheel and the tires of the truck slid away from the smooth steel tracks twice before they caught and went over. Then I was backing off the rails.

The truck was clear of the tracks now, and I slammed on the brakes as the back end canted dangerously downward off the edge of the roadbed.

Then there was a sudden hard jolt as the rear bumper of the truck hit a telegraph pole along the right of way with a force that almost loosened my back teeth. But, thanks to sponge rubber, the nitro didn't explode.

I saw the engine go by only six feet in front of the windshield, slowing down with air brakes screaming.

And then things began to swim in front of my eyes, and something seemed to explode inside my head. I fell into blackness . . .

~§~

I opened my eyes to whiteness, a blurred whiteness that resolved itself into white walls of a room in a hospital.

I turned my head and saw the light of dawn coming through a window. My bed was nearly enough level with the window ledge so I could see other buildings outside. I recognized them and knew I was in the Remmelton Hospital.

It had hurt a little to move my head, and I raised my right hand and found the knuckles and fingers were well covered with bandage. But my left hand was free. I put it to my head and found a bandage there, too.

"Feeling okay, George?" a voice said.

I turned, and there was Roy Burke sitting beside the bed. He hadn't been there before, so I knew I'd dropped off to sleep again. The light at the window was brighter now, too.

"Yeah," I said. "Did they get both of them?"

"They did," said Roy. "One of them alive, and one in several pieces after both the truck and the train had gone over him. You're Remmelton's favorite hero, George."

But I was staring at something on the wall behind Roy Burke. A calendar. It didn't make sense because it was torn off to May, and this was still March. I couldn't have been out cold for two months. It was impossible!

I stared at the calendar unbelievingly, and Roy saw the direction I was looking.

"What date do you think it is, George?" he asked quietly.

"I don't know exactly, but it's the second week in March. Isn't it?"

He shook his head.

"Third in May. That's what we figured, that you—"

"You trying to tell me I've been here nine weeks?"

"No. Not quite nine hours. Listen, you remember what happened last night, early in the evening? And early yesterday?"

"Sure," I said. "I left Denver yesterday morning and—"

There was a quiet knock on the door, and it pushed open. It was the girl who'd called herself Beth Scardale. She wasn't wearing the overalls now, and she was a knockout in regular clothes.

"I heard talking, Mr. Burke," she said. "Is he—"

"He doesn't remember yet, Mrs. Scardale," Roy said quickly. "But he's told me what he does remember, and I can almost put it together now. George, when did you get that bump on the head?"

"Why, when I was running for the train at Wilmot, the division point. I ran smack into a signal post, head down. But why?"

It was very silly that he should be calling her Mrs. Scardale and asking me how much I remembered.

Roy was nodding his head. "I'll start back nine weeks ago, George," he said. "You were on your way back here, after you'd tried to get into the Army. But in Lassiter you met Beth, here, and you fell for each other and were married."

"But—"

"Let me finish, George. You remained in Lassiter for nine weeks. Mrs. Scardale hadn't wanted you to drive a nitro truck, at first. But then you talked her into it. You were broke, and it was a short trip back here by freight, so the two of you started out from there yesterday afternoon."

The girl, Beth, her eyes wide and clear as I remembered having seen them in the light of the match last night in the boxcar, took it up from there.

"You got off the train at Wilmot to buy cigarette papers, George, and you told me to stay on, even if it started, because you might have to get on at the back end. And when you were running to get back on, you got the concussion."

I looked at her wonderingly.

"You mean when I bumped my head on the signal post, it caused a concussion that gave me amnesia or something and I thought I was back two months before when I was heading for Remmelton alone?"

"Some concussions are walking cases, George," Roy said. "The doctor told us about them. When you got back in the boxcar later on, you told Beth your name was Joe Williams and you didn't know her."

"I saw her name on the suitcase," I said. "And I thought she was an imposter. I didn't want to tell her who I was because she'd have known the game was up."

The girl gasped, and I saw there were tears in her eyes now. "I thought you'd gone mad, George, when you didn't recognize me. I tried to remind you by telling you who I was. And then I tried to humor you by playing it your way until I could get you to a doctor and to people who knew you here in Remmelton."

I saw it all now, and as I looked at her, I began to realize that this wasn't just a small problem; it meant everything to me.

I still didn't remember, those two months were still gone, but this girl whom I'd known last night was the girl I wanted to marry was already my wife.

That meant she had loved me, and if the tears in her eyes meant anything, she still did.

"Beth," I said. She came over and sat down on the bed beside me, and put her hand over mine.

"George, don't you remember even now?"

I looked up at her and smiled, so she wouldn't cry any more.

"It doesn't matter, Beth," I said. "I don't remember, yet, but even if I never do, it doesn't matter. I fell in love with you all over again last night, the minute I saw—"

Roy Burke cleared his throat, and stood up.

"You have a leave coming to you for as long as you want it. You'll be out of here in a few days, and you can take a week or a month for a second honeymoon. Then I'll be seeing you."

He tiptoed out and left us alone.

Popular Detective, February 1943

The Little Lamb

SHE DIDN'T COME HOME for supper and by eight o'clock I found some ham in the refrigerator and made myself a sandwich. I wasn't worried, but I was getting restless. I kept walking to the window and looking down the hill toward town, but I couldn't see her coming. It was a moonlit evening, very bright and clear. The lights of the town were nice and the curve of the hills beyond, black against blue under a yellow gibbous moon. I thought I'd like to paint it, but not the moon; you put a moon in a picture and it looks corny, it looks pretty. Van Gogh did it in his picture The Starry Sky and it didn't look pretty; it looked frightening, but then again he was crazy when he did it; a sane man couldn't have done many of the things Van Gogh did.

I hadn't cleaned my palette so I picked it up and tried to work a little more on the painting I'd started the day before. It was just blocked in thus far and I started to mix a green to fill in an area but it wouldn't come right and I realized I'd have to wait till daylight to get it right. Evenings, without natural light, I can work on line or I can mold in finishing strokes, but when color's the thing, you've got to have daylight. I cleaned my messed-up palette for a fresh start in the morning and I cleaned my brushes and it was getting close to nine o'clock and still she hadn't come.

No, there wasn't anything to worry about. She was with friends somewhere and she was all right. My studio is almost a mile from town, up in the hills, and there wasn't any way she could let me know because there's no phone. Probably she was having a drink with the gang at the Waverly Inn and there was no reason she'd think I'd worry about her. Neither of us lived by the clock; that was understood between us. She'd be home soon.

There was half of a jug of wine left and I poured myself a drink and sipped it, looking out the window toward town. I turned off the light behind me so I could better watch out the window at the bright night. A mile away, in the valley, I could see the lights of the Waverly Inn. Garish bright, like the loud jukebox that kept me from going there often. Strangely, Lamb never minded the jukebox, although she liked good music, too.

Other lights dotted here and there. Small farms, a few other studios. Hans Wagner's place a quarter of a mile down the slope from mine. Big, with a skylight; I envied him that skylight. But not his strictly academic style. He'd never paint anything quite as good as a color photograph; in fact, he saw things as a camera sees them and painted them without filtering them through the catalyst of the mind. A wonderful draftsman, never more. But his stuff sold; he could afford a skylight.

I sipped the last of my glass of wine, and there was a tight knot in the middle of my stomach. I didn't know why. Often Lamb had been later than this, much later. There wasn't any real reason to worry.

I put my glass down on the windowsill and opened the door. But before I went out I turned the lights back on. A beacon for Lamb, if I should miss her. And if she should look up the hill toward home and the lights were out, she might think I wasn't there and stay longer, wherever she was. She'd know I wouldn't turn in before she got home, no matter how late it was.

Quit being a fool, I told myself; it isn't late yet. It's early, just past nine o'clock. I walked down the hill toward town and the knot in my stomach got tighter and I swore at myself because there was no reason for it. The line of the hills beyond town rose higher as I descended, pointing up the stars. It's difficult to make stars that look like stars. You'd have to make pinholes in the canvas and put a light behind it. I laughed at the idea—but why not? Except that it isn't done and what did I care about that. But I thought awhile and I saw why it wasn't done. It would be childish, immature.

I was about to pass Hans Wagner's place, and I slowed my steps thinking that just possibly Lamb might be there. Hans lived alone there and Lamb wouldn't, of course, be there unless a crowd had gone to Hans's from the inn or somewhere. I stopped to listen and there wasn't a sound, so the crowd wasn't there. I went on.

The road branched; there were several ways from here and I might miss her I took the shortest route, the one she'd be most likely to take if she came directly home from town. It went past Carter Brent's place, but that was dark. There was a light on at Sylvia's place, though, and guitar music. I knocked on the door and while I was waiting I realized that it was the phonograph and not a live guitarist. It was Segovia playing Bach, the Chaconne from the D-Minor Partita, one of my favorites. Very beautiful, very fine-boned and delicate, like Lamb.

Sylvia came to the door and answered my question. No, she hadn't seen Lamb. And no, she hadn't been at the inn, or anywhere. She'd been home all afternoon and evening, but did I want to drop in for a drink? I was tempted more by Segovia than by the drink—but I thanked her and went on.

I should have turned around and gone back home instead, because for no reason I was getting into one of my black moods. I was illogically annoyed because I didn't know where Lamb was; if I found her now I'd probably quarrel with her, and I hate quarreling. Not that we do, often. We're each pretty tolerant and understanding—of little things, at least. And Lamb's not having come home yet was still a little thing.

But I could hear the blaring jukebox when I was still a long way from the inn and it didn't lighten my mood any. I could see in the window now and Lamb wasn't there, not at the bar. But there were still the booths, and besides, someone might know where she was. There were two couples at the bar. I knew them; Charlie and Eve Chandler and Dick Bristow with a girl from Los Angeles whom I'd met but whose name I couldn't remember. And one fellow, stag, who looked as though he was trying to look like a movie scout from Hollywood. Maybe he really was one.

I went in and, thank God, the jukebox stopped just as I went through the door. I went over to the bar, glancing at the line of booths; Lamb wasn't there.

I said, "Hi," to the four of them that I knew, and to the stag if he wanted to take it to cover him, and to Harry, behind the bar. "Has Lamb been here?" I asked Harry.

"Nope, haven't seen her, Wayne. Not since six; that's when I came on. Want a drink?"

I didn't, particularly, but I didn't want it to look as though I'd come solely for Lamb, so I ordered one.

"How's the painting coming?" Charlie Chandler asked me.

He didn't mean any particular painting and he wouldn't have known anything about it if he had. Charlie runs the local bookstore and—amazingly—he can tell the difference between Thomas Wolfe and a comic book, but he couldn't tell the difference between an El Greco and an Al Capp. Don't misunderstand me on that; I like Al Capp.

So I said, "Fine," as one always says to a meaningless question, and took a swallow of the drink that Harry had put in front of me. I paid for it and wondered how long I'd have to stay in order to make it not too obvious that I'd come only to look for Lamb.

For some reason, conversation died. If anybody had been talking to anybody before I came in, he wasn't now. I glanced at Eve and she was making wet circles on the mahogany of the bar with the bottom of a martini goblet. The olive stirred restlessly in the bottom and I knew suddenly that was the color, the exact color I'd wanted to mix an hour or two ago just before I'd decided not to try to paint. The color of an olive moist with gin and vermouth. Just right for the main sweep of the biggest hill, shading darker to the right, lighter to the left. I stared at the color and memorized it so I'd have it tomorrow. Maybe I'd even try it tonight when I got back home; I had it now, daylight or no. It was right; it was the color that had to be there. I felt good; the black mood that had threatened to come on was gone.

But where was Lamb? If she wasn't home yet when I got back, would I be able to paint? Or would I start worrying about her, without reason? Would I get that tightness in the pit of my stomach?

I saw that my glass was empty. I'd drunk too fast. Now I might as well have another one, or it would be too obvious why I'd come. And I didn't want people—not even people like these—to think I was jealous of Lamb and worried about her. Lamb and I trusted each other implicitly. I was curious as to where she was and I wanted her back, but that was all. I wasn't suspicious of where she might be. They wouldn't realize that.

I said, "Harry, give me a martini." I'd had so few drinks that it wouldn't hurt me to mix them, and I wanted to study that color, intimately and at close hand. It was going to be the central color motif; everything would revolve around it.

Harry handed me the martini. It tasted good. I swished around the olive and it wasn't quite the color I wanted, a little too much in the brown, but I still had the idea. And I still wanted to work on it tonight, if I could find Lamb. If she was there, I could work; I could get the planes of color in, and tomorrow I could mode them, shade them.

But unless I'd missed her, unless she was already home or on her way there, it wasn't too good a chance. We knew dozens of people; I couldn't try every place she might possibly be. But there was one other fairly good chance, Mike's Club, a mile down the road, out of town on the other side. She'd hardly have gone there unless she was with someone who had a car, but that could have happened. I could phone there and find out.

I finished my martini and nibbled the olive and then turned around to walk over to the phone booth. The wavy-haired man who looked as though he might be from Hollywood was just walking back toward the bar from the jukebox and it was making preliminary scratching noises. He'd dropped a coin into it and it started to play something loud and brassy. A polka, and a particularly noisy and obnoxious one. I felt like hitting him one in the nose, but I couldn't even catch his eye as he strolled back and took his stool again at the bar. And anyway, he wouldn't have known what I was hitting him for. But the phone booth was just past the jukebox and I wouldn't hear a word, or be heard, if I phoned Mike's.

A record takes about three minutes, and I stood one minute of it and that was enough. I wanted to make that call and get out of there, so I walked toward the booth and I reached around the jukebox and pulled the plug out of the wall. Quietly, not violently at all. But the sudden silence was violent, so violent that I could hear, as though she'd screamed them, the last few words of what Eve Chandler had been saying to Charlie Chandler. Her voice pitched barely to carry above the din of brass—but she might as well have used a public address system once I'd pulled the jukebox's plug.

". . . maybe at Hans's." Bitten off suddenly, as if she'd intended to say more.

Her eyes met mine and hers looked frightened.

I looked back at Eve Chandler. I didn't pay any attention to Golden Boy from Hollywood; if he wanted to make anything of the fact that I'd ruined his dime, that was his business and he could start it. I went into the phone booth and pulled the door shut. If that jukebox started again before I'd finished my call, it would be my business, and I could start it.

The jukebox didn't start again.

I gave the number of Mike's and when someone answered, I asked, "Is Lamb there?"

"Who did you say?"

"This is Wayne Gray," I said patiently. "Is Lambeth Gray there?"

"Oh." I recognized it now as Mike's voice. "Didn't get you at first. No, Mr. Gray, your wife hasn't been here."

I thanked him and hung up. When I went out of the booth, the Chandlers were gone. I heard a car starting outside.

I waved to Harry and went outside. The taillight of the Chandlers' car was heading up the hill. In the direction they'd have gone if they were heading for Hans Wagner's studio—to warn Lamb that I'd heard something I shouldn't have heard, and that I might come there.

But it was too ridiculous to consider. Whatever gave Eve Chandler the wild idea that Lamb might be with Hans, it was wrong. Lamb wouldn't do anything like that. Eve had probably seen her having a drink or so with Hans somewhere, sometime, and had got the thing wrong. Dead wrong. If nothing else, Lamb would have better taste than that. Hans was handsome, and he was a ladies' man, which I'm not, but he's stupid and he can't paint. Lamb wouldn't fall for a stuffed shirt like Hans Wagner.

But I might as well go home now, I decided. Unless I wanted to give people the impression that I was canvassing the town for my wife, I couldn't very well look any farther or ask any more people if they'd seen her. And although I don't care what people think about me either personally or as a painter, I wouldn't want them to think I had any wrong ideas about Lamb.

I walked off in the wake of the Chandlers' car, through the bright moonlight. I came in sight of Hans's place again, and the Chandlers' car wasn't parked there; if they'd stopped, they'd gone right on. But, of course, they would have, under those circumstances. They wouldn't have wanted me to see that they were parked there; it would have looked bad.

The lights were on there, but I walked on past, up the hill toward my own place. Maybe Lamb was home by now; I hoped so. At any rate, I wasn't going to stop at Hans's. Whether the Chandlers had or not.

Lamb wasn't in sight along the road between Hans's place and mine. But she could have made it before I got that far, even if—well, even if she had been there. If the Chandlers had stopped to warn her.

Three quarters of a mile from the inn to Hans's. Only one quarter of a mile from Hans's place to mine. And Lamb could have run; I had only walked. past Hans's place, a beautiful studio with that skylight I envied him. Not the place, not the fancy furnishings, just that wonderful skylight. Oh, yes, you can get wonderful light outdoors, but there's wind and dust just at the wrong time. And when, mostly, you paint out of your head instead of something you're looking at, there's no advantage to being outdoors at all. I don't have to look at a hill while I'm painting it. I've seen a hill.

The light was on at my place, up ahead. But I'd left it on, so that didn't prove Lamb was home. I plodded toward it, getting a little winded by the uphill climb, and I realized I'd been walking too fast. I turned around to look back and there was that composition again, with the gibbous moon a little higher, a little brighter. It had lightened the black of the near hills and the far ones were blacker. I thought, I can do that. Gray on black and black on gray. And, so it wouldn't be a monochrome, the yellow lights. Like the lights at Hans's place. Yellow lights like Hans's yellow hair. Tall, Nordic-Teutonic type, handsome. Nice planes in his face. Yes, I could see why women liked him. Women, but not Lamb.

I had my breath back and started climbing again. I called out Lamb's name when I got near the door, but she didn't answer. I went inside, but she wasn't there.

The place was very empty. I poured myself a glass of wine and went over to look at the picture I'd blocked out. It was all wrong; it didn't mean anything. The lines were nice but they didn't mean anything at all. I'd have to scrape the canvas and start over. Well, I'd done that before. It's the only way you get anything, to be ruthless when something's wrong. But I couldn't start it tonight.

The tin clock said it was a quarter to eleven still, that wasn't late. But didn't want to think so I decided to read a while. Some poetry, possibly. I went over to the bookcase. I saw Blake and that made me think of one of his simplest and best poems, "The Lamb." It had always made me think of Lamb— "Little lamb, who made thee?" It had always given me, personally, a funny twist to the line, a connotation that Blake, of course, hadn't intended. But I didn't want to read Blake tonight. T.S. Eliot: "Midnight shakes the memory as a madman shakes a dead geranium." But it wasn't midnight yet, and I wasn't in the mood for Eliot. Not even Prufrock: "Let us go then, you and I, when the evening is spread out against the sky like a patient etherized upon a table—" He could do things with words that I'd have liked to do with pigments, but they aren't the same things, the same medium. Painting and poetry are as different as eating and sleeping. But both fields can be, and are, so wide. Painters can differ as greatly as Bonnard and Braque, yet both be great. Poets as great as Eliot and Blake. "Little lamb, who—" I didn't want to read.

And enough of thinking. I opened the trunk and got my forty-five caliber automatic. The clip was full; I jacked a cartridge into the chamber and put the safety catch on. I put it into my pocket and went outside. I closed the door behind me and started down the hill toward Hans Wagner's studio.

I wondered, had the Chandlers stopped there to warn them? Then either Lamb would have hurried home—or, possibly, she might have gone on with the Chandlers, to their place. She could have figured that to be less obvious than rushing home. So, even if she wasn't there, it would prove nothing. If she was, it would show that the Chandlers hadn't stopped there.

I walked down the road and I tried to look at the crouching black beast of the hills, the yellow of the lights. But they added up to nothing, they meant nothing. Unfeeling, ungiving—to feel, like a patient etherized upon a table. *Damn Eliot,* I thought; *the man saw too deeply.* The useless striving of the wasteland for something a man can touch but never have, the shaking of a dead geranium. As a madman. Little Lamb. Her dark hair and her darker eyes in the whiteness of her face. And the slender, beautiful whiteness of her body. The softness of her voice and the touch of her hands running through my hair. And Hans Wagner's hair, yellow as that mocking moon.

I knocked on the door. Not loudly, not softly, just a knock.

Was it too long before Hans came?

Did he look frightened? I didn't know. The planes of his face were nice, but what was in them I didn't know. I can see the lines and the planes of faces, but I can't read them. Nor voices.

"Hi, Wayne. Come in," Hans said.

I went inside. Lamb wasn't there, not in the big room, the studio. There were other rooms, of course; a bedroom, a kitchen, a bathroom. I wanted to go look in all of them right away, but that would have been crude. I wouldn't leave until I'd looked in each.

"Getting a little worried about Lamb: she's seldom out alone this late. Have you seen her?" I asked.

Hans shook his blond, handsome head.

"Thought she might have dropped in on her way home," I said casually. I smiled at him. "Maybe I was just getting lonesome and restless. How about dropping back with me for a drink? I've got only wine, but there's plenty of that."

Of course he had to say, "Why not have a drink here?" He said it. He even asked me what I wanted, and I said a martini because he'd have to go out into the kitchen to make that and it would give me a chance to look around.

"Okay, Wayne, I'll have one too," Hans said. "Excuse me a moment."

He went out into the kitchen. I took a quick look into the bathroom and then went into the bedroom and took a good look, even under the bed. Lamb wasn't there. Then I went into the kitchen and said, "Forgot to tell you, make mine light. I might want to paint a bit after I get home."

"Sure," he said.

Lamb wasn't in the kitchen. Nor had she left after I'd knocked or come in; I remember Hans's kitchen door; it's pretty noisy and I hadn't heard it. And it's the only door aside from the front one.

I'd been foolish.

Unless, of course, Lamb had been here and had gone away with the Chandlers when they'd dropped by to warn them, if they had dropped by.

I went back into the big studio with the skylight and wandered around for a minute looking at the things on the walls. They made me want to puke, so I sat down and waited. I'd stay at least a few minutes to make it look all right. Hans came back.

He gave me my drink and I thanked him. I sipped it while he waited patronizingly. Not that I minded that. He made money and I didn't.

But I thought worse of him than he could possibly think of me.

"How's your work going, Wayne?"

"Fine," I said. I sipped my drink. He'd taken me at my word and made it weak, mostly vermouth. It tasted lousy that way. But the olive in it looked darker, more the color I'd had in mind. Maybe, just maybe, with the picture built around that color, it would work out.

"Nice place, Hans," I said. "That skylight. I wish I had one."

He shrugged. "You don't work from models anyway, do you? And outdoors is outdoors."

"Outdoors is in your mind," I said. "There isn't any difference." And then I wondered why I was talking to somebody who wouldn't know what I was talking about. I wandered over to the window—the one that faced toward my studio—and looked out of it. I hoped I'd see Lamb on the way there, but I didn't. She wasn't here. Where was she? Even if she'd been here and left when I'd knocked, she'd have been on the way now. I'd have seen her.

I turned. "Were the Chandlers here tonight?" I asked him.

"The Chandlers? No; haven't seen them for a couple of days." He'd finished his drink. "Have another?" he asked.

I started to say no. I didn't. My eyes happened, just happened, to light on a closet door. I'd seen inside it once; it wasn't deep, but it was deep enough for a man to stand inside it. Or a woman.

"Thanks, Hans. Yes."

I walked over and handed him my glass. He went out into the kitchen with the glasses. I walked quietly over to the closet door and tried it.

It was locked.

And there wasn't a key in the door. That didn't make sense. Why would anyone keep a closet locked when he always locked all the outer doors and windows when he left?

Little lamb, who made thee?

Hans came out of the kitchen, a martini in each hand. He saw my hand on the knob of the closet door. For a moment he stood very still and then his hands began to tremble; the martinis, his and mine, slopped over the rims and made little droplets falling to the floor.

I asked him, pleasantly, "Hans, do you keep your closet locked?"

"Is it locked? No, I don't, ordinarily." And then he realized he hadn't quite said it right, and he said, more fearlessly. "What's the matter with you, Wayne?"

"Nothing," I said. "Nothing at all." I took the forty-five out of my pocket. He was far enough away so that, big as he was, he couldn't think about trying to jump me.

I smiled at him instead. "How's about letting me have the key?"

More martini glistened on the tiles. These tall, big, handsome blonds, they haven't guts; he was scared stiff. He tried to make his voice normal. "I don't know where it is. What's wrong?"

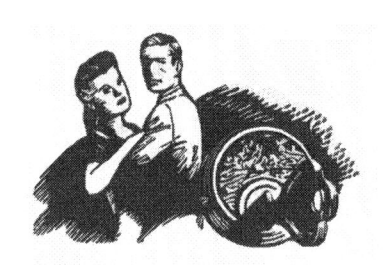

"Nothing," I said. "But stay where you are. Don't move, Hans."

He didn't. The glasses shook, but the olives stayed in them. Barely. I watched him, but I put the muzzle of the big forty-five against the keyhole. I slanted it away from the center of the door so I wouldn't kill anybody who was hiding inside. I did that out of the corner of my eye, watching Hans Wagner.

I pulled the trigger. The sound of the shot, even in that big studio, was deafening, but I didn't take my eyes off Hans. I may have blinked.

I stepped back as the closet door swung slowly open. I lined the muzzle of the forty-five against Hans's heart. I kept it there as the door of the closet swung slowly toward me.

An olive hit the tiles with a sound that wouldn't have been audible, ordinarily. I watched Hans while I looked into the closet as the door swung fully open.

Lamb was there. Naked.

I shot Hans and my hand was steady, so one shot was enough. He fell with his hand moving toward his heart but not having time to get there. His head hit the tiles with a crushing sound. The sound was the sound of death.

I put the gun back into my pocket and my hand was trembling now.

Hans's easel was near me, his palette knife lying on the ledge.

I took the palette knife in my hand and cut my Lamb, my naked Lamb, out of her frame. I rolled her up and held her tightly; no one would ever see her thus. We left together and, hand in hand, started up the hill toward home. I looked at her in the bright moonlight. I laughed and she laughed, but her laughter was like silver cymbals and my laughter was like dead petals shaken from a madman's geranium.

Her hand slipped out of mine and she danced, a white slim wraith.

Back over her shoulder her laughter tinkled and she said, "Remember, darling? Remember that you killed me when I told you about Hans and me? Don't you remember killing me this afternoon? Don't you, darling? Don't you remember?"

Manhunt, August 1953

Murder Set To Music

IT STARTED on a Tuesday evening in early October. It had been a fine evening, up to then. I'd made a good sale and when the phone rang I guessed that it was Danny and was glad he'd called so I'd have a chance to tell him about it.

Danny Bushman and I run a used car lot together. My name is Ralph Oliver. Danny and I have been close friends since we started high school together. He played trumpet and I played sax, and we played together in the, high school band and orchestra, and in our junior and senior years we made our spending money playing at parties and dances.

After graduation we were apart for a year. Danny got a few thousand bucks from his father's life insurance—his mother had died before he entered high school—and he threw it into starting a small but hot dance band, which he called *The Bushmen,* from his own name which, in case you've forgotten already, was Bushman. He wanted me to go with him on it, but I had other ideas. I enrolled as a student at the Wisconsin Conservatory of Music. Both of my parents had died by then too (funny how many parallels there have been in Danny's life and mine, in big things as well as little ones) but I figured I could work my way through by playing evenings. I found that I could, but I also found within a year that longhair, although not for the birds was not for me either, and I quit. And in just the same length of time Danny found out that he was a better trumpet player than a band leader and *The Bushmen,* as Danny put it, went back to the bushes.

For the next ten years we blew for our bread and butter, and managed most of the time to stick together. If not in the same band, at least in bands in the same city.

Something happened then that might have broken up our friendship, but only showed how strong it was. We both fell in love with the same girl, Doris Dennis, who was a singer with Tommy Drum's orchestra, with which both Danny and I were playing at the time. She liked both of us but Danny was the one she fell for. They were married, and still we were friends. All three of us, in fact.

A few months later, Tommy Drum got behind the eight ball and had to break up the orchestra. Almost any musician who's really good, and Tommy Drum was, tries his hand as an orchestra leader once; few of them are businessmen enough to make a go of it.

Danny and I, with Doris kibitzing, had a conference to decide what band might be able to take both of us on, and ended up deciding, with Doris abetting, that we were getting a little old for the game. Most dance musicians quit and get into something else by the time they're thirty, and that's how old we were. And we both happened to be solvent enough for it to be a good time for us to make the break. We'd all been working steadily for quite a while and I had a fairish sum salted. Danny had somewhat less, mostly because he had a weakness for the ponies, but Doris had some savings and wanted to advance Danny enough to make his share match mine, if we could find a good place to put it.

We kicked it around, and the only thing we both knew and liked besides music was cars. So we ended up with a used car lot. Back in the small city Danny and I had come from.

That was almost a year ago, and we were beginning to do all right. At least we were out of the red and into the black, and we made money when we had a good day. A good day is one when we take two good-sales of relatively late model cars; one sale gets us off the nut and a second one is gravy.

It was a quarter of nine when Danny phoned and I was just getting ready to shut up shop. We keep open from nine to nine, with Danny opening the lot in the morning and quitting at dinner time and with me starting after lunch and working till closing, which puts two of us on the lot during the afternoon and one each mornings and evenings. Danny said, "Hi, Ralph. How goes it?"

"*Crazy,*" I told him. "I sold the fifty-three Buick."

"Attaboy. Full price?"

"Full price, except that for cash I promised him four new tires. It's still a good deal."

"I'm flipping," he said. "But I got some good news, too. Guess who's in town?"

"I'll bite. Who? Eisenhower?"

"Better than that. Tommy Drum. He's got a cool combo, and they're opening tonight at the Casanova Club. Need I say more?"

"Did you make reservations?"

"For three. Only you'll have to pick me up and take me there. Doris is at a hen party and she took my heap, so I'm afoot. But I phoned her and she'll join us as soon as her party breaks up, probably around eleven. Can you come right here, or will you have to go home first?"

"I'll come right there. I can wash up and shave there and bum a clean shirt. The rest of my clothes will do."

"Hit it, man. My pad is panting."

We don't ordinarily talk that way, but it came natural to go back to the jive when we were going to see Tommy again and dig his combo. It could be good if he had the right support. Tommy Drum, despite his name, plays a very cool piano.

It took me ten or fifteen minutes to put the lot to sleep and to climb aboard the old Merc I use for my own transportation—although when I'm on the lot it's there too, in case anybody wants to buy it—and another fifteen or twenty to Danny's "pad." He and Doris have a small apartment on the north side. Neat but not gaudy. It's in a small building, only four apartments, two on each floor, and the Bushmans' is the downstairs one on the left. I tried the knob first, thinking Danny would probably have left it unlocked so I could walk right in, and was surprised when the door wouldn't open. I knocked, and then again and louder.

There was only silence on the other side. Could Danny have dozed off? Hardly, and besides he was a light sleeper; even my first light knock would have wakened him. It didn't make sense, that silence. Expecting me any minute, he wouldn't have gone out anywhere.

It had been minutes now, and I began to get worried. Anywhere in that small apartment he must have heard me. But I tried again and still harder, and called out his name.

This got me open the door on the other side of the hall, and a man with rumpled gray hair looking at me through the doorway. I'd been introduced to him once—but didn't remember his name—as a neighbor of the Bushmans. He said, "Oh—it's you," so he recognized me too, and then, "Is something wrong?"

I said, "I know Danny's home—he must be. But—"

He stared at me. "You know," he said, "I thought I heard a kind of thud across there a little while ago. If you think—These locks are awfully flimsy. I think together we could—"

But already I'd thrown my weight against the door, and he was right about the lock; it broke and the door flew open on my first lunge.

Danny, fully dressed except for his suit coat, lay stretched, spread-eagled, on the living room rug with his feet toward the door. I ran to him and bent over him, fumbling to open his shirt at the collar to give him air and farther down to reach in and feel for a heartbeat. The neighbor had come as far as the doorway and I yelled over my shoulder to him to phone for an ambulance. I said a police ambulance because I thought it would get us faster service whatever this was, whatever had happened. And I thought I knew because his otherwise spotless white shirt was dirty just where it would have been dirtied by someone giving him a few kicks after knocking him out. It looked like a going-over.

His heart was okay. I ran to the bathroom and wet a washrag with cold water. I had his head in my lap and was using it on his forehead when the neighbor came back. He said, "They're coming. Is he—all right?"

"He's alive. I think he's been beaten up." Danny was moaning a little now, beginning to come around.

"Is there anything I can—?"

I said, "There's brandy in the cabinet over the kitchen sink. Bring some."

He brought the bottle, a pint about half full. He took the cap off and handed it to me. Danny's eyes were open now, but a bit glazed. His lips opened, though, when I held the mouth of the bottle against them, and he gulped and shuddered when I raised the bottle enough to give him a good sized slug.

Then he tried weakly to sit up but I held him back lightly by a shoulder. I said, "Take it easy, kid. There's an ambulance coming and you'd better lie still. You might have something broken."

Two uniformed cops were coming in the doorway. From a radio car, we learned later, that had happened to be cruising only a few blocks away when they'd got the message.

I beat them to the punch by asking if an ambulance was coming.

"Yeah," one of them said. "What's up?"

"A beating, I think," I told him. Danny tried to say something but I shushed him. "Wait for some strength, Danny. Let us tell our stories first; they're simpler."

But we all three had time to tell our stories before the ambulance came and Danny's was as simple to tell as ours. Or simpler. A few minutes after talking to me on the phone he'd been going to the door to unlock it so I could let myself in when I came, and there was a knock on the door before he reached it. Danny's first reaction had been that he'd misjudged the time and that I was here already and he'd thrown the door wide open. A big than with a handkerchief tied over his face and a hat pulled down over his eyes stepped through the doorway and had swung a right at Danny's jaw that Danny had barely seen coming and didn't have time even to try to duck. And that was the last thing he remembered until he came to, with his head in my lap.

Did he know the guy? No, and he wouldn't be able to identify him if he saw him again. A big guy, maybe six feet and at least a couple of hundred pounds, and that was all the description he could give. Danny thought he wore a brown suit but he wasn't even sure of that. There'd probably been quite literally only a second between the time he'd opened the door and the time he'd gone down and out.

And no, he didn't have any enemies that he knew of and didn't have the faintest idea what it was all about. Either the guy was crazy or it was a case of mistaken identity and he thought he was beating up somebody else.

Danny kept saying he was okay and trying to sit up, but I told him for all we knew he could have some broken ribs and we didn't want one puncturing a lung. When the ambulance came, they were gentle about getting him on the stretcher.

I rode with him to the emergency hospital, but we didn't talk much on the ride. Danny said that from the hospital I'd better get to the Casanova Club fast to be sure of being there in time to meet Doris; she'd be worried if she got there first and didn't find either of us. I said okay, but it was still only half past nine; there was lots of time and I'd wait until they'd at least have given him a quick once over. So that, if there wasn't anything serious—and we were, both beginning to think there wasn't—I could reassure Doris and not frighten her.

It didn't take long, once we got there. I was in the waiting room only twenty minutes when a doctor came in and gave me the news: nothing broken, nothing seriously wrong.

Danny was going to have a sore jaw and some sore ribs, a few bruises other places, but nothing worse. As far as the hospital was concerned he could be released right away, if he felt up to going home, although the doctor advised him to lie quietly and rest another half hour or so before leaving.

"You say as far as the hospital is concerned," I said. "What else?"

"The police," he said. "They are sending a detective around to talk to him."

They let me in to talk to Danny again. They'd stripped him for the examination and he was getting his clothes back on, a bit painfully. He said, "Listen, Ralph, I'm stuck here till some dick comes to grill me, but maybe I can still get to the Casanova before Doris does. And if so, don't say anything—"

"Nuts," I said. "You can't keep this from Doris. It may or may not make the papers, but you're going to be a lot sorer tomorrow morning when you wake up than you are right now. You'll probably need help to get dressed. And your jaw will probably be too sore to chew toast for breakfast. You'll have to tell her *something* and it might as well be the truth. Why not?"

He saw that, and gave in, provided I'd play it down instead of up if I had to be the one to tell her.

I caught a cab from the hospital back to his place to get the Merc, and it was ten o'clock by the time I got it. The Casanova's well west of town, about an hour's drive, but I drove fast and made it well before eleven. I thought ruefully about how much cab fare was going to cost Danny, but there wasn't any out on that.

The joint was jumping. It was a good thing Danny had phoned and reserved a table. Even so, it was a lousy table for our purpose; the room was L-shaped and this one was around the corner and out of sight of the bandstand. No doubt we'd be able to get ourselves a better one later, though; the people who had come mostly for dinner would be starting to leave now.

So I took the table without argument and ordered myself a highball. It might be amusing to listen to the combo before I saw it, to see if I could guess what Tommy Drum had with him. Tommy's piano I'd have known anywhere. The sax was not quite up to it, and I couldn't place it; it could have been any one of a hundred tenor saxes. Smooth tone and no goofing, but weak on improvisation; Tommy's piano could lead him just so far out but no farther. But it was adequate and it was something the squares could dig. The skins were much better but I didn't place the drummer until he took a solo and started to go to town—but in a civilized way—On the Chinese cymbal. It was Frank Ritchie; I'd never played with him but I knew him and had heard him often, always with combos. He was a combo man and didn't like band work. He was right in his element with Tommy; it could have been a great combo with a better sax.

Well I'd identified the drummer and I'd given up on the sax so I left my half-finished drink on the table and strolled out to where I could see the bandstand. I knew the sax after all, although not well. It was Mick O'Neill, a guy Danny and I had played with two or three times for short periods. Danny had never liked him, had almost had a fight with him once, but I got along okay with him. Mick had got his start in. New Orleans and he was strictly a Dixieland man; he was good at that but way over his head in the kind of stuff Tommy Drum was playing tonight. I wondered why Tommy had picked him.

A hand touched my sleeve and a voice said, "Hi, Oliver. Sit down." I looked down and saw it was Max Stivers. Bookmaker and racketeer, I'd heard. I'd met him around a few places.

He said, "This is Gino Itule," and nodded to his companion. "Gino, Ralph Oliver." And I reached across and shook hands with a man built like a beer barrel.

"Sit down," Stivers repeated. "Saw the lousy table they gave you. You can't see from there."

I slid into the vacant seat beside him. "Thanks," I said. "Until somebody I'm expecting shows up." I looked around for a waiter. "I'll have my drink brought over."

"Forget it," Stivers said. "I'll get you a fresh one." He reached a hand in the air and snapped his fingers and suddenly we had not one but three waiters coming toward us. I ordered a rye and soda from one of them and grinned at Stivers. "Real service you get."

"I should. I own a piece of the joint. Say, you're an ex-musician, aren't you? What do you think of the combo that's starting tonight?"

"Came to catch them; they're old friends of mine. So my opinion would be prejudiced."

When the waiter brought my drink it occurred to me that now, while I was sitting with the owner of a piece of the joint, would be a good time to start pushing for a better table, but Stivers stopped me and waved the waiter away. He said, "Take this table. Gino and I are leaving in a minute. And it's bigger; your friends in the band will probably want to join you when they take a break."

That solved that and I thanked him. Racketeers may not be nice people—but they're nice people to know, when they're on your side.

They left a minute later and a minute after that Tommy Drum looked my way and I caught his eye and waved. He didn't wave back or even nod, but his music went into a tricky little phrase that had once been a joke between us. And a few minutes later he ended the number and came over to my table.

I said it was swell to see him again.

"Crazy," he said, grinning err to ear. "How goes the filling station?"

"Used car lot. It goes, somewhat. How goes the combo?"

"You heard it," he said. He shook his head sadly. "My kingdom for a saxophone. You don't want a job again, do you, Ralph?"

"Off it for good, Tommy I'm a car salesman now, and a businessman. Maybe there isn't much dough in it yet, but we're building it up; we'll get there."

"Just evenings, just while we're booked here—a month. You can put in some time on the lot days."

I shook my head. "Sorry, Tommy, but it's out. But what gives? How come you hired Mick? You know he's a Dixie boy."

"Do I, do I? It's a long sad, Ralph. Wingy Tyler's blowing for me—one of the best in the business, short of the real top boys I couldn't afford. Man, can that cat blow. And this morning, two hours or so before plane time for our booking here, he goofs on me. Know what he does, like?"

"What does he do, like?"

"Ruptures his appendix, that's all. Well, the operation went fine; we couldn't wait but I bad the doc send me a telegram. But Wingy's out for the month we're booked here. So there I am in Pittsburg, two hours to plane time, and I run into Mick just when I think I'm going to have to cancel. He says he's going west anyway so he'll come along for the ride and fill in till I get somebody. It's fine with Mick the minute I replace him—you won't be undercutting him. No how, Jackson."

He lighted a cigarette for me that I'd just stuck in my mouth. "Think it over, anyway. Talk to Danny about it; *he'll* tell you not to let an old man down. Where is he?"

"Coming later. So's Doris."

"Crazy. Why don't you people stay home, though? Found both you and Danny in the fun book, and kept calling first one number then the other till I finally got Danny at half past eight."

"You should have called the lot; we were both there all afternoon."

"I looked for it, but I looked under filling stations." He glanced at his watch and got up quickly. "Back to the mountain," he said. "This is supposed to be in the middle of a set, so that's why I told the other boys to stay up there. We'll all be over later. Hasta banana."

I looked at my watch too, wondering about Doris. It was almost half past eleven. Well, half an hour isn't late for a woman.

Danny came in a few minutes later. There was a stocky middle aged man with him and if the man wasn't a cop then he was disguised as one; he wore a shiny blue serge suit, carried a soft black felt hat that the check girl hadn't been able to take away from him, and wore the first pair of high shoes I'd seen in a long time. He had a round face and sad eyes.

Danny introduced him as Lieutenant Andrews.

Danny grinned at me. "I persuaded him to third-degree me while driving me out here. Look at the cab fare I saved."

"He didn't have to talk me into it," Andrews said. "I wanted to talk to you, and to Drum. He's the one playing piano by there, isn't he?"

I nodded, but I asked, "Why to him? He couldn't have had anything to do with what happened to Danny."

He gave me a level look. "Then you know all about what happened to your partner?"

"Of course not. But I see what you mean." I happened to look toward the entrance and I said, "Here comes Doris. Listen, Lieutenant, how's about you and me strolling over to the bar for a few minutes. You want to question me anyway, and that'll give Danny a chance to tell his wife what happened without—well, it would worry her more if there's a cop with him when he has to tell it."

He nodded and we stood up. That's when Doris caught sight of us and I waved to her and pointed to Danny still seated, and Andrews and I started toward the bar. But halfway there he took me by the arm and started steering at right angles. "Let's go out on the terrace instead. I don't drink on duty and besides the bar's pretty crowded."

It was all right by me, and we went out into the cool darkness and sat down on a concrete railing. We could hear the music from here and I heard Mick O'Neill start what might have been a far out wail and then suddenly butter a large ear of corn; I winced.

"All right," Andrews said. "Tell it your way, what happened."

I told it my way and he listened without interrupting. When I'd finished, he asked, "How sure are you it was a quarter to nine when Mr. Bushman phoned you?"

"Within a minute or two. I'd just looked at my watch, wondering how soon I could start turning out lights and closing up."

"I guess it checks," he said. "Mr. Bushman happened to notice the time when he got a call from Mr. Drum, half past eight. He didn't notice any times after that, but the first thing he did was to call the club here for a reservation and—"

"Why didn't he ask Tommy to take care of it? Simpler."

"Says he didn't think of it until they'd hung up. Anyway, then he phoned his wife at the party she was attending, a baby shower, and then called you. That would make it a quarter of nine by the time he called you, as near as matters."

"As nears as matters, but what does it matter?"

"Just trying to reconstruct things. Maybe the exact timing doesn't matter. Neighbor across the hall was watching television when he heard that thud. Thinks it was about the middle of the second half, after the midway commercial break, of a half hour dramatic show he was watching. That would put it between, say, ten minutes of nine and five of nine. Could you have driven from the lot to the Bushmans' place in five or ten minutes?"

"Ten minutes maybe, if I went pretty fast. But I didn't. I closed up the lot, first and that took till almost nine. Then, since I didn't speed, it must have taken me at least fifteen minutes more to get out there. But why? You don't think *I* slugged Danny?"

"No, I don't," he said mildly. "Just not overlooking the possibility. After all, you're about six feet tall and two hundred pounds, like he described the man who hit him. And you're wearing a brownish suit and I'll bet you've got a handkerchief."

I had to laugh. I said, "Put on the cuffs, Lieutenant. You've got me cold. But tell me why I did it?"

"His wife, maybe. You were both in love with her once and maybe you both still are. Mr. Bushman told me that—I mean the fact that you both were in love with her—when he was telling me how close friends the two of you were. But what if you never gave up?"

I said, "I did give up, but even if I hadn't, what would beating up Danny do me toward taking his wife away from him? That's nutty, Lieutenant."

He sighed. "I guess it is. Does your friend have any enemies that you know of?"

"None that I know of and a buck gets you twenty he hasn't any that I don't know of. A few guys who don't like him too well, maybe, back in the old days—all musicians aren't one big happy family, sometimes we get in one another's hair—but nobody who'd still be carrying a grudge"

"Uh-huh. Does he gamble?"

"Nope. Used to a little, just little horse bets, when we were playing, but he's a reformed character now. We both are."

"Yeah? What are you reformed from?"

"Knocking out my friends and kicking them in the ribs," I told him.

He sighed again. "Well, thanks. Guess I had that coming. Shall we go back?"

~§~

When we got inside I saw that the combo had apparently finished the set because all three of them were at the table with Danny and Doris. I wondered for a second if Danny had had time to tell Doris what had happened, then realized he must have had because the combo had played two numbers after Andrews and I had gone out on the terrace.

I stopped Andrews just inside. I said, "Listen, Lieutenant, this is a family reunion, people who haven't seen one another for over a year. If you go asking questions at the table, you'll be a specter at the feast. How about making that corner of the terrace your office and talking one at a time to whoever you want to talk to, like you did with me?"

"Son, I'm tired," he said. And seeing him so closely in the bright light I saw now that his face did look tired, and older than I'd thought at first. "And it's way past my quitting time. Yes, I'll want to talk to everybody there, but I think it can safely wait till tomorrow."

"Good," I said. "That's best all around."

"Yeah. I don't think there's any more danger. The goon who beat your friend up had him down and out; he could've hurt him worse if he wanted to, so why would he come back for more? But I got one more question for you and the fact that I forgot to ask it out there shows my brain is through working for the night."

"Shoot," I said.

"Could your friend by any chance be playing around on the side with a woman who might have a jealous husband or lover?"

"No," I said. "That's one vice Danny hasn't got. And believe me, we're close enough that I'd know it if he was doing any philandering. I'd guess it before Doris would."

"You sound sure. All right, I'll buy it. Thanks, Son, and goodnight."

I went back to the table, said hi to Doris and shook hands with Frank Ritchie and Mick. Danny gave me a raised eyebrow and I knew he was wondering what had happened to the cop, so I leaned over and told him.

And that was an end to serious discussion for a while. For the next half hour it was musicians' talk and old home week and a ball. Then the combo had to climb the mountain for another set, and as soon as Tommy started tickling the keys, Doris looked at Danny, "Mind if I dance one with Ralph?"

Danny grinned at her. "You don't really want to dance with him, Honey. You just want a chance to pump him to find out if I told all. Go ahead."

When we were out on the floor dancing, Doris said, "Danny was right, Ralph. I do want to pump you."

"Sorry I'm such a lousy dancer."

"Don't be foolish. You know you're a wonderful dancer or you wouldn't say that. But about Danny—he's not playing this down, is he? I mean, about how badly he got hurt."

"Only some bruises, Doris. That's the McCoy because I got it straight from the doc, not roundabout. But he may be pretty sore in the morning and maybe he shouldn't open the lot. Tell you what, I'll phone around breakfast time and if he doesn't feel up to it, I'll get to the lot at sine. And if he doesn't feel up to coming in later, it won't hurt me to work the whole twelve hours for once."

"That's sweet of you, Ralph. Do you have any idea who might have done it to him or why?"

"Not a glimmer. Like Danny said when we were talking to the squad car cops, it could have been mistaken identity. Which, in that case, would mean the guy was a professional goon sent to beat up someone he didn't know and knocked on the wrong door or got the wrong building. Either that or the guy was a nut."

"But if he's that, what if he comes back again?"

I reassured her on that by repeating the lieutenant's reasoning, that the man had had Danny down and out and if he'd wanted to hurt him any worse, he could have done so there and then, without taking the added risk of making a second trip.

Then to change the subject I asked her if the dress she was wearing was a new one. It was a strapless black velvet that set off her page boy blonde hair beautifully, and I was sure I'd never seen her wear it before.

She leaned back against my arm and laughed up at me. "It's borrowed, Ralph. You don't think I wore an evening gown to a baby shower, do you? After the shower I explained to Winnie what my phone call had been about, and she loaned me this." She added a little wistfully, "It *is* gorgeous."

That was all there was to say and we danced just one number.

We'd scarcely got back to the table when Mick O'Neill came over from the bandstand. He put a hand on my shoulder. "How about sitting in for a number, Ralph boy? Use my sax. I just wiped the mouthpiece and put in a new, reed for you."

He slid into a chair. I hesitated and he grinned at me. "G'wan, man, I don't care if you show me up. Ride it high and funky."

Doris put her hand on my arm and said, "Go ahead, Ralph," so I nodded and climbed the mountain. Tommy said, "Hi, man. You name it." "You name it," I said, "and start it. But let me wet this reed first." I wetted the reed and blew a few soft arpeggios, and then nodded.

"All right, *Body,"* Tommy said. "I'll take an eight-bar intro and you come in." He swung into a smooth introduction to *Body and Soul,* and we were off.

I took my first chorus reasonably straight, and then started out, not far out but getting farther. Tommy, grinning, gave me a modulation into a new key and a swinging beat, and I found myself and blew. Way out and knowing I'd get back. Tommy looked around at me. "Dig that crazy tenor man," he said. And it sounded good and felt better than it sounded.

Then, when I laid off for thirty-two to give Frank a solo on the skins, I looked toward our table and Danny was sitting there alone, and looking beyond I saw Mick dancing with Doris. I hoped Danny wasn't working up a peeve over that. Not that he minds other men dancing with Doris, but it might be different with Mick if Danny still had a grudge against him. But it was probably all right, I told myself, Danny wouldn't hold a grudge that long; it had been three years ago he'd almost had that fight with Mick. I couldn't remember now what it had been about, and like as not Danny wouldn't remember either.

At the end of the number, Tommy tried to talk me into finishing the set; I told him no, but that I'd be out again within a few days and next time I came I'd bring my own sax and I'd sit in a full set, maybe more.

So I went back to the table and sent Mick, who'd just returned Doris to Danny, back to the combo. Danny said, "Nice going, Ralph," and Doris said "Cool," and I tried to blush modestly.

Danny leaned toward me. He said, "Mick was telling me about Tommy wanting you to join the combo. Why don't you, Ralph? Just white they're playing here, I mean. We could work it out."

"No, Danny," I said. "Remember our promise; we're through blowing for money. Jamming or sitting in, sure. But once one or both of us starts taking jobs oil the side, the lot goes downhill. We talked that out and made it definite."

"But this is different. Tommy's a friend of ours and he *needs* a sax. We can't let a friend down. If we trade shifts on the lot so I work evenings—"

I said, "If Tommy was really in a jam, it might be different. But Mick agreed to stick with him till he gets somebody else. And how many in a crowd like this one know the difference? One in thirty, maybe; Tommy isn't going to lose his booking."

Danny shrugged. "If that's the way you feel about it, okay." Which surprised me a little; I'd expected him to give me more of an argument and if he had, who knows? Maybe I'd have let myself be talked into it. You've got to have principles in business, but that doesn't mean you can't weaken a little *once* in a while.

Doris said, "Ralph's right, Danny. You're going to make a go of that business, but only if you both stick to it tight and don't go goofing off."

And that ended any chance of my being talked into playing with Tommy; I'd look like a fool now if I changed my mind.

We had another round of drinks and Danny danced a couple of numbers with Doris and I danced one, and when I brought her back, Danny was stifling a yawn.

"Chillun," he said, "I better go, I'm the one that gets up early, and it's pushing midnight and an hour's drive from home."

I told him he was going to be sore in the morning and should let me open up for a change, but he insisted that he'd be all right. But he went along with the idea when I said I'd arranged with Doris to phone at breakfast time to make sure he felt up to working.

He told Doris she could stay and come in with me if she wanted to, but she vetoed that. He asked me to explain things to the boys so they wouldn't have to go over to the bandstand and to say good night for them. "If this was a one-night stand," he said, "I'd buck up and stick around. But they'll be here a month; we'll be out often."

"Okay," I told them, "scram before they finish this number then, because it's maybe the last one, and you'll get tied up if you're not gone. Take care of yourself, Danny. 'Night, Doris."

It *was* the combo's last number, it turned out, so it was lucky they'd made their getaway. The Casanova is an early club in an early town. Most people come for dinner and don't stay too long afterwards, so the entertainment is off and on between six and midnight. The club stays open another two hours, until the legal closing time, for those who want to stick around that long, but they have to entertain themselves.

The combo now adjourned to the table I had all to myself and after I'd explained and excused Danny and Doris for leaving early, we entertained ourselves, talking, until they closed.

Meanwhile, I sold another car, although not on a very profitable basis. Tommy brought up that they were thinking about renting a car for the month they'd be here, since they'd flown in and didn't have any local transportation.

He said one car would do for the three of them, even if they fought over it once in a while. I told them what renting a car for a month would cost them—plenty—and pointed out they'd do better to buy a cheap but usable car and resell it when they took off. I told them we had a '49 Ford on the lot priced at four-fifty and said if they chipped in and bought it for that we'd buy it back at the end of the month for four hundred if they hadn't banged it up any, or for whatever price was fair if they'd damaged it any. They said that sounded swell to them and that they'd be down tomorrow afternoon to look it over and would probably drive it away. We wouldn't make anything on a deal like that, but I knew Danny would back me up on it.

"Where are you boys staying?" I asked. "I'll run you home."

I was mildly surprised to learn that they were staying at a motel—Tommy had to look at his key to tell me the name of it—when they didn't have a car. But they'd intended to rent one tomorrow, so it made sense. They'd seen this one oh the way in from the airport in a taxi and because it had a sizeable swimming pool and both Tommy and Mick, especially Mick, liked to swim, they'd had the taxi drop them off there. They'd taken two rooms, Tommy and Frank sharing one and Mick taking the other.

At the motel they tried to talk me into coming in for a nightcap, but I knew that would lead to another hour or two of yak and refused to get out of the car. It was already half past two and I had to get up early to call Danny at breakfast time. But I gave Tommy the telephone numbers of the office on the lot and told him to call early in the—afternoon. If Danny and I were both there I'd probably be able to drop out and pick them up for a look at the car I had in mind for them.

It was three when I got home and I set the alarm for eight and went right to bed.

When the alarm went off I staggered to the telephone, trying to wake myself up as little as possible, and dialed Danny's number. If he was okay, there was no reason why I shouldn't grab a couple more hours of sleep.

But he wasn't okay. It was Doris who answered the phone and she said, "He's pretty stiff and sore, Ralph. He says to tell you he *can* get down there, but he'll appreciate it if you'll swap shifts today and let him have a few more hours."

"Sure," I told her. "Tell him to come in whenever he feels like it, or not at all. It won't hurt me to do the whole thing one day. Sometime I'll take a day off and get revenge."

"Thanks, Ralph. But he thinks he'll be able to come in by afternoon. Maybe sooner."

"He won't need to let me know," I said. "I'll look for him when and if I see him."

So that ended any chance of my going back to sleep. I took a cold shower to wake up and then shaved and dressed. I remembered my promise to Tommy to bring my own sax when I came out next, and decided that I might decide to do so that evening if Danny came to relieve me, so I put my sax case in the car. I stopped for breakfast en route and got to the lot a little, but not much, after nine o'clock.

It was a dull morning. Not a nibble, unless you could count as such a pair of teenagers wanting to sell a jalopy. In our business you don't buy jalopies. You *have* jalopies, ones that you've had to take in as trades to sell somewhat better cars, and you're very lucky if you get out of the jalopy whatever trade-in you had to allow on it. So I had to turn the boys down.

A little before noon another jalopy drove onto the lot, and Lieutenant Andrews got out of it. He didn't look as tired as he had last night but he didn't look exactly cheerful either.

I said, "Sorry, but we can't buy it. Or do you want to trade it in on a better one?"

"Might do that, but not today. Mr. Bushman around?"

I told him Danny was still at home, but might be in later.

"He isn't home. I just came from there. His Missus said he'd left about eleven o'clock. Well, I wanted to talk to her anyway, and I had a chance to do that. Where do you suppose Mr. Bushman might have gone?"

I shrugged. "Some errands, maybe. We're trading shifts today so he isn't due here till one o'clock. Anything new on the matter?"

"Not on our end. Thought maybe after a night's sleep, your friend might be able to remember and tell us something he might have missed before." He took off his hat and wiped his forehead with his handkerchief. "Nobody else has been beat up yet."

For a second I didn't get it and said "Huh?" but I realized what he meant before he went on to explain, "If that was mistaken identity or wrong address, somebody's going to find out he made a mistake."

I said, "Or maybe the right victim won't report it—if he knows he had it coming."

"Could be. You haven't thought of anything to add, have you? Or learned anything new out at that club after I left?"

I told him no to both questions. But then I added, "You said you wanted to talk to the boys in the combo. I drove them home last night so I can tell you where they're holing in—the Cypress Lodge, a motel out on Centralia."

"Thanks. Don't think I'll look them up today, though, if ever. There's no way they could be involved in this that I can see; they were playing at the club when it happened."

"That's right," I said. "And even if they weren't playing at that moment, there wouldn't be time between sets for anyone at the club to get into town and back again. It's at least three quarters of an hour each way."

"I know." He got back into his car and started the engine but instead of driving off he leaned his elbows on top of the door and looked at me.

He said, "I'll level with you, Son. Unless something new develops, there's nothing more we can do on this case. Especially where the victim can't identify his attacker even if he sees him. If it was mistaken identity and if another beating is reported, then we'll have a lead. If it wasn't—"

He hesitated and I prompted him. "If it wasn't, then what?"

"Then we're still not going to get anywhere unless your friend decides to level with us. If a man gets beat up on purpose, he knows why it happened all right. If, for reasons of his own, he won't tell us that, then we can't help him."

"You've got a point there," I admitted. "Shall I tell Danny you'll be back?"

"No, because I won't. I've got something else to do this afternoon, but its paper work and I'll be at headquarters. You have a talk with your friend and tell him what I told you, and tell him to drop by and see me, or else telephone, if he wants to add anything."

"Right, Lieutenant," I said.

Danny showed up a few minutes before one, but I didn't get a chance to talk to him right away because I was talking to a prospect at the time. By the time I was free Danny was busy.

Then there was a lull and I was able to tell him about the lieutenant's call and what he had said.

"Guess he's right," Danny said. "I mean, about there being nothing more they can do about it. And about the fact that if the guy corrects his mistake and beats up the right guy, or already has, it may never get reported to us."

"Uh-huh. How do you feel? Sure you're up to working the rest of the day?"

"Sure. Wouldn't want to climb into the ring with anyone, but nothing hurts any worse when I'm on my feet than when I'm sitting down, so what's to lose working? Any business this morning?"

I told him there hadn't been, but that reminded me to tell him about the deal I'd made—subject to their trying out the car, of course—with the boys in the combo.

Danny approved. "Not much profit if we have to buy it back for only fifty less," he said, "but maybe they won't turn it back. If their next booking turns out to be within driving distance they'll probably decide to keep it. You better run and get yourself some lunch so you'll be free when they call up."

I went to the restaurant across the street and had myself some lunch and when I came back Danny said that Tommy Drum had already called. They were ready.

I hesitated whether to take the Ford—and make one of them drive me back in it if they bought it—or to pick them up in my own car and bring them to the lot. It made sense either way, but I decided on my own car and used it. If we got them on the lot, maybe—if they were solvent enough—they'd fall for one of the better cars instead of the one I'd told them about. By showing them the Ford first I might goof us out of a bigger sale. And a sale it would be, if, as Danny had suggested might happen, they should decide to keep the car and drive to their next booking.

The boys had told me their room numbers but I didn't know where the rooms were located so I parked in front of the motel and walked back. I came to the number that would be Mick's single first and knocked on the door but there wasn't any answer. So I went down the line a few more doors and knocked again. Tommy's voice called out for me to come in.

Tommy Drum was sitting in a chair reading *Downbeat* and Frank Ritchie was sprawled across the bed busily doing nothing. Tommy said, "Hi, Ralph. Did you bring the Ford?"

"No. Thought I'd take you in to the lot. You might want to look at some others too, before you make up your minds. Where's the Mick?"

"In his room, I guess."

"Isn't," I told him. "I passed his door first and knocked."

Tommy shrugged. "Probably went for a walk like the fresh air fiend he is. Doesn't matter. The three of us talked it over last night after you dropped us off and figured it's a better idea for just Frank and I to buy the car. Mick won't be here the full month if I can get a replacement for him, so he'll just chip in on the running expenses and we'll let it go at that."

"Sounds sensible," I said. "Well, shall we take off?"

"Drink first," Tommy said. "I refuse to look at cars on an empty stomach. Want yours straight, Ralph? Or plain?"

He went to the dresser and poured a shot into each of three glasses, handed them around. I said I didn't want mine either straight or plain and took my glass into the bathroom; I poured about half of it out because he'd made it too big a slug for me to want that early in the day when I'd have to go back to selling cars, and I diluted the rest of it with a couple inches of water.

We sat around with our drinks and Frank said, "Let's kill a little time with these. Maybe Mick just went around the block or something. And even the car, he'd probably want to go into town with us."

"I didn't knock loudly," I said. "Maybe he's still asleep."

Tommy shook his head. "He's up long since. We got up around ten and he was swimming in the pool then. Told us which way to walk to find a restaurant for breakfast within a block. He was out of the pool when we came back but he wouldn't have gone back to sleep. Mick doesn't take naps."

We batted the breeze about nothing until we'd killed our drinks and then tried Mick O'Neill's door again with the same result I'd got twenty minutes before, and we piled into the Merc and went down to the lot.

They looked at several other cars but finally settled for the '49 Ford; I'd guessed right the first time on how high they'd want to go under the circumstances. They made out checks and I made out the papers and they had a car. They offered to drive one or both of us to the nearest bar for a drink to celebrate the deal, and I told Danny to go, since I'd already had a drink with them back at the motel.

Alone on the lot, I found myself drowning in prospects looking at cars, but as soon as the boys brought Danny back the rush dropped off and there was not much doing.

At five, Danny said, "Why don't you run along, Ralph? I can take it from here."

"Sure you're up to working all evening?"

"Sure I'm sure. I'll probably be ready to sleep by the time I'm through though, so I'll give the Casanova a miss tonight. You going?"

I said, "Think I'll have dinner there. At six, when they start serving. Then maybe sit in with the boys for a few numbers. I've got my sax in the car."

"Have a ball. See you tomorrow."

"Maybe sooner. I don't spend more than an hour or two at the club, I'll drop by the lot on my way home and see how things are going."

But on the way out to the Casanova I decided I didn't want to eat there after all; I just wasn't hungry enough to do justice to a five-buck dinner. So I stopped at a less expensive restaurant en route and saved myself three and a half bucks by having a lighter meal. It was a quarter after six when I got to the club.

Tommy Drum and Frank Ritchie were playing when I walked in with my sax case; Mick O'Neill wasn't on the stand, or in sight. I started over to them and someone touched my arm and said, "Hi, Oliver. Sit down and have a drink with us." It was Max Stivers, the bookie-racketeer who had bought me a drink last night. The beer barrel shaped Gino Itule was with him again.

I said, "I'd better see the boys first. Hasn't Mick O'Neill shown up yet?"

I had to explain to Stivers that Mick O'Neill was the sax man with the combo and he said no, there hadn't been a sax on the stand yet tonight.

Tommy saw me coming and brought the number to an end just as I got there.

"Where's Mick?" I asked him.

"Don't know. He hasn't shown up. Thank God you got here. I just phoned the lot and Danny said you were on your way and had your sax with you."

I started getting the sax out of the case and putting it together. I asked, "Didn't you stop by at the motel to get him?"

"Sure, and waited around as long as we could without being late ourselves. Then I shoved a note under his door telling him to take a taxi, and we scrammed. Thought maybe we'd find him already out here, but he *wasn't.*"

"You sure he couldn't have been asleep in his room, Tommy?"

"We knocked loud enough to wake the dead, and Mick's a light sleeper. Must have gone somewhere and lost track of the time. He ought to show up any minute."

"It's not like Mick to be late," I said. "Maybe something happened to him."

"I'm a little worried too, Ralph. But let's run off two numbers and call this a set, and if he isn't here by then—well, we can phone the motel and ask the guy who runs it to use his pass key and look in Mick's room. And—anything else we can do?"

"Phone the police maybe and see if there's an accident report or something. But okay, we'll give him till half past before we try either of those. Want to give *Stardust* a spin?"

We gave *Stardust* a spin, and then *Don't Stop.* But we did stop, despite applause that wanted us to keep on.

"Come on," Tommy said, "we'll use the phone in the manager's office."

The door of the manager's office was ajar but the room was empty. We were hesitating in the doorway when Max Stivers' voice spoke behind us. "Something wrong, boys?"

"We were looking for the manager," I told him.

"Green? He's around somewhere. Shall I have one of the waiters look for him? Or anything else I can do?"

I explained briefly and Stivers said, "Sure, take over his office, use the phone all you want. When you've found out, the score, join me at my table, all three of you."

Tommy called the motel first and explained to and then argued with the proprietor. He swore and put down the phone. "Guy won't check the room. Says if Mick's there and won't answer the door it's his business. Says if we call the cops he'll give them the pass key, but he won't use it himself. Guess we'll have to do it that way."

"Let me," I suggested. I was remembering that Lieutenant Andrews had said he had a lot of paper work at headquarters; he might be working late.

He was. I told him what the situation was, listened to what he had to say. I thanked him and hung up.

"He'll take care of both ends of it," I told Tommy and Frank. "He's right at headquarters so he'll check on accident reports. And he'll have the radio operator instruct the nearest radio car to look in the room. He'll call back as soon as he gets anything."

Tommy sighed. "I can use a drink. I'm getting scared now, Ralph. If it was some guys I'd just figure it didn't mean anything, but not Mick. He'd at least have phoned."

I took the boys to Stivers' table. There was a third man there whom I didn't know, but Tommy and Frank knew him and introduced him as Harvey Green, the manager. I told about the call we'd made, and Stivers took over again. He clapped Green on the shoulder and said, "You wait in your office for that call, Harv, so the boys can relax and have a drink." And a snap of his fingers brought a waiter running and got us our round of drinks in a lot less time than we could have got them ourselves.

Stivers tried to keep it from being a wake but none of us felt much like talking and he didn't succeed. Mostly we just sat and nursed our drinks until Green came back and said I was wanted on the phone.

I got there fast. Andrews' voice said. "Bad news, Oliver. Your friend Mick is dead."

My mouth felt suddenly dry. "Dead, how?" I asked.

"Murdered. Beaten up like your partner was, but the beating didn't stop there this time. Hit over the head several times after he was down and out. Probably with a blackjack."

"In his room at the motel?"

"Yeah. I think you boys better come down here, all three of you. The Casanova will have to get by without music, one evening. If anybody out there objects tell 'em it's a police order."

"All right. You mean headquarters or the motel?"

"Make it headquarters. I'm going around to the motel now, but I'll be back here by the time you can make it in from there. Or not much after."

He hung up on me before I could ask any more questions Back at the table I gave it to them straight, without sitting down again. Tommy Drum looked stunned. He opened his mouth, probably to call me a liar or to ask if I was kidding him, then realized I wouldn't possibly be either lying or kidding about something like that, and closed his mouth again.

Frank Ritchie just stood up and said, "All right, what are we waiting for?"

~§~

We took my car, going in, because it was faster. I don't know why we felt there was any hurry, but we did. We didn't talk much, except about one thing. Tommy and Frank had known about Danny's being beaten up last night; it had been mentioned at the table, but played down as something that must have been a mistake. Now they wanted details and I told them the little I knew that they didn't.

I drove to the police station and we all trouped in.

A sergeant at the desk had been alerted to our coming; he showed us into a kind of waiting room and told us Lieutenant Andrews would be back soon. The chairs were hard and uncomfortable, but we sat on them. And waited.

Frank said, "I don't get it. It must have been the same guy who beat up Danny, but who could possibly have a down on both Danny and Mick?"

Neither of us answered him. And that was all the conversation there was until, after half an hour or so, Danny came in. He looked white and shaken, more worried than I'd ever seen him before.

He told us that Andrew had stopped by the lot on his way to the motel and had asked him a few questions and then had asked him to come to the station when he closed the lot at nine. He'd stuck around for a while and then decided to close early and head for headquarters to get it over with.

"Did you phone Doris?" I asked him. And he nodded. Another half an hour and Andrews came in. He put the finger on Tommy first and took him through a door to a smaller office marked *Private*. After a while—I didn't time it—Tommy came back and said the lieutenant wanted Frank next, so Frank went in.

"Are you free to go, or does he want you to stick around?" I asked Tommy.

"Free to go, but where? Nowhere I want to go alone. Maybe when he's through with Frank, he and I can go somewhere where we can have a drink and wait for you guys."

Danny looked at his watch. "May be pretty late when we get through. Here's a thought. Doris is home alone and probably worried stiff. Why don't you go round to my place and keep her company? We can all head there one at a time as the police get through with us here. And there's liquor."

Tommy said it sounded like a good idea but that he'd wait till Frank was through and the two of them could go around together. But he suggested that meanwhile Danny phone Doris and make sure she liked the idea.

Danny nodded and went out into the hallway to use a pay phone. He came back and nodded. "She says it's a swell idea."

We gave Tommy the address of the Bushman's apartment and I tried to give them the key to my Mercury, since their car was still out at the Casanova, but he insisted they'd rather take a cab than try to follow directions in a strange town by night, so I didn't insist.

And then Frank Ritchie rejoined us and said Andrews wanted to talk to me next. A minute later the lieutenant was looking at me across his desk. The chair I sat on was even harder and more uncomfortable than the ones in the outer office.

He said wearily, "Let's start with your running through the day for me. Where you were and when."

I started with my alarm going off at eight o'clock and went through it for him.

He nodded when I'd finished. He said, "At least you fellows tell stories that fit together, as far as times concerned. Not that any of you has an alibi this time."

"What time was Mick O'Neill killed, Lieutenant?" I asked him.

"Give or take an hour, around one o'clock. That makes it between twelve and two. It would have been right around two when you knocked on his door. And he could have answered, and asked you in."

"He could have," I said, "but he didn't. But how about Tommy and Frank? Don't they alibi each other? Unless you think they *both* killed Mick."

The lieutenant sighed. "I don't think anything. But no, they don't alibi each other. About half past one, Mr. Drum left Ritchie in their room at the motel and went out to make that phone call to the lot that brought you out there to pick them up. He didn't make it from the motel office because he was out of cigarettes anyway, so he walked to a store two blocks off and phoned from there. So he could have dropped in on Mr. O'Neill either going or coming. Or Mr. Ritchie could have done it while Mr. Drum was gone."

He got out a crumpled pack of cigarettes, put one in his mouth and lighted it. He said, "And your partner—he hasn't got an alibi either. He left home at eleven and didn't get to the lot until one. Did you ask him what he was doing then?"

"No," I said. "It wasn't any of my business."

"I thought you might have got curious anyway. Well, he says he was just driving around thinking. Does that make sense to you?"

"Why not? He sure had something to think about, after what happened to him last night."

"Yeah. Well, he says when he left home at eleven he intended to drive right to the lot and then he got to thinking that there wasn't any point in showing before one, anyway. Says around half past twelve, just before he did come to the lot, he stopped in at a diner and had a sandwich. We can check that, but it doesn't give him an alibi even if it checks because if Mr. O'Neill was killed at twelve, whoever killed him could still have made that diner by half past, or sooner."

I said, "If you think—Listen, it doesn't make sense. Danny is inches shorter than Mick, and fifty or sixty pounds lighter, and Mick was an athlete to boot. You say Mick was knocked unconscious *before* he was killed with a blackjack or whatever?"

"That's right. And I'll admit I can't see your friend Mr. Bushman doing that, especially picking a fight when he himself had sore ribs and a sore jaw to start with."

"And especially when it could not have been because he thought Mick had beaten him up first, last night. Mick was over twenty miles away when that happened, and playing sax in front of a hundred people."

"Yeah. So more likely the same guy attacked both of them. Who might that have been?"

"I don't know," I said. "I couldn't even guess."

"Nor any reason at all why anyone might have had it in for either one of them, let alone both of them?"

"No," I said. "I wish I could help you, Lieutenant, but it makes nuts." I thought a minute and added, "Maybe quite literally. Last night Danny thought, and I thought with him, that his beating was probably a case of mistaken identity. It's hard to figure it that way now. But our second thought last night—that whoever did it was off his rocker—looks better now than it did then. Nobody could possibly have a sane motive for attacking both Danny and Mick."

"Even a crazy killer would have a motive. One that made sense to him. Could someone have had a grudge against both of them, from way back?"

I said, "It would have to be from way back. There's been no contact direct or indirect between Danny and Mick for longer than the year he and I have been in business here. Probably a year before that would have been the last time they saw one another. That would have been when we were playing with Nick Frazer's band."

"For how long?"

"Danny and I were with Mick for 'bout three months. Mick got taken on two weeks before we left. No connection between his joining and our leaving; we got a better offer, that's all."

"And before that?"

"I'd have to think back to remember times and places but I'd say about three or four times before that Danny and Mick played in the same band, maybe up to two or three months at a time. Always a big band."

"Why always a big band?"

"Any competent musician can read notes and play the arrangements a big band uses. Smaller groups—even small bands, let alone combos—improvise, and when it comes to improvisation, there are different types of musicians. Mick was a Dixieland man, the righteous stuff. Neither Danny nor I swing that way. Did Tommy explain how he happened to have Mick with the combo?"

"Yeah. How did you get along with Mick?"

"Okay. We weren't close friends, but we got along."

"And Danny?"

"They didn't get along very well. But they weren't enemies and neither had anything specific against the other. Just—well, call it a personality clash. Danny can answer that better than I can, and give you reasons, but don't take it seriously because it was nothing serious, believe me."

"I believe you. Mr. Drum tells me he offered you Mick's job last night and you turned it down."

"That's right. Not because Mick would have minded; he wanted me to take it. But when Danny and I bought the lot we decided between us, no more playing. Not professionally, I mean; we sit in on jam sessions once in a while. Or just play together, with Doris on piano."

"She was a singer, wasn't she?"

"Yes. But she plays enough piano to give us a background."

"Going to play saxophone with the combo now?"

I said, "I haven't thought about it."

"Think about it a minute. Won't this make it different?"

"Maybe it will. I doubt if Tommy could get another sax man in town here, even as good as Mick was. He'd probably have to cancel his booking and he's too good a friend for us to want that to happen to. And under those Circumstances I'm sure it'll be okay with Danny. In fact, it would have been all right with him if I'd said yes last night, when there wasn't any emergency involved."

"Uh-huh. Well, just one more question, Mr. Oliver. Can you tell me anything at all that even might possibly be helpful, something I might not have asked the right questions to bring out?"

"Not a thing," I said.

"Okay, that's all for now. You're not planning to leave town, I take it. I'll be able to find you on the lot or out at the Casanova."

"Right," I said. "Shall I send Danny in?"

In the outer office I asked Danny if he thought I should wait for him, but he said it would be silly because we each had a car parked outside and couldn't go together anyway.

I found Doris plenty worried and Tommy and Frank both trying to reassure her by telling her Danny couldn't possibly be in any further danger.

"But why," she wanted to know, "was Mick killed? If we don't know that, how can we know there won't be any second attack on Danny?"

Because, I pointed out again and patiently, the man who'd attacked Danny had had him completely at his mercy; if he'd wanted to kill Danny or even injured him any worse than he had, he could have done so then, in perfect safety.

"That's right, Doris," Tommy said. "You know how I dope it? I don't think that cat intended to kill Mick at all, just to beat him up like he beat Danny. Only Danny went down and out from that first sneak punch—and I'm guessing Mick didn't. Mick was big and tough himself and I'm guessing he put up more of a fight. And got the handkerchief down off the guy's face so he knew who was attacking him, see? So when he did kayo Mick, he went ahead and finished the job so Mick couldn't put the finger on him. Makes sense?"

"Makes sense," I said. "Believe me, if I'm next on his list, I'm going to go down for the count without making a grab for any handkerchief. I'd rather be a live coward than a dead hero."

"Me too," Tommy said. "And because we don't know *why* he put the slug on Danny and Mick, we can't be sure we're not on his list too. Say, Ralph, Frank and I were talking this over on the way here and— Wait, one thing first. You're going to play with us now, aren't you? You're not going to let us down and make us lose that booking, are you?"

Frank said, "It would put us in an awful jam, Ralphie boy. On account that cop ordered us not to leave town, and we'd be strictly on the nut having to stay and not working."

I said, "I want to talk it over with Danny. If he thinks I should—"

"Swell," Tommy said. "Then it's in the bag because I know what

Danny'll say. How's about a drink to that? We're ready for another and Ralph hasn't even had one yet. What kind of a hostess are you, Doris?"

Doris laughed and went out into the kitchen to make a round of drinks and Tommy said, "Attaboy, Ralph. Knew you wouldn't let us down. Now here's what we were talking about on the way over here. What kind of a pad you got?"

"Bachelor apartment. Two rooms and a kitchenette I never use."

"Sleep three?"

"If somebody sleeps on the couch, yes."

"Then why don't we check out of the motel and triple up? Big as that guy is, he isn't going to tangle with three of us at once and if we stick together as much as possible it'll be that much tougher for him to dope a way to get at any one of us alone."

Doris came in with a tray of drinks just as I was saying that it sounded like a good idea to me.

We told her what we'd decided and she said it sounded sensible to her.

"And we'll all save money," Frank said. "We chip in on Ralph's rent, natch, but it probably won't come to as much as the motel. What do you pay, Ralph?"

We were still trying to figure out what one third of eighty dollars was when Danny came in. We briefed him while Doris went out to make him a drink. He approved down the line and said that if I *didn't* help the boys out by playing with them, he'd disown me.

And we worked out a schedule for handling the lot. Danny would work the regular shift I'd been working, one o'clock in the afternoon till nine at night. I'd take the shift he'd had, but shorten it at both ends by not opening the lot until ten in the morning—we never did much business the first hour anyway—and working until three or four o'clock, depending on whether we were busy or not. That would give me two or three hours to clean up, rest a little, and go out to the club with Tommy and Frank in time for the combo to start swinging at six. Because I'd be putting in fewer hours than he on the lot, I talked Danny into agreeing to take two thirds of our profits for the next month, instead of half. I pointed out that with what Tommy would be paying me I'd still be coming out way ahead on the deal. Doris backed me up on that, and Danny gave in and said okay.

Tommy decided he'd better call the club and tell them the combo had a new sax lined up, and that they could count on us tomorrow evening. While he was making the call, I asked Danny if the lieutenant, in talking to him, had come up with anything new.

Danny shook his head. "He isn't through with me, though; just called it off because it was getting so late. He's going to come here tomorrow morning to talk some more. Wants to talk to Doris, too, or he'd probably have asked me to come back there."

We broke it up just short of midnight. I drove the boys to the motel and waited till they'd packed their stuff, then took them home with me. We made our sleeping arrangements, had a nightcap, and turned in.

That was the end of the second day.

Nothing startling happened for the next week. The investigation brought out some things about Mick that we hadn't known, including the fact that he'd really been stashing his dough during the dozen-odd years he'd been playing. He was more solvent than all the rest of us put together, with bank accounts and stocks and bonds adding up to nearly twenty thousand dollars. We'd talked about chipping in for a funeral for him, but when we learned that, we quit talking about it. Or, for that matter, about having the funeral here. It turned out that both his parents were still living, in Cincinnati. His body was flown there for the funeral, as soon as the police released it. Since Mick had been working with them at the time he died, Tommy and Frank thought they ought to go to the funeral, but since the Casanova manager didn't look kindly on the idea of a second comboless evening, they compromised on letting Frank Ritchie represent both of them; I was able to find them a local skin man who was free and who was good enough to hold down Frank's end of the combo for the one evening he'd have to be gone if he flew both ways. Tommy. Drum's piano held the combo together and was irreplaceable so he had to stay. We all sent flowers, of course. Frank came back looking a bit stunned and said he was surprised that a Dixie man could have so many friends. He said cats had come to the funeral from as far away as New Orleans and San Francisco.

Toward the end of the week Danny came out twice and brought Doris, after closing the lot. The second time he brought his trumpet and sat in with us for a few numbers. And we talked Doris into singing a couple of numbers, and the customers really got their money's worth that night.

That was a Wednesday night, and the next night was a Thursday and the night after that a Friday; it was around half past seven and we'd finished our second set and were sitting at one of the tables. With Max Stivers and his friend Gino; Stivers had invited us over again. Had offered to buy us drinks too, but we'd turned them down except that Tommy Drum had taken a coke. When you're playing till midnight you can't start drinking too early and unless there was special occasion for it, we laid off taking our first drink of the evening until ten or eleven o'clock, when a lift would be welcome to carry us the rest of the way. But we'd sat down with them and were batting the breeze with them. With Stivers, anyway, Gino never said much.

Then there was a hand lightly on my shoulder and I looked up and saw Lieutenant Andrews was standing beside me. He said, "Mind if I sit down?"

The chair next to mine was empty and I said, "Sure, Lieutenant." And then corrected myself. "That is, this is Mr. Stivers' table, so I really shouldn't invite you." I started to introduce them, but Stivers smiled. "We know one another, Ralph. Sit down, Andrews. Drink?"

The lieutenant shook his head. "Didn't know you knew these boys, Mr. Stivers."

"Sure I know them. I hang out here. And like music."

"Do any business with them?"

Max Stivers quit smiling. "Is that any business of yours, Andrews? You're not in your territory here. This is outside city limits, way outside."

"Yeah," the lieutenant said. "Forget I asked."

Stivers smiles again. "But since you did ask, the answer is no. None of these boys are horse players."

"Is their friend, Mr. Danny Bushman, a horse player?"

The smile stayed on Stivers' lips but went out of his eyes. He said shortly, "I've met him. I don't know him well enough to know that. Andrews, is this an interrogation?"

The lieutenant sighed and took a pipe and tobacco pouch from his pocket. "No, it isn't. But I was just wondering. And I'm wondering, too, if Mr. O'Neill was a horse player."

Tommy Drum cut in. "I can answer that, Lieutenant. Mick was

down on gambling, all kinds. He wouldn't even match pennies with you."

The lieutenant got his pipe going and didn't ask any more questions, and gradually things got less tense than they'd seemed to be for a few minutes. The conversation got on Dave Brubeck and from Brubeck it got, somehow, to Bix Beiderbecke. Musicians' talk.

I'd just glanced at my watch—Tommy never wears one and he'd put me in charge of keeping time on our breaks—and decided we had a few minutes left before we had to start playing again, when there was another hand on my shoulder and I looked up again. It was a man I knew only very slightly and only by his last name, Hart. He owned a sporting goods store a couple of blocks from the lot and I'd bought a set of golf clubs from him, and once he'd been on the lot and looked at cars, but hadn't bought one.

I said, "Hi," and he said "Hi, Oliver. Don't bother introducing me around; I've get to get back to my table. Just want to ask you one question."

"Shoot," I said.

"Drove past your lot on my way here but didn't have time to stop or I'd have made myself late. But what's the price on that Cad you've got there?"

"Cad?" I said blankly. "There isn't any Cad on the lot. You must've mistaken some other car for one."

"No, this was a Cad all right. I pulled in to the curb and had a close look at it. But I saw your partner was busy with another customer and I'd have made myself late here if I'd waited to ask him. It's a yellow hardtop, late model, couldn't be over a year old. Looked practically brand new."

I shook my head. "It wasn't there this afternoon, when I left at three o'clock. Danny must have taken it in."

He shrugged and said, "Okay, I'll drop by tomorrow sometime. It's sure a sweet car."

He started to turn away but Lieutenant Andrews' voice said, "Just a minute, Sir." And I realized that everyone at the table had been listening to the conversation.

Hart turned back and said "Yes?" politely to the lieutenant. Since they were going to talk anyway, I said, "Lieutenant Andrews, Mr. Hart."

"Glad to know you, Mr. Hart. Just want to ask this. Could that Cadillac have been a customer's car?"

"Not the way it was parked, lined up with the others. A customer wouldn't drive in and park his car that way. It was between an Olds Rocket 88 convertible and a Buick Special. All three of them look like almost new cars." He turned back to me. "When I drop by tomorrow I want to look at that Rocket, too."

"Thanks, Mr. Hart," the lieutenant said.

And then he was looking at me hard, across the table. "Mr. Oliver, was there a late model Buick Special on the lot this afternoon?"

I said, "A Buick Roadmaster. He just got the model wrong."

"Was there on Olds convertible?"

I shook my head.

"All right, let's say he made a mistake on the Buick. Would your partner be likely to have bought *two* almost new, expensive cars in one afternoon without consulting you?"

I said, "It would be unusual, but he's got the authority to. If he got them at a good enough price—"

"Is there enough cash in your checking account for him to have bought them?"

I said, "They could have been trades. Trade-downs. Sometimes a man has an expensive car but goes broke and needs dough. He'll trade it for an older model and a cash difference. Or they could have been left on consignment."

"How does that work?"

"Well, we don't do this often but sometimes we don't want to buy a car outright for what a customer wants for it but if he wants us to we leave it on the lot and try to sell it for him if we can get enough to give him his price and leave a profit for us. We used to do that oftener when we were first starting and didn't have enough cars to make a good showing on the lot."

The lieutenant said, "Uh-huh," and stood up slowly. "Well, I thought I was through for the day but I think I'll want to talk to Mr. Bushman. And if any of you have in mind to telephone him and warn him I'm coming, it won't do any good. If I find those two or three cars gone off the lot, he's going to have to do a lot more explaining than if they're still there."

He looked around the table to take in all of us, and stiffened suddenly. He snapped at Max Stivers, "Where's your goon?"

"You mean Gino?" Stivers asked blandly. "I don't know. I guess I didn't notice him leave."

"You sent him to—" He broke off and swung around to grab me by the shoulder. "Take me to a telephone."

I hurried with him to the manager's office. The door was closed. He jerked it open without knocking and bolted in; the office was vacant. He hurried to the desk and then swore and held up a broken phone cord. "What other phones—? Never mind, if he yanked this cord, he took care of the others. Son, have you got a fast car and can you handle it?"

"Yes," I said. We were already running out. I saw Tommy and Frank starting after us, but we didn't wait.

I led him to the Merc and Tommy and Frank caught up with us and started to pile in the back seat. Andrews stopped them. "*You* fellows got another car?"

"Yeah," Tommy said, "but not as fast—"

"Never mind that. Take your car and find the nearest public phone you can use. Don't waste time calling your friend—call the police. Tell them to get cops on that lot *fast*. Tell 'em they may have to stop a murder."

They were running for the car I'd sold them while I got the Merc percolating and gunned it. I asked, "Do you really think—?"

"Don't talk, Son. Concentrate on driving and I'll do the talking. Your night vision's good?"

"Yes."

"Mine's a little under standard. I'll drive as fast as I have to by day, but at night I don't dare go over forty or so, even on a clear road. You go as fast as you think is safe. Don't worry about tickets. If a cop car gets on our tail, that's fine. I'll ask him to go ahead of us and use his siren. And his radio, if he's got one."

Out of the corner of my eye I could see that he'd taken a gun out of a shoulder holster. It was a flat automatic. He worked the slide to jack a bullet from the clip into the firing chamber and then put the gun back in the holster.

"Watch it, Son," he said, as I passed a car with a rather risky margin of safety against a truck coming the other way. "I've got guts, but I don't want them strewn along the highway. And we aren't going to help your partner any getting ourselves killed. Did you notice Gino leave, how long it was before we missed him?"

"Right after Hart came up and started asking me about the Cad, I think."

"Then he's got a pretty fair start on us. You argued with Mr. Hart a while, and then you and I did some yakking. Even allowing him a couple of minutes to pull out telephone cords, he's got at least five minutes start and maybe ten. 'Course we don't know what kind of a car he's got or how well he can handle it. You're doing fine on this one, but don't try it any faster."

I had to slow down a little as we flashed through a block with lighted stores. The lieutenant said; "That's where your friends will be able to phone from. I'd say it's about a dead toss-up whether or not we get there before they get their call through and get results from it."

I said, "You called Gino a goon. Do you think he killed Mick and beat up Danny? But Danny described his attacker as six feet tall and Gino's built like—"

"Don't talk, Son. Yeah, Gino's built short and broad, but he's got power. Used to fight pro, and used to wrestle. Yeah, he's a goon, for Stivers. People who are beaten up by goons sometimes give wrong descriptions, on purpose. We'll worry about that later. It's funny, I knew Stivers was in on a lot of things, but I never thought he had a part in a hot car racket. And I never thought of your used car lot being used to unload them. It's a natural. Now don't run off the road when I ask you this, but are you sure you weren't onto what was going on?"

I said, "I'm still not onto what's going on. Especially how *Mick* figures in on it."

"I'm beginning to get a hunch on that. Well, Son, we're getting close." He took the pistol out of its holster again and this time kept it in his hand. "You don't by any chance have a gun on you or in the car, do you?"

I told him I hadn't. "Then I want you to stay out of whatever happens," he said. "You just pull up and park in front of—"

We were a block and a half away then, and we heard the shots. Two of them. And we were half a block away when a dark green coupe pulled out of the lot and turned away from us.

It didn't have speed as yet and at the speed we were going I could easily have caught it and boxed it to the curb, but a light turned red in my face and another car pulled out in front of me from an intervening intersection and I had to slam on brakes and barely avoided a smashup. The screeching stop killed my engine and before I could start it again there was another screeching—of sirens. A car with two men in it slowed down alongside ours, and the lieutenant yelled to them to get the green coupe—and to be careful because there was an armed killer in it. The car took off, siren going and red light flashing, and another like it came from behind us and joined the chase.

"They'll get Gino," the lieutenant said. "He hasn't a chance. We stay here."

I had the engine going again now, and I drove onto the lot.

~§~

It was two o'clock in the morning when a doctor came into the hospital waiting room and told us Danny was dead. He said, "Lieutenant Andrews asked me to tell you that he'll appreciate if you'll all wait here a few minutes. He's on the telephone now, but he wants to talk to you."

Doris was crying softly. She had hold of my hand and was squeezing my fingers spasmodically, so hard that it almost. hurt.

Danny had recovered consciousness for a while, and Doris and I had each had a few minutes with him. I don't know what he told her, but he'd asked me to take care of Doris if he died—and I think he knew that he was going to. And he'd made a full statement to the police and had lived to sign it. Anyway, he'd lived longer than Gino.

The green coupe, doing better than eighty, had gone off the road and into a tree when a police bullet had found a back tire. And Pat Stivers was under arrest. The lieutenant had come into the waiting room and told us both of those things before Danny had recovered consciousness.

And now the lieutenant came in again. As he looked from one of us to another—Tommy and Frank were there too, of course—he looked more tired than I'd ever seen him look before.

He spoke to Doris. "Do you want the details tonight, Mrs. Bushman? Or would you rather wait?"

Doris got her sobbing under control and told him she'd rather hear it now.

He said, "Your husband got to playing the horses again; he's been playing heavily for six months now. And he got deeper into debt trying to get out, and Stivers let him do it, gave him credit. As of last week he owed Stivers three and a half thousand dollars. And Stivers decided it was time to close the trap.

"He sent his goon, Gino Itule, to see Mr. Bushman. What happened there wasn't just what your husband told us. Gino wasn't masked and he didn't swing the second he came through the door. He told your husband to see Stivers the next day, and either to bring cash for what he owed or be ready to listen to a proposition about using the used car lot as an outlet for stolen cars until the commissions Stivers would pay him for selling them would cover that debt. Your husband said no to that, and that's when Gino knocked him out and gave him a few kicks to help him think it over.

"When your husband left at eleven the next day he went to see Stivers—and he'd been convinced. But he said you, Mr. Oliver, wouldn't go for it, and he couldn't risk having the hot cars on the lot even when you were off shift because you often dropped in even when you were not working, to see how things were going. Stivers had an answer for that. Gino was still around, and with a broken leg you wouldn't be dropping in for a while."

The lieutenant was looking at me now. He said, "Naturally your partner, because lie was your friend too, wouldn't agree to that. But he had another answer. He said that if Mr. O'Neill was hurt, maybe a broken arm, badly enough so he wouldn't be able to play saxophone for a month then he was certain you'd not let Mr. Drum down, but would agree to join him.

"So he sent Gino to beat up Mr. O'Neill and what happened there was like we figured. Mr. O'Neill resisted and was strong enough to get the mask down off Gino's face. It hadn't been intended as a murder—till then.

"That scared Mr. Bushman, but it was too late for him to back out. He himself had suggested the beating up and that made him an accessory to murder now. Anyway, he could count on you being away from the lot—and far enough away that you couldn't drop in accidentally—all evening every evening. The stolen cars, three or four at a time, were garaged nearby and every evening after you were on your way to the Casanova, Gino would help drive them onto the lot. And off the lot again at closing time. Your partner had sold three of those cars the first week. Four or five more and his commissions on them would have put him in the clear—or so he thought; I doubt if Stivers would have let him off the hook that easily. But that doesn't matter now.

"The blow-up tonight was when, by sheer accident, someone told you about cars being on the lot that you knew didn't belong there—and told you when I was listening and when Stivers and Gino were there too. Stivers acted quick; he saw right at the start of that conversation what it was going to lead to and whispered quick orders to Gino. But Gino wasn't quite fast enough to make a clean getaway. If he had, we might have guessed down the line, but we would not have had positive proof."

"I—I think I understand everything now, Lieutenant," Doris said. "Is that all?"

"Not quite. There's something else I think you should understand. Mr. Oliver's part in this. If he hadn't done what he did, Mr. Bushman wouldn't be dead, might not even have got into serious trouble."

I said. "You're crazy, Andrews. What did I do?"

"Nothing, Son. Nothing at all. That's the whole trouble. You *must* have known your partner was gambling again and getting in over his head. Why, when you assured me he wasn't tangled with some other woman you admitted you and he were so much together you'd know something like that even if his wife didn't suspect it. And he wouldn't have been as secretive about horse playing as he would about that, especially from you. And you mean to tell me he could go that far in debt and worry about it without your even suspecting?"

I said, "I knew he was worrying about something, but—"

"And you knew, or guessed, what. When you found him beaten up that night, you knew he was in over his head, and what did you do about it? Try to talk him into leveling with you so you could help him straighten out whatever it was? Or pretend to believe what he told you, so he'd get himself in deeper?"

I said, "I *did* believe it. And why do you think I wanted Danny in trouble. He was my best friend."

"Until he got married, he was. But you were both in love with the same woman, and I think you still want her. And I think that six months or a year from now, except for what I'm saying, you'd be getting her. Son, you figured it that way. Your Danny was weak, you'd probably saved him from getting into serious trouble more than once since you went to school together. And you knew that if you pretended to keep on being his friend sooner or later his weakness would get him in trouble again and that all you'd have to do was what you did this time—nothing. Am I right?"

"You're *not*. This is slander, Lieutenant. I could—"

"You could sue me, Son, but you won't, because I'm right. You could have stopped things from happening as they did easily, when he first started gambling again. Even after he was beaten up, if you'd talked him into leveling with you. The only trouble he was in up to then was owing money."

Sometime long ago Doris' hand had dropped mine.

The lieutenant said, "And tonight, Son, was the real clincher. You saw Gino leave the table—right after we'd learned that there was a strange Cadillac on your lot. You had more information than I did; you guessed the truth quicker. So what did you do? You kept me busy and distracted as long as you could, explaining how strange cars could have been taken in as trade-downs or could have been taken onto the lot on consignment. You kept me distracted just long enough to let your partner get killed. And there's no charge I can bring against you."

Doris stood up suddenly. "Thank you, Lieutenant. Thank you very much. Tommy, Frank, will you take me home please?"

They followed, and at the doorway Tommy Drum turned. He said, "There isn't any more combo; I'll cancel the booking. The Casanova manager will send you a check."

The door closed behind them. Definitely.

"Happy, Son?" the lieutenant asked.

"Damn you," I said. "Don't call me Son!"

"You'd rather I use all four words of the phrase, Son?"

Saint Detective Magazine, January 1957

The Freak Show Murders

Carney slang used in *The Freak Show Murders*—

Ball Game — Any concession in which the customer tries to win prizes by throwing balls to knock down milk bottles, dummies, et cetera.

Bally — (verb) To give a free show out front (on the bally platform) in order to draw a crowd. (noun) The free show described above.

Bally Cloth — The cloth that hangs from the edge of a platform down to the ground.

Banner — Picture on canvas hung in front of a freak show or other attraction, depicting the wonders to be seen inside.

Barker — The leather-lunged lad who persuades the crowd to buy tickets, and who introduces and describes the attractions on offer.

Blow-Down — The blowing down of a tent by a windstorm.

Blow-Off — (often merely "the blow") The show given in a partitioned-off end of a freak-show tent, and for which additional money is charged.

Canvasman — Employee whose principal job is to help put up and take down tents. He does other kinds of work while the carnival is operating.

Carney — A carnival, or anyone connected with a carnival.

Cooch — A type of dance, and if you don't know what a cooch dance is, better see one.

Doniker — The Chic Sale department. The group of outhouses put up somewhere on the lot.

Flash — The showy, but difficult-to-win, merchandise displayed as prizes at the concessions. Also an act is judged by how much flash it has, which means how spectacular it is.

G-Top — Gambling tent. Not open to outsiders; it's a small tent put up somewhere on the lots where the carneys can play cards or shoot dice among themselves.

Gaff — The hidden secret or gimmick of a trick. Not all acts, of course, have one. There's no gaff to a sword-swallower's act, for example.

Geek — A freak, usually a Negro, who eats glass, razor blades and almost anything else. Don't ask me how they can do it, but there's no gaff about it. A geek can chew up and swallow an old light bulb just as you'd eat an apple.

Gimmick — The same as "gaf" in one meaning. Also, another name for G-string.

Grind — The continuous spiel between ballys whereby the barker keeps customers coming in.

Half-and-Half — A half man, half woman.

Inside Money — Money obtained from customers inside the show through sale of souvenirs, usually, or tickets to the blow-off.

Jig Show — Dance show with colored performers. Negroes with a carney do not resent the term; it's accepted slang and not depreciatory as it would be in some sections of the country.

Nut — The overhead, the expenses. A show or concession is "on the nut" if not meeting expenses; "off the nut" if making money.

Mad Ball — A clairvoyant's crystal.

Mark — A customer or prospective customer, an outsider. "Sucker" used to be the common term; now "mark" is replacing it.

Mentalist — Fortuneteller or clairvoyant.

Midway — The open center area around which the tents are pitched and upon which they all front.

Mitt Camp — A fortuneteller's tent or booth. The term comes, of course, from palmistry, but is applied to any form of mentalism — phrenology, buddha papers, crystal-reading or what have you.

Penny Pitch — A concession in which customers pitch pennies at a board, winning prizes if pennies stop squarely within marked-off areas.

Pincushion — The "Human Pincushion" of the freak show; a man who sticks pins and needles into his skin for the edification of the public.

Pitch — To sell something to a group of marks.

Props — The physical properties of a show.

Side Wall — The straight canvas side of a tent, usually not fastened down at the bottom.

Sloughed — Not permitted to operate. If the law closes a show or concession, it is sloughed.

Slum — Cheap concession prizes; distinguished from flash, the showy but hard-to-get prizes.

Spiel — To talk.

Sucker — Same as "mark?"

Teardown — The dismantling of the show and taking down of the tents to travel to the next town.

Tip — A group of marks. A barker "turns a tip" when he gets a good percentage of them to buy tickets for the show.

Top — A tent.

|

TROUBLE AND MURDER were just about the farthest things from my mind, right then. I was spieling, but my mouth did that for me without my mind having to tell it what to do, and while I talked I was staring out up the midway and thinking how swell it was to be back with the carney again.

It felt good to be standing on a platform with a tip of marks out there looking up with their yaps open while I told them what we had for them inside the top.

"Step right up close, folks!" I told them. "That's it, right up to the edge of the platform. We're going to put on a free show, a big free show, right out here on the platform, and it isn't going to cost you one penny to see it. Not one single, solitary penny—"

And back over my shoulder I yelled, "Colonel bally. Bugs bally."

I hit the bass drum a few thumping boomps while I waited for them to come out from the top. It was going to be a fair-sized tip, for the first one of the afternoon. Usual percentage of kids and suckers.

I gave them the old Pete Gaynor smile and boomped the drum again. Some marks who'd been gawking at the girl-show front turned around and came over.

"Right now, friends, right now, I'm going to call out on this platform a few of the strange people of the Wonderworld top! The most amazing and astounding people you have ever seen. Right out here on the platform to meet you! Here comes one now—"

There's nothing much to barking for a freak show if you've got the gift of gab. It doesn't matter much what you say, just so you keep saying it impressively. You don't even have to yell anymore, because the loudspeaker system does that for you. Brass-lunged barkers are one with Nineveh and Tyre.

"Yes, folks, here he is! The famous *Colonel Toots!* The smallest and one of the most brilliant men alive in the world today! Meet Colonel Toots, just thirty-four inches tall from his heels to the top of his head. A midget among midgets, folks, and a talented and versatile entertainer to boot. Inside the tent, Colonel Toots will show you, I can promise each and every one of you, the most amazing. . ."

I hadn't been looking at them because I'd turned to face Colonel Toots as he came on. But something in the way the Colonel was looking at the tip made me turn around to see what was wrong with them.

What was wrong was that they weren't looking at Colonel Toots nor at me; they were gawking past us, over and around the platform. And I heard voices and excitement back there, now that my attention followed the direction of their gaze.

The ticket man at my right was turning around, too. His head was lower than mine and he could see under the banners into the entrance. I saw him nod that way and start to get out of the ticket box.

He said to me, "Hold it, Pete. No bally."

"Huh? You mean I should let the—"

"Yeah, let the tip go. Won't be opening yet."

He shoved the roll of tickets under his arm and started back at a half run.

I said into the microphone, "Folks, sorry, but we're not quite ready to open yet. Come back in a little while—and we'll show you the best show!"

I realized my tongue was getting loose again and I was darned curious to see what was wrong inside the top. So I cut it short and switched off the mike. Colonel Toots was already gone off the platform.

Bugs, I thought—something's happened to Bugs Cartier. I'd called him for the bally and he hadn't shown up. Of course you never can count on a pincushion; they're a bit off or they wouldn't go around sticking pins in themselves to keep from having to work.

In under the top there was a knot of people gathered around Bugs' platform. It looked like a bigger crowd than it was, because one of them was Bessie Williams, our fat woman. I tried to look over Bessie's shoulder, but Bessie's shoulders aren't made to be looked over; unless you don't want to look in a downward direction.

I could see that the platform was empty, that the bally cloth had been thrown up over the edge and that they were staring at something on the grass under the platform. But Bessie wasn't transparent and I couldn't tell what it was.

Before I could ask any questions there was a hand on my shoulder, shoving me aside. I turned angrily and then curbed the vitriol I was set to hand whoever it was. Because it was Red Lewis, the Haverton copper, who'd drawn the day shift of patrolling the carney grounds. And Red Lewis was six feet four and built along the lines of a more famous Louis. Besides, he had red hair and a pugnacious disposition; not a guy to be cussed out casually without risking a fight.

So I stepped aside, waiting for what was going to happen when he tried to push Bessie. That was going to be worth watching.

But even a copper, it proved, had more sense than to try that. He went around her, shoving his way in between Bessie and Stella Alleman, and I followed his interference and got through.

It was Al Hryner who was under the platform.

He was dead; there wasn't any doubt about that because the back of his head was bashed in. And lying there beside him was a tent stake with dark stains on the end of it.

Red Lewis was glowering at us when he turned. He said, "All right, who done it?"

Stella Alleman, the snake girl, laughed with a sound that was near hysteria. I was behind her, to one side, and I put my hands on her shoulders and said, "Watch it, kid. Don't go haywire."

Somebody, I think it was Bugs, started in to tell the copper what had happened, but I didn't listen. I could feel Stella's shoulders trembling under my hands, and I pulled her back from the crowd, turning her around to face me so her back would be toward the excitement.

"Take it easy, honey," I said, "your mascara is smearing something awful. Don't let a little thing like a murder get you down."

"But why would anyone have—"

"Probably somebody found out Al's dice were crooked, honey. Let's get out of here. I'll buy you a coke."

I took her arm and, before she could object, started to take her out the entrance to the midway. Then I remembered there was a crowd out there and lifted the side wall instead.

"We'll cut through a couple of the tops," I suggested.

But as we cut under the next side wall I rather wished we hadn't. The top next to the freak show is the waxworks—the Chamber of Horrors—and it's not the place to take a girl to make her forget a murder. The place is full of killers and their kills, and some of them are pretty convincing stuff, for wax.

So I hurried Stella toward the entrance, trying to talk fast. "We'll cut out here," I said. "Come on, honey."

But she pulled loose, and when I turned around she was powdering her nose. She said, "I must look awful, Pete. I can't go outside looking—"

So it was all right, and she was over it and not going to take a tailspin. I grinned in relief. There wasn't any hurry now.

"What gave, back there?" I asked her. "Who found him, and what's it all about?"

"Bugs found him," she said. "He—let's see, how did it happen? Oh, yes; you yelled back for Bugs and the colonel to come out for the bally, and Bugs couldn't find his pins—those hatpins, you know. He hunted around and then thought maybe they'd gone between the boards of his platform and were under it. He lifted up the cloth and—well, he saw Al there."

I nodded. Way in the distance somewhere I heard the wail of a siren that meant the rest of the coppers were coming. I realized, suddenly, that Red wouldn't have had time to send for them. I asked Stella, "Who turned it in?"

"Lee Werner, I guess. He went out the side wall and I guess he ran over to the phone in the front wagon."

We went out into the midway by the front entrance of the waxworks. I saw Lee hurrying back toward the freak show. I don't like Lee much, but I felt sorry for him right now. He was the guy who'd be out money on account of this. A Saturday afternoon, too.

He moved past us without noticing, but I said, "Hey, Lee," and he turned. I said, "Tough break. How long'll we be sloughed?"

He ran his handkerchief across his forehead. "God knows, Pete. Maybe later in the afternoon—Stick on the lot. Lord, this kind of weather—"

He looked up at the clear-blue sky and I knew what he was thinking. All week it had rained, off and on. All week had been on the nut, strictly loss, and now came Saturday, the big day of the week and perfect weather. Then somebody has to kill a canvasman. I really felt sorry for Lee. And you can only guess what the law's going to do in a case like that.

Stella and I strolled across to the dog wagon and got a couple of cokes.

I said, "Still prefer the snakes to me?"

"Pete, can't you . . . can't you—"

"Forget? Nope. Can't. I stayed away from the carney three months and missed the best part of the season. I tried four different jobs and three different cities. No go. Here I am back."

"You're carney, Pete. You'd never be happy away from it. But there are other carnivals. Why didn't you get with Royal American or Dodson or somebody else?"

"Nuts to them," I said. "It wasn't the carney. It was you—and those damn snakes. I'm jealous of them. Everything reminds me of them. A thousand miles away I see spaghetti and I think of Black King coiling around you, and wish it was me."

"But you couldn't—"

"I could try, dammit. Say, this Al Hryner—there wasn't any *reason*, was there, for your nearly getting hysterical, was there? I mean, uh, you hadn't fallen for him, or anything, had you?"

She shook her head. "I. . . I almost hated the guy, Pete. Since he's dead now and you can't go starting a fight over it, I might as well admit he's been making passes. But —"

"When did he join the carney?"

"Just two weeks ago."

"Funny," I said. "Alive, the guy was just another canvasman. Dead, he stops the show. Say, let's take a turn on the Ferris wheel. I haven't ridden a Ferris wheel since I was a kid."

She looked at me blankly. "Huh? *Us*, ride a Ferris wheel?"

"Why not? Let's be suckers. Let's ride the merry-go-round and take in the dippyhouse and the jig show. Let's gawk at the geek. The only people who never see a carney are the carneys."

"You're on. Let's." I had her smiling now.

So we gave the merry-gee a whirl, took in Little Harlem and had Stella's palm read at the mitt camp. She wouldn't tell me what they told her there. Then we tried the Ferris wheel.

It was funny, to be up on top of the world like we were when our car was way up there. Looking down on the midway full of toy tents and toy people walking around and knowing that you were seeing the mixing of two worlds down there. The carneys and the outsiders.

And there was an ugly side of each. Lies and gaffs and deceit and never give a sucker an even break, on the carney's part. But the marks, too. It was because the marks were what they were that the carneys had to be that way. It was larceny in their hearts that made them mob the gambling concessions, trying to get something for nothing; lust that led them into the girl shows; morbid curiosity that made them like to see a man stick pins into his skin or a fire-eater put a blow torch in his mouth.

It was the subconscious desire to see a man die that made them stand open-mouthed every evening to watch Vince Piranelli ride a bicycle down that steep, narrow track, loop it in the air, and land in the net. A small net; that was why they watched. He might miss.

It was the ugliness that sent them into the waxworks to see the horrible and gory reproductions of famous crimes and criminals. There was red in that set-up, and they paid to see the red of blood, Bluebeard and Jack the Ripper, and Burke and Hare—they paid their fifteen cents and came. Offer a waxworks of, say, Galileo working on a telescope, young Abe Lincoln doing sums on the back of a shovel, things like that, and what people would pay fifteen cents to get in? A few. But you'd starve.

Then the Ferris wheel went round again and this time, up on top, I forgot all that and saw it as it should be seen. The beauty and pageantry, and brave bright pennants waving in the wind, the brave bright brass of the carney band and the red of their uniforms. The ripple of canvas and the ripple of laughter and the ripple of movement.

Beside me, Stella said, "Gee, Pete. Why didn't we ever think of doing this before? It's... it's swell."

I grinned at her. "Let's get married and buy a Ferris wheel, honey. We'll live in it and keep it running all the time. With walls around the cars and each a separate room but some with windows, so we can watch the world go round."

"And a room for Black King? Can I keep Black King?"

"Sure. But to even it up, we ought to have some pet mongeese, too. I mean, mongooses. Or do I?"

"One mongoose," said Stella firmly. "Then you won't have to worry."

"Unless it has mongoslings. Then they'll grow up and what'll they be?"

"Hey," said a voice, and I looked around and our car was stopped at the exit runway. Red Lewis was yelling at me. "You, Pete."

I got out of the car reluctantly and helped Stella down. We walked over to the copper.

"Opening already?" I asked him.

"No. Lieutenant Helsing wants you, He's in charge over there."

I turned back to Stella. "It's the inquisition," I told her. "Look, you go up to the chow-top and have some coffee and I'll be there as soon as I'm through with the—"

"Better not make a date like that," Red cut in.

And when I turned to stare at him blankly, he added, "I think the looie's going to take you in—for murder."

He wasn't smiling, either.

II

THERE was still a crowd around the freak-show front, although the bally platform was empty and the side wall dropped down, so there wasn't a thing for them to see. But the crowd was bigger than I'd ever seen it. A swell tip, and I could have turned all of them, too, if I could have climbed the platform to spiel. Wouldn't even have needed a bally show.

Except myself.

"Folks, right out here on this platform the one and only Pete Gaynor, living proof of the stupidity of John Law. He's just been told he's going to be pinched for killing a mug he met the night before and never said anything more important to than 'You're faded.' Yes sir, folks, Pete Gaynor, the original and only—"

Yes, it would have been a howl.

Red pushed us through the crowd and past the two coppers who were guarding the entrance, and we went in under the side wall.

I couldn't see any coppers around except one who was standing back against the end platform, the one Bessie sits on. The carneys were gathered around in little groups, talking. None of the groups were around Bugs Cartier's platform. Its bally cloth was folded back, so I could see under it, but someone had put a cloth over the thing that lay there. Somehow, it seemed symbolic of carnival that the cloth was crimson velvet with gold fringe.

Red Lewis was looking about, obviously puzzled. He said, "Wonder where the looie went, him and the others?"

"Maybe the doniker," I said, "but a better guess is they're holding court in the blow-off."

Red glowered at me. "Whyn't you guys talk English?" he wanted to know.

I grinned, because it hadn't occurred to me I was talking anything else. You forget, sometimes.

I said, "The blow-off, my carrot-topped comrade, is where we hold the cooch-blow for the inside money, except that this week in Haverton it got sloughed. Now don't get excited. It's that partitioned-off section of the tent down at the other end. My guess is they'd have decided it was a good private place to interview people."

My guess was right, and Lieutenant Helsing—or, anyway, a heavy-set man with a dull, beefy face whom I took to be the lieutenant—was sitting on the edge of the cooch stage with his round-toed black brogans dangling over the footlights. He looked ridiculously out of place there. Between him and Mae Cole, our cooch gal, being on that stage, I'd take Mae even on a rainy Monday. There were two other coppers standing around, one of them with an open notebook and a well-chewed pencil.

Red Lewis said, "Here's Gaynor, lieutenant," and shoved me forward.

Helsing looked at me expressionlessly and asked, "Why'd you kill this Al Hryner?"

I wanted to laugh, but I didn't. I said, "I bet you ask that of all the boys. I hardly even know Al Hryner I met him last night."

"Where?"

"In the G-top, in a crap game."

"The G-top? You mean the gambling tent?"

I nodded. "Yeah," I said, "and I lost money. Nine bucks But I don't kill people for nine bucks; it's under union scale. Ten bucks is for beating someone up, fifteen for mayhem, and for murder it's twenty-five."

He slid down off the stage and leaned against it instead. "A smart guy, eh?"

I thought it over. Maybe I wasn't being smart.

"Look," I said, "we're getting off on the wrong foot. Seriously, I saw Al Hryner for the first time in my life yesterday evening. He joined the carney while I was away. Two weeks ago, I understand. I came back yesterday. I didn't kill him and I haven't the faintest idea who did."

"What time'd you see him last?"

"It would have been around two o'clock. We ran until a little after twelve thirty. I hit the G-top about one, and was in the game maybe an hour. Hryner was still there when I left. I turned in. My bunk's in the third of those four cars on the siding."

Helsing took a long cigar out of his pocket and stuck it in his face. He said, "When'd you find out Hryner had been using crooked dice to take you with?"

"I didn't know. Was he?"

"You knew, Gaynor. We got a statement on that."

For a minute it left me blank. Then I began to see why the coppers were throwing the book at me. Somebody'd heard my casual remark to Stella, "Probably someone found Al's dice were crooked."

And whoever it was, was deliberately trying to get me in trouble when they reported it. Because from my tone of voice they'd have known I was making a casual guess and not an accusation.

"*Were* Al's dice crooked?" I asked.

Helsing jerked his thumb toward two envelopes that were lying on the edge of the footlights behind him. He said, "Pair in each side pocket. We'll saw 'em to make sure, but I rolled each pair a dozen times and one of 'em gave eight sevens out of twelve rolls."

"Red, transparent dice?"

The lieutenant nodded.

"Those are the ones used in the game last night then," I told him, "but I didn't even know they were Hryner's. The game was going when I wandered into the G-top and I left before they quit."

"Who was still playing when you left?"

I thought a minute. "Besides Al Hryner, just two. Bugs Cartier—the pincushion—and Gus."

"Who's Gus?"

"Gus Smith. Owns and runs the waxworks."

"How much did he and—uh—this Cartier drop?"

I shrugged. "You'll have to ask them. I wasn't keeping books."

"Heavy game?"

"No. Bugs was shooting dimes; he couldn't have lost much. Gus was in the two-bit class. I lost as much as nine bucks because I ran into a bad streak on doubling up when I had the dice myself. Couldn't have been the dice, either."

"Why not?"

"Snake-eyes, threes, and box cars. Dice could be loaded to crap one way or another, but not all three. I must have had the straight pair, because after five craps I got Little Joe for a point, and had nine or ten rolls for it before I sevened out."

Everything was going O.K., I thought. I'd started out wrong, but by now it was going O.K. Only I was in a hurry to get back to Stella, and, anyway, I didn't know any more to tell the coppers.

I said, "How much longer before we can open up?"

"Maybe an hour. But you won't be doing the barking, Gaynor. We're taking you along; the chief wants to talk to you."

"Huh?" I said, and began to lose my temper again, just a little. "You're crazy. Why pick on *me?* Dammit, even if I *had* known the dice were crooked, I wouldn't have done—"

"That isn't why you killed him. Don't play dumb, Gaynor. We got the inside dope and you're the *only* guy around here with a motive. Why'd you leave the carnival three months ago?"

"Personal reasons. And they couldn't have anything to do with Al Hryner because he wasn't around then."

"Sure, they didn't. We know what they were. You left because you were soft on this broad who handles the snakes and she wouldn't give you a tumble and then—"

I felt it coming, and I tried to stop him; I didn't *want* to hit a copper and get myself in a jam. I tried to interrupt. I said, "Shut up, goddam—" But he cut in and kept on.

"—and then you learned somewhere that this Al was making—"

My fist against his jaw bent him back over the footlights of the cooch stage, and then I was grabbed from behind and whirled around. And Red Lewis was wading in before I could get set for him. I saw his fist coming at my face, but I was off balance and couldn't duck. It was a fist the size of a small ham and it had Red's two-twenty pounds back of it. It hit, and the lights went out.

It was two o'clock when Lee Werner, my boss, got in to see me at the Haverton hoosegow. Two in the morning, I mean.

He spent the first couple of minutes cussing, and didn't repeat himself once. Then he said, "Come on, I put up bail for you. God knows why."

"Bail? On a murder charge?"

"You dimwit, there isn't any murder charge against you. You're in for slugging a cop—and why'd you have to pick a looie?"

"I'd slug him again, Lee, if he—"

"Listen, you're going to behave yourself or I'll pull that bail and let you sit here and rot. We pull town tomorrow night, and I'm trying to get this thing squared before then. Lord, I've seen the mayor of this burg and the chief of police, and— Hell, if they wanted to, they could hold *all* of us here until they got that murder settled."

I whistled. "You mean they could hold the whole carney—a couple or three hundred people, just because a canvasman gets killed?"

"Not the whole carney, no. But the material witnesses, and that'd put an awful dent in my show. Lucky our next hop is a short one; I had to promise I'd let 'embe back for the inquest. That's one day we're going to lose as it is."

"And for slugging the looie, how about that? Will I have to come back another day to stand trial for that?"

"We're trying to get the charge killed. Listen, Helsing isn't such a bad guy. I put Stella to work on him, and—"

"You what?"

"Sure. And he's beginning to see the light. He realizes, after he talked with her awhile, that he popped off the wrong side of his mouth. He's apologized to her for it. They're across the street waiting for us."

"*They?* You mean Helsing and Stella?"

"Yeah. I insisted on being the one to come and get you. I knew if you saw Helsing again before I explained, you'd pop off and then it'd be too late—he couldn't withdraw that charge and save his face. And his face ain't so hot now. You did it no good."

I grinned. "Neither is my jaw. But it was the grounds copper, Red, who did that. All right, what we waiting for?"

"You're sure you'll—"

"Positively. If he's apologized to Stella, it's O.K. by me."

"Come on, then."

My release was already arranged and the turnkey let us out. I was broke at the moment, so I borrowed a buck from Lee Werner and gave it to the turnkey. He'd given me a pack of cigarettes early in the evening and there are times when a pack of fags are worth a buck.

Helsing stood up warily when Lee and I walked into the quiet little bar which was right across the street from the station.

I said "hello" to Stella first, and then to Helsing, "Lieutenant, I understand you've taken back what caused it, so I'm sorry I lost my temper this afternoon. Shake on it?"

I put out my hand and he took it and grinned.

"My fault," he said, "but I didn't know Miss Alleman then. Have a drink?"

"The round's on me," I said as we sat down. "My coming-out party. Only Lee'll pay for it and put it on the books. Yes, lieutenant, Stella's a swell gal and don't let the snakes fool you. She was abandoned as a waif and a python adopted her and brought her up, so it isn't her fault."

"Not quite that, lieutenant," said Stella. "My folks were carney and I was brought up in a side show. I liked to play with snakes, almost in my crib, and never acquired the dislike of them that most people have."

"The ones you use have had their fangs pulled?"

Stella shook her head. "They're bull snakes and haven't any fangs to pull. They're quite friendly—anybody can handle them."

"Not me," said Helsing, firmly.

"Anybody can handle them," I said, "but few of us could be as decorative in doing it as Stella is."

After our drinks came, Lee cleared his throat. He said, "Uh—about those charges against Pete, lieutenant—are you—uh—going to press them?"

Helsing looked at me, and for once I decided to keep my mouth shut and let Lee and Stella handle him. They'd been doing all right, so far.

"Just one thing," Helsing said, "before I decide to withdraw them. You got no hard feelings against Lewis, have you, Gaynor?"

I shook my head. "Not a thing. What he did was in line of duty; I swung first."

So that's how it was I was back at the loudspeaker by Sunday and helping with tear-down Sunday night, and making the forty-mile hop to Wilmot. I learned later that Lee had got opened by six o'clock and caught the evening crowd, but that the lost afternoon had cost him plenty.

We put up the top in Wilmot Monday in a drizzling rain that looked as though it would last all week. Lee wandered about disconsolately, without even a hat on, and the rain running down the back of his neck. I felt very sorry for the guy.

III

MONDAY AFTERNOON the rain was harder, and the Wilmot cops came. The chief of police himself, and he was plenty hardboiled. No cooch-blow, no mitt camp, and if we'd had a half-and-half, that would have been sloughed, too. He seemed a little sorry we didn't have one. The police chief's name was Seton, William L. Seton.

It was going to be a bad week; there wasn't any doubt about that. Rain or no rain.

Seton went up and down the midway, asking questions about the set-up on each of the concessions, and he sloughed three of them that were too near to gambling to suit him. He wanted to see the costumes the girls in the girl show wore, or would wear if it ever stopped raining.

Yes, it was going to be a great week in Wilmot. And already some of the wagons were sinking in to the hubs. Shavings fought mud, and the shavings couldn't win.

But Seton said he wasn't going to worry himself about our little murder. It had happened at Haverton, and the Haverton cops could have it. The inquest was for Wednesday morning, he told us, and we'd all better go over there. All of us from the freak show, that is, and any of the others who knew Al Hryner, canvasman, deceased.

Lee Werner did the only thing possible. He introduced Seton to Mae Cole, our cooch girl, and then went away and left 'em, after giving Mae the office. If the chief was susceptible, Mae might talk him into letting her operate. If she did, Lee might make enough profit to wash out last week's losses, because the blow-off was our gravy.

Monday evening it was still drizzling. Only a few kids waded out to see the carney, and none of the shows opened.

The only bright spot was that nobody could find Mae Cole around the lot, and Lee began to hope for the best. Or the worst, depending strictly upon one's point of view.

At nine it was still raining. Not a chance of giving a single show. We got a rummy game going in the G-top and played for nickels until a little after midnight.

Using a flashlight, I picked my way around back of the tents toward the sleepers. I was behind the freak-show top when I remembered the magazine I'd bought that afternoon and had left on Stella's platform. Maybe I'd read a story before I went to sleep.

I ducked in under the side wall, found myself behind Bessie's platform, and went around it. I played the flashlight ahead of me toward Stella's platform and then said, "What the hell?"

Because the snake box was open! Stella kept her snakes in a red tin trunk, specially made with inset screen gratings in the ends. Now the lid of it was wide open, leaning back against the curtain post behind it.

I blinked my eyes and looked again to make sure it wasn't an optical illusion. Stella certainly wouldn't have left it open, and nobody else would have had reason for opening it, unless—unless they wanted to steal snakes. Snakes—good ones—cost money all right. But they're difficult things to peddle to a fence in his right mind.

Just the same I took the rest of the distance to the platform on the double-quick to get that lid down again. I don't know why I thought there was any hurry—unless that lid had just been opened, which was improbable—the snakes would be gone if they were going.

I jumped up on the platform and looked down into the box. Two of the bulls were still in there, the two smaller ones. Black King was gone.

I put the lid down, and I must have slammed it because somebody said, "What's all the noise, dammit?" and I turned the beam of my flash toward the sound of Bugs Cartier's voice.

He was sitting up on his own platform, wrapped in a blanket and blinking sleepily at me.

I said, "It's me, Pete Gaynor. Somebody swiped Black King."

"Huh?"

I jumped down off the platform, my first intention being to go to Lee's trailer and tell him about it. But as my feet hit the soft turf it occurred to me that maybe Black King had escaped because, after all, the lid had been open accidentally. And if so, he might still be hear at hand.

It wouldn't hurt to take a look, at least around and under the platform. I started around back of it, the flashlight held out ahead of me and aimed down at the grass.

But I didn't get there because something heavy smacked down on my wrist and knocked the flashlight out of my hand. I jumped back with an involuntary yowl, thinking my wrist was broken.

The flashlight hit the grass, still burning, but it had twisted in its fall and shone backward on me. Then something hit it a wallop and the freak-show top was in utter darkness.

I kept on backing away, my feet making no sound on the turf by which I could be followed, and I was glad of that. I'm as brave as the next guy, maybe, but with what might be a broken wrist I had no inclination to tangle with a man armed with a tent stake in utter darkness.

But he didn't come after me. I heard the rustle of canvas as though the side wall behind the platform was being lifted and dropped again.

Bugs' voice, still sleepy, said, "What the *hell* are you doing? And what about Black—"

I said, "Got a flashlight, Bugs? Turn it on!" And then I moved again, quick, because the guy with the tent stake might have been bluffing with the sidewall canvas, and I didn't want to locate myself for him by talking and then staying put.

Bugs said, "Sure. Uh." And then a beam of light flashed out from his platform, bracketed me, and then went to Stella's platform.

Bugs was throwing off his blanket and he jumped down and came toward me. He had the flashlight in one hand and a long, sharp-looking stiletto in the other. He said, "*You* hurt, Pete? Where's the guy?"

I told him quickly what had happened, and Bugs said, "Wait a minute," and did what I hadn't thought of doing; ran across to the center pole and plugged in the top lights.

Then, together, we made the circuit of Stella's platform and the ones near it, and even looked underneath the bally cloths. The guy was gone. What made me sure was that just outside the side wall, at about the point where I thought I'd heard it rustle, we found a tent stake lying.

There were what might be called tracks, too, but they were utterly shapeless in the soggy grass, and after a few paces they petered out completely in the well-tracked area around behind the tops.

"Guy's gone," said Bugs. "Say, how's your wrist? How's about getting a doc?"

I'd been wriggling my fingers experimentally and they worked. I said, "I'm pretty sure nothing's busted. Just a bruise. Look, you go wake up Lee Werner. I'm going back to the top. In case—"

I found I didn't know what I meant by "in case" so I went back under the side wall before I had to finish it.

I took a look around for Black King but couldn't find a sign of him. If he was really gone it was going to be another wallop in the pocketbook for Lee Werner; it was he, not Stella, who owned the snakes. Black King had cost plenty shekels, too.

Not a sign of him. I went out the midway entrance and looked under the platform. When I straightened up I saw a man standing just the other side of it.

He said, "Gaynor?"

"Helsing," I said, "how'd you get over here?"

"Just got off duty and drove over. It's only forty miles. Not much doing, huh?"

"Depends on how you look at it," I told him. I was wondering whether I'd better tell him what happened just now. It might mean another investigation that would cost Lee a lot more than the loss of a seven-foot worm.

Helsing said, "I thought this'd be the shank of the evening for you carneys. It's only a few minutes after twelve. Where is everybody?"

Lee Werner's voice from inside the top yelled out, "Hey, Pete! Where are you?"

So Helsing was going to find out anyway, and maybe it would be all for the best. So I said, "It isn't as quiet as it looks, lieutenant. Come on in."

And that way I got a chance to explain to him and to Lee at the same time. Lee surprised me by taking it quietly and calmly.

He insisted on taking me over to Gus Smith first. Gus wasn't a doctor but he'd picked up a bit of medical knowledge—maybe from studying anatomy while he was learning to make wax figures. Anyway, when Gus felt my wrist carefully and said it wasn't broken, Lee believed him. I was already convinced.

Then we routed out all the men who worked for Lee—except Slim Norris, the ticket man, who'd gone in to town and wasn't back yet—and made a systematic search of the top and the area around it. The rest of the carney lot would have to wait till daylight for a systematic search, although we covered it with flashlights and lanterns as well as we could. No sign of Black King.

Helsing stuck by me; maybe because he liked me—or maybe to see I didn't swipe any more snakes.

He said, "How's about the police—I mean, the Wilmot police. You got to call them."

I ducked the issue. "That's up to Lee," I said. "It's his worm got swiped—if it *was* swiped and didn't just escape. It's up to him to make a complaint."

Helsing snorted. "Don't be a dope. You were attacked. The guy who slapped you on the wrist with a tent stake would just as soon have parted your hair with it."

He paused a minute and then added quietly, "Like he parted Al Hryner's hair with it. Remember what the back of Hryner's head looked like."

Neither of us said anything for a minute and then he said, "Well?"

"Well, what?"

Helsing spat disgustedly into a puddle momentarily illuminated by the beam of his flashlight. He said, "You damn carneys. You don't like coppers, do you?"

"Do you know Chief Seton, here in Wilmot?"

"All right, so, off the record, he's a louse. He's still better than having your head bashed in."

"That's a matter of taste," I told him. "Shall we take a look through the waxworks?"

We ducked under the side wall of the waxworks tent and I found the plug that switched the lights on. Then we went around the aisle, taking one exhibit at a time, and looking carefully, using our flashlights wherever there was a dark shadow.

"This stuff is good," Helsing said. He was looking at a life-size wax figure of Pierre Garroux driving his shiv into the back of a man seated at a table. "Only this guy's holding his knife wrong."

"Apache style," I said. "Yeah, this stuff is good. And you won't find Gus pulling any boners like a shiv held wrong. He's maybe the best waxworks man in the country. Only there isn't any money in waxworks since the gay Nineties, and that puts him with Tookerman Shows. He's a bug on authenticity."

"Hey, look—nuts, I thought that was a snake."

We moved down in front of the exhibit Helsing was looking at. It was a cheerful scene in which a murderer was getting ready to hang the victim he had already throttled with his hands. A coil of rope had fooled Helsing.

"Danny Watson," I said. "Killed six people for insurance before they got him, for the murder you see being enacted before your very eyes. It was intended to be taken for a suicide by hanging, but he very stupidly forgot the chair his victim was supposed to have stepped off from."

Helsing looked at me curiously. "Friend of yours?"

I grinned. "Nope, I used to spiel for Gus part of the time last season. Come on, meet the rest of his menagerie.

"Here's Tommy Benno, the bank bandit, in the very act of backing away from the scene of his crime—one of his earlier crimes—with a blazing Tommy-gun in his hands. And, by the way, lieutenant, what ever happened to Tommy? Is he still kicking around loose or did they catch him and burn him?"

"Nobody's heard of him since that Eltinge bank job six months ago," said Helsing. "Half a million bucks, so I guess he's retired all right. That's a darn good likeness of him."

"They're all good likenesses," I said. "Take that next one, Butch Davis. Gus traveled a hundred miles and back just to study Butch in court while he was being tried. Had good photos and descriptions to work from, too, but he still went that far just to look at the guy. That was ten years ago; I read recently Davis was applying for a pardon. Did he get it?"

Helsing shrugged. "Before my time, I guess. I never heard of Butch Davis. No, don't tell me. Let's look for that damn snake instead."

We looked thoroughly. It was no dice as far as the waxworks tent was concerned.

As we went out under the side wall, Helsing brought it up again about the Wilmot police. I listened patiently, and then interrupted.

"Look," I said, "as far as I'm concerned, *you're* the police. You know about it and that lets me out."

"You damn fool, don't you realize that this is part of the same business as the Hryner murder? That this isn't just somebody slapping you on the writ and swiping a snake?"

"All the more reason why it's your baby. The Wilmot police said they wouldn't horn in on the murder. They horned in on everything else from the size of the gimmicks in the jig show to the size of the squares on the penny-pitch boards."

I took him back to see Lee Werner, and Lee looked at it the same way I did. As far as he was concerned, the snake had merely escaped and would be found in the morning. And it was nobody's loss but his; Black King was as harmless as a kitten and wouldn't hurt anybody if he had gone off the lot.

Helsing said, "But dammit—"

Lee ran his fingers through what hair he had left, as though he was going to tear it out by the roots. He said, with pleading in his voice, "Listen, suppose word gets around there's a loose snake around the carney. How many people are going to come if that gets in the Wilmot papers? And will they publish that the snake is nonpoisonous and tame? They will not; they'll make a scare story out of it. And since two weeks ago we're on the nut; we *need* a good play here—or else. Have a heart, lieutenant."

Helsing thought a minute and then shrugged. He said, "Got a phone wire out here?"

"Sure, over in the pay wagon. Want to use it?"

"I'll phone the chief at Haverton. Maybe he'll say it's O.K. for me to stay over here until the inquest. Can you put me up?"

"Put you up?" Lee grinned for the first time in an hour. "Hell, you can have my trailer. I'll bunk with the boys."

Helsing said, "Lead me to the phone. If it's O.K. by my boss —"

And it was.

IV

TUESDAY MORNING and, for a change, it rained.

I heard it on the roof of the bunk car and I turned over and tried to go back to sleep. But the patter of rain on a roof isn't a soothing sound to a carney. If sounds can have opposites, the patter of rain on roof or canvas is the opposite of the patter of silver on a ticket ledge.

So I got up and dressed. Anyway, I wanted to see Stella and to find out if Black King was back. An idea had occurred to me; just maybe, if Black King had escaped and not been stolen, he would have found Stella. Maybe he'd have hunted her out, and had been curled under her bunk while we had looked for him. I don't know whether snakes are that intelligent or not.

But Black King was still gone. Stella was disconsolate; I found her out in the rain, hunting Black King. I helped awhile, and then insisted on taking her into the chow top for coffee. I tried to talk her into a cheerful frame of mind, but I was kind of in the dumps myself, and I suppose my cheerfulness sounded forced. Back in the freak-show top, we found Lee Warner talking to himself. He'd had a quarrel with Ralph Chapman, our prestidigitator, and Ralph had almost quit on him. That would have been bad; with the cooch and the mitt camp out, Ralph was getting the only inside money in the show. At the end of his sleight-of-hand routine, Ralph pitched an envelope of tricks that pulled in quite a few quarters.

"Only two weeks from the end of the season," Lee was moaning, "and all we need is a blow-down."

I left Stella with Lee and went over to talk to Ralph Chapman.

I said, "Listen, Ralph, give the boss a break. The guy's half screwy. He's been taking—"

"Sure, Pete, but so have the rest of us. Dammit, I'm on percentage, and *I* have not been getting rich, either. So why does he got to take it out on me, by calling me—"

"With you," I told him, "whatever he called you is practically a compliment. Now listen, Ralph ." And I went on and got him so mad at me, I knew he'd forget about Lee.

Then I went back to Lee and Stella.

"Where's Helsing?" I asked Lee.

"Drove over to Haverton. Wanted to get his toothbrush or something. He'll be back and stay here tonight again. Then tomorrow, the blasted inquest. Listen, if the weather's good tomorrow ."

"If it is, we'll go early," I told him, "and we'll talk them into getting our testimony quick—or if it's going to drag on, maybe we can get a postponement at noon and get back here in time to work."

Lee said, "It'll probably rain. It looks like an all-week rain to me. All we need is a storm and a blow-down."

"All we need is to keep our heads," I told him. "It can't rain forever. And go easy on Ralph. He's strictly prima donna and you know it."

"What's eating him is that Mae Cole isn't back. He's been making a play for Mae, and he blames me for sicking her on Seton. Hell, Mae can't see Chapman with a telescope."

I whistled. "Mae isn't back? What you suppose happened?"

"I can suppose anything. You know Mae. Maybe she lit out for somewhere. Well, since the blow-off can't run anyway, that'd save me money, for a change."

Late Tuesday afternoon it quit raining. But the sky stayed overcast and the lot, despite tons of shavings the cat-men were pushing around, stayed soggy even in the high spots. The lower areas were swamps.

Tuesday evening, a few intrepid suckers came out to see the carney. We opened up and I was out on the platform grinding all evening. We took in a little. Not enough to get off the nut, but it was less of a loss than if we hadn't worked at all.

Chapman helped plenty. Working to tips of only six or seven marks at a time inside the top, he'd get quarters away from almost a hundred percent of them. Between grinds I asked him if anybody'd heard from Mae Cole.

"She's back," he said. "She's around somewhere. I saw her half an hour ago."

I didn't know whether that was good news or not. Anyway, it was time for another bally out front, so I took Bugs and the colonel and hammered the bass drum until I had the nearest thing to a crowd I'd be likely to get. Colonel Toots did a cartwheel and a headstand for them, and Bugs showed them the long hatpins he was going to stick into himself inside the top, and I told 'em about the myriad other wonders of the Wonderworld.

Three of them bought tickets and the rest wandered off. I kept on grinding. By eleven o'clock we had all we were going to get, and there wasn't any use keeping on.

Stella and I went up the midway for coffee and on our Way back met Bugs Cartier heading out for the entrance.

He waved cheerfully. "Come on, you two," he yelled, "help me get drunk to celebrate."

"Celebrate what?" Stella asked him.

"Getting rich. Look!" He pulled some bills from his pockets. There were five or six of them; the one on top was a five. He held them up gleefully. "I broke the bank at Monte Cristo."

"Monte Carlo," I corrected him.

"All right then, Monte Carlo. Who cares? Let's go in town and get pie-eyed. On me."

"Don't tempt me," I told him, "because tomorrow gives the inquest. Up early we get."

"O.K., be a dope and be sensible." He grinned. "Me, I'm gonna have fun."

"Seriously, Bugs, where'd you get all that sugar?"

He put his finger to his lips and said, *"Shhh!"* And then he walked on and left us standing there. I got a whiff of his breath as he went by—he'd already been drinking.

Stella and I went on more slowly. I said, "I. . . I wonder where Bugs got that dough."

"The G-top? He gambles there a lot, doesn't he?"

"For peanuts. I've never seen him lose or win more than two or three bucks at a time. And he's been working up to half an hour ago. Dammit, I wish—"

"What, Pete?"

"I should have gone with the guy to keep him out of trouble. Somebody'll roll him, if nothing worse. He hasn't got sense enough, even when he's sober, not to stick pins in himself."

"Hm-m-m—I wish you wouldn't, Pete. You. . . you might get in trouble yourself."

That, from Stella, was encouraging. I said, "Would you care if I did?"

She said, "Well—" But never finished it, because I was looking at her instead of where I was going, and I stepped into a mud hole, and that was an end to romance.

Stella's laughter after she made sure I wasn't hurt, destroyed the opportunity, and anyway you can't make love to a girl when you're coated with mud. I scraped off as much of it as I could and then took Stella to her car.

"Up early," I warned her. "The stars are coming out, and that means good weather tomorrow, maybe. If we can get back from Haverton by early afternoon—"

When I left Stella, regardless of the mud I was caked with, I headed for the G-top. Ralph Chapman, Gus Smith, and Shorty O'Hara were there, in a poker game with a couple of the ride men.

Shorty O'Hara—who doubles swords and fire for the freak show—had thrown in his cards, and Ralph and Gus were eying one another warily over a pot that had grown to several dollars. So I asked Shorty, "Seen Bugs?"

"No," he said. "What happened to you?"

"Beauty treatment," I told him. "You've heard of mud packs, haven't you? Was Bugs here at all this evening?"

O'Hara shook his head. "Nope, and I came here as soon as we closed. I asked Bugs then, was he coming, and he said no, he was going to see Lee."

I left the G-top more curious than before. Had Bugs hit Lee for an advance? Didn't seem likely, under the circumstances. And yet where else could Bugs have got that money in so short a time?

There wasn't any light in Lee's trailer, and I went on back to the to the sleeping car. Tomorrow, I decided. I'd pin Bugs down—and then the idea of pinning down a pincushion made me laugh out loud.

Slim Norris, the ticket man, stuck his head out of the upper bunk over mine and wanted to know what was funny.

I told him and asked him if he'd noticed what Bugs had done after the show.

"Dunno, Pete," he said, "but he didn't dip into the receipts. I checked in with Lee right after eleven. Took in only seventeen bucks. Lousy."

But after I was in bed I stopped worrying about it and went to sleep. Wednesday morning was bright and sunny. It was Lieutenant Helsing who awakened me, and he wasn't gentle about it.

"Wake up, you mug. Lee wants to get an early start. Gonna be a swell day."

I sat on the edge of the bunk and started pulling on my socks. "You're getting the carney spirit," I said, "because you're finding out what weather is. Sunshine is money and rain is a kick in the pants."

Helsing grinned. "Shake a leg, then. There's enough money outside to sunburn a lifeguard."

Then his voice turned serious. He said, "Pete you carneys stick together, don't you? And the rest of us are outsiders."

"Hm-m-m—yeah, we do. It's. . . it's kind of a world in itself, a world against the world."

"Look, Pete, here's what I want to know. How far would a carney go—to protect another one? I mean, if you knew somebody with this show had committed murder, would you—uh—perjure yourself at the inquest? Wait, I'll make that easier—let's say you don't *know* who did it, but you could tell something that would maybe be a lead for the police. Would you?"

"That's a tough one," I said. And I stopped to think, so I could give him an honest answer.

Then I said, "I guess a lot would depend on who it was, and what the circumstances were, and stuff like that. Maybe, in some cases, I might keep my yap shut. Like if it happened in a fight, and the guy hadn't meant to kill the other one. But then again—"

"It wasn't in a fight,"Helsing interrupted. "Al Hryner was hit from the back. And a blow that hard was deliberate murder."

I stopped buttoning my shirt and stared at him. I said, "I wasn't talking about Hryner. I was trying to give you a general answer to a general question, and to be fair about it. I don't know anything about the Hryner business I haven't told."

Helsing said, "O.K., don't get your back up. What I'm getting at is that *somebody* with this show—and I don't mean the murderer—must have *some* idea of what happened. Hell, we haven't even found a motive—except the ones I accused you of, once. Nobody will even admit knowing Hryner very well, and we can't find what outfit he was with before he joined your show."

"Lee hired him. Did you ask Lee?"

"Yeah, he says he didn't even ask the guy. You carneys are casual as the devil about stuff like that. How'd he even know the guy was a carney."

"He could tell."

"Hm-m-m," said Helsing. "By the way, you had a fortuneteller with the show in Haverton. What happened to him?"

I grinned. "That's what I meant about a carney being able to tell another carney. If you knew the lingo you'd have asked if the law sloughed the mitt camp. They did."

"Why the mitt camp?"

"Mitt for hand; mitt camp is a palmistry booth. But in carney it's stretched to cover any mentalist act. Hassan Bey pitches buddha."

And I had to translate that for him while we crossed the lot from the bunk car to Lee's trailer. Lee was looking over a list Helsing had given him of those who would have to go over to Haverton to give testimony at the inquest.

"We'll need two cars," he told me. "I'll unhitch mine from the trailer and Gus Smith can take his. You and Helsing ride with Gus and I can manage the rest. Better go tell Gus. And where the devil is Bugs?"

"Huh? Isn't he around?" I'd plumb forgotten about Bugs going into town to get drunk last night.

"I looked inside the top when I got up this morning," Lee said. "Bugs' bedroll was put away, so I figured he was up and around the lot somewhere."

"Damn," I said. "More likely it means he didn't get back last night." And I told Lee and Helsing about my encounter with Bugs the night before.

Lee whistled. He said, "*I* didn't give him any money last night. But if he had some he probably ended up in the Wilmot jail. You go see Gus, Pete, while I go to the pay wagon and phone the hoosegow."

He hightailed off toward the phone and I wandered into the waxworks tent to look for Gus. Gus has one end of the big tent partitioned off into living quarters and a workshop.

I found him making coffee on a primus stove and had a cup with him while I told him about arrangements for going over to Haverton.

He said, "Let's see if Lee found Bugs. Might put a crimp in the plans if one of us has to pick him up somewhere. Where's Lee now?"

I put down my coffee cup and stood. "Back at the trailer, I guess. That's base of operations. Let's see if he found out anything."

We ducked under the side wall and saw there was a knot of people by the trailer. Shorty O'Hara was there, and Ralph Chapman, and Stella, besides Helsing and Lee.

"Of course I'm sure, dammit," Shorty was saying. "No, I don't know what time it was, but I'd guess around three."

Lee saw me join the edge of the group and explained, his face looking worried. "Pete, Shorty here saw Bugs come back last night. He isn't in the hoosegow. I can't figure it out. How tight was he, Shorty?"

"Plenty. He could barely navigate."

Lee said, "Then he sure as shooting wouldn't have been in the mood to get up early this morning. Not if he turned in with a snoot full like that—"

"Where does he keep his bedroll," I asked, "when he isn't in it?" Lee jerked his thumb toward a wagon back of us. Chapman said, "I know where he keeps it. I'll go look." He was back in a minute. "Bugs' bedding isn't there. But, dammit, he isn't on his platform, and that's where he sleeps, isn't it?"

Lee snapped his fingers. "Why didn't somebody think of it? Sometimes he sleeps on the cooch stage in the blow. Go look there, will you, Slim?"

Slim Norris ducked under canvas into the blow-off.

A minute later he reappeared, his face a pasty gray. He was looking mostly at me and there was something I didn't like in his expression.

He said, "The guy's dead."

Helsing and Chapman were running for the canvas. Some of the others followed, more slowly, and Lee sat down suddenly on the trailer step behind him.

His face looked suddenly old, as though the courage had gone out of it. He said, "Slim, was he—"

Slim said, "Yeah" in answer to Lee's unasked question, but Slim was looking at me. He said, "Pete, he was murdered just like you thought'd be funny." I was starting toward the tent, but I turned.

"Huh?" I grabbed Slim's arm. "What you acting funny about, Slim? Like you think *I* killed him or something, and saying—What you mean 'like I thought'd be funny'?"

"Last night." Slim's face was sullen and so was his voice. "You laughed at the idea of somebody pinning down a pincushion."

"Pinning? You mean—"

But what was the use of trying to get the story out of Slim? I let go his arm and went after the others into the top and slid through the slit in the canvas partition that shut off the blow end of the tent.

The curtains of the cooch stage had been pulled shut, but Helsing was holding them apart, and some of the others were crowding around him. I ran up and looked over Helsing's shoulder.

Bugs was dead, all right. He had to be, with a dozen six and nine-inch hatpins stuck into him that way. And one of them embedded so deeply that only the head showed, just above where his heart would be.

V

HELSING had phoned and we sat around waiting for the Wilmot police to get there. Waiting for the inevitable questioning, the inevitable bulldozing we knew we were in for.

None of us talked much.

Lee asked Helsing about the inquest at Haverton.

"I phoned there," Helsing told him, "and it's postponed. Seton will want to do his work here while this is fresh."

"I suppose we don't work today at all," said Chapman bitterly.

Helsing shrugged. "That'll be up to Seton. This is out of my territory."

But from the tone of his voice, and what we'd seen of William L. Seton, all of us knew the answer to Chapman's question. We'd be lucky to get going at all this week. Two inquests to worry about now instead of one.

The Wilmot chief of police brought the coroner and half a dozen policemen with him when he arrived. The coroner immediately took charge of the blow-off part of the top and Seton—with a black look on his face that boded trouble — herded the rest of us into the main part.

He said to a couple of his men, "Tommy, you and George keep an eye on these people. Nobody to go anywhere unless I know about it. Now, which one of you people knows the most about this?"

Nobody spoke up while he glared around at all of us.

Lee said quietly, "Slim Norris found the body when I sent him to look on the cooch stage. Maybe you'll want to talk to Slim first."

"Why'd you send him to look there?"

Lee explained.

"All right. If you don't mind I'll use your trailer. Come on, Norris."

Stella was sitting alone on the tin trunk that still contained two of the snakes. I climbed the platform and sat down beside her. I said, "Don't worry, kid. This'll come out all right."

"But, Pete, who'll be next?"

"Next?" I stared at her, wondering what she meant. And then I got it. "Good Lord, don't get ideas like that. You think somebody's going to bump off the freak show, one at a time?"

"It . . . it sounds silly, Pete, but isn't that what's happening? Three already!"

"*Three?*" I echoed, and for a minute I thought either she or I had gone loco, and then I got what she meant. "Oh, Black King. But, in all probability, honey, he just ran off. There are woods not far from here, and—"

"You think he opened the trunk himself, from the inside? Don't be silly, Pete. Black King was murdered."

"Humph," I said. "Why would anyone do a screwy thing like—"

"For the same reason they . . . he . . . killed Bugs last night. And Al last week. Don't you see it, Pete? Somebody's trying to break up the show."

It was so silly I couldn't help grinning. I said, "Anybody who would try to break up a freak show by murdering the acts one at a time would Hey, Al Hryner wasn't even an act! Murdering a canvasman would be a funny way to start a campaign like that. They'd pick somebody valuable, like—"

I'd started to say "like you," but I stopped, because the idea of anybody murdering Stella wasn't anything I wanted to talk about. Suddenly

I was afraid for her.

Two people who'd been with the show *had* been murdered, and as long as I didn't know why they'd died, who was I to say that the motive might not extend to Stella?

I happened to be looking at the canvas partition of the blow-off when I saw what had been the rosy, cherubic face of the coroner poke through the opening. But just then his face was neither rosy nor cherubic at all. There was an expression on it I couldn't read, further to say that it didn't indicate a pleasant emotion.

He called out, "Mr. Werner!"

I said, "'Scuse me a minute," to Stella and got there the same time Lee did. Just curiosity as to what caused that expression. It couldn't be the manner in which Bugs had been killed, because he'd been in there ten or fifteen minutes, and the pins were obvious.

He said, "Come in a minute, Mr. Werner."

Neither of them paid any attention to me, and I followed through the flap. I was glad to see that the coroner bad thrown the blanket up over the body of the pincushion. He'd taken out the hatpins, too; they were lying in a neat row along the footlights of the cooch stage.

He pointed to something I couldn't see, something lying beyond the blanket-covered body, and said to Lee, "Is—uh—that yours?"

I stepped in close when Lee did and saw what was lying there. A big black snake. Black King. And I could tell by the way he lay there, belly up, that he was dead. A live snake never lies that way, nor a sleeping one.

I heard Lee's breath suck in quickly. He said, "Yes, Doc, that's my snake. It... it disappeared night before last. We thought it just got away into the woods."

"How was it killed," I asked.

The coroner shook his head. "Don't ask me. I'm no herpetologist. I dunno whether I could tell or not, even if I examined it" And by the expression in his eyes I could see that he wasn't keen about finding out.

"Where'd you find it?" Lee demanded.

"Partly alongside, partly under the body. Inside the bedroll. Did—did the deceased—uh—ever sleep with it?"

I shook my head slowly, remembering that Bugs Cartier hadn't liked snakes. He hadn't been exactly afraid of them, but he wouldn't have touched one voluntarily.

I said, "If it had been Bugs who stole Black King, the last place he'd have hidden him would have been in his own bedroll. Whether the snake was dead or alive at the time. And no matter how drunk Bugs was."

"He wasn't drunk the night Black King disappeared," Lee said. "Dammit, Pete—" Whatever he'd intended to say to me, he stopped, and turned to the coroner again. He asked, "About what time would you say Cartier was killed?"

"At least four hours ago, maybe longer. Say between three and six o'clock."

"Will a regular autopsy bring it out closer than that?"

"Maybe. Maybe not. Depends on whether his movements before then can be traced."

Lee looked puzzled. "I don't get it, Doc. How would his movements before three prove what time after that he was killed?"

"Contents of the stomach and esophagus. An analyst can show just about how long the last food he'd eaten had been there and progressed in digestion at the time of death. Then, if tracing his movements can show pretty accurately when it was that he ate the food in question, we can estimate the time of death pretty closely."

"Oh," said Lee. "I've often wondered about that."

As Lee and I went back into the main part of the top I asked him, "What made you so interested in time of death, Lee? Shorty saw him at three last night, and Slim found him about nine this morning. What good would it do to know whether he was killed at, say, three thirty or at six?"

"Guess I didn't have any real reason, Pete. I was thinking about that snake. It... it worries me. *Why* would anybody have put that snake in Bugs' bedroll?"

"That's less important than why somebody murdered Bugs."

"I... I don't know why, but one worries me more than the other, Pete. Because it seems so utterly unreasonable. If somebody had a reason for killing Al Hryner, maybe Bugs found out something about it. Maybe he was bribed last night to keep his mouth shut. Remember that money you told me about. But after Bugs got drunk, the killer decided he couldn't trust Bugs—and I can see why he'd decide that, after the way Bugs flashed the dough. So he waits till Bugs turns in, dead drunk, and—"

I nodded. "I see what you mean, Lee. That part of it can make sense, but the Black King part—it scares me a little."

And then I forgot about being scared, because it was up to me to break the news to Stella about her pet. But she took it better than I'd feared she might.

"I... I had a hunch, Pete, all along, that King was dead." Her voice was quite steady. "I... I'd rather not see him, I guess. But will you see that... that—"

"Sure, honey," I assured her. "I'll see he gets a decent burial."

And, I decided, he would. The police might think me crazy to insist on the point, but a pet is a pet, and Stella had thought at least as much of King as a man thinks of his dog.

Then Slim came under the side wall and crossed the tent to where I was talking to Stella. He said, "You're next, Pete."

There was still that look in his eyes as though he was afraid of me.

Chief Seton had put up the little folding table in Lee's trailer. He sat on one side of it, facing me, and a patrolman with a notebook sat at the end, taking notes. Presumably, I was supposed to stand for the inquisition, but I sat down on Lee's bed instead.

Seton started by frowning at me for what seemed like a full minute. There were several things that it occurred to me to say, but I waited. I was going to let him ask the questions.

When he started it. was with the air of a man who is going to be very thorough.

"Your name?"

"Pete Gaynor. Peter John Gaynor."

"Age?"

"Thirty-six."

"Draft status?"

"Four-F. They wouldn't even let me enlist for noncombatant. I'm slightly hemophiliac."

"What's that?"

"In a way, sort of the opposite of whatever it was made Bugs Cartier into a human pincushion. A hemophiliac is a person whose blood won't clot properly. An extreme case can bleed to death from a pin prick. I'm not that bad, but I've got to be very careful; even a slight scratch can be dangerous to me."

Seton nodded: "I've heard of that, but I didn't recognize the name. Was Cartier's act on the level, or was there any trick about it?"

"There wasn't any gaff. He could stick pins into himself without it hurting, or without bleeding. Not straight in, of course. He just stuck them under the skin, ran them along parallel to the surface, and then out again. Like a needle through cloth."

"He didn't feel it?"

"Not much anyway. It used to give me the willies to watch him do it, though. He'd even take a needle and thread and sew buttons on himself."

"You think he wouldn't have felt it when—uh—somebody stuck those needles into him last night?"

"I've been thinking about that," I said. "I think he would have. His insensitivity was just surface, just his skin. But don't forget, first that he was dead drunk, and second, that if that one through his heart was the first one in, he wouldn't have had a chance to feel the others. That's the way I figure it happened."

"How many people knew he sometimes slept on the stage in the end compartment of the tent?"

"I guess anybody with the show could have known it," I said. "I don't know just which ones did."

"You figure it this way, Gaynor? After he's asleep somebody peels back the blanket and jabs the pin into his heart, and then sticks the others in?"

"It must have been that way. Unless the first one was the fatal one, it would have awakened him, drunk or not. The pins, by the way, look like the ones Bugs used in his act. I think you'll find they were. He used about a dozen of them."

"All at once?"

I shook my head. "Never saw him use more than three at once, but he carried a battery of them for flash."

"And the snake? Berger, the coroner, was just in here and told me about it. How do you figure a dead snake figures in this?"

"I don't," I told him honestly. "I can't even make an intelligent guess about that. But I can tell you when it disappeared, and how."

He listened intently while I told him about the episode of the night before last. I expected a storm and felt relieved when all he said was, "You should have reported it. Do you think that whoever it was knocked the flash out of your hand stole the snake—or just opened the box?"

"I wouldn't even guess. But I'll tell you one thing. The snake didn't crawl into Bugs' bedroll then because he got back in afterward. He'd have felt it. He sleeps in nothing but a pair of shorts—as you found him this morning."

"Hm-m-m," said Seton. "Then you think it was put there, in his bedroll, I mean, *after* he was killed?"

I thought that over a minute before I answered. "Not necessarily," I told him. "If he was as drunk as I think he was when he turned in, it might have been there without his knowing about it."

Seton said, "Getting back to the stealing of the snake, could it have been handled by anybody? Anybody with the carnival, I mean."

"Sure. King was tame and harmless. Wait—I can eliminate one. Ralph Chapman, the magician. He has a horror of snakes and wouldn't have gone near one on a bet. He has what's practically a phobia about snakes."

"But anybody else might have?"

"As far as I know. Most of us have a normal dislike of touching snakes, I guess, but not enough of an aversion to keep us from picking one up if we had an important reason. Only—"

"Only what?"

"Only *damned* if I can figure any reason why anybody, with the carney or otherwise, would have stolen and killed King and put him in Bugs' bedroll. Just doesn't make sense."

"How valuable was this Black King?"

I said, "Not enough for that to be much of a factor. Less than a hundred bucks, anyway."

Seton sighed. He took a cigar from his pocket and bit off the end. He said, "This is a hell of a case. Let's get back to you. How long did you know Cartier?"

"Bugs joined the carney the middle of last season. That was the first time I ever saw him. He's been with some little outfit out on the West coast."

"How did he get with Tookerman Shows?"

"Lee hired him through Bugs' ad in *Billboard*. The carney he was with out there folded, and he stuck an At Liberty ad in the wanteds."

"Know anything about his affairs, his relations with other people around here?"

"He hadn't any enemies I know of," I said. "Kind of a good-natured screwball. Nobody took him very seriously."

"Until last night," said Seton dryly. "Norris, by the way, told me Bugs flashed a roll last night. Tell me what you know about that."

I told him.

Seton asked, "He could have won it gambling?"

I said, "I don't think it likely. It was big money for Bugs; he seldom shot more than a dime or a quarter at a time and, at that rate, he wouldn't have had time enough to run it up to real folding money. It was too shortly after closing. Was there any money in his clothes when you examined them?"

"Not a cent. He might have spent it all or been rolled while he was off the lot, but—"

Seton nodded. "But it's more likely the killer took it. Maybe—took it back."

That talk with Seton made me feel better about things. Helsing was a good guy, but he hadn't shown any streaks of brilliance. I was putting my money on Seton now.

Funny, I thought; twice in two weeks now I'd scratched a copper and found a decent guy under the blue.

Or was Seton just stringing us along? It seemed not, for by two o'clock in the afternoon he told us we could go ahead and open.

We opened, but the crowds were thin that afternoon on the midway. Everybody seemed to work in a desultory way, as if they were waiting for something, not knowing quite what. Colonel Toots was in one of his black, cantankerous moods. He wouldn't put any oomph into the bally.

I did my best to turn the scanty tips, but the percentage wasn't good. It wasn't even fair. If the crowd that afternoon was representative, then Wilmot was going to be a tough town. I wanted to talk it over with Lee to see if he could suggest any way to pep up the percentage; but Lee had gone in to town with Seton, and would probably be gone most of the day.

After a while, during a time when the only marks in front of the platform were ones who'd been there a long time and apparently had no intention of going farther I told Slim to hold down the fort and strolled inside.

Ralph was just finishing his spiel. He had a small tip and made no sales. Disgustedly, he directed them across the tent to listen to the colonel, and came to join me at the ridge pole.

"They're dead, Pete, all of them. Not a live one in this town. I dropped from two bits to a dime and didn't sell any anyway, so I put the price back up. Haven't taken in two bucks all afternoon. What do they want for two bits?"

"Maybe they want Mae Cole," I told him. "Say, did she get to first base with Seton?"

"Don't know. But, hell, if she did, it'd be out now. We're going to have coppers on our necks all the time we're here. I can't work with John Law watching every move. I even dropped a card on the monte."

He stared sourly at the policeman leaning against the opposite ridge pole, who was staring sourly in turn at Bessie, the fat woman. Bessie wasn't staring at anything; she'd gone to sleep.

Ralph chuckled. "The spirit of Wilmot. What a town. For ten lousy cents I'd chuck it and head for Florida. I can play the night clubs there, and there's only three weeks of Tookerman left anyhow."

"That would be a dirty trick on Lee," I said. "He's on the nut. He needs two weeks of gravy to get set for the winter. And Lord, Ralph, you're the only inside money he's getting."

"Nuts," said Ralph. "He won't even get peanuts on his percentage of me, if the rest of this week is like today. And lookit, Pete, there's another reason for scramming. *Who's next?*"

"What you mean?"

"You know what I mean. Al and Bugs. And then maybe you, maybe me, maybe Stella."

I felt something start to boil up inside me and I choked it down. Suddenly— for mentioning Stella that way—I wanted to take a poke at the guy. But if he was on the verge of leaving us like a rat deserting a sinking ship, a poke would be all he needed to make it sure.

I said, "That's silly. Why would anybody kill one of us?"

"Why did somebody kill Al and Bugs?"

"Probably somebody had a reason for killing Al. And the same guy killed Bugs because he found out something he shouldn't have. That won't apply to any of the others of us—at least without our knowing about it."

Yes, I choked down my anger and made myself reason with him. I could call him a rat, or yellow, but that wouldn't help Lee any.

He took a half dollar out of his pocket and it twinkled between his fingers as he back and front palmed it while he talked. He said quietly, "And Black King. Did he know too much?"

There wasn't any answer to that, not any that I could think of at the moment, so I didn't say anything.

The half dollar twinkled a moment and then was gone. Ralph turned his hand backward and forward as though looking for it, and then spread his fingers apart.

He said, "You think I'm a louse, don't you, Pete?"

A minute ago, I had. But it's hard to answer yes when a guy asks you that, quietly and calmly.

I said, "I . . . I wouldn't put it that strongly, Ralph. But, dammit, if you walk out on Lee—"

He nodded. "Come on back to the wagon. I want to show you something. Then maybe you won't think I'm talking through my hat."

VI

I SAID, "Wait a minute," and went out front again. There was a bally going on in front of the girl show and nearly all the people on our end of the midway were over there. It wouldn't hurt to be gone another fifteen minutes or so.

Slim grinned at me. "Can I sell you a ticket, mister?"

"I'll be gone fifteen or twenty minutes, Slim," I told him. "If you want to shut the gate and get yourself a mug of java, go ahead."

"Swell. Help me stay awake, through all this rush of business."

I went back to Ralph and we went under the side wall and back to the big red wagon back of Lee's trailer. I knew Ralph kept his trunk and his bedding there, and slept there. Bugs kept his stuff there, too, but always slept in the top.

I quit trying to guess what Ralph was going to show me, and just followed him as he climbed into the wagon. He crossed over to the roll of bedding and unrolled it, then lifted the top blanket carefully.

I said, "What's the—"

And then the blanket went back farther, and I saw what was lying on the bedding under the center of it. I started to laugh, and the laughter stuck in my throat, because maybe it was as far from funny as anything I'd ever seen.

It was a toy snake, about a foot long, painted bright green and yellow and made up of jointed wooden segments. I recognized it as having come from the marble-game concession up at the front end of the midway. Curley Bates, who ran marbles, had a dozen of them among his flash.

Ralph said, "Somebody put it there this morning. It wasn't there last night."

"But why—"

"I can't even guess," Ralph said. I noticed that his eyes were on me, and not on the toy, and that there were slight beads of sweat on his forehead.

He said, "Uh— Take it, will you, Pete. I . . . I just can't make myself touch the damn thing. It's silly, yes, and I know it's not a real snake and just a toy, but . . . but I *can't.*"

I said, "Sure, Ralph." I picked it up and it wriggled quite realistically as I turned my hand. Then I caught a glimpse of Ralph's face, and stuffed the toy out of sight into my pocket. I know what a phobia is; I'd known phobiacs before.

I asked, "How do you know it was put there this morning? How'd you happen to find it?"

"It *wasn't* there last night. And about noon when I came back to get my sleeve-pull, I noticed that my bedroll didn't look the way I'd left it. I always have the edges neat. I wondered who'd messed with it, and I opened it out to roll it again."

He was rolling it again, neatly, while he talked. I leaned against the side wall of the wagon, my hand still in my pocket and touching the toy snake, and—I began to get scared.

I don't know why. There'd been two murders within a week, and *they* didn't scare me. But there'd been two things that were outwardly much less important than murders, and they *did* scare me. The business about Black King, and now this about the toy snake.

Murder, a man can understand. It's something he doesn't understand that can give him the screaming meamies.

Ralph was lighting a cigarette and his hand shook a little. He said, "I got to leave, Pete."

Well, I had to talk him out of that again. I said, "Don't be a dope, Ralph. Just because somebody plays a joke—" I couldn't quite finish it convincingly, because anybody who understood Ralph's abnormal fear of snakes wouldn't consider that a joke.

Ralph said, "How'd you go for a drink?" And before I answered, he opened his trunk beside the bedroll and pulled out a bottle and a shot glass. He poured some in the glass, spilling a little of it, and handed it to me.

"I'll drink out of the bottle, Pete. Listen, I know why somebody put that there. The toy snake, I mean."

"Why?"

"To let me know what they'd intended to do. What they missed doing. See?"

I didn't. I didn't get it at all, and while I was thinking it over I tossed down the whiskey. Then I asked what he meant.

"Black King. He got put in Bugs' bedroll by mistake—he was meant for mine! Last night somebody put him in Bugs' bedding by mistake, Pete. And this morning they put that . . . that toy in there to let me know what I'd missed. To give me something to think about."

"But that's—" I couldn't quite say it was crazy, because it made a kind of sense. If somebody was deliberately trying to scare Ralph Chapman that somebody was succeeding. His face was a yellowish white—just from *thinking* how close he had come to getting into bed with a seven-foot snake.

Yes, it would have been a dead snake, and even if it were alive it wouldn't have hurt him, but things like that carry no weight against the blinding unreasoning fear that is phobia. Feeling a big, real snake in close contact with him in the dark—whether that snake was alive or dead—would have probably sent Ralph to a sanitarium. Even thinking about it was doing him a lot of no good.

And, understanding how he felt, I couldn't blame the guy, but—

"Ralph," I said, "you *got* to stick it out. Man, you're a trouper; you aren't going to let something scare you into ratting on the show only a few weeks from close."

"But maybe next time it won't be a toy!"

"Phooey." I spoke with a confidence I was far from feeling. "Hey, I got an idea. How's the weasel sack?"

"I got money. Not a lot, but—"

"Look, I know how you feel, after finding that thing, and I don't blame you. But there's an easy out. There are a couple of houses that have furnished rooms to rent within a few blocks of the lot here. For anyway the rest of our stay in Wilmot, why don't you take a furnished room instead of sleeping here? Cost you only a few bucks, and maybe it'd do you good to pretend you're civilized for a while anyway. Get used to sleeping in a bed before you hit the nightclub circuit."

"Pete, that's an idea." There was what seemed to be genuine gratitude in Ralph's eyes, and I knew I'd hit the answer. "Pete, it isn't the days—but I just couldn't face going to sleep here. Wondering who might—hell, there isn't even any way you can lock this wagon from the inside. Have another drink on that!"

"Sure." I held out my glass while he poured a stiffer one than the first.

"I . . . I got rattled, Pete. I should've thought of that answer myself. I don't *want* to rat on Lee if I can keep from it. Even if—"

"If what?"

He hesitated. "Maybe I should have kept my yap shut about this, Pete. Because I'm not sure. But—"

"Get it off your chest. But what?"

"I think Lee owed money to Al Hryner."

I whistled softly. "*Lee* owing money to a canvasman? Hell, Ralph, Lee pays salaries on the dot, and if he covers the others why would he have held out on a canvasman's lousy few bucks? Or—Wait a minute, do you mean gambling?"

For suddenly I remembered Helsing's telling me that the dice he'd found in Al Hryner's pocket were crooked dice. And if Al had got Lee pyramiding in a crap game—but no, that didn't make sense either. Lee wasn't born yesterday, and he wouldn't have shot for big stakes with somebody else's crooked dice. Matter of fact, Lee never gambled heavily anyway—with dice or cards. He didn't have to gamble that way—backing and running a freak show is enough of an odds-on bet for any man.

Chapman said, "It wasn't salary and I don't think it was gambling. I think Hryner had a stake and invested it with Lee."

"A stake? Hm-m-m—it doesn't quite make sense, Ralph. A canvasman having enough money to invest it with a big concession like this. Why, Lee's got ten to twenty thousand tied up in this show. More, come to think of it. Anyway, where'd you get the idea?"

"I heard them talking once, Pete. Didn't get all of it, but got the idea that Hryner had a couple hundred bucks when he came here and—well, it could have been that he gave it to Lee to keep for him, but I got the idea that if Lee could use it, he was going to pay it back with a bonus."

I thought it over and it could be. Lee was hard pressed for running capital lately. Still—"You sure it was only a couple hundred?" I asked.

"I thought Lee mentioned a couple of C's; it *could* have been a couple of G's instead. Whichever it was, Lee won't have to pay it back now. Don't get me wrong, Pete; I don't mean Lee would have killed Al for a couple of hundred bucks."

I grinned. "But you think for a couple of thousand, he might have."

Ralph didn't grin back. He said, "A couple of thousand is a lot of money. And Lee's having to borrow now anyway. He's running in debt to Tookerman, and to Gus Smith."

"Gus? Hell, I didn't think Gus would lend his own mother money."

Ralph said, "The way I get it, he's taking a lien on some of the physical property. The top and the platforms and banners and stuff."

"What would he do with that?" I wanted to know. "Does he intend to run two shows next year? That is, if Lee can't square up?"

Ralph shook his head. "Gus was fair about that. He doesn't want two shows. He'd let Lee operate it next year and settle out of the profits. But until settlement, technical ownership would be Gus'—that is, the physical property, not the concession."

"Well, that's a fair enough arrangement," I said. "Say, we better get back. I'll put on one more bally and then grind awhile before the crowd goes home to eat."

By eight o'clock Lee still wasn't there. But the terror was starting.

It was something difficult to define, something you couldn't put your finger on. I know I felt it, and couldn't tell just why, or just what I was afraid of.

Maybe there's something to this business about mental telepathy and mass hysteria. It couldn't have been exactly telepathy, though, unless it was that the minds of everybody with the show were in tune with each other in some way that left outsiders on the outside. The marks didn't feel it. I watched them to see.

But there was a minute just before I was getting ready to start a bally, when I happened to look across the platform at Colonel Toots. There was terror in his strange little face.

His eyes caught mine and he motioned to me. I put down the mike and went over to him. He said, "Pete, I'm through. I'll stick out this evening."

Knowing I didn't have to ask, I asked anyway, "Why?"

"*I don't want to be murdered!*" His voice rose shrilly at the end of it; so much so that I gave a quick look out front to see if the suckers could hear us. But they couldn't, I guess.

I bent over so I wouldn't have to talk loudly. I said, "Don't get excited, colonel. There's nothing to worry—"

"The hell with you. I'm quitting, tonight. Before somebody cuts off my head."

"*Cuts off your head?* Where on earth do you get a wild idea like—"

"That's what they'd do to a midget, isn't it? To make him shorter! Don't you see it, you dope. How was Al Hryner killed?"

"With a tent stake. But what's that got to do with it?"

"He was a canvasman, wasn't he? Worked with tent stakes. And how'd they kill the pincushion? With pins. They took Stellas snake and I'll bet they were going to kill her with it. There's a crazy guy with this show, Pete. Well, he isn't going to get *me!* I'm—"

"Shut up," I said. "Colonel, you're working yourself up to a case of jitters. Can it. Think about something else, anyway till Lee gets back."

"Yeah, and where is Lee? Would he stay down at the station *this* long? I'll bet *he's* murdered, Pete. Right now he's lying out in a ditch somewhere with—"

Well, I wasn't getting anywhere with Colonel Toots, and by listening to him I was letting him talk himself into the screaming meamies.

I went over and hammered on the bass drum instead, and when I had a tip, or anyway the start of one, I picked up the mike and started to spiel.

After the next grind I pulled out Shorty and Stella for the bally instead of Colonel Toots.

Maybe I shouldn't have. It was Shorty's turn to pop off, and being out on the platform gave him a chance.

He said, "Listen, Pete, I think we better call off the knife throwing for tonight. Agnes is nervous."

"Nuts," I said. "Why should she be nervous? She knows by now you don't miss with those knives. And there's —"

"Sure, I don't miss. But— Grief, I know how she feels with everything that's been going on around here. Suppose somebody pulled something like changing the weighting in those throwing knives?"

"Don't be a dope. You could tell the minute you picked one up."

"Yeah, but something else then. Look, she's going to have a nervous breakdown or something if she keeps on flinching like she's been doing every time I throw one. She's a good trouper, but— Look, Pete, I'll go on swallowing swords and I'll stretch the act there. I'll hold 'em ten minutes instead of five, with the swords."

I said, "All right, all right. But you got to have Agnes around for flash. Have her on the platform with you and have her hand you the stuff you use instead of you taking it off the display board."

He grinned. "Atta boy, Pete. Then it won't matter what I do anyway. They'll watch Agnes' legs instead."

I was pretty thoughtful while I hammered the drum.

Pretty soon, at this rate, we just weren't going to have any show left. No pincushion. Maybe after tonight, no midget. The cooch blow and the mitt camp sloughed. Ralph ready to leave if somebody pushed an oversize worm at him.

Not so good. All we had left besides the colonel and Ralph was half of Shorty O'Hara's part in the show, Bessie Williams, and Stella. And Stella's good snake was gone; now she had only the two four-foot bull snakes to work with, and they didn't have the flash of Black King. Sure, Black King had been a bull, too, but he had flash. You could call him a blacksnake or a python or a constrictor, and get by with it.

When I finished ballying and turned all of the tip I could get inside the top, I strolled back to the entrance and watched inside for a while.

Ralph was doing his act, manipulating the cardboards. His voice sounded jerky and his movements were wooden—for a prestidigitator. The others, too, sat around listlessly. I noticed that Stella's face was utterly blank, and I wondered what went on behind it. Was she, too, sharing the fear that the rest of the performers felt so obviously? Well, I'd see her after close and find out.

Someone behind me said, "Mr. Gaynor?" I turned.

She was a blonde and she was beautiful, but she looked tough. You get used to tough dames in carney, but this one was tougher—if looks meant anything.

Rather warily, I admitted my name.

She said, "The guy at the ticket box said you could tell me where I'd find Lee Werner."

"Went to town this afternoon and isn't back yet. Anything I can do for you?"

"Uh—I guess not. I'll wait." She smiled brightly. "How goes the keeassarney?"

I said, "Ok," and tried to keep from frowning. She wasn't a carney or she wouldn't have used the carney double talk that way without reason. It's showoff outsiders who pop it casually, and carneys never use it unless they want to get something across over the heads of a tip. Outside carney, mostly chorines or chippies use it. This one could have been either—or both.

"He'll be back tonight, won't he?" she asked.

I said, "I think so. I better get back on the platform. You can wait here or look around inside."

"I'll look around inside."

She turned to go in, but just then I saw Lee coming, and I said, "Wait." And then, "Here he comes. How'll I introduce you?"

"Mrs. Hryner, Dotty Hryner. I was Al's wife."

VII

LEE WANDERED UP, looking like a lost soul. He said, "Hi, Pete. How's business?"

"Lousy," I told him. "Lee, this is Dotty Hryner. Says she was Al's wife. Wants to see you."

And, because I was curious what she wanted to see him about, I stuck around.

Lee said, "I suppose your husband told you about the money, Mrs. Hryner?"

The blonde nodded. "He said a hundred and fifty."

"That's right," said Lee. "Or two hundred at the end of the season. He asked me to keep it for him and I could use it if I wanted. And I said I would, but in that case I'd give him back two hundred at the end of the season. Which way you want it?"

"Which way—I don't get it."

Lee grinned. "Sure, you get it. But you can have the hundred fifty right now, or if you want to wait a few weeks till the season's over, you get two hundred. But, of course, you can prove you're really Mrs. Hryner. I suppose you have something to prove that?"

She nodded again eagerly. "I got a letter Al sent me the week he joined up with you." She fished in her handbag, among some papers, and pulled out an envelope. She handed it to Lee and I stepped around to look over his shoulder.

The envelope was O.K. It had "Al Hryner, Tookerman Shows, do Billboard, Cincinnati, Ohio," as the return address. It was addressed to Dotty Wilbur, at an address in Chicago. Postmark was in August.

Dotty caught Lee's glance resting on the name. She said, "That's my maiden name. I was using it because I was with a show in Chi. I used my stage name, naturally."

Without comment, Lee took the single sheet of writing paper out of the envelope. The handwriting was the same as that on the envelope. The letter read:

Dear Dotty: Joined up with Tookerman and I'm handling canvas for Lee Werner, who runs the freak show. The hundred and fifty bucks I had with me I gave to Lee to keep, because, neither of us needs it now. If anything should happen to me, you can get it from Lee.

Doc B. did a swell job and I'm feeling great. Let me know if there's any change in your address or anything. I'll head for Chi at the end of the season and—

The page ended there, and there wasn't anything on the other side when Lee turned it over.

Dotty said, "I lost the rest of the letter. I kept that page because it had your name and address on it. It... it hasn't got Al's name on it, and I never thought about that part because I never thought I'd have to use it, see? But you can compare the handwriting with his name on your records, and—"

"That's all right," said Lee. "You want one-fifty now or two at the end of the season?"

"I—uh—it don't matter much. I can wait till the end of the season. Look, what I really want most is a job. I can cooch. I'm good."

Lee looked surprised. "Huh? Sorry, we got a cooch girl and, anyway—"

"*Please,* Mr. Werner. I know it's near the end of the season, but I've always wanted to get into a carney, like Al was. And getting on with you will give me a start, and next year— But that's thinking too far ahead. Look, why don't you have *two* cooch girls the rest of the season. I'll work for almost nothing. I—"

"Sorry," said Lee. "But—"

I tapped him gently on the shoulder to stop him. I said, "Mrs. Hryner, mind if I talk to Lee a minute alone? I got an idea how we might work you in."

She gave me a dazzling smile that might have swept me off my feet if I went for glamour blondes with too much make-up even for carney.

She said, "Go ahead, Mr. Gaynor. Theeasanks."

Lee winced and I grabbed his arm and pulled him across the tent before he said anything.

Back behind Bessie's backdrop, I said, "Listen, Lee, give her a job. I got a hunch."

He snorted. "That dame? Anyone who says—"

"Hold everything and listen, Lee. There's something screwy about her. Theeasanks or not, she's got no legit reason for wanting a job with you. Anyway, not so bad she'd offer to work for almost nothing. Don't let her walk off till we find out what makes her tick. Do you really think she's Al's wife?"

"His wife or something. That letter was on the up-and-up. I recognized Al's writing. And I do owe that dough. Only I'd rather she'd take the one-fifty and get the hell out of—"

"Shut up," I said. "Listen, we *can* use her. Shorty's wife's got the jitters and won't let him throw shivs at her. I had to tell him O.K., to leave out the throwing routine and stick to swallowing. You know how much that cuts the show, when it's cut already without the blow and without Hassan Bey and without Bugs—"

"Why didn't you tell me? Dammit, Agnes ought to—"

"Don't blame Agnes. Listen, I know how she feels and so do the rest of us. Right now *I* wouldn't let anybody around here throw knives at me for a million bucks a throw."

"*You*, yeah. You're a bleeder. But, dammit, Shorty's her husband. I got a mind to—"

"You got a mind to break up the show? Ralph's on the verge of quitting. The colonel's quit already, but I think you can talk him out of it if you fix things up so he can sleep in a room somewhere instead of on the lot. Now if this dame's willing to take Agnes' spot, and do it for peanuts, what you got to lose?"

"Hm-m-m," said Lee. It was a disgusted-sounding grunt, but I knew he was beginning to see reason.

"Look," I said, "for a few days anyway, until we find out what's what. Tell her you'll try her out on cooch later, but there's no cooch in Wilmot and if she wants to stand in for the knife-thrower while she's waiting, you're killing three birds with one stone. For free."

"Hm-m-m," said Lee. "Guess she's about the right size to wear that costume of Agnes'. Wonder if she's got legs."

"She's a chorine. She must have legs, especially if she wants to cooch. Whyn't you ask her to show you?"

And then before I oversold my product, I said, "I better get back for a bally out front. After you look at her legs, don't forget to soap up the colonel about quitting tonight. And listen, better mention casually to Ralph that you're giving Al's wife the money you owed Al."

"Huh? Why?"

"It'll take a load off his mind, and he's got several. Including this dingus he found in his bed today."

I pulled the toy snake partly out of my pocket so he could see it, and then stuffed it back in before anybody else could notice.

Lee whistled. "Now who the hell would have put that in Ralph's bed?"

"There wasn't a card with it," I told him. "Not even 'Compliments of a Friend.' Better see Dotty before she decides we're calling copper on her and lams."

I went back to the platform and worked awhile.

A couple of ballys later, I yelled for swords, and Shorty came out. But he had his throwing knives with him and Dotty was trailing along after, wearing one of Agnes' costumes. She had gams, all right. If it wasn't for the hardness of her face she'd have been beautiful. Maybe she was, anyway; being in love with Stella I wasn't a judge.

Shorty O'Hara was smiling at Dotty and that meant, unless I missed my guess, that Agnes would pretty darned soon snap out of her jitters and be back in front of the knife board again. By tomorrow at the latest, and sooner if she got a good look at Dotty.

Crowds began to taper off around eleven, and I took time out to walk up to the marble-roll concession. I showed the toy snake to Curley and asked him if it had come from his booth.

He shrugged. "Could have, Pete. I passed out half a dozen of them last week."

I said, "I found this inside a wagon, where a mark couldn't have dropped it. How about the carneys—any of them buy or win one of these from you?"

"No. What you worrying about it for? They cost only four forty a gross."

"It isn't the initial cost, Curley," I told him. "It's the upkeep." And leaving him puzzling over that I went back to the freak show. I hadn't really expected to find out anything, because whoever had put the snake in Ralph Chapman's bed wouldn't have obtained it openly.

By twelve things had tapered off enough that Lee told me to knock off. I took in the mike and the bass drum, and then hung around until the final tip had moved on past Stella's act. Then I took her to the chow top for coffee.

"Pete," she said while we were waiting for Hank to bring on the doughnuts, "did you notice how everyone was feeling tonight? I'm wondering how long—"

I nodded. "Everybody's scared stiff, honey. Even me. How about you?"

"I . . . I guess I'm scared, too, Pete. It's awful to feel that way, and not to know just what you're scared about. Who is the girl taking Agnes' place, Pete? I . . . I don't think I'm going to like her."

I told her about Dotty, and some of my reasons for wanting her to be with the show for a while.

Stella said, "But, Pete aren't you sticking your own neck out? You think having her here may bring—things to a head, but you don't even know what you mean by 'things'? You're groping in the dark."

"Sure, but if you grope long enough in the dark you're bound to catch hold of *something*. It's sitting with your hands in your pockets that gets you nowhere fast."

"But it isn't your job, Pete, to find out what's going on. The police—"

"The police are trying, but they aren't getting anywhere. And, meanwhile, Lee's show is heading for the rocks. I hate to see Lee end up the season with a deficit and not even own the props he'll have to start out with next year. Sure, Gus'll let him run the show and pay back out of the profits, but it's hell to start way behind the nut."

My hand was lying on the table and she put hers over it. She said, "You're a good guy, Pete. If you would —"

"Hold the ifs," I said. "Stick to that I'm a good guy. Good enough to marry, even?"

"If you—Pete, why can't or won't you save your money?"

"What money?" I wanted to know. And then when I saw her face change, I said, "Aw, now, Stella. I was only kidding. Matter of fact, I have got a little ahead, and I've put it where I can't get at it easily and that's why I've been broke a lot recently. Won't you—"

"Where? What did you do with the money?"

"Now listen, Stella, a guy's got a right to—"

"Where?"

I sighed. "All right, it was a fool thing to do, but I lent it to Lee.

Now you see why I'm groping in the dark. If the show folds, well—maybe I get it back some day, maybe not. But Lee was in a tough spot—"

Her hand touched mine again. She said, "You're a dope, Pete. But maybe that's why I like you."

"Then you *will* marry me? That is—if Lee gets on his feet again and we get the show going O.K.? Honest, honey, I—"

And only then was I aware that somebody was standing by our table. I looked up and it was Ralph Chapman, and then I saw something else down at table level and it was the top of Colonel Toots' head.

Ralph said, "Got any idea which way we should head to find rooms?"

It took me seconds to figure out what he was talking about and get my mind on it.

"There's a hotel along the car line that goes by the lot. About ten or twelve blocks toward town. It's the nearest you can get put up at tonight, I guess. It's too late to go looking for rooms in houses."

Ralph said, "We'll go there for tonight then. They run owls on that line?"

I looked to see if Stella had finished her coffee and doughnuts, and she had. I said, "I'll borrow Lee's car and drive you guys to the hotel. Want to come along for the ride, Stella?"

She shook her head. "I'm tired, Pete. Didn't sleep much last night. I'll turn in."

"Come on then. I'll walk you back to the sleeper."

"Take your time," Ralph said. "We'll have something to eat while we're waiting for you."

Walking back along the darkened midway, I tried to bring the conversation back to the point at which it had been interrupted. But the mood was lost and I gave up. We parted amicably, but unromantically.

I knocked on the window of Lee's trailer, told him I was taking the car, and then drove it off the lot and parked it on the side nearest the chow top.

When I went back in, Gus had joined Ralph and the colonel at the table.

I said, "Hi, Gus. Don't tell me you're moving off the lot, too?"

He grinned. "If I was with your show, damned if I wouldn't. I don't blame these mugs a bit." I saw there wasn't any humor in his grin. "Pete, why don't you be smart and play safe?"

"You answered it," I told him. "I'm not smart."

Ralph was just starting a sandwich, so I sat down and called over to Hank to bring me some more coffee.

Ralph said, "Pete, it's none of my business, but did I overhear you saying something to Stella about your investing some money with Lee?"

Well, he'd called the shot; it was none of his business. So I passed it off by saying, "I'm thinking about it."

He persisted, *"You* mean buying a partnership in the show?"

"Maybe. Say, Ralph, remember your wondering about Lee owing Hryner some chicken feed?"

Ralph's eyes widened. "Does he admit it?"

"Sure he admits it; it wasn't any secret. Hryner's woman showed up tonight, and Lee's going to give it to her. Gave her a job, too."

"Hryner's woman? You mean that dizzy blonde Shorty was tossing steel at?" Ralph whistled. "She's three-alarm. What was a canvasman like Al doing with a doll like that?"

"Same as you'd like to do," I told him. "Hurry up that sandwich. I want to get to bed some time tonight."

It was a full hour later, though, when I put Lee's car back by the trailer and headed for the railroad car my bunk was in.

Slim Norris was coming down the steps of the car, and there was a suitcase in his hand. He lurched as his foot hit the cinder path along the rails, and I saw he was drunk.

I said, "Where you going, Slim?"

"Quitting. Hell with it." He backed along the side of the car as I stepped toward him. "Keep away from me, Gaynor."

"Slim, you're tight. Lee know you're walking out on him?"

Without thinking about it, I'd taken another step toward him, and he scuttled away backward, keeping his balance by bracing one hand against the car. "Keep away from me, Gaynor. I'll—"

Then he stepped into a patch of moonlight and I saw his eyes. They were wide with terror. He was afraid, deathly afraid—and of me. It took me a minute to get it.

Then I remembered what he'd said this morning—*had* it been only this morning?—when he'd found Bugs' body. "—murdered just like you thought'd be funny!" Because of that ill-timed wisecrack about pinning down a pincushion, Slim thought *I* was the murderer.

I said, "Dammit, Slim," and then realized that nothing I could say would be able to convince him here and now. Particularly when I was here alone with him in the dark.

I took a step back away from him knowing that would do more good at the moment than anything I could say. Then, with my hands carefully at my sides and keeping my voice calm and low, I tried to reason with him.

I said, "Listen, Slim, Chapman and the colonel are scared to sleep on the lot, too. But they aren't running out on the show. They took rooms at the Burgoyne Hotel, Twenty-first and Hopkins. I just drove them there. You won't be able to get a train out tonight anyway, so why don't you take a room there, too? Then think it over in the morning."

He said, "Well—yeah, but—"

"You're afraid of me because of that remark I happened to make about a pincushion last night. Did you tell the police about it?"

He shook his head:

"All right, in the morning you tell them and get it off your mind. Then you'll feel better about it."

I pointed. "See that light over there? It's an all-night drugstore. You go there and phone for a cab to take you to the Burgoyne. If you still feel the same way in the morning then tell Lee you're leaving and quit like a man."

I saw he was wavering and had sense enough not to press my advantage. Instead, I left him standing there and went on inside the car. I didn't even look out the window to see whether he was taking my advice. It wouldn't matter too much if he didn't; Lee could always get somebody else to take tickets. Just the same it would be setting a bad example. Like starting a run on a bank.

I turned on the dim light and started to undress.

If I'd turned out that light before I threw back the thin blanket to get into bed I'd never have seen it. But I didn't turn out the light because—well, I don't know just why I varied from routine that night unless subconsciously I remembered Ralph Chapman's bedroll and the toy snake that had been in it.

Anyway, I peeled back the covers, standing there dressed only in my shorts. And lying flat in the middle of my bed was a thin and flexible, but very dangerous-looking double-edged razor blade.

VIII

I PICKED the thing up, very gingerly, and then, because I don't like even to hold one of the things, I dropped it onto the window ledge. I stood looking at it with some of the feeling Ralph Chapman must have had when he looked at that toy snake.

The blade wasn't mine, of course. Needless to say, I shave with an electric razor. A nick from an ordinary razor wouldn't be fatal, in my case; I'd certainly know about it and I've got stuff that will stop the bleeding with a bit of trouble.

The blade wasn't mine, and there was no way it could have got there accidentally. It was put there either to scare me, or to kill me. I weighed the odds on which—and there was only one answer. The person who put it there couldn't have known whether it would have killed me or not. The odds were against it, but it was a definite possibility.

A cut from a really sharp blade can be painful—or the pain can be so slight as to be almost unnoticeable. I toss about a bit in my sleep, and with that blade under me I *could* have cut myself on it without feeling enough pain to awaken me, and bled to death in my sleep. Could have, yes, but it wasn't any surefire murder method. I might not have cut myself at all, or the cut might have been one which would have awakened me.

Slowly, I put my shirt back on, and then sat down on the edge of the bed and began to pull on my socks and shoes. I wasn't sleepy any more.

This was hitting close to home now and I had a sudden yen to talk to the police. To Helsing, if I could find him, or to Seton if I couldn't find Helsing. It takes quite a scare to make a carney feel that the coppers are his friends instead of his natural enemies, but right now I felt that way, plenty.

I was through groping in the dark on my own. I saw now that I should have insisted that Ralph go to the police about finding that toy snake. And the minute Hryner's wife had shown up on the lot I should have phoned the police and told them about it—instead of waiting to mention it casually the next time Seton came to the lot.

I should even have told them about Ralph's suspicions of Lee—even though those suspicions had turned out since to be unfounded. Loyalty to Lee was important, but it was more important to stop further murders from being committed. The police should be given all the leads, even if they were false ones. And even false ones were damned few. The further things went, the further I was from making even an intelligent guess as to who was trying to accomplish what.

It had to be one of us, I realized. Someone who knew the freak show well enough to know Bugs sometimes slept in the cooch blow, that Ralph had a morbid horror of snakes, that I had hemophilia.

I left the blade where it was and flicked out the light and left the car. I was going straight down the tracks to the street and from there to the all-night drugstore where I could phone the police.

Sure, my intentions were good. I was through messing with the case on my own—or I thought I was until I stepped down from the car.

And then I didn't move, because I heard the crunch of cinders that meant somebody walking along or across the tracks. I froze, and strained my eyes through the dimness. The footsteps were stealthy; whoever was walking was trying to do so without making any sound. Only the utter stillness of the night defeated that purpose.

Then I saw him—or her—going past the far end of the car I'd just left. A dim white figure—I could make out no details. And as soon as it stepped from the tracks to the path onto the lot, the sound of footsteps ceased.

I hesitated only an instant before I followed. True, I might be following someone on his way to the doniker—but from the attempted stealth of the footsteps, I didn't think so.

And again, I *might* be following the murderer. I might have a chance, a chance that would never come again, to find out what this was all about, possibly to avert a crime and save a life. At the very least I was going to ascertain the identity of that vague white figure.

One long step carried me to the turf along the edge of the cinders, and I ran silently along it to the path into the lot. The path turned through some trees that separated the lot from the tracks. I rounded that turn breathlessly—and just in time to see the white figure ducking under the canvas side wall of the freak-show top. A second later and I'd have been too late.

I ran up to the canvas but I didn't lift it to go under. Anyone inside would have found it too easy to see or hear that. Instead I went flat and crawled partly under.

I lay there with my head inside the tent, wondering whether I was stymied. Because I couldn't see a thing in the deeper blackness inside the top. There wasn't even enough light for me to make out the white figure if it was there.

It might even have gone on through and out the opposite side wall—but no, that was silly. Its purpose must be here inside the top, or it would have been easier to go around the freak show rather than to grope through the cluttered blackness inside.

Then, only a few yards away from me, a light shone dimly. It was a masked flashlight, but I could make out that it was held by a woman, and that the woman was Dotty Hryner.

I wriggled backward so that as little of me as possible—besides my eyes—would show, and I watched wonderingly to find out what she was doing here.

She was standing there doing nothing for the moment except flashing the dimmed light on the mitt camp. I got a side view of her as she stood that way, and of the flashlight. I could see that she had tied several thicknesses of handkerchief across the lens to dim it down—obviously so that the light wouldn't show through the tent, and so no one outside could see that a light was being used.

Yes, that much was obvious, but why she should be interested in the mitt camp was something else again. The little cubical tent of bright-red canvas where Hassan Bey told fortunes had been pitched before we'd learned that the Wilmot police wouldn't let him work. We'd let it stand because it took up space and made the interior look better. But it hadn't been used all week.

The flaps were open, as they always were except when Hassan had a mark inside.

Dotty Hryner went around the outside of the little red canvas tent first, examining and touching everything with minute curiosity. Then she examined the tent from the inside, looking along the seams, and even studying the poles. The two chairs inside were examined carefully, turned upside down, and the seats prodded. Then the little table and the stand for the mad ball.

I watched with increasing, rather than lessening bewilderment. What possible connection could there be between Dotty Hryner—if she *was* Dotty Hryner—and Hassan Bey's mitt camp. Hassan hadn't been with the show this week at all. And Dotty had just—

She must have spent all of fifteen or twenty minutes searching that crimson tent and its contents, and then she moved on, standing now before the platform on which Colonel Toots did his act. She took the bally cloth first, giving it a careful examination all the way around, feeling the seams and the fringe.

Then the diminutive chair on the platform, and— Then I began to get it, partly. She wasn't interested, particularly in Hassan's mitt camp. She'd merely *started* there; she was making the rounds, intending to examine every bit of equipment in the top in equal detail. But for what? Had Al hidden something and told her about it in that letter of which she'd shown us only the first page? Something that may have been the motive for the crimes of the past week?

The more I thought about that the more possible it looked. It was strange that Dotty should have thrown away all of that letter except the first page, and still have kept the envelope. She hadn't shown us all the letter because the second page, the part that had the signature, also contained something she didn't want us to know.

I had an idea.

I wriggled cautiously backward until my head was safely out from under the side wall, and then I looked at my wrist watch's luminous dial. It wouldn't start to get light for a couple of hours yet. And Dotty—from the thorough manner of her search—was probably intending to spend that much time inside the top. Matter of fact, at the rate she was going, it would take her several nights to complete her search. That was undoubtedly the reason she'd been willing to take any kind of a job at any kind of wages to stay on.

I walked quietly until I was out of hearing, and then broke into a run, heading for the sleeping car—the one beyond mine—in which Stella slept. It could have been that Dotty Hryner had started her nocturnal jaunt from that very car, and if so, a spot of counter espionage would be a cinch.

I rapped quietly on Stella's window. Just loud enough, I hoped, to awaken her and no one else. After a moment the window slid up a few inches.

"Pete, what on earth do you mean by—"

"*Sh-h-h,* this is important. This Dotty Hryner—where's she bunking?"

"Right here in the car. Last berth down at the end. Why?"

I told her quickly where Dotty was now and what she was doing. "Can you take a look among her things without waking anyone else? Have you a flashlight?"

"Of course, but—"

"Do it, like a good egg. Maybe we can crack this thing—tonight. What you're looking for is the rest of that letter, the first page of which she showed to me and Lee. I'm going back to watch her; I'll be lying looking under the side wall. If she starts to leave there, I'll run back here ahead of her and whistle a warning."

"If I find it?"

"Bring it to me. I can't guess what to do about it till we see what it is."

She hesitated only a moment. "All right, Pete; we're fools for not calling the police instead, but—I'll do it." The window slid down again.

When I got back and looked under the side wall again, Dotty was still working on the colonel's platform. Yes, she was doing as thorough a job of it as was humanly possible without leaving signs of the search behind her.

She was just leaving that platform and starting toward the next, when there was a light touch on my back. I pulled my head out from under the side wall. It was Stella, and she had a folded paper in her hand.

She whispered, "Is this it? It's signed 'Tommy' instead of 'Al,' but it's the only part of a letter there."

I took it from her, noticing it was the same size and kind of paper as the first page of the letter Dotty had shown to Lee and me.

Stella had a flashlight in her hand and turned it on the letter as I unfolded it. It was the same handwriting as the page I had seen and followed right after it, obviously. It read:

We'll go south. By then it'll be safe.

The stuff, you know what, is hid with the show here, in a swell place. I won't say where on account of where you're staying now. Later, when you're out of that joint, I'll tell you more about it. But nothing's going to happen anyway, Babe. This is a swell set-up and I'm having fun being back with a carney for a while.

Lots of love. Tommy

I whistled softly. Things were beginning, just faintly, to make sense. Al Hryner, whose name didn't seem to be that at all, had hidden something valuable, and that must be what all the excitement was about. At any rate it was what Dotty was hunting for in there now.

Stella whispered, "That letter might be important, Pete. We better go call the police, and—"

I said, "But what if she *finds it?* She'll scram out while we're gone, and maybe we never will find out what it was. Let's wait till she goes back to the car, and —"

I lay down again quickly and stuck my head under the side wall.

Blackness. The flashlight wasn't there anymore. Had Dotty heard us and left? But she couldn't have gone back the way she'd come without us seeing her. Or had she found what she was looking for—right while we were reading about it?

Well, if she'd found what she was looking for, it was my guess she'd have left quickly and without putting things back neatly, as she'd been doing on the rest of her search. Stella's flashlight would show, then, whether the search had been successful.

I took Stella's arm with one hand and lifted the side wall with the other and we went under together. I said, "Give me the—"

And then the beam of Dotty's dimmed flashlight bracketed us. Dotty Hryner was standing behind it with a gun aimed at us. It was a tiny gun, a little .25-caliber, vest-pocket automatic, nickel-plated and with pearl handle. But it was deadly at that range. She was standing right in front of us and I cursed my stupidity for not guessing that she had heard our whispered conference outside and had come over to listen.

There was sullen anger in her face, and fear. It was the fear that frightened me a bit and made me careful. Whatever her game, she had nothing to gain by shooting us; the sound of the shots would bring people running, and it was doubtful if she'd get away. But if she was scared enough she might shoot anyway.

I tried to keep my voice calm and quiet. Rather banally, I said, "Hello, Dotty."

Her voice was shrill and ugly. "Keep your hands up. Damn you, why'd you have to butt in? You—"

"*Sh-h-h*," I said, "you'll wake the elephant on the other side of the lot. Listen—" And I thought fast to think what I could give her to listen to that would keep her trigger finger from getting too nervous. I got it. "Listen, suppose I could tell you where Al — Tommy— hid the stuff?"

"Take me for a sap?" Her voice oozed with scorn. "You'd have lammed with it yourself. That or turned it over for the reward, if you were fool enough to do that."

"I couldn't, Dotty. Come on, I'll show you why."

"Come on where?" She was wavering because I'd put conviction in my voice. The conviction that made me a good sideshow barker. I was telling myself, *Forget this is a gangster's moll; she's just another mark. She'll fall for anything you tell her, like the rest of them.*

I said, "In the next top." And I hoped she didn't know what the next top was; if she'd taken in the show there on her way back along the midway, then she'd be ready for the shock I was going to try on her and my idea would be strictly no dice. Even as a giveaway.

She said, "Turn around. Clasp your hands back of your head, both of you. And walk slow. I'll be behind you and you won't know which one of you this heater's aiming at."

I said, "O.K., Dotty," and followed orders very exactly. So did Stella. I noticed she still had the flashlight in her hand, but that the letter was out of sight; probably she'd stuffed it into a pocket.

We walked that way the length of the freak-show top, Dotty's flashlight behind us dimly illuminating the way. At the side wall, she said, "Wait," came up alongside and lifted the side wall high, standing halfway in and halfway out so we'd have no chance for a break as we went through. That Dotty had taken lessons somewhere; she knew her stuff. And if my hunch was right, she *would* know it.

We went under the side wall of the waxworks tent the same way, and up the aisle between the exhibits. I stopped and said, "Right here. Don't get excited, Dotty. I'm going to take Stella's flashlight so I can show you."

And, without giving her a chance to protest I reached carefully for the flash in Stella's hand, aimed it at a figure that was standing there just the other side of the ropes. A dim, shadowy, unrecognizable figure—until with startling suddenness it leaped into brilliant light as the beam of Stella's flashlight, in my hand, shone full into its realistic, if waxen, face.

And Dotty screamed. *"Tommy!"*

IX

AND BY THAT TIME I had her by the wrist of the hand that held the gun. I twisted and she dropped it without pulling the trigger. But she turned on me with the other hand, clawing like a cat, and kicking at my ankles. But the kicks were ineffective because she was wearing soft slippers, and a moment later I had her other hand pinioned, too.

A voice behind me said quietly, "Nice work, Pete."

It was Helsing. His flashlight went on, and Dotty quit struggling.

Helsing said, "I was in the other tent, watching her. I've been spending every night there. When you butted in I thought you were going to spoil things, but—"

"But my hunch worked," I said. "Al Hryner was Tommy Benno, hiding out here after his last big job—the Eltinge bank. He wrote his moll he was using this as a hideout—probably because he used to be a carney before he turned gunman. And somewhere here he hid the Eltinge loot—nearly half a million bucks!"

I heard Stella gasp incredulously. She was looking at the waxworks figure I had used to frighten Dotty. "But, Pete—*that* doesn't look like Al Hryner. Al's nose was different, and—"

"Plastic surgery," I told her. "On the first page of that letter to Dotty, he said, 'Doc B did a swell job.' But, of course, Dotty hadn't seen that job. She remembered him as he was, and seeing him standing there, as it were, startled her and gave me my chance to get her gun. She probably thought for a second he was still alive."

Helsing stepped forward and pocketed the gun Dotty had dropped, then slipped handcuffs on her.

He said, "Well, I guess this washes up—*the hell it does!*"

There was sudden consternation on his face as he realized, as I, too, was realizing, that it couldn't have been Tommy Benno's woman who had murdered Tommy—or Al—and Bugs Cartier, and who had—

For a moment we looked at one another blankly.

He said, "Dotty here just came into this. Somebody else—one of your mob—found out who Al Hryner was. And killed him and— Hell, it still doesn't make sense, all of it. And who—"

Suddenly it hit me. I knew who it was! There was, with the carney, only one person who could have recognized Tommy Benno in Al Hryner, despite the changed shape of his nose. There was one person with the carney who had *studied* Tommy Benno, studied and analyzed every existing photo and description. Who'd studied the shape of his hands, his chin, his ears, *all* of his physical attributes, in order to duplicate them in wax with the scrupulous accuracy Gus used on each of his wax figures. A change in the shape of the nose might fool even people who knew a man intimately, but it *wouldn't* fool a man whdd made the detailed, feature by feature study that Gus had made. Plastic surgery might fool him at first, but not for long.

I didn't realize I'd said the name out loud, until Helsing said, "Why?" and I was explaining why.

Helsing asked, "But how would he have known that Benno—Al—hid the loot with the freak show? He, must have known because he must have been hunting for it the night you ran into him there and got hit."

I said, "Maybe he saw that letter, or part of it. If he'd recognized Benno he'd have been watching him. Or maybe he read Dotty's *answer* to that letter. That would have been easy; Gus acts as mailman for this end of the midway, the four shows. Front office gives him the mail and he hands it around.

"But the end of the season was coming up, and he hadn't found the money. Maybe that's why he knocked off Al, or maybe Al found him hunting for it. And Bugs, sleeping in the freak-show top, must have seen Gus searching in there. Bugs couldn't have tied it in with the murder, or he wouldn't have been bribed off with a few bucks to get drunk on. But Gus knew the police would make sense of it, if Bugs told, so he played safe by killing Bugs while he was drunk."

"But why in such a goofy way, Pete?" Helsing asked. "With the pins, I mean. And what about the snake in Bugs' bedroll?"

"That's another thing proves Gus Smith did it. He'd given up any real hope of finding it while the carney was running. But he lent money to Lee and took a lien on the props of the freak show. See it? Over the winter they'd be his, and he'd be able to take 'em apart and put 'em together at leisure, and he was sure half a million bucks was hidden in one of them somewhere.

"If Lee paid him back he wouldn't have that chance. So if he could make Lee lose other of his acts—by scaring hell out of them, he could keep Lee from getting off the nut the rest of the season. He swiped the snake to put in Ralph's bedroll—and killed it so it would stay there. But he missed and got it in the wrong roll. Bugs was so drunk he didn't find it. And when Gus found he'd missed, he put a toy snake in Ralph's bedding—and it worked darn near as well. A few more gay little touches like that and there wouldn't have been any performers left for Lee to work with.

"And I know now why he tried to kill me, or scare me out, tonight. Because he learned I was lending money to Lee."

I heard Stella draw in her breath quickly. "He tried to kill you, Pete? How?"

I looked at her and I was suddenly glad—because of what I read in her face—that Gus *had* tried to kill me. It was worth it to learn what Stella's eyes told me. I said, "I'll tell you later, honey. Listen, while you're looking at me that way is the time to ask again. Will you marry me?"

Helsing snorted. "This is a hell of a time and place to—"

"Shut up," I said. "Will you, Stella?"

Stella smiled. "Not tonight, Pete. End of the season—maybe." I started to make a grab for her and remembered Helsing was there.

He cleared his throat. "Now that *that's* settled," he said dryly, "where does Gus sleep?"

But Gus was gone when we went under the partition, and I cussed myself—with Helsing's enthusiastic help—for not remembering that he was within earshot of us if he'd wakened up and listened. And very obviously he had. Just how soon he'd awakened or at what point in our conversation he'd taken French leave, we didn't know. But he was gone all right.

And then, rather quickly, it was dawn and the freak-show top was lousy with coppers again.

Lee was tearing what little was left of his hair, trying to keep them from completely demolishing the top and the props.

He glared at me. "Damn you, Pete—Yeah, they're going to pay for anything they ruin, but how can we get opened again if they make mincemeat out of everything? This is worse than a blow-down!"

Seton had been using the telephone in the front office. He came over to us. "They got Gus," he told us. "Took him off a train in Springfield. But he didn't have the Eltinge bank money with him, so it's still here. We got to keep looking for it until we come across the hiding place."

Lee reached for another handful of hair.

I said, "I know where it is—maybe."

Lee grabbed at me from one side and Seton from the other, and talked at once, telling me to hurry up and say where.

I said, "If I'm right, you guys are making the same mistake Gus and Dotty made. Al's letter said it was hidden with the show, and you thought he meant the freak show. He might have meant anywhere in the carney."

Seton let go of me, and so did Lee. Seton groaned. "You mean we're going to have to take apart everything on this whole damn lot?"

"Maybe not," I told him. "Maybe that makes it easier instead of harder."

Lee echoed Seton's groan. "Look-it," he said. "They're taking the head off the bass drum, and you stand there being coy. Where the hell do you think it might be?"

I said, "Put yourself in Tommy Benno's place, *with this articular carney,* and nobody knowing who you were. What would occur to you as the cleverest place to hide something—even though nobody'd ever appreciate how clever you were?"

Seton stared at me a minute and then said, "I'll be damned," and ducked out under the side wall.

Lee looked at me blankly. "I don't get it. Where?"

I grinned. "Inside the wax effigy of himself. Seton'll know in a minute. *Sh-h-h.*"

A yell from the next tent told me I'd hit the jackpot.

So they quit tearing down Lee's show and we worked like the devil getting it ready to open. And by early afternoon we were ready.

Everybody in the carney was feeling much better now. We had all gone through plenty with the tension and fear that had been working on us.

And just when the crowds started to come in—it started to rain again!

Street & Smith Mystery Magazine, May 1943

Maturity

The Wench Is Dead

I

A FUZZ IS A FUZZ IS A FUZZ when you awaken from a wino jag. God, I'd drunk three pints of muscatel that I know of and maybe more, maybe lots more, because that's when I drew a blank, that's when research stopped. I rolled over on the cot so I could look out through the dirty pane of the window at the clock in the hockshop across the way.

Ten o'clock said the clock.

Get up, Howard Perry, I told myself. Get up, you B.AS. for bastard, rise and greet the day. Hit the floor and get moving if you want to keep that job, that all-important job that keeps you drinking and sometimes eating and sometimes sleeping with Billie the Kid when she hasn't got a sucker on the hook. That's your life, you B.A.S., you bastard. That's your life for a while. This is it, this is the McCoy, this is the way a wino meets the not-so-newborn day. You're learning man.

Pull on a sock, pants, shirt, shoes, get the hell to Burke's and wash a dish, wash a thousand dishes for six bits an hour and a meal or two a day when you want it.

God, I thought, did I really have the habit? Nuts, not in three months. Not when you've been a normal drinker all your life. Not when, much as you've always enjoyed drinking, it's always been in moderation and you've always been able to handle the stuff. This was just temporary.

And I had only a few weeks to go in a few weeks I'd be back in Chicago, back at my desk in my father's investment company, back wearing white shirts, and B.A.S. would stand for Bachelor of Arts in Sociology. That was a laugh right now, that degree. Three months ago it had meant something—but that was in Chicago, and this was LA, and now all it meant was bastard. That's all it had meant ever since I started drifting.

It's funny, the way those things can happen. You've got a good family and a good education, and then suddenly, for no reason you can define, you start drifting. You lose interest in your family and your job, and one day you find yourself headed for the Coast.

You sit down one day and ask yourself how it happened. But you can't answer. There are a thousand little answers, sure, but there's no *big* answer. It's easier to worry about where the next bottle of sweet wine is coming from.

And that's when you realize your own personal B.A.S. stands for bastard.

With me, LA had been the end of the line. I'd seen the *Dishwasher Wanted* sign in Burke's window, and suddenly I'd known what I had to do. At pearl-diver's wages, it would take a long time to get up the bus fare back to Chicago and family and respectability, but that was beside the point. The point was that after a hundred thousand dirty dishes there'd *be* a bus ticket to Chicago.

But it had been hard to remember the ticket and forget the dishes. Wine is cheap, but they're not giving it away. Since I'd started pearl-diving I'd had grub and six bits an hour for seven hours a day. Enough to drink on and to pay for this dirty, crumby little cracker-box of a room.

So here I was, still thinking about the bus ticket, and still on my uppers on East Fifth Street, LA. Main Street used to be the tenderloin street of Los Angeles and I'd headed for it when I jumped off the freight, but I'd found that the worst district, the real skid row, was now on Fifth Street in the few blocks east of Main. The worse the district, the cheaper the living, and that's what I'd been looking for.

Sure, by Fifth Street standards, I was being a pantywaist to hold down a steady job like that, but sleeping in doorways was a little too rugged and I'd found out quickly that panhandling wasn't for me. I lacked the knack.

I dipped water from the cracked basin and rubbed it on my face, and the feel of the stubble told me I could get by one more day without shaving. Or anyway I could wait till evening so the shave would be fresh in case I'd be sleeping with Billie.

Cold water helped a little but I still felt like hell. There were empty wine bottles in the corner and I checked to make sure they were completely empty, and they were. So were my pockets, except, thank God, for tobacco and cigarette papers. I rolled myself a cigarette and lighted it.

But I needed a drink to start the day.

What does a wino do when he wakes up broke (and how often does he wake otherwise?) and needs a drink? Well, I'd found several answers to that. The easiest one, right now, would be to hit Billie for a drink if she was awake yet, and alone.

I crossed the street to the building where Billie had a room. A somewhat newer building, a hell of a lot nicer room, but then she paid a hell of a lot more for it.

I rapped on her door softly, a little code knock we had. If she wasn't awake she wouldn't hear it and if she wasn't alone she wouldn't answer it.

But she called out, "It's not locked; come on in," and she said "Hi, Professor," as I closed the door behind me. "Professor" she called me, occasionally and banteringly. It was my way of talking, I guess. I'd tried at first to use poor diction, bad grammar, to fit in with the place, but I'd given it up as too tough a job. Besides, I'd learned Fifth Street already had quite a bit of good grammar. Some of its denizens had been newspapermen once, some had written poetry; one I knew was a defrocked clergyman.

I said, "Hi, Billie the Kid."

"Just woke up, Howie. What time is it?"

"A little after ten," I told her. "Is there a drink around?"

"Jeez, only ten? Oh well, I had seven hours. Guy came here when Mike closed at two, but he didn't stay long."

She sat up in bed and stretched, the covers falling away from her naked body. Beautiful breasts she had, size and shape of half grapefruits and firm. Nice arms and shoulders, and a lovely face. Hair black and sleek in a pageboy bob that fell into place as she shook her head. Twenty-five, she told me once; and I believed her, but she could have passed for several years less than that, even, now without make-up and her eyes still a little puffy from sleep. Certainly it didn't show that she'd spent three years as a B-girl, part-time hustler heavy drinker. Before that she'd been married to a man who'd worked for a manufacturing jeweler; he'd suddenly left for parts unknown with a considerable portion of his employer's stock, leaving Billie in a jam and with a mess of debts.

Wilhelmina Kidder, Billie the Kid, my Billie. Any man's Billie if he flashed a roll, but oddly I'd found that I could love her a little and not let bother me. Maybe because it had been that way when I'd first met her over a month ago; I'd come to love her knowing what she was, so why should it bother me? What she saw in me I don't know, and didn't care.

"About that drink," I said.

She laughed and threw down the covers, got out of bed and walked past me naked to the closet to get a robe. I wanted to reach for her but I didn't; I'd learned by now that Billie the Kid was never amorous early in the morning and resented any passes made before noon.

She shrugged into a quilted robe and padded barefoot over to the little refrigerator behind the screen that hid a tiny kitchenette. She opened the door and said, "God damn it."

"God damn what?" I wanted to know. "Out of liquor?"

She held up over the screen a Hiram Walker bottle with only half an inch of ready-mixed Manhattan in it. Almost the only thing Billie ever drank, Manhattans.

"As near out as matters. Honey, would you run upstairs and see if Mame's got some? She usually has."

Mame is a big blonde who works behind the bar at Mike Karas' joint, The Best Chance, where Billie works as B-girl. A tough number, Mame. I said, "If she's asleep she'll murder me for waking her. What's wrong with the store?"

"She's up by now. She was off early last night. And if you get it at the store it won't be on ice. Wait, I'll phone her, though, so if she *is* asleep it'll be me that wakes her and not you."

She made the call and then nodded. "Okay, honey. She's got a full bottle she'll lend me. Scram."

I scrammed, from the second floor rear to the third floor front. Mame's door was open; she was out in the hallway paying off a milkman and waiting for him to receipt the bill. She said, "Go on in. Take a load off." I went inside the room and sat down in the chair that was built to match Mame, overstuffed. I ran my fingers around under the edge of the cushion; one of Mame's men friends might have sat there with change in his pocket. It's surprising how much change you can pick up just by trying any over-stuffed chairs or so as you sit on. No change this time, but

I came up with a fountain pen, a cheap dime-store-looking one. Mame had just closed the door and I held it up. "In the chair. Yours, Mame?"

"Nope. Keep it, Howie, I got a pen."

"Maybe one of your friends'll miss it," I said. It was too cheap a pen to sell or hock so I might as well be honest about it.

"Nope, I know who lost it. Seen it in his pocket last night. It was Jesus, and the hell with him."

"Mame, you sound sacrilegious."

She laughed. "Hay-soos, then. Jesus Gonzales. A Mex. But when he told me that was his handle I called him Jesus. And Jesus was *he* like a cat on a hot stove!" She walked around me over to her refrigerator but her voice kept on. "Told me not to turn on the lights when he come in and went over to watch out the front window for a while like he was watching for the heat. Looks out my side window too, one with the fire escape. Pulls down all the shades before he says okay, turn on the lights." The refrigerator door closed and she came back with a bottle.

"Was he a hot one," she said. "Just got his coat off—he threw it on that chair, when there's a knock. Grabs his coat again and goes out my side window down the fire escape." She laughed again. "Was that a flip? It was only Dixie from the next room knocking, to bum cigarettes. So if I ever see Jesus again it's no dice, guy as jumpy as that. Keep his pen. Want a drink here?"

"If you'll have one with me."

"I don't drink, Howie. Just keep stuff around for friends and callers. Tell Billie to give me another bottle like this back. I got a friend likes Manhattans, like her."

When I got back to Billie's room, she'd put on a costume instead of the robe, but it wasn't much of a costume. A skimpy Bikini bathing suit. She pirouetted in it. "Like it, Howie? Just bought it yesterday."

"Nice," I said, "but I like you better without it."

"Pour us drinks, huh? For me, just a quickie."

"Speaking of quickies," I said.

She picked up a dress and started to pull it over her head. "If you're thinking that way, Professor, I'll hide the family treasures. Say, that's a good line; I'm getting to talk like you do sometimes."

I poured us drinks and we sat down with them. She'd stepped into sandals and was dressed. I said, "You've got lots of good lines, Billie the

Kid. Correct me—was that lingerie instead of a bathing suit, or am I out of date on fashions?"

"I'm going to the beach today, Howie, for a sun-soak. Won't go near the water so why not just wear the suit under and save changing? Say, why don't you take a day off and come along?"

"Broke. The one thing to be said for Burke as an employer is that he pays every day. Otherwise there'd be some dry, dry evenings."

"What you make there? A fin, maybe. I'll lend you a fin."

"That way lies madness," I said. "Drinks I'll take from you, or more important things than drinks. But taking money would make me—" I stopped and wondered just what taking money from Billie would make me, just how consistent I was being. After all, I could always send it back to her from Chicago. What kept me from taking it, then? A gal named Honor, I guess. Corny as it sounds, I said it lightly. "I could not love thee, dear, so much, loved I not Honor more."

"You're a funny guy, Howie. I don't understand you."

Suddenly I wanted to change the subject. "Billie, how come Mame doesn't drink?"

"Don't you know hypes don't like to drink?"

"Sure, but I didn't spot Mame for one."

"Hype with a big H for heroin, Howie. Doesn't show it much, though. I'll give you that."

"I haven't known enough junkies to be any judge," I said. "The only one I know for sure is the cook at Burke's."

"Don't ever try it, Howie. It's bad stuff. I joy-popped once just to see what it was like, but never again. Too easy to get to like it. And Howie, it can make things rough."

I said, "I hear your words of wisdom and shall stick to drink. Speaking of which—" I poured myself another.

II

I GOT TO THE RESTAURANT—it's on Main a block from Fifth—at a quarter after eleven, only fifteen minutes late. Burke was at the stove—he does his own cooking until noon, when Ramon comes on—and turned to glare at me but didn't say anything.

Still feeling good from the drinks, I dived into my dishwashing.

The good feeling was mostly gone, though, by noon, when Ramon came on. He had a fresh bandage on his forehead; I wondered if there was a new knife wound under it. He already had two knife scars, old ones, on his cheek and on his chin. He looked mean, too, and I decided to stay out his way. Ramon's got a nasty temper when he needs a jolt, and it was pretty obvious that he needed one. He looked like a man with a king-size monkey, and he was. I'd often wondered how he fed it. Cooks draw good money compared to other restaurant help, but even a cook doesn't get enough to support a five or six cap a day habit, not at a joint like Burke's anyway. Ramon was tall for a Mexican, but he was thin and his face looked gaunt. It's an ugly face except when he grins and his teeth flash white. But he wouldn't be grinning this afternoon, not if he needed a jolt.

Burke went front to work the register and help at the counter for the noon rush, and Ramon took over at the stove. We worked in silence until the rush was over, about two o'clock.

He came over to me then. He was sniffling and his eyes were running. He said, "Howie, you do me a favor. I'm burning, Howie, I need a fix, quick. I got to sneak out, fifteen minutes."

"Okay, I'll try to watch things. What's working?"

"Two hamburg steak dinners on. Done one side, five more minutes other side. You know what else to put on."

"Sure, and if Burke comes back I'll tell him you're in the can. But you'd better hurry."

He rushed out, not even bothering to take off his apron or chef's hat. I timed five minutes on the clock and then I took up the steaks, added the trimmings and put them on the ledge, standing at an angle back of the window so Burke couldn't see that it was I and not Ramon who was putting them there. A few minutes later the waitress put in a call for stuffed peppers, a pair; they were already cooked and I didn't have any trouble dishing them.

Ramon came back before anything else happened. He looked like a different man—he would be for as long as the fix lasted. His teeth flashed. "Million thanks, Howie." He handed me a flat pint bottle of muscatel. "For you, my friend."

"Ramon," I said, "you are a gentleman and a scholar." He went back to his stove and started scraping it. I bent down out of sight to, open the bottle. I took a good long drink and then hid it back out of sight under one of the tubs.

Two-thirty, and my half-hour lunch break. Only I wasn't hungry. I took another drink of the muskie and put it back. I could have killed it but the rest of the afternoon would go better if I rationed it and made it last until near quitting time.

I wandered over to the alley entrance, rolling a cigarette. A beautiful bright day out; it would have been wonderful to be at the beach with Billie the Kid.

Only Billie the Kid wasn't at the beach; she was coming toward me from the mouth of the alley. She was still wearing the dress she'd pulled on over the bathing suit but she wasn't at the beach. She was walking toward me, looking worried, looking frightened.

I walked to meet her. She grabbed my arm, tightly. "Howie. Howie, did you kill Mame?"

"Did I—what?"

Her eyes were big, looking up at me. "Howie, if you did, I don't care. I'll help you, give you money to get away. But—"

"Whoa," I said, "Whoa, Billie. I didn't kill Mame. I didn't even rape her. She was okay when I left. What happened? Or are you dreaming this up?"

"She's dead, Howie, murdered. And about the time you were there. They found her a little after noon and say she'd been dead somewhere around two hours. Let's go have a drink and I'll tell you what all happened."

"All right," I said. "I've got most of my lunch time left. Only I haven't been paid yet—"

"Come on, hurry." As we walked out of the alley she took a bill from her purse and stuffed it into my pocket. We took the nearest gin-mill and ordered drinks at a booth at the back where we weren't near enough anyone to be heard. The bill she'd put in my pocket was a sawbuck. When the waitress brought our drinks and the change I shoved it toward Billie. She shook her head and pushed it back. "Keep it and owe me ten, Howie. You might need it in case—well, just in case." I said, "Okay, Billie, but I'll pay this back." I would, too, but it probably wouldn't be until I mailed it to her from Chicago and it would probably surprise the hell out of her to get it.

I said, "Now tell me, but quit looking so worried. I'm as innocent as new-fallen snow—and I don't mean cocaine. Let me reconstruct my end first, and then tell yours. I got to work at eleven-twenty. Walked straight there from your place, so it would have been ten after when I left you. And—let's see, from the other end, it was ten o'clock when I woke up, wouldn't have been over ten or fifteen minutes before I knocked on your door, another few minutes before I got to Mame's and I was up there only a few minutes. Say I saw her last around twenty after ten, and she was okay then. Over."

"Huh? Over what?"

"I mean, you take it. From when I left you, about ten minutes after eleven."

"Oh. Well, I straightened the room, did a couple of things, and left, it must have been a little after twelve on account of the noon whistles had blown just a few minutes ago. I was going to the beach. I was going to walk over to the terminal and catch the Santa Monica bus, go to Ocean Park. Only first I stopped in the drugstore right on the corner for a cup of coffee. I was there maybe ten-fifteen minutes letting it cool enough to drink and drinking it. While I was there I heard a cop car stop near but I didn't think anything of it; they're always picking up drunks and all.

"But while I was there too I remembered I'd forgot to bring my sunglasses and suntan oil, so I went back to get them.

"Minute I got inside the cops were waiting and they asked if I lived there and then started asking questions, did I know Mame and when I saw her last and all."

"Did you tell them you'd talked to her on the phone?"

"Course not, Howie. I'm not a dope. I knew by then something had happened to her and if I told them about that call and what it was about, it would have brought you in and put you on the spot. I didn't even tell them you were with me, let alone going up to Mame's. I kept you out of it.

"They're really questioning everybody, Howie. They didn't pull me in but they kept me in *my* own room questioning me till just fifteen minutes ago. See, they really worked on me because I admitted I knew

Mame—I had to admit that 'cause we work at the same place and they'd have found that out.

"And of course they knew she was a hype, her arms and all; they're checking everybody's arms and thank God mine are okay. They asked me mostly about where we worked, Mike's. I think they figure Mike Karas is a dealer, what with Mame working for him."

"Is he, Billie?"

"I don't know, honey. He's in some racket, but it isn't dope."

I said, "Well, I don't see what either of us has to worry about. It's not our—My God, I just remembered something."

"What, Howie?"

"A guy saw me going in her room, a milkman. Mame was in the hall paying him off when I went up. She told me to go on in and I did, right past him."

"Jesus, Howie, did she call you by name when she told you to go on in? If they get a name, even a first name, and you living right across the street—"

I thought hard. "Pretty sure she didn't, Billie. She told me to go in and take a load off, but I'm pretty sure she didn't add a Howie to it. Anyway, they may never find the milkman was there. He isn't likely to stick his neck out by coming to them. How was she killed, Billie?"

"Somebody said a shiv, but I don't know for sure."

"Who found her and how come?"

"I don't know. They were asking me questions, not me asking them. That part'll be in the papers, though."

"All right," I said. "Let's let it go till this evening, then. How's about this evening, Billie, are you going to The Best Chance anyway?"

"I *got* to, tonight, after that. If I don't show up, they'll want to know why and where I was and everything. And listen, don't you come around either, after hours tonight or in the morning. You stay away from that building, Howie. If they find that milkman they might even have him staked out watching for you. Don't even walk *past.* You better even stay off that block, go in and out the back way to your own room. And we better not even see each other till the heat's off or till we know what the score is."

I sighed.

I was ten minutes late reporting back and Burke glared at me again but still didn't say anything. I guess I was still relatively dependable for a dishwasher, but I was learning.

I made the rest of the wine last me till Baldy, the evening shift dishwasher, showed up to relieve me. Burke paid me off for the day then, and I was rich again.

III

SOMEONE WAS SHAKING me, shaking me hard. I woke to fuzz and fog and Billie the Kid was peering through it at me, looking really scared, more scared than when she'd asked me yesterday if I'd killed Mame.

"Howie, wake up." I was in my own little shoebox of a room, Billie standing by my cot bending over me. I wasn't covered, but the extent of my undressing had been to kick off my shoes.

"Howie, listen, you're in trouble, honey. You got to get out of here, back way like I come in. Hurry."

I sat up and wanted to know the time.

"Only nine, Howie. But hurry. Here. This will help you." She screwed off the top of a half pint bottle of whisky. "Drink some quick. Help you wake up."

I took a drink and the whisky burned rawly down my throat. For a moment I thought it was going to make me sick to my stomach, but then it decided to stay down and it did clear my head a little. Not much, but a little.

"What's wrong, Billie?"

"Put on your shoes. I'll tell you, but not here."

Luckily my shoes were loafers and I could step into them. I went to the basin of water rubbed some on my face. While I washed and dried and ran a comb through my hair Billie was going through the dresser; a towel on the bed, everything I owned piled on it. It didn't make much of a bundle.

She handed it to me and then was pulling me out into the hallway, me and everything I owned. Apparently I wasn't coming back here, or Billie didn't think I was.

Out into the alley, through to Sixth Street and over Sixth to Main, south on Main. A restaurant with booths, mostly empty. The waitress came over and I ordered coffee, black. Billie ordered ham and eggs and toast and when the waitress left she leaned across the table. "I didn't want to argue with her in front of you, Howie, but that food I ordered is for you; you're going to eat it all. You got to be sober."

I groaned, but knew it would be easier to eat than to argue with a Billie the Kid as vehement as this one.

"What is it, Billie? What's up?"

"Did you read the papers last night?"

I shook my head. I hadn't read any papers up to about nine o'clock and after that I didn't remember what I'd done or hadn't. But I wouldn't have read any papers. That reminded me to look in my pockets to see what money I had left, if any. No change, but thank God there were some crumpled bills. A five and two ones, when I pulled them out and looked under cover of the table. I'd had a little over nine out of the ten Billie had given me to buy us a drink with, a little under five I'd got from Burke. That made fourteen and I'd spent seven of it somehow—and God knows how since I couldn't possibly have drunk that much muskie or even that much whisky at Fifth Street prices. But at least I hadn't been rolled, so it could have been worse.

"They got that milkman, Howie," Billie was saying. "Right off. He'd given Mame a receipt and she'd dropped it on that little table by the door so they knew he'd been there and they found him and he says he'll know you if he sees you. He described you too. You thinking straight by now, Howie?"

"Sure I'm thinking straight. What if they do find me? Damn it, I didn't kill her. Didn't have any reason to. They can't do any more than question me."

"Howie, haven't you ever been in trouble with cops? Not on anything serious, I guess, or you wouldn't talk like that. That milkman would put you right on the scene at close to the right time and that's all they'd want. They got nobody else to work on.

"Sure they'll question you. With fists and rubber hoses they'll question you. They'll beat the hell out of you for days on end, tie you in a chair with five hundred watts in your eyes and slap you every time you close them. Sure they'll question you. They'll question you till you wish you *had* killed Mame so you could tell 'em and get it over with and get some sleep. Howie, cops are tough, mean bastards when they're trying to pin down a murder rap. This is a murder rap, Howie."

I smiled a little without meaning to. Not because what she'd been saying was funny, but because I was thinking of the headlines if they did beat the truth out of me, or if I had to tell all to beat the rap. *Chicago Scion in Heroin Murder Case.* Chicago papers please copy.

I saw the hurt look on Billie's face and straightened mine. "Sorry," I said. "I was laughing at something else. Go on."

But the waitress was coming and Billie waited till she'd left. She shoved the ham and eggs and toast in front of me. "Eat," she said. I ate.

"And that isn't all, Howie. They'll frame you on some other charge to hold you. Howie, they might even frame you on the murder rap itself if they don't find who else did it. They could do it easy, just take a few little things from her room—it had been searched—and claim you had 'em on you or they were in your room. How'd you prove they weren't? And what'd your word be against a cop's? They could put you in the little room and gas you, Howie. And there's something else, too."

"Something worse than *that?*"

"I don't mean that. I mean what they'd do to me, Howie. And that'd be for *sure*. A perjury rap, a nice long one. See, I signed a statement after they questioned me, and that'd make it perjury for me if you tell 'em the truth about why you went up to see Mame. And what else could you tell them?"

I put down my knife and fork and stared at her. I hadn't been *really* worried about the things she'd been telling me. Innocent men, I'd been telling myself, aren't framed by the cops on murder charges. Not if they're willing to tell the truth down the line. They might give me a bad time, I thought, but they wouldn't hold me long if I leveled with them. But if Billie had signed a statement, then telling them the truth was out. Billie was on the wrong side of the law already; they *would* take advantage of perjury to put her away, maybe for several years.

I said, "I'm sorry, Billie. I didn't realize I'd have to involve you if I had to tell them the truth."

"Eat, Howie. Eat all that grub. Don't worry about me; I just mentioned it. You're in worse trouble than *I* am. But I'm glad you're talking straight; you sound really awake now. Now you go on eating and I'll tell you what you've got to do.

"First, this milkman's description. Height, weight and age fairly close but not exact on any, and anyway you can't change that. But you got to change clothes, buy new ones, because Jesus, the guy got your clothes perfect. Blue denim shirt cut off above elbows, tan work pants, brown loafers. Now first thing when you leave here, buy different clothes, see?"

"All right," I said. "How else did he describe me?"

"Well, he thought you had blond hair and it's a little darker than that, not much. Said you needed a shave—you need one worse now—and said you looked like a Fifth Street bum, a wino maybe. That's all, except he's sure he could identify you if he ever saw you again. And that's bad, Howie."

"It is," I said.

"Howie, do you want to blow town? I can lend you—well, I'm a little low right now and on account of Karas' place being watched so close I won't be able to pick up any extra money for a while, but I can lend you fifty if you want to blow town. Do you?"

"No, Billie," I said. "I don't want to blow town. Not unless you want to go with me."

God, what had made me *say that*? What had I meant by it? What business had I taking Billie away from the district she knew, the place where she could make a living—if I couldn't—putting her further in a jam for disappearing when she was more or less a witness in a murder case? And when I wanted to be back in Chicago, back working for my father and being respectable, within a few weeks anyway.

What had I meant? I couldn't take Billie back with me, much as I liked—maybe loved—her. Billie the Kid as the wife of a respectable investment man? It wouldn't work, for either of us. But if I hadn't meant that, what the hell *had* I meant?

But Billie was shaking her head. "Howie, it wouldn't work. Not for us, not right now. If you could quit drinking, straighten out. But I know—I know you can't. It isn't your fault and—oh, honey, let's not talk about that now. Anyway, I'm *glad* you don't want to lam because—well, because I *am*. But listen—"

"Yes, Billie?"

"You've got to change the way you look—just a little. Buy a different colored shirt, see? And different pants, shoes instead of loafers. Get a haircut—you need one anyway so get a short one. Then get a hotel room—off Fifth Street. Main is okay if you stay away from Fifth. And shave—you had a stubble when that milkman saw you. How much money you got left?"

"Seven," I said. "But that ought to do it. I don't need *new* clothes; I can swap with uncle."

"You'll need more than that. Here." It was a twenty.

"Thanks, Billie. I owe you thirty." Owe her thirty? Hell, how much did I owe Billie the Kid already, outside of money, things money can't buy? I said, "And how'll we get in touch with one another? You say I shouldn't come to your place. Will you come to mine, tonight?"

"I—I guess they won't be suspicious if I take a night off, Howie, as long as it wasn't that first night. Right after the—after what happened to Mame. All right, Howie. You know a place called The Shoebox on Main up across from the court house?"

"I know where it is."

"I'll meet you there tonight at eight. And—and stay in your room, wherever you take one, till then. And—and try to stay sober, Howie."

IV

IT SHOULDN'T BE hard, I thought, to stay sober when you're scared. And I was scared, now.

I stayed on Main Street, away from Fifth, and I did the things Billie had suggested. I bought a tan work shirt, and changed it right in the store where I bought it for the blue one I'd been wearing. I stopped in the barber school place for a four-bit haircut and, while I was at it, a two-bit shave. I had one idea Billie hadn't thought of; I spent a buck on a used hat. I hadn't been wearing one and a hat makes a man look different. At a shoe repair shop that handled used shoes I traded in my loafers and a dollar fifty for a pair of used shoes. I decided not to worry about the trousers; their color wasn't distinctive.

I bought newspapers; I wanted to read for myself everything Billie had told me about the murder, and there might be other details she hadn't mentioned. Some wine too, but just a pint to sip on. I was going to stay sober, but it would be a long boring day waiting for my eight o'clock date with Billie the Kid.

I registered double at a little walk-up hotel on Market Street around the corner from Main, less than a block from the place of my evening date. She'd be coming with me, of course, since we wouldn't dare go to her place, and I didn't want there to be even a chance of trouble in bringing her back with me. Not that trouble would be likely in a place like that but I didn't want even the minor trouble of having to change the registration from single to double if the clerk saw us coming in, not for fifty cents difference in the price of the room.

I sipped at the wine slowly and read the papers. The *Mirror* gave it the best coverage, with pictures. A picture of Mame that must have been found in her room and that had been taken at least ten years ago—she looked to be in her late teens or early twenties—a flashlight shot of the interior of her room, but taken after her body had been removed, and an exterior of The Best Chance, where she'd worked. But, even from the *Mirror,* I didn't learn anything Billie hadn't told me, except Mame's full name and just how and when the body had been discovered. The time had been 12:05, just about the time Billie was leaving from her room on the floor below. The owner of the building had dropped around, with tools, to fix a dripping faucet Mame (Miss Mamie Gaynor, 29) had complained about the day before. When he'd knocked long enough to decide she wasn't home he'd let himself in with his duplicate key. The milkman's story and the description he'd given of me was exactly as Billie had given them.

I paced up and down the little room, walked the worn and shabby carpet, wondering. Was there—short of the sheer accident of my running into that milkman—any danger of my being picked up just from that description? No, surely not. It was accurate as far as it went, but it was too vague, could fit too many men in this district, for anyone to think of me in connection with it. And now, with a change of clothes, a shave, wearing a hat outdoors, I doubted if the milkman would recognize me. I couldn't remember his face; why would he remember mine? And there was no tie-in otherwise, except through Billie. Nobody but Billie knew that I'd even met Mame. The only two times I'd ever seen her had been in Billie's place when she'd dropped in while I was there, once for only a few minutes, once for an hour or so. And one other time I'd been up to her room, that time to borrow cigarettes for Billie; it had been very late, after stores and bars were closed.

The fact that I'd disappeared from my room in that block? That would mean nothing. Tomorrow a week's rent was due; the landlord would come to collect it, find me and my few possessions gone, and rent it again. He'd think nothing of it. Why should he?

No, now that I'd taken the few precautions Billie had suggested, I was safe enough as long as I stayed away from her building.

Why was I hiding here now, then?

The wine was gone and I wanted more. But I knew what shape I'd be in by eight o'clock if I kept on drinking it, starting at this hour of the morning.

But I'd go nuts if I stayed here, doing nothing. I picked up the papers, read the funny sheets, a few other things. Back in the middle of one of them a headline over a short item caught my eye, I don't know for what reason. *Victim in Alley Slaying Identified.*

Maybe my eye had first caught the name down in the body of the story, Jesus Gonzales. And Mame's jittery guest of the night before her death had been named Jesus Gonzales.

I read the story. Yesterday morning at dawn the body of a man had been found in an areaway off Winston Street near San Pedro Street. He had been killed with a blunt instrument, probably a blackjack. As he had been robbed of everything he was carrying, no identification had been made at first. Now he had been identified as Jesus Gonzales, 41, of Mexico City, DF. He had arrived in Los Angeles the day before on the SS Guadalajara, out of Tokyo. His passport, which had been left in his room at the Berengia Hotel, and other papers left with it, showed that he had been in the Orient on a buying trip for a Mexico City art object importing firm in which he was a partner, and that he was stopping in Los Angeles for a brief vacation on his return trip.

Mame's Jesus Gonzales? It certainly looked that way. The place and time fitted; less than two blocks from her room. So did the time, the morning after he'd been frightened by that knock at the door and had left unceremoniously via the fire escape.

But why would he have hooked up with Mame? The Berengia is a swank hotel, only people with well-lined pockets stay there. Mame was no prize; at the Berengia he could have done better through his own bellhop.

Or could it be a factor that Mame was a junkie and, stopping in at

The Best Chance, he'd recognized her as one and picked her for that reason? He could have been a hype himself, in need of a jolt and in a city where he had no contacts, or—and this seemed even more likely because of his just having landed from Tokyo—he'd smuggled some dope in with him and was looking for a dealer to sell it. The simplest and safest way to find a dealer would be through an addict.

It was just a wild guess, of course, but it wasn't too wild to be possible. And damn it, Mame's Jesus Gonzales *had* acted suspiciously and he *had* been afraid of something. Maybe he'd thought somebody was following him, following him and Mame home from The Best Chance. If he was the same Jesus Gonzales who'd just been killed and robbed only two blocks from her place, then he'd been dead right in being careful. He'd made his mistake in assuming that the knocker on Mame's door was the man who'd followed him and in going down the fire escape. Maybe his *Nemesis* had still been, outside the building, probably watching from across the street, and had seen him leave. And on Winston Street *Nemesis* had caught up with him.

Nice going, B.A.S., old boy, I thought. You're doing fine. It isn't every skid-row pearl-diver who can reconstruct a crime out of nothing. Sheer genius, B.A.S., sheer genius.

But it was something to pass the time, a lot better than staring at the wall and wishing I'd never left Chicago. Better than brooding.

All right, suppose it figured so far—then how did Mame's death tie in with it? I didn't see how. I made myself pace and concentrate, trying to work out an answer.

I felt sure Mame had been telling me the truth about Gonzales as far as she knew it, or else she would have had no reason for mentioning it at all. Whatever his ulterior motive in picking her up, whether to buy dope or to find a contact for selling it, he hadn't yet leveled with Mame before that knock came. Otherwise she wouldn't have told it casually, as she had, as something amusing.

But the killer wouldn't have known that. He couldn't have known that Mame was not an accomplice. If what he was looking for hadn't been on the person of the man he'd killed he could have figured that it had already changed hands. Why hadn't he gone back to Mame's the same night? I didn't know, but there could have been a reason. Perhaps he had and she'd gone out, locking the door and the fire escape window.

Or maybe by that time she had other company; if he had knocked she might have opened the door on the chain—and I remembered now that there was a chain on her door—and told him so. I couldn't ask Mame now what she'd done the rest of the night after her jittery caller had left.

But if Gonzales was a stranger in town, just off the boat, how would the killer have known he had brought in heroin?—or opium or cocaine; it could have been any drug worth smuggling. And the killer must have known *something;* if it had been just a robbery kill, for whatever money Gonzales was carrying, then he wouldn't have gone back and killed Mame, searched her room. He'd have done that only if he'd known something about Gonzales that made him think Mame was his accomplice.

I killed a few more minutes worrying about that and I had the answer. Maybe not *the* answer, but at least an answer that made sense. Maybe I was just mildly cockeyed, but this off-the-cuff figuring I'd been doing *did* seem to be getting somewhere.

It was possible, I reasoned, that Mame hadn't been the first person through whom Gonzales had tried to make a contact. He could have approached another junkie on the same deal, but one who refused to tell him her contact. Her? It didn't have to be a woman, but Mame had been a woman and that made me think he'd been working that way. Say that he'd wandered around B-joints until he spotted a B-girl as an addict; he could get her in a booth and try to get information from her. She could have stalled him or turned him down. Stalled him, most likely, making a phone call or two to see if she could get hold of a dealer for him, but tipping off her boyfriend instead. Killing time enough for her boyfriend to be ready outside, then telling Gonzales she couldn't make a contact for him.

And if any of that had sounded suspicious to Gonzales he would have been more careful the second try, with Mame. He'd get her to her room on the obvious pretext, make sure they were alone and hadn't been followed before he opened up. Only, between The Best Chance and Mame's room, he must have discovered that they were being followed.

Sure, it all fitted. But what good did it do me?

Sure, it was logical. It made a complete and perfect picture, but it was all guesswork, nothing to go to the cops with. Even if they believed me eventually and could verify my guesses in the long run, I'd be getting myself and Billie the Kid into plenty of trouble in the short run. And like as not enough bad publicity—my relations with Billie would surely come out, and Billie's occupation—to have my father's clients in Chicago decide I wasn't fit to handle their business.

Well, was I? Worry about the fact that you want a drink so damned bad, I told myself, that soon you're going to weaken and go down and get another bottle. Well, why not? As long as I rationed it to myself so I would be drinking just enough to hold my own and not get drunk, not until after eight o'clock anyway. . .

What time was it? It seemed like I'd been in that damned room six or eight hours, but I'd checked in at around eleven and the sun was shining straight down in the dirty areaway my window opened on. Could it be only noon? I went out to the desk and past it, looking at the kitchen-type electric clock on the wall over it as I went by. It was a quarter after twelve.

I decided to walk a while before I went back to the room with a bottle, kill some time first. God, the time I had to kill before eight o'clock. I walked around the court house and over to Spring Street. I'd be safe there.

Hell, I'd be safe anywhere, I thought. Except maybe right in that one block of Fifth Street, just on the chance the police did have the milkman staked out in or near that building. And with different clothes, wearing a hat, he probably wouldn't recognize me anyway. Billie the Kid had panicked, and had panicked me. I didn't have anything to worry about. Oh, moving out of that block, changing out of the clothes I'd been wearing, those things had been sensible. But I didn't have to quit my job at Burke's—if it was still open to me. Burke's was safe for me. Nobody at Burke's knew where I'd lived and nobody in the building I'd lived in knew where I worked.

I thought, why not go to Burke's? He'd have the sign out in the window, now that I was an hour and a half late, but if nobody had taken the job, I could give him a story why I was so late and get it back. I'd gotten pretty good at washing dishes; I was probably the best dishwasher he'd ever had and I'd been steadier than the average one. Sure, I could go back there unless he'd managed to hire a new one already.

And otherwise, what? I'd either have to look for a new job of the same kind or keep on taking money from Billie for however long I stayed here. And taking money from Billie, except in emergency, was out. That gal named Honor back in Chicago was getting to be a pretty dim memory, but I still had some self-respect.

I cut back to Main Street and headed for Burke's. The back way, so I could see if anyone was working yet in my place, and maybe ask Ramon what the score was before I saw Burke.

From the alley doorway I could see my spot was empty, dishes piling high. Ramon was busy at the stove. He turned as I walked up to him, and his teeth flashed white in that grin. He said, "Howie! Thank God you're here. No dishwasher, everybody's going nuts."

The bandage was gone from his forehead. Under where it had been were four long scratches, downward, about an inch apart.

I stared at the scratches and thought about Ramon and his monkey and Mame and *her* monkey, and all of a sudden I had a crazy hunch. I thought about how a monkey like Ramon's could make a man do anything to get a fix. I moistened my lips. Ramon's monkey might claw the hell out of his guts, but it hadn't put those four scratches on his face. Not directly.

I didn't say it, I'd have had more sense; my mouth said it. "Mame had sharp fingernails, huh?"

V

DEATH CAN BE a sudden thing. Only luck or accident kept me from dying suddenly in the next second or two. I'd never seen a face change as suddenly as Ramon's did. And before I could move, his hand had hold of the front of my shirt and his other hand had reached behind him and come up with and raised a cleaver. To step back as it started down would have put me in even better position for it to hit, so I did the only thing possible; I stepped in and pushed him backward and he stumbled and fell. I'd jerked my head but the cleaver went too wild even to scrape my shoulders. And there was a *thunking* sound as Ramon's head hit a sharp corner of the big stove. Yes, death can be a sudden thing.

I breathed hard a second and then—well, I don't, know why I cared whether he was alive or not, but I bent forward and reached inside his shirt, held my hand over where his heart should be beating. It wasn't.

From the other side of the window Burke's voice sang out, "Two burgers, with."

I got out of there fast. Nobody had seen me there, nobody was *going* to see me there. I got out of the alley without being seen, that I knew of, and back to Main Street. I walked three blocks before I stopped into a tavern for the drink I really needed *now*. Not wine, whisky. Wine's an anodyne but it dulls the mind. Whisky sharpens it, at least temporarily. I ordered whisky, a double, straight.

I took half of it in one swallow and got over the worst of it. I sipped the rest slowly, and thought.

Damn it, Howie, I told myself, you've got to think.

I thought, and there was only one answer. I was in over my head now. If the police got me I was sunk. B.A.S. or not, I'd have a hell of a time convincing them I hadn't committed two murders—maybe three; if they'd tied in Jesus Gonzales, they'd pin that on me, too.

Sure, *I* knew what had really happened, but what proof did I have? Mame was dead; she wouldn't tell again what she'd told me about her little episode with Jesus. Ramon was dead; he wouldn't back up my otherwise unsupported word that I'd killed him accidentally in defending myself.

Out of this while I had a whole skin, that was the only answer. Back in Chicago, back to respectability, back to my right name—Howard Perry, B.A.S., not Howard Perry, bastard, wino, suspected soon of being a psychopathic killer. Back to Chicago, and not by freight. Too easy to get arrested that way, vagged, and maybe by that time flyers would be out with my description. Too risky.

So was waiting till eight o'clock when it was only one o'clock now. I'd have to risk getting in touch with Billie the Kid sooner. I couldn't go to her place, but I could phone. Surely they wouldn't have all the phones in that building tapped.

Just the same I was careful when I got her number. "Billie," I said, "this is the Professor." That nickname wouldn't mean anything to anybody else.

I heard her draw in her breath sharply. She must have realized I wouldn't risk calling her unless something important had come up. But she made her voice calm when she answered, "Yes, Professor?"

"Something has come up," I said. "I'm afraid I won't be able to make our eight o'clock date. Is there any chance that you can meet me now instead—same place?"

"Sure, soon as I can get there."

Click of the receiver. She'd be there. Billie the Kid, my Billie. She'd be there, and she'd make sure first that no one was following her. She'd bring money, knowing that I'd decided I had to lam after all. Money that she'd get back, damn it, if it was the last thing I ever did. Whatever money she'd lend me now, plus the other two sums and enough over to cover every drink and every cigarette I'd bummed from her. But not for the love and the trust she'd given me; you can't pay for that in money. In my case, I couldn't ever pay for it, period. The nearest I could come would be by being honest with her, leveling down the line. That much she had coming. More than that she had coming but more than that I couldn't give her.

The Shoebox is a shoebox-sized place. Not good for talking, but that didn't matter because we weren't going to talk there.

She got there fifteen minutes after I did; I was on my second drink. I ordered a Manhattan when I saw her coming in the door.

"Hello, Billie," I said.

Hello, Billie. Goodbye, Billie. This is the end for us, today. It's got to be the end. I knew she'd understand when I told her, when I told her everything.

"Howie, are you in—"

"In funds?" I cut her off. "Sure, just ordered you a drink." I dropped my voice, but not far enough to make it conspicuous. "Not here, Billie. Let's drink our drink and then I've got a room around the corner. I registered double so it'll be safe for us to go there and talk a while."

The bartender had mixed her Manhattan and was pouring it. I ordered a refill on my whisky-high. Why not? It was going to be my last drink for a long while. The wagon from here on in, even after I got back to Chicago for at least a few weeks, until I was sure the stuff couldn't get me, until I was sure I could do normal occasional social drinking without letting it start me off.

We drank our drinks and went out. Out into the sun, the warm sunny afternoon. Just before we got to the corner, Billie stopped me.

"Just a minute, Howie."

She ducked into a store, a liquor store, before I could stop her. I waited. She came out with a wrapped bottle and a cardboard carton. "The ready-mixed wasn't on ice, Howie, but it's all right. I bought some ice cubes too. Are there two glasses in the room?"

I nodded; we went on. There were two glasses in the room. The wagon not yet. But it wouldn't have been right not to have a last drink or two, a stirrup cup or two, with Billie the Kid.

She took charge of the two tumblers, the drinks. Poured the drinks over ice cubes, stirred them around a while and then fished the ice cubes out when the drinks were chilled.

While I talked. While I told her about Chicago, about me in Chicago, about my family and the investment company. She handed me my drink then. She said quietly, "Go on, Howie."

I went on. I told her what Mame had told me about her guest Jesus the night before she was killed. I told her of the death of Jesus Gonzales as I'd read it in the *Mirror*. I added the two up for her.

She made us another drink while I told her about Ramon, about what had happened, about how I'd just killed him.

"Ramon," she said. "He has knife scars, Howie?" I nodded. She said, "Knife scars, a hype, a chef. I didn't know his name, but I know who his woman was, a red-headed junkie named Bess, I think it's Bess, in a place just down the block from Karas' joint. It's what happened, Howie, just like you guessed it. It must have been." She sipped her drink. "Yes, Howie, you'd better go back to Chicago, right away. It could be bad trouble for you if you don't. I brought money. Sixty. It's all I have except a little to last me till I can get more. Here."

A little roll of bills, she tucked into my shirt pocket.

"Billie," I said. "I wish—"

"Don't say it, honey. I know you can't. Take me with you, I mean. I wouldn't fit, not with the people you know there. And I'd be bad for you."

"I'd be bad for you, Billie. I'd be a square, a wet blanket. I'll have to be to get back in that rut, to hold down—" I didn't want to think about it. I said, "Billie, I'm going to send you what I owe you. Can I count on your being at the same address for another week or so?"

She sighed. "I guess so, Howie. But I'll give you my sister's name and address, what I use for a permanent address, in case you ever—in case you might not be able to send the money right away."

"I'll write it down," I said. I tore a corner off the paper the bottle had been wrapped in, looked around for something to write with; I remembered the fountain pen I'd stuck in my trousers pocket at Mame's. It was still there.

I screwed off the cap. Something glittered, falling to the carpet, a lot of somethings. Shiny little somethings that looked like diamonds. Billie gasped. Then she was scrabbling on the floor, picking them up. I stared at the pen, the hollow pen without even a point, in my hand. Hollow and empty now. But there was still something in the cap, which I'd been holding so it hadn't spilled. I emptied the cap out into my hand. Bigger diamonds, six of them, big and deep and beautifully cut.

My guess had been wrong. It hadn't been heroin Gonzales had been smuggling. Diamonds. And when he'd found himself followed to Mame's, he'd stashed them there for safety. The pen hadn't fallen from his coat pocket; he'd hidden it there deliberately.

They were in two piles on the table, Billie's hands trembling a little as she handled them one at a time. "Matched," she said reverently. "My husband taught me stones, Howie. Those six big ones—over five carats each, cut for depth, not shallow, and they're blue-white and I'll bet they're flawless, all of them, because they're matched. And the fifteen smaller ones— they're matched too, and they're almost three carats apiece. You know what Karas would give us for them, Howie?"

"Karas?"

"Fifteen grand, Howie, at least. Maybe more. These aren't ordinary; they're something special. Sure, Karas—I didn't tell you everything, because it didn't matter then, when I said I thought maybe he had some racket—not dope. He handles stones, only stones. Gonzales might have heard of him, might have been trying to contact him through Mame."

I thought about fifteen thousand dollars, and I thought about going back to Chicago. Billie said, "Mexico, Howie. In Mexico we can live like kings—like a king and queen—for five years for that much."

And stop drinking, straighten out? Billie said, "Howie, shall I take these to Karas right now so we can leave quick?" She was flushed, breathing hard, staring at me pleadingly.

"Yes," I said. She kissed me, hard, and gathered them up.

At the doorway, hand on the knob. "Howie, were you kidding when you said you were in love with a girl named Honor in Chicago? I mean, is there a real girl named that, or did you just mean—?"

"I was kidding, Billie the Kid."

The door closed.

Her heels clicked down the wooden hall. I poured myself a drink, a long one, and didn't bother to chill it with ice cubes. Yes, I'd known a girl named Honor in Chicago, once, but—

—but that was in another country, and besides, the wench is dead.

I drank my drink and waited.

Twenty minutes later, I heard Billie's returning footsteps in the hall.

Manhunt, July 1953
Later expanded into the novel, The Wench is Dead, 1955

The Pickled Punks

I

ALL SAMMY the dimwit wanted was to learn about sex. It failed to enter his simple head he might set off a chain-cycle of murder.

Mack Irby stood leaning on a heavy cane, listening to the grind of the talker for the unborn show. The carnival crowd streaming down the midway flowed around him. He listened with ironical amusement on his lean face.

MYSTERY OF SEX read the banner over the front.

"Here it is, boys, the show they been talking about, the show you came out here to see, this is it, the sex mystery exposed, here's where you see it, male and female naked and unadorned, here's where you see everything, I mean everything, right before your very eyes, the naked truth, all on the inside and all for one thin dime."

Burt Evans had done all right by himself, Mack Irby thought, in finding a new talker. The guy was okay.

"Here it is, boys, the show you want to see, this is it, this is where you see it all and learn the naked truth, sex in the raw, stay as long as you like, continuous and now going on, all for only one thin dime, the mystery of sex."

Mack Irby limped only slightly as he made his way to the ticket box. The talker reached to tear off a ticket and then stopped as he saw Irby grinning at him.

"How are the pickled punks?" Irby asked. "I'm Mack Irby."

"Irby? Oh—yeah. You did the grinding here before. Burt told me about you. Go on in and say howdy to him."

"Later maybe. If he's got a tip in there I might queer his pitch on the sex books. I'll be around a few days."

"Not going to ride out the season? You can get a job easy. Model show needs a talker."

"Nah, only two weeks. I'll loaf it out. I got my stake."

"Burt said you got some moolah out of the accident."

"Two grand—not bad for seven weeks."

"Hell no. Anyway luckier than the other guy in the car with you. He was killed, wasn't he?"

"Yeah, Charlie Flack. Well, tell Burt I'll look him up tomorrow. Got a date tonight. So long."

"My name's Barney King, Mack. Okay, I'll tell Burt."

Barney King picked up the mike again. "Here it is, boys, the show you came out to see, the mystery of sex, the naked truth, male and female unadorned . . ."

Mack Irby walked on down the midway and despite the limp and the cane he walked on air. He told himself, *this is it, boy, this is the show you came to see, continuous and now about to start, stay as long as you like, and all for forty-two thousand bucks.*

Forty-two thousand dollars stashed away safely, waiting to be picked up. And almost three thousand more in honest money, the nine fifty he'd put in postal savings earlier in the season and the two grand he'd got from the insurance company, pure lagniappe.

It needed music, that walk down the bright midway. And music it had. The music to his ears that was the overall sound of the carnival. The merry-go-round's organ, the combo of the jig show, voices and laughter and the strident selling spieling grinding over P. A. systems and the crack of rifles in the shooting gallery and singing yelling shuffling, the thud of baseballs and the soft ratchets of fortune wheels and the base drum call to bally.

Try your luck, mister, pitch till you win, the big show just about to start, three balls for a dime, see the strangest people on earth, win a kewpie doll for the little woman, get 'em while they're red hot, pick your lucky number, hurry, hurry, and inside the little woman will show you, win a ham, see the alligator boy, this is the show you came to see, naked and unadorned, every number wins a prize.

Mack Irby walking down the midway, rich.

What a break that accident had been! It had meant the whole forty-two thousand dollars was his instead of only a third of it. Charlie Flack had been tough about insisting on that two-thirds split—but with some justification, Irby had to admit. It was Charlie who knew the ropes on robbing banks, Charlie who'd cased the job, done the brainwork and given the orders. Yes, Charlie had earned the two-thirds split—if he had lived to take it.

Charlie had been a tough guy but a careful one-even a careful driver. That accident the night after the robbery hadn't been Charlie's fault at all. He'd talked Charlie into driving over to a roadhouse near Glenrock for a little private celebration—but they were on their way there when it happened and neither of them had even had a drink as yet.

The other driver had been drunk and on the wrong side of the road and a cop car had seen it happen. That's why there hadn't been any doubt about responsibility and why the insurance company that carried liability for the other guy had settled like a shot.

Of course a broken leg and seven weeks in the hospital hadn't been fun—but what wonderful news it had been when they'd told him Charlie Flack was dead. Only he and Charlie had known where the bank loot was hidden and now only *he* knew. So it was all his, *three*-thirds of that beautiful hunk of moolah.

Maybe he'd inherit Charlie's girl too. He'd know about that pretty soon now—unless someone had snagged off Maybelle already.

He saw that he was about to pass the mitt camp, the little square top with the big palms—human palms, not potted ones—on banners on each side of the entrance and the bigger banner across the top. DR. MAGUS, it read, PALMISTRY, ASTROLOGY, CARD AND CRYSTAL READINGS.

Mack Irby stopped. Right here and now, if Doc wasn't busy, he could get the score on Maybelle. If she'd tied up with somebody else it would be smarter not to look her up at all. Making a pass could cause trouble and trouble was the last thing he wanted right now.

He went to the entrance and called, "Doc!"

Dr. Magus came to the entrance. A little man with a gray goatee, silvery hair, sharp eyes twinkling behind gold-rimmed glasses, dapper. He held out a hand.

"Mack! Good to see you. Come on in and have a drink."

Irby followed him inside. "Just want to ask you a question, Doc. Afraid I haven't got time for a drink—want to catch somebody before they get away."

Dr. Magus smiled. "You have plenty of time, my boy. The model show is still putting on a bally—I can hear them—and that means at least one more show."

Irby laughed. "You win, Doc. Okay, one drink."

"We'll make it a toast to your getting back Luck, Mack."

"Thanks, Doc. How've things been going?"

"Fine. And now I'll spare you asking that question. Maybelle is still free."

Mack Irby stared at him. How the hell had Doc known he'd wanted to ask about Maybelle? The guess that he'd been heading for the model show wouldn't have been a hard one for Doc to make but there were three girls with the model show and either of the other two would have been a more natural guess for Doc.

Trixie Connor because she put out for cash and so would be a sure thing if she didn't already have a date. Or Honey McGlassen because he'd dated her before, nothing steady but half a dozen times maybe. And he'd never once made a pass at Maybelle because she'd been Charlie's.

Suddenly a frightening thought hit Mack Irby. What if Doc, that smart little bastard of a mentalist, really *could* read minds? What if right now he was reading about... Mack tried to jerk his mind away from the bank robbery, from the money and where the money was hidden.

He said quickly, "Thanks, Doc. But I really got to run. Got to see somebody else before I look up—Maybelle."

He got out of there as fast as he could... down the row of hanky-panks. There weren't any marks in front of the milk-bottle game so he stopped there, reminded. He'd need a place to take Maybelle tonight, if he got her, and he might as well line it up now. It wouldn't go to waste. If he couldn't get Maybelle he'd find someone else—after seven weeks continence he wasn't sleeping alone tonight.

Jesse Rau, who ran the ball game, pitched a sleeping top he was always willing to rent for an hour or a night. Ordinarily Jesse and his punk, Sammy the halfwit slept in it, but if he rented it for all night Jesse and the punk would dose down under one of the bally platforms.

Irby said, "Hi, Jess. Got your top rented for tonight?"

"Hi, Mack. Back with us, huh? About the top, I dunno. It's cool tonight and—"

Irby said, "Five bucks?"

He didn't want to argue. Jesse usually got two or three. He put a five on the ledge, knowing Jesse would take it. And what the hell was five bucks tonight?

As he walked away he heard Jesse telling Sammy to get their stuff out of the top.

At the model show, two of the girls were out for the bally, Honey and Maybelle, standing there in thin silk bathrobes that showed every curve of their bodies. As he looked at Maybelle's body he found himself breathing a little hard, almost feeling dizzy he wanted her so bad.

He raised his hand on the chance she'd notice the movement and see him. Miraculously she did. With a finger of the raised hand he made a little circular gesture that meant around behind the top. He caught her slight nod.

He went around behind and waited, taking a long drink out of the flat pint bottle of whiskey he'd been carrying in his pocket.

Then the canvas lifted and Maybelle ducked under it. His arms were around her almost before she could straighten up, pulling her against him, his hands running down the silk of her back, down over her buttocks, cupping them, pulling her so tightly against him that they were almost off balance.

"Maybelle honey, I got Jesse's top lined up. Will you meet me there after the show?"

Her low voice sounded amused. "My God, Mack, you sure don't waste time, do you? What makes you think I want to?"

"Honey, you know I been hot for you all season. You *got* to!"

She fended off his lips. "Now-now, don't mess my make-up or I won't."

"How soon?"

"Hour maybe. Around midnight." She laughed. "You act like a man who hasn't had a woman in seven weeks. Didn't you even make a quick stop on the way here?"

His quick breath told her without words that he hadn't. She laughed again softly. Then, with him holding her as he was, she did a *grind*. And grind has two meanings in show business, one for carney talkers and one for burlesque dancers.

Then, she suddenly pushed him away and went back under canvas.

It took him a minute to get control back. Lord, what a woman. Forty-two grand and a dame like that! He'd take her with him for the winter. Fancy suites in fancy hotels. But for tonight the sleeping top would do. Hell, anywhere would do—the middle of the midway or the top of the Ferris wheel.

In the sleeping top he lay waiting, sweating a little despite the coolness. And worrying. What if she didn't come?

But she came and it was wonderful and later he lay beside her, naked in the cool air.

A foolish thing to do and a hell of a good way to catch pneumonia. But of course that doesn't matter if you're not going to live until morning.

II

BURT EVANS, after he straightened up from the body, stood there listening to be sure no one had heard the thud of the tent stake.

Then, cautiously, keeping close to the sidewall, Evans walked around the penny arcade top to the midway and stood ready to step out into the light, listening first for footsteps. No sound came. He stepped out.

And saw Dolly Quintana coming toward him. She wore moccasins so he hadn't heard her. She stopped and stared at him and the direction of her gaze made him realize what he was still holding.

In concentrating, on walking softly, on listening, he'd made the horrible blunder of forgetting to drop the weapon he'd just killed Mack Irby with.

Almost a fatal mistake, then and there, for Dolly. Then he realized he couldn't safely kill her. She'd stopped, still three paces away, and no matter how fast he moved she'd have time at least to scream. And a scream would bring dozens running.

So he turned and tossed the tent stake back into the darkness, casually as though it were nothing important. He said, "Hi, Dolly, know if the chow top's still open?"

"I hope so." She came forward again now. "Couldn't get to sleep and I'm hungry."

He fell in, beside her. "I can use some coffee myself."

His mind worked furiously. This was dynamite. Dolly was the wife of Leon Quintana, the knife thrower with the freak show, and Quintana was insanely murderously jealous. It was dangerous just to walk or talk

His mind worked furiously. This was dynamite. Dolly was the wife of Leon Quintana, the knife thrower with the freak show, and Quintana was insanely murderously jealous. It was dangerous just to walk or talk with Dolly, yet now he had to stay with her until he had a chance to kill her without her being able to scream, or until he figured another answer. It had to be figured before Mack Irby's, body was found. After that Dolly would have his number—in spades.

Evans wondered if he were strong enough and quick enough to choke her to death, right here and now, without her being able to scream. He glanced sidewise, weighing the chances. Then he heard the shuffle of feet—someone was coming. And they were nearing the chow top already, in any case.

He spoke quickly. "We better not go in together, Dolly, but I want to tell you something. Go in first, take a table away from anyone else. I'll sit near enough to talk to you without sitting with you."

He saw her slight nod and stopped to let her go in alone. When he entered a minute later he saw to his relief that the place was empty except for Dolly at a table way back and Barney King at the counter. He went back and sat at a table next to Dolly's but not facing her. He faced instead so he could watch the entrance and could also keep an eye on Barney and Hank, the counterman, now waddling over to take their orders.

When Hank had gone and was out of earshot he said, "Don't look this way, Dolly, but listen. I'm going to reach over and drop something in your lap: Look at it, but under the edge of the table, out of sight."

He made sure of the entrance and Barney and Hank and then stood up and leaned across far enough to toss into Dolly's lap the tight roll of bills he'd just taken from Irby's pocket. He hadn't counted it but it had looked like several hundred dollars.

He turned away from Dolly again. In a minute he heard her voice, low as his own. "Jeez, two hundred and forty bucks! What the *hell*. . . ?"

"Put it away quick. It's yours if you want it."

"If I *want* it! When Leon never lets me have a penny of my own? With this much I can get away from him. But—*why?*"

"For forgetting you saw me on the midway tonight."

Quiet a moment and then, "Oh." She'd remembered what he'd had in his hand and he'd figured it out.

"Damn right a deal. And I don't care *who* you killed back there. This is *getaway* money. I can get away from Leon now."

He'd suspected she felt that way. He was glad to be sure of it. Because it meant she wouldn't share the money—and the secret along with it—with Leon Quintana. That would have given him one more to worry about.

He finished his coffee as quickly as he could and went out.

Evans was glad he hadn't had to kill her. Dolly was a good kid.

~§~

Dr. Magus woke. Someone was shaking him, saying, "Doc, Doc," in a frantic whisper. A woman's voice. Sounded like Maybelle's.

"Go away," he said. "If I wake up you won't be there."

"Doc, this is Maybelle. I need you."

He rolled over on the bedroll and found he'd rolled against her knees. She was really there, kneeling beside him.

"Doc, somebody killed Mack Irby. You got to help me."

He sat up. "Mack Irby? When? How?"

"It—it must have been half an hour ago. They hit him with something over the head. The back of his head is—*ugh!*"

~§~

He put an arm across her shoulders, pulled her down to sit beside him. "Take it easy, honey. Where do you come in? Were you with him?"

"We were in Jesse's sleeping top. We ran out of whisky and he pulled his clothes on and said he'd wake Pop and get us some. He crawled out and didn't come back; After a while I got worried and remembered a kind of thunk sound just after he'd crawled out and I got to thinking—well, I went out to look and he was dead, just outside. Somebody'd killed him with—well, something like a tent stake."

"Had he been rolled?"

"How would I—all right, yes he was. I wanted to know that too so I felt in his pockets. Just change. And whatever money he'd had wasn't in his coat, either; he'd left that back in the sleeping top. I crawled back in and felt in it too. There was a folder that felt like traveler's checks, but no money."

"Who knows you were there with him?"

"Nobody, as far as I know. But listen, Doc, the cops will find out *somehow*. They'll ask everybody and Honey and Trixie will tell them I wasn't in my own bunk—they hate me."

"But it they don't know you were with Mack...."

"Doc, the cops will figure it. And I can't tell them where I really was—unless somebody'll back up my story and say I was with them all night."

Dr. Magus smiled gently into the darkness. "A light begins to dawn—a lovely light." He cleared his throat. "And far be it from rile to look a gift horse in the mouth, especially when the gift horse is so shapely a filly but—why is it so important to you to keep out of it?"

"Doc, the cops would—well, I've been in trouble before. I got a record. They'd never believe I didn't finger him for the kill."

"What were you in trouble for?"

"Just shoplifting. Three or four times and one time I had over a hundred bucks worth and that made it grand larceny instead of petty. I did six months. Doc, they'll throw the book at me. This is a *murder* rap, Doc. Don't think they don't third-degree women on that, women with a record."

"Ummm—I guess they would, my dear. And on your own story, if you told the truth, they could book you on a morals charge and use it to keep you on ice. But before I stick my neck out to alibi you, you don't mind if I doubt your word on one little thing?"

"I *didn't* kill him. Doc. And I *don't* know who did."

"Those things I believe. You're not a killer, my dear. But money is something else again. Mack might or might not have been rolled before you looked to see. Or his money might have been in his coat. Now since it would be more dangerous for me to give you an alibi if you have any Mack Irby money than if you haven't, will you overcome your maidenly modesty while I make one thousand percent sure that you are not concealing so much as a sawbuck that might have been in one of his pockets?"

She giggled a little. "Okay, Doc. It won't take you long to find out, me wearing only shoes and a wrapper."

"Good. I remove the shoes first... No, nothing in the shoes. And now the wrapper... No, nothing. And now, keeping firmly in mind that money can be concealed, at least conceivably, upon any part of the body by being fastened down with adhesive tape, and that a tightly folded bill can be concealed, well, almost anywhere, and that it is too dark for me to see..."

He missed no inch of surface, no nook or cranny.

Maybelle giggled again. "Doc, no police matron ever gave me a search like *that*."

"No police matron would have the same ulterior motive. And I found no money on you but I found something just the same—I found how badly I want to give you an alibi for tonight. So if necessity arises, wearing a blue uniform, we shall say you spent the whole night here and tell only half a lie. Oh, my dear...!"

And Maybelle, all of whose amours had been with younger and less experienced men, learned a few things that night that she had never known before. Young lust and then experienced lechery, with a murder in between. All in all, it turned out to be quite a night for Maybelle.

III

UNDER BLANKETS in the chill of early dawn; Dolly Quintana lay beside her husband trembling not from cold but from fear. Fear of the very thought of what he could do to her if she ran away and he came after and found her. Not fear of death—she wouldn't be afraid to die, not a clean death.

But killing wasn't what Leon had promised if she ever even tried to run away from him. It was acid—acid thrown into her face to blind and disfigure her so no man would ever want her or even be able to bear looking at her.

And he'd find her, no matter how long it took him. He was crazy jealous, really crazy in that one way although he was sane every other way.

She'd been so fiercely happy when Burt Evans had given her that money and now she was wishing he hadn't. Because the money had meant freedom and now she was finding out she didn't, have the courage to take it.

And if she didn't run away now the money was a danger. Oh God, if he ever found that money. He'd never believe anything she told him, the truth or a lie, about how she got it. Even if he did believe her he'd beat her near to death for holding out on him.

Why had she ever been so crazy as to marry him? Oh, she guessed she'd loved him then but now—now it was horrible when the only times he ever touched her he hurt her because he'd come to be so that the only way he ever had fun sexually was when he hurt her, and now there wasn't any love left for rum, just fear, and she hated to be close to him like now even when he was sleeping.

Oh God, wouldn't it be wonderful just once to have a man make love to her gently, why almost anybody, especially Joe Linder. She could really love Joe Linder and he wanted her too, she could tell, she could feel it just the way he looked at her any time Leon wasn't watching his face.

But don't think about that, it would be awful if Leon found that money, but he wouldn't because she'd stashed it before she'd come back here, not in too good a place and somebody might find it before she could get it back but at least nobody would know it was she who'd hidden it there.

When Leon went into town today like he'd said he was going she could get it from its temporary hiding place and with time to do it in, with Leon gone, she could hide it in a place where it would be safe and he'd never find it in a million years, right in his own trunk, not hers, because she knew he sometimes looked through her trunk. He kept that old cornet at the bottom of his trunk, the one he used to play a long time ago, and he hadn't touched it for years. It was broken too, but he kept it because he was superstitious about it for some reason and the roll of bills would slip right down in the horn out of sight and...

There was a babble of voices from outside, quite a distance away, a lot of people all talking excitedly. Leon must have been partly awake because he heard it too and sat up.

"What the hell's that?" He pulled on trousers and a shirt and went under the canvas sidewall. When he came back he started undressing again. He said, "Mack Irby, that guy used to be talker for the unborn show. Somebody killed him and rolled him last night."

~§~

Cops. The lot was full of cops. There seemed to be dozens of them although actually there were only four.

They got to Dr. Magus a little after ten o'clock. Rather, one of them did. A lieutenant named Showalter. He was big, but not tough outwardly. He was soft spoken, almost gentle.

He was smart, too, but not too smart. Dr. Magus, who found himself strangely interested without knowing why, had managed to make it a conversation rather than an interrogation and had learned more than he had told. Sammy, the boy who worked for Jesse Rau, had found the body.

The police were convinced that a woman had been in the sleeping top with Irby but the lieutenant showed no inclination to doubt Dr. Magus's story that Maybelle had spent the night with rum. He'd already had that story from Maybelle and had come to Dr. Magus merely to confirm it.

The time of death had been set as somewhere between two and three o'clock. There seemed to be little doubt that he'd been killed for his money. How much had he had?

"We know within a few dollars, as it happens," the lieutenant said. "We phoned Glenrock and the boys there checked up. He had a hundred and twenty-seven dollars on him when he was admitted to the hospital. Probably spent about seventy-five of it, ten a week, while he was there—cigarettes, newspapers and stuff—so he left there yesterday afternoon with about fifty in cash and an insurance company check for two thousand.

"He went right to the Glenrock bank and cashed the check—took two hundred in cash and bought traveler's checks with the rest, eighteen hundred. The checks were still in his coat pocket. So he left Glenrock with around two hundred and fifty. Figure his ticket, one meal, a bottle or two of whiskey—maybe fifteen bucks. He'd have had about two thirty-five in cash. That's what the killer got."

Dr. Magus said, "And how disappointing if he knew about the insurance settlement and expected two thousand. But the killer must have been stupid if he thought Irby would carry it all in cash."

The lieutenant shrugged. "Killers sometimes are stupid." He grinned suddenly. "Doc, you're the only guy around here that hasn't acted like I got leprosy, just because I'm a cop. Maybe that ought to make me suspicious of you, but it doesn't. If this was a con game set-up you'd be my first choice, but you don't look like you'd kill with a tent stake. Say, what's an unborn show?"

Dr. Magus smiled. "An unborn show is a collection of fetuses in glass jars. It is also known as a 'punk show' and the fetuses as 'pickled punks.' Whatever the grind is, that's the joint. Usually they're human fetuses in various stages of development, but occasionally there's an animal fetus if it's a freak one.

"Burt's unborn show, the Mystery of Sex, has the fetus of a two-headed calf. But that's just an extra attraction—the pitch is on the human fetuses—male and female, naked and unadorned. Which, of course, they are."

"Fake or real?"

Dr. Magus shrugged. "Probably real because they'd be cheaper to get. It's carney tradition to kid an unborn show man about Goodyear trade marks on the kiesters of his pickled punks but it's just a stock gag. Maybe it would pay to fake a freak fetus, but ordinary ones—hell, anyone who has a friend in the right spot in a hospital or morgue can get all the fetuses he wants for a few drinks or at most a few bucks. Rubber ones would be more expensive."

"That's all there is in the Mystery of Sex show?"

"Practically. Plus a pair of flashy wall charts of male and female anatomy in cross section. And also a table with stacks of sex books on it. That's where Burt's profits come in, pitching those sex books to the marks, once they're inside. That's why the admission is only a dime, to get the marks in so he can sell them books at two bucks a throw."

After the lieutenant had gone, Dr. Magus felt thoughtful but couldn't figure out what he was thoughtful about. It wasn't wondering who had killed Mack Irby. He didn't care about that. But something was stirring at the back of his mind and he wanted to know what it was.

He sat down and pulled over the madball, the crystal sphere in its silver stand, and stared into it. Not because he ever really saw anything there except once in a while when he was a little drunk, and then it always scared him, but looking into it helped him to concentrate. Usually, that is. This time it didn't.

Mid-evening and Sammy was glad because Jesse was drinking and when Jesse started drinking on the job he nearly always closed the place early. And Sammy would be free to wander around the lot while the rest of the carney was still running.

Tonight he was especially glad they might close early because Jesse was mad at him. Jesse had bawled the holy hell out of him this morning and had been mean ever since, all because he'd found a dead man and instead of pretending he hadn't he'd called people to tell them. And how could Sammy have known? That was the bad thing; you never knew what you were supposed to do when something new happened and so many new things kept happening that you were always in trouble because you'd done something wrong.

And if Jesse ever got too mad at him, Jesse wouldn't take care of him anymore and they'd come and get him and put him in a place behind bars because he couldn't take care of himself. He'd been in a place like that for, a long time once and then one day he'd found a door open and had gone away.

And he'd nearly starved to death for a long time until Jesse found him and taught him how to set up the milk bottles for the game and took care of him and fed him. That had been about a year ago, he thought, anyway there'd been one winter since it happened, and he'd been with Jesse ever since.

Maybe tonight if Jesse closed early, he'd have time to spend the fifty cents in his pocket for cotton candy. Mr. Linder had given it to him early this afternoon for running an errand and he hadn't had time to spend it before Jesse had opened the game.

Jesse took another drink and then said, "Okay, kid, let's knock it off. We done enough today."

Sammy remembered something he'd wanted to ask. "Jesse, how old am I?"

"Hell, I don't know. Eighteen, maybe twenty. Why?"

"The cop asked me. I didn't know."

Jesse growled at him. He shouldn't have mentioned the cop—it reminded Jesse about his finding the man dead and telling people. For a moment he thought Jesse was going to hit him again but Jesse didn't. He went away. Sammy straightened things up and fixed the curtain in front of the booth and turned out the lights. Then he was free.

A few minutes later he was eating his first cone of cotton candy. And staring at the bally of the model show. Miss Trixie and Miss Maybelle were on the platform in their silk wrappers. They were both pretty but Sammy watched Miss Trixie. He liked Miss Trixie—she gave him quarters for running errands sometimes. And she treated him nice.

Some of the other women acted like they didn't like him around but Miss Trixie didn't mind. Her silk wrapper was pulled tight around her over her round full breasts. He wondered what they were for. And why men paid money to go in the model show and watch the women pose in just tiny G-strings and cheesecloth bras you could see through?

It had something to do with something called sex, he knew, and something men did to women or the other way around. He'd wondered about it a few times and found, himself wondering again now. He'd asked Jesse but Jesse got mad at him for asking, so he couldn't risk asking anybody else.

But suddenly it came to him where he could find out without having to ask anybody. There was a show called Mystery of Sex right on the lot. It would tell him. And he could have three more cotton candies and still have a dime left to get in.

He bought his second one and with it strolled down the midway to the Mystery of Sex.

". . . see everything, boys," Mr. King was saying. "I mean everything, the sex mystery exposed, red hot, right before your eyes, this is the show you came to see."

Yes, Sammy had come to see. He stepped to the ticket box and put down his dime. Mr. King looked at him and didn't take it. He said, "Hell, kid, you're with it. You don't gotta pay. But—wait a minute, I just thought. You don't want to go in there now. Burt's got a good house and you might queer his pitch on the books, see?"

Sammy didn't see but he nodded. Mr. King said, "Tell you what, Sammy. Come around some afternoon when business is slow and you can go in for as long as you want. But there's nothing in there but pickled punks, kid. Unborn babies. . . What you want to see them for?"

"I don't want to see babies, Mr. King. But I want to see what you said, about what sex is and naked and things like that."

Mr. King shook his head sadly. "Believe you me, Sammy, if you're starting that far behind scratch, what you'd see in there would only confuse you worse. Get a dame to show you some time—that's the only way."

"Show me what, Mr. King?"

"The most wonderful thing on earth, kid. And you look old enough to be showed."

"Would any woman show me, Mr. King? Would Miss Trixie?"

Mr. King chuckled. "I don't know about any woman, kid, and you better be careful who you ask. But Miss Trixie—she would, sure, for enough money. Folding money."

Then a group of people started by and Mr. King looked at them and started talking into the microphone. "This way, boys, this way to the sex show—"

And Sammy wandered off. He had three more cotton candies and then his money was gone. He wondered how much money Miss Trixie would want. A lot, probably, more than he'd ever have. He'd never had even one piece of folding money.

He wandered off the midway, around behind the circle of tops, hoping he could find someone to talk to, someone who wasn't working. There was a light on in one of the trailers, Mr. Evans' trailer. He knocked and when there wasn't any answer he tried the knob and it wasn't locked so he went in. Mr. Evans wouldn't care if he looked at pictures in magazines. He'd let Sammy look at pictures before.

But there weren't any magazines in sight so he opened a cabinet door. And found them and leafed through them. Then he wanted to put them away but couldn't remember just which cabinet he'd opened and found them in. It could have been one of several.

The first he tried wasn't the right one; it had linens in it. The second had books, about a dozen books of different sizes and shapes. He wondered if the books had pictures too. He took one out and looked to see.

It had pictures. The first one he turned to was a picture of a man and a woman naked and in a strange position. Strange, anyway, to Sammy. And he turned pages and saw more pictures, lots of pictures, but they were all pictures of men and women naked together. He studied them and found within himself a growing excitement, a kind of excitement he hadn't known existed. This was it, this was the show Sammy had come to see, here's, where he saw it, male and female naked and unadorned, the mystery of sex, the naked truth.

He looked through the other books too; four more of them had pictures and he studied them but the rest were just printing and he put them back right away.

Then he closed the cabinet carefully because Sammy suspected that if Mr. Evans guessed Sammy had looked at those books he might tell Sammy not to look at them again. But if he didn't know he couldn't tell Sammy not to.

He was glad when he got to the sleeping top to find that Jesse was sound asleep and snoring. He got under the covers quietly so Jesse wouldn't wake up. Jesse didn't.

IV

DR. MAGUS woke to misery and the sound of rain on canvas. His watch told him it was ten o'clock and his aching head told him there was no use trying to go back to sleep. He'd drunk too much, much too much. At the rate he was drinking he'd never live to see sixty. But why the hell did he want to see sixty? What had sixty ever done for him?

At least he'd left himself a pick-up shot in the bottle. He downed it and it stayed down. He slogged through mud and rain to the chow top and put himself outside a breakfast that he didn't want but knew he should eat. He slogged through mud back to the mitt camp but the rain had stopped. He felt almost human now.

What was it, he wondered, that had *bothered* him about Mack Irby? No mystery about why he'd been killed, certainly. Then what bothered him about it?

He realized suddenly that it had been the way Mack had acted that night, Monday night, when he'd dropped into the mitt camp. He'd behaved naturally at first. But then he'd called the shot on where Mack was heading and who he was going to see there. Just a good guess based on observation—he'd noticed looks Mack had given Maybelle back when she'd been Charlie's woman.

A mentalist watches reactions automatically. It's his stock in trade in giving readings. He comes to do it subconsciously even when he isn't working. And Mack Irby had reacted big, just a few seconds after that hit about Maybelle. Fear, it had been—naked fear and a sudden hurry to get the hell away from there.

And the fear certainly hadn't been physical fear so it could mean only one thing. That lucky shot had made Mack Irby suddenly afraid Dr. Magus could really read his mind—and there was something in his mind he was desperately afraid to have read, something damned important.

Mack had had a guilty secret, an important one.

For a moment he toyed with the possibility that Mack had engineered the accident that had killed Charlie Flack—but he couldn't have. If there'd been anything off beat on that accident the insurance company wouldn't have settled so quickly. And hell's bells, cops had witnessed it.

But what then? No kind of petty larceny would get a reaction like that from a man as tough as Irby. If it wasn't a killing, it had to be something big, something with real money in it like a payroll robbery or a bank robbery.

But Mack Irby, tough though he was, just couldn't have been in that kind of a league. But wait a minute—Charlie Flack could have. He'd figured Charlie for a red hot the first time he'd seen him. A bank robber or gangster either of the lam or just holing in with the carney between jobs. And he and Mack had become close friends. He could have taken Mack with rum on something big.

He'd have to talk to Maybelle. She'd known Charlie before Charlie had joined the carnival in the spring. Now that he was dead she'd have no reason not to tell him what Charlie had really been. And it would be easy to get it out of Maybelle by giving her a reading—she'd been wanting him to.

He took another drink of whiskey from the fresh bottle he'd bought when he'd gone for breakfast and decided he felt up to giving Maybelle that reading now.

It was drizzling rain though, and he hated to go out in it. But he sighed and donned galoshes and slicker. He stepped out, intending to start his search at the chow top because she'd been there half an hour ago when he'd breakfasted and might still be there.

But luck was with him. Sammy was going by. He called Sammy. "Sammy, do you know Maybelle?"

"Sure, Mr. Magus."

"Will you find her and tell her I said to ask her to drop in the mitt camp as soon as she's free and has time? Look in the chow top for her first." He flipped Sammy a quarter.

"Sure, Mr. Magus, I'll find her. Say, will you tell my fortune sometime, Mr. Magus?"

Dr. Magus laughed. "I'll tell it right now. You're going to get rich, Sammy."

"You mean paper money, folding money?"

"Lots of it, maybe sooner than you think."

~§~

Giving Maybelle a good reading was almost too easy. She didn't even realize that she told him Charlie had been a bank robber but that he'd reformed and was going straight. She was sure he was. Yes, he was gone from the lot sometimes but that was because he was crazy about fishing. He and Mack had gone on a fishing trip together just the day before the accident—they'd been gone all day. All day—and they hadn't caught a fish.

He sugar-coated the reading by telling her what she really wanted to know, that she was absolutely safe, that the police would never learn that it was she who had been with Mack Irby just before he'd been murdered. A leisurely reading, interspersed with drinks. Dr. Magus felt pretty good when it was over and when she leaned forward and put her hand on his.

"Thanks, Doc," she said. "Thanks a million. I'm not worried any more about Monday night. And listen, any time you want to alibi me again like you did then, just say the word."

Dr. Magus smiled. "Thank you, my dear. I will say the word because I know the word, the perfect word that ends unnecessary words. The word is *now*."

~§~

Burt Evans had not slept well. In the long hours of the night he had come to the reluctant conclusion that Dolly Quintana was too dangerous to him to be allowed to live. Not that he thought she'd ever give him away to the cops—but there was still the explosive situation caused by Dolly's fear of Leon and his psychopathic attitude toward Dolly. Giving her the money had been a mistake, he saw now.

If she stayed, Leon would find it sooner or later, force the truth out of her—and believe only part of that truth, the name of the man who'd given it to her. If she ran he'd go after her and if he ever caught her it would be the same thing.

Dolly must die, and quickly—the end of the season was only ten days or so away—tonight, if possible.

In the long night he'd worked out a foolproof method. He wouldn't have to kill her himself. Leon would only too readily do that if he caught her sleeping with another man.

Joe Linder, talker for the freak show, would be the man. He knew damn well Linder was crazy about Dolly, that if it wasn't for Leon he might even want to marry her. He had a strong hunch Dolly liked Linder. He thought he could set up an assignation between them if he worked it right. Of course Joe Linder would get killed too and that was unfortunate but it couldn't be helped.

He talked to Joe Linder first, right after lunch. Joe listened and was pathetically grateful for what Evans offered to do for him. The first step of Operation Dolly was successful.

~§~

By three o'clock the rain had completely stopped. Evans leaned against the bally platform of the freak show and pretended to watch the cat men putting shavings on the midway, actually watching for Leon to leave. He'd already learned roundabout that Leon intended to go into town and that would give him a chance to talk to Dolly.

He'd be damned careful about it, just the same. He'd been careless last night—he'd left his trailer unlocked. And Sammy had come in and had spent some time there. He knew it was Sammy because the magazines hadn't been as he'd left them. Only Sammy would have got at those magazines. The pornography books had been messed with too, but anybody could have looked at them.

Nobody besides Sammy, though, would have looked through the magazines. It gave Evans gooseflesh to think what might have happened had Sammy got into the suitcase under the bunk. Well, he'd learned;

he'd never again leave the trailer unlocked. How had he ever been so stupid as to do it once?

Three-thirty—damn Leon, wasn't he going after all?

Then Leon came out and Dolly was with him. He swore to himself. That messed things for today. He'd have to wait.

But he watched them walk away and they separated near the main entrance. Leon went on through it and Dolly started off for the show top.

Burt walked to the entrance and stood there until he saw Leon actually board a bus. Then he strolled to the chow top. Dolly had sat at a table with Bess Streeter but he saw that Bess had finished eating. There were only empty dishes in front of her so she'd probably leave before Dolly did. He got himself coffee and took it to a table near them.

When Bess Streeter left, he moved over.

He said, "Don't be scared, Dolly. I saw Leon actually get on the bus, so this is safe. And don't worry about anybody telling Leon we sat and talked together. Everybody with the carney hates Leon and likes you." He watched her closely. "Especially Joe Linder."

Her color mounted. He'd been right. He said, "Listen, I've got something important to tell you. Joe Linder is in love with you and wants to help you get away from Leon. Don't look afraid like that; act as though we're talking casually about nothing important. Can't you?"

"I'll—try."

"Good girl! Here's the way it is—Joe Linder wants to help you get away. But he'll stay with the show himself till the end of the season so Leon'll never connect the two of you, if you go sooner, tomorrow. And at the end of the season Joe'll join you. Will you let him help you?"

"OhmyGodyes!" One word.

Burt Evans smiled. But he said, "Damn it, act as though we're talking about the weather. Here's the plan. Joe's brother and sister-in-law got a little farm in northern California. He's going to spend the winter with them—you too. You'll take off tomorrow or next day, depending when he or I can rig something to get Leon off the lot again. Joe'll give you a letter to his brother. You'll go there and wait for him."

"But—but next season. . ."

"Think Leon could ever find you in Australia? That's where Joe was already planning to go. He's got another brother there, with a carney, and he'd already planning to go. He's got another brother there, with a carney, and he'd already decided to make the jump."

He could hear her breathing. She was damn near crying and he'd better finish his pitch and get away fast. He said, "Take it easy. You and Joe will need a chance to talk this over tonight. I got something for you here that will make it safe as houses." He took a quick look around to be sure no one was watching and then put a tiny glass bottle under the edge of her coffee saucer. "Stick that in your purse quick, out of sight."

He waited till she'd done it. "That's some sleeping stuff. Safe but powerful. Leon always takes at least a drink or two after the last show, doesn't he?"

She nodded.

"Get that in his whiskey bottle and it's in the bag. If he drinks all of it it won't hurt him, but if he gets even a little he'll sleep like a log. Wait till he's sound asleep—this stuff won't put him there. It'll just keep him there when he does sleep. But once he's sawing timber you can count on at least five or six hours while even a bomb wouldn't wake him up.

"Then you go to Joe's sleeping top. He'll be waiting for you and you can fix up the details between you. Okay?"

Dolly nodded. And looked again as though she might cry, so he got away from her quickly before she could.

V

WHEN MAYBELLE left Dr. Magus dressed again. Regretfully, for now after that unpremeditated and delightful interlude he could have slept for a while, and soundly. But fortune beckoned brightly. Everything he'd learned from Maybelle had been on the side of his hunch.

He dressed meticulously in his best clothes, added spats and a panama, took a malacca stick from the foot locker and made his way across newly spread shavings to the entrance.

He enjoyed the cab ride downtown to the office of the Bloomfield *Sun*. He enjoyed the deference his dapper dress gained for him in that office. He was shown to a table and there was given and left with a bound volume of issues for the second half of the year, July 1st to date.

He decided to look for the accident first, knowing offhand only the approximate date, sometime late in July. And he thought it was a Friday. He found it in the issue for Saturday, July 30th—it had happened just before midnight on the 29th. The story was brief and the only things he learned from it that he hadn't known before were the name of the driver of the other car and the fact that he, like Charlie, had been killed.

But he knew the date now. And Maybelle had said that Charlie and Mack had been gone from the lot all day the day before the accident. That would be Thursday the 28th. And since the *Sun* was a morning paper, he tried the issue of Friday the 29th. What he was looking for was there, right on the front page.

MASKED DUO ROBS
UNION CITY BANK

He read it carefully. Two armed men had held up the First National Bank of Union City at 2:25 P.M. and escaped with $42,000 in cash.

Dr. Magus very carefully refrained from whistling and read on. The men had worn handkerchiefs, tied bandit style over their faces, just below the eyes. One had stood guard while the other rifled the vault and the cashiers' money drawers. The money had been stuffed into a musette bag. It had been mostly in old bills of relatively large denominations.

According to the president of the bank the reason for this was that the bank acted as a clearing house for other banks in the county which wanted to exchange such bills for new or smaller ones. Periodically they were sent to the Treasury Department for replacement.

On leaving the bank the men had been seen to drive toward the downtown section of Union City in a dark blue Chrysler sedan. A car answering that description had later been found abandoned on a downtown street and was ascertained to be a stolen car.

That was all.

That was enough. Dr. Magus returned the bound volume to the file clerk with grave thanks and took his departure.

Outside, he took a long deep breath. It all fitted too perfectly to be coincidence. Union City was only about forty miles from Glen-rock, where the carney had played that week, and on the same main highway.

It was even closer to Campton, the town they'd played the week before. Charlie would have started casing the job from there.

It had to be. It was.

Charlie had been killed the day after the robbery, and now Mack was dead, too— and *where was the forty-two grand?*

~§~

Was it, could it be, hidden somewhere on the carney lot? Not the lot itself, of course, but hidden in something that moved each week with the carney? Mack Irby had rushed for the lot the moment he'd been released from the hospital. Why else unless to get the money? Oh yes, Maybelle. But a man with forty-two grand can have his choice of a lot of women as pretty as Maybelle or prettier, In Florida or Mexico or wherever he wants to go.

Who had Mack's trunk? No, it couldn't be there—surely the police, investigating his murder, would have found out who was holding his effects and searched them. And what had happened to Charlie's trunk?

Dr. Magus sighed, realizing what his next step would be. Never before in his life had he gone to a police station voluntarily. He went to one now, asked for Lieutenant Showalter, found him in.

He asked if any relatives had come forward to claim Mack Irby's effects. It seems that he had lent Mack a book on astrology, and he'd just remembered where it was. It was an old out-of-print book, quite valuable to him.

The lieutenant shook his head. "Wasn't any book in his trunk, Doc. I helped look through it, one of the first things after we got out there."

"Do you know if he'd gone to the trunk that evening before he was killed? I'm thinking he might have got it out to give to me and then left it somewhere else."

"Nope. Wiggins, your carney owner, was keeping it for him and said he hadn't seen Irby that night. And he couldn't have gone to his trunk anyway because it was under a lot of other stuff in a storage van."

"Could anyone else have taken the book from his trunk?" Dr. Magus asked. "Not that anyone would steal it alone but if the trunk had been rifled—"

"It hadn't. It was locked and the key was in Irby's coat pocket. It hadn't been opened while he was gone. Wiggins was sure of that."

Dr. Magus sighed again over his lost irreplaceable book, and departed.

Wiggins would be the best person, he decided, to ask about Charlie Flack's trunk. And Wiggins always stayed at a hotel, the best in town, instead of living on the lot. He might be at the hotel now, especially since the carney wasn't playing this afternoon. He asked for the best hotel, found it, found Wiggins in it.

He gave Higgins the same song and dance on an astrology book he'd given the lieutenant, only this time it was Charlie he'd lent it to.

"Sorry, Doc," Wiggins said. "Night of Charlie's death I helped two Glenrock coppers go through Charlie's trunk, just like Monday morning I helped two Bloomfield coppers go through Mack's. Then they took it away."

"You're sure there wasn't a book in it?"

"Almost positive. We went through things pretty fine because they were looking for anything that would show a name and address of some relative they could notify of Charlie's death. But we didn't find any and as far as I know the Glenrock coppers, are still holding the trunk. You could write and ask them to make sure about the book."

"Maybe I will. Thanks, a lot anyway."

"Don't mention it, Doc."

Back in the mitt camp, early evening, Dr. Magus decided to hell with working. Thinking seemed more important. So did drinking. He wanted to recapture the beautiful edge he'd had early in the afternoon and had lost somewhere downtown.

To hell with the twenty or forty bucks he might take in. He was shooting for forty-two thousand—if he could figure out where it was.

He hung out the *Closed* sign and made doubly sure he wouldn't be bothered by closing and lashing the tent flaps. He made himself comfortable and drank and thought.

Chances were poor of his being able to get the money unless it had been hidden with the carnival. If they'd rented a safe-deposit box or left the money, say, in a suitcase checked somewhere, he'd have a devil of a time getting it even if he learned where it was. But he didn't think that was what they'd done with the money.

If a suitcase check or a receipt for a deposit box had been found on either of the men or in their effects, the police would have looked in the box or claimed the suitcase, just as routine procedure, and would have found the money. Besides, he had an idea they'd have liked to keep the money near them, right at hand, if they could figure out a safe place for it.

But where would be a safe place? Where would he hide something on the lot? It would have to be in something at least as big as the musette bag they'd carried it off in. Well, maybe not quite so big—the money had been stuffed into the bag hurriedly and maybe neatly stacked and compressed. . . Well, it would still take, say, half a cubic foot of space.

He thought a while and drank a while.

Later, when he felt just right for it, just drunk enough and in the right mood, he pulled over the madball, the crystal. He stared into it, making his mind a blank. The few times it had actually worked for him he'd done it that way.

From outside the canvas came the carnival sounds, the merry-go-round playing Blue Danube, the voices of the talkers, the crowd murmur, the blend of sounds that added up to a single sound as familiar to him as the beating of his own heart. He let himself hear that sound until he could hear it no longer, until it was part of the night and one with the night, as silent as night itself.

There was a sudden bright flash of light in the crystal, then for a brief instant darkness.

Dr. Magus blinked, and again the crystal was as it had been before, reflecting his own distorted face and the interior of the mitt camp curving upon itself like an Einsteinium universe.

He looked around to see if that flash could have been the reflection of a sudden light somewhere. It couldn't have been. Not even from outside—his canvas had no tears or even thin spots. It was new and whole.

He frowned. Had he really seen that flash in the crystal or had it been the sudden twinge of an optic nerve?

If he'd really seen it and it meant anything, what could it mean?

He tried again and nothing more happened. After a while he gave up and pushed the crystal back. He had another drink and thought some more.

A thought hit him that was so simple and logical that he wondered why he hadn't thought of it sooner. It might lead him to the money even if it wasn't with the carnival. He'd start tomorrow from the logical place to start from, see what he could learn there at Glenrock, at the hospital.

He drank a toast to Glenrock.

VI

STANDING IN THE DARK, looking, watching through the window of his trailer, Burt Evans sweated.

Something had gone wrong. It was after one o'clock—the freak show had closed almost an hour and a half ago—and Dolly should be coming any moment now but Joe Linder wasn't in his sleeping top waiting for her! If Dolly came now Joe wouldn't be there and the whole plan would foozle.

Why wasn't Joe Linder waiting for Dolly? What had gone wrong?

Or could he have missed seeing Linder come in? He didn't think it was possible—he hadn't left the window once since midnight. At midnight he'd gone over to check up with Joe and Joe hadn't been there. He'd come right back and, hadn't left the window since. Joe couldn't possibly be there—unless, well it was barely possible he'd come around the top and gone inside it during the half a minute it had taken him to walk back to his trailer.

Suddenly he had to know, for sure, whether that had happened. If it had everything was still all right. If it hadn't—well, he'd know, for sure, that something had gone wrong.

Quickly he left the window and stepped across to the door and outside, leaving it open behind him so he could get back in quickly. He stood a moment, just outside, hesitating.

What if Dolly comes now, he wondered. Then he had the answer to the problem, at least. He could tell Dolly to go in Joe's and wait and he'd scour the lot to see what had happened to Joe.

He took the first step toward the sleeping top and then stopped as he heard footsteps coming behind him. He turned swiftly and then relaxed as he saw it was only Sammy.

And in that moment of relaxation he thought of something that could explain why Linder wasn't home yet. Just maybe Leon had decided to get into the poker game tonight—if he had and Joe had known it, he'd probably have joined the game too. He'd know that Dolly wouldn't be coming until a little while after Leon quit the game or the game broke up.

By playing in the game as long as Leon did, or a few minutes longer, he'd save himself the suspense of waiting for Dolly in the sleeping top. He'd know to look for her anywhere from fifteen minutes to an hour after Leon left the game. And he could send Sammy to see who was in the poker game.

"Hi, Mr. Evans," Sammy said. "Can I look at pitchers?"

"Not tonight, Sammy. But listen, I want you to run an errand for me over to the G-top."

"Sure, Mr. Evans. I just come from there. Jesse's playing cards."

"Who else is playing?"

"Uh, let's see, there's Jesse and—uh, Mr. King and Mr.—I forget his name, the man who throws the knives."

"Quintana. Who else?"

"The man who runs the fish pond and—uh, Mr. Linder. That's all, I think."

Burt Evans took a deep breath of relief. "Wiggins wasn't there?"

"No, Mr. Evans."

"Okay, Sammy, then you won't have to go back there for me. I just wanted to send a message to him if he was playing. You run along now."

"Can't I *please* look at pitchers, Mr. Evans?"

"No."

"Aw gee, Mr. Evans, I won't bother you none. I'll just—"

Evans' hand lashed out and caught Sammy on the side of the face, a backhand blow. Not hard enough to hurt badly but the sting and the surprise made Sammy take a backward step and fall. He scrambled to his feet and ran toward the midway.

Damn it, Evans thought, why had he done a silly thing like that? He could have got rid of Sammy without hitting him. Now Sammy might go squawking to Jesse and—oh hell, Jesse wouldn't take trouble over a little thing like that. And if Jesse did come to him he'd just tell Jesse about Sammy getting into those pornography books. Then Jesse would beat the hell out of Sammy himself.

Now that he remembered that, Sammy really had had that sock

coming. Just the same, hitting Sammy worried him because it showed how tense he was inside. He'd better start calming down and controlling himself before he made a real mistake.

He went back inside the trailer and resumed his vigil from the window. Joe Linder came back to his sleeping top at about half past one. Dolly came and joined him at two o'clock.

Give them half an hour, he decided. Surely she wouldn't leave before then. Then too they might talk a while first or Dolly might play the old game of pretending reluctance and it was better that Leon catch them in the act. Besides—hell, give them half an hour. It made him feel better about what he had to do.

He checked himself while he waited. He had the razor blade. He had his gun in case anything went wrong. He was wearing crêpe soled shoes that let him walk silently. And the car was ready for a quick getaway if necessary.

Then it was two-thirty, on the head. Evans left the trailer and went around behind the tops until he found the freak show top and the corner of it Quintana partitioned off for sleeping quarters.

He looked around carefully and then took out the razor blade and made a six-inch slit in the canvas. He held the slit open a little and put his eye to it. He could see perfectly—an all-night bulb in the main part of the top threw dim light over Quintana's partition. He could see the bedding, Quintana sleeping on it, lying on his back. And not doped unless a few drops of plain water in his whiskey nightcap had doped him.

He made his voice sepulchral. "Leon Quintana." No movement. He said it again, just a trifle louder. He saw Quintana's head rise.

Quickly now, before he was thoroughly awake. "Your wife is with Joe Linder, in Joe's top."

Quintana was sitting up fast now, turning to look at Dolly's empty side of the bedding. Evans got away from there quickly and silently, back to his own trailer.

He barely had time to get to the window before Quintana was in sight, running. He wore only a pair, of shorts but he had two knives—cutting knives, not throwing knives, one in each hand, held as a knife fighter holds them. He shouldered his way through the flap of Joe Linder's top and there was a yell and a scream.

Evans shuddered.

~§~

Dr. Magus woke to hangover again. But he remembered that today he was going to Glenrock. For forty-two thousand excellent reasons. The thought of going anywhere made him groan but he struggled into clothes—any old clothes until he had a pick-up shot, coffee and breakfast. After that he'd dress for the trip.

He had the pick-up shot inside him when a voice from outside called, "Hey, Doc, you home?"

"I'm beginning to think so. Come on in."

It was Showalter, the lieutenant. He looked at Dr. Magus. "Doc, do you feel as bad as you look?"

"I do not know how I look and do not tell me, please,"

"All right. Listen, Doc, I'm looking for a witness or two to what happened last night. Were you one of the first ones there?"

"One of the first ones where? What happened last night?"

"Dolly Quintana and Joe Linder—Leon Quintana caught them in bed together in Linder's tent and killed both of them."

Dr. Magus swore luridly and at length. "Have you got Quintana?" he asked.

"Sure, and a confession and everything. He didn't even try to get away, just sat there in his shorts, bawling. We got him all right—I'm trying, though, to find some of the people who heard the screams and got there right away—just for the record or in case Quintana might try to repudiate that confession."

"Afraid I can't help you, Lieutenant. I didn't hear a thing. Probably wouldn't have even if I'd been awake. Joe Linder's top is way across the midway from here. I woke up just now, was just getting set to go out for breakfast."

"You look like you need it, Doc. I won't keep you from it. Or come to think of it I'll go with you and have some coffee." He grinned. "I had my breakfast five hours ago."

~§~

In the chow top after his first cup of coffee, Dr. Magus felt a little better. He asked, "Anything new on the Irby business?"

"Forgot to mention it," the lieutenant told him. "That's washed up too. Quintana did it. We found Irby's money in Quintana's trunk, stuffed inside an old cornet."

Dr. Magus looked surprised. "I'll be damned," he said. "I can see Leon committing a crime of passion—but that Irby deal—Has Leon confessed it?"

"No—denies it. But that's logical enough—he probably figured he may get life instead of the hot squat on a *flagrante delicto* kill in hot blood but that he'd get the chair for sure on a cold-blooded murder for money."

"I still can't see him killing Irby, Lieutenant. That really surprises me."

The lieutenant shrugged. "No doubt about it. It *was* Irby's money. Not only just about the amount we figured—two hundred forty-two hundred of it in brand new twenties with consecutive serial numbers. We were keeping this back before; but we learned at the Glenrock bank that Irby had asked for two hundred cash he took out of the check in twenties. They gave them to him from, a stack of new ones fresh from the printing office."

"Sounds as though he did it, all right. Well, I've been wrong about people before. A few times."

"Another reason, Doc, why I figured he wouldn't confess to the Irby kill. He's getting set to try an insanity plea. Here's history of how he knew where Dolly was—claims he heard a voice in his sleep!"

Another cop, a uniformed one, stood in the entrance of the chow top, looking around. He saw Showalter and came over.

"Captain just phoned," he said. "Quintana just killed himself in jail. Know how? Bit through the vein in one of his wrists and let himself bleed to death before they found him. Imagine a guy doing that. Cap said to tell you to come on in, no use looking for witnesses anymore."

Dr. Magus was glad he'd finished his breakfast. He felt a little sick as he walked back to the mitt camp.

~§~

Burt Evans felt lousy, too, but for a different reason. He was nervous, keyed-up, jittery—and worried that he felt that way for no reason at all. All his problems were solved and he should be feeling wonderful. Everything had worked out better than he'd dared hope.

The cops had even written off Mack Irby's murder and wouldn't investigate any further. What a brilliant idea it had been, after all, to give that money to Dolly! Almost as brilliant as his master stroke of eliminating Dolly, the only witness against him, by letting somebody else kill her.

And he'd had luck too—Quintana's committing suicide in jail, especially, so he couldn't keep on denying having killed Irby. Maybe if he'd kept on denying it they'd have started believing him after a while and reopened the investigation.

Now nobody living knew Quintana hadn't killed Irby. And nobody living even suspected the money existed.

Then why was he feeling lousy today? Conscience? Hell, he didn't have any conscience. Of course a good drunk would help him—a knock-down drag-out two-week's drunk—but that would have to wait a week or so until the season was over, until he had that money in a really safe place.

My God the things he could do after that! Hundred-dollar-a-night woman any time he wanted them...

Suddenly, realizing something, he started to laugh.

That was what was wrong with him! He hadn't had a woman for over six weeks now, since he'd found the money. Hadn't even thought about it!

Why couldn't he have, say, Trixie over tonight to spend the night with him? No reason at all—true, he didn't, want to start spending money on the grand scale until he was somewhere else but that didn't mean he had to live now a more celebrate life than he had before he'd found that dough. It wouldn't be acting suddenly prosperous for him to have a woman tonight and a couple of other nights before the big spending could start.

Naturally he was jittery and nervous. But twenty bucks would cure what ailed him.

Burt strolled over to the model show top. He went back inside and called out Trixie's name. She came under the canvas partition that shut off the dressing space.

"Hi," she said. "Haven't seen you for a long time."

"Too long." He dropped his voice. "Busy tonight?"

"Well—I promised someone I'd see him right after we close, but it's not an all-night date. I'll be free by one o'clock."

"Swell, honey. Drop around to the trailer after that. And don't make any other late dates, huh?"

VII

THE RECEPTIONIST at the Glenrock Memorial Hospital checked the card file and told Dr. Magus that she was sorry but the doctor who had treated his son—Dr. Kramer, he'd been the resident physician then—was no longer with them. He'd left only last week to take a position on the staff of Misericordia Hospital in Milwaukee. He could be reached there.

Dr. Magus sighed. "Perhaps I might tall to whichever of the nurses would remember him best?"

"I don't know which one that would be, sir. Maybe you'd better talk to our head nurse, Miss Plackett. She isn't on duty now but she stays here and I think she's in her room."

A few minutes later Dr. Magus was talking to Miss Plackett.

Sharp eyes, sharp nose, sharp manner and tough, no doubt, to work for but, he decided, soft as butter inside. She wasn't in uniform—she wore a navy blue suit.

"Miss Plackett," Dr. Magus said, "I am Dr. Rance Irby. My son, MacGregor Irby—I understand he used the name of Mack Irby—spent seven weeks here, up to last Monday afternoon, with a broken leg and other and lesser injuries. Which of your nurses, may I ask, would be most familiar with the case?"

"I believe I myself would, Dr. Irby. I helped Dr. Kramer the night Mr. Irby was brought in and I am familiar with the progress of the case up to the time of his release. What is it you wish to know?"

Dr. Magus sighed. "Many *little* things, Miss Plackett. Not medical details or anything that could be considered confidential. Perhaps—ah—do you know my son is dead?"

"I know the police came here a few days ago and asked questions about him. They didn't tell us why."

"He was killed—murdered for money he had on him—only hours

after he left here. He returned to the carnival he worked for and met his death there that same night."

"I'm sorry to hear that, Doctor." She wasn't really. But she would be after he got into the song and dance he hadn't started yet.

~§~

He said, "Thank you. Miss Plackett, I'm sure you'll be better able to help me if I explain fully what my problem is—and it's almost impossible to make that particular long story short. I wonder. . . Will you forgive me if I ask you to have dinner with me? It will give us time to talk at leisure."

She declined but not too firmly. They went to a "nice" restaurant only a block from the hospital and he was pleasantly surprised to be able to talk her into a cocktail before dinner.

"I should explain, Miss Plackett, that I am not a doctor of medicine. My doctorate is in philosophy. I am a professor of psychology at U. S. C." He shook his head ruefully. "A psychologist in the eyes of the world but not my own—not until I learn wherein I failed with my own son."

"What do you mean, Dr. Irby?"

"MacGregor ran away from home eleven years ago at the age of eighteen, just out of high school. I have not seen him since nor heard of or from him until yesterday, despite all my efforts to find him. Yesterday I was told of his death, and the circumstances surrounding it, by the Los Angeles Police Department."

"But how did they know to notify you? I mean, if he'd changed his name and—"

"Fingerprints, taken as a matter of police routine after his death. Sent to Washington and found to be those of my son—on record because he'd been arrested during the last year he was living at home.

"I came immediately. Rather, I should say, I started immediately by plane to Bloomfield, to the carnival, but since Glenrock was on my way there, I decided to stop here first to see what I could learn here."

"But I don't quite see what I can tell you. . ."

"I'll try to explain. It's not my son's murder I'm interested in—I understand that his murderer has already been apprehended and that there is no mystery. But there is a mystery, a major mystery, in my son's *life*. Until he was fourteen MacGregor was a normal happy boy, mentally healthy.

"Something happened then—or he had a delayed reaction to something that happened sooner—that changed him. He began to rebel. He began to steal and—to do other things. When I tried to talk to him he was sullen and defiant. He grew farther and farther away from me. And at eighteen he ran away from home. Ever since, I've tried to trace him. Now do you begin to see, Miss Plackett, what it is that I must learn?"

"Why—not exactly."

"I want to know, I must learn, where I made my mistake in dealing with my son, what happened to him inside. Apart from parental love there is the fact that I am supposed to be a psychologist. God help me, the university has been wanting me to conduct a seminar in child guidance.

"How can I and be honest when I don't know where I went wrong in guiding my own son? It's too late to help MacGregor now but for the sake of my own conscience and my integrity as a teacher I must learn the answer."

Dr. Magus took a deep breath. He was hitting his stride now, beginning to feel the role he was playing. And he had his audience. Miss Plackett's nose was still sharp but her eyes weren't.

He said, "How long it takes me doesn't matter. I've arranged for indefinite leave. If necessary I'll find and talk to every friend he had, every woman he knew. I'll trace back places where he lived and worked until I find the answer. Somewhere, sometime, he told somebody something—consciously or unconsciously—that will tell me what I want to know."

"I understand now, Doctor. How can I help you?"

"Thank you, Miss Plackett. What, specifically, do I want to know?" He gestured helplessly. "I don't *know* what you might be able to tell me that might help. Just tell me every slight detail that you remember about him. His personality, his attitudes—anything and everything you can tell me about his stay with you.

"Especially things that would give me leads to other people who might tell me things. Telephone calls he made or received, if any. Incoming and outgoing correspondence. Anything, everything that you remember about him."

Miss Plackett talked. She talked all through dinner.

And said nothing helpful to Dr. Magus.

It was over dessert that he thought of and asked the right question. "Ah—Miss Plackett, was his leg set under a general or a local anesthetic?"

"A general, administered intravenously—sodium pentothal."

"People often talk deliriously when they are coming out of anesthesia. Usually nonsense, of course. But sometimes such nonsense as can come from things that are deep in their subconscious minds, things that are desperately important to them."

"Yes, Doctor. And Mr. Irby did rave a bit when he was coming out I—but I'm afraid that to me it was all pure nonsense and that I don't remember a word of it."

Dr. Magus leaned earnestly forward. "Will you try hard to remember, my dear?"

"I'll try my best." She thought hard. "Some of it was wearing—I remember the word 'Jeez,' a corruption of 'Jesus' I suppose. That and a number—but I can't remember the number."

Dr. Magus took a deep breath. He said, "I punished him once when he was about six for using that very word. I wonder . . . The punishment was that I temporarily deprived him of his toy soldiers. There were, I believe—ah—forty-two of them."

"That's the number, Doctor! He'd say, 'Forty-two, Jeez!' and then laugh. He said that several times. And there was another phrase. . ."

She stared into space. Dr. Magus didn't move a muscle.

"Something about pickles," she said. "No, it was pickle punks or pickled punks. And something about 'it'—whatever 'it' was—being stuffed inside a two-headed calf."

Dr. Magus' smile was beautiful.

~§~

Sammy wandered lonely as a cloud. It was late and the carny had long since closed hut Jesse was playing poker again and Sammy wasn't sleepy. He wanted to find someone to talk to.

Even more, he wanted again to see those pictures of naked men and women doing things. If only Mr. Evans wasn't mad at him! But he was and now he was afraid of Mr. Evans. Mr. Evans would hit him again if he even asked to see pictures, even just pictures in magazines, ordinary pictures.

Or if there was only some way he could get some money, big money, folding money, so he could give it to Miss Trixie, like Mr. King had suggested, so she'd show him those things the men and women in the book did; actually do them with him. But where and how would he ever get folding money?

He walked toward the G-top to make sure Jesse was still playing cards and that it was still all right for him to wander. He looked through the flap and Jesse was still in the game.

When he turned away he saw Miss Trixie. She was already past him and walking fast. She went toward the trailer, Mr. Evans' trailer. She knocked and the door opened and she went in.

Just a few days ago Sammy would have thought she was going there just to talk to Mr. Evans. But Sammy had learned a lot from those pictures and from what Mr. King had told him about Miss Trixie. He knew about women now and he knew why Miss Trixie was going to see Mr. Evans. Or he was pretty sure anyway.

He wondered if they'd let him watch. That would be better than looking at the pictures again. But then he remembered that Mr. Evans was mad at him and had hit him and that he didn't dare even ask Mr. Evans for anything again.

But the shade on one of the windows of the trailer wasn't pulled all the way down—he could see a crack of light between it and the bottom of the window. Maybe he could see, through and watch and Mr. Evans wouldn't know.

Sammy tiptoed over. He hoped he wouldn't have to stand there too long because the night had turned chilly and he was shivering.

He had to bend down a little to put his eyes to the crack. At first all he saw was the edge of the bunk and the wall past it. Then Miss Trixie walked into view. She still had her clothes on except for the coat she'd been wearing. At his angle of vision he could see only from her knees to her breasts. Then she sat down on the bunk, facing his way, and he could see her face too.

Then Mr. Evans came. He was still dressed too, mostly. He had a drink in each hand—he handed one to Miss Trixie and sat down beside her.

Sammy shivered again and wondered if he should go back and get his jacket. But he might miss something if he did.

Mr. Evans moved farther back on the bunk, leaning against the wall. He held his drink in his left hand and his right hand reached behind Miss Trixie and Sammy could ten he was unbuttoning buttons. Then his hand pulled her back to lean against him and slid around her neck and down inside the front of her dress.

Suddenly Sammy sneezed. The sneeze was loud and it was so unexpected that it made his head jerk forward. His forehead hit the window with a resounding thump.

He turned and ran for the concealing shadow of the G-top but he'd taken only a few steps when he heard the door jerk open behind him and knew that Mr. Evans was seeing him run, recognizing him even from behind at so short a distance in the moonlight.

But no footsteps came running after him and he paused and looked back when he reached the shadows. Hadn't Mr. Evans minded after all?

But while he was wondering the door of the trailer opened again and Mr. Evans came out. He'd put on more clothes. He started walking but not, toward Sammy. Sammy could see he was heading around for the other side of the gambling top, where the entrance was. He was going to tell Jesse on Sammy.

How mad would Jesse be? How bad a thing had Sammy done? Maybe an awfully bad one. He turned and ran for Jesse's sleeping top. He'd better be there when Jesse came.

Inside he found the little carbide lantern and got it lighted. He put on his jacket and sat waiting. He didn't dare undress and get in the bedding because if he was naked Jesse's blows would hurt worse if Jesse was going to beat him.

Finally Jesse came. He crawled through the flap and stood up just inside, his head bent to clear the canvas, looking down at Sammy. He was sober but his eyes were cold and hard.

"Get out," he said. Get off the lot and keep going. I'm through with you."

Sammy whimpered. Jesse couldn't really be sending him away for good. That meant hunger and wandering until the police picked him up and put him back in a place again.

Jesse said, "Get going. I mean it. I wasn't going to feed you all winter anyhow and it might's well be now as end of season. Get going." He took off his belt and held it ready to swing. Buckle, end down.

Sammy looked at the buckle and whimpered again. Then he crawled out through, the tent flap past Jesse. Out into the night, the lonely night bright with moonlight and dark with dread.

VIII

SATURDAY MORNING. Dr. Magus woke early, for him, at nine o'clock, knowing he had a big day ahead of him. He'd better operate the mitt camp, for one thing, lest people start wondering why he was working so little.

And there were preparations to be made, none of them difficult but all of them important.

Most important would be getting rid of Barney King tonight for a couple of hours after the show closed. Barney King slept on a bedroll in the unborn show top. He had to get rid of Barney so he could get the two-headed calf fetus, get the forty-two thousand the unborn show.

~§~

Last night after he got back from Glenrock, he'd seen that Barney King was playing cards and he'd taken the slight risk of spending a few minutes with a flashlight in the unborn show top. He'd given the jar and the fetus a quick but careful examination.

The jar was a wide-mouthed five-gallon jar. Pretty heavy but he could manage to get it from the unborn show to the mitt camp and back again; then he'd want an empty cardboard carton to carry it in and rope to tie the carton shut and to carry it by.

Razor blades he had plenty of. But he'd need rubber cement to close the cut he'd have to make to get the money out of the hollow rubber fetus—it was rubber, all right. His examination of it through the glass had convinced him of that.

After they'd put the money inside the fetus Charlie and Mack would have sealed it again, not only to keep the money dry but because water getting in would lower the level of water in the jar and show evidence of tampering. He'd need rubber cement to reseal it for the same reason. He'd go off the lot this morning and get a carton, rope, rubber cement. So much for means.

For opportunity he had to think out a song and dance that would get Barney King off the lot at least two hours. He *might* be able to do the whole operation in half an hour but he'd better not count on it. Furthermore he very much wanted those two hours to be tonight. Tomorrow night there'd be no chance. Tomorrow night was Sunday night and tear-down-packing and moving would start even before the carnival closed. He'd worry about the jar being lost or broken-in the move to the next town and besides the suspense of waiting at least two more nights would be horrible.

He did his errands, put the things he'd bought in the mitt camp and went to see Barney King.

"Your jalopy still running, Barney? Wonder if you could do me a hell of a favor with it tonight after the carney closes. It'll be a drive of about forty miles each way but I'll gladly give you twenty bucks besides your gasoline and any other expenses."

"A double sawbuck I can use, Doc. What's the pitch?"

"Telegram from my brother. He's coming in on a plane tonight, some family business, wants me to meet a one-forty plane at the Springer Airport—guess Bloomfield hasn't got one or else he couldn't get a flight into it.

"I can't even go with you—I got a big deal on tonight that's going to make me a flat hundred bucks— Dame I gave a reading wants a private séance in her house on the anniversary of her husband's death, so it's got to be tonight. So I'll be money ahead to pay you to meet my brother."

"Sure, Doc. Don't blame you. How'll I know your brother, though, and what's his name."

"You'll know him because he looks a lot like me. But don't be surprised, Barney, if he doesn't show up on the plane. He's pretty unpredictable and if he sent me that telegram and then changed his mind about coming, it wouldn't surprise me. But I've got to have him met if he does come." Dr. Magus pulled out his wallet. "I'll give you the money now, Barney. And oh yes, his name. His name is Legion—Harry J. Legion."

~§~

Sammy was hungry. He'd been hiding from Jesse all day and it was late at night again now and the carnival was closing. But Jesse hadn't seen him and he was still all right—except that he was *awful* hungry. Most of the day he'd spent hiding under bally platforms.

Once, in the middle of the afternoon, he'd taken the chance of coming out and walking around—well away from Jesse's booth—long enough to get one errand to run for Dr. Magus, just a short errand that got him a quarter, enough to buy one hamburger sandwich.

But that was all he'd had to eat all day. And if he waited any longer in hiding even the chow top might be closed and he couldn't get anything to eat even if somebody did give him an errand to run.

So he took the risk again and crept out from under the bally platform of the freak show, onto the midway. He'd have to take a chance now, with the carney partly closed already; or it would be too late and he might starve to death and die. And that would spoil his plan.

He'd figured out his plan last night after Jesse had kicked him out. He'd crawled inside one of the trucks and had slept there but before he slept he figured out his plan. He had to stay on the lot, because if he got away from it he might not ever be able to find his way back, so he'd have to stay on the lot but hide from Jesse.

Tomorrow night the carney would move and he'd move with it in one of the trucks but still hiding from Jesse. And in the new town, on a new day, he'd go to Jesse and by that time Jesse would be over being mad at him and would take him back and everything would be all right again.

He'd say, "Sammy, I'm sorry. I thought I'd lost you." At least he could hope Jesse would.

As he walked along the almost deserted midway now he thought how much he hated Mr. Evans for telling on him. It was all Mr. Evans' fault, what had happened to him. Mr. Evans could just have told him not to look into a window, without telling Jesse on him. It was Mr. Evans' fault that he was hungry now. He wandered toward the chow top. It was still open, brightly lighted. He could smell food, frying hamburgers. His stomach hurt.

Suddenly a hand closed around his arm, tight, squeezing hard. It was Jesse. Jesse had seen him from behind and had come up.

Jesse's grip hurt and his eyes frightened Sammy. Jesse said, "I told you not to hang around here, didn't I? Hit the road."

"But Jesse—"

"Get off this lot tonight. God damn you, if I see you again after tonight I'll half kill you! Hit the road-tracks are over that way."

Jesse let go and jerked his thumb to show which way the tracks were and as though on cue a freight engine whistled mournfully in the night far away. Jesse walked on past him and went in the chow top.

Sammy stood there. His plan had failed. And, he saw now, not just because Jesse had found him too soon. Jesse really meant it and wouldn't change, wouldn't ever take him back. And Jesse really would half kill him if he saw him again—he'd meant that too. He had to go, had to hit the road, tonight; now, hungry.

He started in the direction Jesse's thumb had pointed, the direction of the tracks. He found himself cutting off the midway next to the G-top, and he stopped because if he went back that way he'd have to go past Mr. Evans' trailer. But he started walking again—why shouldn't he go past? Mr. Evans wouldn't hit him for just walking past.

Mr. Evans' trailer was dark and it was too early for him to have gone to bed. He wasn't there. Sammy looked at the trailer and his mouth began to water as he remembered that Mr. Evans had a little refrigerator in the trailer and kept food there. Sometimes he made a meal for himself instead of eating at the chow top.

Food. The all-night walk ahead of him would be easy if he could fill his stomach first or find food to take along. He got up his courage and knocked on the door to be sure Mr. Evans wasn't there. Again louder—no answer. He was *sure* now and he tried the door. It was locked but now that he knew no one was inside the pain in his stomach wasn't going to let that stop him.

He threw his shoulder against the door, then harder and again and the door burst open inward. He went in quickly and shut it, then turned on the lights. But the door wanted to swing open now that the lock was broken and he had to put a chair against it. He pulled down the shades so nobody could see him if they went by.

In the refrigerator he found a box of marshmallow cookies and stuffed one in his mouth right away. He could eat them while he looked for more food. There wasn't much more, but in a compartment over the refrigerator he found a box of crackers and the heel of a loaf of bread.

He was starting out with them when he remembered the books. Since he was stealing from Mr. Evans anyway and since he hated Mr. Evans too, why shouldn't he take at least one of those books along so he could look at it all he wanted to? At least the one book that was all pictures, photographs, no printing at all? It would serve Mr. Evans right if he took that too.

But the books weren't in the compartment where they'd been. Mr. Evans had moved them somewhere else or maybe hidden them to keep him from finding them if he came back. He put down the bread and crackers and started looking in other compartments and cabinets and places but he didn't find the books.

He looked under the bunk and there was a suitcase and he pulled it out. Mr. Evans could have put the books in the suitcase. It was locked but he got a hammer he'd just seen in a compartment he'd looked in and broke the lock. That would serve Mr. Evans right too.

He opened the suitcase and on top was a gun, a revolver. He picked it up and it felt nice and heavy in his hand. He'd take that too and then he wouldn't have to be afraid of anybody. He knew how to use it because the man at the shooting gallery had showed him how only a week ago.

He'd run an errand and instead of paying him in money the man had let him shoot a rifle a few times and a revolver like this one a few times. He hadn't hit anything with it but he knew how to shoot it all right. All you had to do was pull back the hammer with your thumb and then pull the trigger with your finger and it would shoot. He put the gun in his pocket and turned back to the suitcase.

There was a knock on the door. Sammy whirled around, his hand going into his pocket and closing around the butt of the revolver, ready to pull it out and shoot if anyone came in.

~§~

Ten minutes earlier, Dr. Magus, from the point of vantage he'd taken for the purpose, had seen Barney King drive away and had sighed with relief.

Now, back in the mitt camp, with the jar that held the fetus that held the money on the ground before him, he sighed again and more deeply.

No one had seen him carrying it around behind the tops. His luck had been in, as it had been all along. God what a break he'd got at Glenrock—that wonderful head nurse remembering and telling him what Mack Irby had said coming out of the anesthetic. Thinking Mack had said *forty-two, Jeez,* instead of *forty-two G's*—and then incredibly remembering and telling him its exact hiding place!

Here it was in front of him and he had lots of time, plenty of time. Why not take a drink now to celebrate? Just one drink now. More later, of course, after the money was in his foot locker and the pickled punk was back in the unborn show. But one now—he very carefully had not taken a single drink all day and—one drink now before he started would make his hands steadier.

He poured a drink into a glass, a measured drink. He couldn't drink from the bottle on an occasion like this. He raised the glass to his lips and sipped, dreaming.

That wonderful moolah, only inches and minutes away. Savor this moment, he told himself. This fleeting instant, this *now*, this anticipation—prolong and enjoy it. Not even the money itself could buy such moments as this.

IX

AFTER A WHILE, after a long while, Sammy decided that whoever had knocked had gone away. And he was glad because he hadn't really wanted to have to kill anybody, not even Mr. Evans.

He took his hand from the butt of the gun and turned to the suitcase again. Maybe the books were under the clothes. He threw clothes out of the suitcase with both hands but the books weren't there.

There was a shoebox, though, and when he picked it up he knew from the weight of it that it held something other than a pair of shoes.

He took off the lid.

He stared unbelievingly into the box. It was money, paper money, in neat stacks. Some of it in packages with paper bands around them, some of it loose. He hadn't thought there was that much paper money in the whole world. It must be an awful lot of money. It must be a million dollars, enough to buy anything.

Dr. Magus had been right—Sammy was rich!

Why he could go to Trixie right now, tonight, if he could find her. And give her a handful of this money and. . .

He put the lid back on the box and stood up quickly, putting it under his arm and going out the door. He didn't have to bother with the food now—he could buy all the food he wanted. With this money and the gun to protect it he could have *anything* he wanted.

Straight down the midway Sammy marched, one hand on the gun, the box under his other arm, not caring now whom he met, even Jesse or Mr. Evans. If he met either of them he'd just point the gun and tell him to go away. Straight toward the model show top he went. If Miss Trixie wasn't there he'd find her no matter where she was.

Trixie Connor put the final touches on her lipstick, standing close to the full-length mirror in the dressing room of the model show. She looked all right, she decided. She had a late date with a mark, a townie, who'd been pestering her with notes all week. She'd decided she could take him for plenty, a hundred bucks if he wanted her to spend all night with him.

She looked at her watch and saw it was time to go. He was going to be waiting in his car over on the McClelland Street side of the lot and he was there now.

She turned out the light, then walked out past the bally platform to the midway.

A voice called her name and she stopped and turned. It was only Sammy, poor half-witted Sammy, coming toward her, almost running. He had a shoebox under his arm and he looked excited.

"Miss Trixie! I was just coming for you. I want—"

"Sorry, Sammy, I'm in a hurry now. Whatever it is, ask me tomorrow." She started walking but he fell in beside her. She stopped to tell him not to but he stopped too and he had already opened the shoe-box and was reaching inside it. He brought out a handful of something. . .

~§~

God, it was *money!* They were right under a light bulb. She could see it plainly, and she couldn't be wrong. He was holding out to her a handful of twenty and fifty dollar bills. A handful of them—there must be almost a thousand dollars right there in Sammy's hand.

She reached out and grabbed the bills—Sammy's fingers released them without a struggle. The quickest glance at the money showed her it was real, not stage money or queer—the bills were all worn ones and they looked right and felt right. She quickly stuffed them into her handbag.

"Sammy, where did you get that money?"

He grinned at her. "I found it, Miss Trixie."

"Let me see that box!" She clutched at it but Sammy held onto it firmly. He was stronger than she.

He said, "I'll let you *see*, Miss Trixie. But it's mine." As she let go he took off the lid and let her look. The light overhead threw light into the box. Trixie gasped.

"Sammy, does anyone know you've. . ." She stopped, realizing that the question was absurd. If anyone knew Sammy had that money he wouldn't have it.

Her mind clicked into overdrive. She did what she should have done a full minute ago—she looked around to be sure no one was watching them and then pulled Sammy back into the shadows between two tops, off the midway and out of the light.

She didn't waste time wondering *where* Sammy had found the money. The thing was to get it from him and she tried the simplest thing first. She put her arms around his neck and pressed herself against him. "Sammy, want to go to bed with me? And have fun?"

"Gee, sure, Miss Trixie. That's what I gave you money for."

"All right. We'll go to a hotel downtown but first let's go back to my place and get a suitcase. We can get in a hotel easier if we've got one. And you can put that box in it so nobody'll see it."

Throwing clothes into the suitcase to fill it, Trixie thought furiously. Let him carry it so he wouldn't be suspicious.

The bottle of whisky—put it in so they could have a drink before they went to bed. And thank God for that little bottle of chloral hydrate she had. She popped it into her purse. She'd get that into the drink she'd offer him and—well, an hour or two after that Trixie Connor would be getting out of Bloomfield on the next plane, train, bus or whatever went out first. And keep going far and fast.

"You carry the suitcase, Sammy. Come on. Let's go."

~§~

Evans looked up from the card table as a hand fell on his shoulder. It was Wiggins. He said, "Hi. Did you know you left the light on in your trailer?"

"When? Just now?" He hadn't left the light on—he was certain of it. Since that time Sammy had walked in uninvited he'd been very careful with the lights and the lock.

"Ten-fifteen minutes ago. I went by and knocked when I saw a crack of light at one of the shades."

Evans tried to keep his face from showing fear, tried to act casual. But he didn't waste any time in throwing in his cards and standing up. He said, "I'd better go check up. Back in a minute."

He walked until he was outside the G-top but broke into a run the second he was outside and saw that not only was the light on but the door was now ajar.

The lock was broken. The suitcase was on the floor, empty. The money was gone. So was the gun.

Blankly, unbelievingly, he looked around. The food out of the refrigerator and cupboard, the empty box that had held cookies...

Sammy!

Only Sammy would have broken in to look for food, only Sammy would have eaten cookies while he searched the rest of the trailer. Sammy on the lam—Jesse had said something about kicking Sammy out.

Sammy must have left after Wiggins had been here and knocked because the door couldn't have been ajar then. So Sammy had left only ten or fifteen minutes ago. He might still be on the lot—he couldn't be far away.

Evans rushed out, not bothering with the door or the lights. They didn't matter now and every second might count.

On the midway he stopped, looking frantically around for someone, anyone, who might have seen Sammy, might be able to tell him which way Sammy had gone.

~§~

He ran for the chow top, seeing it was still lighted. In the entrance he almost ran into Dixie Weber. "Seen Sammy?" he asked.

"You mean Rau's boy? Yeah, just a few minutes ago."

He tried to make his voice sound calm. "Where? Which way was he going?"

"Toward the main gate. He was with Trixie Connor, carrying a suitcase for her."

"Did they have a taxi waiting?"

Dixie shrugged. "I just saw 'em going through the gate."

He gasped thanks and started that way, then whirled and ran for his car instead. Thank God it wasn't hitched to the trailer. He'd have a better chance in it than afoot. Even if they'd had a cab waiting or had been lucky enough to flag one down already, even if a bus had gone by, he might still be able to catch them if he was in his car.

~§~

Dr. Magus shifted the shielded flashlight and looked again to be sure. Yes, the line was faint but unmistakable. The rubber punk had been cleverly cut along the fold under the shoulder so the cut couldn't possibly be seen through the glass of the jar.

He picked up the single-edged razor blade and ran it lightly along the line, then a little harder. It was merely cemented shut with rubber cement, such as he himself had ready to use to close it again. The cut opened.

He dropped the blade and reached his fingers in eagerly through the cut. He touched paper, the crisp wonderful paper of United States currency.

This was the moment of moments. He sighed deeply with satisfaction, realizing now how tense he had just been, realizing that until now, until the very instant, despite all evidence, he had doubted that fate could be so kind to one so undeserving.

Curiously the bills seemed to be tied together and to be tied to something. He pulled.

There was a flash...

X

WEEP NO TEARS for Dr. Magus. He died the best of deaths. He died without even hearing the sound of the explosion that killed him, died so suddenly that there was no time for either pain or realization. He died without *knowing* that he died, and in a moment of supreme satisfaction and happiness. What more could he have asked or wanted?

Weep rather for Burt Evans, owner of the unborn show, the murderer now of five people if one counts Leon Quintana, and all for a shoebox full of money that he now no longer had.

Through the windshield of his car, as he stepped on its starter, he saw the flash, as Dr. Magus had seen it in the crystal ball, but he heard the explosion too. He saw the canvas of the mitt camp billow outward and tear.

In his travail he thought, oh God what now? Had that been the booby trap he'd put inside the rubber calf fetus, the booby trap that had been for Mack Irby in case Mack got back from the hospital unexpectedly and got to the fetus to take the money from it before he could get to Mack and kill him?

It must have been. Somehow Doc Magus had got on the trail of that money and had learned where it was hidden. Rather, where it had been hidden before he'd found it and put it in the shoebox in his suitcase. But how the *hell* could Doc have learned about it?

Well, that didn't matter now. The whole thing was tumbling down around his ears and now he'd have to keep going, on the lam, whether or not he caught up with Sammy and Trixie and the money.

The whole thing would come out now when the police got Sammy and Trixie—and the police would. Trixie was no doubt going to ditch Sammy so the police would have Sammy's story in any case. And they'd get Trixie too in the end—she wasn't smart enough to stay clear of them.

Yes—win, lose or draw in regard to catching up with Sammy and Trixie—he had to keep going now. And unless he got the money back he'd have lost everything. His unborn show, his own money—in the bank but he'd never dare show to try to draw it out—his trailer, even his clothes except the ones he was wearing. He didn't even have much cash on him—most of it had been in chips in that poker game he'd never go back to.

The engine was running now. He jerked the car viciously into gear, turned on the lights and started, circling oft to the other side of the lot, away from the center of excitement where the mitt camp had been.

God, how suddenly everything had gone wrong! Sammy raiding the trailer and finding the money. How could he have foreseen that? Or Doc Magus opening the booby-trapped punk.

It had all gone so perfectly till now, from the time he'd found the money. It had been a few days after the accident that had killed Charlie and hospitalized Mack. He'd noticed that the water level had gone down several inches in the jar that held the calf fetus so he knew it had sprung a slight leak.

When he took it out to fix the leak he'd found the cut Mack had made—and imperfectly sealed—and of course had looked inside and found the money. Wet, naturally—it had been a hell of a job getting it all dry while keeping it out of sight.

~§~

And while he waited for Mack to come back so he could kill him—(before Mack could find the money gone and kill *him*)—he'd worked out and set up the booby trap. And he'd stuck close to the lot so if it ever went off he could hear it and lam with the money before anybody figured what had happened. But things had gone well—he'd got Mack before Mack had a chance to try for the money.

Of course he could have taken the dynamite out any time since last Monday night but it would have been more dangerous to dismantle that bomb than it had been to set it. He'd figured simply to leave it there and after the end of the season bury the whole thing—jar and punk and booby trap all together. How in hell had Doc Magus. . . ?

~§~

He was off the lot now, on the street. He swung around the corner with tires screeching, then slowed down. If Trixie and Sammy were still waiting for a taxi or had started to walk, he didn't dare miss them. He forced himself to drive slowly for three blocks and then speeded up. When he'd gone six blocks, a third of the way into town, he knew they'd caught a cab and hit the floorboards with the accelerator pedal. The needle climbed to sixty and kept on climbing.

Then there was a car ahead that looked as though it could be a taxi. He didn't slow down. He swung out to cut around it and as he pulled level—going so fast the other car seemed almost to be standing still—he looked across into it. It was a squad car. Two startled faces under uniform caps looked at him.

"*Pull over!*"

He held his foot down and shot past them. Behind him their siren started to wail as they gathered speed, but his momentum had given him a full block lead. He *had* to get away from them.

A green light ahead turned red against him. He kept his foot down. But a car came out from the cross street—he had to swing the wheel hard to miss it. He missed it but he swung too sharply. The world tilted, turned upside down and ended in a scream of tearing metal.

~§~

Sammy put down, the suitcase. Behind him he heard Miss Trixie slide home the bolt of the door. He turned to face her.

She looked eager and excited. He felt eager and excited himself. He took a step toward her but she smiled and put up a hand to hold him off.

"Honey, don't rush me. I want to get my breath. Ain't we got all night?"

She walked around him and put the suitcase down flat and opened it. Sammy thought maybe she was going to reach for the money and that was his so he moved over to stop her if she did. But she took out only the bottle.

"Sammy, I'll make us each a drink," she said. "Here's what let's do.

I think you ought to take a bath before we go to bed. Will you do that, honey? Draw a nice tub of hot water and take yourself a good bath?"

"Sure, Miss Trixie."

"And I'll make us each a drink and get undressed, and be in bed waiting for you. Oh—and close the bathroom door, will you? The sound of water running always makes me want to go."

"All right, Miss Trixie." Sammy started for the bathroom and then turned back. "Now Miss Trixie, you wouldn't run off with that money would you? It's *my* money."

She laughed. "I won't. Word of honor as a girl scout."

Sammy went into the bathroom and shut the door. He put the plug in the bathtub and started water running from both faucets. But he was still a little worried about the money. Miss Trixie was nice and he loved her but he remembered the look on her face when she'd first seen the money.

He happened to look up and saw that there was a transom above the bathroom door. The glass was the wavy kind you can't see through but it was open a little. There was a crack at the bottom. And there was a stool in the bathroom. He moved it over and stood on it and looked through the crack. If Miss Trixie really started to undress, then she wouldn't be running off with the money.

~§~

She was making the drinks. She'd already poured whisky into each of the two tumblers on the bureau. Now she had a little bottle from her purse and was putting something from it in one of the tumblers. She must be making something fancy for them to drink. Sammy knew people mixed things to make fancy drinks but he'd never had one. He'd tasted only whisky and beer.

He was getting hot from steam coming up from the tub. He got down and turned the hot water partway off—he could tell now which was the hot water by feeling the faucet. Then he got back upon the stool. Miss Trixie still had not started to undress.

She was kneeling in front of the suitcase, moving the clothes until the shoebox showed. She picked it up and took the lid off, standing up now and looking in and reaching in to touch the money.

He didn't really mind her looking or touching—but what if looking and touching made her change her mind about running away while he was taking a bath? So she shouldn't do it. Maybe it would be a good idea to scare her so she wouldn't. He could scare her with the gun in his pocket and she wouldn't try to run away.

He took out the gun as he stepped down off the stool. He pulled back the hammer with his thumb, like the man had shown rum. He opened the door.

Miss Trixie whirled and from the look on her face he knew she was scared all right. She backed away from him and she dropped the box of money. The money came out and made a pile on the floor.

But he loved her and he didn't want to scare her *too* much. He said, "I ain't going to hurt you, Miss Trixie. I just want to show you that I—"

The gun went off in his hand.

Why, his finger had just been resting on the trigger—it hadn't been pulling hard.

But it went off. The noise it made was awful in that tiny room.

The look on Miss Trixie's face, though, was even more awful. And suddenly her head and shoulders bent forward and she fell down on the floor. She jerked once and rolled over, her head toward him. Sammy let the gun fall. He said, "I'm sorry, Miss Trixie—the gun just..."

She didn't move or answer. Maybe she'd been scared by the noise and had just, fainted.

Sammy got down on the floor by her and put her head in his lap. He saw now that there was a spreading red spot on her dress right between her breasts. And suddenly a lot of blood came out of her mouth.

Sammy whimpered. Her face wasn't pretty anymore and Sammy looked away from it. He saw Miss Trixie's purse where it had fallen too and spilled its contents. The handful of bills he had given her had come out of it and they were lying near the big pile of bills from the box. And a book of matches was lying there too.

There was hammering on the door of the room and yelling outside in the corridor and somebody trying the knob and somebody yelling to somebody else to call the police. Sammy was staring at the money and the matches and thinking that now Mr. Evans would get the money back, and he shouldn't and Sammy reaching for the matches and thinking that he could at least fix it so Mr. Evans wouldn't get the money back. Sammy was striking a match and lighting some money, and flames were getting higher and higher and brighter and brighter...

The Saint Detective Magazine, June/July 1953
Later expanded into the novel, Madball, 1953

Obit for Obie

I

THE FLY seemed to be making a hell of a commotion up there. Its buzz was louder than the sporadic hammer of typewriters. I looked up at it and saw that it was a big horsefly, staying about two inches under the ceiling, flying around fast and not getting anywhere.

Looking up made my collar tight, so I loosened it. It was plenty hot. Must be hotter up there two inches under the ceiling. Damn fool horsefly, I thought, don't you know there aren't any horses in a newspaper office? I wondered if a horsefly starved to death if it didn't find a horse, like the bread-and-butter fly in "Through the Looking Glass" that starved to death if it didn't find weak-tea with cream in it.

Somebody standing by my desk said, "What the blankety-blank are *you* doing?"

It was Harry Rowland. I grinned at him.

I said, "I was talking to a horsefly. See it up there?"

"My God," he said, "I thought you were praying." He stood looking up at the ceiling. "Ed wants to see you."

He moved on to the door. He wore a light tan palm beach suit and the back of the coat was soaked through with sweat over the shoulder blades.

I sat there a few more seconds, getting up nerve to stand and walk. I'd been sitting at my desk doing nothing for half an hour and I'd begun to hope Ed had forgotten me.

Ed is the *Herald's* city editor. A lot of editors are named Ed it doesn't mean anything. I've known reporters named Frank and Ernest, and a girl named Virginia.

I pushed through the heat and entered Ed's office. I sat in the chair in front of his desk and waited for him to look up, hoping he wouldn't. But he did.

He said, "Kid just killed on the roller coaster at Whitewater Beach.

Human interest story—what a swell kid he was, his possibilities. Hell, you know what I mean. Lay it on with a trowel."

"I'm crying already," I told him. "Has he got a name?"

"Get it."

"Had I better go out there?"

"Rowland's going out. Look, get it straight. You're not writing the news story, Rowland is. Burgoyne's writing an editorial. And you Joe—"

"The sob story," I said. "All right. Got a pic?"

"Get one."

He shook with silent laughter.

I went back to my desk. Ed hadn't needed to draw me a diagram; I'd worked for the *Herald* nine years. This was strictly a must job, for dear old Harvard. "Whitewater Beach" was the giveaway. The *Herald* didn't carry Whitewater Beach advertising. The *Herald* never mentioned Whitewater Beach, unless someone was killed or robbed there. Then we went to town.

Whitewater Beach was owned by a man named Walter Campbell. He topped our s.o.b. list. I think it dated back to the time when he'd called Colonel Ackerman, who owned most of the *Herald* a crooked politician.

I picked up my phone and dialed the South Side Police Station. Louie Brandon was on the desk. I asked him what he had on a kid killed at Whitewater.

"Half an hour ago," he said. "Name of—just a minute—Henry O. Westphal, six-oh-three Irving Place, age sixteen, father is Armin Westphal, owner of a hosiery store downtown."

I had that down on yellow paper.

I asked, "Where is he?"

"Haley's. Nineteen seventy-two—"

"I know where it is," I said. "It's an undertaking parlor out on the South Side, the nearest one to Whitewater Beach. "Who made identification?"

"Wallet in his pocket. Parents out of town, for the day. We're still trying to get in touch with them."

"Okay, Louie. Thanks."

I hung up the phone and stood up. Then I didn't know why I'd stood up, so I sat down again. Up on the ceiling, the horsefly was still in business. I phoned the *Herald's* morgue and it was busy. So I phoned Millie, my wife.

She said, "Bill Whelan called. Said I should get you up at four o'clock tomorrow morning. Isn't that a horrible thought, Joe?"

"Sure," I said.

"Oh, I know you don't think so now. But you'd better come right home and get to sleep early, or you'll make an awful fuss in the morning."

"Part of a man's rights," I told her. "He's privileged to make an awful fuss in the morning. Any mail, any excitement?"

"No mail, no excitement."

"Okay, honey. See you at six."

I called our morgue again. This time I got them.

I said, "You haven't anything under the name Henry Westphal, have you?"

"Just a minute. I'll see."

It was routine. She wouldn't have. After about a minute she came back to the phone.

"Yes, we have."

"I'll be damned," I said. "I'll be right down for it."

I went down and got it. It was a manila envelope with half a dozen clippings in it and a photograph—a glossy print. I signed for the envelope and took it back upstairs to my desk. This made it easy; I had something to work on.

It was all high school sports stuff. There were four clippings on football, two on tennis. The kid had been good at both; good enough to rate sports-page ink. The two tennis articles were from the previous summer when he was fifteen. He'd reached runner-up position in the county Junior tournament, after being seeded tenth.

He had a nice backhand and played a hard-hitting close-up game, mostly from the net. He'd been going places in tennis, as of last season, anyway. The football stuff was from the previous fall; he'd been a sophomore then, and had made the first team at South Side High as an end. For a soph he'd been sensational.

I studied the photograph. The date stamped on the back was a year ago, the time of the tennis tournaments. It was a waist-up shot, by one of our own cameramen, of a grinning, good-looking kid in a white sweatshirt with South Side High School lettered on it. It had been blocked down in red crayon, for a half-size halftone.

He looked big, for fifteen, and fairly husky. He had mussed-up blond half and the kind of looks that would make girls nuts about him without being quite handsome enough to make men dislike him. He had a high forehead, too, which isn't supposed to mean anything, but often does.

He'd had a nickname, "Obie."

I put copy paper into the Underwood and wrote, "Under the wheels of—"

Or had he? I wondered. He could have been thrown out and killed or he could have stood up and hit his head against a brace.

I picked up my phone and called Haley's. Rowland wasn't there yet; I didn't think he'd had time, but I asked.

I said, "You've got a kid there, Westphal, killed at Whitewater. Happen to know how he was killed?"

"On the Blue streak. Run over by a car. He wasn't riding it; must have been climbing the tracks, as I understand it."

"Pretty badly mangled, then?"

"Horribly."

I said, "One of our men will be there soon. Rowland, the one I Just asked about. Will you ask him to call Joe Stacy?"

"Sure."

I said, "By the way, is there anybody there who can give me anything more about the accident, or about the boy himself?"

"Well, yes, there is. Not about the accident, but about the boy." Haley's voice had dropped a tone, as though he didn't want it to carry. "I have a girl helping out in the office for the summer. High school girl. She knew Westphal, was in some of the same classes with him. Might be able to give you some information."

"Fine. Will you put her on? What's her name?"

"Grace Smith. Be careful, will you? I mean, it hit her pretty hard. She's been crying. Try not to set her off again."

"All right," I promised.

About a minute later, a girl's voice came over the wire.

"Hello. This is Grace Smith." She'd been crying, all right; I could tell from her voice. It sounded as though it were walking a tightrope and trying hard not to fall off.

I said, "This is the *Herald,* Miss Smith. I'm writing an article about Obie Westphal. I'll appreciate anything you can tell me about him. I have something on his athletic record, but not much else. What kind of a student was he? How did he do in his classes?"

"Oh, he was very smart. He got high grades in everything. He—he was tops, in just about everything."

"Popular with the other students?"

"Oh, yes. *Everybody* was just crazy about him. It's just—just *awful* that he's g-gone."

"What course was he taking, Miss Smith? Do you know what he intended to be?"

"The science course. He wasn't sure, but he thought he might decide to be a doctor. I was in his Latin class last year, second-year Latin. I think he wanted to be a laboratory doctor, the kind that does experiments and research."

"I see. Do you happen to know how he got the nickname Obie?" I asked, after a moment.

"From his middle name. It's Obadiah. Henry Obadiah Westphal. Nobody ever called him Henry, not even his teachers. He even signed his papers Obie."

"Do you know his family, Miss Smith?"

"I met his father and mother once, at a school party. He has a sister, too. She's crippled, I understand. I never met her."

"Older than he, or younger?"

"A little older, I think."

"Paralysis?"

"I don't know. He hasn't any other brothers or sisters, though. I'm pretty sure."

"Did you know Obie pretty well, personally, I mean?"

There was a brief pause at the other end of the wire before Grace Smith answered my question.

"N-not exactly. I mean, he'd never asked me for a date or anything, but I'd danced with him at school dances. F-four times."

The poor kid, I thought. She'd counted them; she knew it wasn't three times or five. Just a schoolgirl crush on the most popular boy in the class. But definitely not funny, now.

I said, "Thanks a lot, Grace. You've been very helpful. Maybe I can do you a favor sometime."

II

I TURNED BACK to the typewriter. The opening lead could stand; I'd guessed right about the wheels. Not that the manner of the accident mattered in the article I was going to write. I had plenty, and it would be easy sailing.

I looked up at the clock; I had half an hour before lunch. I ought to be able to finish it by then.

I did. It came out good, too. While you're writing a story, you can tell, maybe by the feel of the typewriter keys, whether it's good or not. This one was good. It had what a story took. I forgot while I was writing that the real reason for it was that a man named Campbell who owned Whitewater Beach was on the *Herald's* s.o.b. list. I thought about Obie, and wrote it straight, and the tears were there. Maybe *I* wasn't crying, but then my tongue wasn't in my cheek, either.

I finished with a minute to go. I left the last sheet in the typewriter and turned back the roller a little. No use setting a speed record and giving the copyreaders time to edit hell out of it. I could kill another half hour after lunch before I turned it in.

So I went down for a beer and a sandwich at Murphy's Bar, and I forgot all about Obie Westphal. I thought about my week's vacation, starting tomorrow, and the fishing trip I was going to take with Bill and Harvey Whelan, starting at four o'clock tomorrow morning.

It was eleven o'clock then. I was on the early lunch shift; most of us eat at eleven or eleven-thirty or else wait until the home-final deadline at two.

It was twelve when I got back. I sat down at my desk and stared at the sheet in it as though I were concentrating. I was concentrating about fish.

Somebody said, "Hey, Joe, Ed said you should see him soon as you got back from lunch."

Ed looked up when I went into his office.

He said, "That story about the kid killed at Whitewater. You can kill it."

"Fine," I said. "Thanks."

I turned to go out again and he yelled, "Hey, come back here." So I turned back.

He said, "It turned out to be a different kid. A light-fingered kid from the Third Ward, with a detention home record a yard long. He'd pinched this other kid's leather."

"Nice of him," I said. "Now do I write a sob story about the poor little pickpocket?"

He glared at me. Then, abruptly, he grinned.

He said, "Now don't go prima donna on me, Joe. Say, this is your last day before vacation, isn't it?"

"Uh-huh."

"Well, buck up and bear it till two o'clock. Then get that sour mug out of here."

I said, "Thanks," and meant it. The last few hours before a vacation go slowly. Now the four hours I'd expected to suffer were cut in half.

He handed me some sheets of paper.

"Here's some upstate stuff that came in late; the desk won't have time to handle it. Put it in English."

I went back to my desk and yanked the last page of the Westphal story out of my typewriter. I made a pass at the wastebasket with it and the first three pages, but I didn't let it go. Hell, that had been a good story. I wanted to read it over once before I threw it away. I dropped it in an open drawer of my desk, slammed the drawer shut, and reached for the upstate copy.

I started putting it in English.

After a while Rowland came in. He disappeared in Ed's office for a minute, then came out. I called to him and he strolled over and sat down on the corner of my desk.

"How'd the roller coaster business happen?" I asked him.

"Damn fool kid picked the wrong time to take a short cut across the track. Y'ever been on the Blue Streak out there?"

I nodded.

"It was at the bottom of the first hill. You know, where the track dips down to the ground. There's a railing and a danger sign, but the kid must have stepped over the railing and been on the track when the car came down. It made mincemeat out of him."

"Didn't derail the car?"

"Sure, it did. But the car was empty. They were just starting up for the day. They run 'em around a few times empty when they start up. Been a nice mess if that car'd been loaded. Cripes."

I said, "I had a swell story on that Westphal kid. Say, how'd they find out it wasn't him? His parents get there?"

"Fingerprints. They took 'em for routine, like on all D.O.A. cases. His hands weren't hurt at all. They put 'em through for routine, in spite of the wallet. Which shows there's something in this routine business. Only it's tough they'd already phoned his parents."

"But they've gotten in touch with them by now," I said.

"No. They still think their boy's dead. The police found them where they were visiting in Brookville, and they started for the city right away in their car. A four-hour drive. So they won't know till they get here."

"You aren't putting that in the story, are you?"

"Hell, no. That's enough to happen to them. We won't use the Westphal angle at all. And it'll be tough enough on Jimmy Chojnacki's family, if he's got a family, without revealing that he had a lifted leather on him when he was killed."

Rowland is a pretty good guy.

I turned in the last of the upstate stories at one o'clock. I could have made them last until two, but Ed was giving me a break, so I didn't try to stall. I stuck my head in his office and told him I was caught up.

"Swell," he said. "Corner of Greenfield and Brady, on the South Side. Fire. Get over there and phone in before deadline. You can go home from there."

I got in my flivver and drove over to Greenfield and Brady. The fire was practically out when I arrived. It had started in some rags in the corner of a warehouse. It could have been bad, but it wasn't. I found out who owned the warehouse and what the probable extent of the damage was, then hurried to the nearest tavern and phoned in the story.

It was only a quarter of two and I was free. I was on my vacation. I went from the phone to the bar and ordered a beer.

I thought, I'm only a few blocks from Whitewater Beach, and I haven't been there for a couple of years. Why not take a look at it? There was no reason why I should, but there was no reason why I shouldn't, either...

It was broiling hot on the midway at Whitewater. But there were plenty of people there. No matter how hot it gets, an amusement park draws a crowd on a Saturday afternoon.

The Caterpillar, the Tilt-a-Whirl, the Comet, and the Loop-the-Loop were all doing a big business.

The Blue Streak was closed. A cop was standing in the open space between it and the next concession, where you could walk back into the no-man's land between the concession fronts and the fence which enclosed the rides. From one point on the midway you could see back, diagonally through the opening, where some men were working at the bottom of the first dip of the roller coaster. There was a tight knot of people standing at that spot, peering back, as it were, over the cop's shoulder.

I flashed my press pass at the cop, and went on back. I walked to within a few yards of where the men were working, and stood watching.

It was muddy back there. Someone had played a hose over that part of the structure before the workmen had started. It wasn't hard to guess why. The tracks, I saw, had already been straightened if anything had happened to them from the derailment. The men working now were carpenters and painters.

The painters were coating the boards white almost before the carpenters finished nailing them down. They were almost through. The wrecked car was gone, out of sight.

From where I stood, I could see up the steep hill down which the car had come. I could picture it coming down there like a bat out of hell, and the kid, halfway across, turning his head and seeing it coming...

I didn't like it. I had a hunch I might dream about it, only it would be me there on the track. The carpenters were moving away now, gathering their tools, and the painters were taking their last swipes. Pretty soon they'd be running an empty around the tracks, to test. I found I didn't have any special yen to stay there and watch it.

I returned to the midway. I stood there a minute, wondering what the devil I'd come for, and then I went to the parking lot and got my car. I wanted another cold beer. I parked my car in front of the tavern diagonally across the street from Haley's Undertaking Parlor, and went in for a beer. I drank it at the bar, next to the window, and found myself staring across the street at the swanky facade of Haley's.

It wasn't morbid curiosity. I didn't want to see the body; I'd seen bodies. And there wasn't any question I wanted to ask Haley. I decided to have another beer and then go home.

III

A BLUE BUICK SEDAN slid to a jerky stop at the curb in front of Haley's. The man driving it was sitting very straight behind the wheel. He was a big man, well dressed, with graying hair: His face looked stiff.

The woman beside him was crying. I could see that there was a young woman in the back seat, but I couldn't see her face. She seemed to sit there very quietly.

The man got out and went around the front. The woman was opening the door on her side of the car. The man said something to her. I couldn't hear, of course, but it seemed to me that he was trying to persuade her to wait there, but she wouldn't. They went into Haley's together. The girl in the back seat stayed in the car. She still hadn't moved.

It would be the Westphals. They must have been told where they would find the boy when the phone call had reached them at Brookville. Now, for the first time, they'd learn it hadn't been their kid after all.

I ordered my second beer and sipped it.

They came out. The man wasn't walking stiff now, but he wasn't exactly relaxed either. I watched his face. It looked like an utter blank. The woman ran ahead of him, and stuck her head and shoulders into the back of the car. Her face was radiant.

After a few seconds she reached through with a handkerchief in her hand, as though she were wiping tears from the girl's eyes. I wondered if Obie's crippled sister were completely paralyzed.

The man wasn't paying any attention to them. He got as far as the curb in front of the car, and stood there, staring in my direction, but not at me. As though he was not seeing anything at all.

Then he got into his side of the front seat and the woman into hers and they drove away.

I ordered a shot of whisky and drank it, using the rest of my beer as a chaser. I stared at myself in the mirror behind the bar.

After a minute I went out and crossed the street to Haley's. I found Haley in his office, looking pretty busy.

"Where's the girl?" I asked. "Grace Smith, I think her name was."

He frowned. "Threw a wingding when she found out that kid was still alive. I sent her home. She wouldn't have been any good today."

"Overjoyed, huh?"

"A bobby-sockser," he said, as though that explained everything. Maybe it did.

"Was that the Westphals who drove away just as I came up?"

He nodded. "Swell people. Know what Mr. Westphal's going to do?"

"Pay for the other kid's funeral?"

"That's it, on the head. Wanted to know whether funeral arrangements had been made, and I said no and told him what the kid's circumstances were, and—just like that—he said to go ahead and he'd cover it."

"Has the Obie kid turned up yet?"

"Half an hour ago. Missed his wallet and went to the lost-and-found at Whitewater Beach. They figured he would and were waiting for him. He went on home to wait for his parents."

"How do you happen to be in on that?"

He looked at me strangely.

"Why the police let me know, of course. They thought Westphal might head here first when he got to town. And that way, I could tell him for sure his own kid was okay and at home."

"Oh," I said, wondering why I'd wondered.

I said, "Thanks," and started for the door. Then I turned around.

"The other kid," I said. "What was his name? Rowland told me but—"

"James Chojnacki. Mother's a widow; works in a laundry."

"The kid," I said. "Was he about Obie Westphal's size and build?"

"How do I know?" Haley's voice was getting an edge of impatience now. "I never saw the Westphal kid. Nobody thought of questioning the identification—and you couldn't recognize him looking at him anyway."

"You don't happen to know if he was hard of hearing?" I asked.

"My God, no. I should know that by looking at a mangled body. You want to look at him, maybe?"

"No," I said. "No, thanks."

I went out to my car and drove home. We had a good dinner that night to celebrate the start of my vacation, and because it was the last meal we'd have together for a week. Millie was going to visit her family while I went fishing with the Whelans. A nice arrangement because she's not crazy about fishing and I'm not crazy about her family. Also, we're smart enough to figure that a week's vacation from each other once a year—well, you know what I mean.

I packed all my things for the morning and turned in early. The alarm woke me at three-thirty, and I was ready and waiting when Bill Whelan drove up at a few minutes past four.

There was a light rain that didn't look as though it would last long. It was going to be a good day for fishing.

We got to Lake Laflamme a little after seven. We dumped our stuff in Bill's cottage there, got out the boat, and went fishing right away, before we even unpacked.

By noon we had a nice string of perch and walleyes. It was hotter than hell by then, and we figured that was our day's work, so we stayed on the screened-in porch all afternoon. We played two-bit limit stud, and drank.

When supper-time came none of us was in a mood to cook, but we weren't hungry anyway. We kept on playing poker until Harvey Whelan showed too strong a tendency to go to sleep among his chips. Bill and I got him to bed, and had another drink.

Then Bill and I went down to the shore to watch the sun set across the lake. It wasn't bad. It looked like something out of Dante.

We sat there watching until the colors faded. My body was drunk but my mind felt like crystal.

I said, "Bill, I oughtn't to have come."

He said, "You've been like a cat on a hot stove all day, Joe. If you want to go back, all right. There are two of us; you'll be okay. Say, are you in a jam?"

I shook my head.

"It—it isn't a woman?"

"No," I said.

"Anything I—or Harv—can do? Should one or both of us go back with you?"

I shook my head again and stood up. "I'll leave my fishing stuff here," I told him. "I'll try to get back. If not, you can bring it when you come in."

He wanted to drive me in to town, but he wasn't in shape to drive, and neither was I. I walked in to Black Rapids, and caught the bus. I knew I was being a damn fool, but there wasn't anything I could do about it. All the time the whisky kept sneaking up on me, and I felt like the devil. I tried to sleep on the bus, but I couldn't.

It was after midnight when I got back to the city, and there wasn't anything to do but take a cab home. The house, without Millie in it, seemed funny somehow. Black and empty like I felt inside. Everything neat and in order like no one lived there. It seemed wrong, somehow, to unmake a bed and get into it. But I must have slept the instant my head touched a pillow, and it was ten o'clock when I woke.

I woke with a hangover. I got up and made and drank some black coffee. I sat around cussing myself for getting drunk and coming back. I wasn't even sure what I'd come back for. Last night I seemed to remember, my mind had been like crystal. This morning it felt like a stained-glass mosaic without a pattern.

It was a Monday morning and I should have been up at Lake Laflamme, catching walleyes. I listed to myself the varieties of fool I was, and it took quite a while.

Early in the afternoon I went out. I bought all the Saturday, Sunday and Monday papers at a downtown stand that always holds back copies for a few days. I took a booth in a restaurant and went through them.

Apparently there was nothing new; none of the Monday morning papers mentioned the matter. Each of the two evening papers, the *Herald* and the *Times,* considered it covered with a six-inch item on Saturday and nothing thereafter. The *Tribune* and the *Blade,* the morning papers, gave it a few lines on an inside page of their Sunday editions.

None of the papers mentioned the stolen wallet that had been in Jimmy Chojnacki's pocket, or the erroneous preliminary identification of the body. They did have Jimmy's address. I made a note of that.

IV

I hated to do it, but I went to see Jimmy Chojnacki's mother. She was a big, bony woman. She was home alone, and she wanted to talk. Beyond telling her I worked for the *Herald*, I didn't need a reason to get inside and ask questions.

Yes, she said, she was a widow, and she worked for a laundry. She was a sorter at the White Eagle. She was off till after the funeral. And Jimmy was a good boy... Did I want to see his picture?

It was his last picture, taken, she told me, only a few months ago. It was a four-by-six in a folder, with the imprint of a cheap studio on Main Street.

Jimmy Chojnacki had been a fairly nice-looking kid. His face was a bit weak, but not vicious. And he had those deep-set, dreamy eyes some Polish kids have, almost the eyes of a *tsigani* or a seer. But now they'd never see again.

"The funeral," she said. "It's tomorrow, Tuesday, two o'clock in the afternoon, from Haley's Undertaking Parlors. It's—it's a beautiful place. Everything so nice."

"Isn't it expensive?"

"I—I guess it is. But someone is paying. Mr. Haley wouldn't tell me who. Maybe the park management, do you think? But why wouldn't they want me to know?"

I suggested, "Possibly—if it *is* the park management—they think paying for it openly would indicate that they admit responsibility for the accident."

Her face cleared. "Of course, that would be it. Maybe they think I would sue, or something. But it wasn't their fault, was it, Mr.—"

"Stacy," I reminded her. "Joe Stacy. No, Mrs. Chojnacki, I don't see how it could have been their fault. He must have been on the tracks, and there is a railing and a danger sign. Did he go to Whitewater Beach often?"

"Every Saturday. He had a job for the summer, but it was five days only. Every Saturday he went and sometimes Sunday, too. On Saturdays, he went early, mostly. Like last Saturday."

I asked, "Did he go alone?"

"Yes, last Saturday. Sometimes he and Pete Brenner went together, but he said Pete had to work last Saturday."

"Pete Brenner," I repeated. "Was that his best friend?"

"Why—why, I guess so. He was with Pete more than any other boy. Pete works at the fruit market, right around the corner from here on Paducah Street."

I asked, "Did he have a friend by the name of Obie?"

"Obie? I don't understand."

"Westphal, Obie Westphal."

"N-no. Not that I know of."

"He went to South Side High School, didn't he?"

"Yes. Third year. He wanted to quit and take a job, but I didn't want him to. I wanted him to finish one more year, and graduate. I—"

Suddenly she was crying, silently. No sobbing, no motion of facial muscles, just tears rolling down her cheeks. Except that she'd stopped talking, she didn't even seem to notice.

I left as soon as I could, and without asking her any more questions I figured I could find out the rest of what I wanted to know somewhere else. Maybe from Pete Brenner.

I found the fruit market around the corner on Paducah. There was a tough-looking kid, about seventeen, bunching carrots at a table in back. There were more customers in the place than there were clerks, so I got through to the kid.

"Pete Brenner?" I asked him.

His eyes gave me a dusting-over. They weren't shifty eyes, but they were hard and suspicious. He took all of me in before he said, "Yeah."

He was going to be tough to handle. I took the short cut; I removed a bill from my wallet.

"Want to earn a fin?" I asked him. "Answering a few questions?"

"What questions?"

I rolled the bill around my index finger.

I said, "For instance—you went to South Side High, didn't you?"

"Sure. I ain't going back, though."

"You know Obie Westphal?"

"Hell, everybody at South knows him."

"Sure," I said. "I mean, do you know him personally—or did Jimmy Chojnacki know him personally?"

He weighed that one, and couldn't see any harm in it.

He said, "Not much. A little. Last fall Jimmy and me were both out for football, and on the second team. We knew him well enough to say 'Hi' to, but we never went around with him, if that's what you mean."

"Oh," I said, and looked disappointed. "Did you say Jimmy went out for football?" I managed to sound mildly surprised. "Wouldn't he have had trouble with signals? I thought his hearing wasn't so good."

"Hearing? There wasn't nothing wrong with Jimmy's ears. You got him mixed up with somebody else."

"Could be," I admitted.

I unrolled the bill from around my index finger, and gave it to him. I didn't need eyes in the back of my head to picture the puzzled look which followed me out of the store.

I drove from there to Whitewater Beach.

This time there wasn't any cop on duty between the Blue Streak and the next concession. There was a picket fence across, of fresh wood, still unpainted, blocking off the areaway that led to the rear compound.

I walked on down the midway past three more concessions and found an unfenced opening between the Tilt-a-Whirl and a shooting gallery. I stood there a moment, glancing both ways to be sure no one was watching, and went back.

There was the dip where the roller coaster went clear to ground level after the first and highest hill. There was the caution sign and the reconstructed yard-high railing, on which there was now a second coat of paint.

I stood by the railing at its lowest point. I thought, he stood here. The empty car was coming up the hill then. But he couldn't have known it was coming or he wouldn't have started across.

I stood there listening until I heard a car start, back on the platform of the Blue Streak. Over all the other noises of the midway I could hear it plainly. It swung around the curve to the bottom of the uphill pull where a chain caught it, and it started up.

And my vague memory—from the last time I'd ridden the Blue Streak, years ago—was dead right. There was a loud clanking noise all the way up the hill. It was from a ratchet arrangement that was designed to prevent the car from rolling backwards if the chain should break. It was loud as hell.

Nobody could have stood here, and *not* have heard that car coming up the hill. Nobody with normal hearing.

When I saw the car coming over the top, I stepped back from the railing. I closed my eyes, because I didn't want to watch it coming down. But I could *feel* it coming, and I winced and stepped back another step.

I got the hell out of there and had a drink at the nearest tavern. It was getting dusk by then, and clouding up as though it might rain later in the evening.

I drove into town and had something to eat. I tried to remember the street address of the Westphals—it had been in the obit I'd written-but I couldn't. I looked it up in the phone book and drove out there.

It was a big, nice-looking house in a good residential district in Oak Hill. Lights gleamed from several rooms downstairs.

I parked across the street one door away and watched the house.

Nothing happened. Nobody went in or out. At ten forty-five the lights started to go off, one room at a time. By eleven-thirty the house was dark.

I drove home and went to bed.

V

WHEN I WOKE, it was still dark. Something was wrong, and it took me a while to figure that what was wrong was Millie's absence.

I tried to go back to sleep, but I couldn't. The radium dial of the clock showed me it was a quarter to five. I got up and went to the open window, pulled up a chair and sat there looking out at a graying sky across the roof of the house next door.

"You're stalling, Joe Stacy," I told myself. "You're nibbling around the outside, because you're afraid to go in and find out. What you suspect is crazy, but it's so horrible you're afraid to find out."

Sitting there looking out the window at nothing, I added up the crazy things that had made me spoil a perfectly good vacation. I tried to tell myself they didn't add up to much, but I knew better. They were little things, like the expression on a man's face, but they added up plenty, maybe to something bigger than I dared to think.

Outside, the black turned to dull gray. It was going to be a cloudy, muggy day. There wasn't a breath of air stirring.

I felt tired, but not sleepy; I knew I couldn't go back to sleep. I put on some clothes and got myself some breakfast. I sat around and did nothing much until nine o'clock.

It was still too early, but I phoned Nina Carberry. Nina and I had gone together before I met Millie. Now she taught history at South Side High. I hadn't seen her for nearly six years.

"This is Joe Stacy," I told her. "Remember me?"

"A little," she said. Her voice sounded tentative.

"Are you up yet? I mean, were you up before I phoned? Did I wake you?"

She laughed a little. "Yes and no, Joe. I was awake, trying to decide whether I should get up."

"Good," I told her. "How about some breakfast? I want to talk to you about something. May I pick you up in half an hour?"

"All right, Joe. But we'll eat here. My refrigerator is jammed full. And make it at least a half hour."

I killed a little more time and got there at ten. She was still living in the same nicely furnished little apartment. She was still tall and blond, and didn't look any older than she had six years ago. A little more prim and school-teacherish, maybe, but I suppose school teachers can't help that, after a while.

She'd apparently made up her mind, and greeted me as casually as though I'd last been there yesterday instead of six years ago.

"Bacon and eggs?" she asked me.

"That'll be fine," I said. "Can I help?"

"Unless you're in a hurry to talk, you might play some records on the phonograph, while I do the cooking." Something danced mischievously in her eyes. "But I haven't a record of 'Should auld acquaintance be forgot'."

I grinned and walked over to the shelf of albums. I recognized some of them. I picked the album of Bach Brandenburgs and I'd played two of them by the time breakfast was ready.

After we ate she stacked the dishes in the sink. Then we went back into the living room and sat down.

She said, "Well, Joe?"

"You're still teaching at South Side, aren't you?"

"Yes. Is it something about the school, Joe?"

"In a way. I want to ask you some questions, Nina—and I want you to forget that I ever asked them. I don't want you to ask me *why* I'm asking them. Can you do that?"

"I—I think so."

I said, "I can get some of this from the newspaper files, but I don't want to go there this week unless I have to. I'm on vacation and I don't want to explain why I'm not out of town, where I'm supposed to be. Anyway, you might know more details about them than would be in the *Herald* morgue."

"Details about what, Joe?"

"About the accidents," I said.

"Accidents? You mean the boy who fell out of the tower window and the girl who was drowned in the pool and—"

"Yes," I said. "There have been five in three years, haven't there?"

She nodded slowly. She shivered a little.

"I saw one of them happen, Joe. I was coming out of the front entrance when the Harmon boy fell from the window—or the ledge, or wherever he fell from. He hit only five yards from me. It was horrible."

"Tell me what the investigation brought out," I said. "You can skip the details of how he hit, if you don't want to think about them."

"But the investigation didn't bring out anything, Joe. Nobody saw him fall—that is, until he landed. It was during second lunch period; a lot of the students are free then. He must have gone up into the tower and leaned out of the window, or even climbed out on the ledge. They found other boys had done that. And he fell. That's all there is to it."

"They didn't find out if any other students had been up there with him?"

"No, they didn't. Since then the tower door has been kept locked at all times—unless someone has permission to go up there, in which case he can get the key from the office."

"And a girl was drowned," I said. "That was during a swimming class, wasn't it?"

"Yes."

"When I went there, girls and boys didn't use the pool together. A swimming class was for one group or the other. I suppose they still work it the same way."

"Yes. It was a girl's class. There were a lot of girls in the pool. She was swimming in the deep end of the pool and must have got a cramp and gone right under without anyone seeing her."

I could rule that one out, I thought.

I said, "And a boy fell over a railing on the third floor, down the stairwell, and landed on the first floor, on his head. Did anyone see him fall?"

"No. That was two years ago. Wilbur Greenough; he was in my American History class. No, no one saw him fall. They don't even know for sure that it was from the third floor, except by—well, by how hard he hit. It was after school, on a Friday. Most of the students had left, but there were still a few in the building."

"There *was* an investigation?"

"Of course. For a while they discussed putting wire netting at floor levels in the stair wells, but it wasn't practical."

"And there were two others. One was electrocuted, wasn't he?"

"*She.* A freshman girl named Constance Bonner. Last year. I don't know so much about that one. It happened after school, too, in the basement. Apparently, she had reached into a switch box and touched bare copper instead of the handle of a switch. But there was no reason why she should have wanted to throw a switch. Or why she should have gone there at all."

I said, "Remember—you met me down there after school, once."

She colored slightly. "That was a long time ago, Joe. We were young and foolish then."

"Young, anyway," I said. "But the Bonner girl—was there anything to indicate that she couldn't have had a clandestine date?"

"N-no. But there wasn't any proof that she had. She wasn't found until the next morning. If anyone was there with her when she was killed, he'd have run for help, wouldn't he?"

"I guess so," I said. "And there was one other, if I recall. Didn't some boy slip and strike his head on something in the football locker room at the stadium?"

"Yes. A negro boy named William Reed, a junior. He was a very brilliant boy."

"He was alone when it happened?"

"Yes, he was."

I thought, they all were, except the girl who drowned. I could rule that out. But the other four had all died when they were alone. As Jimmy Chojnacki had been alone . . .

We talked a while of other things. We listened to the first movement of the Beethoven Fourth. When I got up to leave, Nina held out her hand.

She said, "Nice seeing you, Joe. Come back again in another six years."

I grinned, and told her that I would.

VI

IN HALEY'S air-conditioned funeral parlor it was cool and comfortable. Outside, it was hot as hell. You could feel, in the brightness of the windows, waves of heat trying to get in at you, held back by the efforts of a whirling little motor somewhere offstage that ran the air-conditioner.

I sat in a back corner, as inconspicuously as possible. The coffin that held what the roller coaster had left of Jimmy Chojnacki was on a flower-banked bier up at the front. It wasn't open; it hadn't been and it wouldn't be.

About twenty-five people were there, and I knew only two of them; Mrs. Chojnacki and the boy who had been Jimmy's friend, Pete Brenner. The tough kid who worked in the vegetable market, and who didn't look tough now. He was dressed in a nicely fitting black suit and one of the whitest shirts I've ever seen. His black hair was slicked down until it gleamed.

Once I saw him looking back at me, obviously wondering what I was doing there.

The organ was playing very softly now, and the heat beat against the windows. Outside, far away but getting nearer and louder, came the drone of a plane going by overhead. Its sound made me think of the horsefly that had flown around the *Herald* editorial room last Saturday morning. My staring up at it and Harry Rowland's saying:

"My God, I thought you were praying."

The minister was praying now. He was a tall thin man with a face like a horse. His voice was good, though. I had his name and the name of his church on the back of an envelope in my pocket. Haley had told me when I came, thinking that I was covering the funeral for my paper. Not to disillusion Haley, I'd written them down.

Out of the corner of my eye, through the glass doors of the hall in which we sat, I saw a man standing. A big man, with dark hair turning gray—Armin Westphal, who was paying for the funeral. He'd come to it, a little late.

I ducked my head again, slid down in my seat to keep out of sight. When the prayer was finished, Westphal entered quietly and took the seat nearest the door.

The organ played, and a fat Italian woman with a face like a madonna, sang. The organist was good, too. He wove little patterns of notes around the melody, as harpsichord music used to be written to fill in for lack of sustained notes. The accompaniment score wasn't written that way, I knew.

"... In the midst of life, we are in death..."

Mrs. Chojnacki was weeping silently.

I knew what I'd wanted to know. Obie Westphal's father had come to the funeral of Jimmy Chojnacki. Another little fact meaningless in itself.

I didn't hear the sermon. I was thinking my own thoughts.

I slipped out quietly when the service was over, while the pallbearers were taking the coffin to the hearse. I drove downtown and had some sandwiches and a few drinks and then drove out to the Westphal house and parked a quarter of a block away on the opposite side of the street.

At four O'clock Mr. Westphal came home, alone in the big Buick, and ran It into the garage. He went into the house and a few minutes later he brought out a wheel chair with his daughter in it and left her on a shady corner of the porch.

Mrs. Westphal came out and sat next to the girl, in a porch chair, talked to her a while and then vanished inside again. Mr. Westphal came out at five o'clock to push the wheel chair into the house.

Nothing happened then, and at eight-thirty I began to wonder. Maybe Obie Westphal wasn't there. Surely in the hours I'd watched the house, then and the evening before, I'd have seen him at least once.

I drove a few blocks to a tavern that had a private phone booth and phoned the Westphal number. A woman's voice answered and I asked:

"Is Obie there?"

"Obie? No, he's staying with his aunt and uncle in Brookville. He'll be back tomorrow at two o'clock. Who shall I tell him called?"

"Thanks," I said. "It's nothing important."

I hung up and went over to the bar.

That was Tuesday...

It was almost noon when I woke up the next day. I had a bad taste in my mouth and I was groggy from sleep. It was hot again and I was soaked with sweat.

It was one of those days. After a shower I couldn't get dry because I'd start to sweat again even before I could get toweled off. I gave up trying to dry myself after a while and dressed anyway. I had a hunch it was going to be a lousy day in more ways than one. It was.

I got to the Union Station in plenty of time for the two o'clock train that came through Brookville. I was reasonably sure Obie Westphal would be on it; whoever had talked to me on the phone had said "two o'clock"; she would hardly have been so specific had he been driving back or coming back with someone else in a car.

The station was crowded and it was like an oven. I leaned against a post and watched the gate he'd have to come through. None of the Westphals—at least none I recognized—were at the station to meet him.

I knew him the minute he walked through the gate. He looked a bit older than the picture of him in the *Herald* morgue, and quite a bit bigger than I'd have guessed him to be, from that picture.

He was a bronzed young giant with shoulders made to order for football. He had clipped blond hair and didn't wear a hat. He was good-looking as hell. You could see how every girl in high school and some plenty older—would be nuts about him.

He carried a light suitcase which he put down just inside the gate. He stood there looking around, and ran his fingers once through his short hair. Then his eyes lighted.

He yelled "Hi, guys!" picked up the suitcase and started toward the station door.

He met two other young men about his age—high school kids. Like Obie, they were well dressed in a sloppy sort of way. One of them carried what looked like a clarinet case.

They stood talking a few minutes and then went into the station. I drifted after them. They had Cokes at the soft drink counter, and Obie paid for them. Then the three of them headed for the door labeled *Men.*

I moved to a bench where I could watch the door without being conspicuous. I watched it for what seemed like quite a while, and when I looked at the big clock on the central pillar, I saw that it *had* been quite a while. I remembered then that the men's room of the Union Station had a door on the other side, leading through a barber shop to the street.

I went into the men's room and they weren't there. I went into the barber shop. They weren't there, either. Not that I'd expected them to be.

I thought, what a, hell of a shadow I'd make.

The cashier was picking his teeth behind the cigar counter bought a cigar and asked:

"Three high school kids come through here from the station a few minutes ago? One of 'ema big blond guy?"

"Yeah," he said. He took the toothpick out of his mouth and grinned at me. "They got in that car that's been parked out front—the one we've been laughing at."

"What about it?"

"Stripped-down flivver with a wolf's head on the radiator cap, and painted on the side—*Don't Laugh: Your Daughter May Be Inside.*

"The big one drive it?"

"Naw, the one with the squealer."

"Squealer?"

"The clary, the licorice stick." He grinned again. "I talk the language. I got a kid in high."

"God help you," I said. "Have a cigar."

I gave him back the cigar I'd just bought from him and went out.

VII

I GOT IN MY OWN CAR on the other side of the street and sat behind the wheel, thinking unkind things about myself, and wondering whether I should drive out to the Westphals. I had a hunch it would be wasted time; he'd be going somewhere besides home with his friends.

And besides, the whole damn thing suddenly seemed foolish. You couldn't look at Obie and think the crazy kind of things I'd been thinking.

I started driving because the inside of the car was hot as a kiln parked there in the sun. I drove aimlessly, or I thought I did, but the car seemed heading south in the general direction of Lake Laflamme. I felt foolish again.

I thought, I'm spending my vacation chasing a chimera down a blind alley.

If I was right, what chance had I of proving it? The whole thing was so improbable, so wild an Irish hunch that I didn't dare even share it with anyone. I hate to be laughed at.

I thought of the cool breezes of Lake Laflamme and I was hungry for fish. Fried fish, fresh off the hook I was lonesome and wanted good guys like the Whelans, who weren't screwballs like me.

In a block or so, I'd be passing South Side High. I thought, it's been a long time since I was graduated from there. I was humming to myself. . . "and her tower spears the sky." From the school song.

It was a beautiful building, all right. I slowed down to look at it, and then I swung the car toward the curb and stopped, with the engine running. I don't know why. But I looked at the high school, set back half a block from the street, a proud building and a building to be proud of, with a straight tower that went eight stones high.

A cold chill went down my back I was looking up at It, and I thought, it must have been from one of that pair of windows just above the ledge that the boy fell last year. . .

Fell, or was pushed. I could picture Nina Carberry coming out the front door there, and the Harmon boy falling, striking the hard unyielding cement. . .

Looking up I could *feel myself* taking that awful plunge. Just as, a few days ago when I had stood at the foot of the first dip of the Blue Streak, I could feel the iron wheels of the speeding coaster car. . .

I thought, if my hunch was right, how many others have there been? What's more important—how many others *will there be?*

I sat there almost half an hour, with the engine of the car still running, and finally I put the car into gear and turned around. I sped back to town.

I compromised with Lake Laflamme only to the extent of eating the best fish dinner on the menu at the best seafood restaurant in town, and then I drove out and parked near the Westphal home again.

A little while after I got there, the jalopy with the wolf's head drove up and let Obie out. He went into the house. A few minutes later his father came home in the Buick and put it into the garage.

I sat there. It began to get dark.

It got to be nine o'clock, and then Obie came out. He stood on the front steps a moment. The light from the street lamp on the corner fell full on his face. He was a good-looking young cub all right. I thought, the girls must be crazy about him. Older women would be, too.

He strolled out to the sidewalk, through the gate, and turned west, coming toward my car, but on his own side of the street. He didn't look across or notice me. It was dark where I was parked, and I don't think he could have told that anyone was in my car.

I waited until he was more than a block past me before I got out of the car and walked after him, keeping to the side of the street opposite from his. He strolled leisurely. I closed lip to within half a block and then kept my distance. The streets were almost empty and I couldn't risk getting closer.

We weren't heading toward any bright-light district. We weren't heading anywhere I knew of unless it could be the freight yards or the jungles.

And that was where we were going. When Obie turned at the next corner I was sure. I held my distance, even though cover was sparse the last two blocks before we reached the tracks. But he didn't turn around or notice me. I even closed the distance a little as he started across the first tracks. But it didn't do any good; I lost him completely the minute we got in among the cars.

It's a big jungle; there are dozens of tracks and thousands of cars. It's over a block wide and miles long. A hundred hoboes could lose themselves in it, and I didn't have a chance once I'd lost Obie.

I hunted for half an hour and then gave up. It occurred to me now that maybe he'd cut across the yards and kept on going, but if he had, I'd never catch up with him now.

I went back to my car. It had a parking ticket on it. I got in it and sat there for a while. Finally, a few minutes before eleven o'clock, Obie came walking back. He went inside. Almost immediately I saw a light go on upstairs and Obie's silhouette against the shade. He was going to bed. I went home...

Bright and early Thursday morning I dropped into Chief of Police Steiner's office. I gave him the parking ticket and a good cigar. He grinned and touched fire to the one literally and the other figuratively. He blew a cloud of smoke.

I said, "Someone told me there was an accident yesterday evening in the freight yards."

He shook his head slowly. "Not last night, Joe. There have been accidents over there, quite a few of them, but none last night."

"Somebody gave me a bum steer then," I told him. "I am interested in accidents, though. Doing a feature on them."

Steiner said, "You ought to see Mike Ragan in Traffic. He's been making analyses of that kind of stuff; got it all tabulated. Going to present it to the common council when the matter of additional street lights comes up."

I said "That won't be up my alley. I'm sticking to non-traffic ones. How's the city record on them, by the way?"

"Pretty high. We rate twelfth in the country on traffic fatalities, but our total accidental death rate isn't too good."

"Think I could take a look through the files on individual accidents?"

"I guess so. You're biting off a job, though."

He was more than right, I thought. I spent the whole afternoon in the record office, going through one folder after another. I was looking for a name, and I found it only once—in a place where I already knew it would be.

Obie Westphal's name was in the reports on the accidental death of Jimmy Chojnacki. It was there only because Obie's wallet had been in Jimmy Chojnacki's pocket.

It was a wasted afternoon. If I'd had any sense I'd have let it discourage me completely and headed back for Lake Laflamme and the big ones. But I'd started there once and turned back.

After supper, it occurred to me that maybe I'd been using my legs too much and my brains too little. Maybe a little intelligent thought would do more good.

So I spent the evening drinking Martinis and thinking intelligently at least, for a while anyway. And, I did get an idea. Not a new one; it was one I'd had all along, but I'd been fighting off trying it. So I quit fighting and decided that tomorrow I'd pay a visit to Mr. Westphal.

VIII

THE BON TON SHOP, Hosiery and Lingerie, was not a large store, but it had a good location downtown. It did a good business. There were half a dozen customers at the counters when I walked in, five of them women and the other an embarrassed-looking man. I felt sorry for him, but only abstractly; personally I enjoy looking at lingerie and am not in the least embarrassed by it. On or off.

I strolled through the store toward the rear where there was a door marked *Private*. It was ajar and I stuck my head through. A blonde at a desk just inside looked up and said, "Yes?"

"I'd like to speak to Mr. Westphal."

She looked across the office and I followed her gaze. Mr. Westphal's desk was in the same room. His eyes met mine and I thought he started a little. Maybe I was wrong; I couldn't be sure.

He said "Come in."

I walked over and took the chair in front of his desk. I wondered how the hell you went about asking a man if his son was a mass murderer.

I said, "I'm afraid, Mr. Westphal, that the matter I want to talk to you about is personal."

His eyes went over my shoulder to the blonde at the typewriter desk and then back to me.

He asked, "Haven't I seen you somewhere before, recently?"

"At Haley's Funeral Parlor, possibly," I said. "I'm from the *Herald*. I covered the Jimmy Chojnacki case."

He didn't say anything for a while. His eyes changed, almost as if a nictitating membrane came down across the eyeballs. I looked down at my hat in my lap and let it go at that. It was his move.

There was another short silence, then his voice raised a trifle.

He said, "Miss Kiefer, you may leave for lunch a little early if you will."

The blonde said, "Thank you, Mr. Westphal."

I didn't look back, but I heard her push her chair back then the click of her high heels across the office and the sound of the door closing.

I figured it was still his move. I waited.

So did he. He won. I looked up. His face was a careful blank.

I asked, "Is it true, Mr. Westphal, that you paid for the Chojnacki funeral?"

"Yes."

"May I ask why?"

His voice was a quiet monotone, a recitation. It was as flat as a glass of beer that has stood overnight. It was a voice that made anything he said untrue, almost blatantly *so*. It was almost as though he prefaced it with "This is a lie." Purposely.

He said, "It was an impulse, I guess. Relief when I learned it wasn't me, son who was killed. And Haley told me the boy's mother was poor."

"That was the only reason?"

"Of course." It wasn't a protest; it didn't register curiosity as to why I seemed to doubt him. It didn't register resentment.

It stumped me. I didn't know where to go from there. Even if I'd had careful campaign of tricky questions worked out, his manner of answering would have thrown me off stride.

I studied his face. That didn't help any either.

All right, I thought. Here goes.

I asked, "Mr. Westphal, have you ever taken your son to a psychologist or a psychiatrist?"

His face still didn't change.

He said, "Yes. Once ten years ago, and once more recently—last year, in fact."

"And he said. . . ?"

"That I was wrong. That I was imagining things. That the boy is normal."

I said, "But you don't agree."

There was just the glimmer of an expression on his face—the ghost of the bleak despair that had been upon it when, from the tavern across from Haley's, I'd watched him come out of the funeral parlor door.

He said, "I hope he is right. I am not sure."

We looked at each other, and there didn't seem to be anything further to say. Or to ask.

I stood up and even started for the door. Then I turned and asked:

"Would you mind, Mr. Westphal, telling me the name of the psychiatrist?"

He said, "The best in the city, Dr. Jules Montreaux. Would you like to talk to him?"

I hadn't thought of it.

"Yes," I said. "But would he discuss it with me?"

"I'll give him permission. What's your name?"

"Joe Stacy."

"Wait."

He looked up a number in the phone book, and dialed it. I listened to his conversation with Dr. Montreaux and before he finished he looked up at me.

"He's free at two o'clock tomorrow afternoon. Will that be all right?"

I nodded.

Into the phone he said, "He'll see you then, Dr. Montreaux. Thank you."

He put down the phone into its cradle. He looked at it and not at me.

He said, "Is there anything else I can do for you, Mr. Stacy?"

I shook my head, then realized the gesture was meaningless since he wasn't looking at me.

"No," I said. "No, thanks, Mr. Westphal."

Very formal, both of us. An executioner isn't flippant to the man he is strapping into the chair.

After that, I didn't know what to say. I didn't say good-bye. I turned and walked quietly out, leaving him sitting there. I wanted to tiptoe out, but I didn't.

I closed the door quietly behind me, went out to my car, and started to drive. I wanted the country, the open air, the quiet. I wanted to think. Or maybe I wanted to run away from myself and not think. I don't know. I just drove. If I did any thinking, it doesn't matter now.

I was out of town on the Bridgetown Road, almost to Harville, when I noticed that I was being followed. It was an old wreck of a jalopy, but not the topless one with the wolf's head on front.

I wasn't looking for a tail, nothing was further from my mind, but I happened to notice it in the rear vision mirror. It kept an even distance behind me, passing cars when I did and staying behind them when I didn't pass. It was Impossible to see who was driving it but I was sure that there was only one man in the car.

By the time I was sure he was tailing me, we were entering Harville. I slowed down to ten miles an hour and pretended to be watching the street numbers. I made a point of not looking back. But the car didn't pass me.

I stopped in front of a house and got out. I managed to look back without seeming to as I closed the door of the car. The jalopy was parked a block behind, too far for me to get a good glimpse of the driver or to read the license

I did what I thought was a nice bit of acting, a double take on the house number, as though I'd read it wrong the first time. I made a pass at getting back into the car and then seemed to decide there was no use moving it and I walked back.

I started briskly back toward the car behind me, still watching house numbers but also, since it was now in the general direction I was walking, keeping an eye on the jalopy.

I figured that by the time he'd realized I was heading for him I'd be close enough to get his license and a look at his mug.

But my acting wasn't so hot, or he was smarter than I gave him credit for being. I hadn't gone more than a fourth of the distance before he shoved the car in gear and got the hell out of there. It was the main drag of Harville, and plenty wide enough for a U-turn. He swung around fast and beat it.

He had an extra block lead on me by the time I returned to my own car and got it started again. A stream of traffic stopped me from making a U-turn for a good two minutes—and that was too long. He was out of sight and I never caught him. My car was a lot faster than his jalopy could have been, but I didn't catch him on the road back to the city. He must have turned off somewhere.

As soon as I was sure of that, I pulled into the drive of a roadside juke joint. There was one thing I had to know. I didn't see how the devil Obie Westphal could know what I'd been doing.

I phoned the Westphal house and asked for Obie. The female voice that answered said, "Just a moment," and a few seconds later a young man's voice said, "Hello."

I put the receiver back on the hook. It hadn't been Obie in that car that followed me. He couldn't possibly have reached home in so short a time.

I knew it couldn't have been the senior Westphal in a car like that, but I called his office to make sure, just—the same. He was there. I told him I'd forgotten exactly what time he'd made that appointment for me to talk to Dr. Montreaux. He told me again that it was for two o'clock tomorrow, Saturday afternoon.

IX

I DROVE the rest of the way back into town thoughtfully, but it didn't get me anywhere. I tried to talk myself into thinking that that jalopy hadn't really been tailing me, after all, but I couldn't make the grade. It had been. And the guy driving it had been plenty fast on the trigger in keeping me from getting a look at him.

It couldn't have been a detective, city or private; they don't drive cars as old and conspicuous as that one, especially on tail jobs. Besides, the tailing hadn't been skillful enough for a pro.

The more I thought about it, the less I liked it. The more I thought about it, the less it fitted into the pattern. It scared me.

Driving home, I tried to think if there was anything I could do before my appointment with Montreaux. It occurred to me that maybe I'd be better off if I could talk his language a bit, instead of making him talk mine. I could hardly learn abnormal psychology overnight, but I could learn a little about it. I could learn the patter, anyway.

I stopped at the main library and picked up half a dozen volumes, the ones that seemed most readable and least technical.

I started one of them while I ate dinner in a restaurant. I kept on reading it after I got home. Some of the case histories sent a chill down my back. At midnight I made myself some sandwiches and coffee and started skimming through the third book.

Looking up at the clock and discovering that it was almost five in the morning was almost a shock. I went upstairs to bed, setting my alarm for eleven o'clock.

~§~

The long-faced receptionist said, "The doctor will see you now." Her eyes followed me across the office, as though she were trying to diagnose what my particular brand of insanity might be.

It was two-thirty and I'd waited there, under her appraising eye, since before two. No one had entered or left the inner office. It was anyone's guess whether the great Montreaux had been playing solitaire or engaged in the contemplation of his navel. I have a hunch it's against medical union rules for a doctor to keep an appointment without making the appointee wait.

Maybe I should have been impressed, but I wasn't. I was annoyed. I was even more annoyed when he said, "Sit down, Mr. Stacy," without looking up from the folder that was open on his desk.

I studied him while he studied the folder. He was a big man, with an impressive leonine head, pince-nez glasses, and a neatly cropped short beard.

He looked the part—too much, I thought. He looked like a Vienna specialist in a yeast ad.

Then he lifted his head and all of a sudden he was human. He smiled apologetically.

"I hope you'll forgive me, Mr. Stacy. I was just familiarizing myself with the case."

"Quite all right, Doctor," I told him. "I understand that you interviewed Obie Westphal twice; is that right?"

"Obie?" He stared at me. "On my records the name is Henry. Wait—I see it's Henry O. Do they call him by his middle name?"

I nodded slowly. "You don't know him very well, do you, Doctor?"

"Know him well? Of course, not. I've seen him only twice. Once as a child of seven."

"Tell me about that, Doctor," I said. "I understand that Mr. Westphal brought him to you then because he had certain—suspicions. What did you discover?"

"That the suspicions were absurd, that the boy was normal. Let's see. Specifically Mr. Westphal feared that the boy might have injured his sister deliberately. It seems that they were climbing in a tree and that the sister fell and suffered a severe spinal injury that paralyzed her."

"Did Mr. Westphal explain why he suspected the boy?"

"Not to my satisfaction. He mentioned that there had been other instances, less important ones, but he didn't explain the details to me. Most of them concerned pets. I remember something about a canary bird and something about a puppy." He paused and looked back at the file folder before him. "The girl herself, his sister, thought the fall was accidental. Or, at least that Henry's part in causing it was inadvertent."

"I see," I said. "And the boy's mother?"

"I don't believe she knew—or knows—of Mr. Westphal's suspicions, if that is what you mean. I have never met Mrs. Westphal. I don't know exactly what excuse Mr. Westphal gave his son for bringing him to talk to me. It wouldn't, of course, have taken much of an excuse the first time, when the boy was only seven."

"And you examined the boy and found him normal?"

"Yes. Definitely."

"May I ask just how you determined that?"

"I talked to the boy, asked him questions and observed his reactions. There was no sign of abnormality."

He leaned back in his chair. I asked, "And the second interview?"

"Quite—ah—similar. I fear that Mr. Westphal has an obsession, that he has permitted his absurd suspicions to broaden and to expand. A year ago he brought Henry to see me again. He told me privately, of course, not in front of the boy—that he suspected his son of having a hand in certain accidents that had happened at the high school and elsewhere."

And elsewhere, I thought. Then there have been, other deaths besides the boy who fell from the tower and the one who fell down the stair well, and the girl who was electrocuted, and...

There was a fly buzzing against the screen of the open window, trying to get in. A big fly. I wondered if it was the one which had been in the *Herald* news room a week ago. It was a silly thing to wonder. Almost as silly as my being here at all.

There were a hundred questions I wanted to ask, but I looked across the desk at Montreaux and I knew it would be useless. He had spoken. He was that kind of a guy; you didn't have to be a psychiatrist to tell that by looking at him, by listening to the tone of his voice.

Suddenly I felt hot and weary and discouraged. I said, "Thank you, Doctor," and stood up.

I went to the Press Bar, near the *Herald,* where the gang from the news room hung out. It was Saturday afternoon now and I didn't have to stay away to avoid explaining things. My vacation was over, practically.

Harry Rowland was there.

He said, "Hi, Joe. How was the fishing?"

"Great," I said. "Caught one this long. And watch out for my sunburn."

"Some sunburn," Harry said. "What'd you do, play poker all week?"

"You could call it that," I told him. "What'll you have?"

We had sidecars...

I got home early that evening, but I wasn't sleepy. The drinks I'd had with Harry hadn't done me any harm, or any good.

It was Saturday night, and my vacation was over. Next day was Sunday and I wouldn't have worked anyway, so my vacation was a dead duck. Monday, back to the mines.

The worst of it, I thought, was that I still wasn't completely convinced that I was wrong. A psychiatrist can make a mistake.

"Ah—Henry, do you have recurrent dreams? I mean, son, do you ever dream the same thing over and over?"

"No. I don't dream much."

"Do you ever feel an impulse to hurt someone?"

"Why no, Doctor."

Obie was smart enough for that.

But Montreaux couldn't be as dumb as that. Or could he? He had a reputation, but that reputation had been achieved by treating neurotics who went to him and *told* him their troubles and their symptoms. Could he possibly unmask anyone, in a casual interview, who chose to conceal his symptoms? Could an ordinary doctor tell that a patient had appendicitis if the patient denied having any local pain and pretended to be perfectly normal?

Forget it, I told myself. Chalk up a lost week to the fool-killer and forget it.

I read myself sleepy and went to bed.

X

I DON'T KNOW what I'd been dreaming; I don't remember my dreams. But it must have been bad. I woke as though something had me by the throat, and yet it was only a noise. It was my electric alarm clock going off, only it was pitch black, the middle of the night. I reached out and smacked the lever. The ringing kept on.

It wasn't the alarm clock. It stopped a few seconds and started again and in those few seconds of silence I noticed that the clock wasn't even humming, wasn't running at all.

I could see now that the luminous hands stood at five minutes after three, but the clock wasn't running. Something was ringing. The doorbell.

Someone was ringing my doorbell at five minutes after three, only it wasn't five minutes after three because the clock wasn't running. But anyway it was the middle of the night.

I got my feet out of bed onto the floor and by that time I was thinking a little bit. I was thinking that maybe Millie had come home a day early, and then I remembered Millie would have her own key and wouldn't ring the doorbell. Maybe it was a telegram. The thought scared me.

I had my hand on the light switch now, but when I clicked it nothing happened. The lamp on the bedside table was out, too. It was pitch dark in the room. And the bell downstairs kept ringing, ringing.

All of it, the ringing and the darkness and the fact that there wasn't any time, that time was standing still, was mixed in with what was left of my dream, whatever it had been. And on top of that: Millie's hurt. Millie may be killed. Something must have happened to Millie. Because that's what a telegram in the middle of the night would mean.

The bell kept ringing as I groped across the room to the doorway to the hall, and through the door into the deeper blackness of the hallway, a blackness that was almost tangible. The doorbell rang again, then stopped.

It seems to take a long time to tell, but all of this was within thirty seconds after the first ring of the bell. Maybe a minute at the outside. It was all happening fast. I was hurrying along the hall to the head of the stairs. Running my hand along the wall to guide me.

My other hand groped for the knob at the top of the banister, and touched it. The doorbell was ringing for what must have been the fifth or sixth time.

It was my hand touching the light-switch button on the wall at the left of the head of the stairs that saved me. I still wasn't thinking coherently, but I did realize that I could go down those stairs faster if there was a light.

I stopped and flicked the switch. Nothing happened. The hall light wasn't working, either. But the fact that I'd stopped to try it kept me from toppling head-first down the flight of steps to the first floor.

For I was leaning slightly backward when I put my foot forward for the first step of the stairs. My bare foot kicked into something that was between me and the step. Kicked hard, because I was still in a hurry to get down there, darkness or no.

The thing I booted went over the edge and bounced noisily down the stairs. At that, I almost lost my balance and followed it, but my right hand was still resting lightly on the newel post of the banister and I grabbed it with my other hand, too, braced my weight against it, and managed to stay on my feet. I think I let out a yell of pain, too, for my big toe felt as if it were broken.

Whatever I'd kicked reached the bottom of the stairs with a final loud bump and the doorbell broke off in mid-ring.

In the sudden stillness I could hear light footsteps race across the porch and down the walk. I heard a scraping sound that wasn't quite the noise of an auto door. But no sound of a car starting.

If I'd run immediately into the front bedroom and looked out the window, I could have seen him. But I didn't. I was too scared and confused, just at that moment, to do anything.

I did know I wanted *light*. I hobbled back into my bedroom, found my trousers over the back of the chair, and got matches out of the pocket. I struck one, and there was light.

I wasn't blind, at any rate. The lights were busted, not my eyes. My toe wasn't broken, either, although it still hurt. I found slippers.

I remembered now that there was an old flashlight somewhere in the dresser. I located it after a brief search. The batteries were weak, but it was usable. I flashed it ahead of me along the hallway and down the steps.

Lying six feet from the bottom of them was the typewriter case I'd used to carry some things to Lake Laflamme. It had jarred open from its fall down the stairs and the contents were scattered.

Fortunately my typewriter hadn't been in it; it was on my desk in the den. The case had been filled with camping clothes, a pair of old shoes, some extra tackle, stuff like that. I'd put it down in the front hallway when I'd come home last Monday and had never got around to moving it or unpacking it.

I'd never taken it upstairs. I'd never put it on the top step of the stairs. Drunk or sober—and I'd been sober last night—I hadn't put it where my foot had found it in the darkness.

I looked out through the glass panel of the front door. The porch and the street were empty. I looked to see if a telegraph had been shoved under the door. I opened the door—I hadn't bothered to lock it yesterday evening—and went out on the porch.

I examined the mailbox and the doorknob to be sure the telegraph boy—if it had been one—hadn't left one of those notices to call Western Union.

There was nothing, no special delivery letter, no telegram, no notice. Just silence and an empty street.

I went back inside and tried the downstairs hall light switch just behind the door. It worked. The electricity wasn't off, then; just the fuse for the upstairs lights had blown.

I walked into the living room, and picked up the telephone to call Western Union. The line was dead.

I put down the phone. Only then did I wake up enough to get scared. It was only then that I got the full impact of that typewriter case on the top step of the stairs, and all the upstairs lights being out. That and the urgency of the ringing bell. It was only then that I realized that an attempt had been made to kill me—*by accident.*

I'm no hero. I was scared stiff. The only consoling feature was that dead telephone. I saw now what it meant. He'd realized that I might miss the trap and not tumble down those steps, or that I might fall and not be hurt seriously—and thus still be able to reach the phone. In either case, I could call the Westphal number, demand that they check whether Obie Westphal was in his bed. If I could phone before he got home and under the covers, I'd have him on a spot. I thought of dressing quickly and rushing out to phone, but I realized he'd be home long before I could reach another phone.

I knew now what that scraping noise outside had been, and why the soft running footsteps had ended at the sidewalk. He'd come on a bicycle, and his home was only a dozen blocks away.

He'd probably be there by this time, sneaking in, getting back into his bed. The scraping noise could only have been a bicycle being picked up from the curb.

There wouldn't be any more danger tonight—that's what the telephone told me. Obie had protected his line of retreat.

But how had he known I was on his trail—or that I *had been* on his trail until—that very afternoon—I'd decided that I was imagining things? Surely not his father. Dr. Montreaux? That was silly.

There wasn't any more danger tonight. But just the same I left the hall light and the living room light on when I went out into the kitchen. I left the light on while I went down into the basement to look at the fuse box.

XI

I FOUND only what I'd expected to find, a blown fuse in the socket marked "upstairs." I hadn't known when I labeled those sockets, so Millie could identify them, that I would be helping a murderer. But had I? He would not have needed to come down into the basement at all.

He could have blown that fuse easily, by screwing a bulb out of the socket in the upstairs hall, when he'd taken the typewriter case to the head of the stairs, and shorting the socket with a pocket screw driver or something.

I replaced the fuse and went back upstairs to the living room. I found a screw driver and took the lid off the telephone bell box. I found what I expected to find there, too. A wire very obviously worked loose from the brass-headed screw that held it down. I fixed it and put the cover back on the box.

I picked up the receiver and got a "Number, please," from the operator. I said, "Never mind," and put it back.

No use making a call now. Obie was home in bed long ago.

Outside the windows, the sky was beginning to turn gray. I looked through the kitchen door at the clock there and saw it was four o'clock.

Thank God there was some beer in the refrigerator. I opened a bottle and sat down to think. I *had* to think.

The first thing I thought of was that the front door was still unlocked, and I got up and locked it. I went around the house checking. There were four downstairs windows unlocked, two of them open.

I started to close and lock the windows and decided to hell with it. It was a hot night and I'd stifle if I closed the house up tight.

I went upstairs to check the lights there—they worked—and I took the typewriter case and its contents with me, and put them away.

Tonight Millie would be coming home. This was Sunday. Sometime today I'd have to go over the house and put everything away that ought to be put away and clean up the bathroom and the kitchen.

Millie wouldn't expect me to clean house, but she would like to find things put away instead of strewn around the way they get when a man lives alone and isn't used to it.

Four o'clock, and I'd slept only two hours. I'd read until well after midnight. I ought to go back to sleep, but I knew I couldn't.

I returned to the kitchen, to the beer. I sat there trying to think, and it got lighter and lighter outside, but it didn't get any lighter inside my head.

I *knew* now that I was right about Obie, but I didn't yet know how he'd known I was checking on him. I couldn't even guess who had been in the car which had followed me yesterday. I thought that if I knew the answer to one question, I'd know the answer to both.

But that didn't seem important compared to the, bigger problem— what I was going to do about it. Go to the police? They'd tell me I was silly. They'd laugh hell out of me, on the basis of what I could give them.

At seven o'clock, when it was bright day outside, my last bottle of beer was gone, but it hadn't made me drunk and it hadn't made me sleepy. I was tired as hell. I felt as though I'd been run through a wringer yet I wasn't sleepy.

I made some breakfast and took my time eating it. Then I went upstairs and dressed. I put on my Palm Beach suit because it was going to be a scorcher of a day.

I thought, maybe I made a fool of myself. Maybe I should have left that telephone alone, and the fuse box and the handle of the typewriter case. There might have been fingerprints smeared all over them.

Hell, that was silly. Obie was third-year high. Kids knew about fingerprints these days before they knew how to spell the word.

I wanted to get out, to go somewhere and do something, but I couldn't think of anything. I couldn't think, period. I went out to the garage and looked at my car and I wondered if a bolt in the steering mechanism might be loosened, or a cotter-pin sheared or something.

I wasn't enough of a mechanic to look and see. I didn't know, I realized, how the steering mechanism worked except for the wheel you turned when you wanted to go right or left. But Obie would know. Kids nowadays knew things like that. And Obie was a bright kid.

No, he wouldn't have messed with my car last night. Some other time maybe. That was one of the cheerful things I'd have to think about from now on until this thing was settled one way or the other.

I got in the car and drove toward town. I slowed down opposite the police station, but I didn't stop. Downtown, I parked and got some more breakfast.

I drank two cups of coffee and didn't feel any less dopey. It came to me maybe I should see Mr. Westphal again and find out for sure whether he had mentioned my name to Obie. But, of course, he wouldn't have. The very thought was silly. But it was sillier that Montreaux—

I got in my car again, then remembered that lingerie stores weren't open on Sunday and that this was Sunday. Tomorrow I was going back to work. Or was I? Could I let go, now that I had a tiger by the tail? *Could* I call the whole thing off and forget it? Sure, but how long before something would happen to me? Or Millie?

That woke me up. I drove home and I drove fast. Nothing happened to the steering mechanism of the car.

I put through a long distance call to Millie at her mother's. In less than half an hour I was talking to her.

"Honey, don't come home yet," I said. "I can't explain over the phone, but it's important. Stay there until I let you know it's all right."

It wasn't as easy as that, but she agreed, finally. I didn't even have to convince her that another woman wasn't involved. Millie and I know each other well enough so she didn't have to ask that.

I hung up the phone and wandered around the house a while. I felt as though I were walking through thick fog. I knew I ought to get some sleep so my mind would work right again. There was *something* I ought to do.

But my mind was like a pinwheel, and my legs were beginning to feel as though they were made of lead. I wanted a drink, yet I was too tired to go out to get one. And eleven o'clock of a Sunday morning is no time to start drinking, when you need all your faculties.

It's funny. My memory stops there. I don't remember deciding to lie down on the davenport in the living room to rest; I don't remember lying down. But when I woke up, it was starting to get dark in the room.

XII

I WENT OUT in the kitchen and washed my face with cold water. By the kitchen clock, it was seven-thirty.

I started to make coffee, then decided I'd be better off to go out and buy a regular meal at a restaurant. I got in my car and started back, only I must not have been thinking for I found myself turning into the street Obie's house was on.

All right, I said to myself. I've got nothing better to do except think, and I can think as well here as home. Maybe better.

I parked a little farther away this time. Lights were on in the house. I thought I could make out the wheel chair of Obie's sister in the shadow of the front porch. Then Obie came out and sat on the top step. Even at that distance there was no mistaking him because of that blond hair of his. He stood up, strolled toward the sidewalk.

If he takes a walk, I thought, I'll follow him again.

Again, as before, he turned toward my car. As before, I sat still to let him pass. I was parked in the shadow of a tree. He might be able, from his side of the street, to see that there was someone in the car, if he looked hard enough. But he couldn't recognize me, even if he knew me by sight—and I doubted that he did.

So I sat there, waiting for him to go by. Then I'd get out and follow him—undoubtedly to the freight yards, as before. Only this time maybe

I wouldn't lose him there.

He strolled leisurely, and didn't even glance toward me. I let him pass, just as I had a few nights ago. I had a hunch that everything that had happened before was going to happen again. It was a lousy hunch. I happened to glance in the rear vision mirror.

There was a car parked behind mine. It was a jalopy. It looked like the car that had tailed me out of town Friday afternoon. There was someone in it. And it wasn't Obie, because Obie was walking past it right now on the other side of the street, paying no more attention to it than he had to my car.

I sat still, very still, until Obie Westphal was almost a block away, headed toward the railroad jungle. Then I got out of my car and walked back to the jalopy behind me.

He sat behind the wheel and waited for me. It was the dead-end pal of Jimmy Chojnacki. It was Pete Brenner, who had gone to school with Jimmy last year, but wasn't going back to school; the kid I'd talked to in the fruit market and to whom I'd given the five dollar bill for very little information.

I leaned my elbows on the side door of the jalopy.

I said, "Hi, Pete." I kept my voice halfway between neutral and friendly. "Want to help me?"

"Help you what?"

I let my voice drop a tone. "Get the guy who killed Jimmy."

Maybe I sounded like something out of a radio serial, but I got him. He tried to stay deadpan, but it slipped. I could see through the mask that he was interested—and scared.

He said, "Go on."

I said, "It wasn't me. I'm just a guy playing a hunch, Pete. But Jimmy Chojnacki was murdered, and I know who did it."

"Who?"

"Obie Westphal."

He said, "You're crazy."

I shook my head.

I said, "Come on. I'll tell you about it."

I turned away; I knew he'd come.

He had the car door open almost before I turned. Something touched the small of my back.

He said, "Don't move."

"I'm not heeled," I said, "and that's what worries you. Go ahead."

"I'll do that." I felt his free hand reach around me, feel first for a shoulder holster, then pat my coat and trouser pockets, and finally my hip pockets. I'd raised my arms slightly. I dropped them down and kept going.

"Come on," I told him.

I went to my car and opened the door. Then I turned. He was close behind me, his right hand thrust into his coat pocket.

He said, "Wait a minute. How do I know you ain't got a gun in the car?"

I grinned. "If I had a gun and any intention of using it on you, would I have left it there when I went back to your car?"

I got in, slid under the wheel. He moved in beside me.

I switched on the ignition. Then I turned it off again. We had time for what I had in mind. Better get part of the talking over with before I started.

I said, "You know that Jimmy was killed at the low dip of the coaster. Ever been there? Know what the track is like there?"

He nodded.

"Then think this over. When you stand by that dip and a car is coming up the hill from the platform, you can hear it coming. You hear the ratchet on the chain that keeps the car from sliding back. It's plenty loud. No one with normal hearing could start across those tracks not knowing that a car was coming.

"Jimmy wouldn't have. You told me his hearing was okay. He was standing there, by the low railing, *with* someone, to watch the empty car come down. That someone shoved him across the railing just as the car came down."

"Jeez," he said. "I never thought of that ratchet clicking. Even when you asked about Jimmy's ears."

I said, "Did you know that when Jimmy was found he was first identified as Obie Westphal because Obie's wallet was in his pocket? It wasn't until later that they checked the fingerprints and found out it was Jimmy, not Obie."

"You're not kidding me?"

"I'm not. Look, Pete, when a guy lifts a leather, what's the first thing he does?"

"Gets rid of it, sure. Takes the money out and ditches the rest."

"Right. But he hadn't got rid of Obie's. Why? Because Obie was with him. Let me give you the picture, the way I see it. He spots Obie—and Obie is a rich kid, comparatively. He knows Obie carries dough. If Obie had been a friend, he wouldn't have done it. But Obie was just an acquaintance.

"So he lifts Obie's billfold. Then something went wrong. Obie turned around and saw him. Obie didn't know his pocket had been picked, I'm almost certain about that. But he saw Jimmy and acted friendly, and stuck with him."

I closed my eyes and tried to picture it, to make it more real and vivid.

"Maybe he offered to treat him to something to eat, or to a ride. Jimmy would have said no because he wouldn't want Obie to reach for his wallet that wasn't there. But he didn't think fast enough to get away from Obie and they strolled back of the midway.

"Maybe Jimmy led the way there—he'd have more chance to ditch that leather before Obie missed it. By that time, I think, he'd have been glad to ditch it, money and all. But they happened to stand by the low railing of the first dip of the Blue Streak as the car started down. And Obie pushed him."

"*Why?* You said Obie hadn't missed his wallet. So *why?*"

"No," I said. "Obie hadn't missed his wallet. When he did, he got a little panicky, because he realized what had probably happened to it, and that his name would be found on Jimmy's body. It was the first time his name had ever been tied in with anybody he'd killed."

Pete Brenner's eyes narrowed to slits.

He said, "You mean Obie's crazy?"

I said, "I've been reading a lot of books about stuff like that. And I don't know what the word I 'crazy' means. The more I read, the less I know. But I think this. . ."

I paused a moment, searching for the right words.

"Obie likes to kill people. Just as some people like to get drunk and some like to paint pictures and others like to play the violin, Obie likes to kill. I think he's killed at least half a dozen people. Maybe more. I think he killed the two boys who were killed by falls at South Side High, and the girl who was electrocuted in the basement.

"I think he's killed bums in the jungle not so far from here. I think he tried to kill his sister, but crippled her instead. I think he killed Jimmy Chojnacki. I think last night he tried to kill me."

I took a long breath, then added, "But I haven't a shred of proof."

XIII

I STILL didn't look at Pete Brenner. He hadn't said anything. That was good enough for me, just then.

I said, "Until tonight I couldn't figure how Obie knew I was after him. Now I can guess. You talked to him?"

"Yeah," he said.

"But you didn't know my name... Wait, you got it from Mrs. Chojnacki. You guess I got your name from her so you got mine from her after I talked to you. That was my slip—I said just enough to get you curious, and thought you'd let it go at that, and you didn't. What did you figure?"

"I didn't know what was up. But, like you said, you got me curious. You made me think something was phony about Jimmy's getting killed, and I wanted to know what. I got your name from his ma. You'd brought Obie Westphal into the conversation, so I talked to him to see if he could tell me what your angle was. He said he couldn't."

Pete hesitated, then resumed. "He didn't tell me about his wallet being on Jimmy. I got your address out of the phone book. That car belongs to a friend of mine. I borrowed it a few times and tried to learn what you were doing. You went to Obie's father's store once. Look, I don't know whether I swallow all that about Obie, but I might play along to find out. What did you figure on doing?"

I turned on the ignition and started the car.

I said, "He started off in that direction a few nights ago, and went to the freight yards, the jungle. I lost him there. It's about a twenty-minute walk. We've been talking fifteen. We can get there about the time he does. Maybe two of us can find him."

I swung the car around in a wide U-turn and tramped down hard on the accelerator.

Pete said, "You mean you want to—look, without being sure, I'm not gonna help you bump him."

"Hell, no," I cut in. "Nothing farther from my mind. But I'd like to trap him into talking, and it won't do me any good unless I have a witness. Even if he talks I want no funny business from you, Pete. Is that really a gun you had?"

"Naw. A pipe. How are you going to get him to talk?"

"I don't know," I admitted.

I parked on a side street just off the jungle.

There was a moon, a bright moon. It was much easier to cover territory than it had been the last time I was here. I felt pretty sure that if he was here, we would find him.

For half an hour, it looked as though I was going to be wrong.

Then, on the far side of the yards, just as we rounded the end of a long string of freight cars, I saw Obie. He was walking toward us, down the passage between two adjacent tracks filled with cars. He was a long way off but I was sure of him because of that light blond hair of his, bright even in the dimness of the cars' shadow.

I grabbed Pete Brenner and pulled him back out of sight. The end car—the one we'd been walking around—was an empty boxcar. Both doors were open. I motioned Pete around to the door on the far side.

"Get in there and keep quiet," I said. "I'll try to talk to him by the door of the car, so you can hear what we say. But don't make any move unless I tell you to."

He nodded, climbed into the empty car and stepped back out of sight.

I went back to the end of the car, and glanced around it. I wanted to time myself so I'd meet Obie opposite that open boxcar door. He was quite a way down the line yet.

I worked fast. I whipped off my necktie and stuck it in my pocket. I turned down the brim of my hat all the way around, then on second thought I dropped it in the dirt and cinders, stepped on it, and put it on again.

I scraped dirt over my shoes, leaving them with a thick layer of dust. I wiped the thickest dirt off my hands, so as not to overdo it, and then used them to dirty my face and the collar of my shirt.

My suit didn't need preparation. I'd slept in it most of the day and there wasn't a crease left anywhere.

I didn't think he knew me by sight, but even if he did, he wouldn't recognize me now if I kept in the shadows. I was reasonably certain he didn't know the sound of my voice.

I listened to the sound of his leisurely footsteps crunching gravel. About two car lengths away. A locomotive hooted. Somewhere in the distance I heard the staccato clank of couplings, the hiss of releasing steam.

I took a long breath and walked around the end of the car.

The timing was good. If I strolled slowly I'd meet him right opposite the open door of the end boxcar. I let myself slouch along. I knew he couldn't see my eyes in the shadow, so I studied him from under the pulled-down brim of my hat.

It scared me, that sizing up. Sure, I'd known he was a football player and an all-around athlete, but I hadn't realized until now, when I was seeing him at close range for the first time, how big he was and how broad his shoulders were.

I fumbled with a cigarette.

I said, "Got a match, kid?"

My voice was a bit hoarse.

"Sure."

He took a book of them from his pocket. He lighted one for me and held it out in his cupped hands. I held the tip of my cigarette into the flame.

He grinned at me in the flare of light, a cheerful schoolboy grin.

My God, I thought. *I'm nuts. This kid has never—*

"Swell night, isn't it?" he said.

I nodded.

It was. I hadn't thought about it till now, and I wasn't thinking too hard about it now, because my mind was doing handsprings, trying to readjust itself to something new. This wasn't, *couldn't* be, the monster. I'd been thinking of for a week. There was a catch somewhere.

"Just get in town?" Obie asked me.

I had to stay in character, now that I'd started it. I nodded.

"How's work here?" I asked him.

He said, "All right, I guess. I'm still in school myself. What kind of work do you do?"

"Printer. Linotype. Say, do you—"

To the south, a locomotive hooted and released steam, and then the clank of couplings drowned out what I'd started to say. The string of cars to my left was moving—the car that Pete Brenner was in was rolling away from us. Both Obie and I stepped back farther from the moving cars. It put his face in the moonlight. I studied him closely.

His eyes were eager and boy-like.

He said, "Let's hop 'em. They're just shifting around."

He ran lightly and grabbed the rungs of a reefer going by us. I hesitated. I almost didn't. If he'd urged me to do it, if he'd even looked around to see whether I was coming, I might have been suspicious again, and afraid.

But he was clambering on up the rungs to the top of the car. It hadn't gathered much speed. It was easy for me to swing up after him. He was sitting on the catwalk when I got to the top. He was lighting a cigarette, cupping his hands against the wind.

He said, "Got to quit this when school starts again. I play football. Ever play it?"

I shook my head. "Haven't the build for it."

Over the noise of the train and the rush of the wind, we had to talk loudly. I flipped my cigarette, a fiery arc into the night, and sat down by the brake wheel.

XIV

SOMEWHERE FAR OFF, another locomotive highballed—three long lonesome wails in the night. Up ahead, the lights of town made a glow in the sky. It was beautiful. And looking at it, I began to get scared all over again for a different reason.

This whole thing, I saw clearly, could have been my imagination. Except last night—what had happened at my place. That was real. Someone *had* blown a fuse, or substituted a blown fuse for a good one. Someone *had* carried that typewriter case to the top of my staircase. Someone *had* rung my doorbell.

Someone had—I started to turn around again. My hand, resting lightly on the brake wheel, saved me from dying the next second.

The push that sent me off the end of the freight car, into the space between it and the car ahead, was so sudden, so hard, so viciously strong that it would have knocked me off the car even if I'd been ready and braced for it. But my left hand tightened convulsively on the rim of the brake wheel. I yelled involuntarily.

I dangled there between the moving cars, only the narrow coupling between me and the roadbed and the crushing steel wheels.

When you're in a spot like that, you don't think. You don't take time out to think what a fool you were to doubt your own judgment and reasoning and to place yourself in deadly danger. You just grab at straws, or brake wheels. You fight to live another second.

I'd *known,* and yet without even thinking what I was doing, I'd asked for it, sitting there on the end of a boxcar right beside him. I'd been so sure he wouldn't recognize me as Joe Stacy, of the *Herald,* who had been too curious about the death of Jimmy Chojnacki, that it had not remotely occurred to me that as John Doe, stranger, itinerant printer, I was in equally deadly danger. I'd forgotten *why* he killed, and how.

All that I thought of afterward. Just then, life was a brake wheel atop a freight car, and I was hanging onto it. Up above, hands stronger than mine were bending back my fingers, unwinding them from their grip on life. I swung, trying to get my right hand up there before he could pry my left one loose.

I looked up and I saw his face. It was horrible. It was horrible because it was so calm, so normal.

Only the tips of the fingers of my right hand touched the rim of the brake wheel. One of the fingers of my left hand felt as though it were being broken.

Then, above and past Obie's head, I saw something swinging down. Even over the noise of the train and the noise of death in some wails in the night. Up ahead, the lights of town made a glow my ears I heard a sound that I sometimes dream about, a sickening, *thud-crunch* sound.

And, like something in a nightmare, Obie's face was coming closer and closer to mine over the edge of the freight car, and the scrape of his body past mine almost, but not quite, wrenched my grip from the brake wheel.

I grabbed again with my right hand and this time I caught hold of the rim in time to look down. I saw Obie hit the coupling and slide off. I saw his head strike the rail, and then the car passed over him.

A hand grabbed my wrist—supportingly, this time—and I looked up again. It was Pete Brenner, bending over the edge of the car. Still in his right hand was the pipe he'd had in his pocket.

I should have known. It wasn't a Dunhill or a corncob. It was an eight-inch length of led pipe. His face was still carefully deadpan.

He seemed to realize, then, that he was still holding the pipe and that he didn't need it anymore. He tossed it over the edge of the car and used both hands to help me back up.

The clank of the couplings, starting at the engine end and coming toward us, told us the train was stopping and we went down the side ladder and dropped off.

We didn't talk at all until we were back inside my car. We didn't talk much then, except that I found out how he had managed to be there just after Obie had pushed me off. Pete Brenner had jumped out of the far side of the boxcar as the string of cars began to move. He'd knelt down and watched our legs under the cars as we stood talking.

He'd seen us run to board the reefer and he'd caught it, too. He'd climbed almost to the top, and hung there on the side, only a few feet from us. He couldn't hear what we said while the train was moving, but there was nothing else he could do. Until he heard me yell as I went over the edge. Then he came on up, while Obie was trying to loosen my grip on the wheel.

~§~

At nine-fifteen the next morning, Harry Rowland passed my desk on his way out.

He said, "Ed wants to see you, Joe."

I got up and went into Ed's office. Ed is the *Herald's* city editor. A lot of editors are named Ed. It's just a coincidence.

He said, "How was the vacation, Joe?"

"Not bad," I told him and let it go at that.

He said, "Give you an easy one to start on. Some kid was killed hopping freights over at the yards last night. Roy Mackin's working on it. We're giving it a quarter column on the front page because his father's an advertiser, runs a downtown lingerie shop. Name's Westphal."

"Yeah?" I said.

"Yeah. You do an obit for the inside section. There's a morgue file on the kid, Mackin says. Football hero and tennis player and stuff. Get a pic. Do a half column or so and make it good or the advertising department will be on our neck. Take your time now and make it good."

"Sure," I said.

I returned to my desk, opened the top drawer and fished around the back of it. It was still there, the story I'd written eight days ago.

It began: "Under the wheels of a Whitewater Beach roller coaster today. . ."

I had to change that.

I took a thick copy pencil and obliterated completely a few words, wrote in others. I made it read, "Under the wheels of a freight car last night at the C.R. & D. freight yards. . ."

I read the rest of it through and didn't change another word.

I called a copy boy over and gave him the story, and a buck.

I said, "Watch the clock. At ten-fifteen go in and give this to Ed. Tell him I just gave it to you, and that I said I was sick and was going home. Got it?"

He grinned. "For a buck, I'll tell him you just flew out of the window in a helicopter."

There are times when there isn't anything else to do but go out and get drunk.

I went out and got drunk.

Mystery Book Magazine, October 1946
Later expanded into the novel, The Deep End, *1952*

NOW AVAILABLE FROM BRUIN CRIMEWORKS—

David Dodge
- *DEATH AND TAXES*
- *TO CATCH A THIEF*
- *THE LONG ESCAPE*

Fredric Brown
- *KNOCK THREE-ONE-TWO*
- *MISS DARKNESS*

Bruno Fischer
- *HOUSE OF FLESH*

Elliott Chaze
- *BLACK WINGS HAS MY ANGEL*

Paul Bailey
- *DELIVER ME FROM EVA*

James Hadley Chase
- *NO ORCHIDS FOR MISS BLANDISH*
- *FLESH OF THE ORCHID*

Coming soon–
The 9 Dark Hours by Lenore Glen Offord

... and introducing CRIMEWORKS *Doubleshots* ➔➔

Double Novel

Edward Anderson's
THIEVES LIKE US & *HUNGRY MEN*

Printed in Great Britain
by Amazon

54900951R10418